'Tis the season when everyone's
merry and bright....
Except for three little girls and six lonely adults.

In *Merry Christmas, Baby* by Pamela Browning,
baby Jessica is too young to harbor bad feelings
herself, but if she could talk, she'd wish the two
grown-ups in her life would sort out their
problems and succumb to the magic of the
season...and to each other.

In *The Nutcracker Prince* by Rebecca Winters,
young Anna is about to realize her dreams...
but at what cost? Her father has come all the
way from Russia for Christmas—and her mother
doesn't even want to see him!

Jule McBride presents a third story of
Christmas—*The Baby & the Bodyguard*.
Pint-sized Amanda thinks Santa had finally sent
her what she *really* wanted. A daddy. But what
Santa *had* brought was a bodyguard—who just
might be her father after all!

A DADDY FOR
CHRISTMAS

PAMELA BROWNING

writes: "Perhaps we most feel the magic of Christmas when we kiss that special person under the mistletoe. Or maybe we feel it during a midnight service on Christmas Eve, when the faces of those we love glow with reflected candlelight. Or possibly it's when our children, their smiles outshining the Christmas-tree lights, find their hearts' desires tied up in red tissue paper on Christmas morning." Jessica's present may not be tied up in red tissue paper, but it's truly her heart's desire.

REBECCA WINTERS

spent Christmases listening to *The Nutcracker*. One day, she says, "I found myself fantasizing about the Nutcracker Prince. I wondered what he'd be like if he really came to life. Naturally he'd be Russian.... And I could see an adorable little girl who yearned for a father's hugs and kisses. But I didn't have a story yet. Not until one day when my daughter came rushing into the house to tell me about her favorite teacher's experiences in the former Soviet Union. 'Mom, did you know that when Jackie was teaching over there she was assigned her own KGB agent? Don't you think that would make the most fabulous Harlequin romance?' " This story will tell you exactly what she thought.

JULE McBRIDE

says, "I'll always remember my childhood winter holidays. We would skate on West Virginia's frozen creeks, warm our toes over the heater vents, then scald our tongues on too much hot chocolate.... Then I grew up and moved to Manhattan—where snow makes the city streets glitter more than all the diamonds at Tiffany's. At Christmastime, shoppers rush, horse-drawn carriages circle Central Park and artists fashion angels from ice outside the Plaza Hotel. As different as the city seems, Christmases remain as warm as those of my youth. After all, Christmas is really about kids and excitement, second chances and the healing power of love. I hope you're warmed by *The Baby & the Bodyguard*."

A DADDY FOR CHRISTMAS

PAMELA BROWNING

REBECCA WINTERS

JULE McBRIDE

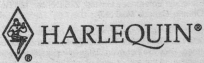

HARLEQUIN®

TORONTO • NEW YORK • LONDON
AMSTERDAM • PARIS • SYDNEY • HAMBURG
STOCKHOLM • ATHENS • TOKYO • MILAN • MADRID
PRAGUE • WARSAW • BUDAPEST • AUCKLAND

HARLEQUIN BOOKS

by Request—A DADDY FOR CHRISTMAS

Copyright © 1998 by Harlequin Books S.A.

ISBN 0-373-20154-0

The publisher acknowledges the copyright holders
of the individual works as follows:

MERRY CHRISTMAS, BABY
Copyright © 1993 by Pamela Browning

THE NUTCRACKER PRINCE
Copyright © 1994 by Rebecca Winters

THE BABY & THE BODYGUARD
Copyright © 1994 by Julianne Randolph Moore

This edition published by arrangement with Harlequin Books S.A.

CONTENTS

With the help of his instant family, could he go from Scrooge to Father Christmas?

MERRY CHRISTMAS, BABY

Pamela Browning

Chapter One

Mariel Evans cruised her car smoothly down the ramp from the interstate highway and peered anxiously at her surroundings.

There was no gas station in sight on this December afternoon two days before Christmas. And an ice storm was approaching from the west, with sleet and freezing rain already falling steadily.

A glance at the gauge reminded Mariel that the gas tank was almost empty, and she knew it would be foolish to attempt to reach the next exit.

Then she saw it—a rusty sign tacked to a tree.

GAS—EATS 2 MI, the lettering said. An arrow pointed left.

In this mountainous part of northern Virginia, Mariel's faithful little Chevy could probably coast the two miles. It might have to.

The rain was falling harder now, and the swish of the car's windshield wipers barely kept up with it. The crackling voice of the radio announcer informed her that this was the worst ice storm to hit the state in thirty years.

This news was hardly reassuring, but the farther north she traveled, the likelier she was to outrun the storm. Now, watching anxiously for the promised GAS—EATS, Mariel proceeded with extreme caution. When the bright red sign of the Magic Minimart came into view, she breathed a grateful sigh of relief, but only until she realized that she'd have to pump her own gas.

Christmas was Mariel's favorite season of the year. Her heart was full of peace and goodwill. So why should she begrudge the Magic Minimart's employees their party?

Through the wide plate-glass window, she saw them inside, whooping it up. The cashier was draped over the cash register, flirting with a guy wearing a Santa hat. A boom box parumpa-pum-pummed "The Little Drummer Boy" so loudly that the music vibrated the concrete beneath Mariel's feet. A man on a ladder was decking the men's room sign with boughs of holly.

And Mariel's fingers were so numb that she couldn't force the gas nozzle to separate from the pump.

"Looks like you could use some help," said a cheerful voice at her elbow. She wheeled around, sure that only a moment ago there had been no one near.

The guy inside wearing the Santa Claus cap couldn't hold a Christmas candle to this roly-poly little man, whose bright blue eyes twinkled up at her over a bushy white beard and a short red jacket.

Before Mariel could say "Jolly old Saint Nicholas," the man had pried her fingers from the handle of the gas pump and was expertly uncapping her gas tank.

"Why, thank you," Mariel said, smiling at him. To look at him made her heart feel happy, as if the sun were shining. Which was ridiculous, considering the fact that rain was dripping down her neck.

"Terrible weather we're having," said the little man.

"I know. And I have to drive all the way to Pittsburgh. I couldn't find a motel room. I guess you'd say there was no room at the inn," she said, trying to make a joke of it.

The little man's eyes snapped with a kind of droll wit. "That happens." He stopped pumping gas and screwed the cap on the tank.

"This is really nice of you," Mariel said. But she couldn't figure out if he worked here. "Do I pay you, or do I go inside?"

"No charge."

"But—"

"It's Christmas," he said with a sage shrug of his shoulders. "Got to get into the spirit of things, you know."

"Well, thanks. And—and merry Christmas." Mariel prepared to get into the car.

"You know, I could tell you a shortcut back to the interstate," the man offered thoughtfully. His beard was rimed with ice.

"Could you? Oh, that would be wonderful!" said Mariel.

"Instead of going back the way you came, take this road in the other direction. When you get to the blinker, turn left, then left again."

"Left, then left again," Mariel repeated.

"It'll be a lot better for you," he said solemnly.

"Thank you. You've been very kind."

"Merry Christmas. And I hope you have a happy New Year, too," he said. He stepped back from the car, and Mariel drove away from the station. When she glanced into her rearview mirror before pulling onto the highway, she expected to see him. But no one was there.

Well. Now to get on with her journey. Even though all that was waiting for her in Pittsburgh was an empty apartment and friends with busy holiday agendas, she couldn't wait to get there. She'd bake cookies for the neighbors, she'd go out and cut lots of pungent evergreen branches to drape across the mantel, and she'd invite the neighborhood kids in for a story hour.

Christmas was always such a magical time. Mariel loved the season and the celebration of it; she looked forward to it all year. If she were granted a pocketful of magic wishes right now, she'd wish for a miracle—that she were already home. She'd wish that it wasn't raining so hard that she could see no more than three feet in front of her car. And she'd wish she could remember if that funny little man had told her how far it was to the blinker. She'd driven miles—or so it seemed—and she hadn't seen a blinker yet.

JAKE TRAVIS DECIDED to take a shortcut back to Tellurian.

He was about ten miles from the new house where he'd been putting the final touches on the finish carpentry so that the owners could move in on the day before Christmas. It was a big deal to them—they wanted to be in their own place for the holidays.

So he'd worked long and hard, and this storm had caught him by surprise. If he'd known it was coming, he would have left for home hours ago.

Old Blue, his aged pickup truck, hugged the curve in the road as he cautiously accelerated for increased traction. If he didn't have to slam on the brakes, Old Blue would do just fine.

Normally Jake took good care of things. That included Old Blue, the only constant in his life. Jake bought beat-up houses and refurbished them, selling them for a pretty penny, moving on when he had to. He didn't even keep a cat.

A truck with four-wheel drive would be nice in this kind of weather. Hell, *brakes* would be nice. Why hadn't he had these lousy brakes fixed last week, when he'd noticed the problem? It was those people, that family. He'd busted his buns so that they could be in their house for Christmas, and now look at him—paying the price for his generosity.

Bah, humbug, he said to himself, thinking that this road didn't look like the shortcut. He couldn't recall the shortcut tunneling through the midst of the forest; nor could he remember its being so dark. Driving this road was like navigating the inside of a cow, and he hadn't passed a house or another car since he turned off the highway.

He pumped cautiously on the brakes, which did little good. He'd have to be careful, the way ice was building up on the asphalt road. Mist swirled ahead of him, graying the land-scape, which was probably just as well. The countryside wasn't much to look at.

What I wouldn't give for a cup of hot coffee, he was think-ing when a rabbit darted in front of his wheels and he slammed on the—Oh, no! No brakes!

BACK TO THAT pocketful of wishes, Mariel was thinking as she noticed with some trepidation that the trees seemed to be closing over the road.

If she were granted three wishes right *now,* she'd wish for snow that lay "roundabout, deep and crisp and even," as in the carol "Good King Wenceslas." And she'd like a cup of hot spiced cider. *And someone special to share it with,* she thought. *Let's not forget that.* At the age of thirty, she'd begun to think that her special someone didn't exist. Or if he did, she'd never find him. Her standards, according to her friends, were impossibly high.

Blap, blap, went her windshield wipers, and then they stalled for a moment. They started again in time for her to see that this road merged with another up ahead, but it was not soon enough for her to avoid the streak of blue hurtling out of the fog.

Mariel heard a sickening crunch of metal. Her car skidded out of control toward the ditch, long gray tree branches stab-bing at the glass of the windshield, and she clung to the steering wheel for dear life until the car stopped spinning.

Silence. Then she was aware of rain drumming on the metal roof, and a rhythmic roar in her ears that she knew must be her own blood pulsing in her veins.

She opened her eyes, taking stock. She was shaken, but she could move all her fingers and all her toes. The car was resting against a couple of trees, the two right wheels sus-pended over the ditch. She unfastened her seat belt and then felt as if her heart had stopped. It wasn't a ditch. It was a deep ravine. Treetops were barely visible below.

Panic sluiced over her, freezing her into inaction. In that moment, she knew sheer terror, knew it intimately. In her mind's eye, she could see her car careening into nothingness and taking her with it. In that moment, she felt utterly alone.

"Don't move!" shouted the man who appeared at her window, and she stared at him wildly, wondering if he was an apparition or—as unlikely as it seemed—a real person.

Whatever he was, he looked very worried. Mariel peered up at him on a slant, taking in high, craggy cheekbones and a squared-off chin, a prominent brow and a lone wet strand of dark hair escaping his stocking cap. The man's brown eyes were intriguingly flecked with amber, and they flickered with concern. Despite the cold and damp, Mariel felt a rush of heat. This man was gorgeous. And—no doubt about it now—he was real.

"Are you hurt?" he demanded.

"I don't think so," Mariel said, tentatively finding her voice.

"Keep still. I'm going to stand back now and take a look at this situation."

He scrambled across a boulder and studied the car. Carefully, and very, very slowly, Mariel clasped her seat belt around her again. The way her car was suspended half in space, she wouldn't be surprised if it lurched suddenly.

Through the rain, Mariel saw that the man was big and broad-shouldered. He wore a red-and-black plaid lumberjack jacket, and he appeared to be fit and strong. Below the jacket, well-worn jeans hugged his calves. He studied the position of the car intently, his brow furrowed in concentration. She tried to breathe deeply in order to calm herself, but without success. Her breath came in shallow little bursts, somehow inhibited by the sheer masculinity of this man who wanted to help her.

The stranger hurried toward her. She started to roll down the window, but he said sharply, "Don't do that!"

She must have looked startled, because his expression softened.

"I can get you out of here. But we don't want to take any chances, and the way your car is leaning against those trees, the slightest movement this way or that could change things real fast. Understand?"

She nodded mutely.

He loped off into the fog, and Mariel thought suddenly that she might never see him again.

The windows began to mist, and she resisted the impulse to wipe them clear with her hand. *If I had three wishes,* she started to think, but before she could clarify them, her rescuer was back with a tool kit and a long length of chain.

"I'll have you out of there in a few minutes," he promised. She only looked at him. Every time she allowed herself to glance toward the ravine, her stomach rolled over.

The man ducked beneath the car. She heard and felt the rasp of the chain against metal, and then he reappeared and wrapped the other end securely around a couple of immense trees.

He yanked at the end of the chain to test it. "I think that'll hold it," he said, coming around to her window again. He bent over and looked at her, and under the influence of his calm gaze she felt her shoulders relax.

"I tied the chain around the chassis in a couple of places. If the car falls, it can't go far," he said.

"What do you want me to do?" It occurred to her that this stranger could be some kind of nut, but he *was* trying to save her life.

He considered, gazing off into the treetops below for a long moment. "I'm going to see if I can get your door open. The metal's kind of crumpled, so it may not work," he said.

Sure enough, it didn't.

"Want me to try opening it from the inside?" she asked, wanting to show him that she was cooperating. It seemed important to her that he know that he could count on her.

"Go ahead."

She tried. The door wouldn't budge.

"I'll roll down the window, and you can reach in and try," she said.

The man nodded. Slowly she cranked the handle, and the window eased down. Fog floated into the car; the mist felt cool against her hot cheeks. The man reached in and exerted a steady pressure on the door handle. His hand was square, and his fingers were long.

"Excuse me for a minute. I've got to go get a tool out of my truck," the man said. He strode away, the red and black of his jacket weaving through the forest until he disappeared altogether.

Mariel almost released her seat belt again, then decided against it. The stranger seemed to be in complete control. She'd be better off following his directions, since he seemed to know what he was doing.

When he returned, he was carrying a tire iron. Again Mariel worried. There were a number of things you could do with a tire iron, and one of them was hitting somebody over the head. Though if that was what he had in mind, he was going to a lot of trouble to do it.

"You can take off the seat belt now," he said briskly. "Then I'm going to pry at the door. Be ready to move fast if you have to."

Mariel braced herself. He pried. Nothing happened to the door, but the car settled against its supporting trees with a tired wheeze. The treetops in the ravine spun sickeningly, and Mariel thought of her three wishes.

"A parachute. A hot-air balloon. And a can opener," she said.

"What?" asked the man.

"Just...um, making a few wishes," she said, feeling foolish.

His look was scornful. "If you're crazy enough to think

that wishes will work, how about wishing for the rain to let up?''

She frowned. Where did he get off, calling her crazy? Nevertheless, she canceled the hot-air balloon anyway, mentally adding ''no rain'' to her wish list.

''You'd think they'd make these car doors with pop-off hinges or something,'' he said.

''I doubt that designers of cars think about all the things that can happen,'' Mariel said reasonably.

''They should,'' he said with a grunt. ''They should sit around and brainstorm all the worst things that could go wrong. They should say, 'What if one of our cars is dangling over a ravine with a woman inside?' All kinds of things can happen, you know. Driving is unpredictable.''

''Life is unpredictable. Nobody makes *life* with pop-off hinges, either,'' Mariel returned.

''Yeah, well, you were talking about wishes. You sounded as if you believed wishing might work.''

''Sometimes it does. I do believe in magic,'' Mariel said defensively.

He paused and studied her for a moment. ''Weird,'' was all he said before inserting the tip of the tire iron in a new place between car door and frame.

''There *are* miracles,'' Mariel said.

''That so?'' he asked, as if he weren't really paying attention. Mariel heard metal bending, but the door still didn't open.

''What do you call, um…well, for instance, springtime? When everything is fresh and new again, and flowers bloom, and grass grows, and—''

He spared her a brief look of disdain. ''I'd call springtime a welcome relief at this point,'' he said succinctly.

Mariel sat back, thinking that what she had here was a realist, not a dreamer. In these circumstances, she couldn't say that was all bad.

''There!'' he said, jabbing the tire iron one last time.

Something bent and snapped, and he peeled the door back. Mariel, seeing an opportunity, started to scramble out of the car.

"Stop!" he yelled, grabbing at her wrist and missing it.

The car rolled slightly forward, and Mariel screamed. He caught her wrist this time, and with a tremendous surge of strength he hauled her out of her seat.

She staggered against him, and he held her in his arms. The wool of his jacket was soft against her cheek, and the length of his body against hers felt warm and reassuring. She clung to him, aware of firm muscles beneath his jacket and his gaze riveted on her face.

"Whoa," he said. "That was some predicament." For the first time, she was aware of his unmistakably southern drawl. It felt gentle on her ears.

"It was close," she agreed shakily, looking back over her shoulder. Her poor little Chevy hung over the edge of the world, its left side sideswiped, one of its headlights dangling from the socket.

"You really are all right?" he asked, and she focused her eyes to see that his face was filled with concern.

"I'm okay. Didn't you see that yield sign where the roads met?"

"I—Well, it was those fool brakes. Should have had them fixed, but I neglected it."

Mariel rolled her eyes in exasperation. "You mean I was in that fix because you were too lazy to take your truck to the garage?" she asked incredulously.

"I had to finish the carpentry in a house where I was working so the owners could move in before Christmas," he said defensively.

"Great," Mariel said through gritted teeth. "Talk about the designers of cars not thinking about all the things that could happen. Didn't it occur to you that brakes are important? That they need to be in proper working order?"

"I didn't think—" he began.

"Obviously," Mariel said, to cut him off.

His jaw was set in a grim line. "I'm glad you're not hurt. I'd never forgive myself if you were," he said, which redeemed him somewhat in Mariel's eyes.

"I don't know your name," she said.

"Jake. Jake Travis. And yours?"

"Mariel Evans," she replied.

"What a way to meet," he said glumly.

"What do we do now? I didn't see any houses, or a place where we could phone for help, did you?" she asked. The fog amplified her voice, and her words echoed back at her.

"No phones, I'm afraid. I must have taken a wrong turn, but how did *you* end up way out here?" He was eyeing her Pennsylvania license plate.

"I followed the directions of a man who helped me at a gas station near the interstate," she said. "I must have gotten them wrong. I have no idea where we are."

"Neither do I, and I live twenty miles away. Well, let's see if Old Blue will crank up." He grasped her elbow and started to steer her past the dank, dripping trees toward the patch of blue in the mist.

"Wait," she said, holding back. "I'd better get my purse out of the car."

"Oh, no, you don't. I don't trust the way it's leaning."

"I can reach in and grab it," she said evenly. She marched toward the car, but he was past her in a minute, opening the damaged door and peering inside.

"I'll do it."

"You're too heavy. If you lean your weight on the car, it's going to move," Mariel argued.

"Who said anything about leaning? Anyway, I tied the frame of the car to the tree as tightly as I could."

"The car moved when I got out," Mariel reminded him.

He heaved an impatient sigh. "All right. I'll hold your hand while you lean in. Don't touch the car, just grab the purse."

"And my tote bag from in front of the passenger seat."

"Okay, okay. Just get on with it," he said. "Hold on to me." He extended his hand.

Reluctantly she reached toward him.

"No, not that way," he said. "You hold my wrist, I'll hold yours. It'll be stronger." He demonstrated, and as her hand held tight to his wrist, she felt the sinews contracting. He seemed as strong as he looked.

As soon as they had a secure grip on each other, Mariel leaned gingerly into the car. Already her little Chevy, which had seen her through a marriage, a divorce and two cross-country trips, seemed alien, different, not part of her anymore. She picked up the purse and stuffed it into the tote bag, and Jake hauled her up and out of the car.

He didn't let go of her wrist right away. His hand was warm, and she felt her pulse beating against his palm. Flustered, she pulled her hand away.

"Let's go get in my truck," he said, so she slung the tote bag on her shoulder and followed him.

Jake's truck wasn't much newer than her own car, but it seemed well maintained. He got in and leaned over the seat to open the door on the passenger side. Mariel climbed in, giving Jake points for the cleanliness and neatness of the cab.

He noticed that she was shivering. "As soon as the engine is warm, I'll turn the heater on full blast," he promised. She nodded. Her relief and subsequent anger with Jake had evaporated, leaving her feeling perilously close to tears. She shoved her hands deep in the pockets of her coat and stared out the window.

Icicles were beginning to form on drooping tree limbs, and Mariel leaned her aching head against the cool window glass. Idly she noticed pale, parasitic clumps of waxy green leaves growing in the treetops, and recognized them as mistletoe. *How appropriate to the Christmas season,* she thought. She had never seen mistletoe growing in the wild before. She'd always been partial to the contrast of the ivory berries against the paler oval leaves. She usually used it liberally in her holiday decorating, and not only for its effect on her love life. She simply liked the way it looked.

But for now, holiday decor was the last thing she wanted to think about. She felt stiff and sore all over, and her head ached. A warm bed with an electric blanket turned all the way to "bake" would feel wonderful at this point.

The truck engine turned over but wouldn't start.

Jake jiggled the ignition key and tried again. Nothing.

"The battery's new," Jake said. He got out and raised the hood, disappearing under it for so long that Mariel began to suspect that the problem was major. When he climbed back in beside her, he looked worried. And when he tried to start the motor again, the battery only clicked a few times and died.

"That's it," he said, a grim tone to his voice. "We won't be going anywhere in Old Blue."

"This," Mariel said wearily, "is a nightmare."

"You said it," Jake answered.

They listened to the rain falling for a while, and then Jake said abruptly, "We can't stay here. It's going to get colder tonight. I think we should strike out and try to find a house. Otherwise..." His words trailed off, and Mariel understood that he considered it dangerous to stay in the truck.

For the first time, she realized their peril. They were lost in the woods, their vehicles out of commission, with the worst ice storm in thirty years roaring out of the west. Without a warm place to stay, they could freeze to death.

Jake regarded her across the wide expanse of vinyl seat. "I passed no place fit for human habitation on the road I traveled, and there's nothing where you came from, either. If we continue the way we were headed, I think we'll come to civilization. There's a major highway in that direction," he said.

"The interstate?" Mariel asked hopefully.

"I think the interstate is the other way. The road I'm thinking of is the highway into the town where I live."

Mariel sighed. "I'm game. I can't see sitting here and waiting for help to come along, when it may not."

"Good," Jake said, smiling at her. He had a nice smile; his teeth were very white. One bicuspid lapped slightly over the adjoining tooth, which only made the smile more interesting. Mariel wished he'd take off his cap so that she could see his hair.

When Jake hopped out of the truck cab, Mariel did, too. "What are you doing?" she asked when he climbed up over the open tailgate onto the bed of the truck and opened a metal box.

"Getting a few tools."

"For what?" she asked. She had to crane her neck to look at him.

"I was a Boy Scout once. We believe in being prepared," he told her, jumping down.

Mariel couldn't resist smiling at him. She wondered how old he was. Thirty-two? Thirty-three? It was impossible to tell, but then he probably couldn't tell much about her, either. She was wrapped in her tan, all-weather coat with the wool lining, her hair tucked under the collar, a red scarf wound up to her ears.

Now she flipped a corner of the scarf over her hair to protect it from the rain.

"Ready?" Jake asked. He shrugged into a small backpack and tugged at the straps until it fitted comfortably over his jacket.

Mariel nodded. With a last look at the truck, which, even though inoperative, represented a dry place to shelter from the weather, she resolutely faced the road. Whatever her fortunes, she had cast them with this stranger.

There was no use looking back. Anyway, it was too much trouble. Her neck hurt.

With the freezing rain stinging her face, and wearing boots that were designed for style rather than tramping along an ice-slicked road, Mariel followed Jake into the eddying mist.

Chapter Two

The road beneath their feet was so icy that it was difficult to keep a firm footing, and Jake kept a covert eye on his companion. She marched up and down the hills like a trooper, thank goodness, and he had the feeling that she was determined not to slow him down.

"So, Mariel, what brings you to this part of the country?"

"My job," she said. "I'm a folklorist for a museum in Pittsburgh, and they sent me to a conference in Roanoke. I was on my way home—I thought."

A glance down at her revealed that her blue eyes were dancing with a kind of rueful humor. He was glad to see it; he had a feeling that she'd need it before this day was over. He didn't look away immediately, because he was suddenly fascinated with her face. He hadn't realized before what a good-looking woman she was.

"What do you do?" she asked.

"I'm a carpenter by trade. Thus the tools," he said, gesturing over his shoulder at the small pack he wore. In it were things he hoped they wouldn't need—matches, leftovers from his lunch, a flashlight, hatchet, hammer, rope, and a Swiss army knife. He didn't want to talk about himself, though. He'd rather learn more about her.

"Tell me what a folklorist does," he said, trying to sound interested.

"I collect legends and catalog them," she said easily.

"How'd you get a job like that?"

"Oh, I have a master's degree in history, and I wrote my thesis on the origins of legends."

"Sounds boring. I guess that's why I never went to college."

She smiled. "It's not boring to me. I'm gathering stories to show how Christmas legends developed. You'd be surprised how many of them evolved similarly in different countries."

"Such as what? And where?"

"Such as gift-givers in all sorts of cultures. We're familiar with the real Saint Nicholas, who was probably a bishop in Asia Minor in the fourth century and is the basis for our Santa Claus. And there was the ancient Roman hag, Befana, who searched the world, leaving candy for good children, stones for the bad. And there was Knecht Ruprecht, a straw-clad German spirit who gave gifts to good children—"

"Sounds pagan to me," Jake said mildly, interrupting her.

Mariel turned wide eyes upon him. "Many of our customs had pagan origins. Take Christmas customs, for instance. People in primitive times lived very close to nature, you see, and they were quite aware of the shortest day of the year, which is December twenty-second. They celebrated when the days started to grow longer, and so we have celebrations of winter cropping up in every culture."

Jake hunched his shoulders against the rain, which was turning to sleet. "The middle of the winter's not much to celebrate, in my opinion," he muttered.

"Oh, but the celebration was to banish the winter doldrums, you see. To cheer everyone up," she said.

A curly blond tendril had escaped the scarf protecting her head, and Jake had the ridiculous urge to reach out and push it back.

"You and I ought to be celebrating, I guess," he said. "We could certainly banish *these* winter doldrums, and that's a fact." His words evaporated into a vapor trail; the air temperature was dropping.

She was silent while they walked another half mile or so. He thought maybe he had offended her, but in his opinion, the whole conversation was silly. Its only merit was that it helped him to know her better.

"I wonder how far we've come." He turned around and walked backward a few steps. The road behind them was shrouded in mist, and a tree limb fell suddenly, startling both of them.

"Strange that no one lives near here," Mariel said, her voice echoing eerily in the surrounding forest.

"I'm sure we'll come upon a house soon," Jake said, with more bravado than he felt. Mariel was still walking pluckily along beside him, but her step seemed less springy, and a tense line bisected her forehead. The veins beneath the skin at her temple were blue; her skin was milky white.

"This isn't supposed to happen at Christmas," she said. "We should be home among our friends and family, our cheeks nice and rosy, comfy-cozy, roasting chestnuts on an open fire."

"Right, but Jack Frost is nipping at my nose, and we'd better not slow down, or we're going to turn into snowmen right here and now."

She glanced at him sideways. "Oh, but you have to keep the Christmas spirit, no matter what happens. That's the whole idea."

"I've never cared much for Christmas," he said tightly. "All that family stuff—well, I never experienced it. As far as I'm concerned, this holiday is one where I get a few days off work, for which, since I'm self-employed, I don't get paid. If I'm lucky, on Christmas Day someone will take pity on me and invite me over for turkey dinner. Then the men of the family and I will watch a football game. Afterward I'll go home to an empty house."

Mariel seemed taken aback. "You're not married?" she asked.

"No. And I've never had any family. I grew up in a series of foster homes. For Christmas I usually got a few pairs of socks and some underwear. There was no Santa Claus for me—ever."

"No Santa? Why that's—that's…"

"That's the breaks of the game," he finished for her. "Do you think you could walk a bit faster? It's getting late, which means it's going to be dark soon."

"You set the pace. I'll keep up," she said stoically, and so he sped up. Walking slightly ahead of her, he was able to hide the expression on his face, which he was sure wasn't pleasant.

He just didn't like thinking about Santa Claus, that was all. The whole idea of a jolly little man who lavished gifts on people who already had everything they needed made him angry. If there really *were* a Santa Claus, he'd give things to people who needed them. The whole Christmas thing was enough to make him Santa Clauseated, which rhymed with nauseated, which was a pretty bad joke, and he already knew there was no point in saying it to Mariel.

THEY HAD BEEN WALKING for about an hour when Mariel spied something that looked like a roof through the trees. At first she couldn't believe her eyes. She'd begun to think they were walking along the most deserted road on earth.

"A house! Over there!" she exclaimed, clutching Jake's arm.

He clapped his hand over hers and broke into a smile. "I knew someone must live along here. Careful, don't trip in that pothole," he said, taking her gloved hand in his and pulling her along. Above them, bare, icy branches seemed to lock arms overhead, creaking and complaining with the rising wind.

A path, almost overgrown with bushes, led to the little

house. Such a funny little house, Mariel thought, and she didn't see any windows or any lights.

Jake stopped so suddenly that she almost ran into him. "It's just an old hunter's blind, not a house at all," he said. "Look, the roof is crumbling."

"Oh," Mariel said on a soft sigh of disappointment.

They made their way around to the hidden side of the structure. "Why, it's nothing but a lean-to," Mariel said.

Jake kicked at a few loose boards. "There's no point in staying. This place wouldn't be any better shelter than my truck. Speaking of which, maybe we shouldn't have left."

"I don't know," said Mariel. "I'm cold and hungry and I ache all over. I wish somebody would come along and give us a lift back to the Magic Minimart where all my problems started, and—"

Jake interrupted her. "No more of your wishes. So far you're batting zero."

They both heard the cry at the same time.

"What's that?" Jake asked in alarm.

"It sounds like a baby crying."

"A baby? Here? No, it could be an animal, or maybe a bird, but a baby? No way," Jake said, as though there could be no doubt. "Come on, we'd better get out of here. This place gives me the creeps." He walked away, his hands deep in his pockets, his boots tramping down the wet brown leaves. The set of his shoulders was resolute, and he didn't look back.

Mariel readjusted the scarf over her hair and groped in her pocket for a tissue. She was stuffing it back into her pocket when she heard the cry again. Not the strong, full-bodied cry of an older child, but the high, thin wail of a small baby.

She looked toward Jake, whose bright jacket was barely visible through the wet tree trunks. She almost followed him. She certainly didn't want to lose him, and she didn't want him to think that she was slowing down. But how could she ignore a baby's cry?

"Mariel! Hurry up!" he called.

Impulsively Mariel pushed aside a rotting, rain-soaked board and entered the hut. It took her eyes a moment to adjust to the gloom, but when they did, she was astonished to see, lying on a bed of dry leaves and wrapped in a sturdy pink blanket, a tiny infant.

The baby's face was red and screwed up into a furious wail. Small fists flailed the air, and beneath the blanket little feet kicked.

"Jake!" Mariel called, falling to her knees and gathering the child into her arms. The baby stopped crying at once and stared, openmouthed, at Mariel.

She heard Jake crashing through the underbrush. He appeared at the entrance to the hut, his eyes wild. "What's the matter?"

For an answer, Mariel slowly rose to her feet and turned so that he could see the child. His eyes widened.

"It *was* a baby!" he said in a strangled voice.

The air between them seemed very heavy.

Jake's cap had fallen off, and he ran his fingers through his hair. It was dark brown and wavy, crisp with the cold, and it sprang up under his fingers as if it had a life of its own.

"I'll be damned," he said. He was regarding the baby with distaste.

"We can't leave it here," Mariel said.

"Of course not," he said. "How did it get here in the first place, that's what I'd like to know." Jake's sweeping gaze took in the dilapidated shelter, icicles forming where water dripped from the roof. His eyes met Mariel's. He looked angry and disgusted.

"Does it matter how she got here?" Mariel asked. She cradled the baby protectively in her arms and pressed her cheek to the top of the infant's head. Despite Jake's dismay, Mariel felt a thrill of excitement. She parted the blanket and counted ten fingers and ten toes. The baby was a girl, and

Mariel thought she might be a month old. She wore a pink flannel nightgown and a dry cloth diaper. She had a curl of pale yellow fuzz atop her head, and she was beautiful.

The baby made little mewling noises, not unlike those of a newborn kitten. Mariel's heart turned over when she realized that she must be hungry.

"Where are her parents?" Jake asked with barely controlled anger. He stomped out of the hut and stared into the woods. Mariel followed, the baby in her arms. They saw no sign of life other than themselves, only wet tree trunks half hidden in fog.

"Hello?" Jake called experimentally, hands cupped to his mouth. The word danced around them in echoes, but there was no answer.

"Is anyone there?" Jake shouted, but the forest only cried, "There...there...there," until the sound died.

"We can't leave this baby," Mariel said again.

Jake threw his head back in exasperation, staring up at the imprisoning branches as if hoping to find an answer. When, after a long moment, he looked back at Mariel, his eyes were grim.

"With the light fading, we can't let the baby slow our progress," he said, in a tone that struggled to be matter-of-fact.

"Of course not."

"And she's an added responsibility. I don't know anything about babies. Do you?"

Mariel bit her lip and gazed down into the chubby little face.

"Well, do you?" he demanded.

"Not a thing," she admitted.

"How are we going to take care of her?"

"We'll have to manage," she said, lifting her chin. "We can do it. We have no choice. We have to get her someplace warm and feed her and—and everything," Mariel said.

"What kind of person would leave a child out in this

weather? I'd like to get my hands on him," Jake said. He pulled his cap securely down over his forehead. "I'd better carry her."

"But I—"

"Your feet were slipping and sliding on the ice, I noticed. I'm wearing work boots with a tread. It's a matter of safety."

"I am perfectly capable—" Mariel began.

"Mariel," Jake said gruffly, "give her to me. You're wasting time."

Stung by Jake's tone, Mariel reluctantly handed the baby to him. The child settled against Jake's chest as if she felt perfectly comfortable there, the pink blanket incongruous against his bold plaid jacket. Mariel solicitously reached over and pulled a fold of the blanket over the baby's face to protect her from the sleet.

"Ready?" Jake said. He held the bundle awkwardly, and his face was stony, unreadable.

Mariel nodded silently, her heart in her throat. She wasn't responsible for the baby's being there, but Jake seemed to be angry with her. This situation was hard enough without having to take that kind of flak.

Making her way at a slower pace, Mariel followed Jake back through the woods to the road. Water dripped from bare branches; patches of dense fog filled the hollows. It wouldn't be long before it was completely dark. The thought of being stranded in these woods in the cold and the dark with sleet falling all around made her shiver.

If she talked, maybe she could jolt Jake into a better mood. If she kept talking, maybe she wouldn't think about the danger.

"Tell me about the town where you live," Mariel said to Jake, struggling to keep her teeth from chattering.

"Why?" His expression was uncompromising, and it only softened slightly when he glanced at Mariel. The baby was snuggled in his arms and wasn't making a peep.

"Because I want to know about it," she said.

"Now? While we're walking along in this sleet? Just after we find a baby in the woods?" he asked incredulously.

"I just want to talk," she said through gritted teeth. When he saw the dark look on her face—the first sign of negativity since they'd started out—he seemed to think better about resisting conversation and began to talk.

His voice was deep and reassuring as they walked through the darkening woods, the sleet cold and wet against their faces.

"Tellurian," Jake said, "is a picture-book town folded into a valley in these mountains, the Shenandoahs. I live on a tree-shaded street in a big, rambling house with old-fashioned plumbing and beautiful hardwood floors and a kitchen with oak cabinets that I built myself," he said, walking briskly to set their pace.

"Go on," she said, keeping her eyes on the road. Ahead was another hill, and she dreaded the climb.

"I buy houses and fix them up, then I sell them. I like working with wood, shaping a board into something beautiful. I like the clean smell of the wood, as well as the feel of it, and I like the way the people who buy my houses admire my handiwork."

"I can't believe you'd put so much of yourself into a house and then sell it," Mariel said breathlessly. They were walking so fast that she was having a hard time pulling enough air into her lungs. Jake was having no difficulty; he swung easily along beside her, planting his feet firmly, the baby hardly any weight at all.

"It's how I make money" was all he said, and she sensed that worldly possessions meant little to him. They walked on, tackling the hill. Mariel was too much out of breath to prod him with more questions. He looked down at her once or twice, and she tried not to let him see how tired she was. Once he slowed his pace slightly, which made walking easier. She sensed he was worried.

I can't let him down, she thought to herself, but at the foot of the hill, she slipped on loose rock and caught his arm, almost knocking him over in the process.

He steadied her, and she peered down at the baby. The infant was quiet, her face barely visible beneath the fold of the blanket. Jake looked at the baby, too, his expression grave.

"Mariel, we're going to have to come to a decision," he said as she leaned against him.

"About what?" she said wearily.

"About which way to go. If it were still only the two of us, I'd say let's forge ahead. But now that we've got this baby, I think we should go back to my truck."

Mariel's head shot up. "We've come all this way and you want to go back where we came from? No way," she said, starting to walk on and expecting him to follow. She hunched her shoulders and concentrated on moving one foot after the other, only to be halted by Jake's imperative tone.

"The truck's a place of shelter from the storm. We don't know how bad it's going to get."

She turned around. He was strong and stolid, standing there with sleet bouncing off his wide shoulders, the baby pressed to his chest. But was he right? *Should* they turn back?

"We already know there's no one for miles in that direction," she said stubbornly. "It's foolish to go back that way."

"We have no idea what lies ahead," he retorted. "Could be better, could be worse. Back there—" he jerked his head to indicate the road along which they'd come "—there's my truck. I vote we go that way."

"A house with heat sounds a lot more inviting. There's bound to be someone in this direction," she argued.

"Don't be stupid!"

"Stupid! May I remind you that we wouldn't be in this fix if you hadn't run me off the road?" Mariel's feet were like blocks of ice now. Her knee and hip joints ached. Never had she felt more miserable.

Darkness was gathering around them, but she saw Jake's brows draw together. Fear stabbed through her. What if he decided to go back to the truck, leaving her to struggle on toward the unknown? Yet she knew in her heart that to turn back would be the wrong thing to do. They already knew there was nothing there, and while the truck might afford a place to shelter from the weather, it wouldn't be warm. She'd rather take her chances on finding a house with welcoming inhabitants up ahead.

Jake was silent for a long time. Too long. Mariel shifted her weight from one foot to the other, wondering if her feet would ever be warm again.

Reluctantly she walked back to where Jake stood and nudged the blanket away from the baby's face. The child looked up at her, blue eyes wide and trusting. In that instant, Mariel felt the full weight of responsibility settle slowly onto her shoulders.

"This baby needs food, Jake. No telling how long it's been since she's eaten," Mariel said, quietly but urgently. She let the fabric fall across the baby's face again, and the child whimpered and nuzzled against Jake's coat.

Jake stared down at the infant in his arms, his brows drawn together. Mariel watched the expressions flit across his face, one after the other—worry, doubt, anguish and, finally, concession.

"All right," he said at last. "You're the one with the college degrees. We'll do it your way."

"What kind of dig is that?" she demanded.

"I didn't mean anything. Let's go." He started walking.

Now that she had convinced him, Mariel felt uncertain. What if they were indeed headed farther into the wilderness? But, no, she instinctively felt that the worst thing they could do would be to turn back.

Quickly, before she could change her mind, she wheeled and caught up with Jake. Anxiously she looked at the bundle that was the baby.

"Do you think she's all right?" she asked.

"She's moving around."

"I guess that's good. I hope wherever we end up, they have clean diapers."

"Dream on," Jake scoffed. After a few minutes he said, "It's getting so dark I can hardly see ahead of us. Can you get the flashlight out of my backpack?" He stopped and turned his back to her, and her fingers struggled with the fastening. He waited patiently, but the baby began to wail.

"You'll have to bend down. I can't reach in," said Mariel.

He bent his knees, and she fumbled for the flashlight. Finally her fingers closed around its handle and she withdrew it and switched it on. The beam bounced around the treetops before settling on the road.

"What else is in that pack of yours?" she asked.

"Some things left over from lunch."

"Anything that would feed a baby?"

"A bit of milk in the thermos."

"We may have to feed her soon." Mariel shone the light on the baby's face as they walked. The infant's eyes were scrunched tightly, and her toothless mouth stretched wider with every wail.

Now that it was dark, Mariel was beginning to feel exhausted. Putting one foot in front of the other was starting to feel like too much of an effort, but she knew she couldn't stop now that she had insisted that they continue in this direction. She wanted to act confident, to make Jake feel as if this had been the right decision.

"I don't see any signs of people," Jake said after they had walked in silence for half an hour or more. The baby had stopped crying after he opened his coat and settled her inside. Mariel supposed Jake was getting tired of carrying the baby, but he hadn't complained.

"Does the road seem narrower to you?" she asked anxiously. She focused the flashlight ahead of them, where the road seemed to become part of the forest.

"I don't know," Jake said. "You look bushed. Want me to carry the flashlight?"

She shook her head. "I'm fine," she said doggedly.

His keen look told her that she didn't look fine, but she was beyond caring. The skin of her face felt raw from the sleet, and the scarf that was supposed to be protecting her hair was soaked through. As a therapeutic exercise, she tried to remember all the warm fireplaces she'd ever known, like the cavernous one at camp where they'd toasted marshmallows on rainy summer nights, and the marble one at the museum, which was used only for patrons' parties in the winter, and the small but cozy fireplace in her apartment, where she would like to be right now.

They walked another hundred yards before the road tapered into a hard-packed dirt track.

"Now what do we do?" Mariel asked in bewilderment.

"We should have gone back to the truck," Jake said tightly.

"We still could," she pointed out.

He glared at her in exasperation. "Look at you. You're barely able to stand up. There's no way you can walk that far."

She stared at him bleakly, knowing it was true.

When he spoke again, Jake's voice was kind. "We'll sit down on that fallen log over there and rest for a few minutes while we figure out what to do."

Mariel's knees buckled just as she reached it. She hoped Jake hadn't noticed.

The infant had been quiet for a long time.

"Is the baby—?" she began fearfully.

"Asleep. I think." Jake opened his coat. The baby's eyes were closed, and her fists were curled against her cheeks like small pink shells.

"Would you hold her while I look around?" Jake asked.

"Of course." Mariel unbuttoned her coat. "I'll hug her inside, next to my sweater."

Carefully Jake transferred the sleeping baby to Mariel's waiting arms, and she drew her inside her coat.

Jake couldn't help feeling tender toward both of them. The baby was so helpless, and Mariel's face was white and strained. He wondered how much longer she'd be able to hold up—and how much longer she would have to.

"You must be freezing," he said, thinking that Mariel was really quite small and more fragile than he had thought.

She nodded. She looked extremely uncomfortable, but not one word of complaint had fallen from her lips throughout this journey, and he had to admire that.

"I won't go far away. Maybe I'd better take the flash-light," he said, picking it up from the log where Mariel had put it.

"I won't be able to see you," Mariel said shakily. Her eyes were like bottomless black pools, and he saw in that moment how scared she really was.

"I'll call to you from time to time," he said, and she nodded. He thought for a moment of leaving the flashlight with her, but what good would that do? He wouldn't be able to see a thing without it.

"Go ahead," Mariel said, wrapping herself around the baby. He saw that Mariel's teeth were chattering, and that she was trying to conceal it from him.

"I hate leaving you here in the pitch dark."

"Just go," she said. "The sooner you leave, the sooner you'll be back."

"Mariel..." He wanted to tell her something to reassure her, but he couldn't think of anything.

"Go," she whispered, her voice barely audible above the sound of the softly falling sleet.

With one last look at both of them—it was a scene that Jake knew would be imprinted on his mind for all time—he turned and forced himself to walk away.

THE FLASHLIGHT made eerie shadows among the trees as Jake walked away from her, and Mariel bent her head down to protect the baby's. She had never felt so completely and awfully alone.

But she wasn't alone. She had the baby.

Jake called to her once or twice, and eventually she saw the beam from the flashlight wavering in another direction. After that, she couldn't see Jake at all.

The baby fussed, and Mariel tried to see her face but couldn't. She felt water dripping off the tip of her nose, and the baby started to cry when it fell in her face. Mariel covered the infant's face with the dry end of her scarf and tried to comfort her, and eventually the cries tapered off into hiccups.

Now that she wasn't moving, Mariel realized the full extent of her exhaustion. She was so tired that she didn't have enough energy to get up off the log, but she thought she should rise and stamp her feet to get her circulation going. She forced herself to stand, surprised at how rubbery her legs felt. Somewhere overhead, a branch cracked under the weight of accu- mulated ice, crashing through tree limbs and landing on the ground behind her.

Mariel sat down again. She was trembling. There might be bears in these woods, or wolves. She hadn't seen the flashlight beam in a while, and Jake hadn't called. She hoped he was all right.

The cold had numbed her face and her feet and her hands. She thought of her parents, who had gone to Africa six months ago to help with famine-relief efforts. They would be warm. They might be on vacation for the Christmas holiday; her mother had written that they might go on a photo safari. It would be adventurous and different, she'd said.

I'll show you adventurous and different, Mariel thought. She wished she'd joined her parents for Christmas, as they'd asked her to. She wished she'd done anything but wander off the interstate and follow the directions of a bushy-bearded man at a Magic Minimart.

She closed her eyes, willing herself to be in Africa. She

saw gazelles leaping across her field of vision, antelopes, and an elephant lumbering toward a river in the distance. The weather was warm, and she was so tired that all she wanted to do was sleep.

Her head fell forward, and it was too much trouble to lift it. She would never open her eyes again, she would sleep here forever, and she would be warm....

"Oh, no, you won't," said a voice in front of her. "Open your eyes, Mariel."

She wanted to speak, but the words wouldn't come out. And her eyes wouldn't open.

"Mariel," said the voice, which was somehow strange and familiar at once.

With great effort, Mariel forced her eyelids apart. In front of her, only a few feet away, stood the little man from the Magic Minimart.

"Who—Who—" she stammered.

"You sound like a frozen owl. Get up! If you don't, you'll freeze to death!" The man's white beard bristled, and his blue eyes were stern.

"But—"

"Hurry up! You have to go find Jake!"

She didn't know what made her follow his instructions; certainly the last time she'd done what he suggested, she'd found herself in a mess. *This* mess. Nevertheless, she struggled to her feet.

"Now get going. No, not *that* way. The other way. That's right. Keep walking through the trees. You'll see the path. Take good care of the baby. She needs you." And with that, the man disappeared.

Mariel blinked her eyes. Had she really seen him, or had he been a dream, like the gazelles and the antelopes?

Her eyes had adjusted to the darkness. She saw a path leading through the trees, a path that she could have sworn hadn't been there before, and she stumbled along it, unsure whether it was the right thing to do. Jake had said to wait for him. And she hadn't heard a sound from him for a long time.

"Jake?" she called, but her voice was so weak that she was sure he wouldn't hear, and she wasn't surprised when he didn't answer.

A MAN ALONE would have a better chance of making it to safety than a man burdened with a woman and a child. Jake couldn't help it; he thought about hoofing it back to his truck, solo. Yet he knew he would never actually do it. Jake Travis was a man who lived up to his responsibilities, and he considered it his fault that Mariel was in this predicament.

He regretted his gruffness toward Mariel back at the hunter's blind, but he'd had to get her moving somehow, and being short with her had seemed like the only way to do it, considering all the commotion she was making over the baby. She sure liked that kid; she didn't seem to mind that the baby might slow them down.

Jake wasn't much for praying, but he found himself doing it. He had to find a place where they could get out of the sleet, a place where they could stay warm. He would probably survive a night in the open, but Mariel might not. No telling what being out in this weather would do to the baby. Jake hadn't mentioned it to Mariel, but the kid hadn't moved much after the last time it cried.

The dirt road continued for fifty yards or so. He veered off the path where a huge fallen tree blocked it, and he changed direction a few times, memorizing his path so that he would be able to return to Mariel and the baby.

The woods were thick here, and icicles had formed on all the branches. When he realized that he had wandered away from the road, he stopped and beamed the flashlight upward. He was shocked to see that he had come up against a sheer rock cliff.

He whistled under his breath. They wouldn't be moving on in this direction, at least. He stood there, taking stock.

Perhaps the downed tree he had passed earlier could form the basis for a shelter. They could dig out the ground beneath the trunk and crawl under it.

"Jake?"

He heard Mariel's voice close behind him. "Mariel, how did you find me?" he asked, because he had taken a circuitous route and had had no sense of her following him.

"It wasn't hard."

As Jake swung around, the beam from his light pinned Mariel's pale face in its glare, and he realized that she was barely able to stand. The baby made no sound, and that frightened him.

"You should have stayed where you were," he said, more sharply than he'd intended.

"I was worried. I called, and you didn't answer." She moved toward him, a wraithlike figure in the fog, and he reached out and drew her to him.

"Looks like this is the end of the road," he said, swinging the beam of the flashlight along the face of the cliff.

Mariel didn't answer, and when he looked down at her, he saw that the light had gone out of her eyes.

"Can you take the baby?" she asked shakily. "I want to sit down someplace."

He reached for the bundle, but as he did so, the dimming circle of light from the flashlight picked out a shadow on the face of the cliff.

"Wait," he said to Mariel, sprinting past her. He scraped his knuckles on the rock as he pulled away brambles. He discovered a waist-high hollow in the wet rock, and when he shone the light inside, the hollow expanded into a small cave. The remains of a camp fire were scattered across the sandy floor.

"Hey! I've found something!" he shouted. A glance at Mariel told him that she was swaying as if her feet would no longer support her weight. He rushed back to her and slid a supporting arm around her shoulders.

"Come on, you can make it. It's a cave, and inside it looks dry."

Wordlessly she let him propel her to the opening, and he carefully took the baby and handed her the flashlight to light her way. She stumbled once as she tried to climb into the opening, which formed a downward chute ending in the larger room of the cave. He felt helpless to assist her, and, since she was carrying the flashlight, he couldn't see her. All was dark.

Light returned when Mariel finally dragged herself into the cave. Carefully shielding the baby's face from the prickly brambles, Jake crawled through the chute. He literally fell into the cave, regaining his balance by grabbing a projecting overhang near the entrance.

The cave was about a foot higher than his six feet, and, judging from the evidence of old camp fires, a place where other people had found shelter in the past. It was dank and damp and smelled of wood smoke, but their having found it was nevertheless a kind of miracle.

The baby stirred against his chest. Mariel sprawled on the sand floor, clutching the flashlight.

Safe, Jake thought. *We're safe.*

Chapter Three

Mariel was shivering violently. A thread of blood trickled down the side of her face from a scratch inflicted by the brambles. She slumped against the smoke-blackened wall of the cave, scarcely able to sit up.

"Mariel? Are you all right? Mariel?" Jake crouched beside her, and the baby in his arms whimpered.

Mariel couldn't answer. She had thoughts, but they wouldn't shape themselves into words. She was thinking *dry,* and *hungry,* and *baby,* and then, finally, *What should we do about the baby?* which made her, with the utmost effort, focus her blurred vision on Jake and the infant nestled in his arms.

"Can you hold her for a minute?" Jake was saying urgently.

With difficulty, Mariel adjusted her position to form a lap, her gaze locked on Jake's. With his face only inches from hers, she was all too aware of the complexity of the emotions flooding his dark eyes. In that moment she wanted nothing more than to sink into their warm depths, but she denied herself that comfort. Right now, there was the baby to think about.

The infant was thrashing her head fretfully from side to side, and her tiny lips were tinted blue. Jake was alarmed about her condition. He had expected her to be rosy and pink, the way she had been when they found her.

"You can't hold the baby against your wet coat," Jake said. Mariel fumbled with her coat buttons with weak fingers until Jake said, "Let me."

Cradling the baby in the crook of one arm, he shed his soggy glove and, one after the other, slid the buttons through their buttonholes. Under her coat, Mariel wore a white lamb's wool sweater that buttoned up the front. The collar of the sweater was damp, but the rest of it was warm and dry. She wore corduroy slacks, and Jake carefully laid the baby in her lap.

Jake didn't know who worried him most, the baby or Mariel. The thing was, neither of them was in good shape. Mariel, with her difficulty in unbuttoning her coat and her vague, slurred speech, was showing symptoms of hypothermia, and as a camper from way back, Jake knew the dangers. Hypothermia, subnormal body temperature, could kill.

He had to raise her body temperature, and the baby's, too. Mariel was a small woman, fine-boned, with little body fat to keep her warm. The shivering would help, it was a good sign, but it wasn't enough.

Mariel's scarf had fallen away to reveal a mass of pale curls tumbling across her shoulders. The scratch on her face was still bleeding, and without thinking, Jake reached out to rub the blood away. His thumb caressed her cheek, and if she hadn't been shivering so much he might have forgotten his purpose. At the moment, all he wanted to think about was the rose-petal texture of her skin.

"The baby," she whispered.

Jake slid his hands between the tiny body and Mariel's thighs. The baby began to wail, and Mariel made a nest of her arms. As soon as the baby felt Mariel's warmth, she quieted.

"Her blanket is so wet," Mariel said, but the words gave

Jake hope—if not for the child, at least for Mariel. She was thinking, and that was a good sign.

Jake stripped the baby's blanket away. A quick inspection told him that the child's long flannel nightgown was damp around the bottom, but dry everywhere else, so he decided it was safe for the baby to wear. But he knew he'd better check Mariel's clothes, too.

"Jake," she said, moistening her lips with her tongue in a gesture that was unconsciously erotic. "I want to hold the baby next to my skin. We could warm each other."

"You want me to unbutton your sweater?" he asked.

"Please." She plucked at the tiny mother-of-pearl buttons marching in a straight row down her sweater front, but it was clear that she didn't have the strength to undo them herself.

Jake hesitated.

"Can you help?" she asked. Slowly he reached out and slid the top button out of its buttonhole. Damn, but the skin of her throat was soft.

It didn't take him long to part the sides of her sweater. Her bra seemed to be made out of cobwebs; he could see through it to the pale pink nipples, puckered from the cold. Mariel was exceptionally well endowed for a small woman, and Jake looked away, entirely unnerved by what the sight of her did to him. He wanted her. It was crazy. In her present state, he could easily take advantage of her, but of course he wouldn't. If only she weren't so beautiful and so desirable and so spirited; if only he weren't so powerfully attracted to her.

He forced himself to attend to business. He slid his arms under the baby and lifted it to Mariel's chest, guiding her arms around it. The baby hid her breasts, and he sighed in temporary relief.

He felt the bottoms of the blue corduroy pants that Mariel wore. The cuffs were cold and wet. He slid his hand upward to check the extent of the dampness, noting that she stiffened slightly as his hand went higher.

Her slacks were wet to the knee. "You're going to have to take these off," he said.

"Wh-what?"

"Take off those slacks. In your condition, it could be deadly to wear wet clothes," he said, clipping his words. He wasn't sure he was making any sense to her; hypothermia victims sometimes lacked judgment and reasoning power.

Mariel's only response was uncontrolled shivering, and that, added to the fact that she obviously was unable to do anything for herself, told Jake that he'd better act swiftly.

"I'm going to pull off your boots and socks and hang them up to dry," he told her. Mariel made no objection, and he slid the boots off her feet, then her cotton socks. Her feet were slim and white, dainty and well formed.

"Now the slacks," he said, reaching under her raincoat. "I'm going to pull these down over your hips. Help if you can."

He unfastened her belt buckle and yanked at the zipper, which immediately caught on a lace flounce in her underpants.

Swearing, Jake wiggled the zipper fastener, which refused to let go. It was firmly stuck.

He glanced at Mariel. Her eyes were open. She was watching him, her chin resting on the baby's head.

"Just what I need," he said tightly. "Another problem."

"Go ahead and rip it if you must," she said, looking embarrassed. He couldn't imagine *why* she would feel embarrassed. She was beautiful, her skin sweetly scented and inviting, her abdomen gently rounded between her hipbones. The triangle of lace that was giving him so much trouble did little to hide the pale curls beneath.

To his relief, when he again tried easing the zipper pull down the slide, the lace sprang free without tearing. In a moment Jake was shimmying the corduroy over Mariel's hipbones. She lifted her hips slightly, her eyes closed.

Jake found it difficult to look at her as if she were an object instead of an attractive woman with considerable sex appeal. He wasn't prepared for the way the sight of her body sent lightning sparking along every one of his nerve endings, and he had to resist to the fullest his impulse to let his fingers stray from their task.

"Tough duty," she said, as he was hanging her corduroys from a convenient rock projection, and he realized that she was trying to make light of the situation for his sake, as well as hers. When he turned back to her, she had already wrapped herself modestly in her coat. Her feet looked shriveled and cold, and that reminded him of his next task.

"I've got to build a fire right away," he said. Mariel's only reply was a nod.

Jake inspected their shelter. The cave was about seven feet wide and perhaps ten feet deep, its walls ledged, its floor a combination of rock and sand. As it played across the back of the cave, the beam of the flashlight picked out a small stack of firewood, which Jake knew was their salvation. It would be impossible to find dry wood outside.

He looked back at Mariel. She was still shivering, but not as violently as before. Her hair was drying in soft, fetching ringlets around her face; the folds of her coat barely hinted at the sweet curves of her body.

Tough duty, indeed, he thought to himself. It was going to be very hard for him to keep his behavior within the bounds of respectability. Mariel Evans was an exceptionally lovely woman. And he was a healthy, red-blooded American male.

MARIEL KEPT her eyes closed while Jake went about the serious business of building a fire. She was shaken by the force of her feelings. Jake's hands had touched her skin as little as possible, and yet, as innocent as his touch had been, she felt physically disturbed by it.

The warmth of the baby against her breasts felt oddly erotic. Jake's scent drifted up from the baby's skin—a woodsy after-shave underlaid by the pungent odor of wet wool. The baby's head pressed tightly against a nipple, engendering a heat that coursed through her veins and made her think about the crisp efficiency of Jake's hands as they had undressed her. The cold must have affected her in a very strange way. Who else in this predicament would be fantasizing about a man whom she had met only hours ago?

For once she regretted her penchant for wispy underwear. It was her secret indulgence. Now she thought she would have been better off with something utilitarian and opaque. Jake had gotten an eyeful, despite his feigned disinterest.

The baby made little snuffling noises, and she realized suddenly that it was rooting against her bare skin, searching for something to eat. It was basic instinct for a baby to do this, she figured. But suddenly she couldn't bear the stimulation of the warm, seeking mouth against her breast, and she abruptly changed position so that the baby's face rested against the soft cable knit of her sweater.

"I need something to use for tinder," Jake said, breaking into her thoughts.

Mariel was grateful for this reminder of practical matters. "Look in my bag. There's a notepad I seldom use."

Jake found the pad and crushed the paper into wads. When he dug into his pack and emerged with matches in a waterproof canister, Mariel thanked her lucky stars that she was sharing this experience with an outdoorsy man who had some survival skills.

The tinder caught fire, and the flames, carefully nurtured by Jake, spread to the kindling. Mariel watched him as he blew on the flames, coaxing them to life. His face was rugged, his nose blunt, his mouth mobile. Not like the baby's tiny rosebud mouth, but well-shaped, the lower lip slightly pendulous, the upper one deeply grooved.

He saw her watching him, but made no comment. When the fire was burning brightly, sending tongues of yellow flame leaping toward the ceiling of the cave, he sat up and removed his boots and wet socks, laying the socks on a ledge above the fire to dry. "How are you feeling?" he asked gruffly.

"Better."

He picked up her hand and closed his fingers around her wrist. "I want to check your pulse. I'm worried about you." He kept his eyes on his watch, and Mariel felt her pulse beating against his fingertips.

"You're fine," he said finally. He dropped her wrist and took a thermos from his pack. He poured milk into the metal cap and heated it over the flames. Mariel slid her feet even closer to the fire and flexed her toes in pleasure.

"Here," Jake said gruffly, holding out the cup of warm milk.

"We should save it for the baby."

"You need it. I'll heat some for her after you're through," he told her.

But Mariel's hand shook so much that she couldn't wrap her fingers around the cup.

"I'll help." Leaning toward her, Jake placed his hand over hers and guided the cup to her lips. She drank slowly, the milk warming her as it went down. It was no more than two or three ounces, but Mariel immediately began to feel stronger, and soon she stopped shivering. The fire was a roaring blaze now, the smoke disappearing into a crack in the cave's ceiling.

Jake's expression was unreadable in the firelight. He knelt beside her, his jacket open to reveal a gray turtleneck sweater that defined the firm pectoral muscles underneath. Mariel drew a long, deep breath, hoping to infuse her addled brain with clarity and judgment. The tingle she felt was not due to the return of warmth to her half-frozen limbs; it was directly attributable to the presence of Jake Travis.

She pulled herself together when the baby began to whimper. "We'd better feed her," she told him, gazing at the bundle in her arms. She wondered what, if any, effect exposure to the cold had had on the child. She looked better now, Mariel thought.

"Aren't babies supposed to drink formula from a can, not cow's milk?" Jake asked anxiously.

"We don't have any formula," she reminded him.

"I don't want to harm the baby, that's all," he said.

For someone who had reacted with anger at his first sight of the baby, Jake had softened quite a bit. He looked so concerned that Mariel's heart went out to him.

"We're talking survival here. We have no choice," she said.

"How much milk would a baby drink at one feeding, anyway?"

"I have no idea," Mariel admitted. They both looked at the baby, trying to assess her capacity.

"She's not very big. Her stomach couldn't hold much," Jake said.

"Three ounces?"

"Maybe," he agreed. "How are we going to feed her?"

"I don't know."

They looked at each other blankly.

"Maybe if we soaked a piece of cloth in the milk, she could suck on it. I saw that in a movie once. Trouble is, they were feeding motherless puppies," Jake said ruefully.

"I carry eyedrops in my purse," Mariel said. "Maybe the eyedropper?"

"It might work."

"Get it, please. There's an unopened package of eyedrops in my cosmetic bag," she said. The baby began to cry, the noise ricocheting off the cave's walls so that no more discussion was possible.

"This must be it," Jake said, holding the box aloft. He tore off the cellophane wrapper.

Mariel raised her voice to be heard over the baby's wails. "The eyedropper should be wrapped in plastic," she said.

Jake held it up for her inspection. "Is it sterile?"

"It says so on the box," she said. "How about the milk? Do you suppose it needs to be sterilized?" She had a vague memory from her childhood of a neighbor boiling baby bottles in a big pan on her stove. She didn't know if anyone still did that.

"Does milk have a lot of germs?"

Mariel didn't know. She shrugged her shoulders.

"I could boil the milk in my thermos lid," he said. "That might take care of it."

"What about the taste? I think boiled milk tastes awful."

"We don't know if she'll drink cow's milk anyway, boiled or unboiled," Jake said. They both regarded the baby, whose face was red from crying. She looked furious.

"If she doesn't eat something, she'll die," Mariel said.

"So back to the question—do we boil the milk?"

Mariel tried to think. She had friends who had babies, but she'd never paid much attention to their care. It seemed to her that her friend Carole had fed her baby canned baby formula, then switched to cow's milk poured directly into the baby bottle from a milk bottle kept in the refrigerator. Had that been at three months? Or had the baby been on formula for six months?

Mariel couldn't recall. She also didn't know the age of this baby, who appeared to be only a month or two old. But then, Mariel didn't know anything about babies. Her college degrees hadn't prepared her for a situation like this one. All she knew was that they'd better make a fast decision.

She decided. "We'll warm the milk and give it to her as it is, but first, you'd better sterilize the thermos lid by boiling water in it, don't you think?" she asked Jake.

"I don't know what I think," he said through tight lips. "Mostly what I think is that we're ill-equipped to take care of a kid."

"I couldn't agree with you more," Mariel said, failing to control the edginess in her tone.

Jake went outside for water. While he was boiling it in the

metal lid, the baby's crying grew louder and more frantic, straining their frayed nerves to the breaking point.

"Can't you keep her quiet?" Jake asked sharply.

"I'm trying," said Mariel over the din. "Hurry up, will you?"

Jake growled, "I'm doing this as fast as I can," whereupon Mariel regretted her own testiness. She turned her attention to the baby again, smoothing the golden hair, rubbing the little back under the nightgown, all to no avail. The baby was hungry, and that was that.

Jake poured out the boiled water, since there was nowhere to keep it, and sniffed the thermos lid. Mariel almost smiled, thinking that smelling it wasn't going to tell him if germs were present, germs not necessarily having odors.

Anyway, what kind of germs were they worried about? Didn't babies put all kinds of things in their mouths, such as key chains that had dropped on the floor, and the dog's chewy pieces of rawhide? And didn't most babies survive such adventures? Someday Mariel would look up the answers to all these questions. She realized that baby care was a great gap in her knowledge.

Jake, apparently satisfied that the lid from his thermos was clean enough, heated a bit of milk and drew some of it into the eyedropper.

"Here," he said, carefully transferring the dropper to Mariel's outstretched hand. She smiled a silent thank-you when their hands touched.

With Jake watching over her shoulder, Mariel dribbled a few drops of milk into the baby's open mouth. The infant stopped crying immediately and looked mystified.

"There, that's better, isn't it?" crooned Mariel. The baby closed her lips around the eyedropper, her eyes never leaving Mariel's face.

The dropper wasn't the best feeding apparatus in the world, because it wasn't suited for sucking, something that the baby expected to be able to do. As fast as Mariel filled the eyedropper, the baby drank, but it was frustrating to watch the baby trying to suck on the hard plastic tube and to listen to her fussing while Mariel refilled it.

"Damned inefficient," Jake said.

Mariel glared at him. "Would you like to try it?"

"No, no," he said, backing away. He watched them for a few more moments. "I feel helpless," he said, giving her the idea that it was an admission that he seldom, if ever, made. "Usually when something needs doing, I can make something to do the job. I'm a fair plumber, a pretty good electrician, and a bang-up carpenter. This has me stumped."

"Me too," she offered, and he grinned at her.

After she had swallowed three or four ounces of milk, the baby stopped eating and puckered her little face as if she were going to cry again.

"Uh-oh," said Jake. "I think something's wrong."

"She has to be burped."

"Burped? How?"

"She's supposed to be patted on the back. I think it brings up the air bubbles."

"Give her to me. I'll try it."

Carefully he took the baby from Mariel.

"You'll have to drape her over your shoulder," Mariel said.

"There, there," Jake said to the baby in a soothing voice.

"She's waiting for you to do something," Mariel told him. She wanted to giggle; Jake, so masculine and rugged, looked absurd with the baby slung over his shoulder. He was holding her as if she were a sack of wood chips.

Jake thumped the baby between the shoulder blades, producing nothing but a startled look.

"Not so hard," Mariel hastened to say, and when Jake experimented with a few tentative taps, the baby obliged by producing a sonorous belch.

"That was pretty good, wasn't it?" Jake asked, sounding smug.

"Better than I could have done," Mariel said, meaning it.

The immediate problem of hunger solved, Mariel reached over and gingerly felt the baby's diaper.

"She's sopping wet."

"Nowhere in this cave have I found a stack of diapers. Have I?" Jake said to the baby, who yawned.

"If my scarf weren't so wet, we might use it as a diaper," Mariel said, though she wasn't at all sure about it's suitability.

The discarded scarf lay in a damp heap on the sand, its fringe clumped together. "It's too stiff and woolly. Babies' diapers need to be soft, like cotton. At least I know that much," Jake said. He was still jaunty from his success at bringing up the baby's air bubble.

"Well, we've got to think of something," Mariel said, staring pensively at the baby, who looked back at her unblinkingly and with great interest. There was trust in that gaze, and Mariel wondered how on earth they were going to meet the complex needs of an infant using only the things they had on hand.

"I know," Jake said suddenly.

"What?"

"What we can use for diapers."

"Is it bigger than a breadbox?" Mariel asked, with more than a hint of sarcasm.

"Never mind. Here, take the baby and turn your head," he told her.

She took the baby, but what he'd said didn't register until he began unbuckling his belt.

"You're not going to take off your clothes?" Mariel blurted out.

"Only my long johns. They'll make good diapers," he replied, seemingly unperturbed.

"Oh," Mariel said faintly. There was nowhere in this cave where he could go for privacy. He'd have to take his pants off in front of her.

"Don't worry—I'm wearing briefs underneath. I often dress warmly at this time of year. In my job, I sometimes have to work in unheated areas."

Mariel could have sworn that she saw the hint of a grin. "Don't we have something else we can use?" she asked skeptically.

"Do you have a better idea, Mariel?"

She realized the futility and folly of objecting to what he had in mind. "No. *No*. It sounds fine. Just do it, okay?"

"Don't look at me, if it'll embarrass you," he said, mollified.

Mariel turned her head away and tried to ignore the sounds of his undressing until she discovered that, by squinting out of the corners of her eyes, she could see him clearly by the light of the fire.

First he shucked off his boots, and then his wool socks, which he hung to dry above the fire. Then, slowly and deliberately, he unbuckled his belt.

She managed to close her eyes before he glanced sharply in her direction, but at the sound of the zipper, she peeked under her lids.

Jake's worn jeans were molded to his body as if they had grown there, and their dampness revealed the firmness of his thighs, the compact curves of his buttocks.

As graceful as a panther, he stepped out of the jeans and dropped them onto the ledge next to his socks. As he pulled down his white cotton-knit long johns, Mariel saw that his thighs were muscled and lightly furred with dark hair. The briefs he wore underneath were brief indeed, revealing a tapering V of hair that disappeared under the waistband, near the well-defined bulge below. She could hardly pull her eyes away as he stood, clad only in turtleneck and briefs, the hard contours of his body limned by firelight and gilded by its glow.

She caught her breath at the sight of him, thinking that she'd never seen a man who so exuded sexuality. Even here, in this miserable cave, Jake Travis had that indefinable animal magnetism that made woman weak, and though it could be argued that she was already weak, her ordeal hadn't caused the catch in her throat when she looked at him, or the tension vibrating just below her skin.

She had been aware of his arresting good looks from the moment they met. His mere touch had been enough to banish her cold-induced stupor. Now that she was being treated to the full impact of his physical presence, she was brought up short by a confusing tangle of emotions.

He caught her staring at him. It might have been her imagination, but he seemed to draw himself up to his full height, a desirable male exhibiting himself more fully to a female who was clearly admiring.

"I thought you weren't planning to look," he said, sounding amused.

"I'm not *looking,*" she lied. "I have to aim my eyes somewhere, after all."

"I never thought about it that way," he said, but she knew he was laughing at her.

Let him, she told herself. She'd have had to be deaf, dumb and blind to ignore the chemistry between them, but she was well aware that in this survival situation it could only make things more difficult.

"I think I'll leave my jeans beside the fire until they dry," he said. She made no comment.

Jake anchored his jeans to a ledge above the fire with a rock, and then he knelt and withdrew a knife from his pack, his movements swift and economical. The firelight emphasized the braided muscles of his thighs and calves as he squatted and spread his discarded long johns across his knees. His hair was dark, and longer than she had thought at first; it had sprung into a shining frame for his face. Intent on his task, he didn't look up, seeming totally unaware that she was observing him so closely.

There was something strange and elemental in this scene.

Mariel could almost imagine that they were cave dwellers in some ancient age, making do with what was available. He was the provider and she the mother of the child who slept in her arms, snug and warm....

She awoke with a start. Jake was shaking her arm, his face contorted with fear.

"Don't go to sleep!" he said.

"I only—"

"It's all right," he said, the sparks fading from his eyes and his shoulders slumping when he realized that she had only been drowsing.

"I must have dropped off for a moment," she began, but he silenced her with a finger across her lips.

"One moment you were wide awake, watching me work, and the next minute your head was nodding and you didn't hear me say your name. I thought—"

"I'm fine," she said. She shifted her position to avoid the rock that was biting into her backbone, wondering how she could have slept while so uncomfortable.

He checked her pulse, holding tight to her wrist. "Normal," he pronounced.

"I told you I'm okay," she said.

"I'm still worried about hypothermia. You shouldn't sleep yet—it could be dangerous."

"I'll try to stay awake," she promised. She nearly told him about the appearance of the man with the white bushy beard in the woods earlier, when she had almost fallen asleep. Jake didn't seem to be in the mood to hear a fanciful story, but she couldn't help musing over what she had seen. Was the little man real? Or had he been a dream?

Jake went back to the fire, squatting there as he contemplated the destruction of his long underwear.

"I wonder what size a diaper is," he mused.

"She's a small baby," Mariel answered. "Cut them into large pieces, and we'll fold them to the size we need." The baby in her arms slept openmouthed, her small puffs of breath stirring the fuzz of Mariel's sweater. Her upturned nose was smaller than the tip of Mariel's thumb, and her cheeks were fat and round. She looked like a little cherub, and already Mariel knew that if it were necessary, she wouldn't hesitate to put her life on the line for this baby.

She would have liked to ask Jake if he felt the same way, but he was making short work of cutting up his long johns, holding up the resulting pieces of fabric for her approval.

"Okay," she said when he had finished. "Let's change her diaper."

"You deserve the honors," Jake said.

"I've never diapered a baby."

"Neither have I," he confessed.

Mariel sighed. "All right, I'll try. We need a clean place to lay her down," she said.

There was only the sandy floor. "Here," Jake said, spreading his jacket over the sand. The inside was warm and dry, and Mariel carefully lifted the baby out of her coat and laid her on the jacket lining. She quickly closed her sweater over her breasts, but not before Jake saw a tantalizing glimpse of her lacy bra.

Mariel unpinned the diaper. The baby awoke, fussed briefly, then saw Mariel's face and began to kick and coo.

"She acts as if life's going on as usual," commented Jake, who looked on from above, his arms folded over his chest.

"Maybe that's why she's here. To remind us that it should," Mariel said briskly, sliding the clean white cotton knit beneath the baby's buttocks.

Mariel's observation took Jake by surprise. For one thing, it made him look at this situation in a new way. For another, it clued him in to Mariel's thought processes. He liked her knack for putting a positive spin on things.

"There," Mariel said, smiling down at the baby. The child waved her fists in the air, and Mariel gathered her into her arms. "Is her blanket dry yet?"

Jake checked. "Nope," he said, hoping that Mariel would open her sweater again.

While he was thinking that, Mariel said, "You'd better put this dirty diaper outside. If only we had something to wash it in, like a pan of some kind."

Jake went back to the stack of firewood and emerged from the shadows triumphantly, a beat-up old tin pot in his hand. The bottom was fire-blackened, but as far as Jake could see, it didn't have any holes.

"I'll set it out to catch water," Jake said, and, to his disappointment, Mariel had already snuggled the baby inside her sweater when he returned.

"Are you warm enough?" he asked her.

She nodded, barely able to keep her eyes open.

Jake regarded her for a moment. Her cheeks were rosy again, and she had brushed her hair behind her ears. She had Dresden-doll coloring, delicate and comely, and her eyes sparkled. It was all he could do not to bend over and kiss her pink lips.

He did lean closer, using the baby as an excuse. "She's pretty, isn't she?" he asked, but he wasn't looking at the baby. He was studying the cleft in Mariel's chin, hoping she wouldn't notice.

"She's a wonderful baby," Mariel agreed. "You like her, don't you?" She watched Jake anxiously for his response. Somehow it seemed important that he love this infant, that he harbor the same tender feelings toward her that she did.

Jake didn't answer right away. "She's okay, I guess," he said reluctantly, but from his tone of voice Mariel knew that he was as taken with the baby as she was.

They sat silently, watching the baby breathe. Smoke curled up from the fire toward some unseen outlet in the cave roof, and sparks danced in an occasional gust of wind that penetrated the sheltering brambles at the entrance. Outside, the sleet continued to fall, holding them prisoner.

"There's half a sandwich in my pack," Jake said quietly.

"We'll split it," Mariel said, and soon he had cut the sandwich into two portions and was handing one to her. Jake heated water in the thermos cap, and they sipped alternately from it.

"I have an apple, too. We can eat it in the morning," Jake said.

Mariel nodded, and after a while he saw her head falling to one side. She jerked it up again.

"Let's talk, so you won't go to sleep," he said.

"You talk," she said.

"That would put you to sleep for sure. Tell me about where you live, your family, your job."

Mariel sighed and shifted position again. "I live in an apartment with a bay window overlooking a gar- den—" she began, but he interrupted her.

"What kind of garden? Vegetables? Flowers?"

"Both, but I love the flowers best. Do you know that the Victorians wrote a language of the flowers? Mistletoe, for instance. It means 'Give me a kiss.'" She stopped talking suddenly, looking flustered.

To fill the gap in the conversation, Jake said, "Is your apartment big? Small?"

"Two bedrooms. And it's not far from the museum where I work," she told him.

"I never knew anyone who was a folklorist."

"I'm surprised. In this part of Virginia, there are probably all kinds of stories the local people tell, legends to be collected."

"Maybe so. I don't run into them much, that's all. I've only been in Virginia for a short time—moved here from Atlanta around Christmastime three years ago, in fact. I think I left Atlanta mostly *because* it was Christmas, because that way I could avoid all the hoopla that I wasn't part of," Jake said.

"Well, my family was small, since I was an only child, but I always loved the 'hoopla,'" said Mariel.

"Must be nice," Jake said noncommittally.

"I guess I was spoiled, in a way. Everything I wished for—no matter how silly—somehow came true at Christmas. A bicycle once, a puppy another year, my grandparents flying in for a visit—all were wishes of mine."

"I think I would have wished for a Lamborghini when I was sixteen, and maybe a football scholarship, even though I never played," Jake said with a grin.

"Well, my wishes had to be within reason. I mean, it wouldn't have done any good to wish for the moon on a silver platter, because it's an impossibility."

"These three wishes you're always making... Now that you're an adult, don't you feel ridiculous doing it?" he asked curiously.

"Why would I? Wishes *can* come true, Jake. Magic *can* happen. There *are* such things as miracles," she said.

"Hogwash," he said amiably.

"Hogwash! Listen, Jake Travis, it was no mere coincidence that you found this cave when we needed it. Or that we happened along when the baby needed us. And let me ask you this—how often do you have milk left in your thermos after lunch?"

His eyes shone mischievously as he bent to stir the fire. "Often, in fact. Sometimes the guys on the job go to a convenience store and pick up a six-pack of cola. Or, like today, it's cold and somebody offers us a hot drink for lunch," he said.

"Okay, so I struck out on that last one. But there's still the cave and the baby. Don't forget that," she said.

"It's probably safe for you to sleep now."

"You're ready to shut me up, right?" she asked him with a glint of humor.

"Not exactly," he hedged, thinking that he could go on listening to her high musical voice all night long. She had a way of talking that slid up and down the scales, a sound most pleasing to the ear. To his ear, at any rate.

"I'm glad to hear that. Tomorrow I may want to talk a lot more. You're a good listener, Jake."

It was a compliment he hadn't heard before, or at least couldn't remember hearing, which amounted to the same thing. He wasn't sure if he should say thank you, so he only nodded his head slightly. Mariel wasn't like any women he knew; most of them were practical and down-to-earth. Not that Mariel wasn't, but she had another, more evanescent quality too, one that he couldn't quite put his finger on. She had a lot of charm, that was for sure.

"There's no place to stretch out except on the sand. If you'd like, I'll hold the baby while you get settled," he said.

"At least we're not out in the cold," she answered as he took the child in his arms.

"And to think it's all because of magic," he said, teasing her.

"I'm glad you're starting to think my way," she tossed back, her eyes sparkling at him, and he knew that she knew that he didn't really believe, and that it was all right. He wouldn't put it past her to work on him some more, and for some reason, he was actually looking forward to it, to sparring with her, to watching her expressive face as she spoke so earnestly.

"I'm ready," she said when she had arranged herself on the sand, and Jake handed the child to her. Mariel tucked the baby inside her sweater again and lay down on her side, flexing her legs to curve her body protectively around the child and pillowing her head on her tote bag.

"Aren't you going to sleep?" she asked, looking up at him. Her eyes were bright and glowing.

The two of them had established a camaraderie, a rapport. He hoped she felt it as strongly as he did.

"I'm going to sit up for a while. I want to keep an eye on the fire," he said, because he knew that he could not lie down beside her without touching her.

The fire crackled and spit, and he saw Mariel tenderly

stroking the pale golden hair on the baby's head. He wished it was him she was comforting.

Mariel seemed to represent everything that he didn't have in his life, everything that other people lived for, not him. He wasn't normally a sentimental guy, so maybe it was that she had taken such care to remind him of the Christmas season, or maybe it was that she looked so Madonna-like with the baby in her arms. He tried to swallow the lump in his throat, but it wouldn't go away.

When Mariel was asleep, Jake got up and brought in the thermos cap, which he had set out earlier to catch water. He heated the water and sipped it slowly, resting on his haunches. After a while, he dropped another log on the fire and lay down as far from Mariel and the baby as he deemed necessary, wrapped in his wool jacket. He was sleeping lightly when he heard Mariel moan. He shot up, instantly alert.

"Mariel?" he said.

"Cold," she muttered, and was quiet.

He felt her corduroys, which were still hanging from the ledge, but they were still damp. All Jake could think of to do was what he had wanted to do all along. He nestled himself against the back of Mariel's body and twined his legs around hers for warmth. She murmured something indistinct, and he reached under her coat and slid his warm hands up along her rib cage. Her ribs seemed not like mere bones, but like a house to enclose her beating heart.

Her heart throbbed beneath his fingertips, and his thumbs brushed the soft underside of her breasts. After a few moments, his breathing automatically synchronized with hers. He smelled the wildflower scent of Mariel's shampoo, blended with the sweet, milky fragrance of the baby, and it was all he could do not to bury his face in the nape of Mariel's neck.

Jake didn't know if Mariel realized he was there, but it didn't matter. All that mattered was her warmth, and her softness, and that neither of them was alone in the dark.

Chapter Four

When Mariel awoke, she didn't know where she was. Her joints and muscles hurt, and a baby was crying.

She opened her eyes. A few feet away, glowing coals were a red eye in the dark.

All at once, Mariel remembered. The accident. Their trek along the icy road. The baby. The cave. Her exhaustion. And Jake. Where was he?

Something moved behind her, and she stiffened in alarm before she realized that it was Jake and that his legs were wrapped around hers. She twisted away as he sat up and said in a groggy tone, "Maybe the baby's hungry." He went to stir the fire, and it blazed brighter.

"You were—" she began.

"I was keeping you warm. You were cold."

"I was asleep," she said, with as much dignity as she could muster.

"So was I," he said. He got up and felt his jeans, which still hung by the fire. They were still wet, and he moved them closer to the flames, his back toward her.

"I didn't ask you to keep me warm," Mariel said.

"You cried out in your sleep." He turned and leveled a serious gaze at her. "I was only trying to help."

Mariel didn't know whether to thank him or not, but at that moment the baby started wailing at the top of her lungs.

Thankful for the distraction, Mariel sat up and studied the infant. She was putting all her energy into screaming, and one tiny pink foot had escaped the nightgown.

Jake was bringing a fresh log for the fire. "Jessica," Mariel said, raising her voice over the baby's cries. "I'm going to call her Jessica."

Jake looked harried. "Is that the most important thing you can think about, with her carrying on like that?" he asked, his eyebrows lifting.

"She has to have a name. We can't keep calling her 'the baby,'" said Mariel. Carefully she spread the baby on her lap and checked the diaper. Soaked. No wonder she was crying.

Jake had already poured milk into the metal cap and set it on a hot rock to warm.

"Diaper time again," Mariel said. Jake's hair was standing up in clumps, and he needed a shave. She didn't look so terrific, either, she imagined. She felt grungy and disheveled, and she needed to relieve herself.

Jake brought another piece of his long johns, took off his jacket, and spread it out. Mariel laid the baby—*Jessica*, she reminded herself—on it.

Jake felt one of the baby's arms. "She's cold. We should keep her covered while you're doing this," he said. He brought the pink blanket, which was finally dry, and folded it across Jessica, who was punching her arms and legs into the air as if against an unseen assailant.

"Your turn for this chore," she said to Jake above the noise. His mouth dropped open.

"I can't—"

"Of course you can," she said, smiling encouragingly.

"I told you, I've never changed a diaper," he said in bewilderment.

"Neither had I until last night," she reminded him.

"But she's kicking," he said, eyeing Jessica's flailing legs. He looked up at Mariel, who had started pulling on her boots while he was voicing his objections. "Where are you going?" he demanded.

"Out." She stood up, surprised that she felt so strong. Her knees gave nary a wobble. She took a few experimental steps, testing them out.

"Why are you going out?"

Mariel regarded him with exasperation.

"I don't see any facilities in here," she pointed out.

It was almost comical, the way he clamped his mouth shut.

"Oh," he said. "Well, uh, when you get outside the cave, turn to your left. There's a chunk of rock that provides shelter from the wind. And you'd better take the flashlight," he said. He was still looking at Jessica's wet diaper, steeling himself to remove it.

She bent, picked up the flashlight, and said sweetly, "Be careful not to stick her with a pin, won't you?" She was rewarded by a perplexed expression, and it was all she could do to keep from laughing when she emerged from the cave.

It had stopped sleeting, but at this predawn hour, it was still dark. Mariel found the boulder, took care of business and, mindful of the scratch on her face, negotiated the brambles at the cave entrance with care. Once safely inside, she switched off the flashlight and sat down beside Jake.

"How'd you do?" she asked. He was squeezing a dropperful of milk into Jessica's mouth, concentrating mightily on the task.

"It'd be a lot easier if you could nail diapers on kids. I didn't poke *her* with the pin, but I stuck myself." He held up his pricked finger for her to see.

"But you survived," she pointed out.

"Barely. So did the baby—barely. That was supposed to be a pun," he said.

"Cute, Jake. Very cute. How much milk is left, by the way?" she asked.

"A few ounces. I'm not going to give her much this feeding. We'll need some for the morning."

"What time is it now?"

"Three o'clock in the morning."

"It doesn't seem like it. I feel so wide awake," Mariel said. She drew her bare legs under her for warmth and watched Jake's hands as they ministered so gently to the baby. They were capable hands, and she would trust them with her life. In fact, she had. She felt a warming toward him and wondered how he felt about her.

"Why did you name her Jessica?" Jake asked.

Mariel was surprised. She hadn't expected conversation. "I've always like the name," she told him.

"Any special reason?"

"When I was in high school, dreaming about a home and family, as many girls do, I chose the names for all four of my children," she said.

He lifted his head and grinned at her. "Four?"

"I was going to have a station wagon, and I wanted to fill it with kids. I'd take them to swimming lessons in the summer, to children's concerts in the park, and all kinds of things. Jessica, Mark, Joanna and Matthew. Those were their names. But—" she sighed "—I never bought that station wagon."

"Regrets?"

"A few. I love my job. I just wish there was something *more*."

"Like a Jessica?" he probed, glancing at her.

"I've thought about becoming a single mother. I haven't quite figured out how, that's all."

"Shouldn't be too hard, for a woman who looks like you," he said quietly.

"Oh, that's not the problem. But there are only so many ways to go about acquiring a child. If a single woman wants a baby, she can be artificially inseminated, but it's too expensive for me to contemplate. Or she can ask a male friend to be the father, but then, what if he expects to be part of the child's life, as he has every right to do? Would I have to invite him to birthday parties and Christmas dinners for the next twenty years? I've never known a man that I wanted to put up with for that long. So that leaves adoption,'' she said.

Jake fed Jessica the last drops of milk from the thermos cap. "I guess you've thought about it a lot."

"And then I find a baby in the woods. It seems—it seems like a kind of gift," she said.

"She belongs to someone," Jake said, turning the drowsy infant over his shoulder.

"But to whom? And why was she there? It's almost as if someone knew we would come along to save her," Mariel said as Jessica twisted her head around to look at her. Jake was patting the baby's back, to no avail.

"She doesn't want to burp," he said.

"She will. Won't you, Jessica, darling? Come on, burp for us," coaxed Mariel.

As if on cue, Jessica brought up a bubble of air and triumphantly waved a fist in the air.

"Let me hold her for a while. You can go back to sleep," Jake said.

Mariel propped herself against the wall of the cave. "I'm not tired. I must have really been out of it before," she said. She was remembering how cozy and warm she'd felt; now she knew that it had been because of Jake's closeness. It had been his warmth, his body heat seeping through her clothes, making her comfortable, letting her sleep.

"You were dead to the world," Jake confirmed. He had derived great comfort from her. He'd have liked her to know that. And yet it seemed inappropriate to talk about it.

"It's stopped sleeting," Mariel said.

"Then we can get an early start. We should leave as soon as the sun rises," he replied.

"Sunrise is only a few hours away."

"That's why I think you should sleep," he said. "You'll need all your energy for whatever happens."

"What do you think will happen?" she asked, looking slightly alarmed.

"I don't know. But if anyone had predicted when we set out during the storm that we'd be spending the night in this cave while trying to figure out how to take care of an infant, I would have accused him of partaking of illegal hallucinogens."

"Have *you* ever done that?"

"No. What kind of question is that, anyway?" he said, halfway offended.

"One designed to find out about your habits."

"Not smart. Besides, I could have lied."

"You wouldn't."

"How do you know?"

"Because you aren't that kind of guy. You were up-front with me from the beginning by admitting that the accident was your fault, that your brakes didn't work. Any lawyer would caution you not to admit liability, but you had to tell the truth. It's in your nature," she said.

He found this conversation fascinating, not only because of where it was going, but also because it covered new territory. Usually women asked if he had been married, if he'd fathered any children, and if there was a serious relationship in his life. Also how much money he made; the answer often caused them to beat a hasty retreat.

"So," he said easily, massaging Jessica's back, "are you always so good at instant character analysis?"

"Most of the time. Men don't like it."

"Why?"

"They don't like being figured out."

"Do I?"

"You're humoring me, so you'll put up with it," she told him.

"Hmm..." he said, sliding the baby into his lap. He moved his forefinger back and forth in front of the tiny face, and the baby's Wedgwood-blue eyes tracked it.

"It's Christmas Eve day," Mariel said, stretching. "It doesn't seem much like it, does it?"

He shrugged. "What's the big deal?" he said.

She stared at him. "Well, tomorrow we will celebrate the birth of Christ, for one thing," she said. "Aren't you a Christian?"

"Supposedly. I lived in a couple of so-called Christian foster homes when I was a kid. They believed in 'Spare the rod, spoil the child,' which forever spoiled Christianity for me."

"They beat you?"

"Me and the other kids who lived there," he said.

Jessica was sound asleep in his lap. She looked sweet and innocent and supremely helpless.

"Well, my experience of religion was Sunday school and church picnics and marching in place in front of the pew when we sang 'Onward Christian Soldiers.' And later, serving as an acolyte and reading part of the Christmas Eve service. Besides," Mariel added, "I can't understand anyone who would hit a child."

"It shouldn't happen. Ever. For any reason," Jake said tersely.

"In my house, it wouldn't. I mean, if I were lucky enough to have a child." She gazed longingly at Jessica.

"If *I* had a child, I wouldn't fill her head with all this Christmas nonsense. Santa sliding down the chimney, bringing gifts for good little girls and boys. What if you've been good and there are no gifts?" Jake asked. He meant the question to be rhetorical, and he was surprised when Mariel shot back an answer.

"The child would be soured on the whole Christmas idea, right? Like you, right?"

"Right." The word was no more than a growl deep in his throat.

"Well," she said, "no matter what you think, it's still Christmas Eve day. And I'm going to keep the season, no matter what." To Jake that seemed like a silly statement, considering that they didn't know what the day would bring. He only hoped she wouldn't break into several choruses of "Deck the Halls with Boughs of Holly" while they were confined to this damn cave.

"I'm going to catch a few more Zs," he told her, thoroughly annoyed with all this sweetness and light.

"Maybe that's a good idea," she agreed, but he thought it was mostly because she didn't want to talk to him anymore.

"Who's going to hold the baby?" she asked.

"I will. In fact, I think we should sandwich her between us. The fire's getting low, and we only have a few sticks of firewood left. It's bound to get colder in here."

She seemed uncertain, looking at him out of the corners of wide eyes.

"Go ahead, lie down. I'll settle Jessica. It won't be much different from before," he said.

With one last, unfathomable look, Mariel lay down and pillowed her head on her tote bag, the way she had earlier. She jackknifed her knees and wrapped the folds of her coat close around her so that all Jake could see was the soles of her boots peeking out from under the fabric.

Carefully he wrapped the baby in the front of his coat; Jessica didn't even wake up. He slid down next to Mariel so that the baby occupied the space between her back and his chest.

"Comfortable?" he asked as he propped his head on his arm. Mariel shifted so that he felt the rounding of her derriere against his thighs. He was unprepared for his sudden arousal, and he leaned away from her under the guise of readjusting Jessica's blanket.

"Well, this isn't the Comfort Inn, you know," Mariel mumbled.

He didn't reply.

"Jake?"

"Hmm?"

"Did you remember to lock the door?"

He felt her shoulders shaking and realized that she was laughing. In a moment, he was laughing, too, and as he did, he realized that the burden of the situation had lightened with her mood.

In his experience, women always took everything so seriously. He had seldom come across one who could laugh in the face of adversity. He wanted to wrap his arms around her and pull her to him.

After a few moments, he heard Mariel's steady breathing. He should have slept, but he didn't. He was thinking that Mariel was a woman he'd like to get to know, and yet their backgrounds were so different. She was college-educated, and he wasn't. She was from a big city, and he was small-town. And if he cared about his own happiness, he'd better nip these thoughts in the bud.

THE GRAY SHAFTS OF LIGHT creeping in through the mouth of the cave woke Mariel first. She lay quietly, listening to Jake breathe. She felt Jessica resting snugly against her back, and she wondered if the bit of milk left in Jake's thermos would be enough for the baby's breakfast. One thing was certain—they would have to find civilization soon.

Civilization...people...home... At her apartment in Pittsburgh, the neighborhood kids would soon be knocking on her door, looking for handouts of candy canes. When she wasn't there, they would be disappointed. She always asked a few of them inside to help her decorate her tree. Would they tell their parents when she didn't answer their knocks? Would anyone think to notify the authorities that she was missing?

She wouldn't be missed at work; she was supposed to be on vacation through New Year's. She had no close relatives other than her parents, who at this very moment might be going about their appointed task of feeding starving children. Little did they know that their own daughter was hungry back home in the good old U.S.A. At the moment, her stomach was so empty that it was nibbling on her backbone.

Jake sighed in his sleep. She wouldn't wake him. The baby would do that soon enough.

Jake shifted position, and she almost spoke to him. Then, her cheeks burning, she was glad that she hadn't. She could feel his erection through her coat. It was pressed hard against her back, and there was absolutely no mistaking what it was.

He apparently wasn't aware that he was pushing against her, and she had no idea whether to move away, thereby waking him and probably embarrassing both of them, or if the proper thing to do under these circumstances was to lie still and feign sleep.

She feigned sleep. She regulated her breathing, trying to keep it even, willing her stomach not to make hungry noises, when all the while her heart was racing and her head was spinning. Not to mention the rest of her, which, heaven help her, was responding the way any healthy woman's body would respond to a sexual stimulus from a good-looking man.

He awoke with a start. Mariel squeezed her eyes shut and held her breath.

Taking the baby with him, he rolled away from Mariel and lay quietly as Jessica fussed herself awake. Mariel didn't move. She remained as if frozen until Jake began to prepare the last of the milk for the baby. Then she sat up and blinked her eyes, smiling with what she thought would pass for supreme innocence.

"Good morning," he grunted, more interested in Jessica than in her. That should have pleased Mariel, but instead she felt slighted.

"How about handing me a clean diaper?" he suggested.

Silently she got up and went to the stack of dry cotton rectangles, folded two together and presented them to him. He unpinned the diaper that Jessica was wearing, looking as if he were all thumbs.

"Those diapers look dry," he said, nodding toward the ledge where they hung. "You might as well fold them up and stuff them in my pack. The way this kid goes through these things, we're going to need them." He slid the clean diaper under the baby's buttocks and drew the fabric up between her legs, pinning the corners haphazardly, his brow furrowed in concentration.

Mariel fought the urge to smile at his awkwardness and did as he suggested. As she was withdrawing her hand from the pack, the apple rolled out. She held it up. "Did you say we could eat this for breakfast?" she asked.

Jake had finished his diapering chores and had begun the slow, laborious process of feeding the baby. Jessica was fretting because she couldn't get the milk fast enough; Jake was concentrating on speeding up the process. He spared Mariel a quick, impersonal glance. "Sure," he said. "My knife's in the pack, too."

Mariel sliced the apple into quarters. She held one out toward Jake, but his hands were full.

"Here," Mariel said, holding the apple to his lips. After a quick look at her, he bit from it, chewed, and swallowed. "There's more," said Mariel, and he opened his mouth, letting her pop the bit of apple into it.

"Thanks," he said.

"Want the other piece?" she said, waving it in front of him.

He eyed it briefly. "Maybe not. I'll save it for a few minutes, and that way it'll seem like I've eaten more than I really have."

"Suit yourself," Mariel said, but she ate her half of the apple all at once, savoring every last morsel. She was just as glad that she hadn't had to feed him the last part of the apple—it seemed too intimate by far for her to be putting food in his mouth. His lips had brushed her fingertips, and it had sent shivers through her, shivers that had nothing to do with the chill and damp of the cave. Maybe he had noticed it, too, since he hadn't wanted her to feed him the rest.

Mariel busied herself with cleaning the knife while Jake finished feeding Jessica. She felt the corduroy of her slacks and found they were still too damp to wear. She moved them closer to the fire, and Jake said, "Are my jeans dry yet?"

She felt them, unable to avoid a mind's-eye picture of Jake peeling them off last night. What was wrong with her? Why wasn't she handling this better? She shouldn't be unnerved by this man—she hardly knew him.

And then she thought about waking up with him, about his erection pressed against her, and she realized that she knew him, knew some things about him well, and that her awareness was normal. But it wasn't comfortable. That was the problem. It wasn't comfortable at all.

"Well, what about my jeans? Dry or not?" Jake demanded.

"Almost," she said, dropping the fabric as if it burned her hands.

Jake ate the last quarter of the apple and stood up abruptly, leaving the baby lying on his jacket, crowding Mariel in her space. She fled to the other end of the cave, keeping an eye on him as she put the knife back in his pack and, for something to do, rearranged the things in her tote bag.

Still facing away from her, Jake pulled on his jeans. She turned her head, her hair falling over her face, as he zipped the fly with a quick flip of the wrist.

After pulling on his socks and boots, Jake took the empty thermos lid outside, which gave Mariel the opportunity to compose herself before he came back with icicles to melt. By that time, Mariel was kneeling by the fire, holding Jessica in front of her like a shield.

Mariel murmured to the baby as Jake pulled a disposable razor out of his pack and began to shave. He had no mirror, but his strokes were swift and sure. He seemed quiet, thoughtful, perhaps even dour.

At first she didn't plan to speak to him, but she couldn't stand the silence. Finally, for the purpose of testing his mood, she observed, "You travel well prepared."

"Habit," he said. He poured water over the razor to rinse it, dried it on his jeans, and returned it to the pack.

"You always carry a backpack?"

"Only when I know I'm going to have to trek miles and miles through a winter storm," he said.

"Seriously," she said, trying to cajole him into the kind of banter that had made them both feel better earlier.

"Things happen. That's why I keep it in my truck. I work far from home sometimes, and I carry the stuff I'll need if I have to spend the night. That's all," he said. He looked at her, then looked away. She had the feeling that he was edgy about being cooped up here with her and the baby, with diapers hung up to dry, nothing but the rocky floor to sit on, and not enough to eat.

As if to verify her thoughts, he said gruffly, "I'm going outside for a minute."

The call of nature or merely a longing for fresh air and a bit of freedom? Mariel didn't know. She tried to think, which wasn't easy on an almost empty stomach. What she thought was that they had to get out of here. Not only for Jessica's sake, but also so that she and Jake wouldn't end up at each other's throats.

JAKE CRAWLED through the tunnel to the outside, toward fresh air. He'd felt cramped all of a sudden: he'd felt crowded. The atmosphere inside the cave was so worrisome and tense. Mariel was beautiful and unconsciously provocative. Had she known what it did to him when she allowed her fingers to touch his lips while she was feeding him that piece of apple? Hadn't she felt the electricity vibrating between them when their eyes met, when they spoke to each other?

Maybe she was too worried about their circumstances to

notice. But he noticed, and that was why he'd put on still-damp jeans. He could no longer wear only his underwear around her without giving himself away, long jacket or no.

He emerged into the cold, still thinking about Mariel, when he suddenly realized the beauty of the scene before him. The ice storm had wrought a miracle. Icicles hung from every tree branch and from every projection on the cliff, glittering in the sun. Each individual needle of the surrounding ever-greens was coated with ice, and it glimmered and shimmered brighter than the tinsel on a Christmas tree. On the ground, water ran in crystalline rivulets; the air was filled with the tinkle of ice as it fell from the trees.

He wanted Mariel to see it. He called her name, his voice filled with excitement.

As Mariel came out of the cave with Jessica in her arms, Jake held back the brambles and helped her get her footing. He watched her eyes widen as an expression of delight spread over her face.

"Oh, Jake, isn't it beautiful?" she murmured, her breath frosty in the air.

"Like a winter wonderland," he agreed in a hushed voice.

"Didn't I tell you about miracles?" she asked him.

"Miracles," he said staunchly, "had nothing to do with this. A winter ice storm, that's what did it. It could have happened on any night."

"But we found the baby last night, and now this," Mariel reminded him.

"And this morning we have nothing to eat. If someone were granting miracles, I think he'd leave us a box of gra-nola, at the very least. Or maybe a few sticks of firewood, since we're getting low," he said wryly.

"Let's gather up our things and leave here as soon as we can," Mariel said.

"Too late," he said, gesturing at the clouds gathering be-hind the mountains in the distance. "Another storm is on the way."

"Another! But it can't be! We just had a storm," she said, though the clouds were all too visible, hunkering on the horizon.

"Just another one of those miracles of yours," Jake said with a sly look that Mariel ignored. "Besides," he said, "you should be happy to have a safe place to ride out this new storm. Remember yesterday? I don't think either of us wants to go through something like that again."

"I'm sick of that cave. And Jessica needs something to eat. We can't stay here any longer. We've got to go."

Jake could see that Mariel was prepared to be stubborn about this, but he was no longer sure that there were houses around here.

"Go? No way. A few hours and the storm will have passed over," he said. He cocked his head and assessed the clouds with an experienced eye before sliding a comforting arm around Mariel's shoulders. "We'll be on our way by early afternoon," he said soothingly.

"What's Jessica going to eat? What are *we* going to eat?" she said, her inflection rising unnaturally at the end of each sentence. She didn't want Jake to notice, but she felt as if she were going to cry.

"We'll have water to drink," Jake said calmly.

"Water! Maybe we can survive for a while on water, but what about the baby? And we only have one stick of firewood left," Mariel reminded him, exasperated that he wouldn't see this her way.

"I was thinking that I'd walk along the face of the cliff and try to figure out where we should go when we leave here. I'll try to find some dry firewood then."

"Jake, let's make a run for it. We can outrun this storm, I know we can!"

"What if we can't? No, Mariel, we're staying where we are."

Mariel gazed down into Jessica's trusting eyes. How long could a baby Jessica's size go without food? She had to make

Jake understand that they couldn't continue to stay in the cave.

"Jake," she said desperately, "can't you see? It's Jessica's life we're talking about. If she doesn't get something to eat soon—real baby formula, I mean—she'll get weaker and weaker, and she may die. We can't do this to her, Jake. We've got to leave. We've got to!"

"And what if we get stuck in a snowstorm, Mariel, the way we were caught in the ice storm last night? What about that? What if *we* die? Jessica has precious little chance of survival without us. Don't you realize that?" He shook off Mariel's arm and disappeared into the cave, emerging in a few moments wearing his backpack.

Mariel's eyes stung with unshed tears. She turned her head away so that he wouldn't see.

"Go back in the cave and try to keep the fire going. I'm going to find some dry wood before the snow starts," Jake said. With that, he stalked away along the track, his boots crunching on fallen icicles and acorns.

Mariel stood stunned, the baby in her arms, her fear a metallic taste in her mouth. She was hungry. So hungry. And suddenly she felt very, very tired.

Jake had disappeared into the forest, and he hadn't even looked back.

Chapter Five

Mariel crawled blindly into the cave, scarcely able to think. But she *had* to think.

For one thing, she had to see if there was anything left from Jake's pack to feed Jessica, anything at all. Jake had been worried about the storm, but there was one thing they hadn't discussed. During their impassioned discussion of the coming storm, neither of them had mentioned that once the snow stopped, they might not be able to get out of here at all. They could be marooned for days.

The temperature in the cave was warm compared to that outside, so she pulled on her dry corduroys, slipped off her coat and zipped out the wool lining. She wrapped the baby in the coat lining and set her down beside the jumble of things that Jake had dumped out of his pack, hemming the baby in between the cave wall and her own tote bag so that she couldn't roll. Jessica suddenly became absorbed in studying her tiny fists, which was all to the good. It left Mariel free to explore Jake's belongings.

She set the empty thermos aside. Next, she inspected the waterproof canister of matches, and a camper's set of interlocked fork and spoon, which almost made her laugh. At the moment, it seemed to be the last thing they needed.

There was also a small roll of cash—also virtually useless

unless they burned the bills to keep the fire going—a hammer, and a rope.

Great, Mariel said to herself, *just great*. He had left nothing that could be useful to her at that point.

Next she rummaged through her purse. In it was a roll of mints, unopened, and an overlooked package of crackers. Deep in the zippered side pocket she found a small packet of sugar.

These things promised some sustenance, but not much. How long until Jessica began crying with hunger? At least, with the ice storm of the night before and the approaching snowstorm, there would be no lack of water.

Mariel had to keep up her spirits or she'd go crazy. She'd taken another look at the scudding clouds overhead, and she knew that the snow would not hold off for long. The fire was rapidly dying; she hoped Jake would be back soon with dry firewood.

She picked up Jessica and held her in her arms, rocking her gently until she fell asleep. Then Mariel placed the bundle in the nest between her tote bag and the wall and crawled out of the cave. How long had Jake been gone? Half an hour? More?

As she stood in front of the opening, snowflakes began to sift from the sky, gently at first, then borne on a biting wind. Mariel's eyes searched for Jake's familiar red-and-black lumberjack jacket among the tree trunks, but she didn't see him.

She wrapped her arms around herself, too cold to stay outside and yet too worried to go back in the cave. Where was Jake? Why didn't he come back?

JAKE WAS HEADING into unknown country, all right. Without a map, with only the sun to give direction, he didn't know if he would run smack into a river, rough terrain or a road. After he stubbed his toe against an upturned stump, he kept his eyes on the ground and wished he were at home watching TV, his feet propped on his favorite footstool.

Adventures like this were tailor-made for television. They did not happen to real people. He shouldn't be following a winding trail through the woods, trying to keep the direction of the cave in his mind while his stomach complained that it hadn't been fed lately. He wondered how long he'd be able to keep up his strength if he didn't get something to eat soon.

There were deer in these woods. And rabbits; he knew that from his disastrous experience yesterday, when he'd tried to brake for one. Jake wasn't a hunter, and he knew nothing about trapping. His survival skills did not include converting live animals into food. Still, if it came down to feeding Mariel...

Mariel. He said her name out loud, there in the silent forest. He liked to say her name.

He shouldn't be thinking about her. One of the benefits of having to gather firewood was that he was able to get away from her.

He needed to figure out what to do. This morning, when he'd awakened, it would have been so easy—and so stupid—to reach for her lush curves and fit himself to them. Warming the baby between them had been his idea, and it was for the baby's benefit. But it was also supposed to serve the purpose of keeping him away from Mariel. It hadn't worked.

Those last few dark hours before light, during the second time they'd huddled on the cave floor trying to stay warm, he'd hardly slept at all. Mariel had; her breathing had been slow and even. That was good. What wasn't good was that he had lain awake, thinking about the tantalizing smoothness of her skin, the creaminess of her breasts, so inadequately concealed by that wisp of a bra, and the curve of her waist, flowing so delectably into the roundness of her hips.

He'd only met her yesterday. What would she think about a man who was supposed to be getting them out of this mess but could hardly think of anything except the details of her body and how longingly he wished to abandon himself to their exploration?

When they had slept together the first time, his hands on her rib cage, her heart fluttering beneath them, it had taken a supreme act of will not to slide his hands upward and under that lacy bra to cup her lush round breasts. He already knew how they'd lie heavily in his hands, how they'd taste sweet to his lips. He had wanted to nuzzle beneath the soft trailing hair on her neck and nibble gently at the fragrant skin there, his breath teasing her ear. He had wanted to hear the soft whisper of her skin against his as she turned within the circle of his arms until the two of them rested front to front, lips together.

He could imagine brushing aside those bikini panties and seeking the silken wet center of her, making her quiver with desire. She would reach around him and pull his hips toward hers, her fingernails cutting into his flesh as she felt him surging against her. He would begin to move, and she would, too, and then—no. He couldn't think about it. He *wouldn't*. If he did, he'd march back into the cave and—What was that quaint expression? Oh, yes, he'd have his way with Mariel.

A dream. All of it. A fantasy that had nothing to do with reality. The reality was that they had to stay alive and find their way out of here after the snowstorm had passed.

Jake looked around, trying to determine his location. The mountain directly above looked like the peak that was known, for some unfathomable reason, as Old Barker. This was a rural area, thinly populated, and the interstate highway that Mariel had been looking for was miles away. He had no idea how to get out of these woods.

The track he was on wound through the dense forest; he saw where a lumber cut had been made through the trees. He jogged along it, and eventually he saw what he was looking for: a tall tree with branches placed so that he could climb it.

He jumped up and gained a grip on a lower branch, sending a thin coating of ice tinkling down the trunk. Then he swung up his legs and pulled himself onto a sturdier branch, dislodging even more ice. He continued upward until he had a fairly good view of his surroundings.

He glanced back in the direction from which he'd come. He saw the cliff and tried to pick out the entrance to the cave, which would be difficult, because it was so small. He detected movement, and that was when he saw the tiny figure in the tan all-weather coat, its drabness broken by a red scarf blowing in the wind. *Mariel,* he thought, a thrill of pleasure rippling through him. He wanted to wave, to shout, but he thought it might frighten her.

Mariel looked no bigger than an insect from this vantage point. Suddenly Jake was afraid she was planning to strike out on her own in the snowstorm. The thought terrified him. She wouldn't do that. Or would she? She was a woman who was accustomed to making her own decisions, after all. Why should she listen to him? He watched the figure that was Mariel, but it didn't move.

He didn't want to take his eyes from her, for fear that she'd disappear, but he couldn't stay there forever. Telling himself that she'd have more sense than to move on alone, he tore his eyes away from the Mariel-figure and scanned the opposite direction. He was looking for a puff of smoke that would indicate a chimney, a driveway that led to a house, a road, a movement, *anything.* All he saw was bare-branched trees, their trunks dark with melting ice.

Then he saw something that wasn't a tree. Neither did it seem to be a house. At first he thought it was part of a distant mountain, but then he looked again. It was…a tower?

He eased himself upward to the next branch for a better view. It was *probably* a tower, he decided, and it seemed to be constructed of gray stone.

His precarious position in the tree afforded him only a glimpse of it. But at least it gave him hope that there was help ahead. That, for the moment, was enough.

He glanced back at the place where he'd seen Mariel, but

she was gone. She'd disappeared. Had she gone back into the cave, or had she left?

He made haste down the tree trunk, stopping to snatch a bit of mistletoe from one of the branches and shove in into his coat's breast pocket. He thought it might amuse Mariel. He had to keep thinking that she'd be there.

MARIEL'S TEETH were chattering from the cold. Or maybe it was fear. She knew that Jake wasn't coming back.

Was she afraid for him? No, she was afraid for all of them. They would die out here. It was Christmas Eve day, and they were going to die.

Jake must have decided that he would go on without her and the baby; certainly it would be easier for him not to have a woman and a child to drag along. So he had walked out into the face of a blizzard. They had argued, and he had been so angry that he'd left.

She looked at Jessica, so pink and sweet, sleeping as if she hadn't a worry in the world. *Poor little thing*, Mariel thought. *Abandoned in the woods, and now this.*

. Mariel gathered a few twigs and pieces of bark from the place where the firewood had been stacked, and she found another log in the far corner of the cave. She noticed with some surprise a previously undetected crevice from which dank air seeped, but she didn't want to waste the precious flashlight battery to investigate what it was.

She tossed the bark on the fire, knowing that it wouldn't keep the flame going for long. But she did want to boil the water in the thermos lid for Jessica. At least she could offer the baby that.

She huddled at the edge of the fire, listening and waiting. Waiting and listening. And still there was no sign of Jake.

ON HIS WAY BACK to the cave, Jake found a good-size fallen tree and rolled it over to expose the dry wood. Using his trusty hatchet, he managed to split off several reasonably dry, seasoned logs.

There was an ominous feeling in the air as he started back to the cave, the firewood in his arms, and he kept his eyes on the encroaching clouds, knowing that if they obscured the sun he'd be in trouble. The sun was his only directional guide. He hadn't taken time to notch the trees as he walked, so he might wander off the track if snow fell hard enough to obscure his vision.

He should feel more successful than he did. He was returning with wood that would burn, wood that would keep them warm until after the snow fell. They would be snug in their cave.

But he, too, was worried about how long the baby could survive without food. As he trudged through the woods, unbidden pictures flooded his brain, freeze-frame images that made him quicken his step. He thought about Mariel carrying the baby through snowdrifts, unable to see in the whited-out landscape. He thought about them falling down, and Mariel unable to get up again, and the baby crying until suddenly the crying stopped.

He was angry with himself for not having made things clear before he left. He should have extracted a promise from Mariel that she wouldn't take the baby and leave. Why hadn't he taken that precaution? Why had he been so rash and bullheaded?

Snow began to fall. *If Mariel and Jessica are still in the cave, I'll never get drunk again,* he promised himself, though it wasn't much of a promise. He hadn't been drunk since a buddy's bachelor party five years ago.

If Mariel and Jessica are still in the cave, I'll never argue with her again, he decided. The whole exercise reeked of "Step on a crack, you'll break your mother's back, step on a line, you'll break your mother's spine," childish doggerel that had stuck with him to this day.

If Mariel is still there, I'll pull her into my arms and kiss her was Jake's final offering. And that was one promise that he fully intended to keep.

JESSICA BEGAN TO SQUALL, and Mariel, giving up on the eye-dropper, used the spoon from Jake's pack to ladle sugar water into her mouth. It kept her quiet while Mariel tried to think.

If Jake didn't come back, she would wait until the storm passed and then dig her way out of the cave. Then she and Jessica would head toward her car.

Not that it would be easy, with snowdrifts covering the road. Considering the fact that they seemed to be in a completely deserted part of the world, she could hardly expect a snowplow to come through and clear it.

After she'd swallowed most of the sugar water, Jessica was due for a diaper change, which Mariel was able to accomplish more easily now that she'd gained experience. She rocked Jessica until she fell asleep and laid her in the nest she'd made from the lining of her coat.

Mariel felt cold; without its lining, her coat wasn't particularly warm. She crept closer to the fire, which was now reduced to a bed of glowing coals.

For lack of anything else to do, she used a bit of precious light from the flashlight and went to look for a scrap of bark, or a bit of paper, or anything else that would burn. And then she saw the log.

There couldn't be another log there. It was impossible. Jake himself had said they'd used the last piece of wood earlier, and Mariel had figured that the log she'd found a while ago, a spindly, meager log, had simply been overlooked. But here was another.

It felt strange to be picking up the log and putting it on the fire, and she wondered how she could have missed it earlier. Then she felt a blast of cool air from the cave entrance and went to check on the weather.

When Mariel emerged from the cave, snowflakes were drifting down in clumps, almost covering the ground. The sky was the shade that her mother had always called tattletale gray, only this sky was telling no tales. Neither were the trees. She saw no sign of Jake.

She thought she had prepared herself never to see him again, but now that she knew that there was virtually no hope he'd return, her heart sank to the pit of her stomach and settled there like a rock.

Well, she couldn't blame him for trying to get out of here. She had no doubt that he'd send someone to rescue her and the baby. In fact, that might have been his purpose in leaving. Now she could only hope that he'd find help—and find it fast. But who could get through in the face of the second major storm in twenty-four hours? Only Santa Claus, she thought, trying to feel lighthearted. Santa Claus and his airborne reindeer, soaring through the sky.

Jake would laugh at her. She was almost laughing at herself. But what if Jake didn't get through to someplace where there were people? What if he was in worse shape than she and the baby were, lost somewhere in these vast, uninhabited woods?

She wouldn't think about that. No point in dwelling on the problems. Time to get on with business. Time to think about how they were going to make it through the rest of the day, and probably longer, without food.

But when she went back in the cave and saw Jessica sleeping so peacefully, it was Mariel's undoing. She didn't mind all of this so much for herself. After all, she was a grown woman, thirty years old, and had experienced some of what life had to offer.

But Jessica was a baby. An infant. She wasn't even old enough to creep or crawl, and she couldn't hold her head up to see what the world was about. She'd never had a chance, and if they died in this awful cave, she never would.

Mariel buried her face in her hands. It was so unfair. So, so unfair...

JAKE STRUGGLED toward the cave, seeing no sign of Mariel. The snow was falling so heavily now that there was no way he would have been able to detect her departing footprints even if they were there.

Then he was at the entrance of the cave, dropping pieces of wood in his eagerness to see within. It was silent inside, a forbidding sign. If Mariel and the baby were in there, the baby would be hungry and she would be crying. Or Mariel would be talking to the baby and he would be able to hear her as he made his way through the opening.

He pressed through the brambles and crawled through the tunnellike entrance. And then, as his eyes adjusted to the gloom of the cave, he saw the flames and the hunched-over shape beside them.

Jake fell into the cave, firewood scattering in every direction.

"Mariel!" he cried, unable to believe that she was there. She was really there. He had talked himself into believing that she was headstrong enough to leave.

The figure rose as he staggered to his feet. "Jake! Oh, Jake!" she said, and the fire was bright enough for him to see the tears drying in salty streaks on her cheeks.

Then, with no warning, she was catapulting into his arms, laughing and sobbing at the same time. She flung her arms around his neck, unmindful of the snow clumped on the shoulders of his coat, and pressed her body tightly against his. His heart began to throb so strongly that he thought it would burst out of his chest.

"I thought you had gone," she said, sobbing into the front of his jacket. "I thought you had left us."

"I wouldn't," he said, wrapping his arms solidly around her and drawing in her warmth. Her sweater was soft, her body voluptuous, her hair tickling his mouth. He moved his head slightly, only to precipitate the uplifting of her face to his. Her eyes were silvery blue, the pupils defined by rims of a darker hue. They were shining with happiness.

"I thought you might be planning to send someone to rescue us," she said in a choked voice.

"I was sure you'd left. I saw you standing outside the entrance of the cave earlier, and I figured you had waited until I was out of sight and had taken the baby, looking for a safer place. When I thought that, I was so scared—"

"You? Scared? I don't believe it," she said, her eyes searching his face.

He enfolded her more tightly in his arms. He could feel her heartbeat, see the pulse of it at her temple. All at once he knew that he would sacrifice his life for her or the baby if need be. He had read about people who did things like that, but before, from his limited perspective, that altruistic mind-set had meant nothing to him. He certainly hadn't thought he would ever feel that way about anyone himself.

"I—I made all kinds of promises to myself while I was on my way back with the wood and thinking you wouldn't be here," he said unevenly.

"Like what?" Her voice was almost a whisper.

"Like—*this,*" he whispered back, bending his head over hers.

Her fingers fluttered at the back of his neck and were still. He fitted his lips to hers, so perfectly, so beautifully, and slid one hand up her spine to weave it into the loose curls hanging below her shoulders.

She sighed, her breath gentle against his cheek, and drew his head down even farther. He deepened the kiss as her mouth opened to his, the textures of her lips and teeth and tongue a powerful aphrodisiac. They were instantly lost in the moment, clinging to each other, pouring themselves into the connection between them. Jake forgot his physical hunger and gave in to a more elemental one, wanting to feast, but not on food. In that moment he realized that she wanted him as much as he wanted her, and he was so wildly happy at the thought that all he wanted to do was to follow his instincts, which would take them both into realms that he had so far only imagined.

She slid her hands into his coat, her fingers finding their way, moving under his shirt, searching for warm skin. He felt as if he were floating in a warm dark world where normal rules didn't apply and where pleasure was the only sensation. He felt her knees buckle and wrapped his arms around her to lower her to the sand.

And then the baby cried.

It took a moment for the noise to register. Time and place seeped back into their consciousnesses; they remembered. The storm. The cave. The baby.

Jake was the first to speak. "Is she all right?" he asked.

Mariel only breathed deeply, a kind of gasp, and then she righted herself. Her hands dropped to her sides, and she closed her eyes for a moment as if to clear her head.

And in that moment, Jake saw that it was regrettably inappropriate in this time and in this place to think that they could relate to each other in any way that didn't ensure their survival and the baby's. While making love might make them feel gloriously and completely alive, it wouldn't solve their problems. It would only make them go away temporarily.

"The noise woke her," Mariel said, sounding like her ordinary self as she backed away, smoothing her hair self-consciously. In a few seconds, she was kneeling in front of Jessica, murmuring sweet nothings in that solicitous voice she always used with the baby and ignoring Jake completely.

Jake waited until his body returned to normal and then bent and retrieved the firewood. Mariel, he had discovered, had a strong motherly instinct. Yet he couldn't help feeling disappointed; he wanted to hold her in his arms, to whisper fiercely that he would never let anything harm her, that he would give his life for her if need be.

But he couldn't do anything of the sort. Mariel was changing the baby's diaper. The storm was roaring outside the cave. Jake made himself wedge a few sticks of firewood on the fire and deposited the rest where the old woodpile had been.

"You know, after you left I found another stick of firewood. And then, just a while ago, another," Mariel said, lifting her head. Apparently she had chosen to act as if nothing had passed between them. Well, he didn't know any better way to handle it, and two could play that game.

"That's impossible. I put the last stick on the fire this morning before I went out looking for wood."

Mariel didn't notice his reluctance to pursue the topic. She went on talking, her hands busy with the baby. "It was strange, and I thought I must have overlooked those two logs this morning," she said.

He detected an unnatural brightness in her tone. She *had* been affected by what had happened between them. The thought gave him hope.

But at that moment he couldn't ignore what she was saying, because it was, he knew, bald fantasy. "Mariel, Mariel…" he said gently, genuinely concerned about her. What was this? Was her mind playing tricks on her?

"Well, it happened," she said flatly.

"It *is* Christmas," he said, hoping to gloss over this disturbing development. He *knew* there had been no other logs this morning. There was no doubt in his mind.

She shook her head and laughed. He was relieved to see the corners of her mouth tilting upward, even though it reminded him that he could still taste her on his lips.

Mariel, quietly efficient, had bundled the baby into her arms and was swaying back and forth, murmuring endearments.

Jake removed his coat and spread it on the sand. "Time for a diaper change?" he asked.

Mariel shook her head. "Not yet."

"Then we might as well both sit on my coat. This storm may take its own sweet time in passing."

Jessica fussed and fretted until at last she dropped off to

sleep. "I scraped up a package of mints and another package of crackers while you were gone," Mariel told him. "And I fed Jessica sugar water."

"She seems okay."

Mariel studied the baby's face, a frown bisecting her forehead. "I think so."

Jake made himself concentrate on other things besides Mariel's closeness. He didn't want her to see how worried he was, so he stood up and began to pace back and forth at the back of the cave. He still couldn't believe her claim that she'd found two more pieces of wood after he left. He kept glancing at her out of the corner of his eye, searching for some sign that she was becoming mentally unstable. She seemed completely normal. And sexy, though he didn't think she realized it.

"How's our flashlight doing?" he made himself ask.

"Almost gone," Mariel said.

He reached down and switched it on, mostly for the hell of it. The circle of its beam was orange and dim.

"Oh, by the way, I found a fissure of some kind in the wall," Mariel said.

"No kidding! It can't be very big," he said, unable to square what she was saying with what he knew to be true. He had thoroughly vetted the cave last night. He hadn't seen any fissure.

"I think we didn't notice it before because it's way at the back of the cave and could have been partly obscured by the woodpile," she said.

Jake, with marked reluctance, took a look. He couldn't believe his eyes when he saw it. Sure enough, there was a crack in the rock.

"Why, there is something here!" he exclaimed.

"Did you think I made it up?"

"I don't know what to think anymore." He saw that the fissure was barely wide enough for him to slip his arm through, and he didn't know what made him do it, but he reached into the crack. As his hand groped within the dark space, his fingers closed around a cylindrical shape. Cautiously he withdrew it, then stared at the object in his hand. Then he reached back in and pulled out two more cans, scarcely able to believe his eyes.

"What are you doing?" Mariel asked. He was blocking her view.

"Bringing home the bacon," Jake replied, in a choked voice as he turned to show her a can of Vienna sausage, a can of date-nut bread, and a can of evaporated milk.

Chapter Six

"Where did those come from?" Mariel asked in sheer disbelief.

He nodded his head toward the crevice. "They were in there."

"Why?" she asked, turning the can of milk over and over in her hands. It was exactly what they needed, and she could hardly believe that it had been there all the time.

"I don't know *why*, Mariel. Can't we simply be grateful that it *was?*" he said, sitting down beside her. He could no longer think there was anything wrong with Mariel's mental faculties, not when everything she'd said had turned out to be true. He was beginning to wonder if his own mind was playing tricks on him instead.

"The milk has to be diluted for drinking. We can mix it with melted snow. It should get Jessica through the rest of the day, at least," Mariel said with a kind of awe.

"The other stuff is for us," he said. "I hope you like Vienna sausages."

Mariel wrinkled her nose. "Under normal circumstances, I wouldn't touch them. But I'm hungry. Very hungry," she added.

"And the date-nut bread," he said. "Actually, I've always liked it, especially when it's spread with cream cheese."

"Did you try sticking your hand further into the crevice? You might find some," Mariel said impishly, and he laughed.

They ate ravenously, and when Jessica woke up, they were ready with milk, which they had mixed with an equal amount of water. The baby was greedy, rooting for the eyedropper and fussing each time Mariel refilled it. Feeding her was a tedious job.

The feeding accomplished, Jake took Jessica from Mariel and balanced the infant on his upraised knees. "Too bad babies don't come with blueprints to tell us what's where and how it works," he said.

"Or instruction books."

"Or user's manuals."

"Do you think we're doing everything right?" Mariel asked anxiously.

"I don't know," Jake said. "But doesn't she seem okay? She's smiling. Look."

"She is! Well, I think she likes us," Mariel said.

"I know she does. By the way, what's the status of the storm?"

Mariel sat down beside him. "Still raging."

"We need to plan what to do when we leave here," Jake said, becoming so serious that Mariel didn't speak but waited for him to continue.

He told her quickly about the tower he thought he had seen when he climbed the tree, and he suggested that they head in that direction when they left the cave.

"Was there any smoke near this tower? Any sign of life?" Mariel wanted to know.

Jake shook his head. "Not that I could tell."

"How about in any other direction?"

"Nothing at all."

"Jake, where *are* we? You're from around here. You should have some idea."

"We're lost, but we're going to get out of here today. I promise you that," he said with an air of determination.

Her eyes were troubled, and Jake reached out and enclosed her hand in his. "I promise," he repeated in a firm voice, and because he sounded so sure, she was, too.

THE SNOW STOPPED before the hour was out, and, fortified by their meager lunch of Vienna sausage, they set out.

With Jake leading the way, they waded through the freshly fallen snow, breaking a trail. Jake carried the baby inside his coat, and Jessica peeped out in round-eyed astonishment.

Mariel smiled at Jessica, thinking what a cute baby she was. Then she laughed at Jake.

"What's wrong?" he asked.

"You look so funny," she said, still grinning. "You look pregnant, carrying her in front of you like that."

"I kind of wondered what pregnancy would be like," he told her, and she laughed.

"How do you like it?"

He made a face. "It's tolerable," he drawled, which only made her laugh again.

"You should stop laughing and talking so much," he said sternly. "You'll get exhausted again."

"Oh," she said, feeling liberated by the sun peeping out from behind the clouds, and the bright snow, and the sky, washed as blue as bottle glass. "Let me enjoy this. After all that time in the cave, I feel as if I can breathe again. I want to dance and sing and play the way I did when I was a child!" She bounded through the snow until she was walking backward in front of him, her eyes sparkling.

"You can dance and sing if you want," he said, trying to keep a straight face, "but I can't. I'm pregnant."

She laughed merrily, the sound reminding him of silver bells.

She looked so beautiful, so carefree, so different from the way she had looked in the cave. At the moment, all he wanted to do was to pull her into his arms and kiss her.

She threw out her arms, as if to embrace everything, and

he thought he had never seen anything as beautiful as Mariel welcoming herself back to the world after an ordeal that both of them had thought might be the end of them.

Then she skipped back to him and took his hand. "I'll behave now. I wanted to get all that out of my system, that's all," she said with uncharacteristic meekness. He wondered if she knew that even the presence of her hand in his aroused him, then decided she didn't. If she knew, she wouldn't do it so casually.

He decided to stick to business. "Mariel, it's not a matter of behavior. It's a matter of conserving your energy in case of a problem," he said.

"You mean, in case that tower you saw was a mirage?"

"I don't *think* it was, but I didn't *think* there was firewood left in the cave, and then there were two more pieces. The things I take for granted don't seem to be true anymore, and things that I thought weren't there, including the food I found in the cave, *were*," he said.

"Magic," Mariel said. "It's Christmastime, you know."

He didn't answer, and they walked on quietly for a few more steps until Mariel realized that Jake wasn't going to rise to the bait. She decided to try a new tact.

"I wonder what it's really like to be pregnant. I don't mean just carrying a baby inside your coat," she ventured.

"It's not as if I would know," Jake pointed out.

"I think it must make a woman feel special to be pregnant."

"I think it must make her feel fat," he said in all honesty.

"A baby is not classified as fat," Mariel said indignantly.

"Did you hear that?" he said into the front of his coat. 'A baby is not classified as fat."

"Wah," said Jessica.

"Oh, my gosh, did you hear that? She said something!" he shouted.

"All she did was get her vocal cords into gear while she was yawning. It doesn't mean anything."

"Knowing what I now know about babies, it probably means 'Change my diaper,'" Jake said, with more than a touch of irony.

"We only have one clean diaper left."

"If you're still in the wish-making business, you should wish for a box of Flubbies, or whatever they call those disposable things babies wear."

Mariel dissolved into laughter. "They're not called Flubbies, but that's close enough."

"I'd hate to turn her over to her parents with a full-fledged case of diaper rash."

"I don't think she has any parents," Mariel told him seriously.

"Of course she does."

"Well, they're not anywhere around."

"She didn't appear out of thin air. She had to come from somewhere."

"Do you suppose she was left in the woods by a stork who was reluctant to risk dropping her down someone's chimney at this time of year?" Mariel asked innocently.

"Well, according to you, chimneys have been preempted by a VIP who has unorthodox ways of gaining entry into people's houses, so what's a stork to do? Look, Mariel," Jake said earnestly, "maybe this baby is the answer to your question. You know, the one we were discussing last night. How does a single woman get a child? We thought we'd covered all the possibilities, but there was one we didn't think about—finding one in the woods in the middle of an ice storm."

She favored him with a keen look to see if he was teasing her, but he stepped up his pace, and the snow was drifted high on this part of the trail, so she had to struggle to keep up.

The glare of the sun on snow was beginning to make Mariel's eyes ache when Jake suddenly stopped walking. "I see something!" he called excitedly over his shoulder.

"A house?"

"I'm not sure if it's a house, but I think it's what I saw earlier."

Mariel plunged through the snow and came to a halt behind him, looking over his shoulder at the tower.

It was visible through the treetops, a high, round gray stone structure rearing up against a bright blue sky. Pale yellow sunlight played over the walls, glittering on the snow frosting clinging to the spaces between the stones. Mariel caught her breath.

"It's a *castle*," she said, dazzled by the sight.

Jake drew her close by slipping an arm around her shoulders, something that she welcomed. She wondered if there was a chance that he would kiss her again, then decided that there wasn't. He had been acting matter-of-fact ever since they left the cave, and in spite of his teasing and their banter earlier, he didn't seem to recapture the highly charged feelings that they'd shared when they kissed. The realization left her with a mounting sense of disappointment.

"It's a castle, all right, unless we're both seeing things," he said.

"But what's it doing here? Where are we?" Mariel asked.

He squeezed her shoulder. "I don't know, but it's shelter. Come on," he said, taking her hand again.

They walked as fast as they could into the very heart of the woods. The track twisted and turned, sometimes doubling back upon itself, so that occasionally the tower was over Mariel's right shoulder, occasionally her left.

And then they came around a curve, and a clearing opened up in front of them. The castle was cupped in a hollow, as if within the palm of a hand. For a brief moment, birdsong trilled through the air, stopping suddenly and leaving them in pristine silence with nothing but the castle to fill their gaze.

The castle was complete with gatehouse towers reaching toward heaven, a huge, nail-studded oaken door, and a sagging drawbridge leading across a twenty-foot-wide moat. Speechless, Mariel and Jake stood and stared.

It looked like something out of a fairy tale. Somehow they expected people or horses to burst through the gate and run across the decrepit drawbridge, welcoming them with a fanfare of trumpets. But nothing like that happened. They saw no one, and they heard nothing but their own breathing.

And then Mariel saw the candle flickering in the gatehouse tower window. "Look."

"Someone's here."

"The candle is guiding us to shelter," Mariel said with certainty.

"If you say so," Jake said doubtfully.

"It's a Christmas custom in some countries to light a candle to guide travelers to a safe place," Mariel said in a rush. "They think that Christ wanders in the guise of a stranger to test the hospitality of people along the way. At Christmas, no one is turned away."

"I'm certainly glad to hear that," Jake said with great deliberation.

"You don't think much of the story, do you?" she challenged.

"At the moment, all I think is that I'm as hungry as a beast. Do we stand out here in the cold, or do we go in and— What did you say? Test their hospitality?"

Mariel knew that, inside, he was laughing at her. She kept her eyes on the candle flame. "We go in," she said, leading the way.

She hesitated at the start of the drawbridge. It was covered with snow, so they couldn't see the actual boards underneath.

"Do you think this bridge is safe?" she asked dubiously.

"You can hold the baby, and I'll go first." Jake prepared to divest himself of Jessica, but her loud wail rent the air.

"Better not," he said hastily, tucking Jessica into the front of his jacket again.

"I'll go first," Mariel decided, but in Jake's mind, the

welcoming horses had become stallions intent on trampling to death anyone who got in their way, and the hounds a yapping horde, sure to tear her to pieces.

"We'll all go together," Jake said, and, mindful of every creak, they made their way across the drawbridge until they stood in the walled outer ward in front of the gatehouse.

It was three stories high, with two elongated twin towers connected by a roofed-over passageway. The top of the walls was crenellated, giving the effect of a giant set of teeth with every other tooth missing. The spaces between the crenellations were banked with snow.

A smaller door had been cut in the massive nail-studded oak door, and a rusty gong to their right presumably notified the occupants that they had visitors.

"Shall I ring it?" Mariel wanted to know.

"Let 'er rip," Jake answered. She picked up the waiting mallet and gave the gong a hard whack, sending a flock of birds fluttering off the battlements in panic.

"I don't think anyone's coming," Jake said after a few minutes had passed.

Mariel walked back to the edge of the drawbridge and looked up at the gatehouse window. "The candle is gone!" she exclaimed.

"Maybe they got a look at us and decided they didn't want to lodge such a scruffy-looking group," Jake said ruefully.

"I don't think that's it. The flame must have blown out."

"Well, do we stay here or go on?" Jake asked, shifting Jessica's weight impatiently.

"We're not in a position to leave. We have to feed Jessica," Mariel said. "We have to go in, whether anyone is here or not."

"Try the door. Maybe it's open."

Mariel pushed at the smaller door within the apparently immovable larger one, and was surprised when it swung open with little effort.

"After you," Jake said, standing back, and so Mariel went in first.

Once inside, she was overcome by the aura of the place; there was a haze of unreality about the castle. Mariel paused for a moment, glancing at Jake to see if he felt what she did, this kind of heightened awareness, as if she were breathing rarefied air.

Jake looked as if nothing were amiss, and so she shook off whatever imaginary effect she thought she'd felt and took notice of their surroundings.

They stood in a passage between the two towers of the gatehouse. Mariel saw a staircase leading up, but it was in deplorable condition, and she didn't see how anyone could have gotten upstairs to light the candle.

Puzzled, she stood on tiptoe to peer through a window in search of an inside stairway, but all she saw was the remnants of one, its boards strewn around the floor. While she was still wondering how anyone could have reached the upper story of the gatehouse with the staircases missing, she was startled to see two long ears waggling at her.

"There's something in here!" she said, turning to Jake.

Jake cocked his head to one side. "Animal? Vegetable? Mineral?"

"Animal, but I can't see *what*," Mariel said as she continued through the passage to the castle courtyard, where she saw a doorway into the first floor of the gatehouse.

The actual door was missing. They could see directly inside. On a pile of straw, backed into a corner, was a goat.

"Bleah-h-h," went the goat.

"That's exactly the way I feel," Jake said in a conversational tone.

"Why, she's scared to death," Mariel said in concern. She didn't know how to behave around a goat; she'd never, as far as she could remember, met one before. She did, however, know that this goat was female, because of her large, swollen udder. The goat was gray and white, with great golden eyes, which were presently rolling around in their sockets to express extreme agitation.

"She's tame," Jake said.

"She probably belongs to the people who live here," she said, looking around for food or water and seeing none.

"Let's go find them." Jake couldn't wait to get to a warm place, where he could relax on a deeply cushioned chair and use the telephone.

Reluctantly Mariel followed him into the castle courtyard. The goat trailed after them, bleating all the while.

They were much too awed by the castle to pay attention to the goat. The courtyard was wide, and snow had drifted into all the corners. There was no sign of any inhabitants.

Mariel sized up her surroundings and determined that this one was small as castles went, with the inner courtyard about the size of two basketball courts. On their left were lean-tos built against the wall; to their right, more of the same.

"The bakehouse," Mariel said as they passed one door. A section of a thatch-roofed building elicited the comment. "That's the stable."

Jake couldn't resist asking, "How do you know?"

"I deal in legends. Legends take place in castles. I took college courses in medieval studies."

"I'm not so much interested in what's what as I am in where the people live."

Mariel pointed to a larger door directly ahead. "I'm sure that's the great hall. That's where people eat and spend leisure time. We should try there first."

Jake followed Mariel's lead, noting the stained-glass windows adorning the small enclosure to their right.

"That must be the chapel," he said. His brilliant deduction should show her that he knew something about medieval castles, too, but Mariel was forging ahead of him, leaving small, neat footprints in the snow.

"I don't see a doorbell," Mariel said as she stood in front

of the door, and Jake had to laugh at the perplexed expression on her face.

"A doorbell? In a medieval castle?"

"Modern people must live here. You'd think there would be modern conveniences."

Jake shook his head. "No mod cons in this place. I don't see any telephone poles, or wires, or signs of any connection with the outside world."

Mariel's face fell, but only fleetingly. "All I hope is that they have a bathtub and water," she said firmly.

Jake knocked on the door, and the sound resounded hollowly within. No one answered. He knocked again, trying not to notice Mariel's look of discouragement.

Finally he said, "There's no one here."

She stared at him. "This big castle, stuck way out in the middle of the forest, and there's no one home? Why would anyone go to the trouble to put it here?" she asked in exasperation.

Jake looked at the blanket of snow, and at the icicles as long and as thick as his forearm hanging from the roofs of the nearby buildings. "I bet they've gone to Florida for the winter. I know *I* would," he said gloomily.

Without saying one more thing, Mariel marched around the courtyard, trying the locked chapel door, poking in corners, and jumping up to peer in windows, which were narrow and few. Jake followed her, being patient and consoling Jessica, whose diaper had reached the saturation point.

"You'll have to break in," Mariel said, looking panicky, when Jake reluctantly told her about the sorry state of Jessica's diaper.

"Bleah-h-h," went the goat.

"At least you didn't suggest that I go down the chimney," Jake said, but Mariel only wrinkled her nose at him.

"Anyway," he said, "this place belongs to someone who might not take kindly to breaking and entering, so maybe it's not a good idea."

"But this is an emergency," Mariel insisted. "Whoever lives here wouldn't want us to stay out in the freezing cold with a baby whose diaper is approaching flood status."

To emphasize her point, Jessica made a sound that was something like "glug."

"Okay, we'll take a look at the door to the great hall," he said.

Mariel found it difficult to keep up with Jake as he strode across the courtyard. The goat cavorted in their wake, something urgent in its manner. Mariel had no time to think about the goat; she was far more concerned about what they would do if they couldn't get inside the castle. Camp in the courtyard? Bed down in the gatehouse? Neither option seemed any more desirable than spending the night in a cave.

Jake studied the heavy door, and in a moment, using nothing more than a hammer and a Swiss army knife, he was pushing the door open. They stomped the thickly caked snow off their boots before Mariel followed Jake inside.

Once she was standing inside the great hall, Mariel realized that no one could be living there. It was long and dreary, dark and musty. The ceiling was vaulted in stone, and occupying one end of the room was a massive fireplace big enough to roast an ox. A dais at the other end held a long table with smaller tables arrayed below it, and a pale winter sun picked out the details of the faded tapestries on the walls.

"It's cold in here" was the first thing Jake said, his voice echoing back from the high ceiling.

Mariel, amazed at the authenticity of the place, was studying the elaborate tapestries. They were embroidered in warm browns and reds, with occasional flashes of yellow and blue here and there. The panels depicted stories—a hunt, the arrival of noblemen amid waving banners, knights jousting.

Jake's spirits were sinking. He might as well scrap the idea of a soft chair and a television set. The most modern convenience he saw was a packet of matches tossed carelessly on the hearth.

"Hello?" called Mariel, thinking she'd better make their presence known, in the unlikely event that someone was around. When no one answered, she looked at Jake and shrugged her shoulders.

"It's not much," Jake said with an audible sigh, "but we call it home. Let's take a look to make sure there aren't any more goats wandering around and to see if there's anything to eat." He took off at a fast clip for the far end of the hall.

"If this is like most castles, we won't find a kitchen. They always put the cookhouse far away from the hall and its apartments because of the danger of fire," Mariel was saying as Jake led the way into the room behind the dais, but she stopped and breathed, "Ooh," when she saw what was there.

"A kitchen," Jake said in an unbelieving voice. "An honest-to-goodness, real-life kitchen."

"With a stove," Mariel said. "And a refrigerator!" Things were looking up.

And in a matter of seconds, she was looking up—at Jake. He wrapped his arms around her, pulling her close.

"We're going to be all right, Mariel. We'll manage here," he said, and she knew then that he was going to kiss her again.

She didn't try to stop him. She wanted it. He ran his fingers through her hair first, tilting her head back before dipping his head and covering her mouth with his. An ache curled up from somewhere below her stomach, making her nipples tighten into hard little points. It was a potent and exuberant kiss, a celebration of their safety. It was a kiss that could have gone on and on, except for Jessica's squirming presence between them.

Reluctantly Mariel leaned away from Jake. "That's one way to raise the temperature in here," she said, holding on to the front of his jacket for balance. "But I think we'd better find a more appropriate heating device."

Jake shook his head, as if to clear it, and although his lips smiled, his eyes reflected a more serious mood.

He moved away and bent to study the stove. "It's run by propane gas, and I'll need to get it fired up," he announced before taking a look at the refrigerator. "This is run on propane, too. There's no electricity, which explains the kerosene lantern and that box of candles on the table."

"With a way to cook, there may be food around," Mariel said.

While she checked the cabinets above the stove, Jake threw open a pantry door.

"A gold mine," he said. "Mariel, look at this!"

Mariel saw a cabinet filled with canned goods of every description. There were baked beans, garbanzo beans and kidney beans. There was noodle soup, cream of celery soup and bouillon. There were cans of tuna and sardines and baby clams. In short, they would survive.

"I don't see any canned milk," Jake said suddenly.

Mariel's happiness turned to dismay. "We have to have it for Jessica. Is there baby formula?"

Jake shoved the cans around. "No. Nothing." His expression was bleak.

"What are we going to do?"

"I don't know."

They stared at each other for a moment.

"Well," Jake said finally. "At least I can do something to improve our comfort level. I'm going to build a fire in here." He handed Jessica to Mariel and headed toward the kitchen fireplace, whose wood box was filled with apple logs.

Even here, far from the door, they could hear the bleating of the goat.

Mariel jounced Jessica expertly. "We'll be nice and warm soon," she promised the baby, who was holding up remarkably well, she thought.

"That goat's probably hungry," Jake said as he built the fire. "I wonder how she ended up here, or if the people who live here left her."

"I don't think anyone has lived here for a long, long

time." Mariel watched as the flames leaped up to embrace the logs.

Jake rocked back on his heels. "Do you want to take a stab at fixing something to eat, or shall I?"

"Before we do anything, I'd better change Jessica's diaper. Maybe you could look around the kitchen for a cardboard box or someplace where she can sleep." She wished fervently that their cursory search had turned up a few dozen clean diapers. Jake's cut-up long johns were really not equal to their task.

Jake returned from his search carrying a drawer that he had pulled out of a cabinet in the pantry. Over one arm was draped a pile of white huck towels.

"Look," he said, tossing the towels down beside Mariel. "These will make dandy diapers. And I didn't find any boxes, but won't this do for Jessica's bed?" He placed the drawer at the far edge of the wide hearth.

Mariel was thrilled about the towels, which could be folded to the right size and were thick and absorbent. The drawer was sturdy and scarred, but suitable. "It's better than nothing," she said.

"Let's eat something before we figure out what to do next." With Jessica settled in her drawer-bed, he and Mariel feasted—there was no other word for it—on canned tuna, smoked oysters, artichoke hearts and beets from the store in the cupboard.

"I hate beets," said Mariel, munching happily.

"Me too."

"This is a horrible dinner," she added as she claimed the last artichoke heart.

"Awful," Jake agreed.

They looked at each other and laughed. Their stomachs were full, and their spirits were rising.

"This might not be such a bad Christmas after all," Jake said, and Mariel smiled.

"There's no such thing as a bad Christmas," she said.

Chapter Seven

While Mariel fed Jessica the last bit of the canned milk they had found in the cave, Jake built another fire in the great hall. When he came back, he said, "Now that we're getting the place warmed up, let's take a look around."

Jake had lit candles in the wall sconces in the great hall, which mellowed it more than Mariel could have imagined earlier. It was furnished sparsely, as great halls should be, with a few wooden chests and a couple of settees for sitting in front of the fire.

With Jake carrying Jessica, they set out to explore the castle. A small corridor off the great hall led to the chapel, jeweled with light from the huge stained-glass windows. Pews were small, and the ceiling was high. On the other side of the chapel was a small room lined with shelves of books. Mariel looked at them more closely. She saw *Ivanhoe,* and a book of recipes, and something called *Your Infant.*

"A book about baby care!" she said triumphantly, gingerly edging it out of its dusty place beside the others.

"It looks awfully old," Jake observed as she leafed through yellowed pages, one of which proved him right by stating the publication date as 1908.

"People knew how to take care of babies then. If they hadn't, you and I wouldn't be here." Mariel hugged the book to her chest as Jake led the way through the corridors and back to the great hall, where a staircase led to an upper gallery.

They were awed by the dusty collection of armor and the display case full of swords. Rooms opened off the gallery, bedchambers furnished in the medieval manner, with immense high beds draped with heavy curtains. Without benefit of fires in the fireplaces, the chambers were cold and damp, and both Mariel and Jake were so uncomfortable with the chill that they quickly returned to the great hall.

After a few minutes of warming themselves in front of the now-roaring fire, Jake started toward another set of steps.

"Shouldn't we explore the tower?"

"Let's," Mariel agreed without hesitation. "At least we'll be able to survey the countryside from the highest point around. Maybe we'll see signs of life nearby."

The narrow tower steps were built into the wall and spiraled to the top. Jake was about to comment on their steepness to Mariel, who was bringing up the rear, but he stopped, speechless, when he stood in the doorway to the tower room.

There were toys everywhere. Dolls were heaped upon rocking horses; toy dump trucks carried loads of blocks; a sled leaned against the wall; a harmonica rested on a child's rush-seated chair.

"It looks as if we've happened upon Santa's storehouse," Jake said wryly. In his arms, Jessica, too young for toys, gawked at all the bright colors.

"I can't for the life of me figure out what's going on," Mariel said, bewildered by the array. "There's no one for miles around, and now we find *this*." She knelt and picked up a stuffed unicorn. "These are new toys, Jake. Not toys that might have been played with by children who once lived here, the children whose mother consulted the baby book, but *new toys*."

"It just goes to show you that Santa Claus lives," Jake said. He bent and scooped something out of one of the dolls' arms. "And he wants Jessica to eat properly. Will we be able to feed her with this?" He held a doll's bottle out to Mariel.

It wasn't the size of a regular baby's bottle, but it was marked for ounces and had an ordinary rubber nipple on top.

"It will work, I think," she said, but then her face fell. "If only we had something to feed her."

"We'll think of something, Mariel."

Mariel was still assessing the contents of the room for usefulness. "I'm taking more than a bottle. Jessica needs clothes, too," she said. She swiftly stripped the baby dolls of their nightgowns and held one up. "This'll fit perfectly."

"And it matches the blue of Jessica's eyes," Jake said approvingly. "Come on, let's go downstairs. I can't figure out what these toys are doing here, and I'm not sure I even want to try."

They trooped downstairs and basked in front of the fire, warming their hands and feeling satisfied with their discoveries. While they were congratulating themselves, they became aware of the piteous crying of the nanny goat in the courtyard.

"Poor goat." Mariel opened the door. "She probably needs to be fed. I wonder what we can give her."

Jake followed her to the door, holding the baby in his arms. "Our discarded tin cans," Jake said helpfully from over her shoulder, earning him a skeptical look from Mariel and a toss of the head from the goat.

"They eat hay," he offered. "Grain, maybe."

"You know this for a fact?"

"I lived on a farm once with some foster parents."

"Wasn't there hay in the gatehouse?"

"What I saw was dirty and trampled. Would you eat it?"

"No, but I'm not a goat."

As it occurred to Jake what was wrong with the goat, a light bulb went on in his head. And then he saw fireworks. Why hadn't they thought of this before?"

"She needs milking," he said in a rush. "And Jessica can drink the milk."

Mariel, looking down at the distressed goat, didn't know whether to laugh or cry. "If we can milk her, it will certainly solve a huge problem. I'm a city girl, however, and I have *no* idea how to go about milking a goat!"

"I told you I've lived on a farm," Jake said.

Mariel grinned widely. "In that case," she said, standing aside, "she's all yours."

Jake confronted the goat, who was regarding him uneasily from the other side of the doorstep.

"First, we'll have to wash her udder," he decided with false heartiness."

"With what?"

"Water. And soap. I saw soap in the kitchen," he said.

"I hate to say this, Jake, but she doesn't look as if she's going to allow you near her," Mariel said. She had stepped forward and was scratching the goat gently behind her ears, a service that was only barely tolerated. The goat, swaying to and fro on tiny, anxious feet, kept tossing baleful glances in Jake's direction.

"How about if you put Jessica to bed while this goat and I make friends?" he said, transferring the baby to Mariel.

Jessica hiccuped. "We'd better leave him to it," Mariel told the baby, who only hiccuped again. Jake thought he detected a hint of skepticism in Mariel's expression as she went back inside.

After Mariel and the baby were safely out of sight behind the closed door, he crouched in the snow and tried to get the recalcitrant nanny goat to regard him as a friend, not an enemy. He put on his most goat-friendly smile. He mimicked her bleat, softly, so that Mariel wouldn't hear. He put his hands up to his ears and flapped them, goat-fashion. But every time he got within arm's length of the goat, she shied away.

He kept saying, "Whoa, Nelly, whoa," even though he

had no idea if the goat's name was Nelly or if you said "whoa" to a goat. He recollected that people talked about saying boo to a goose, but that was another matter. Did you say boo to a goat?

He tried everything he could think of. Nothing worked. By this time, he regretted telling Mariel that he'd once lived on a farm. When he'd lived on that farm, the only cattle his foster father had kept were three geriatric cows. Besides, Jake had been all of three years old.

WHILE JESSICA DROWSED in her makeshift bed and Jake tried to worm his way into the goat's good graces, Mariel read the baby-care book.

The book offered all sorts of advice, one welcome bit about how to prepare goat's milk for drinking.

"'Cool the milk quickly in the icehouse,'" Mariel read out loud, hoping her words would lull Jessica to sleep. "'Bacteria must not be allowed to multiply.' Well, we don't have an icehouse, though at the moment it seems as if the whole world is one."

"Wah," said Jessica.

"I know, I know, but you're stuck with me and Jake. We don't know much about babies, but we'll learn," Mariel said soothingly.

"Nah," said Jessica.

"You doubt it, of course. But you just wait and see. Didn't we find milk for you? And Flubbies?"

"Dah," said Jessica.

"Hmm... I believe that's Russian for *yes*. Anyway, Jessica, you usually make your needs known loud and clear," Mariel said, smiling fondly at the baby.

"Blfdghbf," Jessica said, which Mariel figured was untranslatable into any known language.

Mariel read more of the baby-care book, poring over words such as *colic*, and *cradle cap* as she wondered if she'd ever need to know about them.

When at last Jessica was sleeping peacefully, and after tucking her blanket securely around her, Mariel took soap and water outside to Jake.

When she stepped into the courtyard, Jake was circling the goat, which in turn was trying to circle him.

"She doesn't seem to like you," Mariel said.

"Understatement of the year." Jake slipped on a patch of ice and swung his arms wildly as he tried to keep his footing.

This frightened the goat, who spotted Mariel and trotted directly to her, becoming docile and nuzzling her hand. This only made Jake angry.

"Why does she like you and hate me? And besides, I can't milk her out here in the snow," he pointed out. "I'd have to lie on my belly in order to reach her udder."

"Udderly impossible," Mariel said seriously, for which she received an impatient look from Jake.

"Look, Nelly seems to like you, so why don't you lead her into the stable?"

"Nelly? You've named her Nelly?"

"It was all I could think of. She has to have a name, if we want to be friends with her," he explained.

"Come along, Nelly," Mariel said, holding her hand toward the goat and walking backward across the courtyard, toward the stable. The goat followed, eyeing Jake distrustfully all the while.

Once in the stable, Mariel backed the goat into a corner.

"She's practically begging you to milk her," Mariel told Jake by way of encouragement.

"If that's true, why is she trying to escape?" The goat was scrabbling at the stable wall, sending a shower of stones raining onto the earthen floor. He tried approaching, his hand held out in an attempt to mollify the terrified goat; when that didn't succeed, he clasped his hands behind his back and tried again.

"This isn't working," he said when Nelly rent the air with a terrified squeal.

"I'll hold her head," Mariel offered, grasping Nelly's neck. The goat struggled for a moment and then was still. But when Jake approached her hindquarters with the soapy cloth, she wheeled and tried to wrench away.

Mariel did the only thing she could think of. She began to sing to the goat.

"Silent night, holy night," she began, and Nelly calmed immediately.

"All is calm, all is bright," she went on, heartened by the results. Jake crept closer to the goat, cloth in hand, one eye on the goat's udder, the other on her hooves. At this distance, Nelly could kick him clear into tomorrow if she put her mind to it.

Nelly stood quietly now, Mariel scratching her head. "Sleep in heavenly peace, sleep in heavenly peace," sang Mariel.

"Again," said Jake, reaching for the udder.

Mariel began singing the second verse of the Christmas carol, and Jake sudsed and rinsed, then slowly slid the pan Mariel had brought under the goat and crawled closer for a better look.

"Shepherds something at the sight," Mariel sang.

"Quake," interjected Jake. "Shepherds *quake* at the sight." He was quaking at the sight of this udder. There weren't four teats, like a cow's, but two. That should make it easier, but he had no idea how to express the milk.

"Glorious beams from heaven above," Mariel continued. Jake thought of singing "Glorious streams from udders above," which might get a laugh from Mariel but wouldn't get the job done.

"Don't stop singing," he said, seeing that the goat was virtually mesmerized by Mariel's voice. Mariel sang another verse.

Jake stuck out a hand and curved it around one of the teats. The goat didn't move. Jake squeezed. Nothing happened, except that the goat became startled and almost planted one hind foot on the palm of his non-squeezing hand.

"Silent night?" Mariel sang anxiously. "Are you all right?" She bent to look at him, her brow furrowed in concern.

"I'm okay, don't take fright," he assured her in his chesty baritone.

"Hurry this up, she won't stand still long," Mariel sang, fitting the words to the carol's tune.

"This isn't easy, the fit is all wrong," he sang, wedging himself between the wall and the goat, and Mariel went on singing while he wrapped his fingers around one of the teats again.

This time he followed an instinct that told him he'd get better results if he squeezed from top to bottom. He clamped the top of the teat with the thumb and index finger and pulled. Again, nothing happened, but Nelly remained calm. She seemed to expect him to do this right.

By now, Mariel was starting on another verse of "Silent Night." Jake clamped his other hand around Nelly's second teat and squeezed one, then the other. Much to his amazement, a stream of milk squirted from each, hitting him squarely on the top of one boot.

Hmm… he thought, *I'll have to improve my aim.* The next time, he pointed the ends of the teats straight down toward the stainless-steel pan, and was rewarded by two steady streams clanging against the metal.

He was jubilant. "Did you see that?" he yelled. Nelly promptly kicked the pan, sending the bit of milk flying.

Undaunted, he tried again. Mariel switched to "Joy to the World," and after that, things progressed satisfactorily. Finally, Jake triumphantly held the pan aloft.

"Congratulations," said Mariel, and he beamed.

They fed Nelly from a bag of grain they found in the stable, and on the way back to the great hall he kept one arm companionably around Mariel's waist.

"I'd better get this milk to the kitchen," she said. "I'll want to strain it and cool it, and—"

"Not so fast." Jake carefully set the pan on one of the long tables and pulled her close. "I think I should tell you that you're one of the most versatile women I've ever met. I don't know too many women who look as beautiful when they're keeping a fire going in a cave as they do when they're singing to a goat, and I can't imagine anyone else of my acquaintance keeping her sense of humor. You're very special, Mariel," he said, gazing into those eyes that had captivated him almost from the first moment he laid eyes on her.

"Jake, I—"

He didn't wait for her to finish. Instead, he pulled her into his arms and rested his cheek against her hair, listening to the beating of his own pulse in his veins. He thought that he had never shared so much with any other woman; nor had he ever wanted a woman as much as he wanted Mariel.

She pulled away slightly to look up at him, and he lowered his head until his lips moved lingeringly against hers. Her lips were the sweetest he had ever tasted, full of what he had come to know as the essence of Mariel, and he drank from them as if from a spring that he feared would run dry. He felt his knees go slack, and he knew he would melt into her without any effort if this went on for much longer.

The baby was sleeping. They were alone in the big relic of a castle, and likely to be so for some time. The very thought of saying goodbye to her once they found their way back to the real world made him feel slightly crazy. Then the inevitable would happen; she would leave. Why would a well-educated woman from Pittsburgh want to have anything to do with a simple carpenter from rural Virginia?

He let her go. He dropped his hands, but his face remained only inches from hers, taking in every detail of her expression. For a moment, he thought she was going to fling her arms around his neck and press her body along the length of his, and then it would be all over. If she had done that, there would have been no point in fighting it. Nature would take over, nature and—might as well admit it—passion. He would take her right there on the wooden table, with the baby sleeping nearby.

But she only masked whatever she was feeling and said, "Well. I suppose we'd better see what we can do about cranking up that refrigerator." She reached for the container of goat's milk, and then she bustled away, leaving him to his regrets and his imagination.

MARIEL STEADIED HERSELF against the kitchen counter, hoping that Jake wouldn't follow her.

She had to get a grip on herself. She had no business lusting after Jake Travis. She didn't know who he was or what he was; all she knew was that he looked good in his skivvies and built a decent camp fire. And that he could milk a goat.

Which reminded her that she needed to refrigerate the milk. The refrigerator door was closed, unlike earlier, when it had hung open. She opened it, surprised that the inside light was on and that the air inside was cool. *Funny,* she thought. *When did Jake find the time to turn the refrigerator on?*

Thoughtfully she set the pan inside and closed the door again. Something strange was going on here.

"Mariel, I think we'd better talk about this," Jake said, bursting in the door.

"Did you turn the refrigerator on?" she asked.

"Refrigerator? No. Didn't you?"

"No."

Jake opened the refrigerator door and closed it again. "It's on. You must have done it."

"Didn't you say that it's run on propane gas? I wouldn't even know where to begin."

"When would I have done it, Mariel? You've known where I was every minute." Jake folded his arms across his chest and waited for a reply, which wasn't forthcoming, because she realized he was right.

They stared at each other uncomfortably. Finally Mariel threw her hands in the air and said, "I give up. Neither of us started the refrigerator. It's working. Chalk it up to something, I don't know what."

Jake checked the stove. "While you're chalking, I'm going to make coffee, because the pilot light's on here, as well."

"I'd like a cup of coffee, too," Mariel said, and Jake busied himself filling an old coffeepot while she strained the goat's milk into a glass pitcher. Soon the aroma of coffee filled the air, and she sat across the kitchen table from Jake, who handed her a mug of coffee and stared down into his own mug thoughtfully.

Jake didn't speak, and Mariel was determined that they wouldn't embark on any heavy discussions about their relationship.

"When do you think we'll be able to leave here?" she asked.

Jake lifted his eyes to her face. His expression was impassive as he lifted the mug to his lips. "I don't know."

"Tomorrow? The next day?"

"At the moment, we still have no idea where we are. I can determine direction from the sun, and I think we should probably head west, but the mountain is there. Probably the safest thing to do is to wait until someone comes to rescue us."

"How long will that be? Tomorrow is Christmas."

"No one will come looking for me. I'm pretty much a loner, and all my buddies had out-of-town plans. How about you?"

"Unless some of the neighbors happen to check on me, I won't be missed. Even if they realize I'm not home, they'll think I've gone somewhere with a friend," she said slowly.

His eyebrows shot up. "Any special friend?" he asked sharply.

"My girlfriend Ellie—" she began, then realized that what he wanted to know was if there was a man in her life. "No, not the kind of friend you mean," she finished.

"And Ellie wouldn't wonder where you are?" he probed.

"She'll be with her husband. They were going to her grandmother's in Ohio."

"It looks as if we'll have to depend on someone wandering by if we hope to be discovered."

"How long can we hold out here?"

"If the baby drinks goat's milk, she'll be all right. As for us, there's plenty of food to last a couple of weeks."

"We're lucky," she said.

They drank in silence, each apparently unwilling to say anything more, each thinking private thoughts.

Finally, without comment, Jake went to rinse his cup at the sink. He couldn't see how Mariel studied the way his muscles rippled beneath the gray turtleneck, and he couldn't know her thoughts. She was thinking that she might be safe from the elements. But she didn't feel safe from the most capricious danger of all—her own runaway emotions.

JAKE WANTED to talk to Mariel about what was happening between them. He wanted— But what was the use?

He wanted a relationship. He'd known a lot of women in his life, but he'd never been really close to any of them. Now here was a woman, a woman for whom he was beginning to care deeply, and, thrown into close proximity with her, he was beginning to see how much he'd missed in his life.

When he'd followed her into the kitchen, he hadn't planned to talk about why the refrigerator was running when no one had turned it on. He'd planned a confrontation during which he'd lay his cards on the table.

All that had happened was that they'd had a civilized conversation over coffee. Now she was sitting in front of a fire in the great hall, playing with the baby. Soon it would be time to rustle up dinner. All he could think about was how soft and willing her lips had been when he kissed her.

"Come see Jessica play pat-a-cake," Mariel said, turning to him. Her skin had a golden glow in the firelight.

"How do you know how to play with a baby?" he asked as he sat beside her.

Mariel laughed. "Everyone knows how to play pat-a-cake," she told him, guiding Jessica's little hands through the motions.

"I don't," he said before he could stop himself, and she looked over at him, surprised.

"Because you were a foster child?" she asked.

"Maybe," he said with a shrug.

"Well, here. You play with Jessica," she said, shifting the baby to his lap. She rose to stir the fire with the poker, sending tiny sparks up the flue, and he grinned at her when she resumed her seat beside him.

He looked down at the baby, who blinked at him and kicked her legs. He felt like an idiot, batting the kid's hands together and saying, "Pat-a-cake, pat-a-cake, baker's man," but Jessica cooed, and Mariel smiled. The three of them were warm and safe as dusk grew thick outside the castle windows.

"Everything's going to be all right, isn't it?" Mariel said, tilting her face toward him.

"Not unless we have a diaper handy," he said, grimacing as he felt the dampness seeping through the baby's blanket. Mariel laughed as she went into the kitchen to get a clean one.

A warmth settled around Jake's heart, and he found himself thinking that here in this castle, this strange, out-of-the-way castle, something odd and yet reassuring and wonderful was going on, something he couldn't quite explain. Everything *was* all right—maybe for the first time in his life.

Chapter Eight

"It doesn't seem like Christmas Eve," Mariel said later as they sat in front of the fire, watching over the sleeping Jessica.

"We could hang up our stockings by the chimney with care," Jake told her.

"In hopes that Saint Nicholas soon would be there? No, thank you, I'd rather keep my socks on. Cold feet, you know." Mariel smiled at him, thinking that she had cold feet in more ways than one. Here she was, sequestered with a guy who could have been a pinup, and she was reluctant to let nature take its course. Some might call it stupid; she called it prudent. She'd never believed in rushing into things.

Jake had pulled one of the dusty velvet settees close to the fire, and Mariel was curled up on it. He sat at her feet. Jessica was at the far end of the hearth, where she slept in warmth and safety. Although the castle had many rooms, they had decided to spend the night in front of the fire in order to conserve firewood. They had no idea how long it would last, and Jake wasn't willing to chop down trees that belonged to someone else.

"What do you usually do on Christmas Eve?" he asked.

"My parents and I would go to the midnight service at our church."

"What's it like?"

"Haven't you ever been to one?" she asked in surprise.

"I never lived with a family that did that," he explained. For a moment, Mariel could see Jake as a boy. He would have been vulnerable and he would have been lonely.

"We light candles and sing Christmas hymns. Afterward—in my church, anyway—people hug each other and wish each other a merry Christmas. And then we all go home to sleep, and when we wake up, it's Christmas morning," she said dreamily.

"And then what?"

"Mother and I cook a turkey. And Dad mashes the potatoes. And I bake a cake."

"What kind?"

"Dad likes coconut, and we like to humor him on Christmas, so that's what it usually is. We always have turkey and stuffing and mashed potatoes. I miss them so much at this time of year. I won't be seeing them for six more months."

"Families should be together for the holiday."

Mariel sighed. "It's the first time in my life that I haven't been with my parents for the holidays," she said.

"Even though I don't have parents, I can imagine how you must feel. Not to mention having to spend the night in a cave."

"You know something? That time we spent in the cave—it wasn't so bad."

He focused unbelieving eyes on her. "How can you say that? Your face is scratched from the brambles, we had to care for a baby without the proper equipment or supplies, and we almost starved," he reminded her.

Mariel thought for a moment. "Those things are true," she agreed. "But you left something out. You didn't mention how kind you were to me, or how good it felt to provide for Jessica. You didn't say anything about how it felt when you came back into the cave, after I had been thinking that you had deserted us and you had been thinking that I had left, and we were both still there."

He stared at her, unsure what he should say or do, but she took care of that for him. She reached for his hand across the space between them and squeezed his fingers.

"I need you, Jake. And you need me. Jessica needs both of us. Those truths were brought home to me in the cave."

Jake hadn't known that Mariel realized how important they all were to each other. He didn't know how to react.

"It's almost midnight," Mariel said softly. "Would you like to join me in our own special Christmas Eve candlelight service?"

"I wouldn't know what to do."

"I'll show you," she told him, and got up from where she sat.

He gazed into the flames while she went into the kitchen. He heard her rummaging around, but he didn't want to follow her. He didn't want her to see that he had tears in his eyes or to know that, on this Christmas Eve, Mariel Evans had touched him to the depths of his soul.

JESSICA SLEPT DEEPLY beside the fire, and Mariel insisted that she and Jake repair to the cold chapel for their ceremony. Jake put on his jacket and held Mariel's coat for her. Her scarf was caught in the sleeve, and he pulled it out.

"Don't you want to wear this?" he asked.

She hesitated for a moment, then wrapped it around her head. Jake stared at her, fathomless eyes fixed on her face. To break the mood, she bent to light a candle that she had affixed to a saucer with melted wax.

When she straightened, he was still staring at her as if he couldn't pull his eyes away. "You look…" he began, then stopped.

"I look what?" she asked, something stilling inside her.

"You look beautiful in the candlelight," he finished softly.

This was not the way this was supposed to go. She didn't want to encourage Jake Travis; nor did she want to give herself false hope. Tonight she wanted to celebrate the meaning of Christmas and give thanks for their safety, and that was all.

"Come with me," she said quietly. Taking Jake's hand, she led him through the small corridor to the chapel.

The altar was wide, surmounted by a stained-glass window featuring Jesus, Mary and Joseph. Candelabra holding old parchment-colored candles flanked the altar, and Mariel lit the candles one by one. They cast a warm glow over the room, highlighting the wood grain of the pews and giving enough light to read the print on the pages of the large Bible that stood on the altar.

Mariel cleared her throat. "First," she said, "we thank God for his protection, and we ask for his blessing. Would you like to—?"

Jake shook his head.

Mariel bowed her head, and Jake followed her example. "Heavenly Father, thank you for letting us find Jessica in the woods. Thank you for guiding us to the cave last night and for providing food for us and for Jessica. Thank you for helping us find this castle. We ask your blessing on all of us, and for your guidance in the days to come." She paused. "Is that all?" she whispered to Jake.

"Thank you for the goat," he reminded her.

"And thank you for the goat."

"Amen," Jake said hastily, and Mariel added her own "Amen" to his.

"Now I'll read the Christmas story." Mariel picked up the Bible and leafed through it until she came upon the age-old story, so familiar to her, but perhaps not to Jake, who stood beside her, his attitude cooperative but otherwise unreadable.

"'And she brought forth her firstborn son, and wrapped him in swaddling clothes, and laid him in a manger; because there was no room for him in the inn,'" she read. The story had more meaning than ever for her now, because of Jessica.

When she finished, she laid the Bible on the altar.

"Now we should sing a Christmas carol," Jake said, surprising her, and he started with, "Hark, the Herald Angels Sing." She chimed in with her sweet contralto, and their voices blended so that the notes reverberated from the high ceiling in joyous accord.

"Let's sing another carol," Mariel said, gazing up at Jake, and he smiled and took her hand.

"Your choice this time."

Mariel sang "Away in a Manger," because it had been her favorite when she was a child. She had become unaccountably nostalgic while reading the Gospel, remembering how her father had often read it to her, not only at Christmas but at other times during the year, because she loved to hear about the baby being born in a stable.

"One more prayer, I think," she said in a low voice, and she tried to think of the formal benediction from church, but her mind had gone blank. She looked questioningly at Jake.

"And thank you for each other," he said. "Amen."

Mariel gazed up at him, surprised and touched. "Amen," she said, and he squeezed her hand.

The chapel was no longer cold. The air was warm, warmer than it should have been from the heat of a few candles.

"What time is it?" she asked Jake.

He glanced at his watch. "It's three minutes after midnight."

"Merry Christmas," she said, unwilling to look into his face.

But he had no such compunctions. Slowly he lifted his hands to her shoulders, and slowly he turned her to face him. His gaze was hard and penetrating, the set of his jaw firm.

She shook her head, denying what she read in his eyes, but it was too late.

"Merry Christmas, Mariel," he said, as he lowered his lips to hers.

She let him kiss her, but she held back. She didn't dare let herself participate, because she knew all to well what that would mean.

His lips were warm, and his hands found their way beneath her coat and adjusted to the slender curve of her waist. She wanted to slide her arms around him, to feel the wool of his coat against the palms of her hands, to feel the play of the muscles of his back. But her hands only hung at her sides.

Her mouth parted helplessly as he explored all the warm, sweet textures of lips and teeth and tongue. He kissed her so thoroughly and with so much unexpected passion that her heart trembled beneath her ribs and her skin caught fire.

Stop, Mariel thought. I don't want to do this.

But even as the thought seared her consciousness, she knew it wasn't true. His mouth was insistently seductive, and with supreme effort, she steeled herself to push him away. For one last, sensual moment, she was lost in the scent and taste and touch of him, and then she caught herself, just in time to wrench herself from his grasp.

"No," she said shakily, "I can't." Her boots clattered on the stone floor as she ran from the chapel.

Jake waited for a moment to see if she would return. He didn't know how she'd had the strength to put a stop to the mystical flow of passion and emotion between them, and he didn't know why she would want to. This was something special, this relationship, and he wanted to encourage it, to nurture it, and to embellish it. He couldn't imagine why Mariel wouldn't feel the same way.

He sat down in one of the pews to contemplate the situation, staring up at the stained-glass window of Jesus, Mary and Joseph above the altar. Mary held the infant Jesus in her arms, and Joseph stood behind Mary, his hand placed lovingly and protectively on her shoulder.

A family group. He had a rare flash of insight, unusual for him. He didn't know where it came from. He didn't know why it chose this moment to stun him into understanding. But now he knew what the hoopla of Christmas was all about.

It wasn't only to celebrate the birth of the Christ child. It wasn't just tinny Christmas carols piped into the grocery store, or toys on Christmas morning. It was a celebration of family.

For Jesus's birth had made Mary and Joseph a family. Not just a couple, but a man, woman and child. It was simple, really, because family was the basic building block of society. Nothing could change that. It had always been that way, and always would be.

His thoughts flew to encompass Jessica. She had made them a family, too. A temporary family, maybe, but it was the family that Jake Travis had never had. Families could come in all shapes and sizes. Single parents and their children were families, grandparents who were raising their children's children were families, and sometimes people who were unrelated were families. Like Mariel and Jessica and himself.

He was overcome by this feeling of kinship. One by one he blew out the candles, and then he went to find Mariel.

WHEN SHE FLED from the chapel, Mariel checked on Jessica and found her sleeping blissfully in her drawer on the wide hearth. She didn't want to have to talk to Jake; anything she might say would only make things worse between them. So she hurried into the kitchen and began to fill the huge tin bathtub she had found hanging in one of the pantries.

The castle didn't have adequate bathroom facilities. Toilets and miniscule sinks had been installed, apparently as an afterthought, under stairwells, and every time Mariel used one, the flushing rattled the pipes into a cacophony. She had a fear of causing a miniature Niagara and eventually having to explain to the owner of this castle how she had managed to flood it.

So she was relieved that there were no built-in bathtubs, only this tin tub. She heated water on the stove and poured it into the tub until there was enough for a bath.

Mariel couldn't recall ever having felt so grimy before. She was caked with two days' worth of dirt, overlaid with the smell of a camp fire and the dank odor of the cave, which clung to her hair and skin.

She peeked out the kitchen door and saw that Jake wasn't sitting with Jessica, which surprised her. He was probably still sulking in the chapel, which was fine with her. If he was like most men, his ego was wounded. He'd probably never try to kiss her again. She only wished that thought didn't make her feel so depressed.

JAKE, after coming out of the chapel, was surprised not to find Mariel with Jessica. Jessica was sleeping on her stomach, her mouth open. She looked like one of the dolls in the tower; she really was a lovely baby.

He sat to wait for Mariel. When she didn't return after a reasonable length of time, he made his way toward the kitchen, seeing a glow behind the door as he approached.

The door was ajar, and it didn't occur to him to knock. This was, after all, the kitchen, and he thought that Mariel would be preparing a bottle for Jessica. He had no idea that she would be taking a bath, and when he saw her, he froze, spellbound by the sight of her.

In the light from the kerosene lamp on the table, Mariel's skin glistened like oiled silk. Her hair was dark from the water, and slicked back, making her eyes seem bigger. He was used to her fluffy curls, not this sleek cap; he was accustomed to seeing her wrapped up for cold weather, not totally naked. She was so achingly beautiful that she took his breath away.

Somehow reality evaporated like mist; there was no castle, no baby, they weren't lost, and he knew exactly what he was going to do. Only the two of them existed in the world, and he was going to do what any man would do under those circumstances. He was going to make Mariel his, incontrovertibly and forever.

In his mind he was striding forward, and she was turning her head toward him, slowly, slowly, as if in a dream. Their eyes met, and he was drawn into the warm azure depths of hers as a moth, utterly doomed, seeks the hot blue center of a flame. She smiled and held out her hand, droplets of water scattering like diamonds in the flickering lamplight, and when their hands met, she rose up out of the water like a nymph, smoothly and quietly, and somehow she was in his arms.

He had magically shed his clothes, and their bodies met, melding contours, flowing together. Her breasts brushed against his chest, their nipples wet and warm, and her mouth merged with his in an exquisite mating. He slid his hands down her smooth sides and cupped her bottom, urging her close. She moaned, deep in her throat, and so did he, and he pressed himself against her, lifting her so that she could wrap her legs around him, holding him so tightly, tightly, the two of them wrapped in the enchantment of the moment....

Of course, all this only happened in his mind. What really happened was that Mariel reached for the soap, which was resting on a nearby wooden stool, saw him standing in the doorway and screamed.

"Sorry," Jake said, his dreams bursting like a soap bubble. He retreated, feeling like a fool. She must think he was no better than a Peeping Tom—which, come to think of it, might be the truth. He was so angry with himself that he brought his fist down hard on one of the tables as he was passing, whereupon Jessica woke up and began to cry.

"Okay, okay..." Jake said, rushing to pick her up. If the truth were told, he was glad of the ruckus. At least taking care of Jessica gave him something to do besides put himself down for acting like an idiot.

Mariel shot out of the kitchen, a towel wrapped around her.

"What happened to Jessica? Is she all right?" she shouted, running up the aisle between the tables. Drops of water sprayed everywhere.

"She got scared," he said, trying not to look at Mariel. She hadn't taken time to dry herself, and her flesh rose up in goose bumps. It didn't make her any less attractive to him, unfortunately.

He picked up the baby, who was making more of a fuss than was warranted.

"Time for a diaper change," he said with false cheer. He reached for the stack of towels that served as Flubbies.

Mariel's teeth were chattering. "What was that awful noise?" she said.

"I hit the table with my fist," he said calmly.

"Why?"

"I was angry," he said.

"W-with me?" she asked.

"No," he said, efficiently pinning one corner of the towel together. He was getting good at this diapering business, but Mariel never seemed to notice.

"With the baby?"

"With myself," he said shortly. "Don't you think you'd better put some clothes on?"

Her eyes shot daggers at him. Then she turned and, with the utmost dignity, stalked back into the kitchen and shut the door firmly after her.

Jake had no idea what Mariel's look meant, but he was pretty sure what it *didn't* mean.

Jessica began to cry. It was the wail that he had come to know as her "feed me" persuasion.

"All right, little one," he said tenderly, kissing the top of the infant's head. And then he added, with a kind of wonder that he was saying it at all, considering the way things were going with Mariel, "Merry Christmas, Jessica. Merry Christmas, baby!"

AFTER Mariel came out of the kitchen to dry her hair by the fire, Jake went to take his bath.

Mariel knew he hadn't meant to walk in on her when she was bathing, and she didn't know why she had reacted by screaming. He'd startled her; when she'd looked up and seen him standing there, mesmerized at the sight of her, she'd been momentarily caught off guard. She'd felt foolish afterward. It wasn't as if Jake Travis hadn't seen her body before.

She'd try to reassure him and let him know that she had no hard feelings over it. In fact, it was just the opposite. She was so strongly attracted to him that she felt caught in some kind of spell, unable to resist, though she knew she had no business thinking about him in that way. They had almost nothing in common except the baby and their goal of survival—why, they wouldn't have spared each other more than a passing glance if they had happened to stand next to each other at the bus stop in Pittsburgh.

Pittsburgh. It seemed so far away.

Mariel picked up Jessica and fed her. The baby adjusted to the doll bottle and drank the goat's milk without a peep, and Mariel was so engrossed that she didn't hear Jake when he came out of the kitchen, fresh from his bath. She looked up to see him standing before her.

"Mariel, I think I should sleep upstairs, in one of the rooms off the gallery," he said without preamble.

"It's so cold up there!" she exclaimed in dismay.

"I can build a fire."

"Jessica will wake up again in four hours. I thought we'd take turns feeding her, and if you're sleeping upstairs, you won't hear her cry."

He thought for a moment. "A good enough reason," he said grudgingly.

"We'll toss for the settee?" she said, favoring him with a brisk smile.

"That's not necessary. You can have it."

Mariel nodded toward a window. "I saw blankets in a chest over there."

Jake went to look and returned with his arms piled high with cushions, a comforter, and several woolen lap robes. "These should do," he told her. He tossed the cushions on the hearth and sat beside Jessica. When the baby was asleep, he punched the cushions he'd spread on the hearth into a semblance of a bed.

Mariel held the comforter to her cheek. "This smells of lavender," she said.

Jake ignored her. "I'm going to turn in. It's been a long day," he said. He lay down and tried to carve out hollows in the cushions with his hips and shoulders, his back to her.

"Is everything okay? Was your bath all right?" she asked.

"Yeah. I'm just tired." He threw a lap robe over himself and said nothing more.

Mariel curled up on the settee and pulled the comforter up over her shoulders. It was quiet, the only sound the crackling of the fire.

"Jake?" Mariel said, her voice too loud for the silence.

"What?"

"You know those toys in the tower?"

"I only met them today," he said gruffly, but he sounded slightly amused.

"Don't be funny. Anyway, why do you think they're there?"

He sighed audibly. "For all I know, this is Santa Claus's distribution point for northern Virginia and all points south. Mariel, how the hell would I know what they're doing there?"

"I just wondered," she said. He didn't speak. "Are you comfortable?"

"Mm-hmm" was his muffled reply.

"At least this is cozier than last night," she said.

"I'm not so sure," he answered, leaving her to ponder his meaning. Last night, she thought he meant, she had slept beside him, warmed by his body. It had felt good, *so* good....

Soon she saw his shoulders rising and falling rhythmically, and she knew he was asleep.

After a while, she slept, too, a deep, wintry sleep filled with slippery dreams. Nothing in them seemed concrete; everything was wispy images.

Until suddenly the white-bearded man from the Magic Minimart bent over her, wearing a fur-trimmed red cap and looking as solid as anyone could.

Mariel stared. He didn't fit into this dream. He was too real.

He *wasn't* real—was he?

Chapter Nine

"You made so many wishes, I wasn't sure *what* you wanted for Christmas," said the little man. "I had to guess. How did I do?"

Mariel felt disoriented and confused, and at first she was reluctant to answer. This was a *dream*. She didn't want to participate.

But she knew the man represented Santa Claus. She was in awe of him, the way she'd been when she was a little girl and her parents took her to the city's biggest department store to sit on Santa's knee. The little girl in her felt obligated to answer, even though she was half scared to speak up, just as if she were still a child.

"Well?" Santa said. "Aren't you going to talk to me? I don't have all night, you know."

"I don't like to complain," Mariel said.

He *ho-ho-ho*ed. "Seems to me you made a big fuss the Christmas when you were ten, because you didn't get a chemistry set," he replied.

She had. She was surprised that he'd remembered.

"You did okay this year, but I could have done without the sleet and the cave," she said grudgingly.

"Some things can't be helped. Anyway, don't you think Jessica's better than any of those baby dolls I used to bring you?" And then he winked and disappeared.

At that moment, Jessica started to cry and Mariel opened her eyes. Jake was sleeping, and Jessica had kicked off her blanket. It must be time for her feeding. Jake stirred as Mariel struggled out from the comforter.

"Don't get up," she said, mindful of how tired he'd been. "I'll take the first turn." Still wondering about her dream, she crossed the long hall and went into the kitchen.

The coals in the kitchen fireplace radiated warmth into the room, and Jake had left the kerosene lantern burning on the table. She found Jessica's bottle in the refrigerator, already filled. Jake must have prepared it earlier. Grateful for his foresight, Mariel warmed it quickly in a pan of water on the stove.

Jessica broke into a full-fledged wail as Mariel reentered the great hall, but Jake had already lifted her from her bed and was cuddling her in front of the fire and murmuring consoling words.

"I've got her bottle," Mariel told him. "I can feed her while you go back to sleep."

Jake looked bleary-eyed, but he took the bottle from Mariel. "I'm doing this."

"It's my turn," she protested.

"You go back to sleep," he said. "It's been a long day."

"Jake, I'm wide awake."

"That can be remedied soon enough." He smiled at her, and she sank down on the settee. She pulled the comforter up to her chin, but she didn't close her eyes. Jake was urging the baby to take the bottle, his head bent, his voice low as he murmured encouragement.

They looked so cute together, the man and the baby, and she wished she had a picture of them. But then, she was always wishing something.

That was when she remembered the little man with the beard who had appeared in her dream. Santa Claus. Santa Claus? She forced herself to sit up straight.

"Jake…" she began, but then she knew she couldn't ask

him if he'd seen Santa Claus too. She had no doubt that Jake would seriously doubt her sanity if she so much as hinted that she wasn't sure whether the man was a dream or reality.

Jake looked up at her. "I thought you were going to sleep," he said.

"I told you I'm too wide awake," she said. "I don't think I can sleep anymore."

"In that case, would you mind giving Jessica her bottle? I'll find us something to drink." Mariel moved to the warm hearth, and he carefully transferred the baby to her arms before disappearing into the kitchen.

Jessica drank eagerly, her eyes on Mariel's face.

"A bottle's better than an eyedropper, isn't it, Jessica?" Mariel whispered, and she thought that Jessica smiled momentarily.

She wondered if it was normal to bond with a baby so quickly when the baby wasn't even hers. She loved Jessica so much; before, she would not have believed that she could adore a tiny baby so completely.

"I love you, little Jessica," Mariel whispered, trying the words on for size and liking the way she felt inside when she said them. "I love you."

She was startled when Jake appeared suddenly, holding two steaming mugs.

"What's that?" she asked.

"I dug around in our host's cellar and found several bottles of burgundy, one of which was perfect for my own recipe for mulled wine. I thought we might as well try to be festive," Jake said with a smile. He set one of the mugs down beside her on the hearth and cupped the other between his hands as he sat. He leaned his elbows on his knees and looked ruminative.

"Jessica was a good baby. She drank all her milk," Mariel said after a while, holding up the empty bottle.

"Let me hold her for a while." Jake set his cup aside. "She doesn't look any sleepier than you do."

Mariel handed Jessica to him, and Jake rested her on his knees. Jessica bicycled her legs vigorously, and he laughed. Jessica cooed. He laughed again and tickled her under the chin.

Mariel treated herself to a sip of wine. It was good, warming her all the way down. Jake had spiced it with something—canned oranges from the pantry, perhaps, and cloves and cinnamon. "You two look so right together," she told Jake, and she meant it.

Jake shot her a quick sideways glance. "I was thinking the same thing about the two of you when I came out of the kitchen and saw you holding her. You look like a Madonna. Even your hair. It could be a halo."

"Oh, my hair..." Mariel said disparagingly. Her mother had often said that she didn't appreciate her naturally blond hair, which curled of its own accord, and maybe her mother was right. Mariel had always wanted straight hair, as fine and glossy as corn silk. Most of her friends thought she was out of her mind.

"What I said was meant to be a compliment," Jake said.

"I—well, I do feel comfortable with Jessica. I'll be going home to Pittsburgh after all this is over. Will you let me know how she fares?"

"Of course."

"Where she is, what her parents are like, how they live, all those things?"

"I'll even try to find out what kind of Flubbies she wears," he promised.

"I'm serious, Jake. This has been an experience I could never have imagined. I'll never forget Jessica. Or—" She had almost said "you."

There was silence for a few beats. Jake cleared his throat. "I was thinking that we could keep in touch," he said at last. "Not just about Jessica," he added in a rush, when he saw the fleeting expression of doubt that crossed her features.

"Mmm..." Mariel agreed noncommittally. She wasn't

sure what he meant. Phone calls back and forth between the two of them? Letters? Visits?

She couldn't picture Jake in the city where she lived. She tried to imagine him swinging along her street, wearing blue jeans and his red-and-black lumberjack jacket, and the idea made her want to smile. Jake would feel out of place there, although she was certain that none of the other men of her wide acquaintance would outshine him. She'd be proud to show off Jake Travis to her friends. But she didn't think he'd like being put on display, like one of the artifacts at the museum where she worked.

"You might want to visit me in Tellurian," he said. "I'd show you the house I'm working on, and some others I've finished. We could even go spelunking and reminisce about old times."

"Spelunking?" the word didn't ring a bell.

"Exploring caves," he said, grinning.

"No spelunking," Mariel said firmly.

"When would you like to visit?" He was pushing her, and she didn't know how to deal with it. She couldn't imagine herself in rural Virginia any more than she could picture Jake in Pittsburgh.

"Oh, Jake, I don't know." She was wary of making a promise that she couldn't keep. She was attracted to him, but what did it mean? She needed to sort out her feelings. Right now she didn't know what she felt; all she knew was that she wouldn't mind kissing him again.

He look chastened, and she thought she might have hurt his feelings. She wished he didn't look so crestfallen.

He sat Jessica up in his lap, rubbing her back. She burped noisily. Jake wiped her face gently and then rocked her against his chest.

He's so good with the baby, Mariel thought. *How many men do I know who would share this experience so completely?* She didn't know any men who were this comfortable around babies.

Jessica's eyelids immediately began to grow heavy. Mariel thought that Jake's heartbeat must have a calming effect on the baby, because whenever he held her that way, she became drowsy and fell asleep. Mariel had a notion that it would be a very pleasant way to fall asleep, listening to Jake Travis's heartbeat.

"What do *you* think will happen to Jessica?" she asked idly. The baby's eyes drifted shut, and Jake settled her in her bed before answering.

"After we get back to civilization, we'll have to tell the police how we found her. She was abandoned in the woods, which is clearly a case of child neglect. If they can find her parents, perhaps they'll be prosecuted. Jessica could have died in that hut," he said.

"And if the authorities don't know immediately who her parents are? What will they do then?"

"Call in a social service agency, and they'll see that she's put in a foster home, I suppose," he told her.

"I can't bear the thought of that."

"Why?"

"Because—because I'm so fond of her," Mariel said in a low voice.

"Well, so am I. I'm a product of foster homes myself, and it's not an easy way to grow up."

"I suppose not."

He looked up at her. "Remember what I said, Mariel? Maybe Jessica's the solution to your problem. Maybe she's the baby you always wanted."

Mariel gazed into space for a moment. "There's something I didn't mention," she said at last.

"Oh?" he said, sounding surprised.

She forced herself to look at him. "I was married once," she said. "I could have had a baby then, but I refused. If I'd had a baby, I wouldn't be so alone now, that's for sure." She tried not to sound too regretful. She didn't want his pity.

She only wanted him to know what few people knew about her.

"Do you want to tell me about it?" he asked gently.

Mariel leaned her head back against the stone of the fireplace and gazed at the tapestries, half hidden in the gloom at the opposite end of the great hall. Jake waited while she gathered her thoughts.

"My husband was an officer in the air force, and we lived in California," she said finally, half wishing she hadn't opened this chapter in her life to Jake, but nevertheless feeling compelled to continue. She paused to take another sip of wine, covertly observing him from beneath her lashes, wanting to see how he was responding. His face showed no expression, and his eyes were thoughtful.

"My husband wanted a baby right away, but I resisted, because I thought we needed time to get to know each other."

Jake nodded. "That's understandable."

"Something else upset me, as well. He was drinking too much, and I worried about bringing a child into that situation." She let her sentence trail off, then took a deep breath and went on. "He drank more and more, and in the end he became abusive."

"He hit you?"

"Only once. I left and filed for divorce. He was killed two days after the divorce was final. He drove head-on into a tractor-trailer rig. He was drunk at the time." She bit her lip, remembering how demoralized she'd been by the whole experience. She'd thought she'd never get over the end of her marriage, and her ex-husband's death had sent her into a deep depression.

"I'm so sorry, Mariel," Jake said. He reached for her hand.

"I'm all right now," she said. "I feel as if I missed out on something that was rightfully mine, that's all. I feel cheated out of a home and children."

"I know how you feel. I've felt cheated out of a home all my life," he said.

"What happened to you—all that moving from one foster home to another—wasn't your fault. It *was* my decision not to have a baby," Mariel said earnestly.

"Ah, but, Mariel, I didn't know that all the shifting around wasn't my fault. When I was a kid, I was told I was bad for not eating all my vegetables, for leaving my shoes in front of the TV, for skipping school on the day of a test I wasn't ready to take. Naturally I felt that I must be bad, if I wasn't fit to stay in a foster home. It was easy to blame myself."

"Childhood probably isn't an easy time for anyone," Mariel said softly.

"Probably not. Though I know some people who claim to have had a happy childhood."

Mariel smiled. "I'm one of them. My parents were wonderful."

"Chances are," he said, tracing one of the veins on the back of her hand with his thumbnail, "you'll be a wonderful mother yourself. Since you've had a positive role model," he added.

"I may not get the chance," she reminded him. She bent over, and with her free hand she smoothed Jessica's nightgown. "I hope Jessica's parents will be good to her. I hope she'll be happy," she said wistfully.

The warm wine in her stomach was doing a wonderful central-heating job, and her fingertips were beginning to tingle. But maybe it wasn't the wine. Maybe it was Jake's touch that was sending warm waves of pleasure through her body. Whatever it was, it felt wonderful.

The stone of the fireplace was cool and bracing against the back of her head, and she closed her eyes. The fire crackled nearby, and the faint, sweet, woodsy odor of burning apple logs wafted over them. She still tasted the full-bodied wine on her tongue; whimsically she wondered if it was a magic potion. Whatever it was, it was potent stuff.

She felt Jake's hand brushing her hair away from her face, and she opened her eyes to find his head only inches from hers. She didn't have to read his mind to know what he wanted, because at the moment she wanted it, too. She wanted to be lost in the illusion that this could be more than a one-night stand, that this wasn't really a transient relationship. She wanted to know in her heart of hearts that a simple carpenter from rural Virginia and a sophisticated, college-educated woman from Pittsburgh could find enough in common to fall in love and make it last a lifetime.

If only she could believe! But how could she risk emotional involvement with someone she was sure she would never see again?

He cupped a hand around her face, staring deep into her eyes, and she felt the whisper of his breath on her cheek. Outside the wind blew, and the castle creaked around them. These were realities. She should have refused to be bewitched. She should have fought her way out from under Jake's spell. She should have, but she didn't.

Because in his eyes, there was magic.

Her heart turned over as he began to kiss her expertly and in a leisurely way, as if they had all the time in the world to explore their physical attraction. Maybe they did, she thought fuzzily. Maybe this, too, was a dream, maybe none of this was happening, maybe she would wake up soon.

His mouth tasted of wine and cloves and cinnamon, and his breath fluttered softly against her skin. His face smelled faintly of soap.

His hands rested lightly around her waist, but they began to move upward, exploring her ribs with excruciating slowness. A shiver sliced through her, a delicious tremor of anticipation. One of his hands slid upward and wove through her hair to cradle the back of her head, and the other rested lightly on her back, caressing in small, repetitive circles.

She felt so confused. She loved what he was doing to her, she loved the way she felt while he was doing it, and yet she worried that what was happening wasn't in her best interests. Or maybe it was. Maybe this was what she needed—a fleeting encounter with a man she liked. For too long she had been looking for the right man—preferably a PhD—and a love that would last a lifetime. Perhaps a handsome hunk of a carpenter and a *like* that lasted for a few days was good enough.

Jake shifted his weight so that his chest molded to hers, and he slid his hand lower to urge her toward him. Her head fell back as he traced the outline of her lips with his tongue in a foray that left her breathless.

She didn't know when she began kissing him back, but she was no novice, taking as well as giving, until he moaned with desire. His kisses became wilder and deeper, and soon her kisses matched his.

For the life of her, Mariel could think of no reason now to avoid this; she only knew that she had survived an automobile accident, a trek through an ice storm, a night in a cave, and an excursion through snow to this castle. She had taken on the responsibility for a small baby, and at times, though she would never have admitted it to Jake, she had been frightened out of her wits by their plight.

Now she wanted to celebrate their survival by feeling good again, by feeling alive, by unleashing the passions that had built up between her and this man, this Jake Travis, who might not be a permanent fixture in her life but was, by God, important to her.

She sighed deeply and he trailed a row of kisses down her neck to the hollow of her throat. She slid her hands down over his heavily muscled back, clutching him to her. His hands parted the neck of her sweater, and he lavished kisses in the sensitive hollow between her breasts as he undid the buttons.

His hands moved reverently beneath the soft lamb's wool to cup her breasts, still confined by the transparent lace of her bra. She was trembling as he reached around and unhooked it.

"Mariel…" was all he said, looking deep into her eyes, and she thought that she had never wanted a man so much in her entire life.

Her nipples ached for his touch, and when he rested the tips of his fingers on the sensitive underside of her breasts, she moved closer, until his hands completely encompassed the soft mounds of flesh. She slid her own hands under his clothes, and he moved away for one swift moment to divest himself of his sweater.

His chest was smooth, and bronzed by the firelight, and she slid her hands up over his nipples, gently rubbing until they rose into hard nubs beneath the palms of her hands.

"Ahh," he said, "that feels so good." He helped her to shrug out of her sweater, and her nipples were hot peaks beneath his fingertips.

They fell back against the cushions, her mouth opened beneath his and her hand went behind his neck to urge him closer, closer.

They were going to make love. It was what she had wanted to happen with every fiber of her being, though she still doubted the wisdom of getting involved with someone she'd only have to leave. And now, with the flicker of the firelight the room's sole illumination, and given the attraction that had flowed between them from the first, it seemed only natural and inevitable that they come together.

Jake's mouth was urgent and demanding, and his hands were knowing and insistent. She breathed in his warm, clean, male smell, wondering how it was that men could smell so different from women. Each had his own distinct natural fragrance, too, and Jake's was like no other man's she had known. She tried to identify it, but couldn't; she knew only that it was a woodsy, wild scent, and that it was, at the moment, compelling her to act with uncharacteristic wantonness, as if she weren't Mariel Evans, but a bolder, more seductive, more daring version of herself.

He slid both hands up to fan her hair across the cushions in a flow of spun gold. He gazed down at her, murmuring her name. She thought she had never heard anyone say it so beautifully.

Luminous flecks, so fascinating to watch, surfaced in his dark eyes. His hands cupped her face, and his eyes searched hers. "Oh, Mariel, you are all I've ever wanted in a woman," he breathed.

This is the way it should always be, she thought. She slid her hands between them, fumbling with the fastening of his jeans. He helped by lifting himself away so that she could unzip them, and he slid out of them as she shimmied free of her corduroys.

He knelt before her and slowly rolled her panties down over her hips and legs.

"You are so beautiful," he whispered, his eyes taking her in. He brushed his fingertips lightly across the soft wisp of curls where her legs met. "Lovely," he said, his hand seeking the hot center of her.

Her hands splayed over his flat belly and then moved lower, her fingers encasing his dusky hardness. He was hot, even hotter than she was, and very hard. As he strained against her hands, she felt a rush of heat in her lower abdomen, and she opened to his questing. His fingers found molten honey, and she arched beneath him, guiding the way.

She heard his sharp intake of breath as he lowered himself over her with agonizing slowness, supporting himself on his elbows as he took fierce possession of her mouth.

"Do you...want...?" he gasped close to her ear, and all she could do was cry, "Please...oh, yes...oh, yes..."

He moved a hand beneath her and paused for the space of a heartbeat, an eternity, before rearing back and, guided by her fingers, plunging into her with all his strength. She felt a white-hot throb of joy as he penetrated to her very center, and she gasped with pleasure against his mouth.

Their two bodies were one as, again and again, he rocked against her, his breath harsh against her ear. She felt dizzy, she felt hot, she felt wet and superbly energized. The thought flashed through her mind that somehow, in every past relationship she had ever known, she had missed out on what lovemaking could be, and she felt a sense of loss over those past futile fumblings. She wrapped her legs around him, lost in sensation and riding the sweet waves as they broke over the two of them, dissolving in a crest of pleasure.

She heard him cry out in exultation and heard her own answering sob, and then the sounds merged and were one and she didn't know where Jake ended and she began. As he pulsed within her, she gave herself over to the ecstasy, wanting this moment to go on forever. She had never before felt so wild and abandoned.

He fell against her, spent and sated, her fingers entangled in his damp hair. As he became conscious of time and place, he tried to roll his weight away, but she clutched him tightly around the waist.

"No," she murmured. "Not yet."

He covered her face with kisses, nuzzled her earlobe, and came to rest with his head pillowed on one breast, his finger slowly circling the other.

She couldn't believe it was happening so soon, but she was becoming aroused again. Her nipple rose between his fingertips, a small, swollen berry, and he laughed and took it between his lips, sucking, tasting, kissing. She let him, lazily giving in to the sensations.

"I never knew it could be like that," she said dreamily, and he lifted his head. His eyes were bright.

"I didn't, either."

"You were…wonderful."

"And so were you." He kissed the tip of her nose.

"So, if you feel like doing it again…" she said, because

she already felt him rising against the smooth flesh of her hip.

She was ready for him, but this time it was different. It was more controlled, more knowing, and their eyes seldom left each other's. Once, when she glanced to make sure that Jessica was still sleeping soundly, he tipped a finger under her chin and turned her face back toward him.

"Don't," he said tenderly. "I want to look into the heart of your soul." He held her eyes with his as he moved slowly within her, the flames from the fire illuminating her own reflection in his eyes.

This time he waited for her to climax first, taking in the flush of her face, the widening of her eyes, the gasps that she couldn't, didn't, want to control, and then he sought his own peak. She pulled him close, inhaling the sharp, tangy scent of his skin as he cried out. He buried his damp face in her neck and murmured her name over and over again in a voice husky with passion.

Afterward, he pulled the comforter off the settee and settled it over them in a flurry of warm air, cradling her in his arms when they were both snug beneath it.

"Well," he said, "I guess this proves Santa Claus isn't the only one who's coming," and Mariel dissolved into giggles interspersed with kisses.

"We should get up and prepare the bottle for Jessica's next feeding," she whispered, but he only smiled against her cheek; she could feel the corners of his mouth turn up.

"Jessica will make sure we get up soon enough, and the bottle only takes a few minutes," he said. "For now, let's sleep."

Mariel wanted to stay awake, savoring this experience to the utmost, reliving the joy of these moments over and over. There was no doubt in her mind that this was special, that no two people had ever experienced such passion, and that nothing could ever compare to it.

But it was only two or three minutes before she slept, safe in the confines of his arms.

Chapter Ten

Jake didn't wake Mariel at dawn. Instead, he eased out from under the warm comforter, dressed quietly, and went to the stable. There, he fed and milked the nanny goat who was docile and welcoming. Then he walked into the woods, dug up a beautiful blue spruce tree, and dragged it across the wobbly drawbridge to the castle.

Jake planted the tree in a dilapidated bucket that he found in the stable. He wanted to surprise Mariel with it. It was Christmas Day, and she must have at least one gift; the tree would be the perfect present for the perfect day.

The sun was shining, melting snow and icicles. Avalanches of snow kept sliding from the sloping roofs of the castle buildings, the intermittent dull roars resounding like distant thunder. It looked as if they were in for a thaw, which meant that soon they'd have to walk out of here. The thought that this idyll would soon end, whether he liked it or not, was the only flaw in the perfection of his world on this day.

He carried the tree into the great hall, but Mariel wasn't there. Nor was Jessica sleeping in her makeshift bed. He heard Mariel singing in the kitchen, and hearing her silvery voice cheered him considerably. Christmas wasn't over yet. Not by a long shot.

"Mariel!" he called.

She bustled out of the kitchen, a towel across her shoulder, the baby in her arms. She looked radiant this morning.

"Jake, I—" She stopped when she saw the tree. He thought she would have clapped her hands if she hadn't been holding the baby. "Oh, Jake! How lovely!" she exclaimed.

"It was practically begging me to take it inside to be your Christmas tree." He grinned at her, pleased with himself. Her eyes sparkled as she walked toward him.

"Here," he said, holding out his arms. "Let me see the baby."

He took Jessica into his arms so that Mariel could inspect the tree more closely. He loved Jessica's warm baby smell, and he touched his lips to her forehead. "She smells so fresh."

"I was heating water on the stove, so I poured some of it into the smallest washtub and bathed her. She liked it," Mariel said.

Jake hummed "Rockabye Baby," mostly because he remembered that it had something about a tree in it. Then he remembered what it was, and he didn't hum the rest of it. In the song, the bough broke, and down came baby, cradle and all.

"Who would write a song like that for a baby?" he said indignantly.

"What song? Oh, that rockabye-baby one," Mariel said. "It's an old English folk tune."

She circled the tree. "What a good job you did in choosing this one," she said with satisfaction.

"Sadistic thing," Jake mumbled, holding Jessica more snugly.

"The tree, Jake?"

"No, no. The *song,*" he said. "Sounds like something one of my worst foster parents dreamed up."

"Well, sing Brahms' 'Lullaby.'"

"I don't know that one," he told her.

"I'll teach you. While we're stringing popcorn into garlands for the tree."

"I've never done that."

"It's about time you did. And we'll prop the toys from the tower beneath it and pretend they're for Jessica. Oh, Jake, it will be such fun."

He pulled her to him and buried his face in her hair, unable to embrace her with as much enthusiasm as he really would have liked, because he was holding the baby. Memories of the night before danced in his head.

"Better than visions of sugarplums," he said, his voice husky, and Mariel pulled away and looked at him quizzically.

"The toys, you mean?" she asked.

"Last night, I mean. It was beautiful, Mariel. I'll never forget it."

"Magic," she said. "It was magic."

A smile lit his features. "If that's what you want to call it, that's okay with me."

They walked arm in arm to the fire, which Jake had fed before he left. It was blazing now, the flames roaring. "I found hot cereal in the pantry," she told him. Two large bowls of cream of wheat stood steaming on the hearth, along with two mugs of coffee and two glasses of juice. "It was the best I could do," she explained.

Jake laid Jessica in her bed and picked up one of the bowls. "Let's eat," he said. "Then maybe we should go for a walk in the woods, see if we see any signs of people."

"We could gather berries and things to decorate our tree," said Mariel, her eyes shining. Then her face fell. "We can't. We can't carry decorations for our tree, and Jessica, too."

"I saw a sled in the tower room yesterday," he reminded her.

"So did I. Good, we'll pull Jessica along on that."

She looked so excited and happy that it was all he could do not to lean over and kiss her. He wasn't sure how she'd respond to such a gesture. Passion in the night was one thing, but kisses in daylight were quite another.

He finished his cereal. "That was good."

"I checked the store of canned goods. The prospects for dinner are dismal, unless you like chop suey. I wish we could eat a real Christmas dinner today," she said pensively.

"Is that one of your three wishes?" he asked her with a twinkle.

"It should be."

"Well, one of mine is that we get going on this tree-trimming mission of ours. I'd better run up to the tower room and bring down the sled."

When he left, she was bending over Jessica, the soft womanly curve of her breast outlined by her sweater. The sight of her reminded him that he wasn't so eager to be rescued after all. He'd like at least one more night with her, one more night to hold her close, one more night to—

He stopped in the door to the tower room. He couldn't believe his eyes.

"Mariel!" he called in a startled voice.

After a moment, he heard her mounting the stairs behind him, the heels of her boots rapping sharply on the stones.

"What is it?"

"Look," he said, standing aside, and behind him Mariel gasped.

Not one toy was left in the tower except the sled. And beneath the window stood a pair of tall black boots.

"Where—?" Mariel was as mystified as he was.

"I don't know," Jake said, striding into the room.

Mariel went over and picked up one of the boots. She inspected it carefully. "This boot is damp inside. Feel the lining," she told him.

He did. It was soft and fuzzy and definitely wet. Whoever had worn those boots—someone who wore a man's size 6, apparently—had been tramping around in the snow.

"No one could get in here," he said, trying the latches on

the windows one by one. One swung open when he pushed at it; beyond it was the leaded roof over the chapel, denuded of snow by an avalanche earlier, while he was milking Nelly.

With the practiced eye of a master carpenter, he judged the distance. Someone could climb into this room from the chapel roof if he had a mind to—but who would? And how would he get up there, anyway? The wall on one side of the building was sheer and ended in the moat. The wall on the other side offered no handholds for climbing. There was no ladder that he could see. And, of course, with the snow gone from the roof, there were no footprints.

"Well," Mariel said with remarkable calm, "maybe the toys weren't here in the first place."

Jake turned to her incredulously. "You saw them. *I* saw them. Even Jessica saw them! They couldn't just get up and walk away!"

"Maybe—" Mariel began, but then she bit her lip. Just then Jessica began to cry, and they both hurried down the steps again.

Mariel picked up Jessica and soothed her. "We left you all alone, didn't we? And you knew it, didn't you? Sweet Jessica, how would you like to go for a walk? Outside in the snow? Wouldn't that be fun?"

Jake went outside to prepare the sled for the baby while Mariel got Jessica ready for their walk. After he'd finished, he stood in the middle of the courtyard and studied the tower above the great hall, where the toys had been. How in the world had someone managed to remove them without his and Mariel's knowing about it?

Sure, their lovemaking had made the rest of the world go away, but certainly he and Mariel would have noticed someone hauling toys down the tower stairs. It didn't make sense. It didn't make any sense at all.

MARIEL AND JESSICA, who was wrapped in blankets to the tip of her winsome pug nose, joined him in the courtyard a few minutes later.

"The snow may last only a few more days," Jake said. "From the balminess of the weather, it looks like we're in for a thaw."

"Well, it can't possibly all melt today, and I'm glad. There's nothing like a white Christmas."

Jake had rigged up Jessica's drawer-bed on the sled, hammering in a few well-placed nails to hold it. Now he fastened Jessica securely, so that she wouldn't fall out.

Nelly the goat trotted out of the stable and right up to Mariel, nuzzling her hand. Mariel scratched her ear affectionately, and the goat trailed in their footsteps as they made their way through the gatehouse passageway. But Nelly balked at the drawbridge. They left her behind and headed into the woods, Jake pulling Jessica on the sled. Mariel looked ecstatic.

"Say, isn't that holly growing over there, near that dead tree?" Jake asked after they'd walked half a mile or so.

"Oh, Jake, it will look so beautiful heaped in vases on the hearth!" exclaimed Mariel, her eyes alight with enthusiasm.

"Vases? Dream on," Jake said.

"I saw them in a kitchen cupboard. Or maybe they were big pottery jars. Does it matter? The holly will look so pretty." She ran through the snow, exclaiming over the abundance of berries while Jake, faintly bemused, followed after her, with Jessica on the sled.

Jake cut several boughs of holly with his hatchet. Careful not to prick herself with the points on the ends of the leaves, Mariel stuffed the branches into one of the many large bags they'd found in the kitchen.

Mariel rushed ahead, her hair as bright as the sunshine. "Wait for me," Jake called, because he didn't want her to get too far ahead.

"Oh, I see a fallen spruce tree!" she exclaimed, and with that she was off and running, leaving Jake behind.

"Let's take home some of these big lower branches," she said. "And a few smaller ones." She gathered them as fast as Jake could cut them.

"What are you going to do with those?"

"Drape them all about. The great hall will look so lovely when we're through decorating." She smiled up at him.

"*You* look so lovely now."

"I feel happy. As if I could fly. Watch me." She was off again.

"Look," she called from somewhere up ahead, "I'm making a Christmas angel!" When he reached her, she was lying in a snowbank at the edge of the meadow and energetically moving her arms and legs up and down. She sat up. "Why don't you make one, too? We'll write our names in the snow underneath."

"I'd rather watch you."

To his surprise, she wadded up a handful of snow and sailed it past his head. The next snowball was more accurate and hit him in the chest.

"I wouldn't do that if I were you," he warned. It was too late; she managed to land the next one squarely in his face.

"If you don't want more of the same, I suggest you make your own angel," she said, laughing up at him.

For answer, he bent down and scooped up some snow of his own, molding it quickly.

"Oh, no, you don't," Mariel said, rolling quickly to one side, annihilating the snow angel she had just finished making.

He tried to hit her with the snowball, but it exploded directly to her right, and with that she was on her feet and scooping up great clods of snow.

"We'll see who can make the biggest snowball," she said, but this time he managed to hit her, and she threw a handful of loose snow at him.

"I'll fix you," he said, and he grabbed her by the collar and washed her face with snow until she twisted away and fell in a snowbank, whereupon he lost his balance and fell on top of her.

"Who fixed whom?" she said, grinning up at him, and then they were rolling over and over in the snow. She tickled him, and he retaliated by pinning her down, his hands holding her wrists, his leg across her thighs.

Suddenly it seemed very quiet. All they could hear was the sound of their own irregular breathing.

He was aware of her beneath him, of all her gentle curves, of the bones beneath her skin, of the sublime softness of her lower lip. Her eyes were as blue as the sky, and her skin was pink from the cold. She smelled of evergreens.

"Mariel," he whispered, and then he kissed her, tasting her, tentatively at first, then more forcefully. Her arms went around him, and he felt her warmth through the layers of clothing they wore. With any encouragement, he would make love to her here in the snow, with the whole forest looking on. The heat from his body would be enough to keep them warm.

"If only it could be Christmas forever," he said against her cheek, and she turned her head and looked deep into his eyes. He was dizzy with desire for her, but she pushed him away.

"We're not acting much like angels," she said lightly.

"Do we have to?" he asked, but she was already standing up and bending over the sled to check on the baby.

"What's this?" she asked, holding the thermos he had tucked in the side of Jessica's bed.

He brushed snow off his clothes. "Hot chocolate. For our lunch."

"You brought lunch?"

"A package of saltines and some canned pudding from the pantry." He pulled the cans and crackers out of the blankets around Jessica's feet.

"Let's sit down on that rock over there and eat," Mariel said. Jake could think of things he'd rather do, but even he had to admit that they were impractical. He followed Mariel and endured the peculiar lunch. Mariel insisted on spreading her chocolate pudding on saltines. He ate his separately, watching her and realizing that she was actually enjoying the meal.

"I'll bet we can find some things around the castle to decorate the tree with," Mariel said.

"I noticed scraps of aluminum foil stuffed into a crack in one of the windows. It'll be fine for a star. And if we can find wood, I might be able to make a few ornaments. I used to be a pretty good carver," he told her.

"This part of Virginia is so beautiful." Mariel gazed at the mist-shrouded mountains in the distance. "If this hadn't happened, I would have missed sitting here with you and enjoying the peacefulness of this snowy landscape. Isn't this better than watching a football game in the company of a bunch of guys?"

"You'd better believe it" was Jake's heartfelt reply.

"What would you do tonight if we weren't here?" she asked him.

"Sleep off the effects of a huge dinner. Chop suey at Christmas may have its good points. After an hour or so, we'll have to remind our stomachs that we've eaten."

Mariel made a face and tucked her arm companionably through his. "The chop suey wouldn't be so bad if we only had some rice. And noodles. And maybe a couple of fortune cookies."

"There you go, wishing. Aren't you aware you do it?"

She laughed and shrugged. "No. You know, I dreamed I saw Santa Claus last night," she told him.

"I dreamed I heard hoofbeats on the roof," he said, completely deadpan. He was obviously teasing, but she wanted to be serious.

"No, Jake, I honestly did," she insisted.

"Okay, and what did the old guy have to say?"

Mariel could tell he was humoring her, but she wanted to share this with him; for some reason, it seemed important.

"He asked me if I didn't think that Jessica is better than any of those dolls he used to bring me," she recounted, and her face flushed.

"Ha! I hope you told him that the dolls didn't wet their diapers every fifteen minutes."

"No. He disappeared." Mariel was feeling slightly disgruntled, and she thought she had been foolish to tell Jake about the dream.

"I would too, if I were him. If he hadn't, you might have given *him* the sack of dirty diapers. Speaking of which, it should be fun to wash them by hand. I didn't see a washing machine."

"I can do it," Mariel said. She was disappointed that he hadn't taken her seriously, but at least it made it clear that they were two different types. Jake was down-to-earth, elemental; when he'd told her he didn't believe in magic, she should have believed him.

He took her hand and pulled off her glove, pretending to inspect her palm and fingers carefully. "You'd wash diapers and roughen these lily-white hands? Oh, no, you won't. We'll share."

She smiled at him, feeling better now. "I think it's good the way we divvy up the work of taking care of Jessica," she said, determined to put his previous teasing out of her mind.

"Isn't sharing the modern way to bring up a baby? Isn't that what fathers are supposed to do? I suppose that old baby book you found doesn't tell you that."

"But you're not—" She stopped. She didn't want to hurt his feelings.

"I'm not Jessica's father, you were going to say. No, Mariel, I'm not. And you're not her mother. But living together in the castle, it's almost like we are. I never told you, but after we left the chapel last night, I suddenly knew what

Christmas was all about." He told her how he'd felt when he was looking at the stained-glass portrayal of Mary, Joseph and Jesus. Mariel seemed subdued, so he put his arm around her.

"And you know something?" he went on. "I like being a family, even if it's just for Christmas." He looked away across the field, his eyes on the outline of the mountains rising against the milky blue sky.

"But would you still like it if it was the same old day-to-day routine?" Mariel kept her own eyes on Jessica's face, her dear, sweet, beautiful face.

"I don't know," Jake said honestly. "And it's not something I need to think about, is it?" He stood up; looming over her, he seemed to fill the sky.

Mariel licked her lips, her mouth suddenly dry. His remark had brought her to her senses. She'd been deeply affected by Jake's revelation, and it made her more aware of her own mind-set. She had, without being really aware of it, been thinking about what it would be like for them to be Jessica's parents and to share the responsibility of her upbringing.

Jake reached down and pulled Mariel to her feet. He wasn't wearing his cap today, and his hair fell in an unruly mass over his forehead. It gave him a roguish appeal and emphasized the rough-hewn quality of his features.

"Is everything all right?" he asked, looking puzzled.

"Yes, but I think we should continue our foraging. It'll be time to feed Jessica soon." She turned abruptly and headed into the woods, pulling on the glove he'd removed from her hand and walking too fast for him to keep up with her.

She had to think, and she wanted to do it as far away from those warm brown eyes as possible. Because, now that they were out of any real danger, living together in the castle was too comfortable by far. It was easy for them to fall into playing the role of mother and father to an oh-so-adorable baby. It was easy to think that this could go on forever.

But it couldn't. She and Jake Travis were totally different

types. They led lives so far apart that there was no way to merge them, ever. She'd better face up to that. She'd better not start thinking that it could be any other way, because if she did, she would only be heartbroken.

She picked up some pinecones and gathered a few fallen evergreen boughs. Jake, pulling Jessica in the sled, was narrowing the gap between them when she pointed to a mass of pale green leaves and pearly white berries high in the leafless branches of an old oak tree.

"Jake, look!" she exclaimed, glad of a distraction. "It's mistletoe!"

Jake's gaze followed her pointing finger. "It certainly is."

"Oh, I wish I had some. It would look so pretty on our Christmas tree," she said, but she knew the mistletoe was too high up to reach, and the tree didn't look suitable for climbing.

"I wonder," he said thoughtfully, "if it's the same variety we usually see hanging over people's doorways during the holiday season."

"Oh, I'm sure it is," Mariel told him. "Did you know that mistletoe was revered in olden times as a plant of peace? If enemies met beneath a bough of mistletoe in a forest, custom required them to dispense with their hostilities and observe a truce until the next day."

"Mariel," Jake said, "you don't have to tell me what mistletoe is for. It's for this." And with that he swept her into his arms and kissed her until her knees went weak.

When his lips released hers, she gazed up at him. "What—what was that for?"

"For mistletoe. And for magic."

She struggled to regain her composure. "You don't believe in magic," she reminded him.

He smoothed her hair back from her face, his hand warm against her cool cheeks. "It's getting so I believe in it more and more," he said before kissing her again.

"Jake," she said when he released her lips, deciding that

it was time to lay it on the line, "this is more than I can handle. Last night was wonderful, but now I need some space. Everything's happening so fast." She looked up at him helplessly.

"You think we need a cooling-off period."

'Yes.''

"Don't you know I really care about you? About what happens to you?" he asked fiercely. His arms were still locked around her, and he seemed unlikely to let her go.

"I believe you do," she said, meaning it. "It's just that I'm afraid of starting something that we both know we won't be able to finish."

"Didn't you feel something special last night? Or was it just the same old same old?"

She twisted away from him. "You know it wasn't. You know it meant something to me, too."

"Then why do we have to pretend that it didn't?"

"Because there's no future in it. Can't you see?" she cried. Tossing the bag of forest gleanings over her shoulder, she marched away from him, toward the castle.

"Who says? Why can't there be? Is it because I'm not as educated as you are?" he called after her in exasperation.

Mariel whirled in her tracks. Her voice shook when she spoke. "Let's get this straight once and for all, Jake! I'm well aware that it was *your* skills that saved us in the woods. It so happens that I respect people who work with their hands. But I won't apologize for my education! My father held down two jobs to send me to a state university, and my mother worked in a day-care center. I was lucky. But I don't look down on people who haven't been to college, okay?" She turned her back on him and headed toward the castle.

He hailed her with a shout as she approached the draw-bridge. She didn't think about the bridge's construction—she was too intent on ignoring him. Suddenly, when she was about halfway across, she felt one of the boards snap beneath her feet.

She was flooded with panic as she felt the bridge lurch beneath her and heard part of the board fall into the moat. She was only a few feet from the land at the end of the drawbridge, and she lunged toward it. When she looked back she saw that a hole had appeared in the snow, and through it she spied the rotted edges of the old board. The black water of the moat swirled below.

Jake had already stepped onto the other end of the drawbridge.

"Don't—" she warned him, but it was too late. Jake's strides were long, and by the time she spoke, his boot had struck what remained of the rotted board.

Only then did he realize what was happening. He tried to catch his balance, but, as if in slow motion, he toppled over the side of the drawbridge and into the icy water below.

Chapter Eleven

Fortunately, Jake had had the presence of mind to drop the rope that pulled the sled before he went over the side of the drawbridge. Jessica was safe, and, best of all, she was unaware that anything had happened. She snoozed amid her blankets, bundled tightly against the cold.

"Jake?" Mariel called. She felt frozen in place; she didn't know whether it was safe to move toward Jessica on the treacherous drawbridge. Jessica wasn't in any immediate danger. That couldn't be said of Jake.

Mariel hung over the battlemented fence of the outer ward and peered down into the water. Widening circles told her where Jake had plunged, but he had vanished. Her heart stilled in her chest.

Thoughts chased through her mind; she imagined Jake knocked out by the fall, his body drifting to the bottom of the moat. Did he know how to swim? She imagined him so cold that he couldn't move his arms and legs.

The drop from the drawbridge was a good twelve or fifteen feet, and, despite the thaw in the air, little fragments of ice floated on top of the water, broken off from the thin shell around the edges. As Mariel was wondering how long someone could survive in such cold water, Jake's head popped up.

He saw her immediately. "The water must come out of a

pipe that comes directly from the North Pole!'' he gasped, treading water.

''Are you all right?'' she asked anxiously. She was flooded with relief at the sight of him. And he must not be hurt, if he could joke.

''As all right as someone can be when weighed down by a heavy, waterlogged wool jacket.''

Mariel knew that she had to keep from panicking. She knew that, but the sight of Jake trying to keep afloat in the icy water almost unnerved her.

''Get Jessica off the drawbridge,'' he said.

Mariel took her eyes from Jake long enough to spare a brief glance at the sled, which was still where he had left it. She felt torn, not knowing what to do first. It took her only a split second to come down on the side of Jake, who was in immediate peril.

''Jessica's all right,'' she said distractedly. She looked around for a rope or a pole—anything to help Jake with. She knew she had to find a way to rescue him from the water immediately.

''*Jessica*,'' Jake said in a tone that brooked no resistance and made his meaning perfectly clear.

Maybe Jake was right. Maybe she'd better tend to the baby. Barely managing to keep her senses about her, Mariel ran to the edge of the drawbridge. How safe was it for Mariel to step on the drawbridge and pull Jessica's sled the rest of the way across? Would the other planks bear her weight?

''Stay toward…the middle of…the bridge,'' Jake called. Was it her imagination, or was his voice flagging?

If something happened to her, Mariel knew both Jake and Jessica would be in grave peril. Jake's rescue and the baby's well-being depended solely on her. Yet in that moment, she realized that the baby's safety was more important than either Jake's or hers.

If only she could see the condition of the broken board beneath the snow! She had no idea of the extent of the damage. But there was no time to sweep the boards clean, not with Jake waiting patiently below, so she stepped out onto the bridge.

All one hundred and five pounds of her tensed as she carefully tested each step before investing it with her full weight. Every creak seemed magnified in the crisp clear air, and she waited for the *crack* that would mean that one of the boards had broken beneath her feet.

But finally she was close enough to Jessica's sled to grasp the rope and pull Jessica to safety. When at last the sled stood within the outer ward, she said a silent prayer of thanks and ran to hoist herself up on the wall again so that she could see how Jake was doing.

But now, where Jake's head had broken the surface, there was only dark water reflecting an endless blue sky.

Her heart fell to her boots. What had happened? Had he slipped beneath the water? Was he alive?

"I'm over here!" she heard him say, and when she looked carefully she saw his head, wet and seal-like, at the edge of the moat. He was clinging to a rock that formed part of the foundation of the castle.

"Can you climb out?" she asked frantically.

"I can't get a grip on these rocks! They're too slippery!" he gasped.

She remembered the rope in Jake's backpack. "I'll get the rope," she said. "Can you hang on?"

She thought he answered, "Yes."

This was no time to wait around and clarify things, she thought to herself as she bore Jessica on her sled through the gatehouse passageway and into the castle courtyard. She didn't want to leave Jessica out here in the cold; she wanted to set her inside by the fire.

Nelly the goat greeted her outside the gatehouse and, wagging her tail, capered wildly after the sled. Inside the great hall, Mariel parked Jessica—now awake and gnawing on her fist—in her sled beside the hearth.

"I'll be back," Mariel told Jessica as she fumbled in Jake's pack for the rope. "I'll be back *soon*. I promise." Not that Jessica could understand, but she hoped the baby would know that she wasn't deserting her.

She had been gone for only a matter of minutes, but Jake looked visibly more tired when she returned, his face white, his teeth chattering like a pair of castanets.

"I'm going to tie the rope around this iron ring in the castle wall," Mariel called down to him.

"Have you been p-practicing your c-clove hitches?" Jake hollered back.

"Don't make jokes," she ordered, not knowing what a clove hitch was, but sure that she'd never practiced any.

She fumbled with the knot, taking so long that the plaintive plea rose from the moat: "Mariel...can't you...hurry?"

By way of an answer she ran to the edge of the moat and dropped the end of the rope over the side, testing it from her side of the wall with her own weight. It held to the ring.

The end of the rope dangled above Jake, and she paid it out as quickly as she could, watching as Jake made several unsuccessful attempts to grab it.

"Are you okay?" she asked anxiously. His fingers seemed stiff with cold.

"As okay as...a Popsicle..." he managed to say.

"If you can make dumb jokes, you're fine."

Finally Jake caught the rope and wrapped it around his wrist. Then, with an enormous surge of strength, he hauled himself out of the water and began to pull himself hand over hand up the rope, bracing his feet on the rocks.

When he approached the top, Mariel added her weight to the rope, pulling him up and over the wall. Jake fell to the ground and lay there gasping for a moment. Mariel found a tissue in her pocket and wiped his face. She could hardly bear to think about what might have happened to him.

He rolled over on his back, and it was all she could do not to gather him into her arms and hold him. That would, however, serve no practical purpose, so instead she helped him up. He was soaked through, and his lips were blue.

"Don't you know you're not supposed to *wear* a moat?" Mariel said as he put a wet and dripping arm around her shoulders. She didn't care if she got wet. She didn't care about anything except that Jake was safe.

"I was only trying it on for size. Th-thank you, Mariel. You did a f-fine job," he said, his teeth still chattering. They started toward the gatehouse, Jake walking stiffly at first.

"It was my fault you fell in," she said.

"No."

"I shouldn't have—"

"*No.* Don't blame yourself. Neither of us knew that those boards were rotten. If anyone should have checked it out, I should have. I'm the carpenter in this group, remember?" The color was returning to his lips, and for that Mariel was thankful.

They heard Jessica's wails from the moment they stepped into the courtyard, and they hurried toward the great hall. The baby had kicked off all her covers, and her face was red and wrinkled from the effort of crying. Mariel picked her up and cuddled her close.

"I think I'll take a hot bath," Jake said.

"Good idea. And Jake—I'm sorry for the way I acted in the woods."

"I think we have some things to talk about."

"I think so, too."

"Later?"

She returned his smile. "Later."

While Jake took a hot bath, Mariel went outside and brought in the holly and evergreen boughs, and she shut Nelly up in the stable for fear that the goat would change her mind about the drawbridge and wander into danger.

When she returned, Jake was wrapped up in the comforter on the settee and holding Jessica. The fire was blazing in the fireplace, and their Christmas tree stood ready to be decorated. He was holding the bottle for the baby, who was sucking greedily, the fingers of one hand wrapped trustingly around his thumb.

"I'm none the worse for my winter swim," Jake said, craning his neck to look at her.

Mariel was hovering over the two of them like a mother hen. "Are you sure?"

"Positive. I even made tea and left it on the stove for you."

When she came back, Jake was singing Jessica to sleep with a Christmas carol. He stopped when Mariel entered the room.

"Go on," she said. "I like hearing you sing."

He hesitated for a moment, then went on singing the rest of the verse.

"Doesn't she look happy?" he asked.

"Jessica? Of course."

"Why shouldn't she? Two grown-ups are knocking themselves out to keep her that way." He laughed, clearly enjoying himself.

The comforter had slipped, exposing Jake's shoulder and part of his chest. Mariel stood up, suddenly unnerved. Of course he had no clothes on; there was nothing dry for him to wear. And if she sat here long enough, they would end up making love again.

It was what she wanted. No, it wasn't! If she let it, their lovemaking would become a drug, making her lose track of the rest of her life.

"I think I'll go exploring upstairs for things we can use to decorate the Christmas tree," she said unsteadily, slamming her mug down on the hearth so that tea sloshed over the rim.

Jake turned and stared after her as she fled to the unexplored gallery of rooms above them.

"I thought I'd—" Jake started to say, but she didn't wait to hear what he thought. Instead, she ran past the suits of armor, past the sword collection and into one of the large chambers off the gallery. She slammed the door behind her, cutting him off in midsentence.

AFTER MARIEL ran upstairs, Jake put the sleeping baby in her bed.

Mariel's behavior was erratic, to say the least. She blew hot, then cold, which was different from him—he blew hot all the time. He twisted, trying to get more comfortable. Ever since they had been in this castle, he became aroused embarrassingly often. Maybe he'd better find something to keep him busy. Obviously cold dunks in water wouldn't do it; after his impromptu swim in the moat, he desired Mariel as much as ever.

What could he do? Something to occupy both his hands and his mind, he thought. Carpentry would be good.

He'd make Jessica a proper bed. Or a cradle, so that she could be rocked to sleep.

He inspected the drawer where Jessica slept. With the addition of two curved pieces of wood, it would *be* a cradle. His mind grappled with the problem.

Suddenly there was nothing that he wanted more than to create, with his own hands, a cradle for this baby. He had given Mariel a Christmas tree, and now he wanted to give the baby something, too.

He started to stand up, then fell back. He'd forgotten. He wasn't wearing any clothes.

SHE WAS GOING to have to stop this, Mariel reflected as she sat on the edge of the cold bed in the middle of the cold room and stared out the mullioned window at the tops of trees.

She was sending Jake mixed signals. She was letting him get too close, making the relationship seem all warm and fuzzy, and then finding excuses to put distance between them. She ought to be more mature.

But it had already gone too far. After last night, he would only be hurt if she tried to withdraw, or he'd doubt his prowess—and there was certainly nothing wrong with *that*.

So, why not let it run its natural course? Okay, so she might be falling in love with this guy. He didn't have to know. After they got out of this place, after they no longer had anything in common, it would be over of its own accord. Why precipitate a crisis now?

At least this point of view helped her to feel more cheerful. Now she'd better look around up here and see if she could find something with which to decorate the Christmas tree. Doing that would take part of the afternoon, leaving them less time to get involved in doing other things, such as what was on her mind, and probably on his, right this minute. The memories of the previous evening were very vivid.

She opened a big wardrobe against one wall, looking for scraps of lace, or buttons, or anything else that could be used to trim the tree. In the bottom, below the clothes hanging there, she discovered several bright-colored satin and velvet sashes, red and green and blue, and she held them up to the light for inspection. They would become garlands for the Christmas tree.

After setting those carefully aside, she threw the wardrobe doors open wide, and out tumbled garments fashioned not only of silk, but of velvet, satin and lace, as well.

She picked up one of the articles of clothing and held it up to the light, fully expecting to see moth holes. Though she turned it this way and that, none were evident. In fact, the dress looked almost new.

It was a long-sleeved velvet gown of midnight blue, the bodice joined below the low-cut neckline with golden laces. Bound up with it was a floor-length surcoat of a paler blue, also velvet.

A tissue-wrapped package fell out of the folds, and when she unwrapped it she found a small, pearl-encrusted cap and a pair of soft slippers the same shade of blue as the gown.

They looked as if they'd fit if she stuffed bits of tissue paper into the toes.

Mariel held up the dress. There was no mirror, but the gown looked her size.

Suddenly she was seized with eagerness to try it on. It was cold in this gallery room, but she moved into a patch of sunlight and took off her coat anyway. In a matter of moments she had sloughed off her dirty corduroys and the lamb's wool sweater and was pulling the velvet dress over her head.

It smelled of lavender, just like the blankets from the chest downstairs. When she'd adjusted the velvet-and-pearl cap on the back of her head and slipped her arms through the sleeveless surcoat, she felt as if she were in another age, an enchanted age. She couldn't wait to show Jake.

A search through the clothing turned up a man's red tunic, which she paired with purple breeches and matching soft-soled shoes. A golden surcoat and hat completed the picture. She thought Jake might rather die than be seen in any of it—but he would have to admit, at least, that it would solve the problem of his having nothing to wear.

She burst out of the gallery room as suddenly as she had disappeared into it. She saw Jake wrapped up in the comforter, his bare feet warming on the hearth.

"Jake!" she called. "Look what I found!"

She ran lightly down the gallery stairs and tossed the clothing to him. "These were in the wardrobe upstairs," she explained, whirling for his inspection. His mouth fell open at the sight of her. Jessica, she noticed, was awake, and her expression mirrored Jake's. The baby clearly didn't know what to make of this new Mariel.

"You look wonderful," Jake said when he could speak, and Mariel laughed, the notes echoing back from the vaulted ceiling.

"Evidently the people who own this place entertain themselves with costume parties. Put those on, and we'll trim the tree,'' she said, dancing away when he would have clasped her hand.

"I can't wear these.'' Jake held up the tunic, surcoat and breeches in distaste. "This is a skirt. These look like a pair of panty hose. And this other thing looks exactly like a bathrobe. I'd look like a jackass.''

"But a *warm* jackass,'' she reminded him.

"We can't wear things that belong to someone else.''

"Didn't you say that we'd explain that we had to use their things because it was an emergency? You won't be able to wear your clothes for hours,'' Mariel pointed out.

"There's no underwear,'' he said peevishly.

"Does it matter? I'm going to go cook our chop suey Christmas dinner while you get dressed. Bye.'' She waved her fingers at him as she made tracks for the kitchen.

"Mariel, I can't possibly—'' he was saying, but by that time Mariel couldn't hear him.

Actually, she thought the breeches would do a lot for Jake's legs. A pair of blue jeans hardly did them justice.

"YOU CAN COME OUT NOW,'' Jake called.

Mariel, who had been reading the directions on the chop suey label, set the can on the counter and, mindful of her long skirt, swept out of the kitchen.

"If you aren't a sight,'' she said, barely able to contain her laughter.

Jake glared at her and adjusted his breeches. The surcoat came only to his knees, and his tunic looked as if it might be on backward.

"Well?'' he said.

"You look perfect,'' she said warmly. She went to him and adjusted the front of the surcoat. "The color becomes you, my lord,'' she said, dropping a curtsy.

"You make me feel as uncomfortable as hell,'' he told her.

"But, my lord, 'tis the Christmas season. We should keep

it with good cheer, do you not agree?'' Her eyes danced playfully, and that only seemed to goad him.

"Dammit, Mariel, it's all very well for you to play queen of the castle, but I don't feel much like a king.'' He tugged at the neck of the tunic.

"Nevertheless, there is this strange pagan custom of decorating a tree, and I do believe that we should get on with it. Hast thou found the bit of aluminum foil that thou saidst would do for a star? If so, please do bring it to me,'' Mariel said. She was enjoying this immensely.

"I'll go get it,'' Jake said through clenched teeth, and he stalked away, albeit silently, in his velvet slippers.

He might feel ridiculous, but if anything, Mariel thought the medieval costume accented his rugged masculinity.

Jessica grunted and waved her arms, and Mariel checked her diaper. Amazingly, it was clean and dry. Jake must have changed her.

"Now we're going to deck the halls,'' she told Jessica, and she had already heaped evergreen branches on the mantel and flanked the fireplace with jars of holly when Jake returned.

By this time, he looked more at ease in his costume, and he even managed to grin at her. "I hope we don't get rescued before my clothes dry,'' he said. "I couldn't bear for the guys to see me wearing this.''

"I like the way you look,'' she said honestly.

He picked up her hand and kissed the inside of her wrist, unnerving her completely. "And I like the way you look, as well, my lady,'' he said, making her heart flip over and her knees go weak.

She yanked her hand away. "So,'' she said, too hastily, "see what you can do with those pieces of foil while I pop corn on the stove.''

"I thought we were going to do that in the fireplace,'' he called after her.

She replied over her shoulder, "We don't have anything to pop it in," which was true.

The whole time she was popping the corn, she was thinking about the damp flick of his tongue on the tender inner part of her wrist, and how easily it would have been to let things escalate.

But now the baby was awake. They couldn't make love with Jessica watching. It wouldn't feel right.

Mariel wondered how long it would be before Jessica fell asleep again. A baby couldn't stay awake forever.

WHEN MARIEL WENT BACK into the great hall, Jake had fashioned a big, lopsided star out of the foil and was admiring its position at the top of the tree.

"That's good, Jake." Mariel set down the pot of popcorn and produced a large needle. "Thank goodness for my travel sewing kit," she told him. She also had a long length of thread, which she'd purloined from the torn hem of one of the gowns in the wardrobe upstairs. She began to string the popcorn.

Jake sat at her feet, helping. "About what we said in the woods..." he said uneasily.

"I meant what I said," she told him. "I don't look down on you. There are different kinds of education, you know."

"*I* know. I wasn't sure *you* did," he said quietly.

"So will you quit with the remarks?"

"Yes. If you'll quit dropping popcorn kernels in my hair," he said, grinning up at her. She grinned back. The subject was closed.

The popcorn chains joined the garlands and the holly berries on the tree, along with a few simple ornaments that Jake had whittled from scraps of wood. When they stood back, the three looked so festive that Mariel clapped her hands in delight.

"When will we eat our Christmas dinner?" Jake wanted to know.

"As soon as I heat it up. Want to help?"

Jake shook his head. "I'm going to see if I can knock together a surprise for Jessica. For her Christmas present," he said.

"I'll play with her for a while, so she won't be lonely."

Jake took off for unknown parts of the castle, and soon Mariel heard hammering from somewhere beyond the kitchen.

She picked Jessica up and held her in her lap. The baby seemed to love the caress of velvet against her cheek and Mariel was totally absorbed in Jessica until she heard a knock on the door.

The noise was completely unexpected. It startled Mariel so that she almost let Jessica roll off her lap.

"Jake?" she asked, leaping to her feet with the baby in her arms. She'd heard no sounds indicating anyone's arrival, perhaps due to the hammering from the direction of the kitchen, which had now stopped. But why would Jake come around to the door of the great hall and knock on the outside when he was already in the castle? It made no sense.

Warily she stood up, and, after securing Jessica in her bed, she hurried to the door. Again came the knocking, more forceful this time.

"Who—who is it?" she asked.

"Your friend from the Magic Minimart" was the answer, and it was with surprise that Mariel recognized the voice of the little bearded man.

They were rescued! Someone knew they were here! How and why, she had no idea, but she knew they were safe. She flung the door open, ready to fall into their rescuer's arms.

But she couldn't. He was holding a sack slung over his back and had no arms available for her to fall into.

"Merry Christmas! I thought you could use this," said the little man, and Mariel turned and called to Jake.

"Jake, hurry, there's someone here!" she said excitedly. She turned her back for only a split second, but when she spun around again, the man was gone.

Chapter Twelve

"Someone found us?" asked Jake, appearing at once.

Mariel looked from him to the empty courtyard. She was speechless.

"I thought you said someone was here," Jake said in a faintly accusatory tone.

"He was. He—" she began, but then she saw the sack that the little man had dropped in front of the door.

"What's this?" Jake said, instantly alert. He bent over and opened it. "Food?" Jake said incredulously. "A turkey? A can of coconut?"

"Christmas dinner," Mariel said faintly. "He brought us the ingredients for Christmas dinner."

"Who did?" Jake demanded.

"It was the little man from the Magic Minimart. He looks like Santa Claus."

"And I look like the king of this castle, which we both know I am not. So who was this guy?"

"I can only tell you what he looks like."

"Santa Claus," Jake said, sounding baffled.

"Yes." Mariel felt slightly light-headed. She stepped outside the door, looking for footprints. They had been in and out of this door so many times that the snow was trampled into slush.

"Well, how did he get in? And where did he go? Anyone could see that the drawbridge is out of commission."

"I realize that," Mariel said helplessly. "He can't have gotten far. Let's go look for him."

"We'll need to put on our boots." Jake cast a doubtful glance at Mariel's long skirt. "Do you want to change clothes?"

"There's no time," Mariel said, rushing inside.

"What about Jessica?" Jake looked down at the baby in her drawer-bed as they pulled on their boots.

"We'll take her," Mariel decided swiftly, sliding her arms through the sleeves of her all-weather coat.

Jake bundled up Jessica in one of the warm lap robes, and the three of them set out, rushing across the courtyard. They saw no sign of anyone in the outbuildings; nor was anyone lingering in the gatehouse.

"Let's check the drawbridge," Jake said.

They hurried out of the gatehouse and into the walled outer ward. The melting snow on the drawbridge showed no evidence of anything other than their own footprints, and a gaping hole was still evident where their feet had broken through the rotten wood.

"No one would have crossed the drawbridge when it's so clearly broken," Mariel said with great certainty.

"There's no other way into the castle, other than swimming the moat, and I can promise you that no one would do that willingly on a cold day like this," Jake said, looking around.

Mariel walked a short distance along the outer ward gazing across the moat, toward the trees in the forest.

"'Not a creature was stirring, not even a mouse,'" she quoted.

"If we didn't have the food, I wouldn't believe there had been anyone here," Jake said thoughtfully.

"We might as well go back in. And yet..."

"And yet we don't know what happened," Jake finished.

"At least we won't have to eat chop suey for Christmas dinner."

"Who's cooking?" he asked, eyebrows lifted.

"I am. It's my turn to give you a gift, and Christmas dinner is it."

Surprising her, Jake swept the hat off his head and bowed low in imitation of a courtier. "I accept, my lady," he said. When he lifted his head, his eyes were dancing.

His eyes seemed full of light, and, held in his spell, she stood motionless as he dipped his head and kissed her. His lips were cold and fresh with the tang of winter, but his breath warmed her cheek.

Jessica stirred against her, and Mariel broke away from the kiss. Jake's hands came up to frame her face.

"You're always fighting it, Mariel," he said softly. "Why?"

How could she explain? How could she tell him that she couldn't see herself with this man for the rest of her life? How could she tell him that she was afraid that, after all this was over, they wouldn't have anything to talk about? She didn't want to hurt him.

She only shook her head, willing the silent tears gathering behind her eyelids not to fall.

"We both know it's special," he went on. "It doesn't have to end after we leave this place."

He must have seen the perplexity in her eyes, because he stepped backward and let his hands drop to his sides.

"We'd better go in," he said gently. "We both have work to do."

She couldn't argue with that statement, at least, and so she murmured reassuringly to Jessica and, careful not to look at Jake, walked with him back into the castle courtyard.

IN THE KITCHEN, Jake set the sack of food on the counter beside the stove. While Mariel warmed herself and the baby in front of the fireplace, Jake dug in the sack and pulled out a small stuffed turkey. There were potatoes and milk and butter, so they would have mashed potatoes. There was a can of cranberry relish, a bunch of raw carrots, a can of green beans, and the makings of a coconut cake.

"Oh, I almost forgot," Jake said, after the riches of the sack had been revealed. "I made something for Jessica." He disappeared briefly into one of the keeping rooms off the kitchen. When he returned, he was carrying a small cradle, crafted from a drawer similar to the one Jessica usually slept in.

"I thought she'd like to rock to sleep," he said with an abashed look as he set it in front of the fireplace.

"So that's why you were doing all that hammering," Mariel said, marveling at the cradle. Jake had fashioned wooden rockers from pieces of scrap lumber and had fastened them to the bottom of the drawer.

"If I were making a real cradle for her, it would be wider and longer, so that she'd have growing room. And I'd carve a design with her name into the headboard," he said.

"Maybe you'd better see if you can repair the drawbridge, in case we have any more visitors," Mariel said quickly.

"Good idea. I'll clear out of here while you cook dinner."

"A pleasure, my lord," Mariel said demurely, dropping a curtsy. He only grinned at her and went to get his tools.

"So," Mariel said briskly to Jessica, "you and I have work to do."

But Jessica was already sound asleep.

LATER, Jake came in noisily, stomping his feet and rubbing his hands together against the cold.

"The drawbridge poses no threat," he told her. "Only two of the boards were rotten. Others looked as if they'd been replaced recently. I managed to do a creditable patch-up job, so we don't have to worry about falling into the moat again. Mmm…is that frosting for the coconut cake?"

"Yes. It's only canned coconut, but it's better than noth-

ing. I suppose they didn't have a fresh coconut at the Magic
Minimart," she replied.

Jake leaned on the counter. "Mariel, do you think this guy
was merely a delivery person for the Magic Minimart?" he
asked skeptically.

"Well, what else could he logically be? Meals on
Wheels?"

"Trays on Sleighs."

Mariel shot him an exasperated look. "Whoever he was,
I wish I knew how he figured out that we were here. Or that
we needed food for a decent Christmas dinner. And why
didn't he rescue us? Why did he leave us here?" she said in
a rush.

"Because he gives gifts to good little boys and girls," Jake
said. "Because we've both been good, and he's giving us
the gift of each other."

Mariel stared at him, dumbfounded. "You're not joking,
are you? Do *you* think it was really Santa Claus?"

"At the moment, that theory makes a lot more sense than
believing he's a delivery person for a convenience store. In
case you've never noticed, Magic Minimarts don't deliver,"
Jake said.

He eased up behind her where she stood at the stove and
planted a kiss on her cheek.

She twisted around in his arms. "What was that for?" she
asked.

"For hello. And this one's for how nice it is to come home
to a warm kitchen and the smell of dinner cooking." He bent
his head and kissed her again. It was a kiss that she felt
powerless to resist.

"Now," he said, drawing the word out in that drawl that
fell so pleasantly on her ears, "wasn't that nice?"

"More than nice," she whispered against the front of his
tunic.

"Do you suppose it's like this for people who are married?" he asked whimsically.

"You've forgotten—I was married once," she said, her mood dashed by the reminder of a part of her life that she would have preferred to forget.

"I haven't forgotten," he said. "Was it like this?"

Mariel moved away from him and busied herself measuring out confectioners' sugar. "At first," she allowed. "Not for long, however."

"If I were married, I'd want it to be like this all the time," he said.

Mariel could think of no adequate reply. Because she was happy, too, happier than she'd ever been in her life. But it was a feeling she couldn't trust. It was a feeling that could melt away as fast as the snow, which was thawing even now.

MARIEL INSISTED on using a snowy white linen tablecloth on the table, and where she found the silver goblets, Jake never knew. He only knew that Mariel, wearing her blue velvet gown and with the glow of candlelight gilding her face, was more beautiful than he had ever seen her as she bore the turkey to the table and set it steaming before him.

Jake carved the turkey, taking his time about it and savoring his own happiness. He was almost afraid to admit to himself that he *was* so happy. It was such an unfamiliar feeling.

But now here was Mariel, and here was Jessica, and he felt himself settling into the role of the paterfamilias, and he liked it. He, Jake Travis, who had never had a real family of his own, was finding it comfortable to be the acting head of an acting family.

At the moment they sat to eat, Jessica woke up.

"I'll get her," Mariel said. "You go ahead and start eating."

"No, I'll get her," Jake said, and they both stood at the same time and headed for Jessica's cradle, near the hearth.

The baby was crying lustily, her face red and wrinkled,

her fists clenched. "Is it time for her feeding?" he asked anxiously.

"She just ate two hours ago. Could she be hungry again?"

"I don't know. Do you suppose the cooking odors woke her?"

"Do babies wake up when they smell something good to eat? How can they? It's not as if they ever ate turkey, so how would they know it tastes good?" Mariel asked in a burst of logic.

"I don't know. Maybe she has colic. Do you know anything about colic?" He stared down at the baby, a perplexed expression on his face.

"I read about colic in the baby book, but it didn't say much, except that it makes babies cry," she said. She picked up Jessica and checked her diaper. "Well, she does need a diaper change."

"Here, Mariel, let me do it. You've worked so hard to cook the dinner, and it'll get cold if we don't eat it," Jake said, reaching for Jessica.

"I cooked it for you," Mariel objected. "It's supposed to be your Christmas present."

He saw in that moment that she felt about the dinner the way he had about the Christmas tree and the crude cradle he had fashioned—she had wanted to do something in the spirit of Christmas for the two people most important in her life at the moment.

"Go on," she said, shooing his hands away, and so he went. But he felt uncomfortable sitting at the big table without her, watching her changing the baby's diaper at the other end of the room.

"I'll put her in her cradle," Mariel called to him over the din. "Maybe that will soothe her. I don't know what's bothering her."

"I'm not enjoying this," he said suddenly, almost shouting, because he didn't think she'd hear him otherwise. Mariel was so startled that she wheeled around and regarded him with an expression of mild apprehension, which only made him more determined that Mariel not have her Christmas dinner ruined.

He stood up and strode the length of the hall until he stood before Mariel. "I'll take care of her. *You* eat."

Mariel hugged the baby to her chest. "I don't mind taking care of her, really I don't."

Jake spoke to her in a gentler tone. "Let's bring the cradle to our end of the hall. I can rock her with my foot while we eat," he said, and Mariel, her lower lip caught between her teeth, nodded in silent agreement. Jessica, however, was anything but silent. She was still crying so hard that he could see her tonsils.

He lifted the cradle and tucked it under his arm, smiling faintly at Mariel. "Is this what parents go through? Do babies often interrupt mealtimes?"

"Given the nature of babies, it's entirely possible," Mariel said, trailing after him with the baby, her long skirt sweeping the floor.

They put Jessica in her cradle beside the table, but she continued to scream. Mariel had eaten only a few bites of carrots when she set her fork down, looking miserable.

"I can't stand it, Jake. I can't eat when she's crying."

He had managed a few mouthfuls of turkey since he returned to the table. It was good, but he couldn't enjoy eating, either.

Jake picked up the baby from the cradle. Jessica immediately stopped crying and blinked at him. He wiggled his eyebrows at her; he crossed his eyes. Jessica appeared fascinated.

"You're not going to be able to eat if you hold her," Mariel said.

"If she's this amazed at the faces I make, wait until she watches me chew," Jake said, shifting the baby to one arm and picking up his fork.

He ate slowly, because he held the baby, but Jessica's eyes tracked every bit of food from plate to mouth.

"She likes you, Jake," Mariel said. "She likes you a lot."

"If only I were able to hold your attention the way I do hers," Jake said without thinking.

"How do you know you don't?"

"Oh, come on, Mariel." He couldn't bring himself to admit that her indifference hurt. He hoped she'd take the hint.

She got up and cut the cake, setting the first piece in front of him. "The only thing that takes my attention away from you is the baby," she said. "We *are* alone together here, after all."

"Alone—but sometimes not very together."

"What do you mean?" she asked, sounding as if she really didn't want to hear his answer.

"I mean— Oh, look, Mariel, she's gone to sleep." Jessica's eyes were closed, and she looked peaceful and contented in his arms.

"Now who isn't paying attention to whom?" Mariel said waspishly, and she got up and flounced into the kitchen.

Jake stared at the place where she had been.

"I don't think I understand women," he said to Jessica, who slept on, unaware.

He wondered if Jessica would wake up if he slid her gently into her cradle. He wondered if there was some way to warm the blankets in the cradle so that the cool shock of them after being held against a warm body wouldn't awaken her. He wondered why he was wondering all these things, when what he really wanted to do was go to Mariel and gather her into his arms.

Taking his chances, he deposited Jessica in the cradle as gently as he could. She sighed and made little sucking noises with her lips, lapsing into what appeared to be an even deeper sleep.

He picked up the cradle with Jessica in it and tiptoed to the fireplace, where a steadily burning log threw out an agreeable warmth. He turned around as Mariel came out of the kitchen, her face pale but composed.

"Come here," he said, holding his hand out toward her.

"Where's Jessica?"

"Sound asleep. I think we need to talk."

"You haven't finished your cake."

"I haven't even *started* my cake, but it doesn't matter. We have other, more important, unfinished business. I've taken your comment that we don't know each other to heart, Mariel."

She glided toward him, petite and dainty and looking very much the medieval lady. Behind her, the tapestries on the wall, stirred by a draft, rippled. The candles flickered in their sconces. Jake hoped that she would notice the yearning in his eyes, which was only about half of what he felt in his heart.

"Darling Mariel," he said, taking her hand. "Let's get to know each other better, much better."

"My lord—" she began, but he was tired of playacting. He wanted something real. He swept her into his arms and kissed her, smothering the words upon her lips.

"Is my lady pleased?" he demanded when he released her lips.

She stared into his eyes, and for a moment he wasn't sure what he read in her face. Then, with a playful look, she said, "I could be pleased more," and he laughed in relief and swept her into his arms, mounting the steps to the gallery two at a time before she caught her breath.

"Where—?"

"To my lady's chamber," he told her, and before she knew it, he was kicking open the door to the room where she had found the clothes they were wearing.

"I wanted this to be special. For you, Mariel," he said, and then he carried her into the chamber.

The room had been transformed. Jake had built a roaring fire in the fireplace, and the room was toasty warm. He had lit candles in the wall sconces, and the bed was turned down and waiting for them.

"When did you do this?" she asked as he laid her gently on the bed. The sheets were redolent of lavender, and the fragrance blended with that of the evergreens that Jake had heaped on the mantel.

"After I repaired the drawbridge. We can leave the door open and hear Jessica if she begins to fuss," he said, smoothing her hair. "Mariel, are you happy?"

"I wish—" she began, but he silenced her with a kiss.

"Don't wish anything right now, unless it's for me," he murmured, somewhere in the vicinity of her ear.

She felt a fluttering in her stomach as he bent over her, and a rush of heat rose to meet his lips as he kissed the firm rise of her breasts above the low neckline of the velvet dress.

She was acutely aware of Jake, of everything about him—of the strong, rugged planes of his face, of the yearning in his eyes. Heat radiated from his body to hers, and, lifting his head, he brought his fingertips up to trace the delicate line of her jaw from her ear to her chin.

She had never realized how much she loved to be touched before. Jake's hands, so big and capable, knew all the subtleties of touch, from the quick, deft turn of fastenings to make clothes fall away, to the light brush of fingertips upon skin primed for love.

Time slowed down, became part of her, drifted away on a tide of sensation. She didn't know what time it was or what else she should be doing. She knew only the lazy, languorous exploration of love.

Jake's skin was taut and smooth and golden in the firelight. Her lips trembled slightly, and he brushed them gently with his thumb, his touch like the graze of a butterfly's wing.

"I've never been able to talk to anyone the way I talk to you. Does that mean anything to you?" he asked.

"Where is this going, Jake? What are we doing?" She was so unsure of him, and of herself.

"We're feeling the magic," he said, his eyes solemn with truth. "The magic of Christmas."

"You don't believe," she breathed.

"That was before I met you. Before we found Jessica. Before we ended up in this castle. Before I was truly alive, Mariel," he said with the utmost sincerity.

She swallowed. He was so handsome, and so earnest, and so wrapped up in her. Was she only lost in the admitted thrill of having a man show desire for her?

But this was Jake. Jake, who had sheltered her with his body and guided her to this castle, who had taken on the responsibility for both her and Jessica, when he could have left them in the woods or the cave. Feeling his desire for her was different from feeling his commitment, but both existed.

"So sweet," he whispered, unlacing her bodice with hands that were firm and sure.

By the time he had finished, she was trembling, and as he parted the fabric to reveal her breasts, she said, "Now you," and she helped him out of his surcoat and tunic until he knelt before her bare-chested.

He slid the dress from her shoulders, then bent and took the tip of one breast between his teeth, teasing it with his tongue. He caught her other nipple between his thumb and forefinger and applied gentle pressure until it hardened into a tight round bud. She gasped and arched against him, winding her fingers in his hair.

His lips upon her breast made her undulate with pleasure, and when he felt her body start to move, he trailed a line of slow, erotic kisses upward to her lips. She moaned softly as his tongue slid into her mouth, and she opened herself to it, tantalizing him with the exquisite mating dance of her own tongue, delighting in the play of flesh against flesh until she felt him trembling with desire.

He eased her downward and slid a leg between hers, pressing the hardness of his thigh tight against her. Mariel heard her breath escaping her in sharp gasps, and she felt his hands beneath her, holding her close. She wrapped her arms around him fiercely, wanting to bond him to her, wanting to be part of him, not only now, but forever.

"I think I never knew real passion until now," she whispered against his shoulder.

"Neither did I," he said unsteadily. The pulse of his heartbeat pumped in the vein above his temple, and she impulsively lifted her head to kiss it. He slid his hands beneath her head, twisting his fingers in the silky strands. His breath stirred the tendrils around her face.

Slowly he began to kiss her, breathing little kisses along her jaw, nibbling at her earlobe, probing the sensitive spot at the corner of her mouth with the tip of his tongue. He seemed determined to kiss every inch of her, to explore all of her, and the waiting was excruciating.

His hands moved lower, over the ripe curve of her hips, spreading a warm, pulsing sensation deep into her abdomen, lingering a moment before sliding her dress down. She didn't know how he managed to dispense with the lace barrier of her panties so swiftly, but soon she shivered in his arms, conscious not of the cool air, but of the heat emanating from his body to warm her.

When he slid out of his breeches, she couldn't have looked away if her life had depended upon it. In his nakedness, Jake Travis was magnificent, and she felt as if all her senses had become magnified as he took her hand and placed it on his hardness.

"Do you like to touch me, Mariel?" he whispered, and she said, "Oh, yes," and he smiled and moved himself between her fingers as she kissed his forehead, his chin, his chest, in silent tribute.

"Now I want to touch you," he said, and he caressed the soft curls between her thighs, seeking the silken sweetness within as he drew her into a deep, impassioned kiss. He easily found the sensitive heart of her and stroked gently, so gently, until she was damp with wanting him.

"You are so responsive, Mariel, so ready for love," he

said as he bent down and pressed his lips against her abdomen.

His mouth, moving lower, kindled wildfires in her veins, made her into someone she hadn't known she could be. She could not get enough of him, and she tangled her hands in his hair to pull him closer to the center of her. She felt the whisper of his breath and the warmth of his lips, and then, with the skill of an expert, his tongue found her molten core and coaxed her almost to her peak before stopping.

She moved against him, unable to help herself, and as he positioned himself above her, she wrapped her legs around his, longing to feel him inside her, but still he stroked with his fingers, watching her with half-closed eyes. It was such exquisite pleasure, such delicious sensation, but it was a kind of torture, too, and Mariel longed to be released by her tormentor.

She clung to him blindly, unable to speak, unable to move, totally in his thrall, until with a victorious cry he filled all the emptiness she had ever known with his own hard and satisfying need. She heard him cry out, speak her name, but she wasn't really conscious; all she wanted was to feel and feel and feel, to be entered again and again in time to the elemental rhythm pounding in her veins, to give herself so completely to this man that she would never again be the same person she was now, not ever.

He was much more aware than she, much more ready to pace himself to her passion. They found a flow, a way of giving and receiving happiness, that surpassed the ordinary and approached the sublime.

At the moment when Jake pushed a damp strand of hair away from Mariel's face, their eyes met, completing their union. His eyes were so dark that Mariel could see no iris; all she saw was the reflection of her face, blurred with passion, in their depths. At that moment, with a fusion of spirit, a meshing of bodies, a blending of souls, their climax ex-

ploded inward and outward, leaving them drowning and helpless, safe in each other's arms.

Mariel was limp with exhaustion, but at the same time she
felt a fierce, proud joy in her heart at what she and Jake had
achieved together. They had transcended the boundaries that
usually separate two people and had become one in a state
of mind and body that she knew was the rarest of human
accomplishments. She nestled close to him, as if by main-
taining a connection she could make this moment last forever.

She must have slept, though she didn't know how long.
When she awoke, Jake's arms still held her close. She
thought she would like to lie just this way in his arms forever,
languidly savoring the joy of their mating. She was just beginning, slowly and lazily to figure out the implications of
this feeling when she heard the explosion outside the chamber window.

She was alert instantly. Jake jumped to his feet.

"What was that?" she asked, clutching the covers to her
breasts.

"Gunfire, I think. Someone is shooting outside the castle!"

Chapter Thirteen

Mariel struggled into her sweater and slacks, and Jake raced downstairs to Jessica, who had been awakened by the gunshots. The baby was screaming at the top of her lungs.

Mariel had barely reached them when there was a loud pounding on the door. Mariel looked wildly at Jake, who was zipping up his jeans, grim-faced.

"Who do you think it is?" she said.

"It doesn't sound like some kindly, mild-mannered old gentleman with a beard," Jake replied, his voice muffled by the turtleneck he was pulling over his head.

"Are you going to the door?" Outside, someone was shouting, and they heard another blast of gunfire.

"I'd better, or they'll break it down."

Mariel picked up the crying Jessica and cradled her in her arms. "Hush. Everything's all right," Mariel said, though she did not quite believe it herself.

Jake was at the door now. "Who is it?"

"Open up, open up, we want to wish you a merry Christmas!" was the shouted demand.

Suddenly Jake's features lit with recognition and relief. "It's okay," he said to Mariel. "They mean us no harm."

"But they're shooting guns! What are they doing here?" Mariel said, shocked that Jake was going to open the door without asking more questions.

Jake shot the bolt. "Quaint local custom," he said, smiling broadly. "You'll see." To Mariel's dismay, he flung the door wide.

It was dark, and a full moon illuminated the scene. Mariel could make out one or two grinning male faces, and other people, men and boys, carrying old-fashioned muskets, were milling in the courtyard, laughing and jostling one another.

"Merry Christmas! Merry Christmas!" they shouted when they saw Jake, Mariel and the baby in the doorway.

"Where is Mr. Nicholas? Is he home?" asked one of the party.

"Won't you come in?" said Jake, and Mariel stared at him in disbelief.

"Jake—" she said, but he quieted her with a glance.

"Ah, it's a cold night. We don't mind if we do," said the leader, and Mariel had no choice but to stand back as twelve men and boys trooped past and headed for the fireplace.

The leader looked from Jake to Mariel and held out his hand. "I'm Barney Sims," he said.

"Jake Travis. This is Mariel, and the baby is Jessica. Frankly, we need your help."

"What can we do for you?"

"Mariel, please, will you make us some hot chocolate?" Jake asked. So Mariel listened from the kitchen, Jessica propped against her shoulder, while she stirred hot chocolate and Jake told Barney Sims and his party the story of their accident, being lost in the woods, and their subsequent walk to the deserted castle.

When she came out of the kitchen, she arranged the now-sleepy Jessica in her cradle and carried in a tray holding cups of hot chocolate.

"Funny, I thought it was, when we saw a light on the second floor of the gatehouse. We didn't expect anyone to be here," said Barney.

"A light in the second story of the gatehouse? We didn't—couldn't have—put a light in the gatehouse. The stairs aren't—'' Mariel began, but Jake threw her a warning look. It said, *Don't tell crazy stories.* It said, *Don't tell them something they won't—or can't—believe.*

"Mr. Nicholas, the old guy who owns this place, usually goes away during the winter, but somehow I had a hunch I'd better check on him. He's an old fellow, you know, and healthy enough, but neighbor looks after neighbor around here," said Barney, oblivious of the byplay between Mariel and Jake.

"Neighbors? We didn't see any houses around," Mariel said.

"We came by Jeep. It's not easy to get in and out of this place," he said. That was certainly not news.

"If only we could have found you when we were lost," Mariel said, sitting down on the hearth beside Jake.

"We live on the other side of the mountain," said Barney Sims.

"Can you give us a ride into Tellurian tonight?" Jake asked.

"Wish we could," one of the men said, "but we've got three Jeeploads with just the bunch of us, and bags of mistletoe to take back besides, and no room left over for three more people. What we'd better do is send a Jeep in tomorrow morning. You're safe here for the night, aren't you?"

"Safe enough," Jake said.

Jake went to make more hot chocolate. Mariel leaned forward, eager to talk to the men about their reason for roaming around on Christmas night, shooting off old muskets.

"It's tradition, that's all I know," Barney Sims said, clearly warming toward her. "I heard it started when the old-timers went to gather mistletoe. It grows so high no one could climb up and get it, so they had to shoot it down."

"But why on Christmas Day? Why not before?" Mariel asked.

"The mistletoe's got to be fresh for the big party on Christmas night," said one of the boys.

"Yeah, the women like to hang it up so they get plenty of kissing."

"Aw, Barney, it's not just the women who like the kissing," said one of the men.

As a collector of Christmas folklore, Mariel didn't often find something totally new, and yet she had never heard of this custom before. She borrowed a piece of paper and a pen from one of the men and wrote down everything they could tell her about the origin of the custom of shooting down the mistletoe, scribbling until they said they had to go.

"Look for the Jeep early in the morning," Barney said by way of parting. "We'll get you and your family out of here, safe and sound."

Mariel hung back, busying herself with Jessica, until the visitors had gone and Jake had returned.

"Well," he said with a certain finality. "We're rescued, Mariel."

"Yes," she said in a curiously flat tone, her excitement having evaporated now that reality was beginning to sink in. "I suppose we are."

He waited until she laid Jessica in her cradle before pulling her down beside him on the hearth.

"In a way," he said, gently taking her hand in his, "I've felt rescued ever since I met you."

She tried to pull her hand away. She wasn't up to any declarations right now. Her lips were still swollen from his passionate kisses, and her body was still primed for love.

"Mariel, listen to me," he said. She would have turned away, but he grasped her by the shoulders and made her look at him.

"Mariel," he said. "I never thought I'd be in love with anyone, but what has happened between us has changed my mind. I'm crazy about you, Mariel. When we came out of that cave into a world all fresh and new, it was as if I'd left the dark part of my life behind, too. I don't want to let you go. If we were together, every day could be like Christmas."

"I don't know what to say," she said, helpless under the restless scrutiny of those warm brown eyes.

"Say you feel the same way," he urged. "Say you love me."

"I—I *want* to say it," she told him, and he relaxed his grip on her shoulders and pulled her into his arms. She heard his heartbeat—or was it hers? She couldn't distinguish whose was whose anymore.

"Then why don't you make us both very happy? It's only three little words. Three very simple, easy words. You love me, Mariel. You know you do!" He held her fiercely, and she couldn't see his face.

"If I say it, then we have to do something about it. You have your life, and I have mine."

"We can combine them. I know we can! You and me and the baby—"

"She isn't our baby, Jake," Mariel said quietly. "Have you forgotten that?"

He eased away so that he could look at Jessica and then back to Mariel. "I *have* forgotten, yes, in the same way I've forgotten what my life was like before I had you."

"You were the one who kept reminding me at first that Jessica has parents somewhere," Mariel said, perilously near tears.

"We could have lots of babies of our own."

"It's what I've always wanted, a home and children," Mariel said. "But how can I make any promises? Everything has seemed so unreal, with toys disappearing and roly-poly little men showing up and then leaving without a trace, and men shooting muskets in the courtyard. How can I know if what we feel is real, Jake? How can I?" Tears began to run down her face, and he gathered her in his arms.

"It's real, believe me," he said. "As real as what we feel when I do this."

He kissed her. It was a long, sweet, lingering kiss that spoke of caring and passion and happiness to come. It prom-

ised forever and eternity and a life filled with love. And
magic. It captured all the magic of the hours they had spent
together and made it seem, in that moment, more real than
anything else in Mariel's life.

But the kiss ended. As their life together would end tomorrow.

In a moment, she was sobbing in his arms, and he was
kissing and consoling her, and all she could think of was that
here was an eligible, handsome, kind, considerate man, and
she was a fool for not telling him she loved him. But she
couldn't lie. She didn't know if she loved him or not.

He lifted her in his arms. "Come to bed," he said, and
she made no objection.

He carried her upstairs, this time setting her down gently
amid the rumpled, sweet-scented sheets, adding another log
to the fire before covering her body with his. Sparks flew up
the chimney like golden fireflies, and Mariel held him in her
arms and watched them go, like so many memories turning
to ash.

After a while, he kissed her face tenderly. Her tears were
wet against his lips. Then, because they couldn't help it, because this was to be their last night in the castle, they cou-
pled, slowly and gently, in a celebration of their time together.

To Mariel, who was lost in a haze of desire, the scene had
a dreamlike quality of illusion—Jake's dear, wonderful face
hovering above her, the candlelight and fireglow playing
across the curves and planes of their bodies, shadows leaping
and blending on the wall. There was delicious excitement and
overwhelming passion; there was joy and exuberance, and
finally peace.

That night they slept in each other's arms, waking and
sleeping, making love and just looking at each other, whispering and murmuring all the age-old endearments that lovers
have shared in their mutual enchantment since the beginning
of time. In the castle they were secluded, lost, far away from

mundane worries. Tonight, they didn't have to think about tomorrow and the changes it would bring. Tonight, all they had to do was love.

When the pearly light of dawn crept into the room, Mariel was startled awake.

Jessica, she thought, alarmed. Jessica hadn't cried all night.

Jake was lying with his head pillowed on her shoulder, one hand thrown carelessly across her breast. Carefully she lifted his hand and set it aside, and he whispered her name. Her hair spread across his chest like a golden cloak, and he stirred when she slid out from under the robe covering them.

But he didn't wake up, and, mindful of her responsibility to the baby, Mariel clutched another blanket around her shoulders and crept down the stairs to the great hall.

Jessica was sleeping peacefully, and Mariel realized that the infant had slept through the night. This was a milestone her friends had often mentioned when talking about their own babies.

Mariel went swiftly into the kitchen and warmed Jessica's bottle, wondering as she heated the milk what would happen to the goat when they left. They would have to send someone to get Nelly; otherwise, she might starve. Unless the owner of this place returned, and Mariel didn't know how likely that was.

Mr. Nicholas, the mistletoe shooters had called him. They hadn't seemed to know him well, though they had appeared to like him well enough. Mr. *Who* Nicholas? Mariel wondered. They hadn't given him a first name.

Jessica woke up while Mariel was warming the bottle. As she gathered the baby into her arms, Mariel was glad that she was awake before Jake so that she and Jessica could enjoy this moment of closeness together.

"Jessica," Mariel said, and Jessica seemed to recognize her name. A sense of melancholy settled over Mariel. What was Jessica's real name? Or what name would foster parents give her, assuming that her real parents couldn't be found?

Mariel knew she'd always remember Jessica, how her warm little body snuggled so close, how her tiny, seeking mouth had pushed against her breasts on that first night in the cave. Now that she had sampled motherhood, it was going to be hard to give it up.

She held Jessica over her shoulder and burped her, then settled her in her lap again. Jessica was dressed in doll clothes from the tower room. She looked so pretty, the pink of her cheeks echoed in the pink of the polka-dot flannel doll's nightgown she wore.

When Jessica had drained the bottle, Mariel couldn't bear to put her back into her cradle. Instead, she carried her upstairs to the room she had shared with Jake.

Jake had been up to put another log on the fire, and he was sitting up in bed when Mariel came in.

"Good morning," he said, smiling at them. The sun had risen so that a slat of lemony light lay across the pillow, which he patted invitingly. Mariel climbed up on the bed and laid Jessica between them.

"What time to you think the Jeep will come?" Mariel asked.

"I don't know. Barney Sims said it would be early," Jake replied.

"We should get dressed," said Mariel.

"We should," he agreed, sliding his arm around her and pulling her close.

"Jake…"

"I just want to feel your skin next to mine."

"It leads to other things."

"Only this, at the moment," he said capturing her lips for a kiss.

She pulled away. "We'd better eat breakfast."

"I'm not hungry." He slid a hand around her neck and pulled her down beside him on the pillow. "You mean so much to me. I really do want to keep seeing you," he said, gazing deep into her eyes, as if he were trying to work his way into her very soul.

"We will," she said helplessly, though she knew it wasn't true.

"Wouldn't you like to see each other? Say in a couple of weeks, in order to catch up?"

"I—I'm not sure," she hedged.

Jake was silent for several minutes. "I'm not going to pressure you," he said finally. "But I know—and I hope you know—that I'm not going to change my mind. I'm not going to stop loving you." *And I'm not going to let you get away with this,* he thought. If Mariel noticed the determined set of his chin, she gave no sign.

Between them, Jessica stirred. Mariel sat up and took the baby into her arms.

Jake felt a wave of longing wash over him. "That's the way I want to remember you," he said softly. "With the baby in your arms, looking like a Madonna."

"Please, will you hold her while I get dressed?" Mariel asked. She was on the verge of tears.

Jake nodded, his eyes bright, his look solemn, and she shifted the baby into his arms. Clutching the blanket around her, she slid out of bed.

He watched her as she dressed, and once he said, "You're the most beautiful woman I've ever seen, Mariel," but all she could do was look at him. She didn't want to provide any encouragement for him to think that they had a future together, because she didn't think they did.

Later, she cooked a makeshift breakfast while Jessica watched from her cradle. Jake replanted the Christmas tree in the woods and, using pen and paper borrowed from their visitors, wrote a note to the owner of the castle, scrawling his name and address at the bottom so that he could be charged for the items they had used. He left the note under a salt shaker in the kitchen. Mariel was washing up their coffee cups when they heard the honk of a horn at the draw-bridge. At the sound, she felt a sense of impending doom. She had known it was coming, but she couldn't welcome it.

"Whoever is driving the Jeep probably doesn't want to attempt the drawbridge," said Jake grimly, and he went to talk to the person, who came back with him a few minutes later.

"Mariel, this is Barney's cousin, Hoke Sims," he said, his voice neutral, not giving away his feelings. "He's going to take us to Tellurian."

Mariel said hello, and Jake shrugged into his backpack. He held Mariel's coat for her, and they looked around the great hall one last time. They avoided looking at each other.

"Big old barn of a place, this castle," said Hoke Sims. "Big old *ugly* place, if you ask me."

"Oh, you get used to it," Mariel said.

Jake gave her a sharp look. "I'll carry Jessica out," he said, going to get the baby.

"I want to take a last look around. To see if I left any-thing."

Jake spared her a curt nod, and he and Hoke Sims went out, leaving her alone in the great hall.

Mariel fought to gain control of herself. She wasn't going to cry; she wasn't going to let her emotions run away with her. She blinked back tears, and when her vision cleared, she found herself staring at the tapestries hanging on the wall.

To her regret, Mariel had never taken the time to look closely at the tapestries before. Now, while she was trying to quell her tears, while she listened to Jake and Hoke outside the door, discussing what to do about Nelly the goat, she couldn't help but notice them.

At this early hour, a shaft of light from one of the narrow windows illuminated the wall hangings, making the rich em-broidery gleam. At first, the illustrations on the fabric seemed to be standard tapestry fare—a unicorn surrounded by a group of ladies, a formation of knights and a depiction of a joust, a dancing bear and a juggler in a great hall that resembled this one.

"Mariel? It's time to go," Jake said from the door, propping it open. Jessica was in his arms, wrapped warmly in her pink wool blanket.

"One moment," she called back, wiping her eyes, her back turned to him. "I've been wanting to take a look at these ever since I got here."

She had reached the last tapestry and was ready to turn around when she noticed that it was different from the others. No veiled ladies here, and no knights, just an artistic view of a castle that looked very much like this one. A drawbridge, a moat, a strikingly similar gatehouse and—

"Jake!" she called uncertainly. "Come look at this!"

But the door swung on a cold wind that swept through the hall. Jake had left, presumably to go to the Jeep. She heard the Jeep's motor start up, and she knew that it was no use to call Jake.

She took one last look at the tapestry, which pictured something she knew she would never forget.

"Mariel," called Jake.

She had to leave. Her time here was over. One last look around the great hall, and then she pulled the door firmly shut behind her.

"What took you so long?" Jake asked from the back seat as she climbed into the front seat of the Jeep.

"Just looking around one last time," she said.

"And what did you see?"

"The tapestries. By the way, what did you decide to do about Nelly?" she asked briefly, leaning over and chucking Jessica under the chin. The baby looked so sweet, her cheeks pink and glowing, her eyes wide and wondering.

"I suspect that she belongs to my brother-in-law," said Hoke. "He has a herd of goats, and this one probably wandered away."

"In winter? During two violent storms?" murmured Mariel, who found this hypothesis unlikely.

"We thought that the goat might belong to the castle's owner," Jake said.

"To Mr. Nicholas? No, he's not here enough to keep any animals, though he used to breed some kind of exotic deer," Hoke said. The Jeep bumped over a rutted track, now turned to mud with the thaw.

"Tell me about this Mr. Nicholas," Mariel said.

"Oh, he's a nice guy, but a recluse of sorts. No one sees him much."

"He's away most of the winter?" Mariel ventured.

"Yeah, that's what I've always heard. The rumor is that his family won a lottery in Europe years ago, and the present Mr. Nicholas's father was a student of medieval studies. He built the castle on a kind of a whim, and he lived here for a long time. In fact, I think he was the one who started breeding the deer."

"What kind of deer?" Jake asked.

"Reindeer," Mariel said under her breath, and Jake looked at her sharply.

Hoke, who seemed not to have heard, shook his head. "No one knows. You hardly ever saw them. Maybe a glimpse now and then through the trees, that's all, according to my grandfather, who knew Mr. Nicholas's dad. The deer didn't like to be around people much."

"When do you expect this Mr. Nicholas back?" Jake asked.

"Who knows? He's a hard guy to figure. Kind of eccentric, and all that," Hoke said philosophically.

They rode on another mile or two, and Mariel mulled it all over. There were no firm answers, but she thought she knew who the mysterious owner of the castle was. She didn't think she could talk to this Hoke Sims about it. No, she'd better keep quiet.

"I'd like to hold Jessica," she said after a while, and Jake handed the baby over the seat. Mariel buried her face in the infant's neck, telling herself that her eyes were watering from the cold. Behind her, Jake rode silently, his eyes on the back of her head. They didn't speak to each other all the way into town.

"So," JAKE SAID in front of the Department of Social Services office building as Mariel was about to get in the car she had rented, "you won't change your mind and come see my house?" His southern drawl seemed even more Southern than usual; she had grown so accustomed to it that she'd almost forgotten about it.

"I want to go home," she said, keeping her eyes on the distant mountains.

"The social worker was good with Jessica, don't you think?" Jake asked. They'd had to answer a battery of suspicious questions, but finally, because of their sincerity, they'd been believed. *Yes,* Jake and Mariel had said when interviewed separately and together, *we really found this baby in the woods. No,* they had both said, *we don't know who she is or where her parents are.* Because there was no evidence to the contrary, and because Jessica had obviously been well cared for, the social worker had taken their word about what had happened and found a foster home for Jessica immediately.

"I hope the foster family will take good care of her," Mariel said. She had seen the foster mother and father when they had come to pick up Jessica at the Department of Social Services. They had both had kind faces.

"I'll check up on it," Jake said. "I'll be in touch with you."

Mariel managed a weak smile. "Do you suppose they'll find someone to adopt her right away?"

"They'll have to wait until they're sure they can't locate her parents," Jake reminded her.

"If you hear that they're going to let her be adopted, will you let me know?"

"Of course. Any chance you'd want her?"

"If they'd let a single mother adopt her, I'd certainly think about it."

"You know what, Mariel? You think too much."

She got into the car. "Goodbye, Jake. I hope everything goes well with you," she said, in a tone that was too formal by far.

"How can it?" he said, exasperated. "You know how I feel about you."

"I wish you wouldn't try to make me feel guilty," she whispered around the lump in her throat.

"All right," he said.

He shoved his hands down in the pockets of his water-stained red-and-black jacket and stared at her intently, as if that alone would make her stay.

Mariel tried again to picture him in the city, but he looked even more rugged and rough-hewn here, amid the buildings of the town, than he had in the woods.

She concentrated on putting the key into the ignition and starting the car's engine. When she eased out of the parking space, Jake stood back. She managed a brief smile that he didn't return. He watched her until she reached the corner and turned it. She wondered how long he would stand there.

As for her, she was on her way home, to her snug apartment, her friends and her life. Soon the town of Tellurian was behind her, no more than a dot on the map spread out on the seat next to her.

She never remembered what was between Tellurian and Pittsburgh. It flew by in a blur, less real to her than the castle and the time she had spent there.

When she reached home, Jake's message was waiting on her answering machine.

"Mariel, I miss you. When you decide to come back, I'll be here."

She erased the message. Jake was out of her life. Christmas was over. The magic was gone.

Chapter Fourteen

After a lackluster New Year's Eve spent at a boring party, and an equally uninspiring New Year's Day, during which she tried in vain to find something interesting to watch on television, Mariel tried to resume her former life. She spent too many hours sitting at her word processor, elevating the act of staring at her notes on Christmas folklore to a fine art. Writing about the mistletoe shooters seemed impossible; her hastily scribbled jottings made little sense, and her actual memory of the men and boys who had come calling at the castle on Christmas night was vague.

She certainly had no trouble recalling the hours before their appearance, when she and Jake had made love so joyously in the chamber off the gallery. It was easy to picture the glow in his eyes, and the answering passion that had made her urge him closer and closer, until their bodies blended into one. She remembered every moment as if it had been distilled down to its basic elements, clear and crystalline in her memory.

One Saturday in mid-February, with an air of determination, she sat down at her keyboard and typed *The Mistletoe Shooters* at the top of her computer screen. But, as always when she thought about their interlude in the castle, she found herself adrift in visions of making love with Jake. She wondered if Jake found that happening to him, too.

Not that she would ever ask him. He had called a few times, reporting that Jessica was thriving with her foster family, but Mariel had been pointedly unresponsive. When he left messages on her answering machine, she ignored them.

It was just as well that their connection had been broken, and yet sometimes, when she sat down to her solitary dinner, or when she spotted another tall, rugged, broad-shouldered man in a crowd, she felt a sudden, sharp pain in her heart. She had never dreamed that she was capable of missing someone so much.

But she'd better stop mooning over him. Right now she was supposed to be working, not thinking about Jake.

"Mariel, are you home?" called a voice outside her front door. It was Ellie, her friend and neighbor from down the hall.

"Come in, Ellie, the door's unlocked," she called back.

She heard the latch open and close, followed by footsteps clicking smartly down the hall. In a few seconds Ellie appeared in the doorway to her office.

"I brought you a cup of coffee." Ellie deposited a foam cup from the pancake restaurant around the corner onto Mariel's desk.

"Nice," Mariel said, managing a quick smile of thanks.

"It's a bribe to make you come shopping with me," Ellie said brightly. "We can take advantage of all these President's Day sales." Ellie folded herself onto the futon across from Mariel's desk and flipped her dark hair back from her face. She waited expectantly.

Mariel shook her head. "I don't think so, Ellie. Thanks for asking, but—" She gestured helplessly at the array of papers surrounding her. "Too much work to do. You can see what a mess this is."

"Crazy you. It's the weekend, and you should get out. Are you sure you won't change your mind?"

"I appreciate the coffee. It was sweet of you. Why don't you stay for a while and visit?"

"No, if I can't convince you to come along with me, I'll be on my way. I've had my eye on a lacy teddy since Christmas, and I'm hoping it'll be marked down."

Mariel tried to show interest. "Is it that black one that opens down the front? The one we admired in the window of our favorite boutique?"

"That's it, all right. If I buy it, Leo is in for a sexy night tonight. Did I tell you that we've decided to have a baby?"

"No. No, Ellie, you didn't, but I'm happy for you," Mariel said.

Ellie lifted her eyebrows. "You don't *look* happy, sourpuss. What's the matter? Ever since you wrecked your car in that backwater section of Virginia, you've seemed…well, one step removed from what's going on around you."

"It was difficult," Mariel said.

"I know, I know. Spending Christmas in a cave and a rundown old castle sounds awful, especially since it was with some rustic who probably doesn't even speak standard English," Ellie said, "and finding a baby under such strange circumstances must have been *too* awful for words."

"Oh, but Jake wasn't—" Mariel began, but Ellie wasn't in the mood to let her finish.

"Have they found the baby's parents?"

"I don't believe so," Mariel said quietly, inspecting her fingernails.

"Odd. I can't imagine how a baby could have ended up in the woods. Well, like I said, I'd better go before all the bargains are gone." Ellie stood up and tossed her own empty cup into the wastebasket. "What are you working on that's so important?"

Mariel sighed. "I'm hoping to finish writing down some of the stories I picked up in Virginia. A university press is interested in publishing the final manuscript."

"Great. I can't wait to see what you've been up to for all these years," Ellie said. She blew Mariel a kiss before disappearing out the door.

After Ellie had gone, Mariel stared at her empty computer screen for a while. She shuffled her notes. She pulled a loose hangnail off her thumb. The phone rang, but she ignored it. It was probably Ellie again, wanting her to change her mind about going shopping. She didn't intend to, mostly because she couldn't bear to be around Ellie and her happiness these days—Ellie couldn't stop talking about her wonderful husband and her perfect marriage, and now Mariel might as well steel herself to hear Ellie run on and on about the baby she was planning to have.

A *baby*. And after Ellie gave birth and Mariel went to visit, bearing gifts, if would only remind Mariel of Jessica. And Jake, of course.

Of course. After all, what *didn't* remind her of Jake? Somehow, over the past month and a half, Mariel had managed to relate everything in her life to him. She couldn't eat without thinking about the time she had fed him the apple in the cave, when his lips had brushed her fingers. She couldn't sleep without wishing he was curled around her, his legs warming hers. She couldn't do anything, because all she could think about was Jake.

She stood up and wrapped her arms around herself, suddenly chilled. She and Jake had really had something together—and now neither of them had anything. In the face of adversity, in the space of a few short days, they had somehow managed to build a loving, caring relationship—and she had walked away from it.

She was thirty years old. In her life, she had learned that love wasn't easy to find. You couldn't manufacture it, and you couldn't buy it. Love was a gift. And, when it had been given to her, she had been unable to accept it. She must be the all-time fool, the consummate idiot.

She did what she should have done a long time ago. She marched into her bedroom and raked an armful of clothes off the rod in the closet. She pulled a suitcase from the closet shelf and chucked the clothes into it. She scooped underwear from a dresser drawer, cosmetics from the bathroom shelf. It was enough—it was all she would need for her trip to Tellurian.

Because she was going to Jake, now, today, and she wouldn't look back. There would be no more sitting down and eating a lonely dinner for one in her silent apartment. No more daydreaming at work; she'd call on Monday and request an indefinite leave of absence. No more waking up at night and thinking she heard Jessica crying.

Come to think of it, she thought she heard a baby crying even now. She lugged her suitcase into the hall and stopped to listen for a moment, because it was such a faint sound. Finally, she realized that the noise was coming from the street.

She went to the window and adjusted the blinds so that she could look down from her second-floor apartment into the parking lot. The lot was full, but she made out an unfamiliar pickup truck parked in a visitor's parking space.

Snow had begun to fall, making it hard to see what was going on. She didn't see anyone—until a man carrying a baby walked around the pickup.

The man was tall, and he was wearing a navy wool jacket over faded blue jeans and work boots. He was concentrating on the baby, jiggling it in his arms, his head bent down as if he were speaking to it in a low tone. Mariel's heart stopped beating in her chest.

It couldn't be. But it was.

Mariel flew to the door and tore it open, rushing out on the landing as Jake Travis entered the downstairs vestibule and stomped the snow off his boots. She stared at him down the open stairwell until he instinctively looked up. Jessica looked up, too, her mouth open, her eyes wide. She emitted a small hiccup.

"Jake! What—what are you doing here?" Mariel gasped, unbelievingly. Just when she had been going to go to him, *he* had come to *her*.

"I brought a visitor," he said, turning Jessica so that Mariel could see her better.

"But— How? Why?"

He grinned at her, his eyes merry. "Why not?"

"How did you get here?" Her voice was strangled in her throat.

"In my new pickup. Aren't you going to invite us in? It's cold down here."

"I'm sorry," Mariel said as Jake hurried up the stairs, the baby round-eyed with wonder in his arms. Almost afraid to look at them for fear they would vanish, Mariel led the way into her apartment.

When she turned around, she realized that Jake was taller than she remembered, and she had almost forgotten about the bicuspid that overlapped the adjoining tooth.

He glanced at the white walls of her apartment, with their carefully chosen and nicely framed art prints, at the fireplace with its brass screen, at the gleaming hardwood floors. "Nice place," he said briefly, eyeing her suitcase by the door.

"You got a new jacket," Mariel said, momentarily flustered.

"I figured the other one was past saving after I fell in a moat," he said.

"I can't get used to the way you look in this one," Mariel said.

"You'll have to," he said. He hadn't stopped smiling.

Mariel suddenly remembered her manners. "I'll hang your jacket for you," she said.

"Here, you'd better take Jessica. I can manage the jacket." And then Mariel was holding Jessica in her arms again, was pressing her hot cheek against Jessica's cool one, was inhaling the scent of her soft, sweet baby skin. Memories flooded back, memories of her happiness, and she was overcome by a sense of loss.

Jake found the hall closet and hung his coat inside. He

wore a red turtleneck under a blue chambray shirt, and he looked wonderful.

"I'd bet Jessica is ready for a diaper change," he said.

"Your turn or mine?" Mariel said through a blur of tears, but she laughed with Jake.

She hadn't noticed the diaper bag when he had first come in.

"This time I have all the necessary equipment. Flubbies," he said, digging deep in the bag and producing a disposable diaper with a flourish. "Something called a puddle pad. And a pacifier. Great little gadget, a pacifier. We should have had one in that cave. It works like a plug. Sure wish they'd make one for the other end of babies. Now, that would be something."

Mariel ignored this. "Jessica has grown so much." She marveled as she laid the baby on the couch. She unzipped Jessica's warm suit and felt the little arms and legs. She couldn't believe that the child was actually lying in front of her, waiting for a diaper change.

"And she eats a lot," Jake said. "She eats cereal now, don't you Jessica?"

For an answer, Jessica blew bubbles.

"I brought a bed for her. She'd probably like a nap," Jake said after Mariel had changed the baby's diaper.

Mariel had all kinds of questions, but they had to wait until Jake went back to the pickup and brought in a portable crib, which they set up in Mariel's tiny office.

Jake spared a quick look at the papers spread over the top of her desk. "Doing lots of work, it looks like," he said.

"Let's go into the living room," Mariel said. "I need to know—I need to know all kinds of things, Jake."

She led him into the living room, conscious of him close behind her. When they sat on the couch, he said, "I saw your suitcase in the hall. Are you going away or coming back?"

She might as well tell him she was planning to drive to

Tellurian, that in fifteen minutes more she would have been on the road.

"I was—"

"Because if you're planning to go away for the weekend, you might as well forget it. I have some things to say to you, and I'm going to say them."

"I was—"

"I tried to let you know that I was coming to Pittsburgh this weekend, but you never returned my calls. Now that I'm here, you're going to hear me out, whether you like it or not."

"But I was—"

"Why didn't you call me back?"

Mariel gave up. He had no intention of listening to her— yet. So, first things first. She'd listen. She'd answer questions. And she figured that while she was at it, she might as well be honest.

"I wanted to call you more than once. But it seemed— futile. I thought it would make it all the harder to hear about Jessica and about your life and—well, I was trying to protect myself," she said, hoping he appreciated her candor.

"They haven't found Jessica's parents yet, Mariel. There are no clues, no leads. No one reported a child missing, and no one was seen in that remote area around the time that we found her," Jake said.

"How do you happen to have her?"

"I go to see her every day at her foster parents' house. Sometimes they let me baby-sit. They don't mind if I borrow her for a day or two. But they're going to have to give her up."

"Oh, that's too bad. Jessica seems so happy and well adjusted," Mariel said.

"I'm worried that Social Services won't be able to place her in a home that's nearly as good. I thought—" He stopped talking.

"What, Jake?" she asked gently.

He turned to look at her, golden flecks swimming up from the depth of those deep brown eyes.

"You're coming home with me. We're going to adopt Jessica. We're going to get married."

She felt a bubble of laughter in her throat. The timing couldn't be better. She was already packed.

"I don't want to hear all your reasons why we can't get married. We *can*," he said in a rush.

"I was already—"

"I love you. You love me. We both love the baby. You can't deny it," he said.

Deep within her, Mariel felt a wellspring of love, and hope, and joy. He loved her. She loved him. They both loved Jessica. It was all so simple, so elemental.

"Will you, Mariel? Will you marry me?" As if from a great distance, Mariel watched him reach for her hands, saw him capture them both in his, saw him lean forward and kiss her on the lips. But she didn't feel it. She didn't feel a thing.

"I—I—" she stammered, because even though she had dreamed of such a moment, her dreams hadn't prepared her for the reality of sitting across from Jake Travis and hearing him speak the words.

"I'll always love you, Mariel. When you drove away from Tellurian, I felt like my life was over. I don't want to go on without you. We're a good team. We were happy together with Jessica. So we're going to get married," he finished.

"I was already packed," she managed to say. "I was coming to see you. I was going to leave in a matter of minutes."

He stared at her, then threw his head back and laughed. "Why didn't you tell me?" he asked.

"You didn't give me a chance," she retorted.

"I've got it all planned. You can work on those Christmas legends in Tellurian in my big house, where there's a room that will make a wonderful office for you. We're going to stay in that house, Mariel. It's time to settle down. I can't wait for you to see it. There are four bedrooms, and lots of bathrooms, and a kitchen that I designed myself. And closets, lots of closets. And a large bed that's too big for me. Oh, and a nook off the master bedroom that will make a perfect nursery.''

"I don't believe this is happening," Mariel said, her mind reeling. "I don't believe you're saying all these things."

"What do you want? Shall I go down on my knees to propose?"

"No, you don't have to do that," she said, but before the words were out of her mouth, Jake was on one knee in front of her.

"My lady, my love, will you do you me the honor of marrying me?"

"Oh, Jake, get up. This feels so ridiculous."

"I'm not getting up until you tell me your answer," he said firmly.

For a split second, she wondered how she could help loving this man. How could she not want to recapture the magic she had found at Christmas and hold it close to her heart all the rest of their lives?

"This might help." Jake fumbled in his pocket and pulled out a sprig of mistletoe. Mariel looked blank. She knew what it was, of course, but what was it doing in Jake's pocket in the middle of February?

"Before I tossed my old jacket in the trash, I checked the pockets, and I found this. I kept it as a memento of Christmas, the best Christmas of my life, because I found you and Jessica," he said.

"But why did you bring it now?" she asked.

"To help us recapture the magic," he said, standing up and pulling her with him. He held the mistletoe over their heads. "How's it working?"

"Kiss me, and I'll tell you," she said, lifting her lips to his.

He did kiss her, slowly and thoroughly, but she didn't tell him anything—at least not with words—until much, much later.

Epilogue

Tellurian, Virginia
The Next Christmas...

"Where do you want to drape this garland?" Jake asked, holding up the strand of evergreen boughs and studying it critically.

"How about on the banister?"

"Let's go see how it looks," Jake said. He paused to restrain the two little hands that were reaching toward the bulbs on the Christmas tree. "No, Jessica."

"Give me a heave up," Mariel said, waving at him.

He clasped her hand and pulled. "Up you go," he said, and, once on her feet, she slid an arm around his waist. "Feeling okay?" Jake asked her.

"Wonderful," Mariel said, smiling up at him fondly.

He patted her protruding stomach. "Can't have our little mother overexerting."

"I'm only five months pregnant."

"Since we think you conceived over the Fourth of July weekend, this baby's going to be a real firecracker."

"Have you ever noticed how holidays play a big part in our love story?" Mariel asked, pressing a hand to the small of her back as Jake measured the garland against the banister.

"Yes, and if we're lucky, maybe the Easter bunny will

bring the new baby right after our adoption of Jessica is final.'' Jake adjusted the garland. "How does this look?"

"Terrific. Leave the garland on the stairs, and I'll tie it on with big red bows. I love the way you refinished the banister, by the way. You exactly matched the shade of the stain we put on the floor.''

"I had good decorating advice from my wife,'' he said, swinging around the newel post and planting a kiss on her lips.

"Dadadada,'' said Jessica, crawling over to tug at the hem of Jake's jeans, unwilling to be ignored.

Jake bent down and swung her into his arms. "Leave the red ribbon on the steps, and I'll tie the garland on myself later,'' he told Mariel. "I don't want to take any chances that you might trip on the stairs.''

"I walk up and down the stairs every day,'' Mariel protested. Her new office, where she worked while Jessica napped in a crib with her name carved into the headboard in a cheery yellow-papered nursery, was at the head of the stairs, right next to the master bathroom.

"That's different. Say, isn't it time for me to see those things you've been knitting lately? Why don't you hang our stockings by the chimney with care?'' he suggested.

She smiled at him and lifted her eyebrows. "In hopes that Saint Nicholas soon will be there?''

"Hey, Mariel, you don't have to convince me. Santa Claus is real. Last year I finally got a couple of Christmas presents I'd always wanted—you and this little Christmas angel,'' he said, nuzzling Jessica's neck.

Mariel opened a drawer in the table beside the rocking chair that Jake had lovingly refinished for her, and she took out a tissue-wrapped package.

"Have I ever told you about looking at the tapestry on the wall of the castle right before we left in the Jeep?'' she asked.

"No. Did it look better up close than it did from far away?''

"I thought the tapestries were pretty,'' she protested.

"I was blinded by your beauty, I guess, because I didn't notice them at all."

Mariel crumpled the tissue paper and threw it at him. "Anyway," she said, moving cumbersomely toward the mantel, "I took a good look, and I saw the unicorn part, and the knights-jousting-in-the-meadow part, and there was one other part that I almost missed. It was something I've never seen in any other tapestry."

"Don't be so mysterious, Mariel. What are you trying to say?"

She kept her head turned as she affixed the biggest stocking, Jake's, to the mantel. "In the last tapestry, the one that was closest to the shadowy corner, there was a depiction of a round little man with a long white beard. He was riding in a sleigh pulled by reindeer," she said carefully.

"This was in a medieval tapestry?" Jake said skeptically.

"I don't know that it was an authentically *old* medieval tapestry, but yes, there he was, looking exactly like the man from the Magic Minimart, looking exactly like—"

"Like Santa Claus," Jake finished for her.

Mariel finished tacking her stocking to the mantel and began to hang Jessica's smaller one. "Exactly," she said.

"I've always wondered about the fact that the castle was supposed to be owned by a guy named Mr. Nicholas. And I've never heard from him, even though I left my name and address and offered to pay for the food we ate. Mariel, why are you hanging five stockings?"

"For our family," she said carefully, turning so that he could see her figure profiled against the flames in the fireplace.

"Our family consists of you, me, Jessica, and the new baby. That's four people, which equals four stockings," he said.

She slanted a sly look out of the corners of her eyes. "Don't you realize that I'm gaining more weight than most expectant mothers at five months? Don't you know what I'm trying to tell you?"

Jake stared. His gaze dropped to her abdomen, which strained against her perky maternity top.

"Twins?" he said, as if he couldn't believe it. "Are we going to have twins?"

She walked up to where he stood in the archway between foyer and living room, a mistletoe ball suspended above his head. She put her arms around him, including Jessica in their embrace. "Twins," she confirmed, leaning over her stomach to kiss him on the cheek.

"But that's...that's..."

"The very best kind of magic," she said, and she kissed him again.

There was no forgetting Konstantin Rudenko. Not when her daughter was the very image of him.

THE NUTCRACKER PRINCE

Rebecca Winters

CHAPTER ONE

"SHH, ANNA, HONEY. Remember, we can only sing to the music at home, not during the ballet." Meg Roberts quietly admonished her six-year-old daughter, who was sitting on her lap and blithely singing the words to the "Waltz of the Flowers" a little off-key.

Even though the Saturday matinee performance of the St. Louis ballet company's *Nutcracker* catered to families with younger children, Meg noticed a good number of adults in the audience, as well.

"I'm sorry, Mommy. When will the prince come out?" Anna whispered so loudly it drew a quelling look from an older woman seated in front of them.

Before Meg could caution her again, Anna put a finger to her own lips and flashed her mother a mischievous smile— a smile that never failed to swell Meg's heart with love and pride. Anna's exuberant personality shone through her sparkling eyes, which fastened in rapt attention on the dancers once more.

In the near darkness Meg studied her daughter. Anna's cheeks were flushed with the excitement of attending her first ballet. Though Christmas was only eight days away, Anna had talked of nothing but this day for more than a month; even now, she hugged the picture book of the *Nutcracker* to the bodice of the red velvet dress Meg had made for her.

The well-worn treasure brought from Russia went everywhere her daughter did. With its Russian printing Anna couldn't read the words, but it was the illustrations that captured her heart—particularly the ones of handsome Prince Marzipan fighting the Mouse King. From the very first instant she'd caught sight of his tall, uniformed physique, Anna had remarked on the dark hair and blue eyes similar to her own. Even more poignant, from Meg's point of view, was the fact that her daughter had endowed Prince Marzipan with all the qualities she attributed to the father she'd never seen or known.

The fact that the Prince did bear a striking resemblance to Anna's father made it impossible for Meg to put her own bittersweet memories away, especially since he'd given Meg the book in the first place. It was a constant reminder of the man who, with practiced ease, had made love to a foolish, vulnerable, starry-eyed Meg—the man who'd left her pregnant. But even without it, there was no forgetting Konstantin Rudenko. Not when Anna was the very image of him.

With each passing day Meg grew more troubled as she identified yet another similarity in their coloring and features. Every day she was beset by disturbing flashes of recall that refused to die. Certain facial expressions, the way Anna's head swiveled around when she heard something that interested her, all would trigger long-suppressed memories followed by waves of shame and humiliation. Especially now that Meg knew she'd been set up, lied to, used....

"Look, Mommy!"

The Russian cossack dancers came out to perform their gymnastic feats, and once again Anna forgot where she was and broke into more off-key singing about balalaikas and clicking feet.

"Quiet!" the older woman snapped over her shoulder, and this time several other people turned around, as well.

Mortified, Meg hugged her daughter tighter. "You mustn't talk or sing," she whispered into Anna's short dark curls. "You're disturbing other people. If you make another sound, we'll have to leave."

"No, Mommy," she begged with tears in her eyes. "I haven't seen the prince yet. I promise to be good."

"You always say that, and then you forget."

"I won't forget," Anna asserted so earnestly Meg had to smile. Still, she knew it would be a sheer impossibility for her daughter to remain quiet throughout the rest of the performance.

"You'll have to stay on my lap."

"I will." She wrapped her arms around Meg's neck and gave her a kiss on the cheek before settling down. For a little while, Anna's model behavior lulled Meg into a false sense of security, and they both watched spellbound as the delightful story unfolded.

Then the symphony's brass section announced the arrival of the toy soldiers. Without warning, Anna slid off Meg's lap. "There's Prince Marzipan, Mommy. See?" she cried in ecstasy, pointing to the male dancer who led the march. Her absorption with the Prince made her oblivious to everything else around her, but Meg hadn't missed the furious glare of the woman in front of them.

Luckily by now, other enchanted children throughout the audience had gotten to their feet and were contributing to the heightened noise. Their cheers and clapping made Anna's outburst seem less noticeable. From the glow in her eyes, Meg knew what this moment meant to her daughter, who stood entranced until the Prince leapt offstage after defeating the Mouse King.

The second he disappeared Anna whirled around and climbed onto Meg's lap again. "Mommy," she said in a loud whisper, "I have to *you know what*."

Meg shouldn't have been surprised. The excitement had been too much, and she knew Anna wouldn't be able to wait until the performance was over. "All right. Don't forget your book." Throwing their coats over one arm, she reached for Anna's hand with the other and they made their way past several people to the center aisle.

"Slow down, honey," Meg cautioned, struggling to keep up with Anna who practically ran to the ladies' lounge off the nearly empty foyer. She was still chattering about the Prince when they emerged a few minutes later.

"Can I go see him when it's over, Mommy?" Anna blurted while they stood in the short lineup at the drinking fountain before going back into the concert hall.

"I don't think that's allowed."

"Mrs. Beezley said I could."

"We'll see," Meg murmured, wishing Anna's first-grade teacher hadn't put the idea in her head. Mrs. Beezley's opinions often carried more weight than Meg's.

"Our precocious daughter appears to be enjoying herself," Meg heard a male voice say from behind her. She assumed the man must be talking to his wife and didn't give it further thought as she waited for Anna to finish drinking from the fountain.

"Do you remember that lowly woodcutter's cottage outside St. Petersburg, *mayah labof?*"

Meg let out a gasp and the world came to a sudden standstill.

Konstantin. No. It couldn't be.

But his question, whispered with that quiet, unmistakable sensuality she remembered so well, spoke to the very depths of her soul. She hadn't imagined his voice.

Her body broke out in a cold sweat and she felt herself swaying. She closed her eyes in shock.

He was supposed to be living on the other side of the world, leading a life she would never want or be able to comprehend. Yet her heart beating frantically in her chest told her something vastly different.

He wasn't in St. Petersburg. He was *here*, in *this* theater, and he had just called her *my darling*. If Meg turned around, she'd be able to touch him.

Dear God.

But even as she recognized the reality of his presence, her

body trembled in anger and panic. She was furious with herself for the weakness that brought the memories flooding back. The still-sensual memories of his lovemaking seven years ago—when she'd only been part of a night's work for him.

Her intellectual side had always known he was the enemy, but there was a time she'd been so in love with him her heart had refused to listen or care, had most of all refused to believe.

He knew about Anna.

The knowledge shouldn't have shaken her like this. Of course he knew about Anna. He knew things about people no human being had a right to know, because that was his business. His *only* business.

Which meant he'd been following them, waiting for the perfect moment to seize his property, to seize his daughter....

What better spot than someplace public, where he knew Meg couldn't or wouldn't make a scene because it would alarm Anna? Sick with fear, Meg felt her heart race out of control.

With startling clarity she remembered those terrifying hours she'd spent in the dark—alone—on the dank floor of a Moscow jail, her guards devoid of compassion or pity.

"Meg?" His voice interrupted her thoughts. She didn't know how much time had passed—only seconds, she supposed, but that was long enough to relive the years of heartache. She did not turn around as he began to speak.

"I don't know what you've told her about her father, but now that I'm here, we'll tell her the truth together. Forget any ideas of running away from me, or I will most assuredly cause a scene. Since I know how much you would hate to upset Anna, I expect your full cooperation."

His English was as perfect as ever, formal, precise. The training he'd received in the KGB left nothing to chance. Anyone listening would assume he was from the United States, perhaps the East Coast.

A moan escaped her lips, and the sound caught Anna's attention. She gave up her place at the fountain for the next child. "Mommy? What's wrong?" Apprehension gripped Meg so tightly she couldn't move or breathe; it prevented her from doing any of a dozen things her survival instincts screamed for her to do. No trap ever devised worked as well as the threat to one's own flesh and blood. "N-nothing, honey. Let's hurry back inside."

She grabbed Anna's hand and almost dragged her toward the doors of the concert hall. Meg knew she didn't have a prayer of eluding *him,* but she refused to remain there like a paralyzed animal while he gloated over another easy victory.

"Mommy, you're hurrying too fast," Anna complained, but Meg, whose fear escalated with every passing second, increased her speed.

It didn't matter that there had been drastic changes in Russia since detente. He might no longer be KGB, but he could still be working for the present powers in a classified capacity. Secret police still existed in the former USSR.

As far as she was concerned, he was a dangerous man she'd never wanted to see again—a man who could pass himself off as an American, with no one the wiser—a man who now walked within whispering distance of them and had obviously been monitoring the events of her life for years.

He was a man who would stop at nothing to achieve his objective. And she had an idea his objective now was Anna.

But this time there was one difference. She was no longer that naive twenty-three-year-old who had credited him with a set of values similar to her own. Time and experience had worked their damage, and that vulnerable young creature no longer existed. All that remained of their long-ago nights of passion was Meg's bitterness—and her daughter.

If she and Anna could make it inside before he caught up with them, she could buy a little time to work out what to do. By now she was half-pulling, half-carrying Anna, her own heart pumping hard and fast.

"Meg? Anna?"

At the sound of their names being called, Anna yanked free of her mother and turned around. "Who are you?" she asked, her face bright with curiosity.

Defeated by his cunning, Meg was forced to come to a stop and face the man she'd once, briefly, loved. The man who had fathered Anna. She didn't want to look at him, didn't want to acknowledge him. But Anna was watching them with avid interest, and Meg was afraid to upset her or force his hand too soon.

When she finally dared a glimpse, the intense blue of his heavily lashed eyes almost made her reel. He'd always been the most attractive man she'd ever known, yet he looked different, somehow, from the way she remembered him.

The first time she'd met him, his brown-black hair had brushed the collar of his drab gray suit and trench coat, typical KGB garb. Now he wore his hair shorter and dressed like a successful American businessman in a navy suit and pale blue shirt that enhanced his six-foot height and lean, muscled frame. But the difference she perceived was subtler than that.

Unlike the married middle-aged men at the European-auto dealership where she worked as a secretary/cashier, he'd grown even handsomer, if that was possible, over the past seven years. In his late thirties now, he possessed a virile appeal that her body recognized and responded to without any volition on her part.

"I'm someone who loves you and your mommy very much," he said in answer to his daughter. Anna resembled him in so many attractive ways, Meg was afraid she'd see the similarities right off.

"You do?" Anna sounded amazed and, worse, intrigued.

Meg's eyes closed in growing fury. He meant business. Damn him for his matchless ability to charm his victims. As always, he resorted to ways that had nothing to do with brute force.

With an overwhelming sense of helplessness she waited to hear his response, part of her still denying he had sprung out of nowhere like one of those disturbing dreams that haunts you for years afterward.

"What's your name?" Anna asked softly.

"Konstantin Rudenko."

"K-Konsta... What did you say?"

He chuckled. "Your mommy calls me Kon."

The audacity, the cruel, calculating arrogance of the man, filled Meg with rage.

"It's Russian, like yours."

"You mean I have a Russian name, too?"

"That's right." He pronounced it with his native accent, his voice tender. Then his eyes sought Meg's as if to say, "You've never forgotten me."

"No!" Meg cried out against this threat to her fragile emotions and hard-won independence, but it was too late. In a quick, protective move she placed both hands on her daughter's shoulders.

Anna's young, inquiring mind seized upon the information she'd just learned and carefully imitated his pronunciation of her name. She tried to pull away from her mother. "My mommy told me my daddy lives in Russia, so he can't ever come to visit me," she said in a loud whisper, remembering too late that it was a secret between the two of them. Her mother had told her over and over that no one else must ever know.

"Anna!" Meg chastised her, but the effort was fruitless.

"Well, your mommy is wrong, Anochka," he asserted, using the diminutive of her name.

This time Anna wriggled loose from Meg's grip and moved closer to inspect him. "You look just like Prince Marzipan!"

Quick as lightning she peered over her shoulder at Meg, who was shaken by the stars in her daughter's eyes. "Mommy! He looks like the Prince!" And she immediately opened her book to the page whose edges were worn from constant use. "See?" She pointed out the similarities to him.

In a lithe move he got down on his haunches, making it easier for Anna to show him her proof. A satisfied smile lifted the corners of his mouth, and he fingered one of the curls bouncing over her forehead. "Did you know I gave your mommy this book when she left Russia after her first visit, more than twelve years ago?"

For the second time in a couple of minutes, Meg gasped out loud. Anna's eyes grew huge. "You did?"

"Yes. It's my favorite book, too. That's because we're father and daughter, and we think alike."

His eyes flashed Meg another meaningful glance. "Your mommy was sad because your grandfather died while she was on her trip. So when she went home, I put this book in her suitcase to comfort her because she had admired it. I hoped it would make her feel better and bring her back to Russia one day, because I cared for her even then."

Tears stung Meg's eyes. *Liar,* her heart cried. But she couldn't dispute the fact that this beautiful, overpriced book, which she'd admired at the House of Books in Moscow and couldn't afford, had ended up in her luggage. It was all thanks to the dark, attractive KGB agent, assigned to the foreign-student sector, who had hustled her from jail to the airport.

Meg, along with other seventeen-year-olds on her bus, had been detained because they'd given away blue jeans, T-shirts and other personal articles to friendly Russian teenagers. Unsuspecting, Meg had given her Guess? sunglasses to a young girl—and ended up in prison. She still shuddered when she thought of that nightmarish incident.

During her confinement, one of the guards told her the tour director had just learned that Meg's father had died back in the States. Because of Meg's unwise decision to break the law and consort with black marketers, he informed her, she might not be able to go home for the funeral, maybe not be able to go home at all.

He'd seemed inhuman to Meg, incapable of emotion. He'd left her alone to "think about" what she'd done, and Meg had collapsed on the floor in despair. For hours she'd sobbed out her grief for the loss of her mother a year earlier and now her beloved father. William Roberts was dead, thousands of miles away, and she would never see him again.

But before morning, Kon had come to get her, and she was escorted through hallways to a back door, where a car waited to take her to the airport. She never saw her traveling companions again, and returned to the United States in time to bury her father, the book her only memento.

After her cruel treatment at the hands of other agents under his command, Kon's authority and subsequent intervention had been the only reason she was allowed to return to the States without further repercussions. His gift, totally unsolicited, had caused her to rethink her opinion that all KGB agents were monsters.

Six years later, when she qualified for a new opportunity, arranged through the State Department, to travel to Russia as a cultural-exchange teacher, she looked forward to the experience. Meg had hoped to locate him and thank him in person for his kindness.

She'd seen him again, all right. Naively she'd believed that their meeting was accidental, never realizing that Kon had kept track of her back in the States. The knowledge was almost unbearable. It meant his feelings had never been real. And it meant that on her second trip to the USSR, after the invalid aunt she'd lived with and taken care of had passed away, Meg was targeted. She'd learned about this from the CIA on her return. Kon's every move had been calculated to make her fall in love with him, for reasons best known to the KGB. It had happened before, to equally naive, usually young American men and women—tourists, diplomatic employees and others. What had occurred between Meg and

Kon was, as it turned out, not all that rare. Kon's "love" had been politically motivated; he'd been in control.

And now he'd come for Anna.

"Are you really my daddy?"

Anna's simple question broke the silence. The hope in her earnest young voice had Meg practically in tears. She realized they'd come to the moment of truth. Kon would show no mercy.

"Yes, I'm your daddy, and I can tell you're my little girl. We have the same blue eyes, the same dark brown hair, and the same straight noses." He tweaked hers gently, and Anna giggled. "But you smile just like your mommy. See?"

He whipped some pictures out of his suit-coat pocket. "That's your mommy and I eating ice cream and champagne. I'd just told her I loved her. Look at her mouth. It curves right there—" he touched Anna's lower lip "—exactly like yours."

Anna giggled again before putting the precious storybook on the floor so she could look at the black-and-white snapshot. For once in her life she was struck dumb. So was Meg, who could remember him touching her mouth like that. Then he'd kissed her until she'd never wanted him to stop....

At the time she'd been blissfully unaware that someone was taking pictures of them.

There had to be many more photographs where those came from. Meg had little doubt that a camera had recorded their days and nights together, and she felt a deep, searing pain that the most wonderful experience of her life—loving Kon—could have ended up in the KGB microfilm files.

"Mommy, look! This is a picture of you."

"That's right," he murmured, "and here are some other photos of your beautiful mother and me in front of her hotel and at a nearby museum."

Kon couldn't have come up with a more cunning plan to win over his daughter than this—offering her hungry eyes absolute proof of her parents' relationship.

On both of Meg's trips to Russia, picture-taking had been strictly forbidden, except for the shots taken at Red Square, the military pride of the nation. Which explained why she didn't have even one photograph of Kon to keep in remembrance.

"And here," he said when Anna had finished inspecting the others, "is a picture of your mommy and me at the airport. I begged her to stay in Russia and marry me, but she got on that plane, anyway." His voice sounded desolate, and Meg thought cynically that it was a mark of his consummate acting ability.

By now his arm had gone around Anna's tiny waist and she leaned against his chest without even realizing it. Watching her daughter, Meg felt her heart shatter into tiny pieces.

Anna raised troubled eyes to her mother. "Why did you do that, Mommy?" Tears threatened. "Why did you leave my daddy alone?"

Meg fought for a stabilizing breath, despising Kon for doing this to her. To them. "Because I couldn't have come back to America if I had stayed any longer, and I had responsibilities at home. Classes to teach, commitments to my students."

"You're a teacher?"

After a brief pause she said, "Not anymore, honey. But I was—once."

"Like Mrs. Beezley?" Anna sounded totally puzzled by her mother's admission.

"Yes. I taught high school." But having a baby on her own had forced her to grow up in a hurry, and when she realized the truth of what had gone on while she was in Russia, she gave up teaching Russian and wanted nothing more to do with the country, the language or her memories. Anna was too young to understand, so Meg had never told her about that aspect of her life.

Unfortunately Anna had found the *Nutcracker* book in a box in the storage room where Meg had hidden it. The little girl had fallen in love with it on sight and commandeered it for her own. Meg had never had the heart to take it away from her, but she'd never explained its origins, either.

"Is it true, Daddy?"

With that one question, Meg knew it was all over. Not only had Anna accepted Kon as her father without reservation, but now she was questioning Meg's veracity.

What an ironic fact of life that a mother could give her all to her child for six years, and then a man, whose only contribution had been biological, could come along and in a heartbeat win that child's unquestioned devotion and adoration.

"Yes, it's true. Your mother speaks excellent Russian, and when she wasn't teaching English to some Russian students, we spent every moment of her four months in St. Petersburg together."

Meg's breathing had grown shallow. "Anna...why don't you ask your father why he didn't come to America with me?" She knew her voice sounded brittle.

"But I did come," he countered with a swiftness that took her breath. "You see, in order to leave my country, I had many things to do first, many responsibilities. But I've always known about you, Anochka. I've always loved you, even when I was far away. Now I'm finally here, and I'm going to stay."

For as long as it took to win over Anna. Then he would disappear with her. Meg was sure of it. She wondered when this latent fatherhood instinct had taken over to bring him halfway around the world to claim his child.

"You can sleep in my room," Anna declared, tying up all the loose ends with the simple reasoning of an innocent child. She could have no comprehension of the scattered debris of their separate lives.

"I'd like that," he murmured softly. "That's why I've come—to live with you and your mommy. I want us to be a family. Can I ride home in your car? I didn't bring mine to the ballet.''

"We have a red Toy-yoda. You can sit in the back with me and read me my book while Mommy drives us.''

"We'll take turns reading. Do you like where you live?''

"Yes. But I wish we had a dog. The mean apartment man won't let us have one.''

"Then you'll love Gandy and Thor.'' He bundled her in her winter coat while they chatted.

"Gandy and To—what?''

"Thor. They're my German shepherds, and I've told them all about you. They can't wait to get acquainted. And once they do, they'll play with you and be your friends forever.'' At his words, Anna squealed in delight.

Impotent rage welled up inside Meg. Nothing was beneath him, certainly not the wholesale bribery of his vulnerable daughter. Meg was close to screaming, but the *Nutcracker* had ended and people were pouring into the lobby. For Anna's sake, she had to keep tight control on her emotions until she could be alone with him out of her daughter's hearing.

Konstantin Rudenko was used to being an absolute, unquestioned authority in his own country, but there was no way she would allow him to strong-arm her here, in *her* home.

Meg marched over to her daughter and put a firm hand on her shoulder to separate her from her father. "Let's go, Anna.''

But Anna wasn't listening. Her hands had reached out to explore the texture and hard coutours of Kon's face. For a traitorous moment Meg relived the sensation, the slight raspy feel of those cheeks against hers after she spent the night in his arms. Making love…

"Will you let me carry you to the car, Anochka? I've dreamed of holding my own little girl for a long, long time.''

Anna, who up to this point hadn't liked any man who paid

too much attention to Meg, was obviously mesmerized by his husky voice and the loving look in his eyes. She slid her arms around his neck and let him pick her up, her expression one of sublime joy.

"What does that *noska* word mean?"

"My little baby Anna. That's what the daddies in Russia call their darling daughters."

"I'm not a baby. You're funny, Daddy." She gave him his first kiss on the cheek.

"And you are adorable, just like your mother." He crushed her in his arms, as if he'd been waiting his whole life for this moment.

Meg looked away, pierced to her soul to see Anna's enchantment with a man who wasn't beyond manipulating a child's deepest and most tender emotions to get what he wanted.

She would never forgive him for this. *Never.*

CHAPTER TWO

"WHICH WAY to your car, *mayah labof?*" he asked, repeating the calculated endearment that still had the power to touch her emotionally, though she fought against it. "Anna and I are ready."

Meg was on the verge of shouting that since he'd followed them to the theater, he no doubt knew exactly where her car was parked. But when she saw how perfect father and daughter looked together, with Anna's arm placed trustingly around his neck, Meg's throat choked up and no words would come.

Anna had wanted her own daddy from the time she'd watched her best friend, Melanie, with *her* father. It always made Anna feel left out. Within the last few minutes, though, bonds had been forged that no power on earth could break.

Other people leaving the theater would see at once that they were father and daughter, and Meg noticed how several women's eyes lingered on Kon's striking features.

If anything, it was Meg's relationship to the dark-haired little girl in his arms people might question. Meg's shoulder-length ash-blond hair and gray eyes suggested a different ancestry altogether—yet another irony Meg was forced to swallow. She fastened her coat against the cold, wintry afternoon and headed for her car, parked on a side street around the corner.

She walked several paces from Kon so she wouldn't accidentally brush against him. She felt relieved when he got into the back seat of the car with Anna, keeping some space between them.

He might think he had the upper hand now, especially while Anna clung to him and bombarded him with questions. But once they were home, they'd be in Meg's territory. *She'd* set the rules. They'd have dinner immediately, she decided, and as soon as Anna had eaten, it would be her bedtime.

With her daughter asleep, Meg would be able to have it out with Kon and get rid of him before Anna awakened. As soon as possible, Meg would contact the attorney who had helped settle her father's and aunt's affairs: she would get a court order forcing Kon to stay away from her and Anna.

Since no marriage had taken place and he wasn't an American citizen, she wondered what rights he had where their daughter was concerned. Certainly when her attorney learned the truth of Kon's KGB background, he would do everything in his power to protect Anna from being alone with her father—not to mention being taken out of the country. How she wished her Uncle Lloyd was still alive. He'd worked in navel intelligence and could have counseled her on the best way to proceed.

Meg had no idea how high up in the KGB Kon had risen, but she couldn't imagine him renouncing a system that had dominated his entire life. Of course, political ideologies weren't something she and Kon had discussed when they were together. He'd always managed to find them a place where they could be alone because they were so hungry for each other, could never get enough of each other. Their conversation had been that of lovers.

Evidently when his tactics had failed to get her to marry him—which would have meant turning her back on her own country—he'd had to devise another scheme. He'd decided to come after Anna. But he'd waited until she was old enough to respond to his machinations and his charms.

Maybe he genuinely wanted a relationship with his daughter, but Meg also knew how much he loved his country, how deeply immersed he'd been in its ideology. Naturally he would want Anna to feel the same way, and that meant taking her back there with him.

"Where are my dogs, Daddy?"

"At the house I bought for you and your mother."

"Oh, Mommy!" Anna cried joyfully and clapped her hands. "Daddy has a *house* for us! Where is it, Daddy? Can we go see it now?"

"I think your mommy has other plans for tonight," he told her.

Meg bit her tongue in an effort to keep quiet. She almost ran into a van standing next to the driveway that led to the parking garage of her apartment complex. Kon had deliberately brought up subjects guaranteed to delight a little girl starving for a father's love and attention. If Meg fought with him in front of Anna, it would only alienate her daughter and cause more grief.

And there would be grief.

But by the time Anna awakened the next morning, she would discover her father permanently gone from their lives. Meg wouldn't rest until she had some kind of injunction placed against Kon. Back at the apartment, she would manufacture a reason to run to one of her neighbors so she could phone Ben Avery in private. She didn't care if she had to keep her attorney and a judge up all night!

The second Meg pulled in her parking space and turned off the engine, Anna scrambled from the car, too involved with Kon to be thinking about her mother. "Come on, Daddy. I want you to see my aquarium." She couldn't quite manage the *i*. "You can feed my fish if you want to."

"I'd like that, but first we have to help your mommy," Meg heard him say in a low voice before he shut the rear door and opened the driver's side. She shouldn't have been surprised by his solicitude. Nothing was done without a motive, and she suspected he wasn't about to let her out of his sight.

Avoiding his gaze, she got out of the car, pulled away from

the hand that gripped her elbow and walked ahead of them on trembling legs. She headed blindly toward the door leading into the modern, three-story complex.

It would have done no good to reach for Anna, who still clutched her book in one hand and her father's hand in the other, impatiently waiting to show him her world.

"Melanie lives right here!" she exclaimed as they passed a door on their way down the second-floor hall.

"Is she your friend?"

"Yes, my best friend. But sometimes we fight. You know—" Anna leaned toward him confidingly "—she says I don't have a daddy."

"Then you'll have to introduce us later and we'll prove to her she's wrong."

Anna skipped along beside her father, her face illuminated with joy by his words. "She says my mommy had a *luvver*." This was news to Meg, who could feel her world falling apart so fast she didn't know how to begin gathering up the pieces. "What's a luvver, Daddy?"

While Meg cringed, Kon slowed his pace and picked Anna up in his arms once more. "I'm going to tell you something very important. When a man and a woman love each other more than anyone else in the world, they get married and become lovers. That's why you were born, and we both love you more than our own lives."

"But you and my mommy didn't get married."

"That's because we lived in different countries, which complicated everything. But now that I'm here, we'll get married and live happily ever after."

Meg could hardly breathe.

"Can you get married tomorrow?"

Kon laughed low in his throat. "How about next week at my house? We'll need to help your mommy pack everything and move out of the apartment first."

Terrified of creating a scene that would traumatize Anna and arouse even more interest from her neighbors—many of

whom were just coming home from Christmas shopping with
packages in their arms and had already noticed Kon holding
Anna—Meg practically ran down the hall to her apartment.
She'd hung a large holly wreath tied with a red ribbon on
her door, but hardly noticed it now.

She fumbled with the key, trying to get it in the lock,
Kon's mesmerising power over Anna frightened and enraged
her. He'd learned his seductive techniques through years of
KGB training. He'd learned to consider human feelings ex-
pendable.

"Take me to my bedroom, Daddy. My aquarum's in
there," Anna dictated her wishes, pointing the way as he
carried her across the small, modestly furnished living room
Meg had cleaned earlier that day. The unlit Christmas tree
stood in the corner, a slightly lopsided Scotch pine, but Meg
couldn't afford anything better. Still, the gold and silver balls
among the tiny colored lights looked festive when Kon
stopped long enough for Anna to flip the wall switch so he
could see the effect.

Meg closed the front door, ignoring the triumphant glance
he cast her. He'd made it this far without her interference.
As soon as they disappeared down the hall, she unbuttoned
her coat and threw it over a chair, realizing this might be the
only time she'd be free to talk to her attorney.

Mrs. Rosen, the widow across the hall, was a retired mu-
sician. She could usually be found at home this time of the
evening giving violin lessons. Anna was her youngest student
and had made significant progress in the past year. But
Anna's musical ability was the last thing on Meg's mind as
she let herself out of the apartment, praying the older woman
was in so she could use her phone and ask her to keep an
eye on Meg's door while she made the call. Just in case Kon
had thoughts of an immediate escape....

"Ms. Roberts?"

Meg jumped, surprised to be met in the hall by a man and

woman dressed in casual sports clothes and parkas. They stood in front of her, blocking her path.

The van that had been parked next to the driveway flashed into her mind, and a feeling of inevitability swept over her. Naturally Kon wouldn't have made his move without accomplices. More KGB? Since detente, they were officially known as the MB, but Meg knew very well that despite the chaos in Russia, they could still be dangerous. It was possible some of their operatives continued to function in the U.S. for counterintelligence purposes.

As if reading her mind, they both pulled identification from their pockets.

CIA. Meg swayed on her feet, and the dark-haired, fortyish woman put a hand on her arm to steady her. "We know the appearance of Mr. Rudenko has come as a shock to you, Ms. Roberts. We'd like to talk to you about it. Inside."

Infuriated, Meg jerked her arm free. "Do you actually expect me to believe you're from the CIA?" she hissed. "I know how the MB works. Just like the KGB! You pass yourselves off as anything you like, and you'd double-cross, triple-cross your own families if necessary."

The man, who wore horn rims and looked around fifty, gave her a patronizing smile. "Please cooperate, Ms. Roberts. What we have to tell you should abate your fears," he said with an exaggerated sincerity that nauseated her.

Meg stiffened. "And of course if I refuse, you'll force me back into my apartment at gunpoint. But since you know I'd never do anything to upset my daughter, you're confident I'll do whatever you ask." She turned and reentered her apartment, the two agents close behind.

Just then a door down the short hallway opened and a grim-faced Kon appeared, checking up on her, no doubt, to make sure she was cooperating. Just like old times. Of course back then she'd thought it was because he couldn't stay away from her. In the background she could hear water running and assumed he had talked Anna into taking a bath to distract her.

Meg stared into those damnably blue eyes. "You make me sick," she snapped. "The whole bunch of you! And—" she pointed at Kon "—as far as I'm concerned, if you've forsaken your own country, you're a traitor to all! Now why don't you leave unsuspecting people and children alone? Go find some uninhabited part of the world where you can play absurd war games to your hearts' content. If you battle each other long enough, none of you will be left alive—thank God."

With a nonchalance that stunned her, Kon loosened his tie and removed his jacket. Without taking his eyes off her he tossed it on top of her coat, drawing her unwilling attention to the play of hard muscle in his arms and shoulders. He behaved as if this was an everyday occurrence in his own home.

"Anna's bath will be through in a few minutes, and then she expects to come out and eat dinner with us. She'll be alarmed if she hears you shouting like a fishwife, instead of being cordial to Walt and Lacey Bowman from the auto dealership where you work. Is that what you want?" He pressed the advantage. "Or shall I tell her that you've had to go back to the office on an emergency? There's a vacant apartment down the hall and I have the key. It's entirely up to you where this conversation takes place."

"Mommy? Daddy?" Anna burst into the room unexpectedly, dressed in pajamas dotted with kangaroos, her curls bobbing. But when she saw the strangers, her smile faded, and to Meg's intense relief she ran past Kon straight to her mother. Meg picked her up and held her tightly in her arms. If she had her way, she'd never let go of Anna again.

"Honey?" She strived to keep her voice from shaking. "These are the Bowmans. They work in the sales department at Strong Motors every day after I come home from the office.'' She was improvising, because they'd left her no choice. "You've never met them before.''

The older woman smiled. "That's right, Anna. But Walt and I have heard a lot about you.''

"You're a mighty cute little girl,'' the man chimed in. "You look a lot like your mommy and daddy.''

"Daddy looks like Prince Marzipan.''

The woman nodded. "I heard you went to the *Nutcracker* today. It's my favorite ballet. Did you like it?''

"Yes. 'Specially the Prince!''

Kon's eyes actually seemed to moisten as he lovingly fastened his gaze on his daughter. Meg turned her head away, astounded once again by his incredible acting ability.

"We need to talk to your mommy for a minute,'' the man continued. "Is that all right with you?''

"Yes. Daddy and I can fix dinner. We're going to have macaroni. Daddy says they don't eat macaroni in Russia. It's a...an Amercan invenshun.''

"That's right, Anochka.'' He chuckled in delight. "I can hardly wait to try it. Come with me.'' In the next breath Kon plucked his daughter from Meg's arms and carried her to the kitchen and out of earshot, leaving Meg alone with the two agents. She'd probably never know who they really were or who they worked for. It could be either government—or both.

The older woman ventured a smile. "Do you mind if we sit down?''

Meg's hands tightened into fists. "Yes, I mind. Say what you have to say and go.''

She knew her voice sounded shrill, but she'd been suppressing all that pent-up fear and rage since Kon had first ambushed them in the theater foyer. Right now she was on the verge of hysteria; she was ready to scream the apartment complex down, Anna or no Anna.

Everyone remained standing. The man spoke first. "Mr.

Rudenko defected from the Soviet Union more than five years ago, Ms. Roberts.''

Meg shook her head and let out a caustic laugh. ''He's KGB. They don't defect.''

His brows lifted. ''This one did.''

''If such a thing happened, then it was mere pretense so he could kidnap Anna at some point and take her back to Russia with him!''

''No,'' the woman interjected. ''He became an American citizen this October. After the secrets he exchanged for asylum, he can never go back.''

''Why should I believe you?'' Meg exploded, the adrenaline pumping through her body so furiously she couldn't stand still. ''In the first place, our government no longer needs to make deals with Russian defectors to get information. Not since detente. Now I want you out of here. Out of Anna's and my life!''

''We do make deals when it's a top-ranking KGB official,'' the man persisted. ''One, I might add, who belonged to an elite inner circle and could shed light on highly sensitive issues—give us valuable information about the kidnappings of American citizens, both civilian and military, within and outside the Soviet Union.''

The other woman nodded. ''He never approved of those tactics in the old regime, nor the cruelty to Russians and non-Russians alike. That's one of the reasons he defected.''

Grudgingly, Meg had to admit they were right about one thing. If Kon hadn't intervened, she might still be in that Moscow jail.

''The information he provided has answered questions our government never dreamed would be cleared up,'' the woman went on. ''In some cases, the facts Mr. Rudenko obtained have relieved the speculation and suffering of families who've never learned what became of their loved ones.''

''Mr. Rudenko has done a great service to our country and caused a good deal of embarrassment to his own,'' the man asserted in a firm voice. "Do you remember that news item several years ago about the missing airforce pilot—the son of an elderly woman living in Nebraska? His plane had disappeared over Russia almost fifteen years ago."

Meg's thoughts flashed back to the heart-wrenching story, which had been the main topic of the media at the time. She could still hear the woman sobbing with relief as much as sorrow—relief because the Pentagon had finally received positive proof of her son's death. She remembered the woman saying that now she could die in peace.

"That was thanks to Mr. Rudenko, who was able to provide detailed information about the pilot's incarceration in Lublianka prison and his subsequent death."

Meg's eyes narrowed on the two of them. She simply couldn't trust anything to do with Kon, who never made a move without a motive. She'd discovered, to her cost, that all his apparently generous actions—such as purchasing that book on the *Nutcracker* and putting it in her luggage—had a hidden purpose.

"Even if what you tell me is true," she said, "it changes nothing. There's something strange about a man who would defect as far back as five years ago, then wait until today to show up and declare that he wants a relationship with his daughter."

Her face twisted in pain. "As far as I'm concerned," she continued, her voice rising, "it's a lie, and you're part of it! I don't give a damn which side you're working for. It has nothing to do with me. Now get out of my apartment and don't ever come back!"

"Because of his defection, he had to go undercover at once and assume a new identity," the woman explained calmly, ignoring Meg's outburst. "Out of fear of placing you and your daughter in danger, he has been living apart from you for the past five years and has avoided making contact until—"

"Until he could trap us in a public place where I didn't

dare upset my daughter. Who's just old enough to be seduced by the attention of a long-lost father,'' Meg said bitterly.

The man shook his head. ''Not until the threat of danger had passed and he'd established himself fully in his new life.'' He paused. ''Now Mr. Rudenko has done exactly that. He's written several books on Russia already, including an exposé of the KGB and its methods. That one's coming out in the spring, under an assumed name, of course. The publisher's expecting it to make the *Times* list. So he's doing well financially, and he'll be able to support you and Anna.''

''I don't want to hear any more. Just get out. Now!''

''When you've cooled off enough to ask questions, phone Senator Strickland's office and he'll tell you everything you want to know.''

Senator Strickland? The face of the aging Missouri senator came to mind. He was a politician whose integrity had never been questioned, at least as far as Meg knew. Which didn't mean much. Senator Strickland could probably be bought as easily as the next man.

''Perhaps you don't realize he's on the Senate Foreign Relations Committee and has been cooperating with us since 1988. He knows all about your love affair with Mr. Rudenko and the daughter you conceived during your stay in the Soviet Union. We can assure you that he's your friend and that he's sympathetic to your situation. He expects to hear from you in the near future.''

Meg felt the blood drain from her face. If by the most remote chance they were telling the truth, then not only the KGB but the CIA and her own state senator knew the most intimate details of her private life! The idea was so appalling Meg couldn't think, couldn't speak.

The woman eyed her for a long moment. ''Ms. Roberts, your fear and distrust are entirely understandable, which is why Mr. Rudenko asked us to speak to you—to help you accept that he's a citizen now and wants a relationship with his daughter.''

"You've spoken to me," Meg muttered through stiff lips. "Consider your mission accomplished."

In a few swift strides she reached the door and flung it open, anxious to be rid of the pair and desperate to get Anna to bed before Kon could exert any more influence over her. But the happy sounds of Anna's excited chatter and her father's deep laughter coming from the kitchen mocked Meg's determination to bring this cozy situation to an immediate and permanent end.

She watched till the two agents were out of sight, then quietly shut the door and slipped across the hall to ring Mrs. Rosen's bell. She prayed Kon wouldn't choose that moment to check up on her.

When there was no answer, Meg panicked. She would have started for the Garretts' apartment down the corridor, but didn't dare leave her own apartment unguarded. Besides, the sound of her daughter's tearful voice checked her movements.

Through the closed door she could hear Anna asking Kon if "those people" had made her mommy go to work. Meg didn't wait to hear his response and hurried back into the apartment, her only thought to comfort her daughter.

"Mommy!" Anna cried when she saw Meg. She ran over to her, her distress vanishing instantly. "Where did you go? We got dinner all ready!"

"I think your mother was just saying goodbye to the Bowmans at the elevator. Isn't that right?" He supplied the plausible excuse faster than Meg could think. In an unguarded moment her troubled gaze flew to his. The triumphant expression in those blue depths said he understood exactly what she'd been up to, but that she'd never be rid of him, so why not accept her fate gracefully.

"Come on, Mommy. We're hungry."

Anna tugged at Meg's hand, forcing her to break eye contact with Kon. He followed them into the kitchen at a leisurely pace. Her plan to talk to her attorney would have to be put off until dinner was over.

Whether intentionally or not, Kon's hands brushed against her shoulders as he pulled out a chair for her. She despised the tremor that shook her body when he touched her, afraid he could feel it. But to her relief his attention was focused on Anna. He helped her sit down at the small dinette table, where a plate of cheesy macaroni and broccoli and a glass of milk had been placed for each of them.

"We have to have a blessing first," Anna insisted as soon as her father sat down on her other side. "It's your turn to say it, Daddy. Please?"

"I'd be honored," he murmured in a husky voice, squeezing her small hand in his large one.

Meg forgot to close her eyes as she watched the two identical dark heads bow while he offered a prayer in Russian—a beautiful, very personal prayer that thanked God for preserving the lives of the woman and child he loved, for uniting them at last, for giving him the opportunity to start a new life, for providing food when so many people in Russia and the rest of the world had none. And finally for bringing the three of them this first Christmas together. Amen.

"What did you say, Daddy?" Anna asked, picking up her spoon and scooping up the macaroni.

He lifted his head and stared at his daughter. "I told God how happy I was finally to be with you and your mommy."

Her mouth full of macaroni, Anna declared, "Melanie says it's stupid to believe in God. Wait till I tell her that God let you come to Amerca to be with Mommy and me. I love you, Daddy."

Anna's comments and sweet smile—even more endearing because of the cheese sauce clinging to her lips—combined with the eloquent emotion darkening his eyes was too much for Meg. She found it difficult to maintain the same degree of anger she'd felt before they'd sat down to eat.

His unexpected display of reverence had sounded amazingly sincere. For a brief moment, Meg had been in danger of forgetting that everything Kon did was part of an act. An act that over the years had become second nature to him.

Was it possible he *did* have religious convictions which he'd been forced to hide until now? Could he fake something like that? She didn't know.

His glance switched to Meg. "Did we do the macaroni right?" he asked quietly. "Anna helped me make it. Our little girl is a good cook."

"And a tired one," Meg remarked without answering his question. Tearing her gaze from his, she brushed a stray curl from her daughter's flushed cheek. "I think we'll skip dessert and go straight to bed. You've had a big day, honey."

Anna nodded, surprising Meg who'd been prepared for an argument. "Daddy said I had to go to bed early and get a good sleep so I'd be ready for our trip in the morning."

Trip? What trip? Dear Lord!

Adrenaline set Meg's heart pounding like waves crashing against the shore. Her eyes darted wildly to Kon. He had just finished his milk and eyed her over the rim of the glass, registering her fear with a calm that roused her emotions to a violent pitch.

"Since tomorrow is Sunday, it will be the perfect opportunity for you and Anna to see where I live. It's a two-hour drive from here."

Meg sucked in a breath and pushed away from the table like an automaton. Refusing to let him bait her any further, she turned to Anna and said, "If you're finished, let's run to the bathroom and brush your teeth."

"But I want Daddy to help me. He promised to tuck me in bed. He's going to teach me how to read my *Nutcracker* book in Russian, and I'm going to read him my Dr. Seuss stories."

"Then I'll do the dishes," she said, forcing her voice to remain level. She refused to give Kon the satisfaction of knowing his unexpected appearance had knocked out her underpinnings.

She ignored his curious stare, kissed Anna's forehead and started clearing the table. Acting as if she didn't have a care in the world, she set about loading the dishwasher while they got up from the table and left the kitchen.

By the time she'd wiped off the counters and watered the large red poinsettia her boss had sent her, the apartment was quiet. Removing her high heels, she turned out the kitchen light, then stole across the living room and down the hall, listening for voices.

Meg caught snatches of Anna reading Dr. Seuss's *Inside, Outside, Upside Down*. Occasionally Kon would stop her and make her pronounce the Russian equivalent of the words. Her accent appeared to entertain him no end, and he taught her some more, sometimes laughing deep in his throat at her efforts, but more often than not praising her, calling her his darling Anochka. Eventually there were no more sounds.

Meg shivered as she remembered the times she'd lain in his arms, unable to get enough of his lovemaking, never wanting him to stop calling her his beloved. But it had all been a lie, and the pain of his betrayal was more real than ever. Sweat beaded her hairline.

She entered Anna's bedroom on tiptoe and moved past the aquarium and dresser toward the twin bed. Kon was stretched out on top of the covers, his eyes closed, his arm around the child. She lay under her Winnie the Pooh quilt and had fallen asleep against his broad shoulder, several books, including the *Nutcracker*, still scattered on the bed.

The reading light fastened to the white headboard outlined Kon's features. They looked more chiseled in repose and revealed new lines of experience around his eyes and mouth. She leaned over to study him more closely.

He looked tired, she thought, then berated herself for feeling any compassion or noticing the small physical changes in him since they'd last been together—changes that made him look more appealing than ever. She couldn't allow herself to respond to that appeal or to soften in any way.

Because he was planning to steal Anna.

She couldn't forget that for a second. Right now, with Kon asleep, was the perfect time to alert Ben Avery. He could start proceedings to have Kon legally removed from the apartment. No matter how much it would upset Anna, Meg needed to do this, and she needed to do it immediately. There was no way she would allow Kon to step one foot outside the door with her daughter.

Quietly she retraced her steps to the kitchen and lifted the receiver of the wall phone to call her attorney.

She gasped when she heard a sudden movement behind her. She swung around to face Kon, who stood between the living room and the kitchen, far too close for her peace of mind.

He hadn't been asleep at all!

Heat seemed to pour from her body when she realized what that meant—he'd been watching her the whole time she'd been in Anna's room. No doubt when she'd leaned close to study him while he lay there on the bed exhausted, he'd been aware of her conflicting emotions, and the knowledge compounded her anger.

Anna might think of him as Prince Marzipan, but to Meg he was a devil prince, painfully handsome in a dark, saturnine way. The faint glow from the Christmas tree lights seemed only to emphasize it.

"Whomever you're calling to come and take me away will have to kill me first. I'm here to be with my daughter. But you're Anna's mother, which gives you the ultimate power." His voice trailed off.

Like someone in a trance, Meg hung up the receiver and stared at him, her fear and pain so acute she couldn't swallow. "Maybe that was true, once. But this afternoon you presented Anna with a fait accompli." She spoke haltingly, the tears welling up in her eyes. "How could you have been so…rash? So insensitive? What you told Anna—your declaration of fatherhood—has changed our lives forever!''

"I hope so," he said in a hoarse whisper.

Her hands knotted into fists. "I won't let you take her back to Russia!" she cried. "I'll do whatever I have to do to prevent that from happening. *Whatever I have to do,*" she warned him a second time.

"Your imagination is as predictable as your paranoia, but I have no intention of kidnapping her. Our daughter would despise me forever if I took her away from you. That is hardly the emotion I want to evoke in my one and only child. Besides, I'm very much afraid that Konstantin Rudenko is persona non grata in the former Soviet Union these days.

"If I were to touch the trees of Mother Russia just one more time," he murmured in a faraway voice, "it would be my last act as a free man." A mirthless smile broke the corner of his mouth. "I have no desire to deprive my daughter of her father. Not when I've spent the last six years in near isolation making plans and preparations—so we can live the rest of our lives together, Meggie."

CHAPTER THREE

MEGGIE. The name he called her the first time he'd kissed her...

Suddenly she was that naive, starry-eyed twenty-three-year-old, sitting in the front seat of Kon's black Mercedes as he drove her from the Moscow airport to the hotel in St. Petersburg where she'd be living for the next four months.

Already infatuated with Konstantin Rudenko long before she'd arrived in Russia the second time, she knew she was in love the minute she set eyes on him again. The austere, heart-stoppingly attractive KGB agent had been assigned to guard her and escort her to and from school. Her feelings for him had been growing ever since he'd rescued her from prison on her first trip, giving her that beautiful book....

As before, his word was law and everyone jumped at his slightest dictate. He'd dealt with all the red tape and smoothed her way, making her feel safe and looked after rather than policed. To add to her happiness, she'd learned that part of his duty was to phone her room every morning between three and four o'clock to make sure she hadn't slipped away from the hotel unnoticed.

Being a foreigner on the loose in a Russian city constituted a crime punishable by imprisonment, something she had no desire to repeat.

Once installed at the hotel, Meg couldn't wait for his nightly phone calls to begin. But a problem arose when she discovered she'd been given a middle-aged roommate, a Mrs. Procter who had a master's in Russian from a university in

Illinois. Meg was crushed because it meant that any phone conversations with Mr. Rudenko could be overheard by her roommate.

He, like the agent assigned to Mrs. Procter, would phone and ask her, very formally, if all was well, then start to hang up. But Meg couldn't let him end the calls there, and for the first few nights had tried to engage him in conversation by discussing her students' papers with him—anything she could think of to prolong the contact.

After a few days she'd managed to keep him on the phone as long as fifteen or twenty minutes, occasionally touching on the personal, learning that his first name was Konstantin. But Meg wanted much more from Kon, as she'd secretly nicknamed him, than a nightly phone call. But for that, she needed privacy, which Mrs. Procter's presence made impossible.

The older woman was scandalized by Meg's behavior and expressed her disapproval of what she referred to as Meg's "promiscuous" character. It didn't take long for Meg to realize she couldn't take much more of the unpleasant woman's attitude or presence.

Most important, she couldn't bear it when Kon just drove off at the end of each day after depositing her at the hotel, never lingering to chat for even a few more minutes.

By the end of the second week, Meg had craved his company to the point that she started plotting ways to get him to spend more time with her. That Friday, when he'd pulled up in the parking spot designated for KGB by the hotel, she didn't immediately get out of the car.

With her heart in her throat, she turned to him. Her gaze feasted on his slightly-too-long hair and the searing blue of his eyes, eyes that never revealed his innermost thoughts or feelings.

"If you don't mind, t-there's something important I need to discuss with you. Since the hotel frowns on my being late for dinner, I was hoping you'd join me. Or better yet," she continued in a slightly breathless voice, "I was hoping you might take me to a restaurant, where we could talk in private. So far I've only eaten at the hotel, and I'm eager to see more of the city while I'm here."

A frown marred his handsome features. "What is the problem?" he asked in a businesslike tone, which was hardly encouraging.

"I-it's about my accommodations."

"They are not up to your American standards?"

"No. It's nothing like that. Maybe it's because I've never had to live with a roommate before. But I'm afraid Mrs. Procter and I don't get along too well. We're such different ages and...I was wondering if I could be given a room by myself. I don't care if it's small, and I'd be willing to pay extra for it. All I'd really like is my privacy." *And the opportunity to talk to you all night long, if you'll let me.*

He cocked his head and studied her gravely. She would have given anything to know what he was really thinking. "Come," he said unexpectedly. "Let's go inside. While you eat your dinner, I'll see what can be done."

Her heart leapt. At least he hadn't said no. Elated by that much progress, Meg alighted from the car and entered the hotel with Kon at her heels. While he approached the clerk at the front desk, she hurried to her room on the second floor to deposit her briefcase and freshen up.

So excited she was trembling, Meg applied fresh lipstick and dabbed on some French perfume, then slipped into a coffee-toned silk dress that had a tailored elegance. She brushed her ash-blond hair till it gleamed and fell softly about her shoulders, all the while praying he would find her attractive enough to join her in the dining room for a meal. Their first together...

But her heart plummeted to her feet when she went downstairs to the lobby and was greeted instead by the desk clerk. He informed her that a new room on the third floor had been arranged for her, that she should eat her dinner, then transfer her personal belongings.

Though grateful for Kon's swift help and intervention, she couldn't hide her disappointment; he'd left without saying goodbye. No longer interested in dinner, she went back upstairs ahead of Mrs. Procter, who was at one of the tables in the dining room talking to another teacher from England. No doubt they were gossiping about Meg.

Thankful to be free of that woman, Meg moved everything out of the room before Mrs. Procter learned what had happened and asked a lot of probing questions.

The interior of the tacky, modern hotel was drab and uninteresting, but her new room turned out to be considerably larger than the first one. It contained a good-sized desk with a lamp where she could do her schoolwork. Once again, she was touched by Kon's thoughtfulness and consideration. She could hardly wait until he phoned her that night to thank him.

When she heard a rap on the door, she whirled around, assuming it was one of the hotel staff. But before she had time to reach for the handle, the door opened.

She gasped softly when she saw Kon standing there. He'd never come to her room before. Her heart started to race. Their eyes met and she saw something flicker in his gaze as it swept over her face and body, something that made her go hot and liquefied her bones.

He wasn't indifferent to her. She could see it, feel it.

"Will the room do?" he asked in a husky voice.

She had difficulty finding words. "Yes," she finally managed. "It's perfect. Thank you."

He stared at her through half-closed lids. "There's a club not far from here where we can go for a drink and you can see something of the nightlife. I could spare an hour if you wish."

She swallowed hard. "I do."

"The nights are cold now. Wear something warm."

Scarcely able to breathe with the emotions running rampant inside her, she turned toward the closet for her raincoat.

"I'll wait for you at the car."

She glanced back in time to see him disappear down the dimly lit hallway. A club meant there might be dancing. The need to touch him, to be held in his arms, was fast growing into a permanent ache.

Within seconds she was ready and practically flew down the two flights of stairs and through the lobby, not wanting to waste one precious moment. As she emerged, her eyes went straight to his. She knew her cheeks were flushed with a feverish excitement she couldn't hide.

He was standing next to his car, his hands in his coat pockets—a remote, solitary figure. Evidently he'd been keeping an eye on the entrance, because as soon as he saw her, he stepped forward and opened the passenger door.

Without saying a word, he started the engine and they pulled away from the curb into moderate evening traffic, driving alongside bikes and trolley cars. Meg loved St. Petersburg, called the "Venice of the North" because of its waterways and bridges. Maybe the city looked so beautiful that night because she'd been fantasizing about the man who sat an arm's length away from her. She could hardly believe they were going out together. If she had her way, it would be longer than one hour. Far longer...

He obviously knew the city well. He took them through several narrow, winding alleyways before pulling to a stop behind some expensive-looking cars parked next to a cluster of old buildings.

Her pulse racing, she watched him come around to help her from the car, something he'd always done. But this time there was a subtle difference. This time she felt his hand go to the back of her waist as he guided her through the first set of doors. She could hear sixties' music, of all things, being played inside the building.

His lips twitched in a half smile, transforming the austere-looking KGB agent into the devastatingly attractive man she'd been dreaming about. "You're surprised."

"You knew I would be." She smiled back, so enamored of him, she felt giddy.

"We're not quite as stodgy as propaganda would have you believe."

After helping her remove her coat, which he checked with an attendent, he ushered her through an ornate bar area to another room, where couples were dancing to a live band. The talented musicians and singer made her feel as if they'd just walked into a New York nightclub.

Out of the corner of her eye she saw Kon give the waiter a signal. The man rushed over and within seconds, they were escorted to a free table. Kon said something privately to the waiter, who then left them alone.

Kon seated her, then pulled out the chair opposite. He eyed her with a hint of speculation. "Do you trust me to have ordered something I believe you'll like?"

She lifted solemn eyes to him. "Because of you, I was freed from that awful jail and able to get home in time for my father's funeral. I'd trust you with my life." She spoke with complete and heartfelt sincerity.

For once, something she said managed to penetrate that outer KGB shell and reach the man beneath. She could tell by the way his eyes darkened in color, and the sudden stillness that came over him.

The band started playing an old Beatles tune.

"Let's dance," he murmured in a low voice.

Meg had been waiting for those words. She followed him onto the floor on shaky legs, so eager to be in his arms, she was almost afraid of the moment he'd touch her, afraid he'd know the powerful effect he had on her.

Perhaps he did know how she felt, because to her chagrin he kept her at a correct distance, never taking advantage of their closeness in any way, or letting her think her nearness disturbed him.

Like many of his compatriots in the room, he was a wonderful dancer, and their bodies seemed perfectly attuned. After three dances they returned to their table, where she discovered champagne cocktails and goblets of ice cream that tasted more like lime sherbet.

"What a delicious combination," she marveled, realizing that the entire evening felt enchanted because she was in love with him.

Thirsty from the dancing, Meg drank her cocktail quickly. Then she looked across at him, wondering what he could be thinking to produce such a sober expression. Anxious to lighten his mood, she leaned toward him. "Shall we dance again?" She hoped her question didn't sound too much like begging.

"There's no more time," he told her with a cool, disappointing finality. "I'll get your coat while you finish your ice cream."

She didn't want the evening to end, but had little choice in the matter. He was in charge. Meg supposed it was something of a miracle that he'd taken even an hour from his rigid routine to accommodate her wishes.

"Shall we go?"

She nodded and pushed herself away from the table. They made their way through the crowd to the entrance. This time he didn't touch her as they stepped outside to walk the short distance to his car. In fact, there was a distinct difference between the way Kon treated her now—almost as if he were angry—and the way he'd responded to her earlier in the evening. Was it because he'd revealed something of the man beneath the KGB persona? Maybe now he wanted to show her that it had only been a momentary aberration, that she shouldn't expect it to happen again.

Once they were in the car, driving back to her hotel, Meg didn't speak. The forbidding aura surrounding him prevented her from initiating further conversation. She stared out the side window, dreading the moment he'd say good-night and walk away.

They were almost at their destination when he suddenly made a right turn out of the city, away from lighted streets into darkness.

"Kon? W-where are we going? This isn't the way back to the hotel." But he refused to answer her and pressed forward until they were well into the woods. She started to feel nervous. "I thought you had to get back to...to whatever it is you do."

Still he ignored her and kept driving until they came to a deserted lay-by. He turned off the road and pulled to a stop, cutting the engine. The only sound she could hear was the fierce hammering of her own heart.

Glancing outside, she noticed trees lining the road and saw the stars twinkling overhead. The beauty of the night did not escape her, but she couldn't concentrate on that now. The man at the wheel had become an enigmatic stranger, and she was very much at his mercy.

When she couldn't stand the silence any longer, she turned toward him. The shadowy light from the dashboard revealed the look in his eyes, an unmistakable longing that changed the rhythm of her heart.

"Are you afraid of me?"

"No," she answered in a tremulous voice. And it was the truth.

He let out a smothered curse. "You should be. In the last six years, you've changed from a lovely, spirited teenager into an exciting woman. My comrades envy me because I chose to guard you myself."

She moistened her lips, gratified to hear the unmistakably possessive ring in his voice. "I-I'm glad you did. It saved me the trouble of looking for you."

"Explain that remark."

Meg stared down at her hands. "Just that I've never forgotten your kindness to me. I intended to look you up and thank you. And—I hoped—get to know you better.''

She heard his sharp intake of breath. ''Your honesty is as shocking now as it was six years ago.''

She lifted her head, half turning to face him. ''You said that as if it offends you.''

''On the contrary, I find it refreshing beyond belief. Will it shock you senseless if I tell you how much I want to make love to you, go to bed with you? How much I want to kiss every inch of your face and hair, your beautiful body?''

At those words, she couldn't control the trembling. ''No,'' she murmured, looking into his eyes, ''because I've wanted the same thing since I got off the plane in Moscow.''

Groaning, he said, ''Come here to me.'' He reached out to pull her into his arms, but she was already there.

''Meggie.'' She heard him whisper her name before his mouth fastened on hers. He kissed her with a hunger that obliterated any fears she might have entertained that he wasn't as attracted to her as she was to him.

Overjoyed by the knowledge, she clung to his warmth, kissing him with total abandon, letting sensation after sensation carry her to unexplored dimensions of wanting and need. She'd craved this physical closeness for so long, she was afraid they were both part of a dream. She never wanted to wake up.

In her bemused state she wasn't aware of time passing. Nor did she notice the eventual glare of headlights coming in their direction—until they flashed inside the car.

With a speed and strength she could scarcely grasp, Kon thrust her back to her side of the car, her lipstick nonexistent, her face hot, her body throbbing.

By the time the other vehicle had driven past them, Kon started the engine and pulled onto the road, maneuvering the car with the same finesse and precision that he did everything else, his features schooled to show no emotion.

"Kon— I—I don't want to go back. I don't want the night to end. Please don't take me home yet."

"I have to, Meggie."

"Because of your job?"

"Yes."

"When can we be together again? Really together, for more than an hour?"

"I'll work something out."

"Please let it be soon."

"Don't say anything else, Meggie, and don't touch me again tonight."

His emotions were as explosive as hers. For once, she didn't mind that he was taking her back to the hotel, not when she knew his passion for her was as profound as hers was for him. His unnatural silence after what they'd just shared proved there was no going back to their former relationship.

When they reached the hotel, he remained at the wheel and let her get out on her own. The moment she was safely inside, he sped away, as if in pursuit of another car.

Meg dashed through the foyer and up the stairs, thankful to be going to an empty room. At least she could relive the rapture of the night in total privacy.

But long after she'd showered, brushed her teeth and gone to bed, she lay wide-awake. The adrenaline seemed to pulse through her bloodsteam; she couldn't sleep. The phone was right by the bed and she turned on her side, waiting for his call.

When it came, she'd grabbed the receiver before the second ring.

"Kon?" she cried out joyously.

"Never answer the phone that way again."

Chastened, she whispered, "I'm sorry. I didn't think."

"It's already Saturday. Be ready at ten and pack some warm clothes for the weekend." The line went dead.

Meg put back the receiver and hugged her pillow, delirious with love and longing. Sleep would be impossible now.

To keep from watching the clock, she got out her homework and made up her lesson plans for the following week. When she'd finished that task, she graded her students' poetry, writing notes at the bottom of each paper.

Work was a godsend; it kept her busy until nine, when she put everything away and packed the things she'd need for their trip. At nine-thirty, she left her room and went downstairs to breakfast, nodding to the few teachers she knew. She breathed a sigh of relief that Mrs. Procter wasn't among them.

Promptly at ten, Kon entered the foyer. She felt his powerful presence even before she saw him—like a gravitational pull. She hurried toward him, carrying her overnight bag in one hand, her purse in the other.

To any passerby, he would have looked like the same KGB agent who'd been ferrying her back and forth since her arrival in St. Petersburg. The difference was apparent only to Meg. When Kon gazed at her in that special way, she felt an emotional and physical awareness she couldn't hide. She felt a sensation of falling helplessly toward him, unable to stop.

He couldn't have had much sleep, either, but the relaxed mouth and the darkness beneath his eyes gave him a slightly dissipated air that only added to his attractiveness. Meekly, she followed him to his car and got in while he stowed her bag in the trunk.

They headed out of the city in much the same direction they'd taken the night before. The traffic lightened, and soon after, they reached the forest road.

Meg turned in her seat, admiring his striking profile, and his tautly muscled body. He was as formally dressed as always. In fact, she'd never seen him in anything but a white shirt and dark suit—his uniform, she supposed. He wore it well. Too well. She couldn't keep her eyes off him. "I've never gone away with a man before," she confessed. "H-have you? Gone away with a woman, I mean."

He flashed her a brief but piercing glance. "Yes."

"I should never have asked that question, but this is all new to me."

Naturally he'd had affairs. She knew from their nightly conversations that he was in his early thirties. An unattached male as attractive as Kon would never be without female companionship.

"There haven't been as many women as your fertile imagination is conjuring up," he said in a gently mocking voice. "My work makes it virtually impossible to sustain any kind of lasting relationship. The few women I've known also worked for the Party.

"If it means anything, Meggie, I've never been attracted to a non-Russian woman before. What surprises me is the strength of my feelings for you, how far I've been willing to go to get you alone."

She shivered with excitement. "Th-thank you for being honest with me. If we can have that, I won't ask for anything else."

His long fingers tightened on the steering wheel. "You've never made love with a man, have you." It was a statement, not a question.

"No. Does that make a difference to you?"

"Yes."

She blinked to fight the sudden sting of tears. "I see."

He muttered something in Russian she couldn't quite catch. "We're here, Meggie."

She'd been so caught up in their conversation, she hadn't noticed anything else. Now when she turned her head, she could see they were in the middle of a dense wood, parked outside what could only be described as a lowly woodcutter's cottage.

The reality of the situation came to her with full force. She'd hoped her candor would be enough to make up for her inexperience, but now she knew differently. Kon was a tough, sophisticated, worldly man—and he was probably ready to turn around and take her back to the city.

She couldn't bear that. She bolted suddenly from the car, taking off into the woods.

"Meggie? Where do you think you're going?" he called after her, sounding exasperated.

"I-I'll be right back."

"Don't go too far. It's easy to get lost."

"I won't." *Just give me a moment to pull myself together,* she cried inwardly and kept on running until she was out of breath.

She flung herself against a tree trunk to rest. She felt a rush of embarrassment because she was behaving like anything but a mature woman. She wouldn't blame him if he'd lost complete interest.

That was when she heard him calling her. He sounded angry, upset. Maybe he believed the woman he'd assigned himself to guard had managed to give him the slip. If only he knew the truth—that she *never* wanted to be apart from him. Never.

From the sound of his voice, he was getting closer. If she wasn't mistaken, his tone conveyed real anxiety. Did she dare believe he was actually concerned for her? Could he possibly have feelings for her as deep and as real as those she had for him?

The answer came when he caught up with her as she hurried back toward the hut. "I'm sorry if I worried you," she said when she saw his chest heaving and heard a torrent of unintelligible Russian escape lips narrowed to a taut, uncompromising line.

In the next instant he reached for her, drawing her against his hard body, his eyes a scorching flame of blue.

"*Meggie...*"

The fierceness, the unexpected raw passion in his outcry,

robbed her of breath, telling her what she needed to know. He still wanted to be with her. Nothing had changed.

Blindly she lifted her mouth for his kiss—and was lost. He picked her up in his arms and carried her into the hut, shoving the door closed with his boot.

Her heart streamed into his, and what happened next felt completely natural and inevitable. Drunk on her desire for him, she forgot they were anything but a man and a woman, aching to know the taste and feel of each other.

From that moment on, the barriers imposed by their roles as foreign visitor and KGB agent were cast aside. Their all-consuming need for each other had dictated their relationship. A need that found release and marked the beginning of the rest of their days and nights together. The only thing they'd wanted was to love each other into oblivion....

To think it had all been part of a game plan.

Meg shook off the memories. She thought she'd put that pain behind her forever. But Kon's takeover since his reappearance in her life and Anna's had reopened wounds that would never heal now. She stared at him with accusing eyes.

"Tell me something," she said, not bothering to hide her reaction to the bittersweet memories. "How did you manage to keep a straight face when you asked me to be your wife?"

"Which time was that, Meggie?" he asked quietly. "As I recall, I begged you to marry me every time we made love. Perhaps I should ask *you* a question. Whatever possessed me to keep asking you when I knew what your answer would be?" He managed to sound as desolate as he had earlier, when he'd told Anna about his parting scene at the airport before Meg flew away from him.

He was good at this! He was so good, it terrified her.

"Spare me the deceit, Kon!" She spoke scornfully to mask her uncertainty. "You're a man who did a job for your country. Throughout your career, I'm sure you've managed to infatuate other unsuspecting female visitors like myself. Perhaps you've even fathered other children in the line of duty—'' She stopped suddenly, breathless with anger.

"Why seek out Anna when there are thousands of single women in Russia who would love to marry you and bear your child? From what I understand, women there far outnumber men. You could choose anyone you wanted and have a family if—''

Calmly he interrupted. "The woman I've chosen is standing right in front of me, and the child I already have fell asleep in my arms only moments ago.''

She clenched her teeth. "You *did* choose me, I'll grant you that. My uncle was in naval intelligence, remember? And after he died my aunt told me about the KGB and the way they tried to convert specially chosen foreign visitors. Like me—the niece of an American military officer. Especially since I was obviously interested in Russia and even came back a second time.

"You did everything by the book, Kon. And with all your charm, you came close to succeeding. You tried to woo me away from my country by first befriending me, then seducing me. But in the end, it didn't work. I still went back to the States, and you were probably reprimanded for your failure. So you had me watched, and when you found out I was pregnant, you waited and plotted until the time was right to claim your daughter and return to Russia.''

She could tell her voice was getting louder, but she was fast losing control. "Well, I'm not going to let you do it! We're not married, and if you try to take her anywhere, I'll have you brought up on kidnap—''

"Mommy!'' Anna's frightened cry shocked Meg into silence. Stunned by the interruption, she looked past Kon to see her daughter hovering near the Christmas tree, hugging her favorite doll. The glint of tears on her pale cheeks devastated Meg. "Why are you mad at my daddy?''

Kon moved so fast Meg didn't have time to blink. In one lithe move he gathered Anna in his arms and kissed her nose.

"She's not mad at me, Anochka," he assured her while he rocked her back and forth. "Your mommy is upset, with good reason. I used to live in Russia, and she's afraid that one day I'll want to go back and take you with me."

"Without *mommy?*" Anna asked, as if the idea was unthinkable. Meg was moved to tears.

"No one is going anywhere without Mommy," he stated with unmistakable authority, his eyes never leaving Meg. She wondered how he could carry playacting this far and still sound so convincing. She watched him kiss the top of Anna's head.

"Now it's time for you to go back to bed, because we've got a big day planned for tomorrow, and your mommy and I haven't finished talking yet. You know we've been apart a long time. There are things I need to tell her. Can you understand that? Are you old enough to run to your room and crawl under the covers by yourself?"

"Yes." Anna nodded, making the dark curls dance on her forehead. Her head swiveled around and her eyes, full of pleading, fastened on Meg. "Daddy loves us, Mommy. Can we go see our house tomorrow? The dogs are waiting for me."

Meg stared at her daughter in wonder. How simple it all appeared to Anna's trusting mind. How pure her faith. She didn't know the meaning of real fear or betrayal. Those emotions weren't within her experience—how could she comprehend them? Now that her beloved prince, her daddy, had actually materialized, her child's world was complete.

"I live in Hannibal." He offered the surprising revelation so quietly it was as if his mind had spoken to Meg's.

"It's in the state of Missouri," he added dryly. "It's famous as the home of Mark Twain."

That provoked her to say, "Next you'll be telling me Mark Twain is still alive and entertaining friends at his house on Hill Street."

He gave Anna another hug. "Interesting you'd mention

Hill Street. I live farther up the hill on the same side of the street.''

It seemed the fairy tale was never ending. A KGB agent in the land of Becky Thatcher and Huck Finn.

Meg let out an angry laugh and folded her arms to prevent herself from flinging something at him. ''Anna, it's long past your bedtime.''

''She's right,'' Kon agreed. ''Kiss me good-night, Anochka.''

Meg refused to watch their display of affection and turned on her heel, heading for Anna's room. She was unable to credit the fact that less than eight hours ago Anna hadn't known her father's name, let alone imagined seeing him in the flesh.

She stood by the side of the bed until her daughter scrambled beneath the quilt, but she couldn't avoid the innocent blue eyes staring into her soul. ''God sent Daddy to us. Aren't you happy, Mommy? Please be happy.''

Meg sagged onto the mattress and buried her face in Anna's neck, hugging her daughter close. ''Oh, honey—'' she began to sob quietly ''—if only it was that simple.'' Convulsion after convulsion racked Meg's body, and Anna's comforting pats only contributed to her debilitating weakness.

''It *is* that simple,'' a deep, masculine voice said from the doorway. ''And we're *all* going to be happy.''

CHAPTER FOUR

THE NEXT THING Meg knew, his hand was sliding into her hair and caressing her scalp. It sent a shock wave through her system. Her breath caught, and she released Anna. She was so shaken by his touch she got to her feet and fled from the room in fresh panic.

Kon followed more slowly. "You're tired, Meggie. Go to bed. I'll sleep on the couch. If Anna wakes up during the night, I'll take care of her."

Meg spun around, the cathartic release of pent-up emotion making her feel reckless. But her desire to get everything out in the open diminished when she faced him in her stocking feet. Next to him she felt small and physically weak, emotionally overwhelmed. He seemed even taller, darker and infinitely more dangerous than before.

"Why, Kon?" she blurted, fighting the attraction that was still there in all the old insidious ways. "Why have you really come? Don't tell me it's because you're in love with me. We both know that's a lie. You used me!" she accused him. "I— I'll admit I was the aggressor. In fact, I threw myself at you and made your job pathetically easy. Because of my naïveté, I'll go on paying for that for the rest of my life.

"But why make up stories that will only devastate a vulnerable little girl? If you're really telling the truth and you *have* defected, then the only reason I can imagine for any of this is that you hope to get joint custody—to keep Anna to yourself for six months every year. I couldn't bear that. Do you hear me?"

Her question rang in the air, but for once he didn't have a ready response. While she waited, he lowered himself to the couch and ran his hands through his hair, a gesture she remembered from countless occasions in the past. It drew her attention to his fit, lithe body, which at one time had known hers so intimately....

She shook her head, furious that she could entertain such primitive thoughts when he was more her enemy now than ever before.

Deep in contemplation, she scarcely noticed that he'd pulled a pocket-size tape recorder out of his suit jacket. He placed it on the round marble-topped coffee table, one of the few pieces of furniture she'd kept after her parents had died—one of the few good pieces they'd owned. Her father's schoolteacher salary hadn't supplied much more than the necessities of life. Without winning scholarships, Meg would never have been able to go abroad in the first place.

Suddenly the sound of hysterical sobbing filled the living room. Meg blinked in shock when she recognized her own teenage voice. Her eyes flew to Kon, whose head was bent over the recorder, listening.

Immediately Meg was transported back to that dank Moscow jail cell. She remembered beating the stone floor with her fists in abject despair. The agony of that black moment came rushing in, overwhelming her with its intensity, and she couldn't stop the tears from streaming down her face.

Oh, Daddy. You're gone...my daddy's gone.... I've got to get home to you! They've got to let me out of here! Let me out of here, you monsters.... Daddy...!

To be confronted by her own screams, her own sorrow, was too much to bear. Without conscious thought she flew at Kon, but he'd already pressed the stop button. "Why would you have kept that tape?" She clutched at his arm, shaking him, forcing him to look at her. "What are you trying to do to me? How could you be so cruel?" she lashed out, uncaring that her tears were wetting his shirt.

Catching her off guard, he pulled her onto his lap. He gripped her face in his hands, preventing her from thrashing about by trapping her legs between his. With a gentle stroke of his thumbs, he smoothed the moisture from her lashes. "When I instructed the guard to play back the tape for me and I heard your relentless sobbing, it released a memory buried so deep in my psyche I didn't know it was there until that moment."

His breath warmed her face, but she was too distraught to realize the danger of being this close to him again.

"What memory?"

His body tautened. "Of an icy-cold morning when two men came to my schoolroom in Siberia and told me I was to go with them, that my mother needed me at home. I was eight years old. I remember that very distinctly because my father, who worked with his hands, had made me a sled for my birthday. I loved my father and was very proud of it. In fact, I pulled it to school so I could play with it on the way home and show my friends.

"When I told the men I needed to get my sled, which the teacher had told me to put around the back of the one-room building, they said there was no time, that it would be there tomorrow. I was upset about it, but my fear that something bad had happened to my mother was foremost in my mind.

"They put me in a horse-drawn sleigh and set off in the opposite direction from my house. When I told them we were going the wrong way, one of the men slapped me and told me to be quiet. He said that the state was my family now. That I wasn't to speak about my family again or they would kill my sister and my parents."

Meg's involuntary cry went ignored by Kon. He kept on talking in the same low, steady voice. "But if I was good, they would tell my family I had gone out on the ice over the lake with my sled and had fallen through before anyone could save me."

She shook her head in disbelief. "You're making this up.

You have to be," she whispered, unable to conceive of anything so horrifying. But when she dared to look into his eyes, she glimpsed an unspeakable kind of bleakness, a pain that made her heart lurch.

"I said the same thing to myself while they drove me farther and farther away from the only security I'd ever known. Then came night. They must have put me in a barn, because I was pushed into some straw and told that if I cried, they would kill me. But if I showed I was a man, then it would prove I was worthy of the great honor they had bestowed upon me, the honor of serving the state."

"Oh, Kon!" She broke down, overcome by the enormity of what he'd told her. For the moment the enmity between them was forgotten. She became mother, sister, lover, wanting only to give comfort to the child in him who could not be comforted. It seemed the most natural thing in the world to press her head into his neck and murmur incoherent endearments, much the same way she did when Anna needed consolation.

"I've heard stories of such things happening." She spoke against the side of his neck. "But I never wanted to believe them."

"I'd forgotten all of it," he said, brushing the silvery-blond strands of hair from her face while he rocked her in his arms, "until you were detained. Then your pain became my pain and I couldn't distinguish between them, couldn't tell the difference. It was in my power to keep you incarcerated as long as I desired, regardless of your grief. You'd broken the law and deserved to be punished. That was what I believed. That was part of the KGB's bullying tactics." He gave a deep, shuddering sigh. "But when I heard you call out for your daddy, something inside me snapped. I had to let you go."

The rocking stopped and his haunted eyes met hers. "No child, young or old, should be made to suffer the kind of night I was forced to endure in that barn, knowing I'd never see my family again. Knowing I'd never hear my mother tell me another story. Knowing I couldn't even keep the sled my father had just made for me. Not allowed even the smallest memento of the family I'd loved.''

He was telling her the truth, Meg knew. A strangled sound escaped her throat. He'd wanted to console her during that terrible night. There'd been nothing he could do then, so he'd given her the book, secretly putting it in her suitcase. During her second visit, Meg had asked him about it and he'd been noncommittal. "Just a gift,'' he'd said. Now she understood.

"You wouldn't explain when I asked you before,'' she said. "But it was because you knew how devastated I felt. How alone.''

"Yes. I wanted you to leave with something you treasured, one good memory of my country. And of me…''

Meg lowered her head. "When the customs official in New York opened my suitcase, I saw it lying on top of my things. I couldn't believe it. I knew you had to have put it there, but I didn't understand why, and I couldn't figure out how you knew I wanted that particular book.''

"All the staff at your hotel were KGB, Meggie. That's why the teachers and students from America were put there. It was easier for your guide to monitor your group's activities and report to me. He was careful to make notations on the kinds of things that interested you in the shops, particularly any reading material. Part of an agent's work was to seek out those visitors who might be sympathetic to Soviet communism and win them over.''

Meg shuddered to think that from the time they'd arrived in Moscow until the moment Kon had rushed her to the plane, she and her friends had been collected and examined like insects under a microscope.

"He must have been disappointed when I passed up the free propaganda for a book on the *Nutcracker*. I wanted it badly but couldn't afford it.''

"If anything, he was surprised. Normally American students grab at whatever is given away. Even if it's not free, they have their parents' money to squander. But you were different."

She took a steadying breath and wiped more tears from her face. "How was I different?"

"You were a lovely teenager, independent and spoiled like all of your crowd, but incredibly brave in front of the guards. So free in spirit. Young as you were, you never cowered. A part of me was intrigued by that remarkable quality in you."

She raised her head and their gazes held for a long moment until Meg stirred restlessly in his arms. She felt amazed by his confession, but more troubled and confused than ever. There could be no doubt about the nightmare he'd lived through as a child. But since the age of eight, the KGB had been his family.

Some of what he'd said today, tonight, was the truth. But which part was the lie? *And what was she doing on his lap with her body practically molded to his, their mouths only inches apart?*

Alarmed that her perspective had been clouded by compassion, she pushed her hands against his chest and struggled to her feet. She needed to separate herself from him—to fight off the sensual appeal he'd always had for her.

Something must be fundamentally wrong with her, letting him penetrate her defenses like this! It was all because he'd been able to arouse feelings that were in direct conflict with her fears.

"Your new family did a remarkable job of training you," she said coldly, attempting to put emotional distance between them. "Accosting Anna and me at the theater the way you did was a perfect example of the typical KGB takeover. It comes as naturally to you as breathing, doesn't it, Kon?

"But there's one thing you didn't know. If you try to take Anna from me, I will fight you in court. She's known only me since she was born. It would be cruel to separate us. I won't let you!"

"I've already told you that's not my intention. I want all three of us to live together." A complacent smile curved his lips. "In any event, it's too late for ultimatums, isn't it, Meggie? My daughter and I have already bonded, and I promised her I'd be here when she wakes up in the morning. Surely after spending four months in my company, you learned that I never break a promise."

"You broke *one*," she said icily. When his eyebrows rose she went on, "You'd promised I wouldn't get pregnant. I was foolish enough to believe you."

His eyes narrowed. "You and I both know I used protection. Every single time. But it appears we underestimated our little girl's determination to be born."

"No, Kon. All it means is that I underestimated how far you'd go to make it look like an accident."

His mouth thinned ominously. "Let's get something straight. The second time you came to Russia, it was not my intention to make you pregnant. If that *had* been the plan, I would have taken you to bed the day you stepped on Russian soil."

He didn't need to add that she'd been his for the asking. The humiliation she felt produced a blush she couldn't hide.

"For your information," he continued, "I had many responsibilities, of which you were only one, a quite insignificant one. I should have assigned you to a guard at the lowest echelon. In fact, it was such a routine job that one of my colleagues actually made a comment wondering why I would bother myself with anything so trivial as the surveillance of an unimportant American schoolteacher.

"I won't insult your intelligence by denying that some of the agents did sleep with their targets to obtain secrets. One of the reasons I assigned myself to you was to protect you from just such a situation."

"Why would you do that?"

He sat back against the cushions. "Because there was a refreshing innocence about you when you left Russia the first time. An honesty. Six years later, when I saw your name on a list of foreign teachers coming for a short-term stay, I wanted to see if that innocence was still there." He paused for one breathless moment.

"The only change I could see was that the teenage girl had grown into a beautiful woman. More than ever I wanted to make sure no man took advantage of you while you were in my country."

"I don't believe you, Kon."

He cocked his head to the side and studied her briefly. "Did I ever once force myself on you, Meggie? Have you forgotten that you were the one who rejected me?"

Somehow their arguments always ended with his turning things around so she appeared to be the culprit. Until she met Kon, she'd never been in love. There had been no serious boyfriends in Meg's teens, no prior physical experiences to give her insight or prepare her for the full-blown emotional and sexual feelings she'd had for the man who was Anna's father.

Meg was an only child, born to a mother in her forties and a father in his fifties, both of whom were overjoyed to have a child at last. Being devout Christians who lived on a modest income, they'd sheltered her, pressured her to make the most of her studies, insisted she take advantage of every academic opportunity.

They'd been pacifists who had strongly believed in understanding as the key to world peace. In keeping with their beliefs, they'd enrolled her in a special Russian program from grade school through college. Neither of them lived long enough to realize that this well-intentioned idea would lead her down a path of forbidden passion to the life-and-death situation she faced now, in her own apartment.

"I couldn't give up my citizenship and walk away from my whole life!"

"Certainly not for me," he said beneath his breath, but she heard him and became angry all over again at his power to make her feel guilty. "So I took whatever you were willing to offer, which was as many days and nights in your arms as we could manage. I'm a man, Meggie. You know how it was with us."

"You mean you know how I thought it was with us," she said acidly. "Obviously everything was a lie! You set out to manipulate me and…seduce me. And you succeeded."

His gaze swept over her face and body. Oddly, it reminded her of the way he'd looked at her when she'd been detained by the airport guards.

"You're right. I did set out to win you over. But I've already told you—my success was hardly complete."

Meg, prepared for any excuse except his cold-blooded admission, felt she'd just been slapped.

"Before detente, part of my job was to keep track of foreign visitors, most of whom were tourists. Your uncle's information was correct. If any of them made a second visit, they were kept on a special list and targeted as either possible recruits or possible subversives. Special agents were assigned to scrutinize their behavior. If the same visitor came a third time, he or she was detained indefinitely."

His gaze bore into hers. "Evidently your bad experience in our jail didn't prevent you from returning, which proved what I'd thought about you—that you had an indomitable will. Intrigued by that, I made certain you were placed under my personal supervision."

Meg's head flew back. "And I was naive enough to suppose our meeting again was pure coincidence," she said angrily. "I couldn't believe my luck. Here I thought it might be impossible to track you down so I could thank you for letting me go home to my father's funeral, for giving me that book. Instead, there you were. Right at the Moscow airport!" She struggled to keep her voice steady.

"What was even more astonishing was realizing I'd been put in your charge," she went on after a moment. "In the midst of all that red tape and the endless questions, you once again whisked me away to St. Petersburg. I felt like a princess who'd been rescued by a knight in shining armor. I put you on a pedestal. Imagine putting a KGB agent on a pedestal!'' she exclaimed savagely.

He heaved a deep sigh. "Can this keep till morning? I'm tired. Good night, Meggie.''

Before she could say another word, he'd removed his shoes and stretched out on her couch, turning on his side so his back was toward her. The sight of him made her shake with rage.

"What do you think you're doing?''

"Shh. You'll wake Anna. I thought it was clear what I'm doing. I'm going to sleep.''

Aghast, she cried, "But you can't! Not here!''

He half turned and looked over his shoulder at her, his dark hair attractively disheveled. "If you're inviting me to join you in your bed, I won't say no.''

She refused to dignify that remark with an answer. "I'm calling my attorney, Kon.''

"It's awfully late, isn't it? But you can try," he said in a bored voice. Then he lay back down and punched the bolster a couple of times to get into a more comfortable position.

Meg whirled around and dashed into the kitchen.

The receiver was missing. He must have detached and hidden it while she was putting Anna back to bed.

"Relax. You're perfectly safe with me here. If by morning you still want to call your attorney, go ahead. All it means is that you'll end up meeting Senator Strickland sooner rather than later. Sweet dreams, Meggie.''

She made a noise that sounded like something between a cry and a groan, impotently staring at Kon's back. Within minutes, she heard his breathing change. He'd actually fallen asleep!

What was she going to do? Kidnap Anna from her own apartment?

A mirthless laugh escaped. Short of rendering her daughter

unconscious, she'd never manage. Anna wouldn't stand to be dragged away from Kon when they'd only just been united. And where could Meg take her without being followed?

Physically and emotionally drained, she reflected on comments one of her divorced friends at work had made. Cheryl had talked about how hard it was dealing with an ex-husband who still acted as if he was part of the family. She'd described her feelings of oppression and claustrophobia, and her frequent sense of fear.

For the first time Meg thought she understood a little of what Cheryl had meant. But Meg suspected that if she was to tell her friend about her past association with Kon, about what had happened to her and Anna during the ballet, the other woman wouldn't believe her. Meg could hardly believe it herself.

Yet one of her deepest fears had already been realized. Kon had taken Anna's heart by storm. As for Meg's other fear—that he would insist on taking Anna to live with him for part of the year—only time would reveal Kon's true intentions.

Instead of being relieved by the insight he'd provided about his forced recruitment to the KGB at such a tender age, Meg found that it only deepened her anxiety. After all, Kon had been brutally torn from his own family, with everyone lost to him. Then he'd learned of Anna's existence. What could be more natural than to claim his own flesh and blood to fill that void?

Today's episode at the ballet provided Meg with absolute proof that from now on, wherever he went, whatever he did, he'd make sure his adoring daughter was by his side. And he'd let no one stand in the way, least of all Meg.

Kon was an expert at manipulation and intrigue. What would be the point of contacting her attorney or Senator Strickland, or the CIA for that matter? None of them was capable of giving her the reassurance she needed.

This was a crisis without precedent, one she'd have to

work through by herself. Kon's first step would be to lull her into a false sense of security—then he'd strike. Eventually they'd have to battle it out in court. Perhaps the best thing for now would be to play along until she saw her way clear to thwart him.

A shiver passed through her body. She turned off the Christmas-tree lights, and Kon was no longer visible. But somehow the darkness tended to magnify his presence.

The irony of the situation wasn't lost on Meg. At one time she would have given everything she possessed to see him lying there on her couch. After learning she was pregnant, her ultimate fantasy had been to see Kon walk through the front door straight into her arms.

I was out of my mind, she berated herself, wishing with all her soul that she'd had the wisdom to listen to her aunt.

After Meg had lost both parents, she'd lived with her aunt, Margaret, who'd been crippled with arthritis and suffered from a bad heart. Margaret had been horrified when Meg finally found the courage to tell her about the incident in Moscow, which had resulted in her being arrested and jailed.

Margaret was the widow of Meg's uncle Lloyd, her father's brother and a man with a distinguished career in naval intelligence. He'd died tragically from a slip on the ice when Meg was in her early twenties. Lloyd had been the most vocal in questioning the wisdom of Meg's Russian studies, let alone her traveling to the USSR. Margaret had seconded his opinions.

The brothers had had opposing viewpoints about Russia's threat to the world. Meg's father was not only a pacifist but a political scientist who'd believed language was the basis of understanding other people. He'd argued that there would come a time when the two nations could coexist peacefully. The U.S. would need teachers and ambassadors who understood and spoke Russian, people like Meg.

Uncle Lloyd, on the other hand, had remained adamant that the kind of situation his brother described was a pipe dream. He'd used all the cold hard facts at his command to support his arguments. When Meg told her aunt about the incident, Margaret had reiterated those facts, saying that if Uncle Lloyd had still been alive, he would have made an international incident of his niece's incarceration.

Meg hadn't been able to understand why her aunt was so upset. After all, she'd told her how the attractive KGB agent had intervened and gotten her to the airport in time to make it home for the funeral, how he'd given her a farewell gift.

But the more she defended him, the more her aunt argued. Margaret had finally confided inside information she'd gleaned from her husband about the mission of the KGB, not the sort of thing made public to the American people, details learned from several important Soviet defectors.

When Meg looked back, she felt remorse for having treated her aunt with scorn and disbelief. It seemed that Meg was her father's daughter, and she'd brushed off Margaret's advice, never dreaming that one day the older woman's warnings would come back to haunt her.

About the time Anna was born, Meg's aunt had passed away. Right after that, detente occurred. Stories began to trickle out of Russia about the inner workings of the KGB. To Meg's horror, it appeared that everything her aunt had tried to tell her was true.

And now Kon was here, a new threat to her peace of mind.

Suddenly Meg felt limp with exhaustion. She made her way to the bedroom, where she changed into a loose-fitting T-shirt and sweatpants. Taking the pillow from her bed, she went into Anna's room, needing comfort.

She climbed under the quilt and pulled Anna close, wrapping her arms around her. She caught her breath—the faint scent of Kon's soap lingered on Anna's cheek and hair. With a groan she turned sharply away and smothered her face in the pillow.

The clean fragrance brought back poignant memories of Kon on the last night they were together. She remembered the smoldering blue of his eyes before he made love to her, his insatiable desire for her and the Russian endearments that poured from his soul. Once again, he'd begged her to be his wife, to stay with him forever.

Meg never tired of hearing those words, and she'd told him there was nothing she wanted more—as long as they could arrange to spend half the year in Russia and the other half in the States. Through her uncle's contacts at the Pentagon and Kon's position in his government, surely something could be arranged. Since both of them loved their countries, it seemed the only solution if they were to have a life together.

He'd shaken his head. "What you want is an impossibility, Meggie. The only way we can be together is for you to give up your citizenship and live with me. You have no family now. If you love me enough, you'll do it."

"I think you must know how much I love you, Kon. But what if you grow tired of me? I couldn't bear that," she'd whispered into his hair, clinging to him. "What would happen if you decided you didn't want me anymore and asked for a divorce? I'd be alone, unable to return to the States."

Kon had responded with an anger that was all the more terrible because it was so quiet and controlled. He'd disentangled himself from her body and climbed out of bed to get dressed. Devastated by his reaction, Meg drew the covers to her chin and sat up.

He'd trained accusing eyes on her. "You don't know the meaning of love if you can lie in my arms and talk about marriage and divorce in the same breath. One of the problems in your country—"

"Not just my country, Kon—" she interrupted him, then fell silent. The last magical night they'd shared began to disintegrate.

In a few long strides he was out the bedroom door while she sponge-bathed as best she could, then dressed for the trip to the airport. Kon took her cases to the car and helped her inside, all the while ignoring her questions and overtures. His frozen silence broke her heart.

Once more he was the forbidding and unapproachable KGB agent. He'd rushed her to the airport in record time, instructed a guard to deal with her bags, then walked her to the plane. The way he'd helped her find her seat reminded Meg of the first time she'd left Russia.

Déjà vu except for one thing. She and Kon were alone inside the huge body of the jet. No other passengers had been allowed to board yet. Meg felt torn, and she wondered if a human being could endure this much pain and still survive.

"Meggie…"

She remembered the tortured sound of his voice and how she'd let out a gasp and looked at him. Perhaps it was the shadowy interior that had made his eyes glisten.

"Don't go. Stay with me. I love you, *mayah labof.* We'll be married right away. I have plenty of money. You can have your choice of the finest apartments. We'll live very well. I'll always take care of you," he'd vowed in an almost savage voice before crushing her in his arms.

More than anything in the world, she'd wanted to say yes. She'd molded herself to him, kissing him with all the intensity that was in her. But she was too much a product of her Western upbringing. Fear of what might happen in the future kept her from accepting his proposal.

Consumed by tears and frantic because their time had run out, she'd cried, "Do you think I want to leave you? My life is never going to be the same without you!"

At her words an expressionless mask had come down over his face and he'd held her at a distance.

"Kon, don't look at me like that! I can't bear it. I—I'll save my money and try to come back next year."

"No." He'd ground the word out with a strange finality she didn't understand. "Don't come back. Do you hear me?" He shook her hard. "Don't ever come back."

"But—"

"It's now or not at all."

His implacability had defeated her and she'd slumped against him, sobbing. "With you, I'm not afraid. But if something happened to you, I'd have nowhere to turn."

She heard his sharp intake of breath. "Goodbye, Meggie." He'd let her go and started down the aisle. Any second, and he would disappear from her life forever.

She'd cried his name in panic, but it was like shouting into the wind.

He was gone.

CHAPTER FIVE

"MOMMY! MOMMY!" Meg felt a pat on her face. "Why are you crying?"

Meg awoke from her half sleep with a start and stared at her daughter through bleary eyes, completely disoriented. *It was morning.* "I—I must have had a bad dream."

"Is that why you slept with me?"

After a brief hesitation Meg said, "Yes."

"You should have slept with Daddy. Then you wouldn't have been scared. Melanie says her mommy and daddy sleep together except when they have fights. Then he sleeps at her grandma's. Did you and Daddy have a fight?"

Was there any subject of a delicate nature Anna and Melanie *hadn't* discussed?

Meg expelled an exasperated sigh and threw back the covers to get out of bed, deciding not to comment. Anna must have been up for some time because she'd dressed in her favorite blue velour top with the pink hearts and matching pants. And Meg hadn't even been aware of it.

Anxiety made her reach out and cling to her daughter for an extra-long moment. Anna hugged her back, then struggled to be free.

"We had pancakes for our breakfast but I told him you like toast so he fixed that and said I should come and get you."

Now that Anna mentioned it, Meg could smell coffee. Since Anna didn't know how to prepare coffee, that meant

Kon had taken over. As he always did, commandeering the apartment, her daughter, her life—

But could she really expect him to act in any other way, know any other method—an eight-year-old boy stolen by the state and taught to be the complete authority figure?

Furious to find herself thinking of *any* excuse for him, Meg vented her feelings on the bed, which she'd started to make. Anything to put off the moment she had to face him again.

"Hurry, Mommy. I want to go see our house and the dogs."

"But we'll miss your Sunday-school class," Meg reminded her, already knowing how Anna would react. She couldn't help saying it, anyway.

"Daddy says there's a church by our house. I can go to Sunday school there next week. He says there are six kids in my class."

Meg's movements became so jerky she actually ripped the top sheet, which had caught on the end of the metal frame.

Anna's eyes rounded. "Uh-oh, Mommy. Something tore."

"So it did," Meg mumbled and threw on the comforter before she headed to the bathroom.

"I'll tell Daddy you're up!"

After Anna darted off, Meg glanced at herself in the mirror. A pale, haggard face stared back, but that was just fine with her. She took care of the necessities, then pulled her hair back, securing it with an elastic. She decided against makeup or perfume. For that matter, she'd leave on her sweats. The vivacious young woman who used to do everything possible to make herself beautiful for Kon had died.

"Mommy? Telephone!"

Meg's head jerked sideways. She hadn't even heard it ring. Kon must have reattached the receiver earlier that morning and picked it up the instant it rang.

"Coming."

She hated it that the second she saw Kon standing by the wall with the receiver in one hand, a cup of coffee in the other, her heart thumped crazily in her chest. She avoided his disquieting gaze as she took the phone from him, then turned her back. It should be a sin for a man to be so attractive that her senses couldn't help responding to him. Even her palms had moistened.

"Hello?" She strove to sound calm and normal.

"Am I speaking to Ms. Meg Roberts?"

Meg blinked at the sound of an officious-sounding female voice.

"Yes?"

"Please stay on the line. Senator Strickland would like to speak to you."

She leaned against the doorjamb for support and concentrated on Anna. At Kon's urging the child began to clean up the mess she'd made on the table with her nail polish. She'd obviously been getting ready for their trip.

"Ms. Roberts? Senator Strickland."

She instantly recognized that aging, raspy voice with the sustained pauses. "Yes, Senator."

"I'm calling to offer you my support and assure you that I couldn't be happier about the reunion with that young man of yours."

Reunion? Young man?

"I'd say that any man who would go through this kind of pain, danger and suffering must truly be in love. You realize your young man was one of the Soviets' most important defectors? And then there were the six years of semi-isolation while he waited to claim his American sweetheart and child.... I understand you're having some difficulty with the situation. But Mr. Rudenko deserves a hearing and I damn well hope you're giving him one."

Meg surmised that the two CIA agents had already filled him in on last night's meeting with her and he wasn't happy about it. But she was incapable of making more than a noncommittal sound in reply.

"My wife and I would consider it an honor if you would

plan to join us for dinner soon. I'll have my secretary arrange it with you after the Christmas holidays. You two need time alone to renew the romance and make plans. I envy you that.'' He chuckled amicably.

Meg felt she was going to suffocate. ''Th-thank you, Senator,'' she whispered.

''If there's anything I can do for you in the meantime, you call my secretary and she'll let me know. I'm sure this will be a very merry Christmas.''

The line went dead. In a daze she put the phone back on the hook only to hear it ring again. She could feel Kon's penetrating gaze as she lifted the receiver once more. Clearing her throat she said, ''Hello?''

''Hi.''

Her eyes closed tightly. ''Hi, Ted.''

''Hey? What's wrong? You don't sound like yourself.''

She rubbed the back of her neck with her free hand and walked as far into the living room as the cord would allow, away from prying eyes and ears.

''I—I guess I've come down with something.'' Even if Kon hadn't turned her world inside out, she still would have proffered an excuse not to go out with Ted. She didn't mind lunch with him once in a while, but that was it. He didn't interest her. No man did.

''I'm sorry to hear that. I was about to ask if you and Anna wanted to go sledding with me at the park this afternoon. Afterward I figured we'd get dinner someplace.''

Now he was trying to appeal to her by including Anna. ''That sounds very nice. Maybe another time when I'm feeling better,'' she lied.

''Right.'' The disappointment in his voice was palpable. ''Then I'll see you at the office.''

''Yes. I should be there tomorrow. I'm sure all I need is a good night's sleep. Thanks for calling.''

Aware she sounded nervous, she said goodbye, dreading the short walk to the kitchen to hang up the phone.

"Ted Jenkins, salesman of the year at Strong Motors," Kon said, clearly baiting her. "Thirty years old. Divorced. Frustrated because he doesn't have a relationship with you and never will. Why don't you eat your breakfast while I help Anna on with her snowsuit? Then we can be off."

"How do you know about him?"

"Like any man in love, I made it my business to find out if I had serious competition. Walter Bowman was willing to go in there on the pretext of buying a sports car. Ted Jenkins ended up taking him for a test run, and by the end of the ride, he'd learned enough to give me the information I wanted."

Under normal circumstances, any woman would be thrilled to know that the man she loved cared that much. But nothing about their relationship was normal.

Still, part of her *was* thrilled. And that meant it was starting to happen all over again.... Ignoring the plate of cold toast sitting on the counter, Meg fled from the room. She felt a desperate need to avoid Kon's probing gaze.

He didn't play fair! And she was terrified he would discover the kind of power he still had over her. The wisest thing would be to pretend to go along with his plan for Anna's sake.

Their daughter was determined to see where he lived. Once her curiosity had been satisfied, Meg would tell Kon he'd have to work through her attorney if he hoped to spend time with Anna after today. Any future visits would have to be in Meg's presence.

No matter that he'd somehow gained the confidence of Senator Strickland, Kon wasn't above the law. Her anger made her motions clumsy and she broke a shoelace. She groaned in frustration. Now she'd have to wear loafers instead of running shoes.

"Here's your coat, Mommy. Daddy's outside warming up the car for us."

"Well, wasn't that thoughtful of him," she muttered sarcastically beneath her breath. She was bristling with indignation at the thought that he'd taken her keys off the counter without even asking.

"Daddy says you need a rest, so he's going to drive. He says you've been working too hard, so he's going to take good care of you."

Meg couldn't let this go on any longer. After buttoning her coat, she crouched down to talk to her daughter, who was clutching her doll. "Honey—" she smoothed the dark curls, which bounced right back over Anna's forehead "—I know you're happy about meeting your daddy, but that doesn't mean we're all going to live together."

"Yes, it does," Anna said with complete assurance. "I told Daddy I wanted a baby sister like Melanie's. And you know what?" Her eyes grew rounder. "He said he could give me a sister just as soon as you get married next week. He wants a big family."

Meg gasped out loud and buried her face against Anna's small shoulder. "Anna! Mommy isn't going to marry your daddy."

"Yes, you are," she stated confidently. "Daddy said so. He promised he's going to stay home with us all the time. Don't be scared, Mommy." She stroked Meg's hair.

Meg clung to her daughter for a full minute before getting control of herself. "Sometimes grown-ups can't keep their promises, Anna."

"Daddy will 'cause he's my daddy and he loves me," she argued, sounding close to tears. "Let's hurry, Mommy. He's waiting for us."

She broke free of Meg's grasp and scuttled out of the apartment before Meg could stop her. Afraid of what was already happening to Anna, Meg grabbed her purse from the kitchen counter, locked the door and dashed after her.

Luckily, Sunday mornings were quiet around the complex, especially during the winter. Most of her neighbors were still inside their apartment, and Meg was spared answering difficult questions like, *Why do you look so pale, Meg? Who's the attractive stranger who stayed over at your apartment last night? Why is he driving your Toyota with Anna seated up front next to him?*

Kon got out of the car at her approach, his eyes narrowed on her face. More than ever, she was glad she hadn't dressed up or bothered with makeup. Most likely he was comparing the tired, anxiety-ridden mother to the passionate, love-besotted young woman she used to be.

"If you'd rather drive, I'll sit in back," he offered.

He sounded so reasonable her temper flared. "Why break your record and give me a choice now?" She kept on walking around the other side of the car and climbed into the back before he could help her.

He followed her and shut the door. After a searching glance, which she refused to meet, he went around to the driver's side and got in. Seconds later, they were off.

He turned on a radio station playing Christmas carols and Anna began singing, much to Kon's delight. Meg could see his face through the rearview mirror as he sang with her. She couldn't help but be touched by the adoring expression he cast Anna every so often.

As the Toyota covered the miles, it dawned on Meg that she'd never been chauffeured around in her own car before. It was a novel experience to ride in the back seat and let Kon do the work, all the while keeping their loquacious daughter entertained. Grudgingly Meg admitted that not having to be in charge made a nice change, especially now, with the roads growing icy and wind buffeting the car.

But of course if Kon wasn't in the picture, she would never have gone driving with Anna on a wintry day like today in the first place. Their normal routine was to walk to the church a few blocks away, then come home and fix lunch. Afterward, Meg usually encouraged Anna to practice her violin. Then her daughter would either play at Melanie's apartment, or vice versa, while Meg caught up on some reading or sewing.

Lately Anna had been spending more time at Melanie's because of her fascination with the new baby. This was why she'd become so obsessed with the idea of having a brother or sister of her own and had divulged her fantasies to Kon. So far he'd proved he could grant her every desire. Was it any wonder that Anna adored him? Just the way *Meg* had once adored him?

Unable to help herself, she found her eyes straying to the back of his dark head, the broad set of his shoulders, his incredibly handsome profile. *There ought to be a law!* she cried inside. Abruptly she turned away to stare out the window, but not before his smoldering glance had intercepted hers for an instant. It sent a shock wave through her body, disrupting the rhythm of her breathing.

The force of her own reaction upset her so much she didn't realize that they'd pulled into a rest area and come to a stop.

"I don't have to go to the bathroom yet, Daddy."

Despite Kon's low chuckle, Meg felt nervous, wondering why they'd stopped. He turned in the seat so he could eye both of them.

"We're almost at Hannibal. But before we get there, I have a secret to tell you." His grave tone increased Meg's apprehension. "I know your mother can keep it, but what about you, Anochka? If I tell you something very, very important, will you remember that it is our family secret, no one else's?"

Our family. Meg's breath caught while Anna's eyes grew solemn and she slowly nodded her head.

"When I left Russia, I had to change my name."

"Why, Daddy?"

Meg felt a strange tension radiating from him, as if there was a surfeit of dark emotion he had difficulty suppressing.

"Some people got mad because I left my country," he said in a hollow voice, "and some people in America were mad because I came here. They didn't like my Russian name. They didn't like me."

Something in his tone led Meg to believe he'd suffered. Anna was equally affected.

"We like you, Daddy!" She rushed to her father's defense, her child's heart ready to forgive him anything. "We *love* you, don't we, Mommy?"

"And I love both of you," he said in a husky voice, preventing Meg from refuting him. "So to keep us all safe, I took a different name."

With such important news to consider, Anna forgot to sing along with the carol that had just started playing on the radio, even though "Deck the Halls" was one of her favorites. "What's your new name?"

"Gary Johnson."

Gary Johnson? Meg fought to keep from bursting out laughing. No man in the world ever looked or acted less like a Gary Johnson than KGB agent Konstantin Rudenko. It was ludicrous.

"That's the name of a boy in my class!" Anna cried excitedly. "He's got blond hair and a pet c-coca-too. Mrs. Beezley let us bring our pets to class and Mommy helped me bring my fish."

Kon nodded, seemingly pleased with her response. "Thousands of boys and men in the United States have the name Gary Johnson. That's why I picked it."

"And now nobody's mad at you anymore?"

"That's right. I have lots of new friends and neighbors, and they all call me Gary or Mr. Johnson."

"Can't I keep calling you Daddy?"

Kon undid her seat belt and pulled her onto his lap so he could kiss her. "You're the only person in the whole wide world who gets to call me Daddy, Anochka."

"'Cept when I get a new sister."

"That's right," he murmured, hugging her tight.

Anna finally lifted her head so she could see over the seat, her blue eyes glowing like jewels. "Mommy, you have to call Daddy Gary from now on. Don't forget," she said in a hushed voice.

Anna's remark was so touching, Meg's heart turned over and she averted her eyes. As far as Kon went, though, it would be impossibile for her to call him Gary. In fact, the whole situation was too fantastic: she just couldn't do it. But that really didn't matter, because she wouldn't be seeing him except at visitation times, and then they wouldn't be around other people.

She felt Kon's glance sweep over her. "Your mommy has always called me 'darling,' so I don't anticipate any problem."

Meg couldn't take much more of this farce. She felt as though she'd aged a hundred years since the ballet yesterday.

"I think another snowstorm's coming, *Gary*," she mocked. "If we're going to see your house, then I suggest we get moving."

His brilliant smile twisted her insides. "It sounds as if you're as excited as I am."

After he'd put Anna back in her seat and fastened the belt, he started the car and they reentered the freeway. Hannibal was only six miles farther. "I can hardly wait until we get home," he confided to his daughter, tousling her curls with his free hand. "I've been lonely for my little girl."

"I'm here now, Daddy, and you won't ever be lonely again, will he, Clara?" she said to the doll she'd named after the girl in the *Nutcracker*. "Clara loves you, too, Daddy."

"I'm glad to hear it."

Hard as she tried, Meg couldn't blot out the sound of his deep, attractive voice or the loving look he exchanged with their daughter. Anna's sweet, generous spirit brought a lump to Meg's throat, and it seemed to have affected Kon in a similar manner, because he whispered the Russian word for sweetheart and reached for Anna's hand.

The takeover was complete. Anna would never be wholly

hers again. Meg couldn't bear it and she put a hand over her heart, as if she could stop the pain. *What was she going to do?*

They left the freeway and entered the small town of Hannibal, made famous by Sam Clemens, who had written about his boyhood on the Mississippi in the mid-nineteenth century.

Meg didn't know what Kon had in mind, but supposed that for Anna's sake he would drive them past the riverboat landing in the downtown area, where the Mark Twain Home and Museum were located.

Instead, he took a route that led past all the historic homes decorated for Christmas until they came to the famous Rockcliffe Mansion. They drove another block, then he turned a corner and entered a driveway that needed to be shoveled after last night's snow. They wound around the back of a quaint, white, two-story clapboard house with green trim; it reminded her of the restored Becky Thatcher Bookshop in the historic district.

"We're home, Anochka." He pulled to a stop in front of a detached two-car garage and undid Anna's seat belt.

Anna couldn't keep still, her bright eyes missing nothing. "Where are my dogs, Daddy?"

"On the back porch, waiting for us."

Meg stared at the house in disbelief, then switched her gaze to Kon. He was helping Anna from the car, her doll forgotten. Meg couldn't equate this doting father and family man with the all-powerful KGB agent who, at one time, had inspired fear in the hearts of Soviet citizens and foreigners alike.

She got out of the car, then watched spellbound as Kon told both of them to wait right there while he mounted the steps and unlocked the door.

Anna let out a shriek of delight as a handsome German shepherd came running down the stairs and circled her in the snow, sniffing at her hands and swishing his tail. No doubt Kon had experience with dogs trained in pursuit. This one

had been handled so expertly he didn't bare his teeth or growl
or jump up on her, relieving Meg of any initial worry in that
department.

At Kon's command, the dog came to a standstill and let
Anna pet him. It didn't surprise Meg that her daughter
showed no fear. An elderly couple across the street from the
apartment complex had a friendly golden retriever Anna and
Melanie loved to play with.

"Meggie, come over and meet Thor," Kon urged, his
voice alive and inviting. It conjured up memories of another
place, another time, when she'd lived for nothing but him
and whenever they were apart counted the hours till they
were together again.

For the next few minutes Meg let go of her anxieties about
Kon's motives long enough to become acquainted with the
dog. Thor appeared as ecstatic as Anna to make friends. He
showed his affection with licks and whimpers and a few exuberant barks that made Anna giggle and her father laugh
out loud.

Meg had never heard such a happy sound from him. Forgetting to be on her guard, she raised her head, smiling, and
discovered he was looking at her in the old way, his eyes
fiercely blue and possessive. She felt her body tremble and
turned away.

"Where's the other dog?" Anna wanted to know.

"Gandy's busy inside," came the cryptic reply. "Shall we
go see what she is doing?"

"Follow me, Thor," Anna cried excitedly as she scrambled up the back steps behind her father. Before Meg had
even reached the door she heard Anna's awestruck voice.
Curious to see what had produced such reverence, Meg hurried into the warm, closed-in porch, where she caught a
glimpse of a female German shepherd lying on a makeshift
bed in the corner, with three tiny suckling pups. The new
mother lifted her proud head at their approach.

Thor crept next to Kon, who hunkered down and put his

arm around Anna while they gazed at the beautiful sight. "This is the early Christmas present I told you about, Anochka," he whispered.

"Oh, Daddy!" she squealed in rapture. "Look at the littlest one. She could fit in my hands."

"She's a he." His voice was tender, gently mocking.

Anna absorbed that bit of information and said, "Can I hold him? Please?"

"In a little while, when he's through eating. We musn't disturb them right now."

"What's his name?" she whispered loudly. With Anna, there was no such thing as a quiet whisper.

"I thought I'd leave that up to you since he'll be your dog. The other two we'll find a new home for as soon as they're ready to leave their mommy. But this puppy's just for you."

Once again Anna's eyes looked like exploding stars as she turned to Meg. "Mommy, I'm going to call him Prince Marzipan Johnson."

Meg started to laugh—she couldn't help it—and Kon joined her.

"Why don't we call him Prince for short?" Kon finally managed to say. He got to his feet. "I think we've tried Gandy's patience long enough. Why don't you go inside with Thor and start exploring." He opened another door that led into the house. "See if you can pick out your bedroom."

"*My own bedroom?* Come on, Thor." She put a hand on the dog's collar and they squeezed through the opening together. Meg couldn't tell which one of them was the most excited. But the moment they disappeared, the reality of the situation pressed in on Meg until she could hardly breathe.

"Kon—"

"Later, Meggie. Unless you want to join me in the shower."

She jammed her hands in her coat pockets and fastened her attention on Gandy, who'd returned her attention to the pups. Long after Kon had gone into the house, Meg stood there, willing the image of his hard, fit body, which had once known and claimed hers, to leave her mind.

The bittersweet torture of those memories held her unmoving, and though Anna was calling her, Meg couldn't bring herself to step one foot inside Kon's house. A house she suspected he'd bought with money he'd been paid for selling secrets.

CHAPTER SIX

MEG WAS AFRAID.

Afraid she'd like his home too much. Afraid he'd break down her resolve a little more, until the edges blurred and she didn't know what was phony and what was real. Afraid she'd be like Anna, totally vulnerable and accepting, until—until what? Meg didn't know anymore.

Even if he *had* defected, he was still a son of Russia, a man who loved his country. Now that a detente had been reached, she wouldn't blame him for wanting to return to his birthplace, that isolated village in Siberia for a visit. A place where he'd played with his sled as a little boy, where he'd been happy in the bosom of his family.

He had money and he could travel under an American passport. And he could take Anna with him. What could be more natural than to want to recapture his own stunted childhood through his daughter's eyes, to instill in her his love of Mother Russia? If he had joint custody, he could take Anna wherever he wanted and Meg would never need to know.

Ages ago, she'd turned down his marriage proposal because she hadn't wanted to live in Russia on a permanent basis. That would never change. Kon knew how she felt. She was sure there'd be no warning if he uprooted Anna temporarily.

It was time to have a talk with him.

An excess of nervous energy propelled her into the house. But halfway through the kitchen Meg came to a halt, arrested by the white ceiling-to-counter cabinets in the traditional

British pantry style. Wide cherry floorboards gleamed with a golden patina against white moldings and pale yellow walls, creating a sense of mellow warmth and beauty. It was a classic look that was continued throughout the rest of the downstairs.

The moderately sized house with its old-fashioned, small-paned windows reflected a spare traditionalism. The use of a few period pieces in the living and dining rooms, combined with comfortable, overstuffed furniture covered in a predominantly green chintz, gave it a timeless appeal.

Her eye followed the graceful sweep of the staircase with its hand-carved railing. Slowly she wandered into a study set off by French doors. Two pilastered bookcases on either side of a brick fireplace contained an impressive library of classical literature, with books in several languages, including, of course, Russian.

File cabinets and a desk complete with lamp, computer, keyboard and monitor supplied the only modern touch.

Did the decor reflect Kon's personal taste or had he purchased this charming home as is?

How could she possibly know the real man beneath his KGB-created persona when her only contact with him had been inside a police car, or a hotel or restaurant staffed by KGB?

Or a woodcutter's cottage?

Meg shivered as she contemplated the enormity of what she'd done. Anna had been conceived in a stranger's bed, by a stranger, in a strange land....

Certainly Kon couldn't have taken his lover home with him in those days, wherever and whatever "home" might have been. The normal human experience of a man and woman meeting and getting to know each other had eluded her completely where he was concerned.

According to Walt and Lacey Bowman, Kon had lived here in Hannibal for five years. Had the American government provided him with this house, along with a ready-made identity to hide the fact that he was a Russian defector?

Who was the real Kon?

Was Konstantin Rudenko the name his parents had given him at birth, or had the Soviet government supplied him a new one when they'd kidnapped him for service?

Meg thought she'd go mad trying to answer those questions, and she buried her face in her hands.

Another pair of hands settled on her shoulders. Strong, warm, masculine hands that felt achingly familiar. She should have tried to move away, but her body was being controlled by a force more powerful than her will to fight it. A low, husky voice whispered, "Don't try to solve all the world's riddles right now." It was as though he'd read her mind.

Her breath caught as she felt questing fingers encircle the nape of her neck and gently massage the tense muscles. "You and I haven't had a moment alone until now," he murmured, grazing her earlobe with his teeth. "Much as I adore Anna, I thought I'd lose my mind if she didn't find a way to entertain herself so I could kiss her mother. Dear God, it's been six endless, excruciating years, *mayah labof*."

The heat from his body radiated to Meg's, and those old, familiar longings took over, trapping her despite everything she knew and feared about him. His mouth traveled along her hot cheek, his smooth, freshly shaved skin scented from the soap he'd used in the shower.

"There's been no one else for me since you left me, and I have the strongest impression there's been no one else for you, either. What we shared could never be repeated with anyone else. Help me," he groaned against her lips before drawing her fully into his arms.

Meg tried not to respond, but she felt as if some drug had dulled her power to think, to remember that he was the enemy. His mouth started to work its magic, and before she knew how it had happened, her mouth opened to his. Her passion flared out of control. Just like before...

It was happening again, just as she'd feared. The mindless rapture, this explosion of sensual feeling that left her weak and clinging to him. It had been so long since the last time he'd aroused these sensations that her desire leapt to pulsating life.

Somehow, without her being aware of it, he'd undone her coat and now he was urging her body closer, running his hands over her back, insinuating his fingers beneath the waistband of her skirt to touch her sensitized skin.

With a helpless moan she slid her arms around his neck, and her body arched against his solid warmth, knowing where this was leading, wanting it so badly, she was barely conscious of footsteps running down the stairs and an excited young voice chatting with Thor.

Anna.

Meg couldn't let her daughter see them like this. She shoved her hands against his chest, but Kon must not have heard Anna, because he deepened their kiss, effectively suffocating her cry of panic.

His mouth craved hers with the relentless hunger of a man who'd been deprived too long. To her shame, Meg offered herself in wanton abandon even as Anna came bouncing into the study with an exuberant Thor at her heels.

Mortified to have been caught out like this, Meg tried to pull away from Kon and waited for the inevitable comment from their curious, precocious daughter. But for once, Anna failed to say anything at all.

The unnatural silence must have alerted Kon, who with a low groan reluctantly lifted his mouth from hers. His eyes burned a hot blue as they studied her trembling mouth.

Since he seemed as incapable of speech as his daughter, Meg realized it was up to her to divert Anna's attention.

She took advantage of Kon's temporary weakness to separate herself from him. But she wasn't prepared for the sense of loss she felt as soon as she'd moved out of his arms. Nor was she prepared for the speculative look in Anna's eyes; it reminded her of Kon—the same penetrating gaze. Thor rubbed against Anna's side, waiting.

Heavens, Anna made Meg feel like a lovestruck teenager whose parents had found her in a compromising position with her boyfriend! Before she could think of something to say to defuse the situation, Anna took the initiative.

"Have you and Daddy been making a baby?"

She should have been ready for that one. Her breathing grew shallow as she felt Kon's hands slide to her shoulders. He kneaded them with gentle insistence.

"Not yet, Anochka," he answered calmly. "First your mother has to agree to marry me. Shall I ask her now?"

"No! Please..." Meg begged him, but Anna was nodding solemnly, and Meg knew she herself would have fainted if Kon hadn't been standing behind her, holding her in his firm grip.

"Meggie." He ignored her plea and murmured into her hair, caressing the top of her head with his chin. "With Senator Strickland's help, special arrangements have been made for us to have a private wedding here at the house on Wednesday. A friend of mine who's a judge on the state's Supreme Court will marry us, and Lacey and Walt will serve as witnesses. The only detail left is for you to say yes."

Yesterday he'd placed the noose around her neck. Now he'd drawn it tight.

"I want us to be a family. Anna shouldn't have to grow up without her father the way I did, and I certainly don't want anyone else raising her. Obviously you don't, either, or you would have married before now."

Which was true, but she'd rather die than admit it to him.

"You can quit your job at Strong Motors and be a full-time mother to Anna. This house needs a mother and father, husband and wife. I didn't even want to put up a Christmas tree or decorations until we could do it together."

There was a long silence while Meg tried to absorb what he was saying.

"Anna," she finally said in a shaky voice, "I need to talk to your father alone. Why don't you and Thor go out on the porch and see how the new puppies are doing? But don't touch them."

"Are you going to marry my daddy?" the child persisted stubbornly.

"Anna," Meg said as sternly as she could, "do as I say, please."

But her daughter refused to mind her, and the hint of tears shimmering in her eyes was almost more than Meg could bear. "I want to live with Daddy. I have a pink room and a bed with a tent over it, and a mirror and a little table and...and everything!"

"Anochka..." her father warned quietly. That was all it took for their daughter to grab Thor by the collar and leave the room.

How did Kon do that?

Meg wheeled around in exasperation, noting all at once how incredibly attractive he looked in American jeans and a dark turtleneck. She was determined to ignore her own powerful response to him. "I have no intention of marrying you and we certainly don't need to get married for you to see Anna." Her chest heaved as though she was out of breath. "If you'll tell me what days you want to be with her, I'll drive her here and let you spend time together before I take her home again."

"This is your home now," came the implacable response. "I want both of you here every day and every night for the rest of our lives."

"That isn't possible, Kon. But I'm willing to work out a visitation schedule."

"I'm not."

He was impossible! "It's that or nothing, I'm afraid. You've had your reunion with your daughter. Now I'm taking Anna home. Please give me my car keys."

It shocked her when he reached into his pocket and handed

them to her without a word, a strange smile on that darkly handsome face.

It shocked her even more that he did nothing to prevent her from leaving the house. He stood on the steps and kept Thor at bay while Meg dragged an hysterical Anna through the snow to the car.

"Daddy! Daddy!" she screamed at the top of her lungs as Kon went back inside and closed the door. Her daughter's cries reminded Meg of the tape he had played for her the night before. They had to be tearing him apart, yet he didn't lift a finger to help her. Even though that was what Meg wanted, the pain of the whole thing was almost beyond endurance.

"Don't let Mommy take me away, Daddy!" Anna's heartbreaking plea could be heard for miles, Meg was sure, and the tears didn't stop even when she'd driven away.

Meg found it terrifying that no matter how hard she tried to reason with her daughter, no matter how hard she tried to explain that she could see her father again very soon, Anna cried hysterically all the way home.

"I hate you, Mommy," she said in a hoarse voice when they pulled into their parking spot. "Clara hates you, too, and we're never going to love you again."

Anna's face was flushed and she looked feverish. Guilt almost had Meg restarting the car and returning to Hannibal. But she had to remain firm now or everything would be lost.

Damn you, Kon, she muttered under her breath, fighting back scalding tears of pain and frustration. Before now, there'd never been a discordant note between her and her daughter.

Oh, he was good at his job. Good at creating subversion and chaos! The tears would not be halted now.

Damn you for making me want you, Kon—as badly as Anna wants you. Damn. Damn. Damn!

"MEG? IT'S AN OFFICE aide calling from Anna's school. Line two."

Meg closed her eyes. Anna was probably sick. She'd refused to eat any food after they'd gotten home from Hannibal yesterday, and this morning she wouldn't touch her breakfast before Meg drove her to school.

"Thanks, Cheryl."

With a trembling hand Meg picked up the receiver and pressed the button, her headache so fierce she didn't know how she was going to make it through the rest of the day. Four aspirin still hadn't done the trick, and now she was starting to feel nauseated. If this kept up, she'd have to go home.

"Yes? This is Meg Roberts."

"Hi. This is Carla Morley. I'm helping out today because Mrs. Hixon is home with the flu. I'm just checking with you to see if it's all right if Anna's father drives her home. Anna didn't feel well when she got to school this morning and had me phone him in Hannibal when we couldn't reach you at lunchtime. He drove here as fast as he could."

How did Anna know his phone number unless he gave it to her when Meg was unaware?

"The problem is, you haven't put Mr. Johnson's name on the emergency card, but he said that was because he was out of the country until recently. But as I explained to him, I can't give him permission to take Anna off school grounds unless you give your consent."

Dear God. "Just keep Anna there. I'll be right over. And thank you for being so conscientious." Meg's voice shook. It was entirely possible that without Carla Morley's intervention, Kon could be halfway back to Hannibal with Anna—who was so upset with Meg right now she would have willingly accompanied him anywhere.

Cheryl flashed Meg a look of concern as she hung up the phone. "Is something wrong with Anna? You're as white as a sheet."

"Sh-she's sick." It was the truth. And there was no way she could tell anyone about Kon right now, not even Cheryl. "I'm going to have to take her home. Would you mind covering for me?"

"Of course not. You shouldn't have come to work this morning, anyway. Go home and stay there until you're both better."

"Thanks, Cheryl. I'll cover for you next time."

On her way out of the car showroom, Ted tried to engage her in conversation, but Meg told him Anna was sick and she couldn't stop to talk. He went out to the back lot with her and helped her into the car, telling her he'd call later to see if there was anything he could do.

Meg thanked him for his concern but told him it wasn't necessary. Then she didn't give him another thought as she drove the seven miles to Anna's school. Fortunately for her, the storm predicted the day before had failed to materialize. The streets were relatively free of snow, and she broke the speed limit getting to her destination. She parked in the school-bus zone to save time and leapt from the car.

With pounding heart she dashed into the main office, where she discovered Anna sitting on Kon's lap, her curly head resting against his chest. The sight of father and daughter never failed to jolt Meg; they looked so *alike*—and so right together.

Kon's enigmatic gaze rested on Meg. Her sigh of relief at finding her daughter safe quickly changed to one of consternation when she saw Anna's flushed face. "Honey, Ms. Morley said you were sick."

"I don't feel good." The small, weak voice sounded odd to Meg's ears. Caught up in a welter of emotions, she ran directly to Anna, who surprisingly offered no resistance when Meg reached for her. There was no more "I hate you, Mommy," to make her feel worse than she already did.

Ms. Morley flashed her a commiserating smile. "There's

a bad flu bug going around. Quite a few of the students are out with it this morning.''

"That's probably it,'' Meg murmured indistinctly. Kon had risen to his full, intimidating height and she could feel his eyes on her, challenging her to make a scene in front of the other woman.

"Luckily today's the last day before Christmas vacation,'' the aide said amiably. "She'll have the whole holiday to recuperate.''

Meg couldn't get out of there fast enough. "Thank you, Ms. Morley.''

"Think nothing of it. As soon as Mr. Johnson got here, he was able to calm her down. Seeing her daddy made all the difference, didn't it, Anna?'' The woman smiled at Anna, then Kon, obviously charmed by him. "Merry Christmas.''

Meg silently blessed the woman for not bringing up the authorization issue. No doubt Ms. Morley dealt with many divorced parents throughout the school year and had learned to be discreet.

"Merry Christmas,'' Anna called back in a voice that sounded much more cheerful than before.

"How did you know your father's telephone number?'' Meg asked Anna the minute they were out of the office. She was acutely conscious of Kon at her elbow opening doors for them.

"I told Ms. Morley that Daddy lives in Hannibal and I said his name was Gary Johnson—like he told us. She called him for me.''

To Meg's chagrin, Kon sent her a withering glance. "Our daughter is very bright and resourceful,'' he began in Russian. "If you're not careful, your paranoia is going to alienate her.''

His rebuke made Meg feel small and mean. And guilty, of course, because she was always prepared to think the very worst of him. She realized that, ironically enough, the incident verified at least part of his story, which put him at a moral advantage. That call had proved he was in the phone book, that he had been established for some time.

"Can we go home now? I didn't get to hold Prince yesterday and he misses me."

"I'll take care of him for you, Anochka." Kon had spoken before Meg could manage a word. She felt her world disintegrating a little more—Anna no longer considered their apartment home.

Perhaps Kon noticed that the blood had drained from her face. When he opened the passenger door of Meg's car for Anna, he said, "Right now both you and your mother need to get to bed."

Anna stared up at her with concern. "Are you sick, Mommy?"

"No," Meg hastened to reassure her as Kon fastened the seat belt. "I'm just a little tired."

"Is Daddy coming with us?"

"That's up to your mother," he inserted smoothly, throwing the onus on Meg, who continued to be the villain in this cleverly orchestrated piece.

"Don't go away, Daddy!" Anna started to cry again, deep, heaving sobs that poured from her soul and washed her cheeks in tears. Meg felt suddenly, completely, helpless.

She slumped against the car door, all the fight gone out of her. She didn't have the strength to battle Kon and her daughter, too. In a dull voice she said, "Your father can follow us home in his car if he wants."

Like magic Anna's tears subsided.

Meg expected to see a triumphant expression on Kon's face as he walked her around to the driver's side of the car.

But as he opened the door for her, a brief glint of what looked like pain darkened the blue of his eyes. It fragmented her emotions even more because she had to wonder if he could summon emotion like that at will—just for effect.

"I'll be right behind you, Anochka."

"D-do you p-promise?" Anna's halting question ended on something between a cough and a hiccup.

Meg's hands curled tightly around the steering wheel. She didn't recognize her daughter when Anna behaved like this, when she became this anxiety-ridden child who constantly feared her father would disappear from her life. Her normally trusting and vivacious personality had undergone a complete change.

Apparently Kon was not immune to Anna's fragile condition, either; he unexpectly opened the back door and got into the car. "I'll ride with you and pick up my car later."

Before Meg could fathom it, Anna had unfastened her seat belt and climbed into the back with Kon, flinging her arms around his neck. Meg could see them through the rearview mirror, and her heart seemed to expand with something that felt like pain as she watched the tender way Kon was comforting their daughter. He rocked her back and forth in his strong arms, whispering endearments.

And that was when it came to her. He *loved* Anna.

Emotion like that *couldn't* be faked. Some sixth sense told her that in his own way he adored his little Anochka as much as Meg did. And Anna loved him back just as fiercely. If Meg had held on to the vain hope that this was a passing phase from which Anna would recover once Kon was out of sight, she'd better let go of it now.

The drive back to the apartment was silent, with Meg deep in her own thoughts. When she pulled into her parking spot and got out of the car, she saw that Anna had fallen asleep with her tearstained face half-buried in Kon's neck. The night before, Anna had cried for hours before she'd passed out from exhaustion.

He maneuvered himself and Anna from the back seat without disturbing her and followed Meg into the building.

There were few people around this time of day, for which Meg was thankful. She opened the door of the apartment, and Kon carried Anna to her bedroom. Meg trailed behind them and stood in the doorway, watching the deft way he discarded Anna's parka and shoes and tucked her into bed. He lightly caressed her cheek with the knuckles of one hand. Then abruptly, he straightened and started toward Meg, his expression inscrutable.

A little frightened of the tension between them, she hurried into the living room, feeling far too susceptible to his presence. She wondered if she was on the verge of an emotional breakdown.

"We can be married the day after tomorrow and never have a recurrence of what happened today. But if you're too selfish to think of Anna's best interests, then be warned that I do intend to have a relationship with her."

"What about *my* best interests?" She jerked around, her ash-blond hair and pleated black wool skirt swinging.

He studied her features, the hectic color in her cheeks, her glittering gray eyes, the curves beneath her oyster-colored silk blouse. "You're not in love with anyone else."

"That's beside the point," she lashed out.

"It *is* the point, Meggie. If you'd stayed in Russia, we'd be married today and Anna could easily have a sister or brother by now."

"You're talking about a period of time that's come and gone. I was a totally different human being then! We couldn't possibly have worked anything out because you were already married—to your country. And…and I was afraid." Her breath quickened with the force of her emotions.

"I defected," came the swift rejoinder. "Surely that should tell you something."

"Why?" she cried. "*Why* did you defect? It doesn't make sense for a man in your position. And please don't insult my intelligence by telling me you were overcome with love for me!"

His dark brows furrowed. "I may have been a government

agent, but I'm still a man, Meggie. One, moreover, who became enamored of a young American woman to the point that I took many dangerous chances, many risks, to spend time with you. When you left, I...contracted a disease.''

CHAPTER SEVEN

A DISEASE?

Meg's anxious gaze darted to his. "D-did you become ill?" she whispered, her hand going to her throat, where she was positive he could see the hammering of her pulse.

He shifted his weight. "It's a term used by agents to refer to burnout. I'd never had a sick day in my life, and suddenly I went into a depression that left me emotionally ill for months. I lost weight, suffered from insomnia and battled a restlessness I'd never known before.

"As I once told you, there'd been a few other women in the past, mostly other agents working on assignments under me. One relationship lasted a little longer than the rest, but I was always able to move on without becoming emotionally involved."

She hadn't known about the relationship that had gone on longer. How *much* longer? Had he asked that woman to marry him, too? A shaft of pure, unadulterated jealousy left her feeling weak and vulnerable. Until he added, "For some inexplicable reason, it wasn't that easy to walk away from you.

"A comrade suggested I take a leave of absence and go on vacation. So I went to the Urals to do some climbing and fishing. But what should have been a two-week retreat lasted all of two days, and I returned to my post because this restlessness was eating me alive.

"I plunged into my work with such ferocity even my peers tended to stay away from me. But by then I was diagnosed as suffering from severe clinical depression and, oddly enough, the only pleasure I found in life was to follow your movements—through another agent living in the United States.''

Meg rubbed her arms, suddenly chilled to the bone, though in reality the apartment was pleasantly warm.

"On one particularly bleak day, the agent telephoned me to say that the beautiful Meg Roberts was pregnant.''

He said nothing further for a long moment, apparently lost in recollection. Then he resumed, speaking in a low, rapid voice.

"No one could have been more surprised than I, because I'd taken precautions against that happening.'' His eyes narrowed on her mouth. "Since I gave you no opportunity to be with another man while in Russia, and since I had irrefutable proof that you hadn't been with another man after leaving the country, I knew you were pregnant with *my* child.''

She bowed her head to avoid the possessiveness in his eyes.

"The knowledge that a baby we'd made together was growing inside you took hold of me. It was as if I were there with you, sharing this miraculous experience, and it brought me out of the wretched blackness that had been engulfing me daily.

"When the agent supplied me with a picture of Anna taken while she was still in the hospital nursery, I almost lost my mind. I couldn't be there to hold her, to inspect her fingers and toes, to kiss her soft skin and watch her nurse at your breast. That was the moment I decided to defect.''

"Kon...''

"At that point the government was in turmoil, and detente was looking like a real possibility. The changes reshaping my country made me take a long, hard look at my personal life, at my future. All those years I'd served the KGB and that was the only life I'd known.

"But Anna's birth forced me to ask questions about what I wanted for myself." He paced the floor, then came to an abrupt halt. "Don't be deceived by what I'm telling you, Meggie. Russia will always have a claim on my soul. I've been given the finest education in the world, the best lodgings, exceptional pay, diversion when I needed it. And above all, Russia is my homeland. But I found myself wishing that I *belonged* to someone and that someone belonged to me."

He picked up her family photographs from an end table by the couch and studied them for a while. "I don't even know if my parents and sister are still alive. I know nothing about them. They believe I'm dead because this is what they were told thirty years ago. That part is finished."

He put the pictures back and flicked her an indecipherable glance. "I need my daughter. Being with her for the last two days has already filled part of that void in my life."

She sucked in her breath. "If that's how you felt, why didn't you approach me as soon as you arrived in the States? We could have worked out visitation." When she thought of the years that had already gone by...

"When I got out of Russia, I gave your government classified information. The normal procedure was for me to go into hiding. Eventually I was set up with a new identity.

"Since then, the international picture has changed, and the threat isn't the same anymore. But because I know how certain factions of the old guard still think, how the Party mind still works, and because I wanted to make absolutely certain that you and Anna remained unharmed, I waited until now to approach you."

He eyed her steadily. "It was a risk to stay away so long knowing that at any time you could become involved with another man and get married, providing Anna with a stepfather. But it was a risk I had to take because I knew that one day, one way or another, I'd eventually have a relationship with her—and, I hoped, with you."

He gazed at her, a dark, brooding look on his face. "That

day is here,'' he said quietly. "But the choice is yours—do we work out a visitation system, when Anna's already traumatized by everything that's happened? Or do we get married and give her her rightful father and mother?

"In a world where the traditional family unit seems to be disappearing, we're in a position to give her the stability millions of children are denied. The stability I was denied," he added hoarsely.

Maybe she was a gullible fool, but Meg suddenly had the intense conviction that he'd been speaking the truth. Probably because he was so open about telling her that his bond to Russia would never be broken....

"I won't, you know," he murmured, voicing her fears about kidnapping aloud. "Perhaps marrying me is the only way to erase this irrational idea you have that I'm going to take Anna away."

"But you love Russia. I know you do!"

"Yes, but I can't go back, Meggie. My life is here with you. I earn my living at home and I keep a low profile. As my wife, you won't have to work unless you choose. We'll be together twenty-four hours a day. It's what we both wanted before you left Russia." In a low voice he added, "But whether or not you sleep in my bed will be up to you. How does that sound?"

How *did* it sound?

Terrifying, her heart cried. How could she live in the same house with him, year in and year out, wanting him in all the ways a woman wanted a man, yet always feeling afraid he would miss his country, his old life? He said *now* that he couldn't go back, that it was over, but what if he changed his mind? It was all too easy to see how that might happen.

"It's a little matter called trust, Meggie. A rare quality our daughter seems to have in abundance. Apparently she didn't inherit it from you."

Meg reeled from his bitter words. Ignoring her, he took a few strides to the kitchen and reached for the phone.

"Who are you calling?" Meg asked in confusion.

In even tones he said, "I'm simply phoning for a taxi. I need to be driven to my car. The school called me before I could feed and water the dogs. I need to get back to them."

"But if you're not here when Anna w—"

"As I said," he broke in with that arrogant hauteur left over from his KGB days, "visitation has its flaws when we try to function as parents from two separate households." He started punching the buttons.

When she thought of the state Anna would be in when she found him gone, Meg realized she couldn't go through that kind of emotional turmoil again. In a panic she cried, "Wait!"

A tense silence stretched between them. Kon still held the receiver in his hand. "If you're offering to drive me over to Anna's school, it isn't necessary. She needs the sleep and there's no one to mind her." He finished punching the last two numbers.

Her head reared back. "Damn you! You know that isn't what I meant!"

She watched him hang up the receiver, and even from a distance, she could see the glimmer of satisfaction on his face. She despised him for it.

"From the moment you hijacked us at the ballet, you knew you'd win. It was just a matter of time. An agent never accepts losing."

He frowned. "This isn't about agents or ideologies. This is no game, Meggie. I'm fighting for my life, for you and Anna. Without you, I have no future."

His voice throbbed with naked emotion, and it tore her apart. His words rang with undeniable conviction, bypassing logic to speak to her soul, successfully destroying the last fragile barrier she'd raised between them.

"AND SO, BY THE POWER vested in me, I now pronounce you husband and wife, legally and lawfully wedded from this moment on. What God has joined together, let no man put asunder. You may now kiss the bride.''

Had it been only two days since she'd agreed to marry him?

From the time Kon had slipped the solitaire diamond ring and wedding band on Meg's finger, he'd kept hold of her hand. As the final words of the ceremony were pronounced, his grip tightened possessively.

The soft, pale pink chiffon of her calf-length wedding dress flattered her coloring, but she was positive Kon could detect every fluttering heartbeat through the thin material. Meg refrained from looking at him, fearing that she'd see a gloating look in his eyes, a look of victory.

In fact, from the time she'd entered Kon's living room with Anna for the late-afternoon ceremony and had acknowledged Judge Lundquist and the Bowmans—whom she'd learned were not husband and wife, having adopted the fictitious name as part of their cover—she had ignored her husband-to-be. Now she closed her eyes as she turned to him for the ritual kiss.

But when she felt his warm mouth unexpectedly brush the backs of both her hands instead of her lips, her eyes flew open in astonishment. She'd never heard of a groom kissing the bride's hands before and wondered if it could be some kind of Russian wedding custom.

Until he suddenly lifted his dark head and his scorching blue eyes trapped her confused gaze. ''Finally!'' His triumphant whisper told her he'd been aware of her refusal to look at him until now. Before she could react to his subterfuge, his mouth captured hers and he took full advantage, deepening their kiss, demanding a response that stirred her senses in spite of her attempt to remain unmoved.

''It's time for my kiss, Daddy,'' Anna demanded, pulling at his sleeve. The others chuckled quietly.

Meg was shocked back to reality for an instant when Kon broke their kiss. He scooped Anna from the floor and embraced them both, first kissing his daughter's cheeks, then returning to Meg's unsuspecting mouth, which he kissed so thoroughly she was in danger of forgetting there were other people in the room. Not only that, it seemed Walter Bowman had been filming the proceedings with a camcorder, a revelation that made her flush with embarrassment.

The ringing of the telephone, followed by Lacey Bowman's announcement that Senator Strickland was calling to congratulate them, brought Meg's senses under some semblance of control. She pulled away from Kon on unsteady legs, then bowed her head for a moment, ostensibly to rearrange Anna's crushed nosegay, but actually to take a few steadying breaths. After that, she straightened the collar of her daughter's taffeta dress. Finally she followed Kon into the study to speak to the senator.

The older man did most of the talking, which was just as well, because Meg was so bemused by her new status as Kon's wife she couldn't talk with any coherence. Especially not when Kon's arm slipped around her waist and he held her pressed against his side as if she belonged there.

Anna's voice calling them gave her the excuse to break away from Kon's grip while he finished the conversation with the senator. He seemed reluctant to release her, though, and she felt his gaze on her retreating back as she escaped.

"What is it, honey?" she asked as she hurried into the living room, trying to steady her breathing.

"Look!" Anna squealed happily. "It's Prince Marzipan!"

At first Meg thought she was talking about the puppy. Then her attention was drawn to a large nutcracker—almost two feet high—that her daughter had lifted from a box sitting on the coffee table, the red and green wrapping paper in shambles.

"An early Christmas present from Walt and me," Lacey Bowman murmured in an aside. "Since she loved the ballet, we thought she might like one as a memento."

"See, Mommy?" Anna rushed over to show it to Meg,

her face glowing with joy. ''He looks like Daddy! And his mouth opens and closes! Watch!'' She took hold of the handle and worked the jaw of the beautifully hand-crafted nutcracker. Meg suspected it had been carved and painted in Russia, rather than Germany. The detailing of the soldier's cossack hat and uniform was unmistakable.

By now Kon had reentered the living room and come to stand behind his daughter, placing his hands on her shoulders. When Meg sensed his nearness, she raised her head and gasped softly at the similarity between the dark hair and blue eyes of the toy soldier and Kon's own striking coloring. The contrast of his olive complexion against the midnight blue suit and white shirt was almost dazzling.

He stood tall like the nutcracker, the personification of a dark and dashing Russian prince. Meg's heart took up its crazy thumping and she could easily imagine him in a cossack uniform and sable hat, a handsome, impossibly romantic male figure astride his horse.

Her husband.

She swallowed hard and turned a flushed face to the judge, who winked at her, then proposed a toast to the happy family. Meg drank the champagne Lacey served each of them. Kon declined his drink to pick up Anna—nosegay, nutcracker and all. Teasingly, he helped her to a champagne glass of cranberry juice so she could feel part of the celebration.

Despite Meg's attempt to harden her heart against Kon, his devotion to their daughter pierced her armor. She couldn't deny that, though Anna had always been a happy child, Kon's appearance in their lives had added another dimension of loving; even in the short time that had elapsed, his presence had boosted Anna's confidence and made her feel that much more secure.

On Monday evening, when she'd awakened from a much-needed sleep to learn that her mommy had decided to marry her daddy after all, Anna's almost hysterical reaction to everything Meg did or didn't do immediately disappeared.

Instead, an inner glow seemed to radiate from her, and she was at peace again. She cooperated willingly with all the packing and work involved in moving an entire household to a new town. Meg noticed that their impending marriage had produced such a calming effect on Anna the difference in her behavior was like night and day.

Everyone at the wedding could see how delighted she was with her daddy, and Walt kept the camcorder on Anna. Right now she was discussing the merits of her new nutcracker with Kon, both of them hamming it up a bit for the video. Lacey finally told Walter to stop taping and join them in a final congratulatory drink. Meg felt too nervous to swallow more than a few mouthfuls of champagne.

Before the ceremony, she'd dreaded the arrival of Walt and Lacey, who'd been in league with Kon from the beginning. But now that they'd finished their toast and were making plans to leave, Meg found she'd actually enjoyed their undemanding company and special kindness to Anna, and she didn't want them to go—for once they did she'd be alone with Kon. Her husband—who posed more of a personal danger to her peace of mind than ever before.

Anna hugged Lacey and thanked her for the nutcracker before she and Walt left the house in a flurry of goodbyes and Christmas wishes.

Kon shut the door behind them, then turned around, his glance sweeping over Meg's face and body. It reminded her of the many times in Russia when his gaze had said he could hardly wait to get her alone. That look had always left her shaken and trembling, and she felt no different now. Finally, to her relief, he turned to his daughter.

"Now that the wedding is over and we are an official family, I thought we'd celebrate someplace exciting."

Anna's eyes worshiped him. "Where are we going, Daddy?"

"With your mother's approval, I'd like to take us to dinner at the Molly Brown Theater to watch the Christmas show.

There'll be singing and dancing and all your favorite Mark Twain characters. How does that sound?''

While Anna pleaded for her mother's acquiesence, he waited for Meg's reaction. The show catered to families with small children, and there would be other people around to act as a buffer, so Meg couldn't think of a better way to fill the next few hours. "I—I think that sounds lovely."

Kon appeared pleased by her agreement and glanced quickly at his watch. "We need to leave now if we're going to be on time."

"I'll find my coat." Anna dashed from the room and Meg hurried into the hall to catch up with her. She couldn't tolerate being alone in the same room with Kon while she was still trying to forget the taste and feel of his mouth, the passion he evoked whenever he touched her.

Over the past few days she'd managed to cope with his presence, not only because there'd been so much to do—dresses to buy and arrangements to make for the move—but because Anna and Melanie were constantly around, acting as unofficial chaperons.

And, of course, Anna had told everybody in the apartment complex about the wedding, which had prompted a number of people, including Melanie's family, the Garretts and Mrs. Rosen, to drop by with fruitcake and cookies and offer their congratulations.

Kon, who looked upon his daughter with fatherly pride whenever she played her violin for him, had taken an instant liking to Anna's teacher. He'd assured Mrs. Rosen that he'd drive Anna into St. Louis every week so she wouldn't miss her lessons. He'd also promised Anna they'd go early enough for her to spend time with Melanie. Naturally that won Melanie's overwhelming approval and devotion.

In fact, she'd spent most of Tuesday staring at Kon, following him around, plying him with questions. He answered them with infinite tolerance and good-natured humor while he dismantled the aquarium, taking care to put the fish in jars Anna had filled with water for the transfer to Hannibal.

Meg knew Anna would miss her friend, but she could tell it was going to be much more of a wrench for Melanie. The movers would be coming after Christmas to load their belongings; by New Year's, Meg and Anna would have left the complex for good.

In an effort to smooth the transition for both girls, she'd invited Melanie to come the following weekend for a sleepover. That had naturally initiated a whole new series of conversations and plans and made the move less upsetting.

Persuaded by both Kon and Anna, Meg had resigned from her job without giving the usual two-week notice; she hoped that because business was slow during the Christmas holidays, her boss wasn't too angry with her.

Inevitably Ted had heard about Meg's impending marriage to Anna's natural father, and he called her to find out what was going on. Unfortunately Kon happened to answer the phone first, telling Ted she was too busy to talk and would call him back after they'd returned from their honeymoon.

Meg had no intention of going on a honeymoon with Kon and could just imagine Ted's reaction to that inflammatory piece of news. She decided that in a few days she'd write him a note explaining the situation. He was a nice person, and Kon had no right to intentionally offend him.

"Cold?" his deep voice murmured near her ear, startling her out of her reverie. She hadn't realized Kon had followed her and Anna into the hall. "Maybe this will warm you." His nearness made her knees go weak. Meg turned around to see Kon holding up an elegant black cashmere coat lined in black satin. "Try it on, Meggie."

As if in a trance, she put her arms into the sleeves and tied the belt around her slender waist.

"Mommy, you look *beautiful*."

"She does, doesn't she, Anochka," Kon murmured as he shrugged into a formal, dark blue topcoat. He gazed openly at Meg's ash-blond hair gleaming silvery gold against the soft black of the coat. At the question in her eyes, he smiled. "Consider it an early Christmas present."

"Thank you," she whispered, and averted her head, filled with a strange, terrible pain. Kon had decided to defect because of the many problems relating to his work in the KGB, but mostly because of Anna. And in order to have his daughter, he had to take Meg, too.

Meg didn't deceive herself. After all these years, Kon *couldn't* still be in love with her. Love had to be nurtured, and they'd been apart too many years. She had no doubt he'd told her that he hadn't been involved with another woman to spare her feelings.

He could shower her with gifts and convincingly act the lover, but it was for one reason only—she was the mother of his child. Anna was the key. He would never have come to Missouri to marry her otherwise.

Because of the way they'd once felt about each other, it was all too easy for Kon to claim that his love for her had never died, that it was too powerful and intense to die.

The unpalatable truth was that any woman who happened to be his child's mother would be the recipient of Kon's generosity. He'd waited six years before making his appearance; he'd even confessed that he'd taken the risk that she'd be married by the time he deemed it safe to present himself. That hardly sounded like a man deeply and passionately in love.

She thought back on his admissions about the other women in his life, agents working under him. Apparently none of them had gotten pregnant, and she supposed that was why he'd felt nothing lasting, why he hadn't married during all those years in the KGB.

Little did she realize when she first went to bed with him in that cottage seven years ago, her life would be irrevocably changed, that her chance to find love with a typical American man—the kind of love her mother had found with her father—would pass her by.

"Pretend to have a good time for Anna's sake, will you? It is our wedding day, after all." He spoke in a low, brusque tone meant for her ears alone as they left the dogs guarding the house and went out through the back door.

The change in his demeanor shocked her into realizing that her thoughts had been visible enough for him to read. For Anna's sake she made a mental note to avoid alienating him further.

She could tell he was still attempting to suppress his anger as he opened the front passenger door of his car. It was a Buick, the kind of car an American man named Gary Johnson might drive. Meg couldn't help but wonder what kind of car Kon would have chosen if he hadn't been forced to exist as this invented persona.

Anna's happy chatter coming from the back seat made the uncomfortable silence between the two of them even more marked. Thankfully, Meg noted that their daughter seemed oblivious to any undercurrents as they drove on streets relatively free of snow to the dinner theater situated near the riverboat landing. Kon let them out in front, then found a parking spot and joined them.

After the numbing cold outside, the building felt warm and inviting. It also looked filled to capacity, but the hostess, dressed in an 1850s' period costume, showed them to a table Kon had reserved. Located on the first level, it allowed Anna an unimpeded view of the stage show.

The next few hours flew by as they ate a delicious dinner and sat entertained by one of the actors, who did a wonderful impersonation of Mark Twain. A professionally staged musical production presented songs of the '20s through the '50s and ended with some renditions of Mississippi river music that enchanted Anna.

Meg would have loved it if she'd been here with anyone but her husband, on any day but her wedding day. Kon lounged, apparently relaxed in his seat at her side and appeared to be enjoying the performance. But when the house lights dimmed for the final act and she dared a glance at him, she saw a haunted, faraway look that hardened his features and told her he was seeing something else, thinking of another time, another place.

Perhaps for the first time since the ballet, Meg truly understood how much he must miss his country, how much he'd given up to be with his daughter.

Six years was probably an eternity to a man deprived of Russia's beautiful language and age-old culture. How lonely he must be for people like himself, his compatriots. How could he stand to live here when he was a product of a fabulous and colorful history that had produced the czars and contributed so much to world culture—to literature, music, dance and theater?

Meg had fallen in love with his country. She knew better than most how much he must be yearning for the woods and mountains of his homeland. Seven years ago he'd spent many, many hours driving Meg through rural villages and long mountain roads. Unless she specifically asked that he take her to a café or a museum, he had always headed for the countryside.

It was probably natural, since his first recollections of childhood were of Siberia, of frozen tundra in winter and wildflower meadows in summer. His home had probably been little more than a mountain hut, where life had been hard, maybe even primitive, but where there had been love....

"Tears, Meggie?" Kon mocked in quiet menace as he unexpectedly turned his head and caught her staring. "Have you suddenly realized how much of a prisoner you are now that you're legally tied to me? Are you thinking that the walls of your new home are no different from the walls of that jail cell in Moscow?"

Kon was so far off the mark she was stunned. She lowered

her head to search for a clean napkin so she could wipe her eyes before Anna noticed anything was wrong.

"Gary?" A vibrant female voice spoke up just as the houselights went back on. Both Meg's and Anna's heads swiveled around as a tall, curvaceous brunette still in costume put her arms around Kon's neck and lowered her face to his. "I thought it was you. No other man that gorgeous has ever sat in this audience before."

"Sammi."

Meg was shocked that the beautiful woman's name came so easily to Kon's lips. Not only that, the two of them were so familiar with each other he actually caressed her cheek with his lips before getting to his feet.

With his arm around the actress's waist, he gazed down at Meg. She was so shattered by feelings of jealousy she could hardly move—and Kon knew it! She could tell by the way his eyes glittered. "Sammi Raynes, meet my wife, Meg, and our daughter, Anna."

Meg could tell the woman was sizing them up, trying to figure out how Kon could have a daughter this old.

"You mean you went and got married on me while I was on tour?" she cried, extending a friendly hand. "You heartbreaker!" Then she turned to Meg once more. "How do you like that? This character told me he'd be waiting for me when I got back. Your marriage happened awfully fast, didn't it?"

"Actually, K—Gary and I have known each other for a long time." Meg caught herself barely in time.

The woman's eyes flicked back to Kon. "You're a deep one, you know that?"

She was probably much closer to Kon's age than Meg was. She'd clearly had more than a casual interest in him and was putting up a heroic front. But Meg had no doubt that the actress's face had paled beneath all her stage makeup.

Had Kon been sleeping with her? And for how long?

Meg had been so focused on her own problems and fears she hadn't given any real thought to the women Kon might have met *after* defecting. Just as she'd surmised earlier, his statement that there'd been no other women since Meg had been another little fabrication, another part of his strategy. Kon wasn't the celibate type and had never pretended to be. Naturally he would indulge himself when the opportunity arose. Few women could remain immune to his virile looks and charm, as no one knew better than Meg.

Dear God, she was still in love with him. She always would be.

The woman called Sammi walked around to Anna's side. "Did you like the show, honey?"

Anna nodded. "We came here 'cause my mommy and daddy got married today."

"Today? Is that why you're wearing such a pretty dress?" When Anna nodded again, she looked at Kon for confirmation.

"That's right."

"Well, congratulations. If I'd known that before the show started, I would have asked the director to announce it. Here. Have a lollipop." She pulled one from her pocket and handed it to Anna, who asked her parents if it was all right before she accepted it.

A warm, genuine smile lit Kon's features as he smiled at the actress, and something unpleasant twisted inside Meg. She'd never seen Kon smile at *her* in quite that way, not even during those carefree days in St. Petersburg when they were alone and away from prying eyes, where he could be himself.

"Thanks, Sammi. It's always good to see you," he murmured.

"The feeling is entirely mutual."

She broke eye contact with Kon, then cast a speculative glance at Meg. "You're a lucky woman. Take good care of this marvelous man. There's no one to compare to him."

She was right, Meg acknowledged, and her pain deepened. How did Sammi know so much about him? It seemed that

Kon had allowed this particular woman to see a side of him he'd never shown Meg.

Kon gave her a final hug. "One day soon we'll invite you for dinner."

"I have a new puppy you can hold," Anna offered, easily managing to talk around the lollipop still in her mouth.

"A new puppy, too? There's so much excitement at your house, I bet you can hardly get to sleep at night."

Anna giggled and Meg warmed to the woman in spite of her own distress. "I enjoyed the show very much, Ms. Raynes. We all did."

The actress smiled her thanks and moved away. Kon walked some distance with her while they talked in private. As Meg stared at their dark heads bent toward each other, a horrible envy rose up in her. Needing to expend her nervous energy, she jumped up from the table and helped Anna with her coat before slipping on her own. Ready to face the cold, they had started making their way through the crowd when Kon intercepted them.

Meg felt his eyes on her, trying to draw her gaze, but she couldn't look at him. She waited as he picked up Anna, then followed them out of the theater to the car. She made sure she didn't walk close enough for him to touch her.

"Are we going to get our Christmas tree now?" Anna asked cheerfully.

"I think we've done enough for one day, Anochka. How about tomorrow morning, after you've had a good night's sleep and a hot breakfast?"

"Okay. Who was that lady, Daddy? I saw you kiss her."

"She's a good friend."

"Do you love her, too?"

Unconsciously Meg held her breath, waiting for his answer.

"If you mean, do I love her the way I love you and your mommy, no."

"Does she love you?"

Kon crushed her in his arms. "There are all kinds of love, Anna. I met her several years ago when her little boy got lost during a family picnic. The whole town ended up looking for him. I happened to be the one who finally found him, asleep under some bushes near the Mark Twain Cave."

Meg's heart lurched in her chest.

"What's his name?" Anna persisted.

"Brad."

"How old is he?"

"Eight."

"Doesn't he have a daddy?"

"Yes, although his daddy doesn't live with them."

"How come *you* found him?"

"I was lucky."

Anna's arms tightened around Kon's neck. "I'm glad you're my daddy."

"So am I," he whispered.

So am I, Meg's heart echoed wildly.

CHAPTER EIGHT

WHEN THEY REACHED the house, Anna cuddled her puppy, then climbed the stairs to get ready for bed. Kon said that as soon as he'd taken care of the dogs and turned out the lights, he'd be up to kiss her good-night.

But the minute her curly head touched the pillow, Anna's eyes closed and she fell sound asleep, hugging the nutcracker in her arms.

Meg hung the beautiful party dress in the closet and tidied the room. When she felt it was safe, she carefully removed the nutcracker from Anna's now-slack grip and put it on the white French-provincial dresser. It matched the canopied bed and night table. The room was a fairyland of pink and white eyelet, everything a little girl's heart could desire.

After Christmas, when the movers delivered the belongings from the apartment to Kon's house, the room would be filled with all of Anna's things, including the rest of her dolls. So far, the only large item they'd brought with them was the aquarium, which Kon had immediately set up under Anna's supervision.

Meg wandered over to the tank and watched the fish, remembering the day she'd purchased the aquarium, never dreaming where it would finally end up. Since she knew Anna needed some kind of pet and animals were forbidden in the apartment building, fish had seemed a good solution.

Now her daughter had three dogs to love. And a father who returned all the love she gave him, yet could be firm with her when the occasion warranted. At first Meg had been afraid he would spoil Anna, but time was proving her wrong. He was very much in charge of their daughter, not the other way around.

Was it all a sham? Or could she dare believe that Kon would never have taken Anna away from her, even if they *hadn't* married?

"Meggie?"

There was a husky timbre in his voice that made her tremble. She lifted her head to see Kon's dark shape in the doorway.

"Yes?"

"Now that Anna's asleep, I'd like some attention."

Her fingers clung to the edge of the tank. "I—I'm coming."

Her mouth went completely dry as she followed him out to the hallway and shut the door. She noticed with alarm that he'd changed out of his clothes and was dressed in a blue-and-black-striped velour robe. She wondered, aroused yet half-ashamed, if he wore anything underneath.

It didn't matter that this same man had made love to her seven years ago. He was still an enigma to her, more now than ever. A virtual stranger. She wanted to trust him, but it was so hard....

"Before the wedding I told you the choice was yours to sleep in my bed or not."

Her nails cut into her palms. "But now that we're married, you've decided to do what you want, forget the promise you made."

"In a manner of speaking, yes. I want you in my bed, Meggie. I won't make love to you if you don't want me to, but I need you lying there next to me. Don't deny me that, *mayah labof.*"

"I'm not your darling," she gasped, so breathless she felt dizzy.

"You are. You always will be."

"No more lies, Kon. Please God, no more lies," she

begged, the tears streaming from her eyes. "You said you wanted a relationship with Anna, and now you have it. Isn't that enough?"

"I wish I could say it was. But it isn't." His voice trailed off.

"And if I refuse?"

"Don't. I've waited too long."

"So now that you have me where you want me, you're flinging the mask away. Is that it?"

"There was never any mask," he said calmly, his hands in his pockets. "I begged you to marry me before you left Russia. I asked you to marry me as soon as I saw you at the ballet. You're my wife now. There's nothing to keep us apart."

"Nothing except the fact that I don't even know who you are," she half sobbed. "I don't know the first thing about you. I've never met your family. In Russia you were a highly placed, feared KGB agent, and I'll never know if our affair was part of a secret plan or not. You said your name was Konstantin Rudenko. Is that the name your parents gave you or one the KGB made up?"

Her hysteria had reached a momentum, and she couldn't stop herself. "In my country you pretend to be an ordinary American citizen named Gary Johnson. He lives in a dream house, drives a Buick and behaves like Mr. Niceguy to his unsuspecting community. How can I know the real you? Have I ever met him? Where did the child, the teenager, the young man go? Or were they ever allowed to exist? *Who are you?*" Her frantic voice broke.

His face darkened and he shook his head. "I don't know, Meggie. It's why I came for you. To find out."

The admission seemed to come from someplace deep within him, and it was the last answer she'd expected. It threw her into such confusion she didn't know how to react or what to say. It drove her to the guest room, between his bedroom and Anna's. She'd slept there the night before, tossing and turning as she anticipated her wedding day with alternating feelings of excitement and dread.

Kon stood in the doorway. "Can we start finding our answers in bed? That's where we once communicated without any problems—one man and one woman. Can we go from there?" He grasped the doorjamb as if for support. "I swear I won't touch you, Meggie, if that's the way it has to be. Only lie with me tonight." His voice throbbed with raw longing.

"After this many years' separation—" he switched to Russian so easily Meg was scarcely aware of it "—let me have the satisfaction of at least looking at you throughout the night, smelling the flowery scent of your hair, knowing you're within arm's reach. I'm begging you, Meggie."

Speaking to her in his native tongue, in that particular tone of voice, tore down her last, pathetic defense. It brought back too many memories, memories that suffocated her with their sweetness.

Meg grabbed a nightgown from the dresser and hurried into the bathroom to change. Her heart pounded at every pulse point until she thought it might explode. This vulnerable, pleading side of Kon had left her utterly vulnerable, too.

He was still standing in the doorway when she came back into the room. He followed her with his eyes as she hung her wedding dress in the closet.

The short walk to the bed felt like a hundred miles. When she got under the covers, Kon turned off the light and moved toward her.

"Meggie?" he whispered.

"I—I don't think—"

"If I stay with you tonight," he interrupted her, "then you don't have to be afraid I'll kidnap Anna. That is what you're terrified of, isn't it?"

No, her heart cried. *I'm afraid of something much worse. I'm afraid you'll never love me the way I love you.*

The mattress dipped as he slid beneath the covers, and though their bodies didn't touch, she could feel his warmth and smell the soap that lingered on his skin. She had no idea if he'd disrobed and wished her mind couldn't see what the darkness blotted out.

"Talk to me, *mayah labof.*" His low, velvety voice reached out to her like a soft night wind. "Tell me how long it took you to forget me after you left Russian soil. Had some other man fallen in love with you by the time your plane landed?"

Oh, Kon. She smothered her groan in the pillow and hugged the side of the bed.

"I watched your plane until it disappeared in the clouds, then drove back to the cottage like a demon possessed and drank enough vodka to send myself into oblivion. Or so I thought. But nothing was strong enough to wipe out your fragrance on the sheets and pillows. Dear God, Meggie—the emptiness after everything we'd shared... I didn't particularly care if I lived or died."

"Do you think I felt any different?" she blurted. Whether he was still acting a part or not, his words unlocked memories and they came flooding back with an intensity so fresh she felt as if she were reliving the nightmare. "I kept thinking that if the plane crashed, it didn't matter, which shows you the instability of my state of mind, considering that there were hundreds of other people on that flight.

"I had no one to go home to, and I'd left my heart behind. At one point during the trip home, I even found myself wishing I was dead because I couldn't bear to imagine you with another lover, particularly one of your beautiful, dark-haired Russian women. I always saw them staring at you with hungry eyes whenever we went out in public."

"Meggie!"

"They did, Kon, and you know it, so don't try to deny it. I had no idea I could be that jealous."

A heavy sigh escaped. "Think what you will, but I had

eyes only for the exquisite blond creature who got off that plane in Moscow and caused complete havoc with my comrades as she passed through control. Every agent there would have given six months' pay for the privilege of being assigned to you. When they found out you were under my supervision, I acquired enemies.''

If any other man had said that to her, Meg would have scoffed. Instead, she shuddered. He was probably exaggerating but...how would she ever know?

"Thank God your plane didn't crash," he murmured. "Tell me what exactly happened when you arrived back in the States. What you did. How you felt."

Why did he ask these questions when he already knew the answers?

Her eyes closed tightly as if to ward off the pain. By the time she'd passed through customs and the CIA had finished with her, allowing her to go free, she'd walked away feeling as if she'd been skinned alive and her heart torn from her body.

"When the plane landed in New York, I was singled out from the others and taken to a place for a grueling, two-day debriefing."

She heard his sharp intake of breath. "Because of me," he said. "Because they knew of our association."

"Yes."

"And that's when you were warned off for good."

"Yes." Frantically wiping tears from her cheeks, she said, "Up until they told me that I'd been targeted specifically by you, I had every intention of saving my money and returning to Moscow the following summer to be with you."

"Now you know why I told you never to come back," he muttered fiercely.

"It...it was a good thing I had so much to do after they released me, or I would have gone mad remembering my aunt's warnings. As it was, I had trouble sleeping and lost weight. I suppose what saved me was the necessity of finding an apartment and getting things out of storage. And, of course, looking for a job.''

"You didn't go back to teaching."

"No. I wanted nothing to do with anything that could remind me of you. So I took the first job that offered decent pay.''

"Strong Motors?"

"Yes.''

"Tell me about the pregnancy. When did you first discover our baby was growing inside you?''

Taking a steadying breath, she said, "As I told you, food didn't interest me and I slept poorly. When a month passed and my condition seemed to get worse because I felt tired all the time, my friend at work urged me to see a doctor.

"I fought against taking her advice, but then I started to be sick to my stomach in the mornings and realized something was wrong. So I consulted my family doctor over the phone. When he heard the symptoms, he sent me to see an obstetrician.

"I was furious when he suggested I could be pregnant, because I knew you'd taken precautions. That was when he gave me a lecture about no contraceptive method being one hundred percent reliable. After the examination the obstetrician told me I was definitely pregnant. I didn't want to believe her.''

A heavy silence hung in the air. "Did you...''

"No, Kon. I never considered an abortion, if that's what you're asking. Whatever happened between us, our baby was an innocent victim. I would never have done anything to harm it. In fact, I experienced a miraculous sense of responsibility when I learned I was pregnant. I had a reason to go on living. I followed the doctor's advice so the baby would be born strong and healthy.''

"Thank you for telling me that.'' His whisper reached her ears. "Don't you know I'd have given my life to have been there for you?''

Could he sound that sincere and still be lying? She didn't know anymore.

"When I saw Anna's baby picture," he began, "I started working on a plan to defect, one that would expose the fewest people to danger. That had to be my first priority. Of necessity it was elaborate and had to be timed to the split second."

"How did you finally get away?" She couldn't help wanting to know the answer to that question.

"I can't tell you."

Rage welled up in her all over again, and she shot straight up in bed, pushing the hair out of her eyes. "And you still expect me to trust you?"

Kon raised himself on one elbow, as calm as a panther at rest, but capable of springing at the slightest provocation. "Don't you think I'd like to be able to tell you what I went through to join you and Anna?"

"I don't understand why you can't. I thought a husband and wife were supposed to share everything."

"So did I," came his mocking reply. "But the matter of my defection falls into another category altogether. I have to keep quiet to protect others who put their lives at risk to help me."

There was too much to absorb. "Do you think you're still under surveillance by your government?"

"Actively, no. But I'm on a list."

She had difficulty swallowing. "Does that mean you could still be in danger?"

"From which government?"

His question chilled her. "Don't tease me, Kon."

"Maybe it's better we skip the subject altogether."

"Why would you be in danger from my government?" she persisted.

"Perhaps because they don't trust me any more than you do." He reached out for her pillow and pulled it to him, burying his face for a moment.

The vulnerability and despair in that gesture made her avert her eyes. "Even after you gave them information?"

He lifted his head. "You once said it yourself. A man who could turn his back on his country is a traitor to all."

The words she'd thrown at him. They sounded cruel. If no one ever trusted him, how lonely his life must have been for the past six years. How lonely it would continue to be for the rest of his life.

He slid from the bed, still dressed in his robe. The tie had come loose, though, allowing her a glimpse of his well-defined chest with its dusting of dark hair. "I knew it was too much to hope that we could start over. But fool that I am, I had to try. Good night, Meggie."

He strode to the door, then paused. "I'll give you an early Christmas present now—by promising that I'll never ask you to sleep with me again."

"WHERE ARE WE GOING to put the tree, Daddy?"

"Wherever your mother thinks is best."

They'd gone shopping that morning. Meg had left it to Anna to entertain Kon while they'd gone into store after store, looking for more tree decorations. The lights and ornaments from the small Scotch pine they'd dismantled at the apartment would only cover part of the eight-foot tree they'd purchased.

But now that they were home, Meg couldn't go on ignoring Kon. Anna listened to every word and nuance of meaning, observed everything that passed between her parents. So Meg stated that the best spot might be in front of the living-room window. Everyone driving by would see their tree. All they had to do was move the table and lamp to a different place.

The suggestion met with wholehearted approval, and Kon, dressed in jeans and sweater, set up the perfectly shaped blue spruce in a matter of minutes. As soon as Meg untangled a set of lights, Anna, with Thor at her heels, handed them to her father and he strung them on the tree. The three of them worked in complete harmony. Anyone peeking in the window would see the ideal family happily at work.

No one could know of the brooding blackness in Kon or suspect that after he'd left her room last night, Meg had lain awake in agony, part of her wanting, aching, to go to him and crawl into his arms.

But something intangible had occurred during their conversation. The man who had devastated her by promising he'd never ask her to sleep with him again was not the same man who earlier that night had begged her to lie next to him, just to know she was there.

Lacking the confidence to face him in case he rejected her attempt at reconciliation, she remained in her bed, alone. She spent the rest of the night trying to sort out her own confused thoughts and feelings.

Every time she attempted to put herself in his place, she felt physically ill. She could imagine his sense of isolation, the inevitable gloom and depression that must have weighed him down after leaving Russia to settle in a country as foreign and unfamiliar as the United States.

The CIA had given her some things to read, articles about defectors years before; she remembered that one theme had dominated the rest. They lived with the consequences of displacement for the rest of their lives.

Perhaps that explained why Kon had become the exemplary father, throwing himself into the role so completely. Perhaps that way he could forget for a short period what he'd left behind. It would also explain why he'd wanted Meg in his bed last night, to blot out for a brief time the pain of his actions.

In all honesty, she had to admit she couldn't blame him for those very human needs and drives. If their positions were reversed and she could never return to the United States, it would be a horrifying experience, one she'd have to sublimate somehow, just as he was doing.

"Mommy, you forgot to open the last box."

Startled out of her tortured thoughts, Meg tore off the cellophane and handed the lights to Anna. In an unguarded moment, her glance darted to Kon, who seemed to stare right through her, as if his thoughts were far removed from the scene in front of him. Cold fear spread through her body—there was such unhappiness in his look, and a kind of bleak resignation. Meg couldn't stand it. She excused herself to start dinner.

During the next few days a feeling of domestic tranquillity existed, on the surface, at least. But Kon had withdrawn emotionally from Meg, and she was paying a bitter price. Upset and confused by this remote stranger who'd never treated her with such indifference before, she needed to do something, anything, to relieve the tension between them.

It was on one of her trips with Anna back to the apartment to finish cleaning that Meg scanned a batch of Christmas cards sent to her and came across one from Tatiana Smirnov, her old Russian teacher. The woman's newsy letter triggered an idea for a special Christmas present for Kon, one she hoped would let him know she understood the loneliness of his self-imposed exile and wanted to make up for it in some small way.

When Kon came to pick them up, Meg told him that as long as they were in St. Louis, she and Anna had a few more presents to buy. He dropped them off at a local mall, indicating that he needed to take care of some business and would be back for them in a couple of hours.

The minute he was out of sight, Meg explained her secret to Anna. Then she hailed a taxi and gave the driver an address that took them across town to an art gallery Tatiana had mentioned in her letter. A shipment of arts and crafts from Russia was up for sale. Meg and Anna spent a good hour studying the paintings, icons, dolls, hats, scarves, eggs—all kinds of memorabilia from bygone eras.

As many times as Meg went over everything, her eye kept

going back to one particular oil painting. It depicted a mountain scene with a meadow of wildflowers in the foreground. Her gaze followed the dirt road that ran past an old barn, then disappeared. The painting's title, printed in Russian, convinced her. *Urals in springtime.*

Anna was taken with several of the icons but preferred the one of the Madonna and child. The combination of colors— gold and royal blue against the black of the shiny wood— drew the eye, and Meg told the saleswoman to wrap it up along with the painting.

Out of Anna's hearing she also whispered to the clerk to include the nesting doll sitting on the display table. The pink-and-black stylized figure of a Russian peasant woman hid seven versions of the same woman, each one smaller than the one before. They all fit together, and Anna would be delighted when she discovered the surprise.

The clerk put it in a sack, and when Anna wasn't looking, Meg stuffed it into her tote bag. The purchases cost more than a thousand dollars and took most of Meg's meager savings. But the situation between her and Kon had grown so precarious she would have done anything to extend the olive branch.

They took another taxi back to the mall, where they stopped to get their gifts boxed and wrapped in beautiful Christmas paper at a gift-wrapping booth. Then they window-shopped until Kon came for them.

Though Anna was bursting to tell her father what they'd done and wanted to give him his presents right then and there, she managed to contain herself. But her eyes sparkled like blue topaz, and Kon's gaze slid to Meg's several times in silent query. The amused glimmer in his eyes made her heart turn over, their enmity temporarily forgotten in the face of their daughter's excitement.

On Christmas Eve another winter storm blanketed the area with snow, delighting Anna. Along with the dogs, she followed her father outside, watching while he shoveled the driveway and then built her a snowman. As Meg gazed out at them from the dining room window where she was setting the table for their Christmas dinner, she saw that a couple of children close to Anna's age had come by to help.

There were joyous shouts mingled with the dogs' barking, and Kon seemed to be having as much fun as the children who hovered around him.

Seeing him like this, Meg had to ask herself again—what if he was exactly what he seemed? A man who'd willingly made certain choices. A loving father. A new American citizen who embraced the land he'd chosen. A man who still loved a woman, although seven years had passed. What if there were no ulterior motives and everything he'd been telling her all this time was the absolute truth? Tears stung her eyes....

Meg couldn't sleep that night. Long after she'd slipped downstairs at midnight to put her presents under the tree, she lay wide awake in the large bed, staring into the darkness as the tears ran down her face.

Early Christmas morning Anna ran into Meg's room with both dogs at her heels, bubbling with excitement. Daddy was already up fixing breakfast, she said. According to him, Santa had come, and as soon as they'd eaten, they could go into the living room and see what he'd brought.

A feeling not unlike morning sickness assailed Meg as she got out of bed and staggered to the bathroom. After spending most of the night crying until she wondered how there could be any more tears, she was sure that facing Kon, let alone Christmas day, was almost beyond her. But she had to, for Anna's sake.

The shower revived her a little. She brushed her hair and secured it with combs at both sides, then added blusher to her pale cheeks, followed by an application of lipstick. She pulled on a cherry-red sweater dress she'd had for a couple of years. Her low black patent pumps would be comfortable to walk around in and still look dressy.

"Just keep coming toward me," Kon murmured as she started down the stairs, the camcorder in his hands. "Merry Christmas, Meggie."

"Merry Christmas," she said when she could find the words. The sight of his dark, handsome features, his snug-fitting forest-green sweater and charcoal pants, his lithe movements left her breathless.

Anna stood next to her father in a new dress of red-and-blue plaid, a glowing look of anticipation on her face. "You have to kiss Daddy, Mommy, 'cause Daddy says it's a tradition."

"Only if she wants to, Anochka."

Meg needed no urging to close the distance between them and rise on tiptoe to brush her mouth against his. Kon would never be able to guess at the depth of her hunger for him, the kind of iron control it took not to devour him in front of their daughter. It was no use pretending that she didn't remember every second of those months when he'd been her lover.

His passion had electrified her, bringing them both a fullness of joy she hadn't known was possible.

Heaven help her. She wanted to know that joy again.

CHAPTER NINE

"CAN WE GO IN NOW, Daddy? I've eaten my eggs and drunk all my milk."

"What do you say, Meggie? Are we ready?"

She lifted her eyes to surprise a bleak look in his. It was only there for a moment, but she couldn't have been mistaken and it only added to her torment.

With a nod she put her coffee cup back on the saucer. "Why don't I get the two of you on tape first?"

Not waiting for a reply, she jumped up from the table and grabbed the camcorder from the counter, preceding them into the living room.

The next hour flew by. The dogs crouched close to Anna, who squealed in ecstasy over the new dollhouse and tea set Kon had set up for her. Meg had hidden the nesting doll in Anna's stocking, along with a candy cane and an inexpensive Little Mermaid watch.

Anna shook everything out, then examined the strange-looking toy first. "What is it, Mommy? An old lady?"

Meg laughed because her daughter didn't know what to make of it. Kon's delighted chuckle joined hers, and he threw Meg a quizzical glance, as if to ask her where she'd found the Russian treasure. The sound of lazy amusement in his voice as he talked to his daughter reminded her sharply of other times and places. A time, seven years ago, when she'd been madly in love with him and free to express that love. A night at her hotel in St. Petersburg, when he'd been lounging on the floor at her feet, just like this. Only now it was Anna's face he caressed, her bouncing curls he tousled.

"Watch this, Anochka."

In a deft movement that fascinated Meg, as well, Kon pulled the two halves of the doll apart. Anna saw a smaller version of the same doll inside and cried out in wonder.

"Open it like I did," Kon urged.

Within a few minutes fourteen halves lay spread out on the carpet, and Anna sat there with a frown of concentration on her face, trying to put everything back together again.

Meg decided now was the time to give Kon her present. "I hope you'll like this," she said in a nervous voice, wondering too late if it was the wrong thing to give him. Maybe he wouldn't want a reminder of everything he'd left behind.

He took the package from her hands and sat up to remove the paper. Anna was too aborbed with the dolls to notice how quiet the room had become, but Meg felt uncomfortably aware of the unnatural stillness. She held her breath while Kon studied the canvas. What was he thinking?

"I-it's a scene in the Urals. You must be missing Russia, and since you said you liked to hike there, I thought—"

"Meggie..." Where he gripped the edge of the canvas, his knuckles stood out white.

"I have a present for you, too, Daddy."

Anna dropped the doll parts she was having problems fitting together and scurried around the far side of the tree to fetch the package.

When she handed it to him, he put it to his ear and shook it, making Anna giggle. "I wonder what my little Anochka has given me."

Anna couldn't wait any longer. "It's an...an icon, isn't it, Mommy?"

Kon's grin slowly faded to be replaced by a sober expression as he carefully lifted the wooden plaque from the tissue and reverently traced the halos of gold with his index finger, his head bent in solemn concentration.

Anna squeezed past the dogs and knelt down next to her father. "That's the baby Jesus with his mommy," she pointed out. "I liked this one the best. Mommy said it came from Russia. Do you think it's pretty, Daddy?"

He drew Anna roughly into his arms and buried his face in her dark curls. "I love it," came the husky reply. "I love it almost as much as I love you."

Several Russian endearments whispered in hushed tones brought tears to Meg's eyes, and she covered her emotions by busying herself opening a box of candy from her boss, and another from Ted.

"Where's Mommy's present?" Anna finally asked.

"Your father already gave it to me," she said before he could reply. "Remember the beautiful black coat I wore to the theater the other night?"

Anna nodded.

In a quick movement Kon got to his feet. "Actually, I do have another gift for your mother, but it didn't arrive in time for Christmas."

"No, please." She gathered a basket of fruit—from Mrs. Rosen—in the crook of her arm and headed for the kitchen to check on the turkey, avoiding the intensity of his gaze. "I don't want anything else. You've done too much for us already."

Relieved that he didn't follow her, she was able to get preparations under way for Christmas dinner. Anna brought her dollhouse into the kitchen and, chattering away, put a different nesting doll in each room. She gave the dolls exacting instructions on how to behave. If they didn't, she said, the nutcracker, who stood guard on one of the kitchen chairs, would have to punish them.

Eventually her new friends from across the street traipsed through the house to see her presents and look at the puppies still confined to the porch. They were all fascinated by the nesting doll, and at one point Kon had to intervene so everyone could take turns assembling the various parts.

Finally the children grew tired of even that game, and at Kon's suggestion they decided to play outside in the snow, leaving Meg in peace.

Once everything was cooking, she went to the living room to clean up the mess, but Kon had gotten there before her and the room looked immaculate. He'd put the painting and the icon on the mantel and had started a fire in the grate. She felt compelled to find him and thank him.

When he wasn't in his study she called to him from the foot of the stairs, but there was no answer. Nor was there any sign of Prince, or Thor and Gandy, whose other two pups had been given to a family across the street. Whirling around, she ran out the back of the house, but no one responded when she called and both cars were still in the garage.

Maybe everyone was in the front yard. She ran down the driveway, almost losing her balance in her heels while she shouted for Anna. Whichever direction she looked, there was no one in sight. Nothing but snow. Freezing air lodged in her lungs as she beheld the lone snowman with one of Kon's ties around its neck.

Silent testimony to a kidnapping?

A growing dread gnawed at her insides, and she raced across the street without thought of boots or coat, praying she was wrong, praying Anna was at the neighbor's house. But when the children answered the door, they said Anna had gone off with her daddy and the dogs.

By the time Meg reached the house to get her car keys, she was hysterical with fear. She backed slowly out of the driveway and drove up and down the icy streets, past the local parks, asking people if they'd seen a man and a little girl walking a pair of German shepherds and a puppy. No one had.

Realizing there wasn't another second to lose, she sped home as fast as she could and dashed into the house, her only thought to contact the police and prevent Kon from leaving the country with their daughter. He could be anywhere by now, following another elaborate plan of escape.

With tears gushing down her cheeks, she clutched the receiver and punched in 911. When she explained that her daughter was missing, the dispatcher asked for her address and said a couple of officers would be arriving shortly.

To Meg, the next few minutes felt like centuries. Though she knew it was hopeless, something made her go out to the street and call Anna's name at the top of her lungs.

Soon the two neighbor children and their parents joined her and volunteered to start a door-to-door search. Meg thanked them, but didn't tell them she suspected Kon was behind her daughter's disappearance. That was a matter for the police. A cruiser finally drove up in front and two officers followed her into the hallway to get a statement.

"Just calm down, ma'am, and tell us why you think your family is missing. How long have they been gone?"

"I don't know. An hour or so. I was busy in the kitchen before I realized I couldn't hear voices. Even the dogs are missing."

"Maybe they went for a walk."

"Naturally I thought of that, but I've been driving around the neighborhood and there's no sign of them. No one has seen them. Our other car is still in the garage."

"Maybe they stopped at a neighbor's home. It is Christmas Day, you know."

She took a shuddering breath. "You don't understand. My husband—"

"—is right here." A chilling male voice that could only be Kon's cut her off abruptly.

"We've been at Fred's house showing him the new puppy, Mommy. He has a bottle with a ship in it and a marmalade cat who's so fat she just sleeps." Anna rushed through the hall to explain and gave her mother a huge hug while the dogs circled them, whining a little. Meg couldn't speak. She simply clutched her daughter closer.

One of the officers nodded to Kon. "Your wife here got a little nervous because you and your daughter had been gone a while."

She'd seen pain in Kon's eyes before, but nothing could compare to the look of raw anguish she saw there now. The inner light faded completely, as if something in him had just died.

Another kind of fear tore at her heart. *What had she done?*

He glanced at the officer. "You know how it is when you've only been married five days. We don't like to be out of each other's sight."

Once again, Kon's superb playacting was in evidence and he handled the awkward situation like a master. But Meg knew nothing would ever be the same between them again.

He slid his arm around her shoulders and pulled her close, pressing a fervent kiss to her temple. "Fred Dykstra was on his front porch and he called to us. His house is two doors down. He's a retired widower from the railroad and he lives alone. When he saw Anna, he invited her in to give her a chocolate Santa."

"I'm sorry," Meg whispered in agony. "I—I didn't realize…"

He rubbed her arm. "When he helped me move in, he had to put up with my talking about you and Anna all the time, and he wants to meet you. So I was coming back to the house to ask if we could invite him for dinner. That's when Anna and I saw the police car and bumped into Mrs. Dunlop, who said you were looking for us. I'm sorry if you were worried."

This time he lowered his mouth to hers in a gesture the officers would interpret as a lover's salute. In reality Kon pressed a hard, soulless kiss against her lips, a kiss that made a mockery of the passion they'd once shared. "I make you a solemn vow that I'll never be that thoughtless again, Mrs. Johnson."

Meg knew he was saying one thing while he meant another. She couldn't seem to stop shaking. No amount of sorrow or remorse for her actions would put them back on the same footing they'd achieved that morning. Before she'd called the police.

"We'll be going, then." The officer smiled. "Merry Christmas."

"Sorry to have troubled you. Merry Christmas." Kon's

fingers bit into her upper arm before he released her to see them to the door.

"Anna, run out to the porch and take off your boots, honey. You're getting water on the floor."

"Okay, Mommy. Here, Thor. Here, Gandy."

Meg was halfway up the stairs when she heard Kon's footsteps and realized there was no hope of escape. He followed her into the bedroom and shut the door too quietly. He didn't say anything, merely watched her through narrowed eyes.

"I—I'm sorry," she began haltingly. "I know that sounds inadequate but—"

"Just tell me one thing," he demanded coldly. "Did you give away my cover?"

She shook her head in denial, staring at the floor. "No."

"The truth, Meggie. If you even hinted that I might have abducted her, we'll have to move and I'll be forced to take on a new identity. As it is, I'll have to get hold of,...certain people to report the incident. The decision might well be out of my hands already."

His words made her more frantic than ever. "No, Kon. When I phoned 911, I only said Anna was missing. I told the Dunlops the same thing."

"But you were on the verge of telling them all about me when I walked in the hall. Don't deny it."

She struggled for the words that might placate him. There were none. "I won't," she finally murmured.

"You've missed your calling, Meggie."

She lifted tearful eyes to him and shrank from his cold, hard face.

"No Mata Hari of my acquaintance could have pulled off a more convincing act than you did this morning when you tried to give me back a little piece of my Russian soul. To include our innocent little Anna in the subterfuge was pure genius. My compliments, *beloved*." He said the endearment with a particularly cruel twist that brought a moan to her lips. "You actually had me convinced there was hope."

Unspeakable emotion—anger and something else she

couldn't define—tautened every muscle and sinew of his body before he strode swiftly from the room.

When she thought about what she'd done and the possible consequences to Kon's safety after the years it had taken him to establish his new identity, Meg collapsed on the bed.

"Mommy?"

Meg could hear Anna's footsteps on the stairs. She jumped up from the bed and hurried into the bathroom to wash her face so her daughter wouldn't suspect anything.

"Can Fred come to our house for dinner? He's nice."

As far as Meg was concerned, a guest would provide the diversion she needed to get through the rest of the day. Kon had extended the initial invitation and would have to be on his best behavior.

"Of course he can, honey. Why don't you take the dogs and go back to his house and bring him over? He can spend the day with us and sit by the fire. You can show him your toys."

"Can I go right now?"

"Yes. Don't forget your hat and boots."

"I won't."

Meg followed her down the stairs and busied herself in the kitchen until she heard Anna and the dogs leaving.

Realizing Kon needed to be told about Fred, she hurried to his study. But the glacial look he shot her when she appeared in the doorway froze her into stillness.

"Where's Anna?"

Meg tried to swallow, but her throat felt swollen. "I sent her over to Mr. Dykstra's to bring him back for dinner. That's what I was coming in here to tell you."

He leaned back in his chair and watched her through shuttered eyes. "I'm glad she's out of the house for a few minutes. What I have to say won't take long, but I don't want her privy to it."

"D-did you pho—"

"I don't intend to answer any of your questions," he cut in brutally. "All you have to do is listen."

"I'm your wife!" she cried, aghast. "You have no right to speak to me like that, no matter what's happened."

"I forgot." He smiled with cold disdain. "Yes, you're my wife—who five days ago in this very house swore before God to love and honor me, be my comfort, my haven, my refuge—"

"Stop it!" she shouted. "I can't take any more."

He sucked in a breath and got to his feet. "You won't have to. I'm leaving."

"What?"

"Your name is on my bank account. You can draw out funds any time you need to. There's enough to keep you indefinitely. The house is in your name, as well."

"What do you mean?" she asked, panicking. "What are you talking about? Where are you going?"

His mouth thinned. "If I told you, you wouldn't believe me, so there's no point."

"H-how long will you be gone?"

"If it were up to you, I'd never come back, so it really doesn't matter."

She let out a groan. "Don't say that. It *does* matter. You can't do this to Anna."

"She'll recover. I was torn from my family when I was young, and I turned out all right. The Party has given me several commendations. Besides, she has *you*."

"Kon...don't do this." She suddenly felt afraid for him. "Have I put you in danger?" When he didn't reply, she asked, "Do you hate me so much for what I did that you can't bear the sight of me any longer? Is that what this is all about?"

"I'll leave tonight after Anna has gone to sleep." He went on talking as if she hadn't spoken. "As far as she has to know, I've gone to New York on business."

"What business?" Her voice shook.

"Have you finally decided to show a little interest in my writing career?" The contempt in his question devastated her. "Did you think that was made up? That I defected to a life of luxury, living off the proceeds of the information I brought your government?''

Before they were married, she'd assumed exactly that. But too late she knew it wasn't the truth.

In a dull voice she asked, ''What is it exactly that you write? Walt Bowman, or whoever he is, said something about the KGB and…'' Her voice faded.

One dark brow lifted. ''When I'm gone, you can search through my study to your heart's content and figure it out for yourself. At least when we part this time, Anna will have some videos to help her remember her father. It's more than I was given when I was taken away.''

Meg could feel him slipping beyond her reach and didn't have the faintest idea how to hold on to him. In desperation she said, ''I thought you loved Anna. I thought you defected because of her, for her.''

''Does it really matter what either of us thought when it's abundantly clear I got here six years too late?'' His eyes bored holes into her.

''Now, if I'm not mistaken, I can hear Thor and Gandy, which means Anna and Fred are almost at our front door. Shall we greet our guest together, *mayah labof?*''

''MRS. JOHNSON? Senator Strickland here.''

Thank God. Meg's hand tightened on the receiver and she sat up in bed, praying Anna had finally gone to sleep and hadn't heard the phone ring. Today—the day after Christmas—had been a waking nightmare, one she never wanted to live through again.

''Thank you for returning my call. Thank you,'' she murmured. ''I'd almost given up hope that you'd even get your messages before you went back to your office next week.''

''I have a secretary who monitors my calls in case of an emergency. She phoned me at home when she heard your name.''

''Please forgive me for bothering you this late, but I'm

desperate.'' Her voice wobbled despite herself. "I need your help."

"This sounds serious. By a strange coincidence, my wife and I were just talking about you newlyweds on our way home from a concert tonight. We were trying to decide on a date for that dinner I promised you."

Meg groaned with renewed pain. "Senator—my husband left me last night."

There was a prolonged silence on the other end of the phone. "A domestic quarrel?"

"No. It was something that goes much deeper. I don't even know where to begin. I've been out of my mind with grief, and my daughter is inconsolable. I've got to find him and tell him I love him." She broke down sobbing and it took her a minute to get control of her emotions and her voice. "He has to come back to us. *He has to*."

"Tell me what happened."

More hot tears streamed down her face. "I drove him away with my paranoia. I accused him of planning to kidnap Anna and take her back to Russia." In a few words she explained why she'd called the police. "All this time I've refused to believe what was before my very eyes. I have to go to him and beg his forgiveness."

"Did he leave in his own car?"

"Yes."

"I'll get on it as soon as we hang up, and when I have any information, I'll contact you, but I doubt it will be before morning."

"Thank you. I'm in your debt," she said fervently.

"If I can effect a reunion between the two of you, then I'll hold you to that at campaign time. Meanwhile, don't give up."

"I'll never do that," she vowed. "I fell in love with him when I was seventeen. I'll always love him."

"That's the most painful kind of love, first love," he said kindly. "Your husband told me he was similarly affected when he met you for the first time."

Meg blinked. "Kon told you that?"

"Mmm. Tell me, are you familiar with the story in the Bible about Jacob who loved Rachel?"

Her heart began hammering. "Yes."

"When your husband and I talked, I told him his plight struck me as being very much like Jacob's. He loved Rachel on sight and worked seven years for her. And even though he was tricked into marrying Leah because of the laws of the land, he loved Rachel so much he worked another seven years for her. Few women will ever know that kind of devotion from a man."

After a slight pause he went on, "Despite the laws of his former country, your husband has worked close to seven years for you, putting himself in grave danger. It hardly stands to reason that you've lost him now, no matter how dark things look at the moment."

"Thank you," she whispered tearfully. "I needed to hear that. Good night, Senator."

The minute she hung up the phone, she got out of bed and crept down the stairs to Kon's study in search of a Bible. If memory served her correctly, she'd seen one with his collection of books when she'd gone in there earlier to go through his papers. Naturally his work was stored on disk, but she found enough correspondence in the file cabinets to realize he wrote not only about the KGB but about the beauty, the culture, of Russia.

When she found the Bible, she sat down at his desk and opened it to Genesis 29. Verse 20 had been underlined in black ink and she skipped to it immediately.

And Jacob served seven years for Rachel; and they seemed unto him but a few days, for the love he had to her.

Suddenly the letters blurred together. She laid her head down on the table and wept.

CHAPTER TEN

"I DON'T WANT to go to my new school, Mommy. Prince will cry, and what if Daddy comes home and can't find me?"

It was going on three weeks since the Christmas holidays. Every single one of those days, Meg had been listening to Anna's tearful arguments repeated over and over again like a litany.

If Meg hadn't gone to Anna's new school with her every day and stayed in the building to work as a volunteer aide—so Anna could check throughout the day to make sure her mommy was still there—Anna would never have gone at all.

In truth, Meg wouldn't have let Anna go if she hadn't been able to spend the better part of the day with her at school. The yawning emptiness of the home Kon had created for them was unbearable without him. His absence affected everything and everyone, especially the dogs. They kept returning to Kon's study and whining, the sound eerily human, when they couldn't find him.

From the first night after his disappearance, Anna had crept into Meg's bed with her nutcracker and she'd been sleeping there ever since. Meg knew it would create more problems down the road, but she drew comfort from Anna's warm little body next to hers and didn't try to make her sleep on her own. It wouldn't have worked, anyway; Anna couldn't tolerate even a brief separation from her right now. Kon had been too wonderful a husband and father in the short week they'd lived together as a family. It was no wonder that Meg and Anna had gone into mourning and refused to be consoled.

Meg had no doubts that Senator Strickland had done everything in his power to discover Kon's whereabouts. Lacey Bowman had phoned Meg the morning after the senator's call. The only information the CIA would give Meg was that Kon was no longer in the country.

Because of Anna, Meg couldn't give in to the pain of that excruciating revelation. She had to go on pretending he was away on an extended business trip with his publisher and would come home just as soon as he could.

Every time the phone rang, Anna ran to get it and cried, "Daddy?" This happened so many times Meg thought her heart would break. She had to admonish her daughter to say hello first or she wouldn't be allowed to answer the phone at all.

So far, there'd been two disastrous sleep-overs with Melanie, who was so taken with Prince she never wanted to go home. But Anna was no longer the vivacious friend she used to be and refused to share her puppy. This, in turn, created fighting and unpleasantness. After Melanie left, Anna confided to Meg that she didn't want Melanie to come to her house anymore. Jason and Abby across the street were her friends now. Meg decided to let it go for the moment. She'd arrange something with Melanie in a few months' time.

Violin lessons were out, after Anna cried all day and night over having to leave the house to drive to St. Louis. It was too far away and her daddy might come home.

By the end of January, there was still no sign of him, and Meg had to face the dreadful truth that he might never come home. The more she thought about it, the more she believed he hadn't gone back to Russia at all but was looking for another place to live.

Kon spoke several European languages and could easily have relocated in Germany or Austria or even France. The American government would have cooperated with the country he'd chosen, giving him the proper papers and credentials to start over again.

And it was Meg's fault. She felt as though her heart had died.

Since Anna's inability to deal with her loss seemed to be growing worse, Meg's family doctor advised her to consult a good child psychologist and referred her to a colleague who practiced in Hannibal. Their first appointment would be the next Saturday at eleven. Meg recognized that she was in need of help herself and decided they could both benefit. She prayed counseling would help them; she could think of no other alternatives.

On Friday night after dinner, Meg broached the subject with Anna, who didn't like the fact that her mother had a doctor's appointment. Yet she had no choice but to go along, since she wouldn't let Meg out of her sight. Meg was in the process of explaining why they had to see this doctor when the doorbell rang.

"Daddy!" Anna shrieked, and toppled her chair in her haste to get to the front door. The dogs got there even faster, barking more loudly than usual.

Meg's adrenaline kicked in the way it always did—because there was a part of her that never gave up hope, either. But there was no point in telling Anna that if her father *had* come home, he would enter through the back porch from the garage. He wouldn't ring the front doorbell.

In all probability, it was Jason or Abby. Meg expected them to come running through the kitchen to play with Prince, who needed Kon's firm hand to learn obedience. Or it might be Fred, who'd become a welcome visitor and friend and had more influence with Anna than anyone else these days.

Meg was halfway to the front hall when she heard a woman's voice speaking a torrent of Russian. *"mayah malyenkyah muishka,"* she repeated. "My darling little mouse," she said over and over again.

What on earth?

Meg emerged from the dining room in time to see an elderly, heavyset woman dressed in black envelop Anna in her arms. The stranger's long gray hair was fastened in a bun, and she wore amber around her neck and wrist. Tears streamed down her ruddy cheeks, and she held on to Anna as if she'd never let her go.

"Anochka." A deep, commanding, familiar voice sounded from the front porch. "This is your babushka, but you can call her Grandma Anyah."

"Her name is just like mine!"

"That's right, Anochka. It must be fate. She's come all the way from Siberia to live with us."

Kon.

As Meg mouthed his name, he stepped into the hallway. The sight of his tall, lean body and striking face was so wonderful she could only stare and go on staring. His dazzling blue eyes were trained on her now, but there was a humble look in them she'd never seen before.

"Meggie, may I present my *matz,*" he said in a tremulous voice.

His mother.

"She's my belated Christmas present to you. She doesn't speak any English, but we'll help her learn it, won't we?"

Meg didn't answer the unspoken plea in his unshed tears, because love had lent her feet wings. She threw herself into Kon's arms so hard it might have knocked the wind out of a less solid man. Like a powerful waterfall, her avowals of love, her pleas for forgiveness, cascaded down on him, submerging him so completely he could be in no doubt that she belonged to him heart and soul.

Meg could tell the exact moment Kon knew that trust had come to stay. He groaned his satisfaction and, in full view of his mother and Anna, found Meg's questing mouth and kissed her with all the fiery passion of those halcyon days in Russia long ago. Once again they were free to give in to their hunger, their longings. Meg forgot everything but the feel of his arms and mouth, the warmth of his hard body melding to hers.

"Are you and Daddy making a baby?"

Anna!

Kon had the presence of mind to break off their kiss faster than Meg did, but he refused to let her go. He rocked her in his arms as he rested his chin on her shoulder and spoke to his daughter.

"Tomorrow, your mommy and I are going to sit down with you and explain about babies. Right now I want her to meet *my* mommy."

In a lightning move he turned Meg around, sliding his hands down her arms before wrapping his own around her waist from behind and squeezing her so every part of their bodies touched.

"Mama, this is Meggie. My wife." His voice broke as he introduced them in Russian.

Kon's mother was still holding Anna as she lifted her head from her granddaughter's curls.

Meg gasped softly when the brilliant blue eyes so like Kon's wandered over her face and hair in a friendly yet searching perusal.

It wasn't just the eyes. Her bone structure was similar to Kon's, and Meg could see flecks of dark among her gray eyebrows that testified where he'd received his black-brown hair.

Slowly the older woman put Anna down and cupped Meg's face with her hands.

"*Mayah Doch,*" she said like a benediction.

My daughter.

Meg nodded before returning the greeting. "*Mayah Matz.*"

Then they embraced. Meg formally kissed both cheeks, feeling an overwhelming tide of love and happiness. She held her mother-in-law in her arms for a long, long time. This wonderful woman who'd given birth to Kon, who'd thought he was dead all these years. This woman Meg had always wanted to meet...

Who knew the hardships, the deprivation, she'd lived

through? How Meg would have loved to witness the reunion of mother and son!

There were too many questions she wanted answered, but now wasn't the time, not when everyone's emotions were spilling over. The dogs were no less thrilled as they rubbed their heads against Kon's legs in joyous homecoming.

"I'm glad you're home, Daddy. I've been waiting and *waiting* for you."

"So have I, Anochka, so have I."

By now Anna was in her father's arms, the healing after separation already begun. He whispered the special endearments he reserved for his daughter.

Anna was exactly where Meg longed to be. He was their safety, their rock, the light of their lives. Their love.

Slowly, over one gray and one dark head, Meg felt the burning heat of Kon's desire reach out to her, and she read the unspoken message in those smoldering eyes. Like her, he was barely holding on to his control until they could be alone.

But there were his mother and Anna to consider. By tacit agreement they decided to see to their comforts first. Meg's time with her husband would have to come later. Like Jacob and Rachel, they'd waited this long and could wait a little longer. But only just a little.

She answered his unasked question in a husky voice. "We'll put your mother in the room I was using before you left. It's all made up and ready for her. She'll enjoy the privacy of her own bathroom, and Anna will love having her grandmother next door."

He lowered Anna to the floor, his chest heaving with the strength of emotions he was having difficulty holding in check. "Where are your things?"

She could hardly breathe. "Where do you think?"

"They're in your room." Anna giggled. "You're silly, Daddy."

He tousled her dark curls and muttered in Russian, "Our little pitcher has awfully big ears."

Meg replied in kind with a straight face. "She takes after her father."

"And my Dimitri takes after *his* father," Anyah added. Kon grinned at Meg's astonishment.

The moment also gave Meg a glimpse of the older woman's sense of humor. It warmed her heart as nothing else could have done, and she hugged her mother-in-law once more before fastening loving eyes on her husband. "Is that your real name? Dimitri?"

"Da," his mother answered for him. "Dimitri Leudon-ovitch."

"How do you like it, *mayah labof?*"

"Enough to give it to our son when he's born."

She watched him swallow several times, and he looked at her with fierce longing.

Meg smiled into his eyes. "You've been gone forever, so you'd better plan to make up for lost time."

Anyah patted Meg's arm. "I can see you are good for my Dimitri. He needs to be loved by a woman like you, a woman to match his passion."

Her blunt, outspoken manner brought a blush to Meg's cheeks. To cover her embarrassment she said, "Did you know he was your son when you first saw him?"

"Da." She nodded, eyeing him with motherly pride. "No child in Shuryshkary had such a face and blue eyes like my little Deema's. And you see the way his hair grows into that widow's peak, and the shape of his ears, like a seashell?"

Her weatherworn hand reached out to touch his left eyebrow, as if she, too, couldn't get enough of him. "See the little scar covered by the hair? He got that scar and the one on his left shoulder when he fell out of a tree. I think he was four. He always loved the trees and begged his papa to take him up into the mountains we could see from our house."

Kon still loved the trees and the mountains, Meg thought, reacting with a shaky breath. She'd noted all those physical characteristics of Kon's when they'd made love. Particularly the scar on his shoulder, the one he couldn't remember getting, the one she'd kissed again and again because she loved everything about his magnificent body.

Right then Kon's eyes captured hers—hot, glowing, blue coals that let her know he was remembering the same thing she was.

Meg cleared her throat. Switching to English, she asked, "Where is Shuryshkary?"

"In northern Siberia at the foot of the Urals."

"That explains so much," she whispered.

Kon nodded his dark head and they communed in silence. But not for long, because Anna inserted herself between her parents and grandmother. "What's that sure-scary word mean?"

Kon chuckled. "It's the town where I was born, Anochka."

Unable to contain her curiosity any longer, Meg cried, "How did you ever find your mother?"

"When the idea first came to defect, I managed—with the help of another agent who owed me some favors—to get into my file. Once I read the details, I found out my mother was still alive, and I negotiated her escape with the help of your government. But like the situation with you and Anna, I had to wait all this time before I felt it was safe to bring her here. Unfortunately there were problems that prevented her from arriving on Christmas Day as we'd originally planned."

"Oh, Kon…" Her voice shook. Now that she had answers, his behavior on Christmas Day and his subsequent disappearance made complete sense. She lifted pleading eyes to him. "Can you ever forgi—"

"All that's over, Meggie," he broke in. "Today is the beginning of the rest of our lives."

"Yes," she whispered, and linking her arm through her mother-in-law's, she said in Russian, "Are you tired? Would you like to go upstairs, or would you like to freshen up for dinner first, then take a tour of your son's house?"

The older woman looked thoughtful. "We flew all the way from San Francisco today and ate a big meal on the plane. I think I would like to get acquainted with my little grand-daughter, then go to bed.''

As they started for the stairs, with Anna and the dogs running ahead of them and Kon trailing with the luggage, his mother said, ''Anna is very much like Deema's sister, Nadia, used to be. Bright, inquisitive, full of life.''

''Nadia died of a lung disease before her fourteenth birthday,'' Kon explained under his breath in English.

Meg's chest constricted. ''And your father?''

''One day he went logging and his heart gave out. That was five years ago.''

''How has she survived all these years alone?''

''Scrubbing floors and toilets in civic buildings.''

''How old is she?''

''Sixty-five.''

''She's wonderful, Kon.''

''She is. So are you.''

Much later that night, when the house had finally fallen quiet and the lights were turned off, Kon entered their bedroom, where Meg had been impatiently waiting for him.

''The last time I looked, Mama was reading the *Nutcracker* to Anna. She's actually picked up quite a few words from our bedtime stories.''

''What could be more natural, my darling?'' Meg whispered. She reached eagerly for him as he shrugged out of his robe and slid into the bed. ''Mrs. Beezley told me she was exceptionally intelligent for her age. Mrs. Rosen said the same thing about her talent for the violin. She inherited those qualities from her father.''

''And from her mother. She's also inherited the sweetness of her spirit from you,'' he murmured against her mouth, kissing her breathless. ''When I left them, they were communicating with amazing facility.''

Meg couldn't contain her emotions. ''That book has been like a magical link between all of us, my darling.''

He smoothed the hair from her forehead, staring into her very soul. ''That's because the *Nutcracker* is magical. When

Mama embraced me and started talking to me about the past, dozens of memories came flooding back. One of my strongest impressions was of her reading the *Nutcracker* to me when I was a child. That's why it made such an impact on me— and why I wanted you to have that particular book when you left Russia. It symbolized hope and love for me, Meggie. *Our* love. Now it has all come together in a living reality." His voice broke before he claimed her mouth once more and drew her fully into his arms.

"I've yearned for you, Meggie. I love you with such a terrible hunger it frightens me."

"I'm frightened to think I almost lost you again."

"I won't lie to you, Meggie. After I left the house at Christmas, I'd pretty well lost hope for us. But I had to try again."

"Thank God you did! I love you so much! Kon—" She gasped in ecstasy at the first touch of his hand against her flesh. The pleasure was almost unbearable. "I can't believe this is happening. Am I dreaming?"

"Does it matter?" he asked in a husky voice. "We're together at last. Any more questions or explanations will have to wait, because nothing else is—or ever will be—as important as you here with me.

"Love me, Meggie," he begged, the pain of longing in his voice and body echoing hers. She gave herself up to the only man who would ever be all things to her—guardian, friend, lover, husband, father of her children.

Not many other women had traveled so far from home, on so strange and precarious a path to their ultimate destiny and fulfillment.

But she'd do it again for the love of one Konstantin Rudenko, the prince of her heart and, most assuredly, of Anna's.

**Sexy Santa reminded Cyn of a Christmas past and
a thief who'd stolen her heirlooms—*and* her heart!**

THE BABY & THE BODYGUARD

Jule McBride

Prologue

"So, how are my three busiest elves this morning?" Analise Sweet smoothed the skirt of her green wool Chanel suit, tapped a perfectly manicured red nail on top of a file folder, then ensconced herself at the head of her laquered boardroom table.

Evan Morrissey merely grunted. The numbers cruncher for Too Sweet Toys' retail division was already seated. His eyes remained riveted on rows of figures that indicated holiday sales trends. Judging from his expression, they weren't good.

"My, my, I do believe Evan is the Grinch himself," Analise teased. Standard protocol dictated that her meetings begin with friendly joking, but the Wall Street transplant had never really adjusted.

Bob Bingley had. The thirty-something man chuckled, ran a hand over his shock of white-blond hair, then sprawled in the leather swivel chair nearest Analise. "It's three weeks till the day, and this particular elf is tired of working 'round the clock." He tweaked his mustache. "I'm ready for the parties, if you want the truth."

"Did I ask for the truth, darling?" Analise smiled at her favorite office prankster. When their eyes met, Analise decided he was almost perfect for her daughter. Unfortunately Bob was a womanizer, and Cynthia had already been played for a fool. The last man had left her a single mother—and worse. "Clayton?"

As usual, elderly Clayton Woods, devoted family friend and head buyer, was positioned in front of the boardroom's wall-to-wall window. He didn't respond, but leaned on his cane and glared across the Rockefeller Center complex through a pair of binoculars. *Poor Clayton. He's taken my separation from Paxton nearly as hard as I have.*

Outside, couples skated on the Rockefeller ice rink. Analise could see their foggy breaths and catch bright snatches of their bobbing hats and blowing scarves. The twinkling bulbs on the center's huge blue spruce lit up the cloudy winter day, making her feel wistful for Christmases past.

After all, she'd been married thirty-five years ago, on Christmas day, 1959. Then four Christmases past, she'd discovered her daughter Cynthia had fallen in love with a man named Jake Jackson. On Christmas Eve, when Analise and Paxton had been away, Cynthia had caught the jewel thief and his two cohorts stealing the Sweet family heirlooms, including Analise's lucky Christmas necklace. Although two men had gone to prison, one had absconded with the jewelry.

The necklace had been of ruby and emerald links, and Analise's husband had added a new link every Christmas since their marriage. Now the necklace was gone. Not that Analise would have received her thirty-fifth link this year. Last December twenty-fifth she'd walked out on Paxton.

"There's Paxton!" Clayton clutched the binoculars. "Eileen's bringing him coffee."

At the mention of her husband's assistant, Analise tried not to bristle. "Of course Paxton's in his office. He works there."

In response to her censuring tone, Clayton placed the binoculars aside and hobbled toward the table. "Ever since he left, this company's been a mess," Clayton said defensively. "I'm worried, if for no other reason than I own such a large share of the stocks. We're in a ridiculous situation, with him and Cynthia handling marketing, while we—who are right across the ice rink—handle the toy store."

"And never the twain do meet." Bob sighed, eyeing the building opposite. "Unless Cynthia and I—" he glanced at Analise "—running the gauntlet between you and Paxton counts as communication."

"Now, now, Too Sweet is fine," Analise said soothingly.

"Why doesn't he just come back?" Clayton groused. "This split has caused rumors of takeover, you know."

Analise forced herself to smile. Paxton hadn't returned because she'd walked out on him, not the other way around. But that was too personal to divulge to her executives. "May we please get into the holiday spirit?"

"Oh, but we are, Analise." Bob's blue eyes twinkled naughtily. "I have the perfect plan. We'll punish Paxton for leaving, by hitting him where it will hurt most."

"And just where might that be, Bob?" Analise noted that even Grinchlike Evan was now perking up.

"Well—" Bob leaned forward conspiratorially "—we'll steal the central, key element in the biggest marketing campaign he's ever launched."

Evan chuckled. "You are thoroughly incorrigible."

"Ah—" Clayton leaned back and steepled his fingers. "So we cutthroats would steal the star baby? The three-year-old spokesperson, mascot and figurehead of our own beloved toy company, Little Amanda? That *would* ruin Paxton's special promotion!"

"If it hit the tabloids," Bob added reasonably, "it would increase our holiday sales."

"Why, you know how people are drawn to a good tragedy," Evan said, picking up the thread.

"And once Little Amanda was returned," Clayton continued, "sales would absolutely skyrocket."

Bob sighed with satisfaction. "Why, it would look more like the Fourth of July than Christmas."

Analise's lipsticked mouth dropped open in feigned terror.

She playfully scrutinized Bob, Evan and Clayton, in turn. "Now, gentlemen." Her voice lowered to a stage whisper. "Do you honestly think I should kidnap my very own granddaughter?"

The members of the group maintained a long, wicked silence, while contemplating the ludicrous suggestion. Then, suddenly, everyone burst into merry laughter. Or *almost* everyone...

Part 1

Chapter One

Tuesday, December 13, 1994

"Little Amanda needs a bodyguard." Paxton Sweet sounded furious. He shook Anton Santa's hand, then draped the bodyguard's garment bag over a chair. "I'm sorry about interrupting your Caribbean vacation, and I want to thank you for stopping by in the evening." Paxton gestured wildly around his office. "During the Christmas season we work nonstop."

Santa grunted and glanced around. Dolls tumbled from an overful box beside the door, inflatable Teenage Mutant Ninja Turtles bobbed on cabinet tops. Windup beetles, yo-yos, and gum banks littered Paxton's desk. And on the windowsill, next to a Barney doll with a torn ear, was a framed picture of Cynthia Sweet. Just looking at it made Santa feel vaguely murderous.

He had no intention of taking this job, although he almost wished it was Cynthia who needed protection. Then he'd take it...and kill her, himself. No, his reasons for entering the office, once he'd realized the address led to Too Sweet Toys, had nothing to do with Little Amanda, whoever she was. "Well, Mr. Sweet," Santa finally returned tersely, with a hint of a drawl from his long-lost Southern roots, "sunning myself in the Caribbean is less of a vacation, and more my everyday life-style. At least, when I'm between jobs."

"Call me Paxton."

"Paxton," Santa repeated, feeling his chest constrict. Was he really in the office of the man he'd once hoped would become his father-in-law? "You can call me Santa."

Paxton scrutinized him, clearly liking what he saw. "You *look* like a bodyguard," he said, sounding pleased with himself.

Feeling edgy, Santa rubbed the razor-thin scar on his jaw. "I *am* a bodyguard."

"I've been looking all over the place for you! Everybody says you're the absolute best in the business. Top of the line."

"The most expensive, too," Santa added dryly, making Paxton smile. Santa blew out a sigh as Cyn Sweet's father dug a file folder from a locked cabinet, then began to remove the toys from his desk, so he could better display whatever it was he meant to display.

While he did so, Santa studied him. Paxton had never seen him. Nor had he seen Paxton. But Santa recognized him from an oil painting above the piano in the Sweet family's living room. The last time he'd seen the sixtyish man with the thick silver hair, Anton Santa—along with Matthew Lewis and an unidentified man who remained at large—had been stealing the Sweet family blind.

If the man only knew. Santa stared into the wintry darkness, through the window, which was decorated with paper snowflakes, thinking that he hated Christmas. Christmas in Manhattan was worse. And Christmas anywhere near the Sweet family would be like slow death.

"Will there be anything else this evening, Paxton?"

Santa glanced in the direction of the voice. A fiftyish brunette in a blue flannel suit hovered in the doorway.

"Yes, Eileen." Paxton smiled. "Go paint the town red *and* green."

The woman chuckled lustily. "I'll get right on it, boss."

As soon as she left, Paxton finished cleaning his desk and

arranging the materials. "What you've got to understand," he said, "is that our three-year-old Amanda is no ordinary child."

Santa fought not to roll his eyes. Kids were kids, weren't they? "How's that, Mr.—er—Paxton?"

"Well, this year we're running a special promotion, all surrounding a ghostwritten book, called *Little Amanda's Perfect Christmas.*"

"Well now, that sounds real special." Santa hadn't meant to sound so cynical, but the past four years had left him bitter.

"Yes!" Paxton clearly hadn't caught Santa's irony. "The story's about a little girl who's been so bad all year that she only has the twelve days until Christmas to atone for it. She needs to be extra nice, so that Santa will bring her toys."

Santa forced himself to look interested.

"She helps her friends decorate a tree, then takes them to *The Nutcracker* ballet. She goes caroling at a shelter for homeless children, too. So, Little Amanda—the real Amanda—will be involved in such activities over the next twelve days, just like in the story!" Paxton's rising excitement suddenly fell flat. "And now we get these."

Curiosity got the better of him. Santa rose lithely from his chair, crossed to the desk, then stared down. There were three notes, composed of sharply cut red and green letters, probably taken from magazine pages with an X-Acto blade. All three said, "Take Amanda off the Promotion or She Will be Kidnapped!"

"So these are the notes," Santa drawled noncommittally. "They're a bit juvenile." He hadn't seen anything so nonthreatening since the notes left by The Grinch Gang, the jewel thief ring of which he'd been a part. The college boys had seduced security information from young heiresses at New York University, like Cynthia Sweet. Then, they'd stolen family valuables during the Christmas holidays, pawned them during spring break and used the cash to tide them over in high style, during the longer summer vacations. At every theft, they'd left a bottle of good champagne and a note to the victims, wishing them a happier new year. Four years ago the Sweet family had received no champagne, of course, since The Grinch Gang had been interrupted in the act, thanks to Cynthia.

"I knew you'd be as worried as I am when you saw them," Paxton finally said.

Something in the man's voice actually made Santa want to take the job. But he couldn't. Not that he'd see Cyn. Last he'd heard she was married to a man named Harry Stevens and living in Alabama. Even if she saw him, she wouldn't recognize him. He was a master of disguises. As the chameleon par excellence, he bore no resemblance to the young man she'd once said she loved.

"Look—" Santa suddenly decided to soften the blow. "I protect senators, stalked movie stars, star witnesses with mob contracts on their heads—"

"That's exactly why I requested you!"

I'm a bodyguard, not a babyguard. "Usually, there's a lot of danger involved—"

Paxton's Adam's apple bobbed up and down when he gulped. "Have you ever taken a bullet for anyone?"

Your damn daughter, who left me for dead. "On occasion."

Paxton paced the length of his window, which overlooked the Rockefeller tree, making the paper snowflakes flap in his wake. He pivoted and stared at Santa. "You have to take the job! I—I'll pay double."

Santa chuckled. "You already were, because of the holidays."

"I mean double the double!"

"Sorry, Mr. Sweet. I can't—"

"Granddaddy!" a little girl squealed.

When Santa turned, his whole body tensed. The child who flew past him was nothing more than a blur. Because Cynthia Sweet herself was standing in the doorway. A thick, luxurious *faux* fur coat was wrapped around her fabulous figure, and her lush blond hair hung free, just past her shoulders. Shopping bags dangled from both her wrists until she gracefully set them down.

When her coat fell open, he caught a glimpse of her suit. The skirt was short and her long, perfect legs went on for miles, all the way down to her trademark spiked heels. She was exactly as he'd remember: Rectangular face. Wide, full lips. A body to die for. *One I very nearly did die for*, he mentally corrected. Now she seemed even more beautiful than the last night he'd spent with her, the one and only night they'd ever made love.

For an instant, he was sure—maybe even hoped—she'd recognize him, but she didn't. In her eyes, which were still as bright, shiny and green as Christmas lights, he read nothing more than surprise at seeing a stranger. Of course, she'd never expect to find him in her father's office, and when it came to identifying people, context played a larger part than most people assumed.

"I picked up the elf outfits from the seamstress, Daddy," Cyn finally said. "Then Amanda and I went out for dinner."

She's still a daddy's girl. Santa realized he'd been holding his breath and slowly exhaled.

"Mr. Santa," Paxton said, "I'd like you to meet Amanda."

Only years of masking his personal responses and reactions gave him the power to turn away from Cyn. He did so just as Amanda leapt on top of Paxton's desk. From the back, the little girl's head was a mass of blond waves. When she whirled around, her eyes were the same bewitching green as Cyn's.

Then he noticed the tiny cute mole beside her pouty upper lip. His grandfather had had it. His father had had it. He'd had it, too, until a doctor had insisted on removing it.

For the first time in his life, Anton Santa couldn't move. The plush red carpet seemed to take flight beneath his feet, like a reindeer-driven sleigh. He felt downright woozy. Was he really being hired to protect a baby he and Cyn Sweet had made four long years ago…a daughter he'd never known he had?

TIME STOOD STILL. Cyn Sweet held her breath and clutched her shopping bags as if she were drowning in rough seas and they were her only lifeline. How had she been able to speak? A thousand unwanted impressions were still flashing through her mind.

First, it was crazy, but she could swear Jake Jackson was in her father's office. He wasn't, though. The strange sensations sweeping over her could have nothing to do with the man who *was* there, either.

She summed him up in a heartbeat. An aura of self-containment clung to him like a second skin. He was clean shaven and tanned a deep bronze, even though it was winter. The medium-brown eyes weren't special, and his too-short, slicked-back hair was also an unremarkable dark brown. Given his tailored brown wool suit, he was possibly rich. Still, the jacket hung so loosely that she'd barely recognized it as a Valentino Uomo original.

The expression was aloof, distanced and unreadable, something she'd learned to hate in a man. Very definitely, she was falling in distrust at first sight, but that may have had nothing to do with the stranger, specifically. Cyn knew better than to trust men, categorically.

In the next heartbeat, images of Jake Jackson flew through her head. Fury had shaded her memories of Jackson, the thief who'd loved her then betrayed her. Where once she'd thought him the most handsome man alive, she now remembered his long blond hair as scraggly and obviously dyed. He'd had a scruffy, unbecoming beard and a mustache that had almost covered a mole beside his lip. Four years ago, the mole had seemed sexy, of course. Now she mentally added a hair that grew from the center of it, just to remind herself that she hated him. He'd been overly pale, reed thin, and had usually worn sunglasses with his leather jackets.

No, the man in her father's office in no way resembled Jake Jackson. In fact, the two were as different as night and day. This man was all business. The other had been a hellion and a rebel, just the sort an overly protected, well-to-do college girl might use for her one brief fling with danger. Was the stranger wearing Jake's brand of cologne? *Eau de Bad boy.*

She realized Paxton was staring from face to face with a perplexed expression, as if sensing strange energy in the room. "Amanda, Cyn," he finally repeated, "this is Anton Santa."

Amanda's giggles cut through the tension. "You're Mr. Santa, so is Santa Claus your daddy?"

The man's brown eyes narrowed, as if he'd heard enough Santa jokes to last him a lifetime.

"Now, Amanda," Cyn said quickly, "please don't tease Mr. Santa."

As soon as she'd spoken, she was sorry. The man shot her a look that made her feel as hot as fire, then as cold as ice. He turned to Amanda, with a grimace that Cyn supposed was his best attempt at a smile. "Maybe I am related, sweetheart," he said gruffly.

The faint Southern accent gave Cyn pause, but she bit back a smile, nonetheless. The man—probably a manufacturing VP, she decided—clearly didn't have much experience with kids. In spite of that, Amanda was charming the Uomo trousers off him.

In her twenty-eight years, no man had done more than play Cyn for a fool, but give Amanda ten seconds, and she'd wrap even the toughest cases right around her pinkie. Anton Santa, with his panther-about-to-kill posture and blank expression, was very clearly a tough case.

Amanda reached up and squeezed the poor man's biceps. "Are you my new bodyguard, Mr. Santa Claus?"

"You didn't!" As soon as Cyn imagined Anton Santa as a personal sidekick, he became a lot less "medium." Had her initial, very strange reaction to him really been attraction? "You didn't hire—"

"Yes." Paxton glared at her pointedly. "I intend to ensure that you and Amanda are safe."

Cyn gulped. Between the Christmas promotion, shopping and running the gauntlet between her parents, her next two weeks were going to be busy enough. She couldn't have a tall, gruff bodyguard shadowing her, too! Especially not one who made her feel so oddly uncomfortable. "No offence, Mr. Santa—"

"Just Santa." His voice was both rough and unsettling.

"Sorry—er—Santa, but we really don't need a bodyguard." Her eyes shot to Paxton's. "I talked to Bob Bingley. He said kidnapping Amanda was a joke cooked up during one of Mother's meetings. We simply can't involve—" She glanced at the man. His eyes now seemed hazel, hard to define. Changeable and arresting. Were they dark or golden? "A third party in our family infighting," she finished in a rush.

"Some joke." Paxton sniffed.

Cyn stared him down. Her father didn't take the warnings any more seriously than she did. He'd merely followed through with his own threat to hire the best, most expensive protection money could buy. His game plan was to make her mother feel like an idiot.

"I think I need a bodyguard!" Amanda sounded more excited about Anton Santa than about the Santa who came down the chimney. "People are gonna kidnap me and lock me up and everything!"

Was it her imagination, or could she feel the bodyguard scrutinizing her? Cyn glanced his way and caught his gaze roving over her face. He shoved his hands deep into his trouser pockets, then leaned idly against a file cabinet. It was strange, but she could swear she saw coldhearted fury in his eyes, in spite of his relaxed body language. She turned away and almost glared at Paxton.

"You know how they are about office pranks." She felt Mr. Calm, Cool and Collected's eyes drop from her face to her stocking-clad legs, and wished she'd worn a longer skirt. "Sometimes their jokes go too far. Bob probably sent the notes himself. He just won't admit it now because of all the ruckus you've caused."

Her eyes narrowed when they landed on her father's sleeves. He was missing both cuff links, as usual. When her mother left, it had become clear who'd been dressing him all those years.

"Well—" Paxton smiled wanly. "Mr. Santa was just saying he won't take the job."

Cyn sighed in relief. "Then things are—"

"I do believe I've changed my mind," Santa said.

Paxton began wringing his hands. "You said the threats seemed juvenile!"

Santa shook his head. "True, but I've been around a long time...."

Santa's voice had changed! Previously it was so gruff that Cyn was convinced he ate gravel for breakfast. Now it sounded silkily persuasive and as clear as a bell!

"Long enough to know that even the most ridiculous threats can be very real." His casual shrug suggested that even death couldn't faze him. "Better safe than sorry."

"Daddy, everything's fine," Cyn insisted, wishing Santa wouldn't encourage her father. "It was a practical joke taken—"

"Too far," her father finished, not looking convinced.

Cyn sighed. It wasn't the first time her father had gone overboard. He'd told lies on her own behalf that had left her a pampered widow, when she wasn't one, for instance. Paxton had a warm heart and good intentions, but his childish streak was a mile wide. It was why he'd started a toy company.

"You're a single mother!" Paxton exclaimed urgently. "I simply can't leave you and Amanda unprotected. If this is a false alarm, fine. If it's not, you'll have someone to watch over you."

"You live alone, then?"

Cyn's gaze shot to Santa's. The question was simple—just the sort a bodyguard might ask—but something in the man's eyes seemed almost suggestive. Cyn was so taken aback that words failed her. She felt her knees go a little weak.

"She was widowed over three years ago," Paxton explained.

"Her husband died?" Santa prodded.

"Very unfortunate." Paxton shook his head. "A car wreck."

"Please, Mommy!" Amanda piped in, seemingly unconcerned about her father's death. "I really want him!" The way she said it, Santa could have been a Ken doll.

Cyn shot her father a quelling glance. "I live alone," she said. "I like it that way. And I *can* take care of myself." She put her hands on her hips. "I can answer for myself, too."

"Such a talented woman," Santa remarked, making her mouth drop open in astonishment. The man's lips curled in what might have been a smile. He turned to Paxton. "Yes," he said softly, "I can certainly see why you'd want to keep two such charming ladies safe."

It was obvious he didn't find her at all charming. He was railroading her father and talking about her as if she weren't there, too. "I said I don't need—"

"You're gonna be bodyguarding me?" Amanda interrupted. She bounced on the desk, her dimpled cheeks bright with barely contained pleasure.

"He is." Paxton sounded decisive.

"Yeah." Santa nodded as Amanda jumped off the desk.

If she really put her foot down, Cyn knew she could dissuade her father. Instead, she found herself wondering what being guarded entailed, and wishing she wasn't so inclined to indulge Paxton since her mother had left him. Fortunately, her father's whims always ended as quickly as they began. Santa wouldn't be around long.

"So, I'm your boss," Amanda said precociously. "Right?"

"Guess you could say that."

Santa's voice sent a sudden shiver down Cyn's spine. It had turned gravelly again. Like his brown hair and eyes and suit, it should have been unremarkable. It was an ordinary baritone, touched with the slightest hint of a drawl. And yet, it was as changeably sexy as his eyes. The man was hardly nondescript, but there was something fluid about him. It was as if she kept reaching for him but couldn't quite grasp him.

"I'm the boss and you gotta carry me." Amanda's arms shot into the air.

An awkward moment passed. Santa's face tightened, looking more unreadable than ever. Cyn felt sure he was going to deny the request.

"Well, Amanda. I guess I do."

Cyn watched in surprise as the man lifted Amanda into his arms. "Wait a minute!" Maybe one last protest would put an end to this! "We're not in danger. Between the doormen, elevator operators and lobby attendants, my building's as secure as Fort Knox. I can't have a strange man underfoot during the day. I've work to do, both here and at home." She stared at her father, looking for support, and got none.

"I'll be there day *and* night." Santa glanced over his shoulder but kept walking.

Amanda yelled, "Stop at the door!"

Santa halted and shifted Amanda on his hip. While she swooped down to lift a doll from the overflowing box, Santa's eyes remained fixed on Cyn's.

"Okay, you can go again, Santa Claus," Amanda said, cradling the doll against his chest.

Santa chuckled. "Why, you little thief." He glanced

quickly at Amanda with seeming approval, then looked at Cyn again.

"Day and night?" Cyn echoed.

"I always move in with my clients." His leisurely gaze dropped down the length of her body, then slowly traveled upward again. "Sometimes I consider it a perk of the job."

The way he'd just looked at her made Cyn want to kill him. "And do you in this particular instance?" she asked tartly.

"Probably not," he said. Then he breezed over the threshold without a backward glance.

"WHAT HAS MY FATHER gotten me into?" Cyn fumed under her breath. The new bodyguard, still carrying Amanda, had the audacity to precede her through the outer door to her building. Worse, the doormen were nowhere to be seen and she'd somehow gotten stuck hauling Santa's heavy garment bag and a camel coat that was every bit as tasteful as his suit. Just as the door swung shut in her face, she nearly yelled, "You're a real gentleman, Mr. Santa."

He smirked, kicked the door partially open with his foot, then kept walking. She swung his garment bag, wedged it in the crack, then nudged through, using her shoulder. "Thank you so very much."

"You're so very welcome," he drawled. He glanced over his shoulder, then looked pointedly downward, at where his bag touched the floor. "Watch the bag. It's a Louis Vuitton, and I'd sure hate to see it soiled."

Her eyes narrowed as he turned away and began walking down the corridor. Jennifer, the lobby attendant, flashed her a quick smile of sympathy. "If you didn't want it *soiled*, then perhaps you should have carried it yourself." Cyn sped her steps, hoping to keep pace with him. "What's in it? Lead?"

He was far ahead now, but she heard his infuriating chuckle. She also realized that her initial estimation of him as average had been dead wrong. Outside, temperatures were hovering somewhere around subzero and the man hadn't even bothered with his coat. He hadn't shivered, either.

Now, still holding Amanda, he somehow managed to shrug out of his suit jacket. His shoulders were broad, accentuated by stylish thin suspenders. They tapered to a narrow waist, a perfect behind and long, lean-looking legs. Handcuffs were affixed to an unused belt loop. Beneath that loose-fitting suit, his body was very definitely not medium.

And then she saw the holster. "I will not have a gun in my apartment!"

"Maybe not," he called, without turning around. "But you sure need something. Your place is wide open. Where are all those doormen you were talking about?"

She forced herself to keep moving. Her high heels were skittering across the polished tile floor, and the exertion of dealing with him and carrying his luggage was making her short-winded. "I don't know—" He was a good ten feet in front of her now, so she had to raise her huffy voice. "They're usually right—"

"Which floor, Amanda?" His voice was soft, but it carried. Every time he addressed Amanda, rather than her, his tone became as sweet as honey. Cyn had never felt so annoyed in her life.

"Penthouse," Amanda and the elevator operator said simultaneously.

Apparently, the operator hadn't seen Cyn. The mirrored elevator doors slid shut just as she reached them. She scrutinized her reflection. She was well coiffed. Her green suit was tasteful and flattering. When her gaze dropped to the man's luggage, she jabbed the up button so hard she nearly broke a nail. "Once I get upstairs," she muttered, "you're history."

And then she smiled. Amanda was too young to carry keys, which meant the bodyguard was locked out.

WITHIN MERE MINUTES, Santa would feel prepared to see her again. It was enough time that he could wrap his invisible shield tightly around himself. He quickly cased the apartment, ignoring the wreath on the door, the lighted, ornamented tree in the living room, the red stockings hanging from the mantel, and the profusion of other homey Christmas decorations, all of which made him feel vaguely uncomfortable.

The front door, he found, opened onto the overly Christmassy living room, which led to an unsecured terrace. The dining room, kitchen, den and study were on one side of a hallway. Four bedrooms were on the other. Cyn had bad locks, one fire escape, no window bars, and in this case, "penthouse" only meant one of two top-floor apartments in a brownstone that would be easy to scale. Santa could do it with his eyes shut.

"Given her experience with thieves," he muttered as he began to pace, "you'd think she'd buy a decent dead bolt."

"Where's Amanda?"

He was walking the perimeter of the living room, mentally listing the new items he'd need, since he intended to secure the place, whether Amanda was really in danger or not. He turned around easily and smiled in Cyn's general direction.

"Your daughter—" Santa let the phrase hang in the air, as if to point out that she might be his, too. "Said she had to go change, in order to model her favorite nightgown for me."

Cyn gasped. "Do you mind telling me how you got in here?"

He shrugged. "I picked the locks."

"There were three of them!"

He seated himself gracefully on her cream velvet sofa. "I *did* leave the door open for you."

She remained in the doorway, with his bag in one hand and his coat in the other, her chest heaving. Her skin was flushed, more from fury than exertion, he thought.

"Why do you keep looking at me that way?" She sounded almost as curious as she did angry.

Because we used to be lovers. "What way?"

She sniffed, then kicked the front door shut with one of her high heels. "Like you hate my guts," she returned haughtily, as if the fact that he might didn't bother her in the least.

"I don't hate you," he said, even though the thought had entered his mind at least a thousand times. Did he? he wondered. He sure wanted to rail at her…right after he tasted her sweet-smelling skin again. He even wanted to tell her the truth.

But as near as he could tell, Cyn Sweet had kept a few secrets of her own. Namely, Amanda. "Nice spread," he finally said. It was an understatement. Her uptown penthouse would appraise at over a million.

She sighed. "Would you mind telling me what you've got against me?"

Where do I begin? The list is as long as your legs. "Not a thing," he said lightly. Looking at her, he realized that he'd have to attempt civility. Otherwise, she really would throw him out. He knew the dynamics between Paxton and Cyn well enough to know that she'd get her way if she really wanted it. So why hadn't she done so earlier, in her father's office?

"Do I look like a doormat?" She stared pointedly at his belongings, which were in her hands.

He couldn't help it. He looked her up and down, then tilted his head as if considering. "Well, you sure don't have *welcome* written on you." So much for being civil.

She dropped his bag with a thud, tossed his coat on top of it, then stared at him, looking thoroughly puzzled. Cyn Sweet—with her cheerleader good looks and helpful personality—was definitely not used to having people dislike her on sight.

Why was he torturing himself this way? When he'd seen

Amanda, he'd been sure she was his. Now he was beginning to wonder. In the elevator he'd gotten Amanda's birthday, and the timing was right. Still, she could belong to Harry Stevens, Cyn's husband. Santa had to know, but staying here might actually jeopardize his secret investigation.

Maybe he wanted to stay, since the situation was so strangely coincidental. But then, Santa didn't believe in fate. He still wanted Cyn, of course, but his fantasies were so ravenously vengeful that *how* he wanted her could hardly be called lovemaking. Finally, being in Cyn's apartment when she didn't recognize him made him feel as if he had power over her. Wielding it, he felt he was delivering the punishment she deserved. She hadn't given him the benefit of the doubt. She'd married someone else, and possibly to give Santa's own child a name.

"Are you going to apologize or not?" she asked impatiently.

He told himself he was staying merely because Paxton Sweet was paying him a bundle. "I'm sorry." There was nothing he hated more than groveling, but he had no choice. "Guess you just rubbed me the wrong way."

"I didn't rub you at all," she said levelly, making it clear she wasn't going to, either.

He nodded, as if agreeing to a hands-off policy.

"I love my father," she continued. "And if he thinks you should be here, I'm willing to let you stay. I figure this whim will pass. Until then—" she pointed "—your room is the first on the right, nearest the front door." Her lips suddenly twitched into a near smile. "That way, if any kidnappers come, maybe they'll take you first."

He almost smiled back. "Do you really think they'd mistake me for Amanda?"

"If I'm lucky."

Cyn was as high-handed and imperious as she'd ever been. And yet there was something in her eyes…a sadness that hadn't been there before. He sure hoped he'd caused it. "I'll stay wherever you like."

He only half listened as she ran down a list of house rules, which included him wearing a robe. She told him to help himself to anything in the kitchen, and that she worked at the office part-time but didn't keep regular hours. The pre-packaged speech reminded him that Cyn had grown up with maids, housekeepers and chauffeurs.

"First thing tomorrow, I'll install a new security system," he said, when she'd finished.

"My security is fine."

At that, he almost chuckled. "Well, Ms. Sweet—"

"I guess you can call me Cyn."

He stretched his legs over her carpet. "Well, Cyn, you never know when unwanted elements might penetrate—" he swept his arm over his own lap "—into your very living room."

"You say that almost as if you're such an element," she remarked with a smile.

"Maybe I am."

"No maybe about it," she said lightly.

Amanda pranced into the room and whirled in a circle, showing off her long white gown. Then she lunged into Santa's lap. "I'm the boss and you have to put me to bed!"

Santa rose without bothering to gauge Cyn's reaction. Was the little girl in his arms really his? "Sure, sweetheart, point the way."

Cyn's spoiled her rotten. Amanda had more toys than were offered for sale at Too Sweet. Her walls were pink, the can-opied bed lacy and ruffled. Just looking at the room, and feeling Amanda snuggle against him, he suddenly felt as if his heart might break. Whether it was because he'd never had a childhood himself, or because he may have missed part of his own daughter's, he didn't know.

As he pulled back Amanda's covers and leaned to slide her beneath them, he felt Cyn's eyes on his back. His sixth sense told him she was directly behind him, in the doorway. He even knew that her arms were crossed over her chest.

"Now you gotta kiss me," Amanda whispered. "Okay?"

He clamped his jaw shut, since his face felt quivery. Amanda was so beautiful. Was that why he now doubted she was his? Could rough-and-tumble Anton Santa have helped make someone so perfect? Her green eyes were twinkling, and her blond hair, which was as fine as silk, now spread across her pillow. He suddenly realized he'd never kissed a kid before.

"You don't gotta, not if you don't want, Mr. Santa Claus."

Santa just wished Cyn wasn't standing behind him. He had few vulnerabilities, but he meant to keep the chosen few hidden from her. He leaned slowly and kissed Amanda's cheek. Her skin was smooth and cool, like fine china. His throat felt as dry as dust. "Night, Amanda."

"You're gonna shoot 'em when they come here. Right?" Amanda murmured excitedly. "Like on a cop show."

"Yeah," he said softly.

Amanda's blond brows crinkled. "You don't gotta go home for Christmas, do you?"

He shook his head. "No."

"You're gonna get in big trouble from your mom and dad."

"They're dead." The look of surprise and sorrow on the little girl's face made him want to double over. How could he have been so insensitive? Amanda was just a kid. "It's okay," he quickly added. "It was a long time ago."

"Oh, Mr. Santa!" she exclaimed in a soft, breathy voice. She sat up, hugged him tight and pressed kisses against his shirt.

"Night," he managed to say, turning away.

He didn't look at Cyn when he passed her. He just couldn't bear to, somehow. He was nearly out of earshot, when he heard Amanda say, "Please, can I call him daddy? Please, Mommy?"

He cocked his head, listening for Cyn's response. He heard none.

"I need a daddy and I don't got one! And he doesn't got a mom *or* dad."

He heard whispers and hushed rustling. After a moment, Amanda's voice rose. "I'm gonna tell him your secret!"

"Fine, then," Cyn said.

Santa's jaw dropped open in astonishment. What was Amanda using for blackmail? And was she really his daughter? The Santa mole was a possible giveaway, but Amanda also happily engaged in doll theft and now blackmail. Definite proof of the Santa genes, he thought dryly.

"I'm turning off your light now, honey," Cyn said.

Santa quickly gathered his bag and coat and headed for the room Cyn had indicated. It was early, but he didn't want to see her again. Not tonight.

"I wouldn't have imagined you'd go to bed at seven-thirty."

It was Cyn. He turned in his doorway. Their eyes met and held. "I need to sleep," he said gruffly. "I've been traveling a long time."

For a moment his last words hung in the air, as if they meant something special. He wondered if he would tell her his true identity, or if she would discover it. Would he then tell her about those four long years of traveling?

"Somehow," she said softly, "I imagine you have."

Santa breathed in sharply, feeling sure she'd recognized him after all.

"ON THE FIRST DAY of Christmas my true love gave to me…" Cyn sang along with the CD. She'd meant to finish wrapping copies of *Little Amanda's Perfect Christmas*, which would be given away tomorrow, during the Christmas tree decoration promotion at the toy store. Instead, she found herself

leaning in the living room window, sipping mulled cider. Outside, dry flurries spiraled in the dark air but never landed. It was so cold, the cement of the sidewalk below looked white.

Inside, warm yellow light seeped from beneath the body-guard's door, which meant he'd lied. He was wide-awake. But why had he been in such a hurry to escape? The man really was as mysterious as the North Pole Santa, she thought wryly. After all, *he* was the one who'd been uncivil.

Seeing him with Amanda, she'd felt herself warming to him. She felt sorry for him because he had no family to visit at Christmastime, too. Maybe a man like Santa—one who kept his cards close to the vest—was better than the more flirtatious type, she decided now, wishing she could quit comparing him to Jake Jackson....

Like Santa, Jake had had no family. At least he'd *said* his father had died in a work-related accident, and that his mother had died of cancer. Unlike Santa, Jake had sure been outward. He'd had a heavy Southern accent, thicker than mo-lasses, but his every word had been nothing more than smooth talk. Only after she'd slept with him had she started to worry about his many small evasions. Only then had she started wondering if they'd added up to him seeing another woman.

That was why, four long Christmases ago, she'd followed him. He'd already kissed her goodbye, since she was sup-posed to meet her parents in Puerto Rico for a tropical Christ-mas, but when she'd reached Kennedy, her plane was snow-bound. Like a thief in the night, she'd stolen back to Jake's place in the Village and waited for him.

She'd tailed him and another man over perilously icy roads, right to the house she'd just left, the one she'd shared with her parents. At the high wrought-iron gates, they'd met a third man, the one who'd gotten away. He was already wearing a red-and-green ski mask.

That a group called The Grinch Gang had been playing

local heiresses for fools was old news, but she was so shocked at finding herself a victim that she'd waited another fifteen minutes before calling the police from her car phone.

No. Admit it, Cyn. You were considering not turning Jake in. Now she turned away from the window, hardly wanting to think about what happened after she'd made the call. She glanced at Santa's door again, just in time to see his light go out. The darkness left her feeling bereft.

"You can't make me feel safe," she whispered. *I doubt you'll make me forget Jake Jackson, either.* "Even if you're the best of the best." After all, there were no locks for the mind. No chains or bars to keep away the fantasies. No cage that could withstand her dreams. And even if there were, her jewel thief was as slippery as Houdini.

Why can't I stop thinking about Jake? Perhaps because it was Christmas again. Or because the bodyguard made her think of danger, and Jake was certainly the most dangerous thing she'd ever known. Anton Santa would never know her secret, but it was her attraction to him and her memories of Jake that had made her decide to let him stay. She could have dissuaded Paxton, and she was positive the notes didn't signify real danger.

But other threats were always real. That Jake would be released from prison and come to claim Amanda, for instance. It was all the more terrifying, since Cyn still found herself wanting to make excuses for him because he hadn't had parents. And yet, it wasn't his background but his lips that had almost made her lie for him. If he ever came back, she was sometimes sure she wouldn't be able to resist....

How could she? No other man had set her nerves on edge in the exact way Jake had—until today. And that was the real reason Anton Santa had to stay.

Because maybe he could make her forget.

With relief, he realized America was in the room.

Part 2

Chapter Two

"What are you doing to my apartment?" Cyn croaked. She'd hardly forgotten about Anton Santa, but now she wished she'd come into the living room in something other than her red silk robe after she'd checked on Amanda.

The new bodyguard turned away from two jeans-clad workmen who were standing beside her fireplace. "Exactly what I was hired to do," he said calmly. Had his eyes really flickered with contempt? It almost seemed as if he were testing her, or as if he harbored a secret he thought she should know.

As her gaze flitted around the room, her lips parted in horror, then pursed again. The windows were covered with white wrought-iron bars, which weren't entirely unattractive. A complicated-looking, dowel-style lock secured the terrace door, and parts to a keypad alarm system were sprawled over her floor. Her mild annoyance rose to outright anger. "I have no intention of living in a fortress, Mr. Santa!"

"You'll live any way I tell you to," he said simply.

Their eyes met and held, neither wavering. The various parts of him—his short hair, practical dress shoes and non-descript tie—should have made him look like a G-man. But his hooded hazel eyes seemed to smolder with hidden emotion. The slacks to his loosely tailored gray suit—the jacket of which was neatly draped over a chair—hugged and accentuated his slender hips. Thin, narrowly striped suspenders curved over his crisp white shirt, showing off his powerful shoulders.

For the first time she decided he had a little Latin blood. It was in the eyes, which were more heavily lidded than she'd previously thought. He turned back to the workmen, as if satisfied. That gesture, showing a complete lack of regard for her opinions, made her anger rise to the level of pure fury.

"Wait just a minute!" Unfortunately, her voice was too sleep-creaky to carry much authority.

He turned his head to the side, as if she didn't merit so much as direct eye contact.

She tossed her hair over her shoulders with two quick jerks of her head. "By the time I'm dressed, I want those bars off my windows, that mess off the floor, and these men out of here! My father hired you, I didn't! And I can't have you waltzing in and rearranging my life to suit his—and your—whims!"

One moment, he wasn't even looking at her. In the next, he'd crossed the room. He grabbed her elbow firmly, turned her, then began propelling her down the hallway. "Go ahead and install the front door keypad," he said over his shoulder.

"Just who do you think you are?" she sputtered.

"Whoever it is, I'm sure you'd be surprised," he said cryptically.

"Let go!" His chest was flush against her back and he was breathing down her neck, making it tingle. She tried to wrench around and face him.

In a quick reflex he tightened his grip, pulling her even closer. Cyn clutched her robe lapels against the collar of the high-necked gown she wore beneath, feeling exposed. Without her high heels, he was taller than she and when she craned her neck to look at him, her gaze settled on his jaw. She realized a hairline scar ran the length of it.

"You will *not* rearrange my life," she repeated. "And you *cannot* manhandle me from room to room, either!"

In the kitchen, he pulled out a chair and shoved it beneath her behind. He stared at her for an instant, licking his bottom lip as if the gesture might keep him from smiling. "I can't? I believe I just did."

She blinked as if that might somehow make the man vanish. Not that he noticed. The timer on her coffeepot had ensured that coffee would be waiting when she awakened, and Santa was now pouring a cup, without offering her any.

"I see you know where my cups are," she said huffily. "I take it you've already pawed through all my cabinets." When he glanced over his shoulder, his lower lip curled slightly, as if to say she amused him. She sighed. "You wanted to make sure my cups and saucers didn't pose a serious threat to our security, right?"

He turned and leaned against the counter. "No," he said calmly. "I made myself breakfast. Not everyone sleeps until noon."

Somehow she couldn't imagine Anton Santa puttering around a kitchen. She rolled her eyes. "It's only nine."

He glanced at a clock. "Ten after."

Her lips suddenly quivered with impending laughter. What would it take to get a rise out of him? Had any woman ever gotten under his skin? "You seem to have a lot of hidden talents," she said coyly.

"Like knowing how to tell time?" He shot her another trademark Santa glance that was so hard to define. His lips parted slightly, but he didn't really smile. His head tilted to the side, but he didn't quite cock it. His eyes were just about to roll heavenward, but they never did. That look both chastised her for baiting him, and yet it urged her on, since it also said she'd never best him.

"Yeah," she finally said. "Why, the next thing I know, you'll be tying your own shoelaces."

"Only time will tell," he drawled, still sizing her up with

his eyes. His own seemed to say that she was playing with fire and she was about to get burned. To her surprise, he placed the cup of coffee, he'd poured, in front of her. His lips twitched. "I had mine at five-thirty."

"This morning?" she couldn't help but ask, appalled.

This time, he did roll his sexy eyes, almost flirtatiously. Or was that just wishful thinking? "No. Five-thirty last night."

Her brows drew up into points. "You really don't like me, do you?" She toyed with the rim of her coffee mug, deciding she would get a rise from this standoffish enigma of a man one way or another. His sudden smirk seemed to say that she was welcome to think whatever she pleased.

"Why?" she prodded, lowering her voice. "Judging by your suits, you do all right for yourself, so it can't be because I'm a spoiled rich kid."

When his eyes dropped from hers to the lapels of her robe, she wondered if it was intentional or accidental. Either way, his gaze lingered on her breasts, as if to point out that she wasn't a kid at all, but a woman. The tips of her breasts constricted and stiffened against her nightgown, and she sucked in an audible breath. His jaw tensed, his facial muscles hardened and his eyes rose again in a leisurely fashion, as if he meant to make no apology for looking. There was an extremely awkward silence.

"You don't really think Amanda's in danger, do you?" she finally managed to ask. His gaze remained so steady that she felt the sudden urge to jump up and tickle him.

"Like I said, I've been around." His voice made her think of tightly coiled metal that was about to spring free. "And no threat should be taken lightly."

But it was Santa she shouldn't take lightly. His strangeness had worn off, and she could see *him* now. The powerful, sensual virility in his gaze and body carried both threats and promises. "And just how long have you—" The back of her throat went dry. Her gaze dropped from his eyes over his rounded, muscular shoulders. "Been around?"

He shot her the trademark Santa look again, and she felt a little silly. Surely she was imagining he desired her. She could bait him all she wanted to but he'd never rise to it. As soon as she blinked, he turned to the refrigerator, took out a carton of half-and-half and placed it beside her mug.

"Now, wait a minute, Santa." She squinted at him. "How do you know I take cream?" Something about his air of suave cool made her smile. "Do you have ESP? Before you became a bodyguard, you were a professional psychic, right? You had a big glass ball in which you could read the future and a book of spells...."

This time he gave her enough of a smile that she could see his polished, gleaming, straight white teeth. There was another difference between him and Jake. Jake had had crooked bottoms.

"I'm sure I'd be good at anything I undertook."

She wasn't certain but thought he was implying he was a good lover. *He probably is.* Her smile faltered. "You're sure about that?" Her voice was raspier than she'd intended.

"Absolutely."

She decided he had to be attracted to her. Their combined physical energy seemed to make the very air vibrate. "So how did you know I take cream?"

He leaned quickly, so his lips were next to her ear. "Because I've been around a lot longer than you think." His breath sent a tingle down to the toes of her bare feet.

"And what else do you *think* you know about me?" She couldn't decide whether his self-containment was making her angry or not.

"Ms. Sweet," he drawled softly. "Before you ask, you should be damn sure you really want to know." With that, he pivoted and strode from her kitchen.

"You're a strange one, Anton Santa. You really are." Cyn

was still staring from the carton to the empty doorway when Amanda bounded over the threshold.

"Mommy, Mommy," she said breathlessly. "How can Santa Claus get in now?"

For a second, Cyn didn't know what she was talking about. Then she remembered the bars, dowel and keypad. She chuckled, thinking of Anton Santa. "Amanda," she said, "maybe the real question is whether or not we can get out."

"MORE CHRISTMAS CAROLS," Santa muttered. This time they were Musak. He reclined on the guest room bed, bunched the pillows beneath his head in preparation for a long wait, then coiled the phone cord around his finger. While he patiently waited for one of his old college friends who now worked at the census office to come on the line, he simultaneously listened to "Rudolph the Red-Nosed Reindeer" and the running shower.

He was glad Cyn was performing her morning ablutions, since it was buying him time to make calls, but he wished he could quit imagining how she looked, scrubbing herself beneath those water jets. He could nearly see her long, well-toned arms stretch as she sudsed her hair. Slender, foam-tipped fingers kneaded her scalp. A round water drop glistened on her collarbone. It grew heavier, then slowly snaked toward the dark, hard, beaded tip of one of her breasts. Santa's slacks tightened and he all but squirmed. *Quit torturing yourself. Hell, she's just a woman.* He blew out an annoyed sigh. Their encounter in the kitchen had left him with enough unwanted arousal to last him a week. He hardly needed fantasies.

"Census office," a woman said.

Good. Something to occupy my mind, other than Cyn. "Right. I'm holding for Josh Meyers."

"He'll be right—" The woman didn't even finish before she put him on hold again. Just opposite him was a large mirror in which he could see himself. The room itself was chic and contemporary, done in blue and black, with steel and glass tables. Anyone would have been comfortable in it. Even him, if it weren't for the fact that it was in his ex-lover's apartment.

"Anton? Sorry to keep you on hold."

"No problem. I know you're not really supposed to—"

Josh's chuckle cut him off. "Anything for a buddy."

Santa smiled. "I just wanted to see what you could tell me about a man named Harry Stevens. He used to live in Alabama. I need his marital statistics."

"You sound pressed for time."

Santa mustered a good-old-boy laugh. "Yeah, but I promise to call and converse soon. Maybe I'll even head down to D.C."

"That'd be great," Josh said. "Hold on a minute and let me see what I can give you."

Santa listened as the water was turned off. Now Cyn was stepping from the shower, fully naked, and into a thick woolly towel. He could smell her everywhere, he thought, and hear her steps. Last night she'd nearly driven him crazy, singing along with those sappy Christmas carols. Santa sighed again, thinking he'd really hate her if he found the proof that she'd withheld from him the one thing he'd never really had—a family.

Winter was always tough. His mother and father had both died in winter. Christmas was even worse. During the season, everyone on earth seemed to have somebody. Not that he gave a damn if he didn't, of course, but the impending holiday was why he'd grabbed the New York job. When the referral service that managed his schedule called, he hadn't even asked questions. He liked to keep moving. This time of year, he moved even faster.

But now he'd stopped. And he was reclining on a bed in Cyn Sweet's apartment of all places. After their exchange in the kitchen, he was beginning to think that neither he nor she were particularly likable people. She was as spoiled as ever.

He was acting edgy. *But I have every right to, because of Amanda.* Still, he could remember a time when they'd both been open, thoroughly likable and deeply in love.

"Anton?"

"Josh?" The severe cold had been affecting the lines, and the phone suddenly crackled. "You still there, Josh?"

For a moment the two waited for the static to clear.

"Yeah," Josh finally said. "Harrold Stuart Stevens married Cynthia Anna Sweet…" Santa grabbed a notepad and began writing the pertinent dates as Josh talked. "The daughter, Amanda, was born September 17, 1990."

It was a close call, but Amanda could be Harry's. "What do you have for the guy's death date?" Santa felt a little disappointed. He'd gotten this much from Amanda.

"Death date?"

"Yeah," Santa said. "He died in a car wreck."

"Hang on."

"We wish you a merry Christmas, we wish you a merry Christmas…" Santa sang along with the Musak in spite of himself. Then he tilted his head and stared into the mirror, trying to recall the particulars of his Jake Jackson persona. After all, given the palpable, sensual energy coursing between him and Cyn, she was bound to recognize him sooner or later.

He half hoped it was sooner, though he wasn't sure why. Maybe it was simply because high drama and heart-stopping action made him feel so alive. If Cyn recognized him, sparks would surely fly. Especially if Amanda really was his.

He decided he didn't *look* like Amanda's father. The reflection staring back at him was clean shaven, shorthaired and in a suit. It was definitely the no-frills Santa. He sighed, wondering how anyone could have loved Jake Jackson. Especially Cyn. She was a golden girl. Spoiled, no doubt, but made for life's finer pleasures.

Long-haired rebel Jake Jackson could have given her none of them. He'd been as lean and mean as Santa had been back then. A scruffy kid who was out to prove himself. His hair, mustache and beard had been blond and he'd had a penchant for hip leather jackets and motorcycle boots. He'd worn sunglasses so often that Cyn probably couldn't even remember his eye color. Yeah, Jake had been a far cry from the clean-cut straight arrow who was now staring back at Santa. And if Cyn's taste ran to the Jake Jacksons of the world, the real Santa didn't stand a chance.

"Great," he murmured aloud. He tried to tell himself that the last thing he wanted was a second chance at Cyn Sweet. "We Wish You a Merry Christmas" broke into "Deck the Halls."

"You say this guy died in a car wreck?" Josh asked.

Santa sat up. "He didn't?"

Josh chuckled. "According to this, buddy, Harry Stevens is alive and well and still living in Alabama."

After a long moment Santa murmured, "Do you have an address and phone?"

"Sure do."

Santa started scribbling again.

"You visiting family for the holidays?" Josh asked.

"No." Santa thought of Amanda. "Well, I'm not sure yet."

"Well, merry Christmas, Santa."

"You, too, buddy."

He hung up still thinking that Harry Stevens could be Amanda's father. But why would Cynthia and her father take it upon themselves to claim the man was dead?

"AMANDA?" Cartoons played on television, the door was wide open, and all Santa's senses went on alert. He hadn't been on the phone but ten minutes. Now he slipped noiselessly into the living room. Involuntarily his hand slid over his chest toward his holster, and he wished he hadn't removed it in deference to Cyn's wishes.

"You can't catch me!" Amanda shrieked. She shot from behind the Christmas tree, a fast blur of a man on her heels.

Santa easily lunged between Amanda and her attacker. In a second flat, he'd gripped the man's parka and lifted him clean off the floor.

He turned his head slightly to the side. "Go to your room, Amanda," he said with deathly calm.

Amanda wavered uncertainly by the door to the guest room. Her white velvet dress was embroidered with holly berries. Its sash had come untied, her white leggings sagged at the knees, and her little black patent leather shoes gleamed. In spite of the circumstances Santa found himself thinking she looked as pretty as a picture.

"Go."

She streaked down the hall like a bolt of white light.

"Now—" Santa glared at the culprit. He was blond, blue eyed and about five-ten. He looked twenty-five or thirty and scared spitless. "Who are you?"

"Get your hands off me!" he yelled, trying to squirm away from where Santa held his collar. Suddenly he pushed both hands against Santa's chest.

"Oh, brother," Santa muttered as the man bolted for the door. He threw out his foot, catching the other man's ankle. The poor fellow crashed into Cyn's Christmas tree, then leaned forward, in an effort to regain his balance. He tripped over a wrapped present, then went sprawling across the floor.

"Please don't try to get up," Santa said, sounding bored. The man rolled over, raking his fingers through his hair. It was strewn with strands of silver tinsel.

"What is your problem?" The man sounded furious, but it was clear he didn't intend to fight.

"How did you get in here?"

"I let him in!"

Santa turned toward the hallway. Cyn's hands were on her hips. She was either going to laugh or start shrieking.

Amanda peeked out from behind her. "For heaven's sake! He's the delivery man from Bloomingdale's."

"Bloomingdale's?" Santa repeated. For a long moment he and Cyn gawked at each other. She was wearing a red suit today, with another short skirt. She had on high heels, too, the kind that made him want to let her walk all over him. "Never leave the door open," he finally said.

"I had to get my wallet," she protested, still gaping at him.

"Next time, leave him in the outside hall, then lock the door," Santa said, fighting to maintain his cool. "And then you go get your wallet."

"If you hadn't put in that newfangled keypad, perhaps I would have."

"I could sue for this!" The man was clearly trying to salvage some semblance of his destroyed dignity.

"You could." Santa shot him a quelling glance.

"But maybe I won't," the man quickly added. He warily watched Santa as he struggled to his feet.

Amanda giggled. "You still got tinsel in your hair, mister!"

"You were the one who insisted I play tag with you," the man returned tightly.

At that, Santa was glad to see that Amanda had the decency to blush. But then she giggled again. "I was winning!" she squealed.

Cyn's shoulders started to shake with laughter. "I'm so sorry," she said, rushing forward. One of her perfectly manicured hands slid inside her wallet, and she pulled out a hefty-looking number of bills. "So very sorry," she repeated, pressing the money into the man's hands.

The tip seemed to help some. "Merry Christmas" the man said grudgingly, heading for the door. "And have a happy New Year."

Santa shut the door and activated the lock from the inside. Behind him, Cyn's chuckles gave way to full-scale laughter.

When he turned around, she was crumpling against the wall, indulging her shoulder-shaking giggles.

"Heavens," she gasped, between fits. "I'm sure glad you're here to protect us."

He decided to let her get it out of her system. It would take more than a barb like that to unman him. Amanda hadn't joined in. She was staring at him, looking as guilty as sin. After a moment she crept uncertainly to his side. She placed her tiny hand in his and squeezed tightly.

"It's okay, Mr. Santa Claus," she said in comfort. "It could have been a robber or a mugger." Her voice rose hopefully. "Maybe next time it will be."

The words sent Cyn into another bout of hysterics. The situation made Santa feel a little ridiculous, but he had to admit it was good to hear Cyn laugh—really laugh—again. She nearly staggered across the room, teetering on her high heels, then collapsed in an armchair, sighing. Watching her cross her long, elegant, black-stocking-clad legs, Santa almost sighed himself.

"I'm gonna go get my coat by myself now, like a good girl," Amanda said, releasing his hand. "Mommy says we've got to go to a promp-tion at the store."

Promp-tion? Oh. Promotion. He glanced down. The little girl barely came to the level of his thighs. He felt a sudden urge to lift her into his arms again.

"I just bet those kidnappers are gonna come to our promp-tion," she crooned, still clearly trying to soothe him.

"Oh," Cyn managed to call out as Amanda flew past her, "but don't you think we should give him the day off, Amanda? After all, he's been working *so* hard this morning." At that, she started laughing so uncontrollably that she actually snorted.

"Very unladylike," Santa muttered under his breath. He tried to tell himself that her hysterics weren't annoying him. He was merely anxious to complete the day's agenda so he could call Harry Stevens and have a nice little chat.

When he could no longer stand it, he said, "You'll need your coat, Ms. Sweet."

His tone sobered her. She opened her mouth, undoubtedly to offer some tart response, then clamped it shut. "Whatever you say, Santa," she finally conceded weakly.

"Right," he said, sounding more agreeable than he actually felt. "I'm glad to see you're getting the picture."

"Now, Amanda," Cyn said, "every time someone comes up, you reach in the box and hand them an ornament. Then, when they take the ornaments to the elves, the elves will hand them a copy of your book. Okay?"

Amanda crossed her arms defensively over her sash. "I know what to do."

"I know you do." Cyn smoothed the velvet hem of Amanda's dress, then glanced anxiously around Too Sweet Toys, feeling sure the promotion had drawn in needed customers. All three levels, the glass walls of which faced the Fifth Avenue side of Rockefeller Center, were crowded with shoppers and their children.

The long-needled pine she and Paxton had ordered from upstate rose to the high first-floor ceiling. Ladders had been placed around the tree, and workers in elf costumes—mostly unemployed actors and actresses—were ready to place ornaments on the higher branches. Cyn caught a glimpse of both her father's assistant and her mother on the escalators. Eileen was going up; Analise was headed down. Kids sprawled and squirmed in the many colorful armchairs that had been placed throughout the store for tired shoppers.

Suddenly Cyn's nose came level with a pant leg. She sucked in a quick breath, then slowly raised her gaze. It traveled over the finely woven, expensive fabric, then inadvertently stopped at the apex of the man's thighs. She gulped.

"I'll stick close to Amanda."

Cyn craned her neck and found herself peering into Santa's eyes. They were every bit as powerful looking as his thighs.

Realizing that he was towering over her, her mouth went dry and she forced herself to stand. Not that it helped. In her heels, she was nearly his height, and now her gaze met his, dead-on. The way her knees buckled almost made her wish she was staring at his pant leg again. The man was definitely growing on her. In fact, she was beginning to think more about him than Jake Jackson.

"The store's so crowded...." She smiled as kindly as she could, hoping to atone for laughing at him earlier. It had clearly made him furious. "I'm so glad you're here. I really am."

She thought he nodded, but it was hard to tell.

"You're not much for conversation, are you?" she prodded just as the first toddler, a little girl, ran up to her daughter. Amanda handed her a gleaming silver bulb.

"You know—" Cyn felt foolish, but felt compelled to continue. "Like I would say something, and then you would, and then I would." She blew out a quick sigh. "Guess you just don't like to talk."

At that, Santa actually grinned. "Depends on who I'm talking to."

"So the problem's just me?" she asked coyly.

"I'm working."

He sounded more annoyed that he actually was, she decided. Something in his eyes made her sure he was beginning to crack a little. "Well, I'm going to go say hello to my mother." She pointed toward the opposite side of the first floor.

"You're not my client. You don't need to clear your comings and goings with me."

She felt almost as if she'd announced she was going on a date. She arched her brows. "I'm not your client?" If Paxton had hired him, it was as good as if she had.

"No." He glanced down just as Amanda handed a little boy a bright blue origami ornament. "Your daughter is."

Cyn squinted at him, wondering why he always used such

an odd intonation when he said "your daughter." She decided there was just no talking to the man, and glanced around the crowded store again. As a mother, she couldn't help but give ear to those occasional stories about mothers who'd lost children in public places. "You'll watch her, won't you?"

"With my life."

He sounded so serious that she gulped. "You would, wouldn't you?"

"It's my job."

It was hard to turn away from him, but she did. Before she'd reached her mother's side, Bob Bingley steered her past an armchair. He pushed her behind a counter, saying, "Sorry, but we need you on register one, Cyn." He wiggled his brows. "Or should I say 'doll face'?"

"If you want to die," Cyn returned playfully. The store was the Sweets' lifeblood, and Cyn easily began ringing up purchases. As she worked, her eyes kept drifting back to her baby and the bodyguard.

They were an odd couple. Santa towered behind Amanda, with an erect posture, his hands held loosely at his sides. Even from where Cyn was, she could feel his eyes sweeping back and forth across the room, in watchful protection. Sometimes, his gaze seemed to want to stop on her, but it never did.

Men had occasionally come on to her like gangbusters. But not this one. Because he was always watching Amanda, talking to him was even more difficult. She found herself wondering how she might arrange to spend some time alone with him. Just to see if he warmed to her....

He's a bodyguard, all right, she thought, as she gift wrapped a Barney doll. Santa's suit was so nondescript as to make him invisible. When she'd first seen him, she hadn't even noticed his good looks. Now the adults in the store barely noticed him at all. But the children did, she realized with surprise. They gravitated toward him somehow, as if sensing he was keeping them safe. Just watching him, noting how good he was at what he did, she felt a chill creep along her spine. *Don't worry. No one will ever take Amanda. Jake Jackson's in jail.*

Her discomfort passed. Once again she was aware of the lively Christmas music. The kids rushed to the elves and pointed toward where they wanted their ornaments hung. Some opted for the lower branches and hung the decorations themselves. In return, each received a wrapped copy of *Little Amanda's Perfect Christmas.*

"Thank you for shopping at Too Sweet!" Cyn smiled brightly and extended the elegantly wrapped Barney doll.

"So far the best day for sales yet!" Bob Bingley called. He raced past her, a ribbon of calculator tape trailing over his shoulder.

"Have you seen your father?" Analise leaned against the counter.

Cyn continued to ring up purchases. "You're looking for Dad?" Were her parents speaking again?

"Looking to avoid him," her mother admitted.

Cyn sighed. If she knew more about her parents' difficulties, maybe she could help fix them. "He's staying on the third level," she said, handing a bag to a customer.

Her mother smiled. "Good. Then I can lean here for the whole of two seconds before Bob requires me again."

"Thank you for shopping at Too Sweet," Cyn said cheerfully to a woman about her age. She lowered her voice as she reached for the next batch of merchandise. "Why are you and Daddy fighting, anyway?"

Analise shrugged. "What I want to discuss is your bodyguard."

Cyn chuckled. "I believe he belongs to Amanda." She glanced in his direction again. Santa was helping Amanda untangle the hanging wires on some of the ornaments. Even from here, it was clear that Amanda's hands were too little and his were too large. Illogically Cyn thought she could almost stretch her arm across the room and fix things for them.

"Well, with that build, I think he might make even a grown-up girl feel safe."

Cyn reached under the counter, groping for more gift boxes. "Or like she's in dangerous trouble," she said to her mother.

"So you like him?"

Cyn shrugged as she punched out the flattened sides of a box. "I don't think he likes me."

"Who wouldn't like my daughter?" Before Cyn could respond, Analise gave her a quick kiss on the cheek. "Bob calls," she said, heading toward the escalators and waving over her shoulder.

A full hour later Cyn felt a tug at her skirt. She glanced down. "Amanda?" When Cyn raised her gaze to Santa's, she realized he looked vaguely embarrassed.

"I gotta go to the potty right now and Santa Claus can't guard me there," Amanda said in a distressed tone.

"Come on. I'll take care of you." She hoisted Amanda to her hip and headed toward the employees' bathroom. Unable to help herself, she glanced over her shoulder and shot Santa her most flirtatious smile. "Coming, Santa Claus?"

"Right behind you."

"You could walk beside us," she offered.

He sped his steps until they were walking side by side, in perfect rhythm. When his hips grazed hers, warmth seemed to infuse all her limbs.

Until Santa leaned against a wall. "Just don't get lost in there, ladies."

"And run the risk of never seeing you again?" Cyn raised her brows and stared boldly into his eyes. "No chance." She playfully slammed the door.

As coy as she was by nature, she couldn't quite believe the way she'd looked at Santa. Even at her age, she wasn't above practicing the proverbial come-on look in her mirror.

Her eyes had been beaming out rays of pure lust, and she knew it.

As she helped Amanda, she wondered what he'd say when she came back out. Perhaps he'd actually pick up the thread of the flirtation she'd begun. But to her disappointment he'd vanished. He'd taken up his post by the tree again. Since Amanda ran ahead, there was no real reason for Cyn to follow. Except that she wanted to.

Only after all the ornaments were hung did Cyn come anywhere near Santa again. "Can Mr. Santa please do the star at the top?" Amanda begged.

Cyn could almost feel Santa holding his breath. Christmas clearly wasn't his cup of tea. She looked at him pointedly. "Mr. Santa?"

"Please, please, please!"

He exhaled audibly. "Sure."

Without waiting for him, Amanda marched toward one of the ladders, quickly dispensed with one of the elves, then climbed upward and seated herself on a rung. Her dangling ankles curled around the ladder's sides. She crooked her finger in Santa's direction, then smiled, showing her dimples.

"I do believe your client wants you," Cyn said wryly.

"That she does."

Cyn watched him head for the tree. He took the star, agilely climbed the ladder, then hung it. As he did, all the children in the store applauded. Cyn wasn't positive, but she was fairly sure he would prefer to be back in whatever sunny country he'd just come from.

When he came down, Amanda grabbed his hand. Her face was lit up with pure prideful pleasure. She glanced from Santa, to the tree, then to the other children. When she craned her neck to look at Santa again, her gaze seemed to say she owned him. Cyn felt her shoulders begin to shake. *You poor, poor man,* she thought, as Amanda led him toward the counter.

He gingerly removed a teddy bear from an armchair and eased himself into it. "May I rest now?"

Amanda clasped her hands in front of her and smiled sweetly. "You can do what you want," she said, wriggling onto his lap.

Cyn realized she wasn't the only person getting a juvenile crush on Santa. Her daughter had fallen—head over patent leather heels—in love. Cyn leaned around the arm of the chair and tugged Amanda's elbow. "Why don't you go see Grandmama? Mr. Santa's been standing for a while. He might want a break."

Amanda reached for her, just as a shopper jostled Cyn from behind. Cyn found herself teetering, then turning, and suddenly—without understanding how it happened—she was sitting on Santa's spare knee. An uncharacteristic flush rose to her cheeks.

Amanda giggled. "I already told Santa that I gotta get a daddy for Christmas," she announced.

Everything in her daughter's eyes made clear just which daddy she had in mind.

"But I can't call him 'daddy,' even though you said it's okay. He's not my daddy and I'm not a liar. Now I gotta go." In a flash, Amanda tore toward Analise.

"I—I'm sorry," Cyn managed. Her head was still reeling from her daughter's lengthy speech, and her heart was beating double time. She started to get up, but Santa's hand caught her waist. *This is a definite role reversal. What's he doing?*

"Now, wait a minute, Santa—" She'd meant to sound playful, but failed miserably. She felt unbalanced, even though the thigh that supported her was as hard and steady as a rock. "First you won't even talk to me, and now you're—"

He chuckled. "It's Christmas. I thought everybody wanted to sit on Santa's lap."

This is my fault. I'm the one who was coming on to him.

"What?" She was glad her voice wasn't quivering as much as her insides. "Are you going to ask me what I want for Christmas?"

"Now, what could it be?" he drawled. "You've already got your two front teeth."

She relaxed right up until she remembered she was seated on his knee. "The better to bite you with," she returned.

He raised his brows and gazed into her eyes, letting the remark hang in the air. "I didn't mean it like that!" she exclaimed, lightly punching his shoulder.

"Like what?" he asked innocently.

She shot him a smirk. She wasn't about to let him embarrass her into silence. "You know," she said, poking his chest with her index finger. "Like when people kiss and accidentally bite each other."

His lips were twitching all over the place, as if he were fighting not to crack up. "Well, one should watch those slips of the tongue."

She feigned confusion. "I keep all my slips in my drawers." *What am I saying?*

"Funny," he said. "Most women I've known don't tuck them in."

Cyn couldn't help but shake her head. "Sorry, Santa. You lost me on that one." She tried to scoot casually off his lap.

He held her tight. "Drawers as in bloomers," he drawled. "And why are you wiggling away? Not three hours ago, you were desperate to see if I was capable of conversation."

"You call this conversation?" Her cheeks were getting warmer by the second. The undeniable, volatile chemistry cooking between them seemed about to explode. It was no accident that they'd somehow gone from slips to drawers.

"Sure," he said. "You know. I talk, you talk, I talk."

"Whatever it is," she managed to say. "I definitely mean to keep my slips in check." Watching Santa's face, she wondered if she could. The man smelled like clean winter weather, the day of a first snow.

"What a shame," he murmured.

For the first time Cyn realized that shoppers were gawking at them. Nevertheless, she relaxed against his chest, as if his proximity wasn't affecting her in the least. "And I thought you were just wondering what I want for Christmas," she said levelly.

"But, Cyn—" He bent so close his lips touched her ear. "Have you been good this year?"

She leaned back, only to find that his penetrating eyes were judgmental, as if she'd been bad. Her mouth went dry. She felt as guilty as she had when she was a kid on Santa's lap. After all, like most kids, she'd been bad much of the year. She thought about how she'd considered not turning in Jake Jackson. *But that was four years ago!*

"I've been good," she finally protested, feeling suddenly annoyed.

His eyes narrowed, as if he didn't believe her. "Yeah?"

"Yeah." She forced herself to smile. "Better than a man like you would ever deserve," she added tartly.

"Probably true." He chuckled softly, even though his gaze seemed somehow veiled and a little sad now. "Probably true."

"Mommy!"

Cyn turned away from Santa. She felt relieved at the intrusion, until Amanda crawled onto her knee and swung mistletoe above her head.

"Okay, Mr. Santa Claus," Amanda said. "You gotta kiss Mommy. I'm the boss."

Santa grinned. "Where'd you get that?"

"Granddaddy," Amanda squealed.

Good going, Dad. Cyn sucked in a quick breath. Her first impulse was to run. Then she decided to play it cool. After all, she'd been making a play for the man. He'd just shocked her by responding. She raised her brows archly, shot Santa a smile, then jutted her chin forward, offering him her cheek.

"Oh, goody!" Amanda hopped down.

"A quick peck won't kill you," Cyn said.

"To make Amanda happy, of course," he returned.

"And only Amanda," she said. "I do assure you."

When Santa's thumb grazed her chin, white-hot fire seemed to pour into her veins. *He's supposed to kiss my cheek!* Instead, he turned her face, and his lips quickly claimed hers. One instant, she was merely sitting on his knee. The next, she was curled into his shoulder, her chest crushed against his.

It was a full-service kiss, with no preliminaries. She could feel Santa strain against his own desire, every touch of his mouth making clear he wanted more. It was almost as if he'd known and wanted her for a long time, years even. He seemed to be drinking her in…hungry for her.

Suddenly she wrenched away and stared into Santa's eyes. Her breaths came in great gasps. For the second time in two days she could swear Jake Jackson was in the room. Except this time she was sitting in his lap and he'd just kissed her.

"Oh, Mr. Santa Claus," Amanda said breathlessly. "That was just great!"

"Glad to oblige," he said casually.

Jackson slipped from Cyn's mind as quickly as he'd entered it. Hadn't Santa felt anything at all? She managed to shut her gaping mouth and pat his shoulder. "Thank you so much for doing that," she said sweetly, "and all for the sake of my little girl."

Then she stood slowly, brushed her crinkled skirt and sashayed away, as if she had somewhere important to go. She made sure her heels beat a steady, rhythmic tattoo on the tile floor, and hoped she looked thoroughly unaffected.

But her insides quivered like jelly. Her knees wobbled like rubber, and her lips felt as swollen as a prize fighter's. Her heart was soaring, though. Because she'd finally found a man in this world who could kiss as wickedly as Jake. And Anton Santa, thank heavens, was honest in the bargain.

"WONDER WHAT'S GOING ON between those two," one of the Too Sweet executives murmured as he watched Cyn approach. Even from across the room, he'd felt the fireworks. Now, he wondered if this, too, might play into his hands, somehow. Maybe he was about to find out. Cyn was coming at him like a magnet.

He hadn't sent the notes, of course. Still, when they'd arrived, he was sure the story would reach the press. It hadn't, and that had been terribly disappointing to him. After all, he'd researched Too Sweet carefully. The family and company were so intertwined that every time personal tragedy hit, the stocks plummeted, making the place ripe for takeover.

Not that a kidnapping was necessary. Bad press was all he needed, even if he'd prefer not to leak it himself. Nevertheless, he did have enough dirt on the Sweet family to cause a stir. He'd heard the rumors about Cyn's torrid affair with a convict, and about Harry Stevens. And the holidays would be the perfect time to republish materials from The Grinch Gang's trial.

He just wished today's promotion hadn't been so successful; it meant the company was getting stronger by the day, rather than weaker. Suddenly he had a flash of inspiration. *That's what I'll do....*

When Cyn reached his side, he realized her lips were kiss swollen, and that she'd beat a truly hasty retreat across the room. She also looked as if she'd never been happier to see anyone in her life.

"It's good to see a friend, right now," she said.

He smiled. "It sure is."

Part 3

Chapter Three

Thursday, December 15, 1994

Santa stepped from the shower onto a bath mat woven with a Santa Claus face, then knotted a woolly red-and-green holiday towel at his waist, wishing Cyn had just left his room alone. He wished he hadn't kissed her, too, since the lingering taste of her lips had kept him awake. Now every cool, dripping-wet inch of him felt singed, as if she'd touched him with burning need.

"But no," he whispered. She either felt sorry for him, or wanted to let him know that his kiss hadn't affected her. She'd employed all her decorative talents, and now his room looked fit for Kriss Kringle. She'd replaced his bathroom water glass with a Frosty mug, switched the previously blue towels to red and green, then hung a wreath of rope pine, complete with red velvet bows on his door. Paper reindeers were now taped above his headboard, flying in the direction of the hallway. And the closest avenue of escape, he thought.

"It's no wonder a man can't sleep around here," he muttered aloud. When he'd opened his eyes at five-thirty, he'd found himself staring into the spray snowflakes on his mirror. He'd read all the morning newspapers, but had forgone his usual police procedurals. Instead, he'd read through Cyn's scrapbooks, yearbooks, and photo albums for two hours while ensconced between Christmas-tree-print bedsheets. The only thing Cyn seemed to have forgotten was to hang some more mistletoe.

He opened the bathroom door and headed toward his closet to choose a suit. Just as he decided on navy, a sheet of lined, ragged-edged paper shot beneath the door and slid across his bare feet. He agilely retrieved it from the carpet, then squinted. "Aw," he said softly. It was a crayon drawing.

He wasn't sure but thought it was of him in a Santa suit, and it was signed with a word that resembled "Amanda," except that the *d* was backward. At the bottom, in Cyn's writing, it said, "Hope you like Amanda's decorations in your room!"

So, it was Amanda's idea, not Cyn's. He should have felt relieved, but he didn't. He'd imagined Cyn riffling through her decorations and thoughtfully deciding where to place them. He'd imagined her breathing in his scent while she'd hung those ridiculous reindeers, too. He'd imagined her *wanting* him.

He sighed, crossed the room and gingerly wedged Amanda's drawing in the bedroom mirror's frame, next to a snowflake. Then he returned to the bed, sat down and glanced around, trying to remind himself that he hated Christmas. But how could he keep hating it when a little girl—maybe his little girl—drew such cute pictures for him? Or when her beautiful mother helped her decorate his room?

"Get ahold of yourself, Anton," he murmured. He grabbed the phone receiver with more force than was necessary, then dialed. *What if she's not my little girl?*

The most annoying thing was that his morning researches had rendered countless photographs of the supposedly deceased Harry Stevens. He'd attended high school with Cyn and they'd clearly been close. Worse—he was far better looking than Santa, at least in Santa's own humble opinion. Fury had coursed through him when he'd realized Cyn had always kept Harry waiting in the wings. Not that he'd found wedding pictures.

But if Harry Stevens had done something terrible—which might be why Cyn had pretended he was dead—then she may have destroyed evidence of their nuptials. *Good*. As it was, Santa had seen more than he'd wanted to. The snapshots of their senior prom had nearly turned his stomach. Santa absently rubbed the scar on the underside of his jaw, as if to remind himself of why he should steer clear of Cyn. Then he glanced at his calf and the circular two-inch scar left by the second bullet.

Harry Stevens didn't pick up until the sixteenth ring.

Santa went directly into his spiel, using his thickest Southern drawl. "Mr. Stevens? Now, you are Mr. Harrold Stevens, aren't you? Well, I'm B. D. Whittacker—talent agent out of Atlanta. Perhaps you've heard of me?"

Santa stopped for a breather and allowed Stevens to say that he'd never heard of him. Instead, Stevens said, "I'm not sure, but I do believe I may have heard that name."

The worst thing was that Stevens was just trying to be polite, and Santa wanted to like him. "Well," he continued, "down here in Atlanta, we've been following the Too Sweet promotion in New York City, and I was hoping to speak with you—and your wife, of course—about using your little Amanda for a commercial. Not a big contract, just a local baby food, mind you, but a start..." Santa paused, almost hating himself for laying it on so thick.

"I'm sorry, you must have the wrong—"

Santa's heart dropped to his feet. Stevens didn't know what he was talking about. Did the man even know Amanda existed? He'd have to, if the census reports were right.

"Oh!" Stevens chuckled. "You mean Amanda?"

"Do you always forget you have a daughter?" Santa returned gruffly.

"It's my ex-wife I try to forget," Stevens said smoothly.

Santa couldn't help but feel a little defensive on Cyn's

behalf. Still, he was mad. She'd pretended Stevens was dead. She'd kept the man waiting in a wedding tux, when she'd been seeing Jake. Now it appeared that Amanda was Harry's child. As soon as he hung up, he was going to call Paxton and quit.

"My daughter lives with her mother." Stevens continued so easily that Santa was sure Amanda belonged to him. "Look, I was just leaving, to catch a plane home for the holidays." Santa could almost see the amicable, sandy-haired Harry smiling. "But would you like me to give my ex-wife a call? Or perhaps I could give you the number for Too Sweet Toys."

"Why, that's mighty nice of you." Santa suddenly wished Harry didn't have those sandy-blond blue-eyed good looks. "Just let me get a pen."

He held the receiver in the air and mentally counted to five. It was a shame Stevens was headed out of town. Santa'd had every intention of calling back later—from Puerto Rico, after he quit. He'd play a confused bureaucrat who needed to clarify Stevens's supposed death records. He swung the mouthpiece to his lips again. "Could I possibly have a number where I could reach you? In case I can't find your wife?"

The man was amazing. He actually gave Santa his parents' number in Utah. Stevens had just given the New York area code when thudding steps flew past Santa's door. "Thanks, I've got it," Santa said, sensing that something was wrong. He covered the mouthpiece.

"But I haven't fini—"

"Amanda?" Cynthia called out. "Amanda?"

"Thank you, Mr. Stevens," Santa said curtly, hanging up. Then Cynthia screamed his name.

"WHAT'S WRONG?" Santa asked calmly. Even though he was searching Cyn's eyes, he was aware that her red robe was untied and that she wore a short silk nightie underneath. With relief, he realized Amanda was in the room.

"He was here," Cyn whispered in shock. "The front door was wide open, and this note—" She waved her hand; an envelope and sheet of stationery were pinched between her thumb and finger. "This note…"

He didn't wait to hear the rest. He bolted into the hallway, the thick red carpeting feeling soft beneath his bare feet. He tried the door to the other tenth-floor apartment. Locked. At the elevator, he pressed "down," then ran the length of the hall. The entrance to the roof and metal fire door were locked. *Good in this case, bad in case of a fire.*

Someone chuckled. "Don't tell me you're going down, sir?"

Santa whirled around, hardly needing a reminder that he was clad only in a towel. "Jim." As he jogged toward the elevator operator, he realized a frightened Cyn had shut her door. "Who came up?"

The middle-aged man hit the Stop button, removed his cap and ran his fingers through his thick dark hair. "No one," he finally said.

"Someone must have."

"Toby's the only other person on this shift. He called in sick. So—" The man's jaw dropped. "There was no one to cover me when I, er, had to take a quick break."

"You took one just now?"

"Yes, sir, just now."

"How long?"

"No more than five minutes, tops."

Santa sighed. Cyn's eyes had held pure terror. He could only hope she was overreacting. "No visitors are to come up without calling from the lobby," Santa muttered. "How could anyone have gotten past Jennifer?" He stepped into the elevator. "Take me down."

Jim merely stared at him. "In that, er, outfit, sir?"

Santa glanced down at the red-and-green towel. The words "Merry Christmas" were emblazoned across his privates. He grimaced but nodded.

Unfortunately, the trip to the lobby was a dead end. He accomplished little more than a few raised eyebrows, whispers and chuckles at his expense. Jennifer's phone wasn't working properly, due to the weather, and she was unable to offer a good description of the only person who'd used the elevator. He'd said he was a delivery man going to an apartment on the fourth floor, but she'd been busy talking to repairmen.

"Thanks for waiting, Jim," Santa said gruffly when he returned.

Jim laughed. "You kidding? I got some pointers. You sure know how to create a stir with the ladies." He pointed.

Santa raised an eyebrow. Sure enough, three well-heeled female tenants had stopped to gawk.

"And a very, very Merry Christmas to you, too," one yelled before she doubled in a fit of giggles. There wasn't much mistaking which part of his anatomy had caught her attention.

The last thing he heard, as the door slid shut, was one long, ear-piercing wolf whistle.

WHEN THE DOOR HANDLE jiggled, Cyn put her eye to the peephole. Then she threw open the door. "Did you find him?"

Santa shook his head. "Did you get a look at him?"

"No. I just saw the elevator doors close." Her shoulders slumped, and she leaned against the wall. Only then did her eyes drop from the safe, comforting vision of Santa's face down the rest of his body. It was a good thing the wall supported her; otherwise, her knees would have buckled. She tried to tell herself that worrying about Amanda had left her feeling faint, but she knew the way her heart thudded against her rib cage was due to Santa's attire. The towel rode low and knotted beneath his navel. It rose, just slightly, where it pulled across his hips, too.

Worse, Santa mistook her shocked expression for rawboned fear. He grasped her shoulder and squeezed with comforting pressure. It was a sweet, soothing masculine gesture. He clearly wanted to force all his own considerable, inner strength into her body. It was working, too. "Everything will be fine," he said in a near whisper.

His voice was so reassuring that she believed him. Out of the corner of her eye, Cyn caught a glimpse of Amanda. She was staring at Santa from the hallway, with her mouth gaping and her eyes popping out of her head. "Run and watch your cartoons, honey," Cyn called weakly. No doubt, she appeared as awestruck as her daughter. Amanda took one long, last look at Santa, then fled as if the hounds of hell were on her heels.

"Guess she's not used to seeing men so scantily clad," Cyn managed to say. Between the frightening circumstances of the morning and Santa, she felt thoroughly unnerved. Blood whirred through her veins so fast that her ears were actually ringing, and her face couldn't have felt warmer if she'd downed a whole jar of red-hot chili peppers.

Santa chuckled softly. "And you are?"

She mustered a weak smile and evaded him by glancing toward her Christmas tree. Then she forced herself to fix her eyes on his again. They looked as darkly smooth and gold as roasted almonds. She gulped. "This is really no time to flirt. I'm scared."

His expression softened. It held so much concern that she was sure she'd misjudged him. Unlike other men—unlike Jake—this one could be trusted. He squeezed her shoulder again. His hand was so warm...but it was creeping toward her collarbone! She leaned farther back. Behind her, the wall felt solid and real. It steadied her.

"Just wanted to help straighten you out," he said quietly. She didn't realize her robe had nearly fallen from her shoulders until he lifted her lapels and gently snuggled them against her throat. Ever since he'd kissed her, the man had become a whole lot less standoffish. The role reversal was unnerving her. When she was the aggressor, she'd felt in control.

His fingers grazed her neck. "Thanks," she nearly squealed. She tried to skeddaddle backward, but hit something hard. The wall. So comforting a moment before, it now made her feel trapped.

"I like to think of myself as a full-service bodyguard," he finally returned.

As much as she was trying to fight it, her gaze dropped over his powerful shoulders. His smooth chest was tanned to a delicious bronze, and the dark hairs swirled, then tapered southward, in an ever-narrowing V. She drew in an audible breath and glanced down as he lithely grasped both loose ends of the tie to her robe. Even though Amanda was in the den and the kidnapper's note peeked from her pocket, she half hoped he meant to undress her.

"Wouldn't want you to catch a cold," he drawled as he knotted her robe in front.

How could this man excite her so much in the midst of such horrible circumstances? And how could he make her want to laugh? Why wasn't he attending to the note in her pocket? "If anyone's going to catch cold," she said, regaining her equilibrium, "I do believe it's you, Santa."

Their eyes met and held. His wry half smile made his mouth look lopsided. "So you noticed the outfit?"

The fact that he had tiny laugh lines around his eyes suddenly seemed more important than it should have. "I'm sure it will be the primary order of business at the next tenants meeting."

"When you left it in my room," he drawled softly, "I just assumed it was what you wanted me to wear."

"As a sort of uniform?" She looked him up and down, as if considering, wishing her throat didn't close like a trap every time her gaze landed on his glowing naked skin.

He nodded.

"Well, it is seasonal," she offered, her gaze meeting his

again. The fool man wore a towel with the same ease and commanding air he did his suits. "Especially the holiday message."

He glanced down. "A number of people wished me a merry Christmas, in return."

"Why, all you're missing is a bow for your head." She tried not to notice how his fresh-scrubbed skin smelled like a forest full of Christmas trees.

"I'm sure we could round one up."

"But then you'd be so chilly," she countered quickly.

He chuckled. "I *am* feeling the draft," he conceded.

She felt compelled to check him for goose bumps. There weren't any. Actually there were, but they rose on her own arms. A shiver zigzagged down her spine. She had to get him into one of his suits, she thought. Pronto. "Well, I guess you can go change now!" she trilled.

His eyes widened at her voice. She'd meant to sound brightly perky, as if casually conversing with a nearly naked man was her usual morning activity. Instead, due to all her pent-up anxiety and excitement, she'd nearly shrieked.

His eyes crinkled and twinkled. "I should, huh?"

"Well, yes." Her mouth felt so dry she could barely talk. "Don't you have to investigate or something or maybe—"

His smile turned into more of a smirk. It said he knew he'd thrown her off balance. "Don't worry—" His mock gravity almost made her smile back. "I don't intend to run around like this all day."

"That's good." She blew out a shaky sigh, wishing she hadn't sounded so breathless. "It is ten below out there, you know."

"True." Santa wiggled his brows. "And I've got no one to keep me warm on these wretched New York mornings."

"Well—er—oh heavens," she suddenly rambled. Could she possibly recoup some sense of dignity? "I'm sorry, I don't know why I was nearly yelling a minute ago. I was so scared and then, you're—"

His eyes seemed to dare her. "I'm?"

Nothing less than Santa's presence could have taken her mind off that terrible note, she thought. Why couldn't she simply fade into the wood of the door? "You're—well," she managed.

"I *do* feel well this morning."

She was starting to feel a bit hysterical. "Well, I just don't know what's come over me." She tried to clear her throat and nearly choked. "I mean, yelling like that and all."

He merely scrutinized her, and smiled that cryptic Santa smile. "I could make a few guesses," he said pointedly.

She felt herself blush to the bottoms of her Clairol roots.

"But I won't."

"Nothing you could say would bother me in the least," she managed, wishing it were true.

His smile became kindly. Then it vanished by degrees until he looked as serious as he had when he'd said he'd guard Amanda with his life. "Why don't you sit down and relax a minute?" he said softly. "Fix yourself something hot to drink, while I change. Then I'll need to see the note."

Her mouth dropped open in astonishment. His every word, she realized, had been calculated. He'd intentionally offered her a diversion. In the next heartbeat she found herself liking him for it. She did feel calmer now. By the time he was ready, maybe she could look at that note again. She nodded. "Okay."

He swiftly stepped closer, so his rock-hard thigh touched hers. She felt the warmth of his large hand press against the small of her spine. Heat shot right through her back to her stomach, then spread through her whole body. "We'll figure all this out," he said. "Trust me."

For a second she thought he might try to kiss her, but he didn't. "I do trust you," she said in surprise. *And it's been a long time since I trusted a man.*

Sadness seemed to touch his eyes, as it sometimes did. "You should have trusted me always," he said levelly.

"When I first met you, I admit I didn't."

He looked as if he were going to say something more. Instead, he turned and headed for his room. His back was every bit as enticing as the front of him, and though her towels were heavy and thick, they truly left very little to the imagination. When her eyes settled on his legs, she wondered how he'd gotten the scar on his calf. Bullet wound, she decided, just as his door shut.

"I saw Mr. Santa in a towel, Mommy!" Amanda squealed from the hallway sometime later.

Cyn realized she was still staring at Santa's door. "So did I, honey," she said with a sigh. "So did I."

HE DRAPED HIS navy jacket over a kitchen chair. Cyn was seated and gazing wanly through a window. Amanda's cartoons blared from the next room. "You should eat."

She hadn't bothered to change, and her robe had nearly come untied again. Santa could see a hint of cleavage and her lacy nightie. She started toying with the rim of her coffee mug and glanced at the kidnapper's note, which was on the table. "I just don't feel like eating, Santa."

"I'll make you a bagel." He pulled one from the bread box, popped it into her rickety toaster oven, then placed the cream cheese on the table, suddenly wishing he could make her smile again, even if he wasn't Amanda's father. The events of the morning had been so swift that he'd barely been able to process that. Now he tried to tell himself it was for the best. What kind of father would he make, anyway?

"I'm toasting you a bagel," he finally said playfully. "Don't look so impressed by my culinary talents."

She smiled then, but only because it was expected. He continued gazing into her eyes, wishing she didn't look so vulnerable and beautiful. It was rare for Cyn to not be in complete control. Her softened features made him want to take her into his arms, to offer comfort rather than take his revenge. He served the bagel. "Should I change back into that towel?"

"Oh, please, no," she said chuckling. "I think I've had enough excitement for one morning."

At that, he grinned. He was pleased to see her lather an unhealthy amount of cream cheese onto her bagel, too. She actually started nibbling, while he looked at the note. This one was on heavy white stock and the words were typewritten with a pica electric. It said, "I'll steal the closest thing to your heart."

"Could mean anything and it doesn't specifically mention Amanda," Santa finally said. "It's probably not the same person."

Cyn put down her bagel as if she'd suddenly lost her appetite again. "No, it's not."

His gaze shot to hers. "You know who sent this?"

Her jaw clamped shut and her green eyes turned as hard as glittering emeralds. He grabbed the chair nearest hers, scooted it beside her, then sat. He was so close that their knees touched. "Who?" he repeated.

"Jake Jackson." Her voice sounded low and lethal.

Santa's lips parted in defensive protest, but he quickly caught himself and remained silent. After a moment he decided he might have laughed, if she hadn't sounded so deadly. After all, Jake Jackson wasn't even in the running for the suspect list. He felt a gut-level twinge of guilt. His being here, without her knowing his identity, was beginning to feel like a bad joke gone way too far. Worse—not a half hour ago, she'd said she trusted him. And Amanda wasn't even his baby.

He realized Cyn was watching him carefully. "Jake was a past lover of mine," she finally said.

His first impulse was to demand to know just exactly how many lovers she'd had. To hear himself described so off-handedly as a past fling was unnerving. *I've got to leave. Right now. Today.* He forced himself to nod.

She exhaled shakily. "A few years back some college guys were romancing heiresses—" She paused and pursed her lips as if she'd just tasted something foul. "They called themselves The Grinch Gang."

He shifted in his chair uncomfortably and fought to keep the irony from his voice. "I remember the story." Did she really think Jake Jackson would come back into her life, to hurt her or Amanda? Four years ago she'd lain in his arms, gloriously naked and so full of trust.... Or so he'd thought.

"Did you see me on TV? Or read the papers? Most of them printed the text of the trial." She grimaced, a slight flush staining her cheeks. "Heiresses being played for fools make good copy for the tabloids, I guess."

Santa didn't trust his voice. Lengthy segments of the trial had been replayed on newscasts. He'd seen her, all right. While he was on his back in a hospital bed, his calf and face undergoing reconstructive surgery, she'd positively blasted him. He felt himself getting furious all over again. He leaned forward casually and placed his elbows on the table. "I seem to remember seeing something about it," he finally drawled.

She reached over and squeezed his arm, as if thanking him for his support. Beneath his crisp white shirt, tingles skated along his skin. No matter how angry he felt, he still wanted her. It amazed him. He cleared his throat. "So you think it's this Jackson character?"

When she tilted her head, a lock of sleep-mussed hair fell over one of her eyes, making her look as mysterious as she did sexy. "During the trial, Jackson was hospitalized," she said slowly. "I had followed him to my parents' house. I saw him and two others robbing us, and called the police."

She slid a hand beneath her robe lapel absently. Apparently, her nightie strap had fallen. The simple, guileless gesture nearly took away Santa's breath. Didn't she have any idea what she was doing to him? "Why did you follow him?"

"Because I was an idiot," she said.

Unfortunately, that didn't really answer his question. At the trial, she'd said she'd trailed him because she hadn't trusted him all along. Santa didn't buy it. "Jackson," he continued casually. "He was the guy who got shot, right? A couple of rookie cops came in on the scene, and it turned out that one of the robbers had a gun."

"The man who got away with our jewelry," Cyn affirmed. "Some cash, too."

"So it wasn't Jackson who had the gun?" he prodded, feeling oddly triumphant.

"No," she conceded, sounding almost as if she wished it had been him. "But the jerk sure deserved everything he got, including getting shot," she added with uncharacteristic menace.

"Well, maybe he learned his lesson," Santa said. "Maybe he even reformed in jail. I mean, why would the man come back to haunt you?" Did Cyn secretly hope that Jackson still loved her? *Maybe he does.* Santa blinked, as if to make the thought vanish.

She shrugged. "Matthew Lewis—he was the only defendant present at the trial—got really mad at one point. He jumped up and screamed that they—all of them—would come back someday. He said—" Her voice suddenly broke. "That they'd steal the closest thing to my heart." Her eyes shot to his and misted with tears. "And that would be Amanda. Now, wouldn't it?"

"So it could be either Lewis or the man who got away," he said, trying to sound reasonable. "Why does it necessarily have to be—" He almost couldn't say it. "This other guy, Jackson?"

"It just is," she snapped.

"That doesn't make sense, Cyn," he returned softly. A thousand warring emotions were pulling him every which way but loose. He wanted to defend himself, he wanted to make her see reason. And yet, at moments—so drawn in by her lovely eyes—he nearly forgot he *was* Jake Jackson. Hell, hearing her vehemence, he was ready to kill Jake, himself. Worse, he wanted to take her into his arms and hold her tightly. "I'm going out of my mind," he muttered.

Her eyebrows shot upward. "Excuse me?"

"Nothing." He got up and crossed to the kitchen counter, as far away from her as he could get.

Unfortunately, her bare feet, complete with their dainty pink-painted toenails, pitter-pattered right behind him. She nearly leaned against him while she rinsed crumbs from her bagel plate. His hands itched to touch her soft thick hair and the silk of her robe. His eyes flitted over her, yearning to see every last inch of her skin. His mouth went dry with both desire and the urge to tell her the truth.

But the truth no longer mattered. He didn't love Cyn. She hadn't trusted him. He didn't want a woman who bolted when the going got tough, either. Besides which, he wasn't even Amanda's father.

She hates Jackson now, and when she finds out the truth, she'll hate me. The thought flashed through his mind, but he assured himself that wasn't the reason for his silence. He wanted to rectify the past, perhaps, but he didn't want her back.

He absently touched the scar on his jaw, thinking he had so many motivations these days—some even running at cross-purposes—that he couldn't keep track of them all. And he didn't have to. He wasn't telling her. Period. And he wasn't going to stick around until some telltale sign gave him away.

She turned from the sink and reached past him, to grab a dish towel. "I know Jackson's been here," she said as she dried her hands. "The man's as slippery as an eel. When I went out this morning and saw the door wide open, I just knew it. I could sense it. I could *feel* him. In fact, I've felt his presence for a few days." She stared intently at Santa. "I never really believed in such things before, but do you think it could be some sort of premonition?"

Santa's eyes roved over her face. If only her eyes were less green and her lips were less full... "Well, maybe he was here," he said gruffly.

Cyn placed her hand on his arm again and gazed at him trustingly. "But he's gone now, isn't he?" she asked softly.

He could smell soap and the fragile scent of yesterday's perfume. "Yeah." He swallowed hard. "I guess."

Without moving away from him, she said, "You know something funny?"

That you're about one second away from being kissed? His lips parted, and he licked them. "What?"

"Don't take this wrong." She came a step closer and their thighs brushed.

The only wrong thing I'm going to take is you...in my arms. "I'll try not to," he managed to say.

She cocked her head and glanced upward, scrutinizing him with a quirky, flirtatious smile. "Heavens, Santa," she teased, poking his chest with her finger, "it's not a test."

He dipped his head and grinned, his mouth just inches from hers. "Well, if it is," he found himself drawling, "I sure hope I pass."

She leaned more of her weight against the counter. "You remind me of him a little."

His stomach balled in a knot. "Who?"

"Jake Jackson," she chided, playfully rolling her eyes.

He didn't even want to laugh this time. He cleared his throat. "Comforting, I remind you of a burglar."

She flashed him a quick smile. "Well, he was a cheat and liar, too."

When she shifted her weight again, the silk of her robe whispered against his fingertips. "Let's not forget that," he murmured.

"And a convict," she added.

He drew in a quick breath. "Thanks."

Although she was gazing into his eyes, she suddenly

seemed to be staring right through him. For an instant, Santa almost felt as if he'd vanished.

"It's so very strange," she continued, sounding almost whimsical. "You don't look like him, or talk like him, even though you've got a bit of a drawl. You sure don't dress like him. And he was skinny, without a single muscle to speak of. He was a night owl, too." She frowned. "I just can't imagine him with a suntan. And he was so much shorter…"

Shorter? I'm the exact same damn height. "The man doesn't sound particularly appealing," he finally said.

"Try boy," she quipped. "And not nearly as appealing as you."

Boy? I can't believe I'm now being compared to myself. Did she really just admit she's attracted to me? "So do you always date unappealing men?" It was increasingly difficult to match her teasing tone.

She shrugged. "He was a jerk and I was young and stupid."

Actually, she hadn't been all that young. She'd been twenty-four. She was acting as if their whole affair were easily summed up in a sentence, too. *Boy, jerk, young, stupid.* "But now you're old and so very wise," he said roughly.

She didn't notice his tone. "There's just something about you. I can never quite put my finger on it. And—"

He glanced down, both wishing she'd move away from him, and that she wouldn't. "Hmm?"

Her cheeks colored slightly. The silk of her robe still whispered against his fingertips, as if calling him closer. Pressed against his muscular thigh, her hand felt soft and warm. "When you kissed me the other day—" She paused and swallowed. "You know, at the store…"

As if he could forget. Just a breath away, her lips seemed to beg for his. He swallowed around the lump in his throat. "Yeah," he repeated gruffly, "at the store."

"It just made me feel like…well, like…"

I've had all of this I can take. "Like this?" He grabbed

her waist, feeling amazed at how small it was beneath the slippery robe. As he pulled her in front of him, he covered her lips with his own.

He'd taken her by surprise. He could feel it in how her thighs turned hard and unyielding against his, and in how her shoulders tensed against his chest. For a full minute her confused arms remained rigidly suspended in midair, while one of his circled her waist, keeping her close. His free hand raced up her back, under her soft hair, and cupped her neck.

Then her shoulder gave, curling into the crook of his. Her thighs went as soft as a pillow and nestled against his legs. Her arms crept around his neck. And the warm spear of her tongue began to tussle with his. He nearly moaned when he felt her long fingers knead the muscles of his shoulders.

In her bare feet, she was shorter than he, and as he plunged his tongue deep between her lips, he felt her strain upward on her toes. His hands automatically dropped down the length of her back, until he cupped her behind, almost lifting her. It had been so long since he'd felt her.... He almost leaned back, so he could see her face. Instead, he continued drinking her in, feeling as though he'd never stop.

His desire for her had been tightly wrapped inside him for too long. Now it unfurled like a sail taking wind. He was ready to make love to her. Nothing mattered. Not the time or the place or the fact that she didn't know who he really was.

She was kissing him so deeply that he could barely breathe now. And when she arched against his growing arousal, his hands began to rove over the soft rise of her backside. He lifted her quickly, and turned, so that her back, rather than his, was against the counter.

She drew away, with a shaky intake of breath. He let her slide down the length of him until her feet touched the floor again. Her green eyes looked as soft as water, and her lips were as swollen as ripe red berries. Her mussed hair looked like hell. And sexy beyond any words Santa could think of.

"I want you," she finally whispered, sounding breathless.

He wasn't sure what he'd expected, but not that. Cyn had changed. She'd always been an unconscionable flirt, but never quite so bold. Now she was all grown-up, a woman conscious of her needs and desires. And he liked it. He glanced toward the doorway. The sound of Amanda's cartoons suddenly seemed to fill the kitchen.

She blew out a soft, satisfied sigh. "I don't mean now," she nearly whispered. "I think I just mean that I'm glad you're here. The holidays are always a little hard for me."

He was somewhat taken aback. "Glad to be obliging," he drawled, feeling a little breathless himself but determined not to show it.

She chuckled, and a teasing glint winked in her eyes. She poked his chest playfully with a finger, yet another new gesture he was getting to know intimately. "But the real question is whether or not you want me, now isn't it, Santa?" She gazed at him expectantly.

His mouth dropped open in mock astonishment. "Are you always so blunt?"

"One of the things I've found out in the past few years," she said, "is that life's too short."

"For old-fashioned courtship with the hired help?" he asked with a smile.

"You really don't have to answer me, Santa." She wriggled out from between him and the counter.

She was almost to the door when he said, "Cyn?"

She turned and raised an eyebrow.

"Just so your mind will be at ease..." he began softly.

She giggled like a schoolgirl. "Just so I can sleep nights?"

"Why, I'd hate to think of you tossing and turning," he said, drawing out the words, "and all because you couldn't quit wondering."

"Well, you better hurry up and tell me," she teased. "Because I've got to take a load of clothes out of the dryer."

His brows shot up in genuine surprise. "You mean, a woman like you does her own laundry?"

She rolled her eyes heavenward, then fixed her gaze on him. "Impressed?"

He smirked back. "No."

Her laughter filled the room. "Those clothes of mine are probably burning up by now," she singsonged.

"I don't know about the clothes," he said, his gaze never leaving hers. "But I sure am."

Her smile spread into the sexiest grin he'd ever seen. "Yeah?"

"Yeah. And I want you." He gazed deep into her eyes. "Something fierce."

She quickly held up her index finger, touched it to her tongue, then waved it in the air. "Pssst," she said. "Why the very air in here sizzles."

"But Cyn," he continued, feeling an odd mixture of anger and desire, "I don't have to have everything I want."

Her face fell just a little and, as much as it hurt him, he felt almost glad. "Don't tell me. Santa is above involving himself with his clients."

"That's right," he said softly. "I'm here to do a job."

She shot him a false smile, then whirled around and headed for the door again. "Pardon my saying so," she called over her shoulder. "But you don't look all that busy to me."

"A minute ago," he called at her retreating back, "I sure felt pretty busy. Didn't you?"

"Look, Paxton—" Santa blew out a very loud, annoyed sigh. He had to get away from Cyn. He couldn't be in the same room with her without touching her. He had to get away from Amanda, too. The beautiful little girl wasn't his. And now she represented his most secret dreams...of the family he wanted but would probably never have. "I hired a temporary rent-a-cop to stay outside Cyn's door. And there are at least five other guys with my qualifications.''

Paxton's hands shot to his hips. He was facing away from Santa, staring through his office window at the Rockefeller Center tree. ''Name one.''

''Strauss.''

Paxton snorted. ''Mr. Santa!'' He turned around and stared into Santa's eyes. ''Strauss is protecting the President of the United States! When we couldn't find you, we tried him.''

When Santa leaned back in the office chair, something stabbed him in the back. He glanced behind himself; it was the handle of a ''say and tell'' toy. He sighed again, thinking that Carpenter was in South America, Gibson had slipped two disks playing tennis, and O'Conner never worked Christmas. ''Hudson,'' Santa suddenly said. ''Naomi Hudson.''

Paxton's jaw clenched.

''She's a woman,'' Santa said. ''But I assure you, she's good.'' With a woman, he wouldn't have to worry about Cyn. After all, Carpenter and Gibson both had legendary reputations with the ladies.

''I don't care that she's a woman,'' Paxton said defensively, ''but she works full-time for a senator in Texas.''

Santa frowned. ''I haven't talked to her in a while,'' he admitted.

''With all the work I have to do this time of year, I can't worry about Cynthia and Amanda,'' Paxton said. ''You have to stay. Especially since this morning's note looks like a real warning.''

''I'm sorry,'' Santa said. ''I can't.''

Paxton's eyes narrowed. ''Just what has Cynthia done to you?''

What hasn't she done? Santa couldn't help but take the opportunity. ''In researching the background, hoping to get to the bottom of this, I've come up with certain...'' He paused. ''Discrepancies.'' Was it his imagination, or did Pax-'on look as guilty as sin?

"What kind of, er, discrepancies?"

"Harry Stevens isn't dead." Santa tilted his head and scrutinized Paxton. The man was hiding something. He could sense it. "When I work for people, I don't like being lied to about the facts. Turns out your daughter also had an affair with a convict."

"He wasn't a convict then! She didn't know!" Paxton plopped in his desk chair so quickly that it nearly swiveled in a complete circle. He righted himself, looking resigned. "Harry used to be a good friend of hers," he said, leaning his elbows on his cluttered desk. "He merely gave Amanda a name."

Santa wanted to rise to his feet but didn't. His chest felt as if it were being squeezed by a vise. "The kid," he said, fighting for control of his voice. "Amanda." He crossed his arms, as if the gesture might still his beating heart. "She's really Jake Jackson's daughter, isn't she?"

"You know about the case?"

Santa forced himself to nod. "Is she?"

Paxton's eyes widened. The man looked positively stricken. "I just don't know," he finally said. "Please, Mr. Santa, my daughter's been through the wringer. There was a lot of press at that trial." He waved a hand in the air. "Cynthia was devastated—just what you might expect when a young, vulnerable, sensitive girl has been betrayed like that."

At twenty-four, Cyn had been overprotected; still, she wasn't a girl.

Santa wasn't sure why, but he felt guilty. "So why did you declare Harry dead?"

Paxton shrugged. "It just seemed the cleanest way to end everything and explain Amanda."

Paxton was lying. Santa was sure of it. It would be easy enough to get Amanda down to a lab for a DNA test. And yet, somehow, Santa didn't want to do that. He wanted to hear the explanation from only one source. Cyn Sweet's lips.

He simply couldn't believe how devious the members of the Sweet family were. "Whose child is it?" he finally asked.

"I really don't know," Paxton repeated, sounding almost sincere.

Santa thought about the way Cyn had been teasing and toying with him. Just how many men had she come on to in that way? He doubted she'd had an affair right after the trial, but it could be the truth.

"Will you stay?" Paxton's eyes were pleading him.

Sure. I'll seduce the information out of your daughter.

"I'll pay double what you're getting now."

"Fine," Santa said.

Part 4

Chapter Four

Friday, December 16, 1994

"Dad, I didn't *do* anything!" Cyn exclaimed, twirling the phone cord around her pinkie. She retied her robe, then glanced toward the TV, wishing Amanda was watching in the den, rather than the living room. Fortunately, her daughter was thoroughly engrossed in *Sesame Street*. "In fact—" Cyn lowered her voice "—I haven't even *seen* Santa since last night, when he left to—"

"To storm my office!" Paxton barked so loudly that Cyn leaned away from the earpiece and grimaced. "And quit his job! For what I'm paying, things must be pretty darn bad, if he wants to leave. I demand to know why things aren't working out."

Because he kissed me and I kissed him back so hard we could have made love. Her ego still stung from his rejection. How could he kiss her with Jake Jackson's verve and passion, then say he wouldn't act on it? And why had he tried to quit on her? Just where had he been all night? "I don't know why he wanted to leave. Santa can be a little—er—standoffish," she said in self-defense.

"I'd call it respectful, young lady," her father countered. She was sure Paxton was thinking of Jake Jackson, who hadn't respected her in the least.

"Daddy, when I'm sixty, are you still going to be calling me 'young lady'?" She hardly felt inclined to discuss what was going on in her own apartment. Or not going on, she thought, feeling frustrated.

"Don't change the subject," he said levelly. "If you ask me, you could do a lot worse than Anton Santa."

She gasped. "Worse than! For what?"

"You know exactly what I mean, Cynthia Anna."

Paxton never called her that unless he was truly mad. "All I need is for you to start playing matchmaker," she returned huffily, wondering what had gotten into her father. Usually she could do no wrong; now he was actually taking Santa's side. *I don't always have to have what I want,* she thought, mentally mocking Santa.

"Well, maybe you need a matchmaker." Her father's voice gentled. Knowing what was coming, she had to fight not to pitch the phone across the room. She grabbed it from an end table and cradled it against her stomach. "After all, you can't raise Amanda alone. You need someone. And you haven't—"

"Haven't done such a good job matching myself up?" she asked tartly. Her father was definitely making veiled references to Jake, and she was starting to feel like a pressure cooker that was about to blow.

"Santa's responsible," her father said. "He's protecting you and Amanda and you've got to appear appreciative, at the very least. He's just not the sort of man who'll put up with nonsense."

A quick image of Santa, clad only in his "Merry Christmas" towel flashed through her mind. She almost chuckled. "And he's good-looking and wears tailored suits, instead of leather jackets," she added, not bothering to hide her irony.

"He does dress nicely." Her father suddenly sounded agreeable.

Cyn's hand tightened around the receiver. "And so he must be the man of my dreams? Practically every man in

New York wears suits, Dad!'' Except Jake Jackson, she mentally amended.

"I don't see what you've got against him." Paxton's voice rose again.

"Why, not a thing." The words were delivered more sarcastically than she'd intended. "Maybe I should just marry him tomorrow."

"Maybe you should." This time it wasn't Paxton. It was Santa.

She whirled around. "Do you always eavesdrop?" Hot color seeped into her cheeks. Before she'd met Santa, she hadn't blushed in years. Only Jake had flustered her to that point. It was positively infuriating. So was his opening line. He meant to continue a flirtation, even though there'd be no follow-through. "How long have you been standing there?"

He smiled pleasantly, his eyes looking like dark round globes beneath his thick lashes. "Long enough."

"Well, you shouldn't creep around!" The receiver slid downward. She caught it between her jaw and her shoulder. "I didn't even hear you come in!"

His eyebrow arched in a way that was barely perceptible. "Should I take that to mean you were listening for me?"

The nerve of him. "All night," she returned drolly.

His powerful shoulders rolled slightly in their sockets, like a shimmying dancer's. "Twisting and turning and waiting and wondering…"

It was so true, she felt embarrassed. "Don't flatter yourself," she snapped.

He leaned forward idly, resting his elbows on the back of an armchair. "I'd much rather flatter you."

"Be nice to him!" Paxton warned over the phone.

"You could flatter me by vanishing," she said with a scowl.

"I said, be nice!" Paxton shrieked.

This time Santa clearly heard him. "I—I…" She didn't know who to address first, her father or Santa.

"Be nice to me," Santa mouthed, wagging a suntanned finger.

"I am being nice," she said into the mouthpiece.

"And let me know when you're off the phone," Santa said.

"Does Santa need to use the phone?" Paxton asked. "If he does, it's probably important. We'd better get off, Cyn."

Her lips parted in wonder. Santa's self-satisfied smile made him look like a cat who'd just lapped up the last of the cream. "Daddy, we need to go over the final plans for this evening's promotion!"

"Santa has an important call to make," her father returned.

Her eyes widened and she sighed. "Love you, Daddy."

"Love you, too," he said. "And be nice to Santa. I'll be watching you at the drawing for the tickets to *The Nutcracker*, to make sure you're behaving."

She hung up and glared at Santa. It was difficult. She could still feel his lips on hers. Her thighs suddenly tingled, as if he were pressed against her again. His sharply tailored, double-breasted chocolate suit made his eyes look darker. But, she had to remind herself, the first time he'd kissed her without mistletoe, he'd tried to quit his job. "When did you get so buddy-buddy with my father?"

Santa shrugged, looking genuinely puzzled. "He seems to like me."

She nodded as if he had just confessed to armed robbery. "Just what did you do to him?"

"The regular snow job." He flashed her an irresistible, glistening grin that made his eyes twinkle.

She sniffed. "And *he* fell for it," she said, as if to indicate that *she* hadn't.

Santa gazed at her steadily. The grin slowly tempered to an amused smile. "You're jealous."

As soon as he said it, she knew it was true. Her father had never taken someone else's side. "I thought you'd quit," she remarked lightly, wishing the man couldn't read her quite so easily.

"Changed my mind."

"Would you like to tell me why?" Had he really come back for her? she wondered. Maybe he'd worried all night about his ethics regarding clients, but couldn't get their kiss out of his mind, so he'd come back. Maybe she was being too hard on him. "Why?" she repeated softly.

He chuckled. "Every time I say no, your father pays me double. It's starting to add up."

That figured. "Good," she said with a lightness she didn't feel. "I was afraid you'd reconsidered your client-involvement policy." She eyed the armchair, wishing she could sit down. Her fool knees were buckling again.

"Oh," he drawled softly. "That, too."

"Ah—" She sucked in a quick breath, hating him for thinking she was that easy. "But in the gray light of another chilly New York morning, I'm sorry to inform you, I've cooled considerably."

They stared each other down for a solid minute. Everything in his eyes said he knew she was only saving face. "Didn't you say you had a call to make?" she asked innocently, holding out the phone.

He was still sizing her up with his eyes. "Sorry," he drawled. "*My* call's private."

She couldn't help but wonder whether he was phoning a woman. Given his looks, she imagined he found plenty to call. "Well," she said. "I hope you don't expect me to leave the room."

She wasn't sure but thought his shoulders were beginning to shake with laughter. He turned on his heel and headed for his room. "I guess I can play the gentleman. Once." He glanced over his shoulder and winked at her.

Now that Dad's on his side, I'm doomed, she thought.

She stared at his closed door, feeling more curious than ever about who he was calling. Was it a woman he'd been with the night before? As much as she hated herself for it, she found herself dragging the living room extension down the hallway and into the kitchen, away from the TV. She shut the door.

Don't do it. So far, your jealousy has gotten you nowhere but in a heap of trouble. She tried to keep reminding herself that the last supposed "other woman" she'd researched had led her to The Grinch Gang. Nevertheless, she very quietly picked up the receiver.

"Santa, I'm going to have to put you on hold for a minute," a woman said. The line went blank and Cyn held her breath. She felt like an idiot. What was she doing?

"Oh, Cynthia," Santa singsonged. "Who's eavesdropping now?"

Caught red-handed! She considered hanging up, but that would be even worse than an outright admission of guilt. "It *could* have been Amanda," she said coolly.

"But it wasn't," he returned. The last thing she heard before she hung up was Santa's resounding belly laugh.

"Ho, ho, ho," she muttered. Still, she knew it took an extremely powerful man to reduce her to such juvenile tactics. Mulling things over, she almost convinced herself that Santa hadn't come back for the money, but because of her. Hadn't he?

"Sorry, Santa, just one more minute." Right before his friend put him on hold again, he heard her perkily answer the other line, saying, "Sally Steele, Riker's Island."

He'd spent the previous night rifling through desks at Too Sweet. He'd been determined to find stray bits of cut magazines, an X-Acto blade, or the typewriter on which the last note had been composed. He'd found zero. He'd paid for the rent-a-cop to watch Cyn's place out-of-pocket, too.

He removed his cuffs from where they were looped over his belt, tossed them onto the mattress, then leaned back on his pillows. Cradling the receiver against his shoulder, he decided that seducing information out of Cyn would be a piece of cake. She was angry, but only because he'd rejected her yesterday. Nevertheless, her supposed premonitions about sensing Jake Jackson's presence were making him nervous.

Why was it so important that he hear the information from between her lying lips? he wondered. As much as he fought it, he thought of her around the clock. He kept imagining the moment when he'd take her. It would happen quickly, without feeling, but sometimes now, the fantasy ended all wrong. She realized who he was, they forgave each other, and everything was hunky-dory. Why hadn't he simply pushed Paxton harder for the truth?

And how long could he wait? He was being jerked around like a lapdog. First he was Amanda's father. Then he wasn't. Then he was again. What was he going to do if he found out he was? Take Amanda from her mother to live with him? How could such a thing work? *Excuse me, would you mind watching my little girl…while I take a bullet for the Speaker of the House?*

The line clicked on. "Sally?"

"Hey there, Santa Claus! Haven't seen you out at Riker's Island lately. Guess you've been good this year."

If he wasn't careful, Amanda's nickname for him was going to stick. "Hey there," he said.

"What can I do for you?"

"Besides leave your husband?"

She giggled. Sally loved her husband more than life, and both of them knew it, but she always flirted with Santa. "It would be too cruel to leave him before Christmas," she chided. "But is there something else?"

"I'm checking on an inmate. He was arrested on a B and E four years ago. The name's Matthew Lewis."

"Guess you've been sunning yourself in the Caribbean again." Sally laughed. "Don't you watch the news?"

He sat up. "No, I've been reading the papers, though. Did he escape or something?"

"As far as I'm concerned, you're the escape artist," she said flirtatiously.

Santa chuckled. "Sally, honey, you're married."

"So true." Sally blew out a mock beleaguered sigh. "The guy you're looking for was released on a holiday pardon from our humble Riker's two weeks ago."

"He's been out for two weeks?" Santa repeated. That meant Lewis could have sent all the notes. Having worked with The Grinch Gang, Santa knew the man was skilled enough to get into Cyn's place, too. Prison might have hardened him and made him mean enough to steal Amanda. Maybe this time he wouldn't get caught.

"Should I call you back with an address for him?" Sally finally asked. "It's hard to find people this close to Christmas, but I'm sure I can track down his parole officer."

"That would be great," Santa said, giving her Cyn's number. "I owe you one."

Sally's ribald laughter cackled over the line. "Keep saying that," she said coyly, "and I just might try to collect."

"I'm sure you'd take it out in blood," he teased.

"I was thinking more in terms of flesh," she joked. "As in your hide. But perhaps your firstborn would do."

He thought of Amanda. "Oh, please, Sally," he said, "not that."

"Don't tell me there are little secret Santas out there," she said laughing. "Ones you've never told us about."

"Sally," he said before he hung up, "when I know, you'll know."

"I CAN'T STAND TO HAVE a man watch me cook," Cyn said, tightening a red-and-green apron around her waist. She shot him a taunting smile, then shoved a tray of cookie sprinkles in his direction. She'd changed into black wool slacks and a white silk blouse, through which he could see hints of a lacy camisole.

"Nothing worse than a feminist," he returned playfully,

seating himself at the table. The aroma of freshly baked cookies filled the warm kitchen and made him think of home, hearth and family. Glancing between Cyn and Amanda, he wondered yet another time if this really *was* his family.

"What's a fem-nist?" Amanda lathered a cookie with icing, getting more of the green goo on her hands than on the cookie. She pushed it toward Santa, who was now on sprinkle detail, apparently.

"A mild annoyance," Santa teased. He chuckled, gazed into Amanda's adorable green eyes, then picked up her cookie. Instead of sprinkling it, he naughtily popped it into his mouth whole.

Amanda gasped, staring at him, slack jawed. Then her rosy cheeks dimpled and she giggled. "Mommy, Santa Claus don't help us bake right."

"It's *won't*, not *don't*, and men never do, honey," Cyn replied over her shoulder as she put another tray into the oven.

When she turned around again, Santa surveyed her with the most penetrating gaze he could muster. She leaned against the same counter where they'd kissed the day before. "But don't forget, there are some things *only* men can do in a kitchen," he said. Judging from the way she pursed her lips, she too was now thinking about kissing him.

"Yeah," Amanda said brightly. "Men can come and they fix the sink when the water goes everywhere."

"Right, Amanda," Cyn said, leaning against the counter and giving Santa the once-over, as if she couldn't have made the point better herself.

Still, he was pleased to hear that her voice sounded a bit faint. She was thinking of kisses, all right. The corners of his lips twitched. "Men can fix all kinds of broken-down things."

Completely forgetting Amanda, Cyn's eyes widened. "I sure hope you aren't implying that I'm somehow broken-down."

He shrugged. "No, but are you now implying I could fix you?"

"Put me in a fix is more like it," she said coyly, clearly unable to stop herself from rising to the bait.

"And then there's your father—" He grinned and leaned his elbows on the table, enjoying himself. "Who's trying to *fix* us up."

Cyn suddenly chuckled. She crossed her arms over her chest. "Well, I'm not *fixing* to let him."

Santa glanced at Amanda, who now looked thoroughly confused. "Granddaddy's a fem-nist," she piped in as she finished icing the last cookie.

Cyn's eyes narrowed to a squint. "How's that?" she asked as he leaned forward and sprinkled tiny pink stars over Amanda's cookie. The gesture won him endearing smiles from both Amanda and Cyn.

"Granddaddy calls and don't let me watch cartoons," Amanda groused, jumping up from the table.

Ever the patient mother, Cyn automatically repeated the won't-not-don't rule, then said, "How would that make him a feminist, Amanda?"

"He was 'noying me," Amanda said promptly.

Cyn's laughter seemed to make the kitchen even warmer. "No, what a feminist is—"

"I'm gonna get my dress to wear by myself," Amanda announced, interrupting her.

Cyn smiled. "You go pick out a dress. I'll call you when the next batch is ready for icing."

"If Santa Claus doesn't eat them all," Amanda said, shooting Santa a coy glance that she'd clearly copied from her mother. "I get in trouble. Mr. Santa should be in big trouble."

"As soon as you leave to pick out your dress," Cyn said gravely, "I mean to explain the rules to Santa."

"Rules?" As soon as Amanda had gone, he picked up another cookie and took a large bite.

"We don't eat without asking." Cyn tossed a dish towel over the lip of the sink and stared pointedly at his cookie.

There were some remarks even he wouldn't touch with a ten-foot pole. Still he couldn't help but imagine his mouth sliding over Cyn's smooth skin. When he said nothing, her face suddenly went from wintry pale to berry red in a second flat.

"You are so crude!" A faint, shocked smile curled the corners of her lips.

"*I* didn't say a word," he drawled.

"You don't have to. Is your mind always in the gutter?"

He downed the rest of the cookie and reached for another. "Perpetually, when I'm around you."

"You have a whole tray of sprinkles to finish," she said, suddenly sounding like a drill sergeant. "And I suggest you get to work. Otherwise, you'll disappoint Amanda."

Was Cyn really going to try to implement her own hands-off policy? Good luck, he thought. Given the energy between them, her resolve would never last. "Hmm," he finally hummed, picking up a container of sprinkles. "If I concentrate real hard on decorating, then maybe you won't be so likely to read my gutterlike mind."

"I sure hope I can't," she returned archly. "I'd probably collapse from the shock."

His gaze dropped from her face and lingered momentarily on her blouse. Looking at how the scalloped lace edges of her camisole formed heart shapes over her breasts, his smile almost faltered. "No probably about it," he said softly.

Her sharp breath seemed overly loud in the quiet kitchen. She grabbed the dish towel, dampened it, then strode to the table and began mopping in and around his elbows, as if he weren't even there.

"Missed a spot," he prodded as he put down the pink star sprinkles and reached for the tiny blue dots. When she glanced his way, he pointed at a glob of green icing.

"Thank you," she said a little huffily, swiping at the green smear with more force than was needed.

"Anytime." After a moment, he cleared his throat and watched her busy herself, cleaning up the kitchen. He'd debated for some hours about whether or not to tell her about Lewis. He didn't want to see fear in her eyes again. But he couldn't protect people who weren't aware of the danger they were in, either.

"Cyn," he said. "We need to talk."

She folded the dish towel, slapped it over the sink again, then rinsed dishes, as if she meant to ignore him. When they teased each other, there was always some truth in what was said. He wondered whether their words would heat up into a real argument or a kiss. This time he hoped they could simply talk.

She finally turned around. "Now, what do you want to discuss?"

"You might want to sit down for a minute."

"You mean, right next to you?" She chuckled. "Forget it, Santa. Our knees might touch or something. And even though you seem ready to forget it now, I am your client. Right?"

"If I happen to forget I'm sure you'll be the first to remind me."

Her smile broadened into a confident grin. "Why, Santa—" She was mocking his drawl now. "I'd just feel so downright wretched if I accidentally compromised your ethics."

His eyes never left hers. "Ms. Sweet as sugar," he returned, "it's not my *ethics* I'm worried about."

That stopped her cold.

Out of the corner of his eye, he saw a wisp of smoke. "And Cyn?"

She crossed her arms over her chest. "What?"

"I do believe your cookies are burning."

In the next instant, she went flying around the kitchen like a spooked bird. She looked so upset when she slammed the tray onto the counter that he said, "Sorry."

"It's not your fault," she quickly returned, as if not about to admit that he'd captured her complete attention. "Besides," she said as Santa rose and came up behind her, "Daddy likes them that way."

"Burned?"

"Crunchy," she corrected. A flicker of awareness sparked in her eyes. Santa was sure she was thinking what he was. That they'd been standing in this exact spot when they'd kissed the previous day. "So, what is it?" Her businesslike tone was as crisply brittle as her cookies.

He suddenly wished that he could protect her and Amanda, not just from Lewis, but from all the harm in the world. His mouth opened slightly and he licked his upper lip.

"Don't tell me," she teased. She was clearly aware of the emotion in his gaze but read it incorrectly. "You're going to propose to me now." She smiled wickedly. "It always happens after men have known me three or four days."

"I wish I were," he found himself saying softly.

Her eyes met his dead-on, and widened. "It's—it's something bad," she rambled. "I can tell, it's something bad. Dammit, Santa, what is it?"

Somehow, he wanted to be holding her when he told her. "Matthew Lewis is out of Riker's Island on a holiday pardon," he said.

She all but crumpled against the counter. The expression in her eyes had gone from viciously teasing, to fearfully surprised, to helplessly vulnerable—all in a heartbeat. "Jake Jackson," she demanded. "What about Jake?"

He should have expected that. And he didn't want to lie. He was digging himself in deeper with every single falsehood he uttered. But seeing the expression in her eyes, he knew he'd tell a million lies to erase it. "I think he's still in prison," he managed to say.

She gasped. "Think?" Those beautiful green eyes pleaded with his.

"Know," he corrected. He waited for her to say something more. She didn't.

"Come here," he nearly whispered. Before his arms were even around her shoulders, her face was pressed against his chest. Her body curled against his, feeling so right he was almost convinced they had never been apart.

He tried to remind himself that she hadn't been there for him. That she'd left him, lying on her parents' lawn with two gunshot wounds. She might have deprived him of his very own daughter, too. The woman who was asking for his strength now hadn't given him hers. Cyn was demanding his trust but hadn't trusted him.

Santa knew he was supposed to be seducing information out of her. Instead, he was almost sure he could fall in love with her all over again. But even if he could, he thought, he'd never forgive her.

"BUY NOW! Lotto tickets are distributed with every purchase!" Bob Bingley grandly barked commands over Too Sweet's loudspeaker. "At exactly seven o'clock—that's just five minutes from now, folks—we'll dispense the very last ticket and the drawing will begin. That ticket might be a winner! So make your final purchases now!"

As Cyn and Amanda headed for the makeshift stage on the ground floor of Too Sweet, Cyn wished that the elf hadn't called in sick. A flu bug seemed to have half of Manhattan under the weather. She leaned and adjusted her green leggings. The next thing she knew, she thought, she'd be dressed as Santa Claus.

She shot Amanda an encouraging smile as they took positions on either side of the air-driven lotto machine. Inside the transparent plastic, bright red and green balls printed with silver numbers whirled and tumbled.

How does Amanda stand this? Cyn wondered, plastering

a smile on her face. Their matching elf outfits were bright green and consisted of pointy-toed, Aladdin-style slippers, thick leggings, and squarish, shorty dresses. What Amanda referred to as the Robin Hood hats had gargantuan red plumes. With Anton Santa staring at her protectively, Cyn felt more than a little idiotic.

She heaved a sigh of relief when the drumroll sounded. Over and over, Amanda pressed a button and the balls shot upward, landing in their ball-size pockets.

"Nine," Cyn called over the microphone. "Seven. Four..." There were to be twenty winners, each of whom would receive three free tickets to *The Nutcracker*, so that parents could accompany the child. Cyn wished all the kids present could win. "Six. Seven..."

As she called out the numbers, she glanced at Bob, who was recording them all. Then her gaze returned to Santa. No matter how hard she tried, she couldn't keep her eyes off him. He could be so sweet, when he wanted to be.

"Mommy," Amanda said in a stage whisper.

Cyn started. "Three," she called into the microphone, still watching Santa. "One..." She'd done her best to cold-shoulder him on their way out of the apartment, and now she was glad. In the few days she'd known him, he'd sent out more mixed messages than the post office. First he'd kept her at arm's length, which had made her want to flirt with him. When it had led to a kiss, he firmly rejected her, then tried to quit his job. Now he was seemingly ready to offer her comfort.

"Mommy!"

"Lucky number one again," Cyn said promptly. "Two. Nine..."

"That's us!" someone yelled.

Cyn's eyes darted over the crowd, settling on familiar faces—Eileen, Bob, Evan, Clayton. Somehow she half expected to see Matthew Lewis. Lewis made her think of Jake. *I've got to stay away from Santa,* she thought. "Three," she called. "Seven again! Five..." After all, Jake Jackson had taught her enough about mixed messages to last her a lifetime. She wouldn't have a man in her life who blew hot and cold.

"And now for the last lucky number!" she said brightly a few moments later as Amanda pushed the button. "Number nine!" She blew out a quick sigh, trying to forget that Santa's call this morning had been to a woman. She grinned at the crowd. "That wraps it up! Have fun at *The Nutcracker!*"

Amanda preceded her down the steps and right into Paxton's arms. "Good job, Amanda!" he said.

Meaning to avoid Santa, Cyn hurried toward the employees' door. Glancing over her shoulder, she realized the man in question was right behind her. Paxton was following, too, with Amanda on his hip.

She needed to take a roll of wrapping paper home, so she ducked into a walk-in closet that served as a supply room. The place was a mess, cluttered with tumbled stacks of boxes and scattered bows. Cyn smiled. A disaster area meant that today's sales were good. Just as she glanced over the pickings—gold foil, red foil, and red-and-green wreath print— she heard steps. Then the door behind her shut.

"What exactly did I do wrong?" Santa leaned casually against the door. Even though they were at opposite ends of the storage closet, he was a mere four feet away.

"Not a thing." She ignored him and bent over. Her hands fumbled over the various papers, even though she'd already decided on red. Suddenly she stood up straight. Just how short was her skirt? She forced herself not to grab at the hemline nearest her backside, and glanced at Santa. *Pretty short, judging by his expression.*

A loud series of raps sounded on the door. *Saved,* she thought, watching Santa cross his arms over his broad chest as if he didn't intend to budge.

"Are you in there, Cyn?"

She smiled at Santa as if to say that he wasn't going to

get away with trapping her. "Yes, Daddy!" she called brightly.

"Santa?" Paxton called.

"Right here."

Then the worst imaginable thing happened. The lock turned over. Her father had locked the door from the outside! What in thunder did he think he was doing?

Santa had the nerve to chuckle. "Your Daddy's sure got a juvenile streak," he remarked.

She sighed. "Why else would a man start a toy company?"

He shrugged. "The real question's why my favorite elf ducked in here to hide."

Favorite elf? His eyes gave her the once-over. She wished she was clad in anything other than a felt dress, and that the supply room was larger. "I'm not hiding," she said pointedly.

"Does Cyn not want to join in our reindeer games?" he drawled.

She grabbed a roll of paper, feeling so flustered that she accidentally picked up the green rather than the red. She wanted the man, there was no doubt about it. But she was just as sure it would be a mistake. She stalked toward the door. "I'm an elf, not a reindeer. Remember?" She pounded on the door. Hard. "Dad?"

"Sorry," Santa said softly. "But I think we're at his mercy."

Her gaze met his. "Let's wait it out, like adults, shall we?"

He threw both hands in the air. "Is it something I said?"

She arched her brow as if she had no idea what he was talking about. Still, she'd made such a point of avoiding him that he couldn't have missed it.

He shot her a knowing smirk. "You know what I mean."

"All right," she said levelly, leaning her shoulder against the door. "I'll tell you."

He turned so he was facing her. "Please do."

"Number one, you're toying with me," she said, leaning even closer. "Number two, you blow hot and cold, and I don't like that in a man. And number three," she said, her voice rising, "I don't play silly games." She flashed him a quick smile. "Reindeer or otherwise."

The fact that he was still smiling truly annoyed her. "I'm sorry I blow hot and cold," he said. "But you know something?"

"What?" She just couldn't help but ask.

"Right now, I'm blowing hot."

Before she could even respond, the fool man was kissing her again. She dropped the wrapping paper, and her arms flew up in protest. As his lips claimed hers, one of her hands somehow wound up on his shoulder. The other, fortunately, remained rational. With it, she began pounding on the door, as if to save her life.

It flew open in the next heartbeat.

Thank heavens, she thought, just before she realized they'd been leaning on it. She and Santa tumbled outward, sprawling toward the floor. Having no choice, she clutched him for support, but he was airborne.

His lips never left hers, but he somehow managed to twist his muscular body so that he hit the hard tiles first. Her hat lurched off her head and then, because of the plume, floated slowly downward. Santa kept rolling, until he was right on top of her.

Cyn wrenched away, only to find that she was trapped by Santa's weight. "Daddy!" she nearly shrieked. She looked up, into Paxton's eyes. He seemed to be towering over her.

"Something wrong, dear?" Paxton stared down at her calmly. In his arms, Amanda clapped excitedly.

"Look at what this man just did to me!" Cyn burst out, her eyes shooting Santa daggers. She unpinned one of her arms and tried to pull down the hemline of her ridiculous elf outfit. It was bunched nearly to her waist and she now realized that one of her slippers had come off in the melee. "Just look!"

"What?" Paxton was all innocence. "Oh, I suppose I should thank Mr. Santa. After all, he just broke your fall with an astounding display of professionalism and expertise. Excellent job, Santa," he continued as he began ambling away. "Excellent." He glanced over his shoulder, suddenly chuckling. "Oh, and Santa?"

The man was staring deeply into her eyes, and the full length of his body still covered hers. Cyn was sure he could feel her heart pounding against his chest. He finally glanced at Paxton. "Yes, sir?"

"Do keep up the good work."

I'M DEFINITELY getting out of shape. Across the river, in New Jersey, a man grunted and leaned against a wall, debating if he should contact Club Med or buy a StairMaster. Then he lugged the heavy typewriter up the rest of the stairs. "What a workout," he muttered when he reached his bedroom. He dropped the typewriter onto the mattress. It was so heavy that it bounced.

He fished through the odds and ends in his bedside drawer. When he found the key to his walk-in closet, he hoisted the typewriter into his arms again, carried it inside the closet, then shoved it behind a row of shoes. Then he locked the closet.

Things were getting serious, all right. Anton Santa had scrutinized the contents inside every drawer in the Too Sweet corporate offices. Santa had also looked at every typewriter. Worse, the last letter that had been sent hadn't even been mentioned in this morning's meeting. It hadn't made the papers, either.

He wanted that toy company! If it were run as something other than a family business, it could become a franchise. He'd make a fortune. Contrary to what the other execs thought, bad press always lost Too Sweet money. But the notes hadn't generated publicity.

He sighed. Maybe it was time he truly took matters into his own hands.

Part 5

Chapter Five

Saturday, December 17, 1994

Santa glanced at his clock. He'd finished the papers and his police procedural by six-thirty this morning, and was halfway through a thick forensics book now. He finally dog-eared the page and stood and stretched, hoping he'd given Cyn enough time to dress. It was ten, but he still hadn't heard the shower. One more look at her in a bathrobe, he thought, and he'd attack her.

How anyone could sleep past five or five-thirty was simply beyond him. The cartoons hadn't even come on until eight. "Ready or not, here I come," he chanted.

He flung open his door and found himself staring at the empty living room. He ambled in the direction of the blaring cartoons, only to find the den vacant, too. He tilted his head, listening. *Nothing.*

Both Cyn and Amanda knew better than to leave without him, he thought. Had someone forced them to? He crept down the hall. No one was in Amanda's room. Her bed had been made and the toys she'd played with the previous night had been put away.

He checked all the rooms, then warily pushed open Cyn's door. The room was a mess. Struggle or mere slobbishness? It was hard to tell. He circled her bed cautiously, half hoping the twisted sheets indicated a struggle, since he was neat to a fault. *How could I ever live with this woman?* He squelched that thought and squinted at her covers. Mere slobbishness, he finally decided. He didn't know if he felt relief because Amanda was probably safe, or because the mess meant his and Cyn's personal habits were so different.

In spite of the circumstances, he leaned and ran a hand over the sheets. They were of pink satin and so tangled that he could easily imagine they'd spent the night together. The whole room smelled like a woman who'd bathed and perfumed just for him, and the vanity was strewn with feminine trappings—powder-tinged makeup brushes, tiny crystal vials, delicate colored bottles, and crystal sprayers with pumps. Her blouse of the previous day had been sheer enough that he recognized the lace camisole on the floor. He had to fight not to pick it up.

He strode into her private bath and crouched down. The tub was dry, which meant she definitely hadn't showered. Suddenly his eyes widened, and he snagged a bottle from the lip of the tub. He scrutinized it so carefully that it might have been evidence at the scene of a murder.

"I'll be damned," he whispered, shaking his head. Cyn Sweet dyed her hair. The label really said Blonde. And all this time, he'd thought of her as a natural.

When he stood again, one of the soft silk stockings that hung over the shower rod fluttered against his face, then trailed over his shoulder. "She still wears garters, too," he murmured. *And I've got to get out of here.* He turned abruptly, reentered her room proper and checked the closet opposite her bed. He found nothing but rods hung with clothes that smelled of Cyn. "Cyn?" he called, heading toward the kitchen. "Amanda?"

Her folded note was hidden under an angel-shaped refrigerator magnet. It said, "Don't worry, we weren't kidnapped or anything."

He rubbed the scar on his jaw while he stared at the note.

He was angry at himself for becoming so engrossed in his book, and furious at her. In fact, what he was feeling was out of proportion with the situation. He felt as if he'd just raced back in time. It was four years ago, and he was running through her parents' front door. She took one look at his face, then turned and fled toward a cop cruiser. He felt abandoned.

He sighed. The kidnapper had a line on Cyn's daily activities, judging from how the last note had been delivered. He or she could have forced Cyn to write the note.

"More likely you just took off." He grimaced in the direction of a window, as if he might actually see Matthew Lewis, trailing Cyn and Amanda down the crowded avenue below. How could Cyn have left when they knew the man was out there somewhere?

"Why did you do this?" But he knew why. Last night, after the promotion, Paxton had insisted they all have dinner, and her father's matchmaking tactics had clearly infuriated Cyn.

She was sweet as sugar during their meal at The Russian Tea Room, of course. But as soon as Paxton was out of sight, her smile had vanished and she'd closed up like a clam. Santa wondered, as he had the previous night, what exactly had caused the rift between Paxton and his wife. *Who knows?* he thought now. *Women are impossible.*

He headed back down the hall to get his coats. As he shrugged into a gray suit jacket, he suddenly chuckled. "Some things never change," he said. He knew exactly where she was.

"WHAT DO YOU THINK, honey?"

Amanda was perched on a raised platform in her cotton undershirt and underpants. She shrugged. "Is she gonna come with my stuff?"

Cyn turned one way, then another, sucking in her stomach. "The lady from children's will bring your things in just a minute," she murmured, deciding that the emerald dress clung like a second skin. Too obvious. "Maybe I should try the red again."

A woman rapped on the door to the spacious dressing room, then nudged inside, her arms piled high with clothes. "Sorry for the delay, but we've brought up everything you liked from downstairs." She laid the clothes on a chair, while Cyn stripped back down to her slip.

"Did you like the red one better?"

Amanda pawed through her own pile. "I like black."

"It was better?" Cyn asked thoughtfully. She'd awakened this morning, deciding that she wanted to look smashing for *The Nutcracker.* After all, Amanda was going, which meant Santa was going. As she preened, Cyn told herself she just didn't want him upstaging her in one of his dashing suits.

"The black is for Mr. Santa," Amanda said, as if reading her mind. She marched up to her mother and craned her neck upward.

"Who said it was for Santa?" Cyn asked wryly, staring down. She realized Amanda had put on a sweatshirt backward and chuckled. "Here, honey, raise your arms." She turned it around, thinking the top was positively adorable. It was green, with Rudolph appliquéd on the back. A puffy Santa Claus adorned the front. When the string that hung from his cap was pulled, his eyes blinked.

Amanda stared in the mirror for less than a second. "Goody," she said. "We'll buy it." She tossed it onto her pile and found the matching leggings.

"We can?" Cyn laughed. "The next thing I know, you'll be asking for a gold card." She flashed Amanda a grin. "Please do me a favor though, and don't ask before you're at least five."

Amanda plopped down on the platform and wriggled into the pants, with a concentrated expression. "You're so very definitely my daughter," Cyn said wryly. She could swear that Amanda had been dressing herself before she could even walk. Suddenly she felt a twinge of loss. If anything ever happened to Amanda, she couldn't bear it. A lump formed in her throat and she swallowed. She forced herself to tug on the red dress again.

Staring at it, she realized she should have listened to Amanda. The black dress was the one, hands down. She stepped out of the red, reaching for it. The sleeveless velvet sheath could be worn with opera-length gloves. It would have Santa's eyes popping out of his head.

"Mommy?"

Cyn glanced down and had to fight not to laugh. Amanda had donned a black velvet dress, too. The scoop neck came down to her navel. It seemed to point out that her baby was years away from having breasts. Cyn felt relieved, somehow.

"I gotta get a dress for Santa," she nearly wailed.

"Well, we're going to concentrate strictly on you now, honey," Cyn said soothingly. "Shopping takes practice."

"We practice lots," Amanda said glumly. "I wanna be a knockout."

A knockout? Did they use terms like that on *Sesame Street?* "Sure, honey," Cyn managed to say.

HE FOLLOWED their trail from Barney's to Macy's to Bloomingdale's, back to Barney's, and then to Bergdorf Goodman. He found them in Saks. By that time, he was so steamed, he didn't let the sales personnel stop him. He rapped once on the door, then flung it open, thinking, *Hell, Cyn, I've seen you stark naked before.*

Amanda screamed.

Santa gulped. Cyn was fully clothed, and Amanda was scared to death. She scurried toward a corner, clutching a green wad of velvet against her undershirt.

She whirled around. "You gotta say who it is!" Amanda's mouth gaped and her green eyes were wide.

What he'd taken for modesty, apparently wasn't. A furious Amanda flung down the dress and put her hands on her hips.

He guessed it was all right to be in her underclothes in front of a man, just so long as she was acquainted with him.

"Sorry, Amanda," he managed to say. He glanced at Cyn, who was clearly enjoying his discomfort.

"Try the blue one, honey," she said to Amanda.

"He can't see it," she whined in protest.

Santa felt like an idiot. "I'll wait outside."

"I don't care!" Amanda stomped her foot. "It's ugly."

"Sweetheart, anything'd turn pretty if you put it on," he said soothingly. That helped. She smiled just enough that her dimples started to show.

"Santa, why don't you wait outside," Cyn said, sounding tired. "We need to get this over with."

Her tone put him on edge. "I have been charging all over Manhattan," he said softly. "Do you know how many women's clothing stores there are in this town?" He shot her one long, penetrating look, then glanced pointedly over the shopping bags in the dressing room. "But of course you do."

"Well, why didn't you just stay home?" she returned saucily.

He didn't want to argue with her in front of Amanda, but he wasn't going to let her get away with a stunt like this, either. She couldn't play silly games, not when she might be endangering Amanda. "Whatever's between us is between us." His voice was soft yet carried a warning. "But you don't jeopardize the safety of yourself—" he glanced quickly at Amanda "—or others because of that." She looked so guilty he almost wanted to retract the words.

"We were just shopping," she said defensively.

"Shopping," he echoed, trying not to sound as disgusted as he felt.

She folded her hands primly in her lap. "Well, we had to finish Christmas shopping."

His eyes trailed from one shopping bag to another. He fixed his gaze on hers again. "Everything you've bought is for yourself," he chided.

Her blush told him it was the truth. Suddenly her lovely green eyes narrowed. "How did you know where to find us, anyway?"

The same way I know you take cream in your coffee. I know you inside out, lady. "Just a lucky guess," he drawled, his eyes never leaving hers.

"Mommy's sorry, Mr. Santa Claus," Amanda said tearfully.

When he looked down, the little girl—so very probably his little girl—looked like her whole world was about to collapse.

"Mommy was bad and she won't do it again," she vowed. She looked as if she were making a life-and-death oath.

Cyn looked at Amanda for a long time, then at him again. "I really am sorry," she said, sounding genuinely contrite.

He nodded. "I'll be outside."

"Santa Claus?"

He turned at the door. "Yes, Amanda," he said, more sternly than he'd intended.

"We got somethin' not for us, 'cause Mommy let me. You got a present you can't have till Christmas. Okay?" Her eyes begged him to say that everything was all right between them.

His heart skipped a beat. This kid was bringing him to his knees. "Thank you, Amanda," he said softly.

Outside, he took a seat in an armchair facing the dressing room. The man next to him was asleep and snoring. *My sentiments, exactly.* That women could shop for an entire day would never cease to amaze him.

It was a good thing he was patient, he thought. After all, waiting was his job. It was good that he could hide his feelings, too. Otherwise, he would have given Cyn a tongue-lashing that neither she nor Amanda would be likely to forget. But he could wait—through all the hours of shopping, and until he heard the truth about Amanda from Cyn's own lips.

Another full minute passed before he realized his heart was pounding. He blew out a long, relieved sigh. *They're safe,* he finally thought. *My girls are safe.* This time he didn't even consider that neither might belong to him.

MORE WAITING. Santa glanced at his watch, then stared at the football game again. His team was winning. Was he really missing the play-offs because of a ballet? Between shopping and *The Nutcracker,* he was sure he'd fall asleep like that poor fellow in Saks. Not that he'd ever been to a ballet before, of course.

"Ta-da," Cyn called out.

When Santa turned around, he forgot footballs even existed. Cyn's thick blond hair was pulled into a French twist. Springy silken tendrils framed her face and wound around the dangling clusters of her pearl earrings. Her wide, full lips were glossed a kissable, glistening pink.

But it was the dress that caused an almost uncomfortable tightening in his groin. The black strapless velvet sheath was long enough to look classically elegant, but short enough that no man—least of all, him—could ignore those sexy, perfectly shaped legs. Black gloves stretched all the way up her arms, and a single strand of gleaming pearls looped all the way down, past her waist.

It was almost impossible to imagine that this was the same woman who'd left him for dead just four years ago. But he remembered, all right. She moved behind an armchair and rested her palms on the back of it. Even though he wanted to tell her she looked lovely, he found himself gruffly saying, "Aren't you going to freeze?"

Her face fell, but she recovered quickly enough to shoot him a false smile. "Since when is my body temperature any of your concern?"

As of right now. "As a bodyguard," he said, rising lithely from the sofa, "bodies always concern me." He strode across the room and stood in front of the chair.

"Ah—" She tossed her head, showing off the long, smooth touchable column of her throat. "But temperatures are another matter."

"Perhaps, but whatever perfume you're wearing is sure making mine rise." He decided that it had been easier to remember the past and why he should avoid Cyn when he was on the other side of the room. Why had he moved?

When she leaned her elbows on the chair back, he was half-sure she was intentionally accentuating her cleavage for his benefit. "It should," she said. She reached out coyly and grasped his tie between her gloved thumb and fingers. "It's called Flame."

What had come over the woman? She was driving him crazy. His every muscle and sinew tensed with need. He wanted her. Getting close would be the easiest way to find out about Amanda, too. And yet he knew it was a mistake. If they made love, she'd realize who he was. Unfortunately, he *liked* to play with fire. Besides which, it was she, not he, who was going to get burned. If she really thought he cared about his client ethics in this particular case, she had another thing coming.

Ever since he'd arrived, they'd circled each other as warily as caged tigers. Judging from her behavior of the moment, she'd decided to pursue him again. He was fairly sure she was no match for him when it came to boldness. His gaze dropped to her breasts. After a moment he blinked and looked into her eyes.

"Since I'm going to be so chilly—" Her voice was lazy, and she lightly tugged his tie. "I'd ask you to keep me warm..." She rolled her head around her shoulders, as if she were desperately in need of a massage. "But..."

He leaned forward, placed his hands on either armrest and brought his lips within inches of hers. She dropped his tie as if it had just caught fire, and he nearly smiled. "But?" he prodded softly.

"But—" She wriggled her elbows on the back of the chair, as if getting comfortable. "I have a coat."

"I doubt it's as warm as I could be," he said, wishing his own voice wasn't starting to sound so husky.

"But it's fur," she countered.

"Not very politically correct," he remarked dryly, even though an image of Cyn in nothing but fur flashed through his mind.

"I've had it nearly ten years," she returned guiltily. "And it *is* warm."

"Like I said—" He leaned an inch closer. "So am I."

She leaned away from him in a barely perceptible movement. The wafting scent of her perfume was so overwhelmingly feminine that he didn't exhale for an instant. It made him think of how mysterious women really were—of top drawers crammed with lace and hidden compartments that contained love letters and cloth diaries full of secrets.

He had no idea how long they merely gazed at each other. "I dare you to come around this chair," he finally said.

She blinked. "What in the world for?" she trilled. She'd been going for casually flirtatious. She sounded breathless.

"You know what for."

Faint pinkish color stained her wintry pale cheeks. "Can't you just escort Amanda and myself like a normal person?" she asked.

He chuckled and raised an eyebrow. "I take it a normal person is a man who isn't attracted to you?"

She smiled, obviously feeling as attracted to him as he was to her. "Well, yes."

He was about to say that normalcy was highly overrated, when he heard steps bounding down the hallway. He glanced toward the door.

Cyn leaned over the chair and whispered, "Tell Amanda she looks like a knockout."

"A knockout?" he managed to ask. Cyn's minty-smelling breath lingered by his ears.

"Yes," she hissed, just as Amanda appeared.

She stood uncertainly in the doorway. She was wearing a blue velvet dress, with a full skirt and wide sash. A tiny matching pocketbook hung from her white-gloved hands, which were clasped nervously in front of her. Two small blue bows held her wavy curls back on either side. It was on the tip of Santa's tongue to tell her she looked cute as hell. Instead, he crossed the room and knelt in front of her. "Wow," he said, "you're—er—a knockout, Amanda."

He didn't know what he'd expected, but it wasn't to have her glare at him suspiciously. "Mommy told you to say it."

He mustered his best dumfounded expression. "Well, she didn't. Was she supposed to?"

"I'm a knockout," Amanda said proudly, not bothering to answer him.

Once their coats were on and they were headed out the door, Santa caught Cyn's hand and guided her arm through his. "And so are you," he whispered.

She smiled up at him. "I knew you'd come around."

"CAN YOU HOLD the pocketbook, Mr. Santa Claus?" Amanda asked as the houselights dimmed. She snuggled down in the seat between her mother and Santa.

"Sure, honey," he said gruffly.

Cyn fought back a chuckle as she watched Amanda's teeny blue bag vanish beneath one of Santa's hands. He set it so gingerly on his knee that it could have been a kitten. Clearly, he wasn't quite sure what to do with it. Cyn nestled back in her own seat, ready to watch the show. *If I can keep my eyes off Santa.*

Even when she wasn't looking, she was conscious of every inch of him. It was almost as if she'd known him before. And tonight, entering the theater on his arm, she'd felt more like a woman than she had in a long time. He was so controlled and strong and handsome in his charcoal suit, starched shirt and silver silk tie that she'd felt smaller and infinitely more delicate.

She trained her gaze on the stage longer than she'd thought she could. After all, she was still waiting for her own nut-cracker, wasn't she? With a sigh, Cyn imagined she was Clara. She received the nutcracker from her uncle and was astounded when he became a handsome prince. Cyn's heart thudded with fear as the rats, with their long noses and tails and colorful costumes, leaped across the stage.

And yet, as the first act became the second and third, she found she wasn't thinking of herself, but of Amanda. As she watched Clara's transformation, from a naive girl to a young woman, Cyn hoped that her daughter's initiation would be more gentle than her own. *Damn Jake Jackson.*

She glanced at Santa, and her lips parted. The man seemed as engrossed in the ballet as he had been in the play-offs. Were his thoughts anything like her own? Did he feel faint twinges of sadness as he watched Clara's first glimpse of love? Did he wish he could be that young, just one more time? In some sweet, soft part of Santa, did he wonder if he could ever become her prince?

Cyn's eyes narrowed. For the first time, she wondered if he'd ever been married. Had he ever been madly in love? What had his life been like before they'd met, just a few short days ago?

Santa turned and looked at Cyn, as if he'd felt her gaze. She glanced down at the top of Amanda's head quickly. Less than a second passed before she raised her eyes again. He was staring back steadily.

After a long moment, she smiled and turned her attention to the stage.

But she could still feel those eyes.

Their caress was so strong and bold and real, it was as if his hands were actually touching her.

"IN YOU GO, SWEETHEART," Santa said.

Cyn removed her gloves, shoved her hands deep into her

coat pockets and leaned in the doorway. She watched as Santa attempted to slide Amanda between the sheets. Her daughter had slept while she and Santa slipped her into her nightclothes, but now Amanda seemed unwilling to relinquish him.

Her small pudgy arms were flung around his neck and her legs remained wrapped around the waist of his camel coat. Santa pried her loose ever so gently, clearly trying not to awaken her. Then he seated himself beside her on the canopied bed and tucked her in. He remained there, simply watching her, as if he'd forgotten Cyn entirely.

Why is it that every time I see him with Amanda, I think I could fall in love with him? Cyn wondered. She tried to tell herself that it was only because the dainty, feminine room made him look so much more masculine. His hands seemed larger and darker against the tiny pink throws, his back seemed broader beneath the frilly canopy, and his feet—clad in shiny dress shoes—looked adultly male next to Amanda's girlish pocketbook, which had fallen to the floor.

A tug of sadness pulled at Cyn's heart. She'd barely dated in the past four years. It had seemed best to focus on Amanda, to try to give her everything in the world. But she hadn't given Amanda the thing she most wanted. A daddy. Right now, seeing such a strong man watch over her little baby, the absence of a father almost hurt. *Jake Jackson isn't coming within a mile of Amanda, no matter how much she needs a dad.* Cyn sighed. She was a daddy's girl, herself. She was approaching thirty, but she simply couldn't imagine a life without Paxton, or her mother.

Amanda had accepted Santa so easily. What would happen when the threats were gone and he left? Even now, Cyn feared the effect on Amanda. *And on myself.* In a few short days Cyn had come to want him. Maybe that was fine, she decided. If she made love to him, he would leave. He would be a man who briefly touched their lives—without leaving heartbreak in his wake.

She sucked in a sharp breath. As if remembering that she was watching, Santa gently smoothed the hair on Amanda's forehead. He leaned, retrieved Amanda's pocketbook from the floor and placed it on her bedside table carefully. Then he reached for her lamp. Its shade was scalloped and its base was a pink porcelain ballerina. The tutu seemed to shrink beneath his hand as he turned out the light.

"Sleep well, Amanda," Cyn heard him whisper in the darkness. "And dream of a nutcracker prince." The whole room grew quiet and seemingly smaller and Cyn felt oddly self-conscious.

"It was a big night for her," Cyn whispered as she and Santa tiptoed into the hall.

"For me, too," he said softly as he opened the coat closet. He looked sleepy, and the dim light transformed his eyes so that they softened to a gleaming gold. He stepped behind her. When he removed her coat, his fingertips grazed her bare shoulders and glided gracefully over her skin.

"So, did you have an all right time?" she murmured, facing him in the hallway's dim light. Was it her imagination or were his hands really luxuriating in the sensual feel of the fur?

He nodded as he hung her coat for her, then shrugged out of his own. "It made me think of lost childhoods," he said in a dreamy-sounding drawl.

"And lost first loves?" she asked, before she'd really thought it through.

He hung up his coat, then leaned against the door frame. "Those, too."

There wasn't much light, but it caught in his slicked-back hair and streaked it with a gold that matched his eyes. She smiled. "Just how many lost first loves can one have?"

His eyes suddenly seemed so all-knowing that she nearly flinched. His lips parted slightly, then closed, as if he'd been about to say something but then changed his mind. "Only one," he finally said.

She tilted her head, wondering what he'd decided not to say. "Who was yours?" Her voice lowered huskily.

He merely stared at her, as if he could do so forever. A look she could swear she'd seen a thousand times in his eyes now touched them. It was of sadness, longing and desire—all combined. "Who was yours?" he countered softly.

Jake Jackson, she thought, wishing there was just one other name...one other man. One other time when she'd been touched to the depth of her very being. "Bad topic?" she suggested. She tried to tell herself that the raspiness of her voice was caused by sleepiness, not Santa. And yet, she knew she wanted him.

"Afraid so," he murmured. He leaned lithely and touched her pearl necklace. His fingertips lingered against her collarbone, then he lifted the strand just inches into the air. He thoughtfully turned it one way and another, as if watching how the pearls caught the light.

The thought flashed through her mind that she'd thrown her pearls before swine, with Jake Jackson, and yet when Santa carefully replaced her necklace all she could think of were those tanned fingers that remained on her skin.

Say something, she thought illogically.

"Good night, Cynthia."

He said it, but he didn't move away. Instead, his fingers traced across her upper chest, then slid up the column of her neck. Just when she remembered to breathe and sucked inward, his hand turned and cupped her chin.

Her lips parted. Slow heat curled in her stomach like trailing smoke, and fire seemed to lick its tongue into the corners of her body. Her mouth went as dry as cinders. *He's going to kiss me,* she thought. *Oh, how this man's going to kiss me.*

He leaned and pressed his lips against hers with an astonishing gentleness. She'd expected feverish fury and fiery intensity. She'd expected to feel his whole body crush against hers. Heavens, she'd expected the kiss they'd shared in the kitchen. But the almost chaste, steady pressure of his lips was even more intimate. She realized she was holding her breath.

He leaned back. "Sweet dreams," he murmured softly.

Her heart was hammering, her knees were wobbly, and she still hadn't breathed. Santa's golden eyes flickered as if lit by inner fires, and his broad shoulders looked strong enough to carry the weight of the world. Cyn exhaled shakily. "Ah, Santa," she managed to whisper, "who needs to dream?"

Part 6

Chapter Six

Sunday, December 18, 1994

"A fine dinner, as usual, Cynthia," Paxton said. He took a last quick bite of cheesecake, then leaned back and sipped his espresso. He tilted his head toward the CD player, as if listening to the soft classical music. "You'll make a man a fine wife, someday." He glanced mischievously in Santa's direction. "Won't she, Santa?"

"Perhaps sooner than she thinks," Santa drawled from the head of the table, where Paxton had insisted he sit. She'd dimmed the lights, and Santa's eyes danced in the candlelight. For a second his penetrating stare made her feel particularly transparent. She could swear he knew her innermost secrets.

"Amanda needs a father figure," Paxton continued.

"Now, Daddy," Cyn protested weakly. Her gaze drifted to where his shirt cuffs peeked from beneath his suit sleeves. As usual, her father was missing a cuff link. She wished he'd concentrate more on dressing himself and less on marrying her off. She simply couldn't believe how Paxton had warmed to Santa.

"Well, they always say that second marriages are the best," Santa said to Paxton, picking up the thread.

Is it my imagination or does Santa know something about

Jake and Harry? "So glad you could come, Daddy," Cyn piped in, for what had to be the umpteenth time. Why wouldn't her father take the hint? Not that she wanted to be alone with Santa. All her five senses longed for him, but her sixth sense kept screaming, "mistake." She'd avoided him today, since he hadn't attended church with them. Instead, he'd rifled through drawers at Too Sweet again.

Paxton sighed, placing his napkin beside his plate. "I'd glance in on Amanda, but I don't want to wake her."

"You won't," Cyn said quickly. "You know how soundly she sleeps."

Paxton ignored her and turned to Santa. "Real cute, isn't she?" he prodded.

Santa's eyes, which had seemed so nondescript just days ago now steadily met Cyn's, making her whole body tingle. "Cyn or Amanda?" he finally asked, his gaze never leaving hers.

Paxton chuckled. "Amanda."

Santa nodded. "She sure is." Everything in his expression made Cyn sure he was thinking of her. And not in terms of cute, exactly. She appreciated the easy way in which he humored her father. Still, she was starting to feel testy.

"Next time Mother can't make dinner, I'll call," Cyn said, more pointedly than she'd intended. Her parents traded Sunday night dinners, and this one belonged to Analise. Cyn wished her mother hadn't worked tonight, too. She half expected her father to come right out and beg Santa to marry her.

"Yes, Amanda *is* cute, isn't she?"

"I think you said that, Daddy," Cyn reminded.

"As a button," Santa said. From the opposite end of the table, he shot Cyn a grin, as if to say he was as aware of Paxton's machinations as she was.

"Heavens!" Cyn cleared her throat loudly and looked at a clock. "How time flies!"

Paxton scrutinized her, then Santa. "Oh!" he exclaimed guiltily. "I guess you two want to be alone."

Cyn's cheeks warmed. "That's not what I meant! I mean—er— I just need to start cleaning up...."

"I'm no fool," Paxton said, sounding pleased. Feeling flustered, Cyn slammed her demitasse cup onto its saucer.

Santa smirked, seemingly enjoying her discomfort. "I'll walk you to the door, Paxton."

Cyn busied herself by gathering up the dessert plates. She was nearly to the kitchen when she heard Paxton say, "You'd be a good man for my daughter, Santa."

Santa's laughter rang in her ears. "You just don't quit, do you, Paxton?"

In the kitchen, Cyn put her hands on her hips and sighed. As much as she loved to cook, she'd also managed to dirty every dish in the house. She headed toward the dining room again and collided with Santa. He caught her in his arms, and once more she felt sure he was going to kiss her.

Instead, he said, "You rinse. I'll carry." With that, he playfully marched her back toward the sink.

"Sorry about my father," she said.

"You sure rushed him out." Santa's breath whispered by her ear.

"I'd had about all the male bonding I could take," she managed to say. Feeling Santa's broad chest press against her back, she half wished he'd responded differently to her father's last words. He could have said he was Mr. Right, for instance. Instead, he'd laughed.

"The Super Bowl is male bonding," he said, depositing her in front of the dishwasher. "What your father engages in is old-fashioned matchmaking."

Watching him amble back down the hallway, Cyn almost wished it had worked. He was obviously attracted to her, and she was fairly sure he wasn't bothered by the ethical question of their involvement. Ever since he'd tried to quit, his eyes had flickered with invitation. On the one hand, a casual affair, which was all a traveling man like Santa could offer, seemed perfect. And yet, Cyn wasn't sure she was capable of it. She'd end up wanting more. She sighed and started cleaning with a vengeance.

"Why doesn't a woman like you have a cook?" Santa asked moments later. He grabbed a towel and began hand-drying the sterling silverware.

She shrugged. "I like to cook." When she glanced at him, she realized he'd removed his jacket. His suspenders were off his shoulders and hung in loops by his thighs. "Besides, I love turkey dinners." She smiled. "I even make them in the summer."

He leaned casually against the counter, while he polished a serving spoon to perfection. "At least someone to clean up..."

She placed the last pot in the drain board. "Why?" she asked saucily. "When I have you?"

"Ah—" he drawled. "But do you have me?"

She decided not to pursue that one. "Honestly, I don't really like having people around all the time. My mother always did."

He chuckled. "Is that a not-so-subtle hint?" He slapped the towel over his shoulder and crossed his arms over his chest. "Just what am I getting in the way of?"

"Oh," she managed to say lightly, "of my many dates." *What am I saying? What dates?*

He grinned wickedly. In the next instant, the towel snapped off his shoulder and he playfully swatted her behind. "Meet me in the living room." He shoved away from the counter with his hip.

He'd nearly reached the hall before she asked, "What for?"

"You know." He turned in the doorway. "I'll take you out, squire you around town. We'll have dinner. Take in the show..."

"A show in my living room?" she asked archly.

He turned and strode down the hall with such lean-looking long strides that her heart started to race. "Always," he called over his shoulder. "If you're there, sweetheart."

"I guess we could watch TV," she yelled.

Another throaty chuckle floated to her ears. "I was thinking more in terms of fireworks."

"So, IS THIS WHERE you bring all the girls?"

For a moment, Santa kept staring through the living room window at the snow flurries. Would it ever really snow? And did he dare seduce her? Wouldn't she realize who he was? He forced himself to turn around.

He watched her smooth her crepe cream dress beneath her behind as she sat daintily on the sofa. She sat right in the middle, too, which meant she intended for them to get cozy. Her thick hair was drawn into a soft, seductive knot. He almost wished he'd extinguished the candles and turned on all the lights. "It might be more to the point," he finally drawled, "to ask if this is where you bring all the boys."

"Ah—" She flashed him a quick smile, then glanced at the two glasses of wine he'd poured and left on a coffee table. "Many a man has lost his virtue here," she said. The tremor in her voice almost convinced him it wasn't true.

"Not to mention his heart, I'm sure." Santa's own skipped a beat, and he wondered just how much truth there was in what she'd said. He was a little jealous by nature, and he couldn't help it.

"A man's heart," Cyn returned lightly, "is the very last thing I need." She picked up a glass and took a quick sip of wine.

He crossed the room and sat next to her on the sofa. She looked as lovely to him as she had the previous night. Through the transparent sleeves of her dress, her skin glowed. "So, it must be a man's hand you're looking for...." he said in a teasing whisper.

She smiled. "Oh please. Not that."

He burst out laughing. "Just what part of a man do you *want*, Ms. Sweet?"

Her smile broadened. "Do you really want to know?"

He managed to straighten his face. "Actually——" He casually laid his arm along the back of the sofa, above her shoulders. "I'm afraid to ask."

She took another sip of wine and replaced her glass on the coffee table. Then she turned and looked at him boldly. In the dim candlelight, her eyes seemed as darkly green as a forest at midnight. Just looking, he felt himself getting pleasantly lost. "You should be," she said, holding his gaze.

Many times, he'd noticed that Cyn had grown up. But this was too much. How many men had she talked to this way? He knew he hadn't been her first lover. And yet, she said there'd only been one other man, one time. All along, he'd assumed it was Harry Stevens. Maybe it wasn't.

When he said nothing, she leaned forward again. When she lifted her wineglass, her stocking-clad knee brushed his slacks, begging the question again: Could he possibly make love to her without her recognizing him? She took a sip that left her mouth wet and glistening. The classical CD fell silent between movements of a symphony, and in the sudden, hushed quiet, her glass tinkled against a coaster.

Without even thinking, he leaned forward as she leaned back, and his arm left the sofa and curled around her shoulders instead. In a second, her cheek was pressed against his chest. "I've lost my fear," he said huskily. "Just what part of a man do you want?"

The hemline of her dress had risen and how her long, perfect legs twined at the ankles suddenly captured his whole attention. He wasn't sure, but he thought he felt her smile press against his shirtfront.

"What part of a woman do you want, Santa?" She poked his chest lightly with one of her long, polished nails.

He chuckled softly. Everything about her—her playfulness, her nearness, and her scent—was arousing him. The pressure of her hip against his was warm. "Depends on the woman."

She snuggled closer, nuzzling her cheek into his shoulder. "What about me?"

"You?" He dipped his head and breathed in the clean, fresh scent of her hair. As he brushed his lips across her thick bun, he thought about removing her hairpins. Heat coiled in his abdomen and his whole body felt heavier. His slacks began to tug perceptibly. *My face is different. My hair's another color. I'm more muscular. But my inner self, the way I am when I lose control, when I make love...*

"Who else but me, silly?" she finally murmured.

When he inhaled, his mouth went dry. He licked his lower lip, knowing he couldn't take much more of this. Not the constant teasing. Not the soft, almost accidental touches when they brushed past each other. Not the way her legs could twine around his waist if he only pulled her on top of him. He wasn't wondering about Amanda at the moment. He had to know if he was her father, but right now, all he knew was that he wanted Cyn.

Finally he said, "You're not the kind of woman that I could break down into parts." He dropped his arm from around her shoulder and slid his fingertips down the length of her arm.

She giggled throatily. "So the whole of me is greater than the sum of my parts? Isn't that some law of chemistry?"

"Philosophy, I think," he murmured. He tightened his arm around her, thinking that he was nearly ready to make love, even though he hadn't even kissed her yet. "But chemistry will certainly do."

"Is that a compliment, Santa?"

"No, sweetheart," he said, kicking off his shoes. "It's an invitation."

"Am I supposed to RSVP?" Her voice lowered so that it was barely audible. She kicked off her high heels.

"Immediately."

When she sat up, he wished he was still wearing his suit jacket. As it was, there was nothing to hide his aroused state. Her gaze flitted toward his lap, and rose immediately to his eyes. The sheer vulnerability he saw in her face made him sure he was making a dangerous mistake. Her confidence was gone. So was the jaunty smile that preceded her saucier come-on lines.

"I don't want—"

She was speaking so quietly that he had to lean forward to hear. He glanced toward the hallway. "Are you worried about Amanda?"

She shook her head. "She's a sound sleeper and my door locks."

"Condoms?" he asked softly.

"I have some."

Bad sign, he thought. Who was she keeping them for? After a long moment, she licked her lower lip and swallowed. "I just don't want any serious involvements," she whispered in a quick rush. "I really don't."

He tried to tell himself that he just wanted to know whether or not he was Amanda's father. But right now he didn't care. He tried to remember that moment, four years ago, when she'd deserted him, but couldn't. He was ready to take her on any terms she offered. Shadows wavered across her skin, just as her resolve seemed to waver. "But you want me?" he said.

She nodded. "For just—just one night."

Why doesn't she want something more? Is it because I'm Amanda's bodyguard? Because I'm living in the apartment with her? Because I remind her of Jake Jackson? His warring emotions were tugging him apart. He reached out and touched her cheek. "No strings attached," he assured softly, wondering if he meant it.

Even in the dim light, he could see the flush that was beginning to stain her cheeks. She had the embarrassed look of a woman who wished that things would quickly be decided, one way or the other.

"Yeah—" She smiled quickly, clearly trying to banter but failing. "No tomorrows and all that."

His chest closed around his heart like a vise. "And no yesterdays," he said gruffly. Beneath his fingers, the skin of her cheek felt as soft as silk. His gaze never leaving hers, he dropped his fingertips lightly to her chest, just inches above her breasts.

"Heaven knows," she whispered, her voice catching. "There are a few yesterdays I'd like to forget."

He caught her hand and rose lithely from the sofa, pulling her with him. "Maybe this will help," he said, claiming her lips.

SANTA LOCKED THE DOOR and turned around. Hints of lamplight shone through her window into the intimate darkness. Cyn was standing by the window. One of her long arms hung rigidly at her side; the other lifted a corner of the curtain. *Ah, Cyn*, he thought, wanting to tell her that he liked her just the way she was. *This new you is just a disguise. I can see that you're as soft and sweet as you ever were.*

She'd warmed to his kisses in the living room, but now, in her bedroom, she seemed tense. He crossed the room and approached her from behind. His arms circled her waist and his hands rubbed slow circles on her abdomen. When he hugged her tightly, and she felt how aroused he was, her back stiffened and then slowly relaxed. Together, they stared through the window. He could hear her swallow. "It's cold out there," she finally said.

Her hand was trembling and the curtain fluttered. "That's why I'm in here tonight," he said. "With you."

She turned in his arms, letting the curtain fall. "To keep me warm?" She gazed into his eyes, her voice tremulous.

He drew her closer, pressing her against the length of his body, and kissed her, slowly probing her lips. "Ah, Cyn," he chided softly as he leaned back, "don't tell me you're scared."

He smiled, feeling glad it was dark, knowing there was less chance he'd be discovered this way. "Brassy Cyn," he murmured, nuzzling his cheek against hers. He began to let down her hair. His other hand roved over her back. When her hair cascaded around her shoulders, he raked his fingers through it, caught it in fistfuls then let it fall again.

"It's been a long time," she said breathlessly.

For an instant, his hand froze on her back. "How long?" *Four years?*

"Too long." Her hands cupped his chin. "How'd you get that scar?" she asked huskily.

He was surprised to find that the question didn't even anger him. He smiled. "Knife fight."

Her chuckle caught in her throat. "Somehow I doubt it," she whispered as her hands dropped to his chest. As she began to unknot his tie, his lips settled on hers again.

He tried to remind himself that he was supposed to make love to her quickly and without foreplay. But as he kissed her, his hands dropped gently from her hips, to her thighs. He lifted the hemline of her dress with nothing more than his fingertips, until skin met skin and he was touching the bare silken inches that lay above her stockings. As he loosened her garters one by one, she drew in a quick breath against his mouth.

He was more adept than she was. Slower, too. Within moments she was rising on her tiptoes and arching against the most intimate part of him. And yet, in her fury to undress him, while he kissed her, she suddenly seemed to forget her own pleasure. She fumbled with his buttons, tugged at his shirt without managing to remove it, and nearly ripped the cuff links from his wrists. Santa let her. Until she reached for his zipper.

"Cyn," he said softly, "we have all night."

"Sorry." She leaned back in his arms.

"Don't ever be sorry," he whispered, "but you're coming at me like this is something you want to get over and done with."

"I'll admit that ever since I first saw you, that's pretty much how I've felt." The sheer frustration in her soft voice made him smile. She slid open the ends of his shirt, ran her nails through the curling hairs on his chest, then pressed her face against him. She smiled against his skin. "You're the most controlled person I ever met," she murmured.

His eyes had adjusted and he could just make out her features. He wondered if making love to her might get her out of his system for good. She was so incredibly beautiful that he somehow doubted it. Still, he did mean for this time to last him the rest of his life. *That's what I want, isn't it?* That, he thought, and to push any other men she may have had from her mind forever.

Will she know who I am?

"Santa?" she whispered throatily, sounding a little bereft.

"I'm right here." A soft sigh escaped her, just as his mouth captured hers again. He lifted her and carried her to the bed.

"I want you," she whispered against his cheek, as his hands deftly removed her remaining clothes, then his own. When her hands glided over his back, he swallowed a moan and drove his tongue deep between her lips.

He shut his eyes, and while his tongue dueled with the wet, warm spear of hers, he fought for control over the depth of passion this woman could arouse in him. As his hands rose and fell over the contours of her flesh, he told himself he wouldn't relinquish his whole self. Some part would remain distanced and detached. Untouchable.

But then her thighs parted. In the darkness, they looked like silver, glistening fish in deep, mysterious waters. As his palms roved slowly over them, toward the most feminine, intimate part of her, he felt as if he were drowning. She moaned when he began to touch her, and he felt his control slipping away.

But she'll know...she'll know.

"Santa..." she murmured. Her silken thighs relaxed, parting more for him. All he could think was that she was so open and that he was touching her. Her sighs suddenly caught on the air. She whimpered. "Anton..." And then she cried it out. "Oh, Anton."

His heart nearly broke. He'd never heard her say his real name. And to hear it spoken with such need... "Say my name again," he whispered.

She grasped his shoulders, arching to both meet his touch and to kiss him. "Anton..."

"Oh, Cyn." His own voice was nothing more than a ragged sigh. She captured it with her lips as she rocked against him. He found a condom, then rolled fully on top of her. For a long moment, he merely hovered above her.

How can you not know who I am?

As he slowly sank into her, he almost wished that she would discover him. If she didn't, he might tell her. What if—driven by desire—he confessed the truth?

"Anton..." This time, his name came in a short, quick gasp, as she caught his rhythm.

He drove into her steadily, repeatedly, kissing her neck, her cheeks, her breasts...until her skin turned damp and warm and until he felt her losing his rhythm and straining with all her might for her own. Against his mouth, her breath came in fits and starts. She held it, then let it go in shudders that urged him deeper inside her.

Damn you, Cyn. Tell me you know who I am.

Her legs wrapped around his back like a vise. He was a controlled man, but now, caught in the tangle of her arms and legs, crazy images started flashing through his mind. He could no longer damn her, but only kiss her, over and over again.

For an instant, he was almost sure they were lying in a

warm field of dew-damp grass and yellow spring flowers. A thousand white butterflies took flight. They hovered just above the flowers, like angels. When the tiny palpitations of Cyn's body closed around him, her flesh fluttered as gently and as urgently as those wings.

When she rocked against him, uttering one long soft whimper, the last vestiges of his control gave away. He was with the one woman on earth who could make everything vanish—past, present and future. The one woman who could take all the parts of him—heart, body and soul. And with one final kiss that seemed to go on forever, Santa completely lost control.

"WHERE'D YOU GET the scar on your leg? Another knife fight?" Cyn murmured.

"Yeah," Santa said softly.

She glanced dreamily at her digital clock through heavily lidded eyes. "It's after two in the morning," she whispered huskily, stretching her long legs against the length of his, and nuzzling her face against him.

"Hmm."

She smiled, hearing that hum rumble deep within his chest. When he nodded, she didn't see but only sensed it. She rolled to her back, luxuriating in how she felt. Her limbs were limp and languid, her whole body warm. Hours had passed, but time seemed to stand still. No man had ever loved her the way this one had. Certainly not Harry, her one love before Jake Jackson. And not even Jake Jackson himself.

Thinking that, she realized she wanted no secrets to come between her and Santa. "Santa?"

"Hmm?"

"You know when I told you about Jake Jackson? I mean, about going out with him?"

This time Santa didn't hum. Had he fallen asleep? Heaven knew, she was about to. She reached across a scant space between them, then grazed her fingertips from his thigh to his chest. Tiny muscles leapt to life beneath her touch, assuring her that he was still awake. She folded her hands beneath her breasts, then blew out a long, satisfied sigh.

"You were saying?" he finally murmured.

"I didn't tell you the whole story."

He rolled toward her slowly, scooting so that they barely touched. She could feel his breath on her shoulder. "What happened?" he asked, now sounding almost fully conscious.

"I—" She started to admit that she'd loved Jackson, but then decided that wasn't exactly wise, given the circumstances. "He's Amanda's father."

"Really?" Santa's voice lowered. "I thought Harry Stevens was her father."

She sighed. "Harry was just an old friend. And, after all the publicity of the trial, we thought it would be better if another father was somehow named." She took a deep breath, then exhaled.

"We?"

"Daddy, mostly. Mom thought it was horrible to lie, and it was. It is. But I didn't want Amanda to know her father was a criminal. I thought it would really hurt her. And Dad didn't want my name raked any further through the mud. Amanda knows anyway," she said unhappily. "She has ears."

"Amanda knows Jake Jackson is her father?"

Was it her imagination, or did Santa sound mad? She hoped he wasn't. Even if he was, she meant to say her piece. She was determined to ensure that this relationship begin in a completely honest way. And it was the beginning of something Cyn now knew she wanted to last. He raised slightly on his elbow. She nodded. "Amanda threatens to tell people all the time," she finally said softly. "When she doesn't get her way."

When Santa didn't respond, she continued. "After Harry Stevens agreed to give Amanda a name, he wanted to marry me—for real. I mean, we did marry, but he wanted for us to live as a couple. I didn't love him, though. It could never have worked. For Amanda's sake, I wish it could have. Harry's change in attitude caused a rift between us, so my father declared him dead. That way, people would think I was a widow and there wouldn't be questions.'' Cyn sighed in relief. ''Jake was really bad news,'' she admitted. ''I should have known it all along. He told small lies. He'd be late to meet me and arrive with explanations I shouldn't have believed.''

Cyn glanced at Santa. In the darkness it was hard to make out his expression. ''I'm glad that part of my life is over,'' she continued. Looking at Santa, she knew it was. Jake Jackson was the furthest thing from her mind.

Santa rose stealthily from the bed. ''The switch is on the right wall,'' she said sleepily, thinking he was headed for her bathroom.

He wasn't. She heard him rummaging around on the floor, gathering his clothes. By the time she realized he was actually dressing and flicked on her bedside lamp, he'd already pulled on his slacks and shirt. She squinted against the light. ''Where are you going?''

His expression was unreadable. ''To sleep.''

''You can sleep here for a while,'' she murmured, wishing a pleading tone hadn't crept into her voice.

His fingers slid deftly from shirt button to shirt button. In a fluid movement he tucked in his shirttails and zipped his trousers. He folded his suit jacket almost mechanically. Then, instead of resting it over his arm, he dangled it from the hook of his finger and swung it over his shoulder, making her wonder why he'd folded it in the first place.

She gulped and sat up. ''Did I say something wrong?'' He merely stared at her, and her heart began to thud. When her hand flew to her chest to cover her heart, she realized she was sitting there, stark naked. Moments ago it wouldn't have mattered. Now she knew it did. She grabbed the sheet and pulled it up, clutching it against her breasts.

"You knew I had had a past lover when you slept with me," she said, trying to keep her voice level. *Is that what's wrong? Why did I bring up Jake?* "You think I'm dishonest," she tried, starting to feel angry. "But you don't know what it was like. I was an overprotected kid, and I was pregnant by a man I simply couldn't have in my life. A criminal..." *I'm losing him. I'm going to lose Santa.* "Can't you understand that?" she asked, trying with all her might not to wail.

Why is he staring at me like that?

Was this really the same man who'd loved her body so completely? She'd been so amazed she could almost believe their lovemaking hadn't happened. The self-consciousness she'd felt in the past—the tiny worries about how she looked and sounded, about her scent and the dampness of her skin—had all been forgotten. He'd touched her thoroughly, matter-of-factly, with complete, loving acceptance.

But now, there was nothing more than cold judgment in his eyes. Or was she imagining that? "You just don't understand..." she repeated.

He pivoted gracefully on his heel and strolled toward her door. His soft drawl floated over his shoulder. "Maybe I understand more than you think I do."

Part 7

Chapter Seven

Monday, December 19, 1994

Cyn was waiting for him in the predawn hour, which was when the fool man got up. Outside it was still pitch-dark, and the light in the kitchen had taken on a yellowish cast. She'd barely slept and her eyes felt itchy. Not his, apparently. At precisely 5:30 a.m., Santa breezed into the kitchen. He looked so relaxed, she felt sure she'd conjured their night together in her dreams.

But I didn't. He made my knees weak and my head spin and my heart beat out of control. He touched me in the way only Jake could...so much like Jake that I just can't believe it. Except Santa's in a whole other league. I've been with him and now I'll never stop wanting him.

He nodded, headed straight for the cabinets and fixed himself a bowl of cereal. He was showered, shaved and wearing a fresh deep amber wool suit. His sparkling white shirt looked so crisp Cyn was sure she could snap it like a cracker. He turned, watching her as he munched. "Unusual to see you up at this hour," he finally remarked, between bites.

She'd spent the past few hours stewing, mentally rehearsing sweet apologies and speeches that were downright mean. Now she was so unnerved by his control that she couldn't remember them. "You're a pretty up-front guy, right?" she asked, keeping her voice level. She drew her chilly bare feet beneath her in the kitchen chair, and wrapped her robe more tightly around herself. "I mean, you always call things pretty much as you see them?"

He crunched his cereal and nodded. She realized his gaze wasn't anywhere near as ambivalent as she'd previously thought. Those eyes of his smoldered beneath his heavy eyelids. "Are you really going to pretend that last night didn't happen?" she finally snapped, wishing that each movement of his hands and hips and lips didn't remind her of it.

He leaned and placed his bowl in the sink behind him, without breaking their gaze. "You don't want serious involvements," he said softly. "Remember?"

She exhaled huffily. "Maybe I changed my mind." She sounded haughtier than she'd intended, as if determining the course of their relationship was entirely up to her.

"You should have thought of that before you laid down your ground rules," he returned gruffly.

Play it cool, Cyn. Don't let him get the best of you. Once he does, you're a goner. As angry as she was, her gaze roved over the broad shoulders she'd clung to during the night, then dropped to the chest she'd nuzzled against. "You're not mad about all the family secrets I told you, are you? I mean, a man in your line of work has undoubtedly heard worse."

He shoved his hands deep into the pockets of his trousers. Her eyes followed the movement inadvertently, and alighted on the space where the fabric tightened across his hips. He shrugged. "Yeah—" He caught her gaze when she raised it. "I've heard it all."

"Well then, hear this," she said calmly. "In the past couple of hours I decided—" *I want to marry you. Oh, don't say that!* Something in his expression—a warning, perhaps—stopped her.

He looked alert, but his brown eyes seemed sexily lazy. She decided he was intentionally trying to look bored.

"Don't tell me you couldn't sleep?" he asked.

She uncurled her feet beneath her. They slapped the tile floor when they hit it. "I think you're afraid."

He merely surveyed her with that trademark Santa look, where his lips parted but he didn't speak, and his eyes looked heavy but he didn't roll them heavenward. Everything in his gaze said there was nothing he feared.

She tossed her head so that her loose hair fell behind her shoulders. "You travel a lot, and you're used to being on your own," she said. "Having things your own way..."

"So, I'm afraid?"

"Maybe." As if to undercut her own seriousness, she managed to shoot him an unconcerned smile.

"Of what?"

"Loving me."

He chuckled softly. "Don't kid yourself."

She shrugged, as if it didn't matter to her one way or the other. "Well, I know why I wouldn't fall in love with you." She wished the smile she'd plastered on her face wasn't making her cheeks tingle.

He sighed. "Do tell."

"Oh, well—" She busied herself by picking up crumbs— some real, some imaginary—from the tabletop. "You're a globe-trotter, and you're involved in a dangerous business. I mean—" She clapped her hands together above a saucer, dusting off the imaginary crumbs. "You could get shot at any moment."

"My, my, don't you sound bloodthirsty."

He sounded annoyed now. She suddenly hoped she could make him every bit as irritated as she felt. "Not at all," she returned lightly. "But I think it's sweet that you don't want to involve yourself with a woman on account of that."

"Cyn" he said flatly, the veneer of banter vanishing. "That has nothing to do with—"

"Well then, what does?"

He didn't look particularly happy about being caught in

her verbal trap. "You said you wanted to sleep with me, for just one night. So, I did. That's all."

"That's all!"

"That's—" He paused and swallowed. When he spoke again, his voice was unnervingly calm. "That's right."

"Right after you kissed me, when the note concerning Amanda came, you tried to quit." Her voice leapt upward and she couldn't rein it in. "When I needed you most, you walked out. Do you *always* leave when people need you?"

"That's enough," he said levelly.

"Apparently, *I'm* not," she returned in a steely tone.

He was clearly trying not to react, but his expression softened. "You're my client," he nearly whispered.

She rolled her eyes. "Amanda's your client."

"I'm an up-front guy," he countered. "And I'm calling it like it is."

It was clear he'd taken his position and didn't intend to budge. But she didn't, either. In those long, cold, wee hours of the night, Cyn was just too sure she'd finally found a man she wanted to be with. He was amazingly strong, but he could be so caring and gentle....

They were still staring each other down when the phone rang. "Who could be calling at this otherworldly hour?" she muttered, reaching it first.

"May I please speak to Anton Santa?"

She held out the phone. "It's a woman," she said, not bothering to hide her pique.

When he reached for the receiver, his fingertips grazed the back of her hand. She wanted to hang up the phone and feel the strength of his arms around her again. She wanted to be held. He turned his back to her. "Yeah? This is Santa."

Cyn crossed her arms over her chest and listened to his hmms and sighs. After a moment, she decided that something was wrong. "Thanks for calling as soon as you got the information, Sally," he finally said. "I owe you one."

"What is it?" she asked as he hung up and turned around.

His eyes were even more disturbing than the call. She was almost sure that he was considering offering her comfort again. *It's bad. I can feel it.* A shiver of both fear and longing raced down her spine.

"I got an address on Matthew Lewis." Santa's voice gentled for the first time that morning. "He's nearby. At a house in Jersey."

"I'M COMING WITH YOU!"

"You're staying with Amanda and the rent-a-cop," Santa called over his shoulder, listening to Cyn's flat boots thud after him, through the parking garage. He turned the key in the driver's side of his rented sedan. Just as he opened the door, Cyn elbowed him with such force it nearly took away his breath. Before he could grab her, she'd scooted in and slid across the seat.

He glanced over the items she'd brought with her: oversize pocketbook, picnic basket and thermos. He removed his handcuffs from where they were looped over his belt and tossed them onto the seat, next to the car phone. Then he got in and slammed the door. Hard.

He felt half-inclined to tell her he was Jake Jackson, if for no other reason than that she'd hightail it back to the apartment. But he meant to tell her in his own good time. Like when he figured out what he wanted to do about Amanda, for instance. If he'd ever felt he was exacting revenge by keeping his identity hidden, it was doubly true now. When he told her—and he'd have to, since Amanda was his daughter—Cyn would never recover from the blow. Not after he'd made love to her. He tried to tell himself that he didn't care. She was a liar and two-timer and he didn't want her back.

"I know what Matthew Lewis looks like," Cyn finally announced breathlessly as she rummaged in her pocketbook, pulled out a plastic band and drew her hair into a loose ponytail. She pulled on a little black knit hat, then stuffed her stray hairs beneath it. "And you don't."

"Fine," he said, wishing she didn't look so cute in her ridiculous undercover getup, and thinking he knew damn well what Lewis looked like. If Cyn came with him, Lewis might see the two of them together, and identify Santa. After all, the man had seen him clean shaven and in a suit. As soon as Santa had left the hospital, he'd questioned him. Well, Santa thought as he turned the key in the ignition, he'd just make Cyn stay in the car. When the sedan roared to life, he felt half-inclined to squeal out of the garage. Instead, he somehow managed to calmly back out of his space.

"I bet this'll be kind of fun," she said as he pulled onto Eighty-eighth Street. "I mean, a stakeout and everything. I made some turkey sandwiches, either with or without mayo, and a whole thermos full of coffee, with the cream separate, of course, since I know you like yours black."

He hit the brake at a light and slowly turned his head, staring at her pointedly. His gaze dropped slowly over her outfit and, suddenly, he had to fight not to smile. She was wearing all black—tights, hooded sweatshirt, suede coat and hat. She looked like an adorable thief in a TV movie. Since it was daytime, she looked pretty obvious, too.

"Maybe you like peace and quiet when you drive," she said, after a moment. She made a show of primly folding her hands in her lap, then glanced away from him and stared through the windshield.

He took the FDR, doubled back into midtown, then took the Lincoln Tunnel. He didn't know which was worse, her silence or her chatter. He didn't know why he was so furious, either. After all, hadn't he suspected Amanda was his daughter, all along?

But hearing Cyn say the words had changed everything. He was a father. She was a liar. And he didn't have the slightest idea what to do about any of it. Oh, he'd claim Amanda. He had no intention of letting her go through life believing her father's name was Jake Jackson. Still, once he claimed her, what in the world was he going to do with her?

He drove in silence for some time, trying to tell himself he hated Cyn, even if having her had only made him want her all the more. Being trapped in the cramped, closed confines of the car made things infinitely worse. Not a second passed without him feeling conscious of her nearness. He could pull her silly hat from her head, release her hair band, and all that disheveled, luxurious hair would cascade around her shoulders. Beneath the scents of bath powder and perfume, Cyn's own scent filled the car. Resting one hand lightly on the wheel, Santa cracked his window with the other. The chilly rush of air smelled like burning leaves, but it didn't help.

Because he was thinking about Cyn, he made a wrong turn and landed on an expressway. He braked at a tollbooth harder than was necessary, rolled down his window and handed over the money, thinking that maybe he could start a securities business in the city. Images of picking Amanda up and dropping her off at Cyn's flashed through his mind. *What a mess.*

Cyn. Was that really what he was mad about? Threads of their conversation kept replaying in his thoughts. Had she really had the nerve to accuse him of walking out when she'd needed him? That was rich. She'd left him lying in her parents' yard with two gunshot wounds. As badly hurt as he'd been, he'd chased after her. He'd saved her life, too. Now he pulled off the expressway and tried to get his bearings.

"Such cute decorations," Cyn remarked pleasantly. As Santa wound down the circular streets, he couldn't help but follow her gaze. "Oh, look! Look at that!"

She pointed excitedly at a house with candles in the windows. A German shepherd, wearing a green bow for a collar, thumped his tail on the front porch and pawed the door. In another yard, a huge plastic Santa sat on a sleigh, driving a team of reindeer. In front of a quaint two-story stone place, tall brass lanterns tied with red bows marked either side of a brick walkway. Dark smoke plumed from chimneys, then trailed through the whitish winter sky. Wreaths hung from nearly every door.

He hazarded another glance at Cyn, thinking that she'd deprived him of this. Of some homey little neighborhood somewhere with her and Amanda. Of holidays with a family he could call his own. Maybe he and Cyn would even have had other children by now. Four years had passed, three Christmases where Amanda had squirmed on Santa's lap and torn crinkling shiny paper from her presents. *Damn.*

"I just love the decorations," Cyn crooned softly. "Don't you?"

He didn't know whether it was her proximity to him in the seat or the fact that he was breathing in her perfume with every breath, but he found himself nodding. "Yeah."

She whirled around, laughing. "Was that a yes, Santa?"

"Can't a man like decorations?" he asked gruffly.

"Absolutely." Her eyes were twinkling but he was fairly sure her attitude correction was a ploy. She was still furious. Cyn didn't take no for an answer when she wanted something. And she wanted him. *Too bad,* he thought. He battled another sudden urge to reveal himself. The information would go down like a bad medicine, but it would definitely cure Cyn of her desire for him.

He pulled to a curb. "See the brick place down there? The one with the lit-up dogwood tree?"

Cyn nodded.

"That's Lewis's mother's."

She scooted up and peered through the windshield. "Can't we get any closer?"

He shook his head, then leaned and stretched his arm over her knees. When he did, she nearly jumped out of her skin. He wished he didn't want to smile at the proof that her new-found perkiness was nothing more than show. He slowly opened the glove compartment and took out his field glasses.

"Oh," she murmured. "You were just getting your binoculars."

"Don't worry," he said as he raised them to his eyes. "I won't attack you."

"WHERE DO YOU FIND the patience for this stakeout stuff?" Cyn asked hours later. She raised her arms above her head and yawned lazily, looking at Santa.

"I'm a patient man," he returned. He polished off the last bite of his second turkey sandwich and washed it down with a gulp of coffee.

You sure are, she thought. Images from their night together touched her mind, but that wasn't the only reason she had to know him better. Paxton liked him. Amanda felt as strongly about him as she did, herself. Santa had seemed less perturbed by her presence as the day had worn on, too. "Don't you start feeling like you just have to *do* something?"

"No." He glanced at her. "Like what?"

"We could make out," she teased. "After all, we *are* parking. It's cold in here, too. We haven't turned on the car or the heater forever."

He shook his head in mock censure. "You're a woman with only one thing on her mind."

She curled her legs in the seat and turned to get a better look at him. She felt all rumpled and he looked as dapper as he had at the crack of dawn. "Are you trying to tell me you're less focused?" she asked, as if she felt sorry for him.

He relaxed in the seat and tilted his head, his eyes roving over her face. "Maybe I have only one thing on my mind, too."

She arched her brows and stared back at him innocently. "What?"

"Making sure Amanda's safe," he said levelly.

Cyn gulped, wishing they were here for some other reason. "I know you will," she said, meaning it. Santa was so patiently diligent about his work that Amanda could have been his own daughter. Could he ever truly accept Amanda as his own? And, after having Amanda to herself for so long, how did Cyn really feel about sharing her? With Santa, she thought, perhaps she could.

Her eyes drifted over him as they had a thousand times that day, and she thought, as she had each time, that he seemed like the strongest man in the world. While she was looking at him, his whole body suddenly tensed.

"There he is," Santa whispered.

She whirled back toward the windshield and gasped. "How did you know it was him?" Her blood boiled as she watched Lewis cross the yard and get into a compact car. Was it her imagination or did he look nervous?

"Is it him?" Santa asked.

"Yeah," she said, staring the man down. An almost murderous hatred pumped through her veins. The sensation couldn't have been more intense if she had seen Jake Jackson himself. After all, Lewis was one of the men who'd nearly destroyed her life four years ago. And now he might be coming after Amanda.

Santa started the car, then pulled out, keeping a good distance away from the compact. Cyn fell silent and glanced between Santa and the other car. He was good at tailing people. Half the time she was sure they'd lose the man, but they never did. The longer they drove the more anxious she became. Suddenly all the lovely Christmas decorations seemed a little menacing.

"Damn," Santa muttered under his breath.

Something in his voice made Jake Jackson's face pop into her mind. *It's only because we're tailing Lewis.* "What's wrong?" she asked, her heart pounding.

"Er—nothing." He sounded surprised, as if he hadn't meant to curse out loud. He sighed. "If I'd known we'd be following him, I wouldn't have let you come."

"I'm not going to get hurt," she said defensively. Why did he think she couldn't handle herself? She felt touched. He was worried about her, which was a good sign. Up ahead, Lewis pulled to a curb. Santa backed into a driveway.

After a moment his wry chuckle filled the car. "Just don't make me take another bullet for you," he said. "Okay?"

She leaned across the seat and playfully poked him in the ribs. "*Another* bullet?" she teased. "Have you been having fantasies about protecting me or something? I mean, I don't remember that first one."

He flashed her a quick grin. It seemed to light up the dreary winter afternoon, but it didn't completely hide the sadness in his eyes. What was it in this man's past that haunted him?

"Maybe you just didn't see it coming," he finally said.

"STAY PUT," Santa said roughly, feeling desperate to ensure that Lewis and Cyn didn't get within view of each other. "And I mean it this time."

"But, Santa—"

He shot her a long, penetrating glare to communicate his seriousness. He had a hunch about what was happening. It had come from a thousand subtle impressions: the way Lewis squared his shoulders, fidgeted with his hands, tensed his thighs, paused before he rang a doorbell. Santa felt he was standing at the most precarious impasse he'd ever encountered. Should he keep Cyn away from Lewis...but at the risk of not capturing the man who might be threatening Amanda?

"I mean it," he repeated, grabbing his cuffs.

"Whatever you say." Cyn sounded resigned. She wasn't happy about it, but everything in her expression said she meant to stay in the car.

Santa quietly shut his door, then casually ambled toward the house Matthew Lewis had entered. It was a shingled two-story, surrounded by boxwoods. A rough-hewn wooden deck had been added onto the back, and at either end were stairs that led into the backyard. It faced a privacy wall that presumably hid an alley.

As Santa neared the house, Lewis stepped onto the deck with another man. Looking at them, Santa could bet his bottom dollar that the second man—a man Santa had only seen in a mask—was the one who'd escaped from the Sweets'. He was also the man who'd pulled a gun on the cops. He was wearing only jeans and a flannel shirt, and his hands were shoved deep into his pockets for warmth. When he spoke, his breath fogged the air.

As soon as the men turned their backs, Santa bolted through the yard at a silent crouching run, then stealthily crept beneath the deck. He squatted down, glanced up through the spaces between the boards and listened.

"What are you doing here?" It was definitely the man who'd gotten away. Santa recognized the voice. The man bounced up and down as if he were cold, making the boards above Santa creak. "This is my mother's house. We could have met somewhere."

Oh no. Santa drew in a breath and glanced over his shoulder. He could hear Cyn's boots crunching over the frozen grass from a mile away. Fortunately, the men above him were too engrossed in each other to notice. Santa tried not to think about the last time Cyn had taken it upon herself to follow him into a dangerous situation.

"I kept trying to get a number for you, but couldn't. I tried every John Christopher in the tri-state," Lewis groused. So that's the man's name, Santa thought just as Cyn crept up beside him. When he realized she'd brought her pocketbook, he nearly rolled his eyes. "So, I just started coming by here every day," Lewis continued.

"Guess you want your part of the last haul," Christopher said. "That's why you came, right? You knew I was going to keep it here."

Santa shot Cyn his steeliest stare, then pressed his finger to his lips. Small puffs of her breath clouded the air, and her cheeks, which looked even paler than usual against the black of her hat, had turned red in the cold. For the briefest instant, he shut his eyes. Why couldn't the woman have just stayed in the car?

"No, you don't understand!" Lewis's voice rose. "We've got to give it all back!"

"Keep your voice down," Christopher growled. "My mother's in the kitchen, making a ham, and she'll hear you." He stamped his feet on the deck as if that might warm them. "The stuff was way too hot after the trial to pawn," he continued. "So, I've still got it." His voice lowered, persuasively. "Did you really think I'd try to rip off a partner?"

Santa watched Cyn's eyes widen in disbelief. She was clearly starting to get the picture. The two men were talking about the Sweet jewelry. Santa glanced upward. Through the cracks in the planks of the deck, he could see the soles of the men's shoes. Christopher started pacing. "Wait here," he finally said. "I'll get them. You can take your share."

Above, steps sounded. A screen door snapped shut. A storm door slammed. The boards creaked as Lewis walked to the edge of the deck, leaned his elbows on the railing and stared out over the yard. He now had the same view as Santa and Cyn. The yard sloped toward the privacy wall. Brown dirt patches peeked through the frozen whitish grass. A concrete birdbath had been disconnected from its base and overturned.

Honor among thieves, Santa thought, shaking his head. Lewis hadn't choked up Christopher's name or revealed that Christopher had kept the jewels at his mother's.

"He's not listening to me," Lewis said to nothing but the thin air.

"You're not just going to sit here, like this, are you?" Cyn finally whispered, looking furious.

He had half a mind to clamp his hand over her mouth and drag her back to the car, since he was beginning to suspect that this had nothing to do with Amanda. It was about the Sweet robbery, and nothing more.

"We have to do some—"

"Shut up," he mouthed, just as Christopher returned.

"But we—"

This time Santa did silence her. He deftly reached around her shoulders, drew her against him and pressed his palm over her lips. She tried to wrench away, but in her effort to stay quiet, the move was completely ineffective. Santa felt her lips purse against his skin. *Good. She's not going to talk. I'll hear everything I need, get her out of here, then come back.*

He gazed down at her eyes, which were riveted on the deck above them. He glanced up again. Christopher was holding out a bag. Gazing through the cracks, it was hard to tell, but it looked like a regular brown bag. The large sandwich kind.

"Well, take it," he said angrily.

"You're not listening!" Lewis burst out. "We never should have stolen these things. We've got to return them. We could just mail the bag back anonymously. You won't get caught."

"Get caught?" Santa imagined that Christopher's mouth was gaping open in astonishment. The brown paper bag swung down with his arm and dangled at his side. "Did you get reformed in jail or something?"

"As a matter of fact," Lewis said stiffly, "I did."

Christopher's low chuckle sounded menacing. "And here you are," he taunted. "Out on a holiday pardon, and just dying to play secret Santa to the Sweet family. Why, Matt, where's your little red suit?"

"Leave me alone," Lewis said just as Cyn tensed in Santa's arms. "If nothing else, I'll return my half."

"I don't think so," Christopher countered. "The Sweet family has undoubtedly collected and spent the insurance. They're never going to see this stuff again."

Cyn wrenched quickly in Santa's arms. "Oh, yes, they are!" she shrieked, scrambling toward the stairs.

"Oh, Cynthia," Santa muttered. He bolted after her.

"Don't move a muscle!" She charged up the stairs, digging in her pocketbook. "Don't even think about it."

"Who the devil are—" Christopher began, instinctively dropping the paper bag. He began backing away stealthily.

"It's Cynthia Sweet!" Lewis exclaimed, sounding as pleased as he was dumfounded.

"And she's got a gun," Christopher said flatly.

Sure enough, she'd gotten his gun out of the glove compartment. Fortunately, since Cyn had a gun, the two men were more interested in her than in him. Santa watched her train the weapon inexpertly on them, while she slung her pocketbook over her shoulder. The safety was on, and he was positive she'd have no clue about how to release it. At least he hoped not.

She bent with graceful agility, scooped up the paper bag, then glanced inside. "My class ring! The little diamond studs Daddy gave me for my sweet sixteen! And Mom's necklace!" she exclaimed, glancing over her shoulder at Santa. She looked at him a second too long.

Christopher barreled across the deck, lunging for the gun. Christopher knew how to use it, too, Santa thought as he raced forward. Cyn's arm flew upward. Santa caught both her hands, then the gun and, completing the arc, tossed the weapon far behind him, in a stand of trees.

"What's going on out here?" The screen door swung open and a fiftyish woman peered out, wiping her hands on her apron.

"Get back inside," Christopher said, his gaze still riveted on the bag in Cyn's hand.

"I will," the woman said. "But this time, I'm calling the police."

The second the door slammed shut, Christopher charged at Cyn again. She swung her pocketbook at his head, and when Santa leapt between the two, the bag caught him square across the jaw. Christopher took the opportunity to sucker-punch his ribs. He wrestled Christopher to the ground, anyway, then hauled him across the deck. Reaching for his back, he grabbed the cuffs and hooked Christopher to the railing.

When Santa turned around, Cyn was staring at Lewis with her hands on her hips and murder in her eyes. And Matthew Lewis was beaming at her.

"You all stayed together," he said, shaking his head.

"What?" she demanded in a tone that was nearly as menacing as Christopher's.

Santa found himself wishing the earth would open, and swallow him up. "There's something I think I should tell you, Cyn," he said quickly.

"We can talk in the car," Cyn said. "Right now, I want to know what this cretin has to say in his defense."

"You and Jake stayed together," he repeated, nodding at Santa.

Her eyes narrowed. "Jake?"

Lewis chuckled. "Or should I say Anton Santa?"

Cyn gasped. She pivoted around slowly and stared at him. Long moments passed. She tilted her head. Her eyes widened, then she squinted.

"It's true," Santa began, keeping his voice calm. "I can explain every—"

"I almost didn't recognize you, because of the weight you've gained," Lewis interrupted, in a booming voice. "How are you, Anton?"

"This is the craziest thing I ever heard," Cyn murmured, sounding more puzzled than angry. Santa blew out a long sigh and waited for whatever was about to come. He'd let her get it out of her system, then he'd explain. She was still looking at him oddly, as if unable to make out any resemblance between him and Jake Jackson.

"Look, Cyn," he said. "It's not what you think."

"Oh, it isn't?" she finally bit out. "Well, Jake..."

"It's Anton," he managed to say. "Anton Santa. That's my real name."

"Well, Jake or Anton or whoever you are," she snapped. "I just wanted to inform you that your partner in crime or suspect or whoever *he* is—'' Cyn raised her finger and pointed ''—is getting away.''

Santa whirled around. Sure enough, the cuffs were dangling from the rail and Christopher was halfway over the privacy wall. Santa glanced at Cyn again, just in time to see her pivot on her heel and storm down the stairs.

''Cyn, wait,'' he called, just as a siren sounded in the distance. Who was he going to lose—Cyn or Christopher? His gaze shot from one to the other. Then he leapt over the deck railing and sprinted across the grass.

...

Part 8

Chapter Eight

Tuesday, December 20, 1994

'Twas five days before Christmas and all through the house, not a creature was stirring, not even a mouse. Santa was reclining on Cyn's sofa, with his hands folded on his belly and his feet propped on her coffee table. He stared at the lighted-up Christmas tree, then at the door, then at the tree again, wishing Cyn would come home. As he listened to the early morning silence, he told himself he had no right to be furious. He'd spent more than a week pulling the wool over *her* eyes.

But what was a mere week, compared to the three long years he could have been Amanda's father? By the time he'd recaptured Christopher, Cyn had vanished with the car. Then he'd had to wait for the warrant to search the Christopher place, in order to get a ride back to the city in a cop cruiser. He'd grilled Lewis and Christopher, of course. Still, by the time he'd reached Cyn's apartment, Cyn, Amanda and the rent-a-cop were gone.

It wasn't until midnight that he'd found Analise, with Amanda and the cop at the Plaza Hotel. Not that he'd gone there. Cyn had gone elsewhere, but Analise hadn't known where. As long as Amanda was with the rent-a-cop, she'd be fine. Besides, he meant to give Cyn time—not much more, but some—so she could mull over their unusual situation. And boy, he thought wryly, was it unusual. Maybe they were even now.

I should have chased Cyn, not Christopher. "No," he muttered. "I had to do my job." And he'd wanted the Sweets' belongings returned, so that the past was laid to rest and he could get on with his life—as Amanda's father.

He just wished Cyn's place didn't feel so empty without her and Amanda. He couldn't help but miss their early morning sounds: the whoosh of the water jets in Cyn's shower, the patter of Cyn's bare feet on the kitchen tiles, and the cartoons blaring when Amanda turned on the TV.

The cheery holiday decorations made their absence more intense, too. Every red and green knickknack reminded him of it. The apartment felt as empty as the hotel in Washington where he'd spent the previous Christmas. And the one in Singapore, the Christmas before that. And the one in North Dakota...

I've been traveling a long time. That's what he'd said the night he'd arrived. Now he found himself waiting for Cyn to walk right through that door, without anger or malice, and accept him back into her life...their lives. Not that she would. But he'd been traveling too long. And Anton Santa wanted to come home.

Another hour passed, during which Santa decided he was tired of waiting. He'd waited in countless hotel lobbies, on platforms and stages, beside closed doors during corporate meetings, and in parked cars outside the gates of mansions. He'd waited in crowded airports from Amsterdam to New York to San Francisco. All over the world, he'd waited.

Now, never moving, watching Cyn's door, Santa decided that he'd never been waiting for the people he'd been hired to protect. Never for a high-ranking Swedish official, or a low-level French dignitary, or to take a bullet. No, all that time, in all those places, he'd really been waiting for Cyn

Sweet. And what he'd been waiting for was her love.

Just as he realized that, the key turned in the lock.

REMEMBER THAT HE'S AS slippery as an eel. He'll try to persuade and cajole, but don't listen, and stay as calm and cool as he is, Cyn thought. She'd left Analise and Amanda with the rent-a-cop, then she'd gotten her own room at The Carlyle. She'd wanted to be alone, and she'd wanted to think.

Now she felt as if she were about to confront the devil himself. Her hands were shaking so badly that she could barely manage the electronic keypad. "No doubt he was trying to keep me out of my own apartment," she muttered just as her keys rattled against the door. One by one, the dead bolts clanked, turning over. She took a last, deep breath, then flung open the door.

He was there all right, just as she'd known he would be. She stormed inside, slammed the door behind herself and leaned against it. He was seated on her sofa, in a soft-looking cream wool suit, as casually as you please. She realized, with a quick shock, that even under the circumstances she couldn't help but react to the way he looked. *How can I be attracted to someone so horrible? What's wrong with me?*

For long moments she merely stared at him. How could it be that this man was also Jake Jackson? They looked nothing alike. Their voices were different. And yet his kisses had told her the truth. Oh, how they'd told the truth, if she had only listened. All night she'd wondered why Jake Jackson would carry handcuffs and seemingly arrest John Christopher. Now she didn't care how Jake had come to be here. She just wanted him away from her daughter.

"About time you showed up," he finally said. "Where's Amanda?"

His voice, which was every bit as soft as it was gruff, more than hinted at the South now. It had become pure Mississippi Delta. His more clipped, nearly Northern, accent had been nothing but a calculated ruse. Her lower lip began to tremble.

"Where is she?" he repeated. The words rose and fell in an almost lilting cadence.

She shook her head. She was looking at Anton Santa but hearing Jake Jackson's voice. "In a safe place," she finally returned. Everything in her voice indicated that Amanda wasn't safe with him. *Stay cool, Cyn.*

He crossed his long legs. The perfectly tailored lines of his elegant suit made him look somehow draped across her sofa. His hands remained calmly folded in his lap. He could have been on an ad page in *GQ*. "With a kidnapper running around," he said, "I'm not sure The Plaza's so safe."

Her lips parted in astonishment. Clearly he meant to evade the issue of his presence in her life. "You got your kidnappers," she snapped. She reached for the doorknob just to steady herself. "And if you knew where we were, why did you ask?"

He lifted one of his shoulders in a graceful shrug. "Lewis and Christopher aren't involved." His voice was unnervingly gentle. "As for The Plaza—" His lips stretched into what might have been a smile but wasn't. "I wanted to see if you'd tell the truth."

I wouldn't tell the truth! She pushed herself off the door, then fought the impulse to fly across the room and punch him. She had to keep her distance. Even now there was a chance she'd wind up in his arms. The only comfort was that he didn't know she'd stayed at The Carlyle. That meant she could escape his clutches if she wanted to. "Whether *I'd* tell the truth," she finally repeated, assuring herself it was anger, not desire, that made her voice turn raspy.

He nodded. "In four years—" he began tersely. She watched him clench his jaw, then swallow. When he spoke again, his tone was as even as her hemlines, and as silky as the fabric of her dresses. "In four years," he continued, "you never bothered to mention that Amanda was my daughter."

She tossed her hair over her shoulder with a quick jerk of her head. "Sorry—" She wasn't about to let him think she was shocked to find he had another identity, or that she wondered why he was now carrying handcuffs. "But Riker's Island isn't exactly one of my haunts."

He rose so lithely from the sofa that she gulped audibly. Fortunately he didn't head for her but strolled idly to the window, making her wonder how she'd ever thought him ordinary. He lounged against the bars he'd installed, his whole body looking dangerously lean and sensuously languid. He carried his weight in his hips, not his shoulders, and now they swayed outward, barely perceptibly. He looked as restless and calmly predatory as a caged cat.

"So...Santa, Jake, Anton...where all have you been?" she asked with mock politeness. "Or should I say, 'where have you *all* been?'"

"You mean, where did I go after I took the bullet that could have killed you?"

It was the last thing she expected. Her wry chuckle filled the room. "You seduce me, rob my family, then try to tell me you saved my life!" It was so ludicrous that she relaxed against the door, crossed her arms over her chest and stared at him, openmouthed. "I can't wait to hear this one."

"Good," he said levelly, without bothering to look at her. "Because you're about to."

"Well, get on with it," she quickly returned. "Because your time's running out."

Now he did glance her way. His muscular shoulder rolled against the bars and he barely turned his head. His profile nearly took away her breath. The nose was straight, the jaw firm, the forehead high below his slicked-back hair. When his eyes, which looked nearly black today, shifted from her face to the stocking-hung mantel, they looked mysteriously deep. How could a liar and a thief manage to look so arrogant?

"I used to be a cop," he began slowly. "Undercover."

He looked directly into her eyes, but she was too shocked to respond. During the night, the possibility had occurred to her, of course, but she'd rejected it. The man was too dishonest. If he'd been an undercover cop, he would have called her during the trial, to explain. He turned back to the window.

"I was pulled out of the academy before I'd even graduated. They set me up in an apartment in the Village." A faint smile touched his lips. "But then, I guess you remember that."

Her mouth went dry, as she thought of the apartment where she'd made love to Jake...to Anton. He sounded totally serious. Could he be telling the truth? *No way.* Watching him lounge against the window bars, it was easy enough to imagine him in a cell. The detective in charge said her testimony had put him away, too. After Jake left the hospital, he'd gone straight to jail. *Don't listen to him!*

"...and I was enrolled in a class in every school in the city. Columbia, NYU, the midtown CUNY. They were already pretty sure that the people burglarizing the outlying areas were students. Which they were—" He glanced at her. "Lewis and Christopher were enrolled at NYU."

"I had classes with them." She shot him a steely stare, hoping to communicate that she didn't believe a word he said.

He turned fully away from the window, leaned his head against the bars and shoved his hands deep into his trouser pockets. His gaze was as unflinching as hers, but his voice remained calmer. "You have no reason not to believe me."

"Oh, no!" she exclaimed. "And why is that?"

"Because nothing else makes sense."

She sighed, then tried her best to sound bored. "So, you grew your hair long...."

"It was long already."

"But you dyed it, and grew a mustache and beard and lost a lot of weight...."

"Gained," he corrected. "Since then."

"I can't believe I'm hearing this," she said flatly.

His gaze still met hers dead-on. His low, throaty, almost

bitter chuckle filled the air. "Oh, but sweetheart," he continued. "It gets even better."

No matter how much she wanted to, she couldn't tear her eyes from his. He was so self-possessed. All her senses heightened when she took in his casual attitude and understated elegance. Only his eyes alerted her to the emotions that seethed beneath his surface. "I'll just bet it does," she said coolly.

"Sometimes truth's stranger than fiction."

"Especially when we get to the part where you save my life." She blew out a piqued sigh.

"You followed me...." His voice lowered a notch. "Because of you, two rookie cops who didn't have a clue what was going on stormed into your parents' house."

A lump lodged in her throat and she swallowed, knowing that much was true. She arched a brow in his direction. *Whatever he's going to say is a lie.* "Go on."

He shook his head. "Why *did* you follow me?"

"I was wrong to call the police?" she snapped. Her eyes widened. "I was just supposed to sit there while you carted off all of our worldly possessions?"

"The only thing that got carted off was me," he said flatly. "On a stretcher." He suddenly shrugged, as if the rightness or wrongness of her actions didn't concern him. "The two cops burst in, Christopher pulled a gun, and one of the rookies fired a shot, hitting me instead of Christopher. The bullet grazed my jaw."

He absently rubbed a thumb across the scar now, as if to prove it. Had she really nearly gotten him killed? "So you took a bullet for Christopher." She spoke in an overly innocent tone, realizing she'd just caught him in one of his infernal lies. "That's not exactly saving my life, now is it Jake...Anton?"

He looked as if he wanted to kill her. "Well, after that shot was fired, you suddenly hopped out of the front seat of a cruiser and ran toward the house. Why did you do that, Cyn?'' It wasn't a question, it was a demand for an answer.

Because I was afraid you were going to be killed. And I was going to save your life. But then you flew through the door, with blood on your face, and I got scared. More scared than I'd ever been. She sighed shakily but didn't answer him.

''And Christopher, either because he wanted revenge because you'd turned us in, or because he needed to fire some cover shots, so he could get away, aimed right at you.''

That's why you ran into the yard? All she remembered was seeing his face, feeling scared, hearing a shot and seeing him leap into the air. She'd turned and fled. Now she realized that it explained the scar on his calf. ''You're lying,'' she said weakly.

''Feel guilty yet?''

If I believe this, every word of it, I have no excuse to keep him from Amanda. Her heart suddenly thudded in her chest. Her worst nightmare had just come true. Jake Jackson had come back to claim their daughter. And for a second time he'd stolen into her life under completely false pretenses.

''You're lying,'' she said with resolve, her voice as cold as the winter day.

''You just can't face it, can you?''

''You can tell ten million lies—'' She strained to keep her voice level. ''But you'll never get within sight of Amanda again.''

He crossed the room silently, looking every inch the predator. The sheer energy radiating from the man had her backing herself up against the door. He stopped right in front of her. Then he sprawled an arm alongside the door; his elbow claimed the space next to her head. He leaned so close his hips grazed hers. ''You want to repeat that?''

''You're not getting anywhere near my daughter!'' Her voice sounded high-pitched and thin. Her mouth went dry and her breasts suddenly felt full and heavy. With his lips so near and his breath warming her skin, there was just no way she could fight her body's traitorous response.

"Need I remind you," he drawled, "she's my daughter, too."

He *had* come for Amanda. And she had to be strong. "You steal into my life," she returned coldly, "and each time, you pretend to be someone other than who you really are. Now, like four years ago, what you intend to do is rob me. Cop or no cop, you're a thief."

"And you're a liar," he countered, leaning just an inch closer. "What about your marriage that never was? Or poor, dead Harry? Or how you live as a grieving widow? Or about how you mean to deny me rights to what's mine?" His eyes now looked as dark as a starless night. "Sounds to me like you're the thief, Cyn."

Whose heart did she hear beating, she wondered, suddenly feeling dizzy. Her own or his? "You've used me one too many times," she managed to say huskily. "This time, to get to Amanda. Last time—" His eyes held her spellbound. She forced herself to blink. "I—I don't know why."

"It was my job," he nearly whispered.

"And you did it so very well." The words caught in the air as if each one had a barbed hook buried deep inside it. "I bet you enjoyed it—seducing a rich, extremely overprotected college kid until you made her…"

"I did enjoy it." His hand dropped to the sleeve of her luxurious coat. "But what was it that I *made* you do?"

Everything in his dangerously dark gaze reminded her that she'd always gone willingly into his arms. Her mouth had become so dry that her throat ached. "Nothing," she croaked.

"Did I make you love me, Cyn Sweet?"

The truth made her feel a little faint. She clenched her jaw. "Did you use me, Jake Jackson?"

"Anton Santa," he corrected. His eyes narrowed. "I had no family, no money and nowhere to go," he continued persuasively. "I'll admit, I liked the excitement of my job, and that I was hungry...." The last word hung in the air as his gaze roved over her face. "To make good," he finished abruptly.

"You did use me," she said in shock.

His jaw hardened and his eyes seemed to judge her. "What did *you* love? The man you see now? The man I am? Or some scruffy bad boy from down South? Some guy with a motorcycle and a leather jacket, of whom your parents would never approve."

She licked her lips against their dryness. "Touché," she whispered.

"That's why you didn't recognize me," he continued with that hypnotic voice.

"What are you talking about?"

"You didn't recognize me because you were in love with a myth. And then, when you felt betrayed, my looks got all scrambled up in your mind. Maybe you couldn't even remember what I looked like at all."

Cyn's mind raced while she listened to him. "You're sending the notes!" she burst out. "You sent them so that you could get this job, so that you could see Amanda—"

He gasped. "What?"

She stared at him, not knowing what was truth and what were lies, and only knowing that perhaps none of it mattered because she still craved his lips.

His eyes widened, as if all his questions had suddenly been answered. "Why did you follow me?" he demanded again.

She decided to tell him. Maybe the truth would hurt him. Maybe he'd realize what he'd lost by betraying her. "I thought you were with another woman," she said.

"And where were you last night?"

Did he think she'd been with another man? "At The Carlyle." As much as she wanted to let him wonder, she wasn't about to appear dishonest. "Alone."

"Oh, Cyn," he whispered, his expression softening.

"Don't 'Oh, Cyn' me. You've no excuse for not calling me during the trial. You could have explained."

"I was in the hospital, doped up, with my whole head bandaged. My boss wanted my cover kept a secret, so that I could go after Christopher when I got out."

His every word was making her furious again. "You could have made someone tell me the truth."

"I was about to—" His voice was raspy, tinged with longing. "When you announced your engagement."

She sucked in a quick breath. Maybe he'd really loved her. But if she believed it, she'd have to forget the past, and he'd take Amanda. "You sent those notes!" she accused again.

His hand savagely cupped her chin and he leaned so close that the tips of their noses nearly touched. "There are bad guys," he said softly. "And they're out there and they're real. But I'm not one of them, Cyn."

His mouth settled on hers with a quick vengeance, as if a kiss could convince her. She wanted to wrench away but couldn't, not when his lips probed hers farther apart and his hand dropped into her hair in the softest caress she'd ever felt. She found herself weakening against the door, softening against his strength, and kissing him back.

It wasn't fair that no other man had ever felt so right or fit so snugly against her. It wasn't fair that only he could kiss her with such dangerous, almost primal need. Her knees nearly buckled beneath her as he drew back then pressed his lips to hers again. Completely against her will, she felt herself arch toward him as his tongue plunged between her lips. Her breasts tingled with awareness, the aching tips straining against the lace of her underwear.

I can't do this! She violently jerked away. His hand cupped the back of her head swiftly, before it connected with the door. They merely gazed at each other, their breaths coming in gasps.

"Would it really be so terrible," he finally said, "to have me in your life...to have a father for Amanda?"

"We have a life." A pleading tone stole into her voice. "A good, stable life. And you used me. I can't forget it."

His gaze dropped from her eyes to her lips, then to her chest. He sighed. "C'mon, Cyn," he said calmly. "Get away from the door."

She stepped away before she'd thought it through, then watched him get his coat. *He's leaving. Good.* As he opened the door, her relief was replaced by heartfelt terror. She assured herself it wasn't because she was losing him, but because she needed him to protect Amanda. "Where are you going?" she asked uncertainly.

"Where do you think?" he returned. "To get my daughter."

"STOP! STOP RIGHT THERE! At least wait! You can't just..."

For the second time in two days, Cyn was chasing him through the parking garage. This time, her high heels clicked and clattered against the concrete. She was running. Hard.

He'd already learned that she didn't take no for an answer, so he unlocked the passenger door first, then held it open for her. She whooshed past him breathlessly, in a rush of that sweet-smelling perfume. Once she was inside, he slammed the door.

"Do you mind telling me what you—er—what you—" She gasped as he slid into the driver's seat and started the car. Too winded to continue, she threw her head back against the headrest and gulped down long, deep breaths while he pulled out of his space and onto Eighty-eighth Street.

"I mean—" She whirled around to face him. "Once you *get* Amanda, just what exactly do you intend to *do* with her?"

"You know," he said, glancing at her. "I was kind of hoping you'd help me figure that one out."

Her expression softened a little. "Oh," she murmured in surprise.

His hands tightened on the wheel. "If it hadn't been for some very strange coinci—"

"If it *was* a coincidence."

"I didn't send the notes." He sighed. He didn't believe they'd met again, by coincidence, either. The first notes had been juvenile, and Paxton had a childish streak. Was it possible he'd known that Jackson and Santa were the same man? Had Paxton sent the notes, in hope of reuniting his daughter with the father of her child? If so, why hadn't he admitted it when he'd been asked directly about the identity of Amanda's father?

"As far as I knew," Santa finally said, "you were still married to Harry Stevens. I would never have come here. But now that I have...now that I've seen Amanda, I can't just walk away."

"You mean, you're not going to tell her when we get to The Plaza?" Cyn asked.

The sheer hope in her voice made him mad all over again. What right did she have to deny him his daughter? "When I saw Amanda," he managed to point out reasonably, "I thought she might be mine. I've known that she is for over twenty-four hours, and I haven't told her." He braked at a light. "Eventually, I mean for Amanda to know she has a father. An honest one who cares about her." The light changed and he pressed the gas. When he glanced at Cyn, she looked a little flushed.

"All right," she finally said. "I can never forgive you for using me...but all right."

He was so surprised, he nearly missed the circular entrance to The Plaza. He concentrated on driving for a moment, until he'd braked again. He stared ahead at the long line of limos and cabs that were also waiting for the parking valet. "You'll let me tell her?" he finally asked.

For long moments, she didn't say anything. He glanced through his side window. Various ice sculpture angels were displayed in front of the hotel. As beautiful as they were, they were nothing next to the flesh-and-blood woman beside him. When he glanced at her, she tilted her head and gazed at him.

"Amanda was told that Harry Stevens was her father," she said softly. "Then she overheard the truth." She shot him a sad smile. "Mom certainly never approved of the way Daddy handled things. I mean, having me marry Harry was sort of his idea. And Harry—because he wanted to marry me, for real—agreed. It was Daddy who later sort of declared him dead. And then one thing led to another," she finished in a rush.

Santa nodded. He'd heard all this before. "So?"

"Well, Amanda heard Mom and Dad arguing about it, and then she found out about…Jake. Amanda thinks Jake, who is in jail, is her father."

For the first time, how things might look from Amanda's point of view really sank in. "How could you let her think a criminal's her—"

"Santa, that's what *I* thought!"

At least she was calling him Santa now, he thought. Maybe Cyn could forgive him, too, in time. "Well, she can't go through life thinking that."

Suddenly her eyes shimmered and looked misty. He almost hoped she'd break down and cry, so he could pull her close, under the guise of comfort. She gulped audibly and blinked. "I just need to think it through," she said softly.

Was it the truth? Or was she buying time, while she figured out how to get him out of their lives? He shook his head, as if to clear it of confusion. If nothing else, she was the mother of his child, and he was going to trust her. He had to.

"Amanda's so young," she continued. "I don't want her to be any more confused than she already is. Maybe we should even bring in a counselor. I want to decide when to tell her." Cyn scooted across the seat and one of her long slender fingers reached up and traced the scar on his jaw. "Can you understand that?"

He nodded. The last thing he wanted to do was to confuse his little girl. "Why didn't you stop Paxton from telling all those lies?" he asked. "Why did you let him make such a mess of things?"

"I'd been through the ordeal of the trial. You were gone. I was twenty-four, unmarried and pregnant," she said, a hint of bitterness touching her voice.

Everything in her tone said he'd broken her heart. He expected her to say it outright. Instead, she scooted back across the seat. "You'll have to leave my apartment as soon as possible." The farther away from him she got, the more her voice seemed to harden with resolve. "There can be nothing between us. First, because I'll never want a man who lies to me. And second, because this is going to be confusing enough for Amanda as it is."

"I'll leave as soon as Amanda's safe," he said gruffly. He tried to tell himself that he'd gotten what he'd wanted— Amanda. To hell with Cyn.

He realized horns were blaring all around him and glanced through the windshield. Sure enough, all the cars in front of them were gone. One glance into Cyn's eyes, he thought, and the whole world ceased to exist. *Forget it. Just concentrate on getting Amanda.*

"MOMMY! I ATE THREE candy bars and watched lots of TV!" Amanda flew into Cyn's arms. She was getting heavy, but Cyn managed to swing her around in countless, dizzying circles. Then they collapsed on the bed in The Plaza's suite.

"Tickle fest!" Cyn exclaimed, wiggling her fingers against Amanda's ribs.

"Grandmama and Granddaddy are gonna take me to the Christmas trees from around the world!" Amanda broke into a fit of giggles. "I won't go if Mr. Santa can't." Amanda rolled away from Cyn and shot a guilty glance at the rent-a-cop. "And Mr. Thomas is gonna come."

Cyn glanced up. She'd left Amanda with Mr. Thomas and

her mother, but both her parents were in the suite. Together. In the same room. For a moment the only sound came from the TV. *It's a Wonderful Life* was on. Cyn blinked, then looked at Santa. He seemed surprised, too.

"Santa Claus!" Amanda lunged off the bed and shot toward Santa. He caught her in his arms and settled her on his hip.

Cyn's heart dropped to her feet. *He lied. He's going to tell her now. Why did I listen?* The seconds ticked on, feeling like eternity.

"Why, hey there, you knockout you," Santa drawled.

"Now that we've spent the night here, do you mind telling me what in the world we're doing at a hotel?" her mother asked, gazing between Santa and Cyn. Cyn watched her mother smooth the skirt of her suit, then recline in an armchair. She could feel Santa's gaze on her back; it nearly raised the hairs at her nape.

Her father wiggled his brows. "Now, Analise, it's not nice to pry," he chided.

"I just want an explanation." Her mother smiled wickedly.

"It's so long and involved you wouldn't want to hear it," Cyn said in an embarrassed rush. Did her parents really think she'd gotten Amanda out of the house so that she could sleep with Santa? A guilty flush warmed her cheeks. Little did they know. She inadvertently glanced at Santa. The way she caught him looking at her, they might have come from making love. When she looked away, it was straight into her mother's merry grin.

Cyn had a few questions, too. She wanted to ask her parents what they were doing together, but then she decided she might hex the situation by asking if they were a couple again.

"Well, wherever you've been," her father began, "we waited until you arrived to do the honors."

"Honors?" Analise asked.

Paxton grinned. ''The police called yesterday evening and asked me to identify a few things.''

As if sensing what was to come but not daring to believe, Analise leaned forward. ''My necklace?'' she murmured.

''Not just a necklace,'' Paxton returned softly. ''A chain of time…the Christmas and anniversary gift that marked off each of our many wonderful years together.''

Analise gasped. ''They really found it?''

Paxton circled around her chair, pulling the necklace from his pocket. He leaned slowly, looped it around her neck, then clasped it.

''Oh, Paxton,'' she whispered.

He place his hands gingerly on her shoulders and leaned close. They looked so romantic and wonderful together that Cyn pressed a hand to her heart. The whole last year of their estrangement seemed to slip away.

''I knew you'd want to see it again,'' her father murmured. ''The other items were all recovered and they're in the safe.'' With every word, he seemed to be asking Analise to come home.

''I hope there were some cuff links in the bottom of that bag,'' Cyn whispered softly, looking at her father's open shirtsleeves.

Paxton patted Analise's shoulder. ''Matthew Lewis was released on a pardon, and he went to John Christopher's house. Santa followed him and found Christopher. He was the man who got away.''

''I helped catch him,'' Cyn pointed out.

Analise's throaty laughter filled the room. ''Well done, you two. Now, if only Jake Jackson stays in jail. Somehow, I doubt that man will ever reform, no matter how much time he serves.''

Cyn was about to hazard a glance at Santa when Paxton chuckled. ''Oh, he just might, Analise. I mean, you never know.''

The twinkle in her father's eyes nearly convinced Cyn he

knew the truth. But that was impossible, she assured herself. The way Jake—Anton Santa, she amended—had stormed back into her life was just making her paranoid. The fact that he'd betrayed her twice wasn't helping, either.

She felt a warm hand rest on her shoulder and nearly jumped out of her skin. It was Santa. When she glanced up, Amanda—who was still in his arms—waved at her. Her chest constricted, but she managed to smile. *I'm going to lose my baby to this man.*

Her mother's voice brought her back to reality. "I've got to go."

"So soon?" Paxton cleared his throat. "I thought you and I were taking Amanda to the museum."

"You all run along," Analise said, her voice catching.

"I thought that necklace was supposed to be lucky," Paxton returned softly.

Analise's gaze alighted on Cyn's eyes, then fluttered upward to take in Santa and Amanda. "Oh, who knows?" She flashed Paxton a sudden smile. "Maybe it will turn out to be a lucky year, after all."

Part 9

Chapter Nine

Wednesday, December 21, 1994

The phone's shrill ring pulled Cyn from a deep, disturbed sleep. Maybe all of this—Jake's return, his transformation into Anton Santa, the fact that she'd actually slept with the man, and the threats against Amanda—had been nothing more than a nightmare, she thought groggily.

"No such luck," she muttered, her fingers fumbling over her sweat-damp, tangled sheets. She accidently knocked the receiver to the floor, scooted and leaned to retrieve it, then barked, "What do you want?"

She quickly recovered. "I'm sorry. It's just that it's—" She glanced at the clock. "Twelve o'clock." Midnight? She squinted at her curtains and could see light peeping through. Noon!

She bolted upright just as her father said, "Your mother and I taught you manners, young lady. Would your highness mind telling me what's wrong?"

She shut her eyes, feeling thoroughly disoriented. "Please, Daddy," she whispered hoarsely. "I'll call you back in five minutes. I promise." She opened her eyes long enough to hang up the phone.

Then she stumbled into the bathroom and rinsed her face.

It barely helped. All night she'd either wanted to creep into Santa's room and make love—or storm in and kill him.

What a strange few days it had been, she thought, squinting at her reflection. Jake Jackson had waltzed right back into her life as Anton Santa, and now he wanted to play Daddy to Amanda. "No play about it," she muttered, trying to force herself to face the facts. "He *is* Amanda's father."

Yesterday she'd accompanied Paxton, Santa and Amanda to the exhibit of Christmas trees from around the world. She'd wanted to avoid Santa, but she couldn't bear to leave him alone with Amanda. The worst thing was that he was the perfect daddy. He'd piggybacked Amanda through the museum, held her hand and let her buy postcards at the gift shop. Because of his world travels, he was able to tell funny stories about the kids he'd seen in every country for which there was a tree. Her little girl adored him.

But what about his lies? Cyn wondered as she brushed her teeth. Wouldn't he betray Amanda eventually, just as he'd betrayed her?

She rinsed her mouth, gulped down a healthy amount of cold water, then glared in the mirror. She looked downright horrible, but with a life like hers, who could concentrate on beauty sleep?

How come I didn't recognize him? She headed for the phone again, thinking of the reasons Santa had enumerated. Her image of Jackson had definitely colored him in memory—and not favorably. *Did I not recognize him simply because I didn't want to?* Now she couldn't see anyone *but* Jake when she looked at Santa.

Suddenly she cocked her head. No cartoons! "Amanda?" she yelled. She ran across the room and flung open her door. "Santa? Amanda?" *He's taken her. He's gone and he's taken her with him,* she thought. *But he wouldn't do that. Not Santa.* She ran to the phone again.

"Paxton's at your mother's office," Eileen said, when Cyn got her father's assistant on the line.

"Is Santa with Dad? Is Amanda there?"

"I don't know." Eileen sounded harried.

"Thanks, Eileen." Cyn hung up and tried her mother.

Her father answered on the first ring. "Paxton Sweet here."

"Daddy?" Cyn perched on the edge of her bed and coiled the phone wire around her hand nervously.

Her father sniffed. "I certainly hope you're calling to apologize," he said, a little huffily.

"Is Jake there? Does Jake—oh, heavens, I mean Santa," she corrected in a rush. "Is Santa there? Does he have Amanda?"

"Jake!" her father burst out. He lowered his voice, as if there might be other people in her mother's office. "For once in your life, you've got a respectable man after you, Cynthia Anna Sweet. You may choose to ignore it, but I've seen how Santa looks at you. He has a profession, character, he adores Amanda…"

Cyn was waking up fast. As her father ticked off Santa's attributes, it was right on the tip of her tongue to tell her father that his oh-so-respectable golden boy *was* Jake Jackson. She bit her lip as if to keep herself from talking. If anyone heard that piece of news today, it was going to be Amanda.

"When are you going to straighten up and fly right?" her father finally finished.

"Is Santa there with Amanda or not?" she asked, trying to stay calm.

"He most certainly is," her father returned. "Humph. I take it you're still in bed?"

Her father sure was in an uncharacteristic bad mood. "I couldn't sleep very well," she said in a conciliatory tone.

"Well, the early bird gets the worm. While you've been sleeping, Santa has been doing his job. He's found the kidnapper."

Her mind was suddenly reeling. As soon as she'd agreed

to let Santa tell Amanda that he was her father, he'd found the kidnapper! Was he that anxious to leave her apartment? Had he known who it was all along? Had he merely waited until he'd gotten what he'd wanted—namely, Amanda—before he exposed the person who'd sent the threatening notes? Didn't Santa care about her at all?

"I'll be right there!" Cyn exclaimed.

Only after she'd hung up did she realize that she'd forgotten to ask the identity of the culprit.

"CLAYTON?" CYN GASPED. She scrutinized the elderly man in front of her as if she'd never seen him before in her life. *Clayton, who'd always bought her ice creams when she was a kid? Clayton, who was so involved with the store that he was almost a member of the family?*

Sure enough, Clayton Woods was seated behind her mother's desk, with the notes in front of him and Amanda on his lap. Analise was all but petting Clayton's hand, in order to soothe him. Paxton kept a firm hand on his head buyer's shoulder.

"It was—it was me. Me, Cynthia," Clayton said brokenly. "I'm so—so sorry. I—"

"There, there," Analise crooned softly, patting him with one hand and twining the fingers of her other through the links of her Christmas necklace. "Take a few deep breaths, dear. Paxton, why don't you run and get Clayton something to drink?"

"What about some nice hot tea, Clayton?" Paxton asked, scurrying toward the door. "I should have brought Eileen with me. We need to make some tea!"

"Heaven's, Paxton—" Analise sounded suddenly angry at the mention of Eileen. "Why don't you get it yourself? It amazes me that you can't even make a drink without your assistant."

Something in her mother's tone gave Cyn pause. So did Clayton's guilt. Still, even that couldn't erase Santa from her thoughts. He was leaning casually in the windowsill, with his arms crossed over his chest and a self-satisfied smile on his face. He was looking right at her.

Clayton seemed barely aware of the people present. Not even of Amanda, who flung her arms around his neck and gave him a sloppy kiss on the cheek. "It's okay," she murmured. "You can kidnap me, Uncle Clayton, and you don't have to write any letter."

The older man shook his head, as if confused. "I just had to heal the company." He glanced at Cyn.

"The company?" she managed.

"There're rumors of a takeover attempt," he said more firmly. "When we were joking in the board meeting, I just thought…"

Out of the corner of her eye, Cyn could see Santa. She could feel his gaze rove over her. In spite of the circumstances, she hoped she didn't look as underslept as she felt. She tried to focus her attention on Clayton. "Thought what?"

She tried to tell herself she should be angry, but she knew Clayton nearly as well as she knew her own father. Clayton had gotten a little absentminded and addled in the past few years, but he was still like family. Besides, all she really felt was relief. And Santa's eyes.

Clayton ran a hand over his bald scalp. The tufts of gray hair on either side looked springy and uncombed. He blew out a shaky sigh. "I thought maybe—" He hazarded a glance at Analise, then at Paxton, who breezed in with Clayton's tea. "Well, I thought maybe you all would have to interact. If you just got back together, even enough to have a good working relationship, the company might pull through. The talk on Wall Street is that someone's desperately angling to get inside…." Clayton's eyes seemed to plead for mercy from those who loved him.

Paxton squinted. "You've actually heard that down on Wall Street? Not secondhand?"

Clayton nodded sheepishly. "I go down there every once in a while," he said, his breath becoming more even. "Bob's there all the time, too. He loves to hit the Seaport and schmooze the ladies after work. Anyway, a few days after our meeting, I ran into an assistant from Holmes and Furrows and she said someone was actively pursuing us, but she didn't know who."

"Get Evan on it," Paxton said to Analise. "He knows practically everybody downtown by name."

Analise sighed. "According to Evan, someone's been buying up the employees' stocks."

Paxton gasped. "And you didn't tell me!"

"We weren't exactly speaking," Analise returned defensively.

"Well, we are now," Paxton said. "And we're going to pull together on this one. You, me, Clayton and Cyn have the lion's share of the stocks in the store."

"I haven't sold a one," Clayton quickly said.

"Of course you haven't," Analise said matter-of-factly.

"Me, neither," Cyn said.

"I wouldn't sell my store," said Amanda, making Clayton crack the first hint of a smile.

There was a long silence. Then Clayton said, "Can you ever forgive me, Cyn?"

"You really scared me," she said, speaking honestly. "I can't deny that. But I'm relieved to know the truth."

"When Mr. Santa arrived, I knew you'd feel safe, and then when you two got along so well, kissing at the store, under the mistletoe and all..."

Cyn's face was getting hotter by the minute. Santa seemed to be enjoying her blush immensely. "Mr. Santa has been of great help," she admitted in a businesslike tone.

"I only wanted your parents to start talking again," Clayton repeated.

Paxton clapped his back. "Well, Clayton—" He smiled at Analise. "Maybe your scheme worked." Paxton turned and winked at Cyn. "And just think, Clayton," he continued, with a quick glance in Santa's direction. "If you'd never sent those notes, my future son-in-law wouldn't even be here."

"Daddy!" Cyn nearly shrieked.

Santa's low belly laugh suddenly filled the room. "Why Cyn, didn't your Daddy tell you about the marriage he's arranged for us?"

SANTA CAUGHT CYN'S WRIST as she rounded a corner in the hallway near her mother's office. She'd been walking so fast that she swung toward him, still moving on sheer momentum, and nearly crashed into a water fountain. "Aren't you going to congratulate me?"

"What do you want, Santa?" she asked drolly. "A medal?" The woman was clearly in no mood for pleasantries. Her eyes were flashing and her lips were stretched into a thin line. "Or perhaps I should simply be pleased, since you've caught a man I consider to be my uncle." She raised her brows archly. "But then, maybe it's you who should congratulate me. After all, you and my father have arranged my marriage." Now Cyn smiled sweetly.

He was fairly sure her pique was due to the fact that she still wanted him and wished she didn't. "Can't you take a joke?" He playfully tightened his grip on her wrist. Beneath his fingertips, he could feel her pounding pulse beat.

"I'm merely worried about my father," she returned lightly, withdrawing her hand from his and placing it on her hip. "He seems to think you're so wonderful—" She lowered her voice. "And he's going to be upset when he finds out the truth."

Somehow Santa doubted it. "He's not going to dislike me for having been a cop."

She shook her head. "When he finds out you and Jake Jackson are one and the same, he'll be crushed."

He tried to assure himself that he only wanted the go-ahead to tell Amanda the truth. Then he was leaving. "Do you think

he'll be crushed,'' Santa said softly, ''because you were?''
Why do I keep hoping she'll admit she cares for me?

"I was not!" She heaved a quick sigh. "I just don't like
the way you're snowing my father. I'd appreciate it if you'd
quit acting so buddy-buddy."

Eileen rounded the corner. Apparently, feeling as if he
couldn't do without her, Paxton had called and told Eileen
to rush over. "Hello, you two," she said pleasantly.

The way she said it, they might have just been caught
kissing. Both he and Cyn smiled dutifully at Paxton's assistant until she'd passed. Then he said, "There's no reason for
you to be jealous, Cyn. I get along with your father and I
think it's a good thing. It'll be good for Amanda."

"Jealous?" she burst out, as if it were the craziest thing
she'd ever heard.

"You don't want to share your dad," he said calmly.
"And you sure don't want to share Amanda." In spite of her
anger, he couldn't help but notice her kissably pursed lips.
He almost wished he'd just arrived in New York. He would
be playing it cool; she would be flirting mercilessly.

"I don't mind sharing," she finally said with a toss of her
head. "It's all a matter of who I'm sharing with."

He reached for her hand again, lifted it quickly, then
pressed it against his chest. "Sometimes—" He gazed deeply
into her eyes, wishing she'd be more reasonable. "We've
shared pretty well."

"Oh, please," she whispered miserably. "Don't remind
me."

"Can you really forget?" He drew her a fraction closer.

"Believe me—" The huskiness of her voice seemed to
belie her true emotions. "It's as if I've been stricken by a
case of total amnesia."

He chuckled softly. "A serious medical condition." He
realized she was almost in his arms. "Maybe I should jog
your memory."

"The only jogging I'd like to see you do is in sweatpants.

And of course—'' She shot him an innocent smile. "You'd be running far away from me.''

"Still convinced I'm a bad guy?''

"More than ever.''

"If I'm already condemned, then I've got nothing to lose.'' He swiftly pulled her against him and delivered a fast, wet kiss. Then he tilted his head and looked into her eyes again. "How was that for bad?''

Her glistening lips almost curled into a smile. "Pretty bad,'' she conceded softly.

She's giving in as surely as if she'd cried uncle. He chuckled. "I can get worse.''

"I'm well aware of that,'' she said throatily, a deep flush now spreading over her features.

"Not as aware as you could be.''

Her jaw clenched and her eyes turned cold. She all but leapt back a pace. "I don't want you taking off with my daughter again.''

"She's my daughter, too.''

"Not yet.''

Santa leaned against the water fountain. "She always has been my daughter, and she always will be my daughter,'' he said, wishing he didn't think of taking Cyn to bed every time he looked at her. "She doesn't become my daughter simply because you say so.''

But when would it all come true? Would there really be a day when Amanda would fly into his arms, calling him Daddy? He could easily open a business in the city and find an apartment. He'd decorate a room for Amanda that would be every bit as enticingly little girlish as her room at Cyn's.

Finally Cyn sighed. "Now that your case is solved, I assume you'll be moving out of my apartment.''

Didn't Cyn—in some small part of herself—want him to stay? Wasn't she having occasional fantasies about the two of them getting together and parenting Amanda? He guessed not.

"Well, are you?"

"You seem to have forgotten something." He drew an envelope from the inner pocket of his suit jacket and held it up for her to see.

"I—I thought," she stammered. Was it his imagination or did her gaze really flit to his as if she wanted his support again? "I thought Clayton was the one who—"

"Clayton didn't leave the typewritten note," Santa said.

Her eyes darted down the hallway as if seeking the culprit. "Who left it?"

"I don't know." He leaned closer to her. "But you can count on one thing."

"What's that?"

"That I'll be staying at your apartment until I find out."

CYN MANAGED TO AVOID Santa through the afternoon promotion and dinner. When they'd finally gotten home, she'd gone to the one place where Santa wouldn't follow—at least not in the early evening—her bedroom. Now she felt trapped.

Why should I be stuck here while he and Amanda watch movies? she fumed, momentarily forgetting that she was in self-exile. It was nearly Amanda's bedtime, which meant she'd been cooped up for hours. The longer she'd sat on the edge of her bed, the more she thought of things she needed to do.

If it weren't for Santa, she would be cleaning, baking, wrapping presents and planning a menu for Christmas morning brunch. She could read her magazines, which were on an end table in the den. She, not Santa, would be cuddling with Amanda on the sofa, watching videotapes.

"I can't live like this," she muttered. She got up, opened her door, then headed down the hall. *I'm not going to vanish simply because he insists on being here. I'll just sit down, pretty as you please, and watch television with my daughter!* Unfortunately, when she reached the den, a tape was rewinding.

"*Beauty and the Beast* is over, Mommy," Amanda said.

Cyn's gaze drifted from her daughter to Santa. "Oh," she said wryly, "I wouldn't be too sure about that."

Cyn did a double take, just as Santa drawled, "I take it I'm the beast and Amanda's the beauty?"

"Boy, aren't you quick." She had to fight to keep her voice light, since she couldn't take her eyes from him. He was wearing a white hooded sweatshirt and jeans. She'd never seen him in casual clothes, at least not since he'd been Jake Jackson. Throughout the day, she'd tried to remind herself that Santa had rights with regards to Amanda, but she could barely force herself to be civil, no matter how good he looked.

"*Beauty and the Beast* is over, Mommy," Amanda piped in, sounding confused.

"Yes, it is, honey," Cyn said, just as the tape stopped whirring. She crossed the room and returned it to its box, glad for the excuse to turn away from Santa. He looked as elegant as he did masculine in his suits, but his jeans left less to her imagination.

"I *was* a beast—" Santa's soft voice filled the room and seemed to take the very air from it. For a second, Cyn couldn't breathe. "But then Amanda kissed me and turned me into a prince."

Amanda giggled. "We gotta do *Aladdin* now."

"It's nearly bedtime," Cyn said quickly, wishing she didn't get so nervous and anxious when she was in the same room with Santa.

"Bedtime's not for another hour," Santa said. He seemed well aware that she'd been hiding to avoid him. Sure she couldn't take another second of this pins-and-needles feeling, she strode to the window and drew the curtain cords. The floor-to-ceiling curtains rattled on their rods and swept open.

"Snow!" Amanda shrieked. "It's snow, Mommy! Snow!"

In an instant, Amanda was at her side and hugging her leg.

It was coming down hard and had been for some time. At least three inches had accumulated on the ground below. Just looking at it, and touching her daughter's shoulder, Cyn's anxiety vanished. She felt nearly as excited as Amanda. The first real snow! "C'mon—" She lifted Amanda into her arms. "Let's bundle up and make a snowman."

"On our roof?" Amanda asked breathlessly. "Can we?"

"Yep." Cyn breezed past Santa, with Amanda on her hip.

"I'll get a carrot for the nose," Santa called softly behind them.

Sure enough, he was waiting for them at the door. He'd put on soft-looking gloves and pulled a leather jacket over his sweatshirt. A carrot peeked from one coat pocket, and a hat and scarf from the other.

They headed to the roof and he flung open the door. The three of them stopped on the threshold and huddled together against the sudden rush of wind, as if some silent communication had passed between them.

"You just don't wanna mess it up," Amanda nearly whispered.

Cyn double-checked the high safety fence that enclosed the perimeter of the roof, then her gaze followed her daughter's over the blanket of glistening, untouched snow. There were no footprints or dirt smears or slushy tracks. The old tar roof had been transformed into a winter wonderland.

"I always love the first snow," Cyn found herself saying.

"Snow's a magic trick," Amanda said.

"It's like you've just discovered a whole new world," Santa said.

To hear such sweet words spoken so gruffly almost made Cyn smile. She was sure Santa was thinking of *their* new world. The one that was glimmering and beckoning at the edges of her consciousness...calling to her to give him another chance, and to let him be a father.

"You first, Amanda." Cyn gave her daughter a tap on the behind.

Amanda bolted from the threshold and zigzagged through the snow with her arms outstretched, leaving a trail of pint-size footprints. When she'd nearly reached the fence, she whirled around, collapsed in the snow and waved. Cyn chuckled. Amanda looked so adorable—sitting in the snow in her ski pants and parka, with her knit hat pulled nearly all the way down to her eyes.

She glanced at Santa. He was leaning against the door frame and gazing into her face as if he'd been doing so for some time. He pushed himself off with his shoulder, stepped onto the roof, then turned and extended his hand with a flourish. "Ready?"

She smiled at his mock courtly gesture. Why couldn't the man always be this charming? she wondered as she placed her mittened hand in his gloved one. Even though he'd come to take her little girl, it was difficult to stay angry. "Lead the way," she said grandly.

He moved back a pace and she stepped over the threshold.

For a moment he merely grinned. "Bet you can't catch me," he whispered, leaning close.

He suddenly dropped her hand. Then he—like Amanda—flew across the roof, leaving Cyn to contemplate how his large footprints left a winding path right next to her daughter's.

"You better watch out!" Santa yelled just as the season's first snowball left his glove. It smashed against the door frame next to Cyn's head.

"You better not shout!" Amanda called. She started singing the well-known Christmas carol.

Cyn wondered whether or not Santa Claus *had* come to town. "Well, Mr. Santa sure has," Cyn murmured. She sucked in a breath of the harsh wintry air, wondering how things would work out.

When the next snowball broke against the door frame, Cyn took off, too. She bolted toward Santa and her daughter, flying alongside the trail of footprints they'd left in the snow, her own heels kicking up great sprays of powdery dust.

What was it about running through a first snow that made her feel so free and happy and alive? She only knew that it did. Because as she ran toward Amanda and Santa, all kinds of images flashed through her head. She thought of Eskimo kisses, and the hot chocolates they might share when they were good and cold, and of wrapping paper crinkling on Christmas morning. She thought of something else, too. Of the warmth that existed nowhere on earth—except in Anton Santa's embrace.

Part 10

Chapter Ten

Thursday, December 22, 1994

The typewriter could be anywhere.

Santa's breath fogged the air as he took in the Rockefeller Center tree, the ice rink, then the life-size, decorative gold angels that were grouped around Rockefeller Plaza. He crossed Fifth Avenue, where adults—who were parents, just like he was now—waited in long lines in front of the windows at Saks. Their bundled-up kids clung to the red velvet queue ropes with little gloved fists; they looked inside with such wide-eyed wonder that Santa imagined their eyes might be attached by springs.

In the windows, elves busily hammered toys, a little red choo-choo train chugged along its track, and Santa Claus squeezed down a chimney. The other Santa decided to take a walk, since he had plenty of time before Too Sweet's evening promotion, which was a caroling trip to a home for children. He ambled on down Fifth, as if he might actually find the missing typewriter on the sidewalk or on display inside the Godiva chocolate shop.

Where was it?

And who would send such a note? Santa could only hope the culprit didn't intend to kidnap Amanda on Christmas. He'd spent all morning rifling through the employees' drawers at Too Sweet again, analyzing the personnel files and rechecking the typewriters. The perp had to be someone who worked for the company, someone who was intimately acquainted with both the promotion schedule and Cyn and Amanda's habits. But who?

And what am I going to get Cyn for Christmas? He paused in front of the Warner Brothers Studio Store. As a crowded, glassed-in elevator rose, he realized that a larger-than-life Superman was pushing it upward. He smiled and kept walking. Choosing an appropriate gift for Cyn was plaguing him nearly as much as finding that fool typewriter. Somewhere— in this city that had everything, including Superman to push the elevators—the appropriate gift had to exist.

It couldn't be something too big. After all, he didn't know whether she'd gotten him anything or not. Besides which, he hadn't even kissed her for what felt like eternity, at least not so that she was kissing him back, which was the only kind of kiss that counted. Although they'd played in the snow like schoolkids the previous night, they sure weren't lovers.

And yet the gift couldn't be too small, either. Perfumes and scarves and gloves didn't seem right. Neither did chocolates. A new blouse might be nice, but Cyn had closetsful. Her toaster oven was embarrassingly ancient, but he simply couldn't bring himself to buy the mother of his child an appliance.

If he only knew where he and Cyn stood, then he'd automatically know what to buy. All he knew was that he had to touch her again, to kiss her and to make love to her. He could still hear her cries of pleasure as surely as if she were standing next to him on Fifth Avenue.

But could he really love her again? It was hard to tell. His feelings about her were getting all mixed up with his fantasies about having Christmas with a family. Maybe those sappy commercials they showed on television this time of year were getting to him. Every program he watched was interrupted countless times by moms, dads and kids who called relatives, opened packages and hung stockings.

It made him feel as if everyone but him was having the picture-postcard family Christmas that he'd always wanted. He'd been so far from attaining it for so long that he'd never even admitted he wanted it—until Amanda. Still, could Cyn be the right woman? He hardly believed that a child could keep an adult relationship together.

He was so lost in thought that he nearly stopped in the street, while a crush of shoppers bustled around him. When a bag swung against him, he sidled closer to the storefronts.

Great. I would come to a dead halt right in front of Tiffany's. He stared in the window. A tiny gold pen for her appointment book? he suddenly wondered. He could have it engraved, which would make it more personal. But with what message? *To Cyn. Christmas 1994.* Hardly.

The door swung open. "Coming in, sir?" the doorman asked.

Santa nodded. A great whoosh of wind from the avenue propelled him inside. Pressed on by the crowd, he ambled past the gleaming glass countertops. Every dazzling jewel imaginable stared back at him, making him think briefly of The Grinch Gang. Then one particular ring captured his attention.

It was perfect. Santa didn't know much about diamonds, but it was rectangular, set in a no-nonsense thick gold band. It looked bold. Classic. It was so simple that it made all the other rings seem overly flashy.

If Santa *was* going to ask Cyn to marry him someday, it was the ring he'd buy. After a moment a hand appeared beneath the glass and withdrew it. Santa felt a little piqued, as if someone had just snatched away his own personal prize.

"I do believe this is what caught your eye, sir?"

Santa glanced up.

A clerk smiled back. "She must be a very special lady, if

you're considering this one,'' the man said, holding out the ring.

Santa didn't know what to do, so he pinched the band between his thumb and finger and smiled down critically, as if ''diamond buyer'' were his middle name.

''Lovely suit,'' the clerk continued conversationally. ''Christian Dior?''

I've come a long way from my past and childhood, Santa suddenly thought, looking into the clerk's eyes, which held an unmasked appreciation for the well-dressed, cosmopolitan man and potential client in front of him. Santa glanced at the ring again.

''It's part of our Imperial collection,'' the man continued. ''It's known as the Giancarlo gem because it was cut last year in Amsterdam by Giancarlo, of whom I'm sure you've heard.''

Santa nodded as if Giancarlo from Amsterdam were his best friend.

''It's an absolutely flawless diamond....''

''What it would be is presumptuous of me,'' Santa said flatly. But then he thoughtfully turned it one way and another, and slowly raised it to the light.

''DOES EVERYONE HAVE their music?'' Analise asked as she hurried down the hall of the Harrison House, clutching a stack of song booklets.

''I've got mine,'' Cyn called. ''We'll do 'Holly Jolly Christmas' first.''

''Mr. Santa Claus and me gotta share,'' Amanda piped in.

''Paxton?'' Analise's voice rose. ''We've got to find Paxton because he has the sack of gifts.''

A man leaned in a recessed window at the home for children, watching and listening. Santa, who was carrying Amanda, looped an arm casually around Cyn's shoulders and headed toward him. *What a happy little family they'd make,* the man thought, feeling annoyed. But not for long, he assured himself. One thing had led to another, and now he had no choice but to kidnap Amanda. After all, the notes hadn't garnered any negative press.

Still, kidnapping Amanda tonight would be impossible. There was a time when taking her would have been as simple as stealing candy from a baby. In fact, whenever the child was bored at Too Sweet, she'd often come to his office to round up stray toys. Now Anton Santa and Cynthia were sticking to her like glue.

There was definitely no way he'd get to her tonight. The many volunteers from the marketing and promotion departments filed past him. Unwittingly, most of them had sold their Too Sweet stocks to him. And who could blame them for wanting to sell? he wondered. The company wasn't worth nearly what it had been the previous year. He'd make it a fortune, though, once it was his.

His jaw suddenly clenched when he saw Paxton kiss Analise's cheek. The two were more intimate than usual, which was striking sheer terror into him. If they had a good heart-to-heart, his cover would blow sky-high.

Yes, time was running out, but all he needed was to strike one final blow at the company. With any luck the bad news of Amanda's disappearance would give the papers every reason to republish the particulars of Cyn's past, too.

Someone tugged his sleeve, and he turned.

"Hiding?" Cyn lowered her voice conspiratorially. "Playing the Grinch and trying to escape your caroling duties?"

"Me?" he joked. "Never."

"Well, c'mon," she said, pulling him forward. "Amanda's waiting for you."

"Oh, is she?" he returned, fighting to keep the irony from his voice. He only wished it were true.

"YOU CAN SING, SANTA," Cyn said. It was almost as amazing as the fact that she'd accidentally spied him in Tiffany's that morning. She just wished she'd been close enough to see what he'd bought. Paxton and Analise were ahead of them, heading down a long hallway and toward the stairwell. Amanda was snugly tucked between her grandparents, clutching their hands.

Santa's fingers tightened on Cyn's shoulder. "I mean, really sing," Cyn continued. As "Holly Jolly Christmas" had given way to "Frosty the Snowman" and "It's Beginning to Look a Lot Like Christmas," his smooth baritone had almost shocked her into silence.

"So, you like my fa-la-las," he teased.

How did that terse macho drawl manage to produce such clear liquid notes on other occasions? "Don't tell me," she said drolly. "You have yet another secret life."

He tensed beside her, breaking their stride, then relaxed again. "Other secret life."

"Oh, you know—" She smiled at him. "You accompany the New York Philharmonic in your spare time." His face became so serious that she was sure he was still hiding things from her. She desperately hoped he wasn't. No matter how much she wanted Amanda to herself, she also found herself wanting to give Santa a second chance.

"Close," he finally said.

Cold fear knotted in her stomach, making her realize how much she wanted to trust him—both with her and Amanda. "Close?"

"Backup for Pavarotti," he said gruffly.

Cyn giggled in relief. "A backup singer? I thought that was for people like Diana Ross, when she was with the Supremes."

"Ah, Cyn—" He grinned. "You're showing your age."

The way he said it made her feel that she was getting older by the minute—without a man. Without him. "I'm all of twenty-eight," she protested.

His face became stern. "And you're right."

"About what?"

"I used to sing with the Supremes," he said gravely as he

swung open a fire door. Above them, the rest of the carolers passed through the upstairs doorway. As it slammed shut, Santa looked deeply into her eyes. "Can you still respect me?"

Her lips quivered with laughter. He put his arm around her shoulders again and began slowly taking the stairs. "Well," she said, her voice growing husky. "I guess I can live with your wretched past, as long as you never dressed up in one of those spangle gowns."

Santa turned and leaned his back against the stair rail, pulling her with him. His hands crept beneath her red blazer and settled on either side of her waist. She could feel their warm pressure through her blouse. "You think you could?"

She rested her fingertips against his chest. "What?"

"Live with it?" he asked softly.

One look in his eyes told her that he was no longer referring to his supposed past as a pop singer. She was pretty sure he didn't mean *live with it*, either, but *live with him*. "We've gotten ourselves into a pretty complex situation." She wanted to do whatever was right for Amanda, which meant not involving herself with Santa. Nevertheless, her fingers crept farther upward, over his pin-striped shirt.

Gazing into his eyes, she wondered what he'd been doing at Tiffany's. She'd gone there to pick up a gift for him. It still wasn't engraved, and she didn't even know if she'd really give it to him. After all, she'd also bought him a tie.

"Yeah," he finally said. "Things are complex, all right."

"We'll just have to see how things go," she murmured. *Between us.*

He cocked his head and smiled. "Well, there are certain things I've come to feel I can't live without."

"Like what?"

His hands slid around her back in a tight, intimate circle, and he nipped her lower lip lightly with his teeth before covering her mouth with his own. Cyn shut her eyes, feeling languid in his arms, and teased him with the flickering of her tongue. After a moment, she forced herself to lean away. "They're probably at 'Silent Night' by now."

He chuckled. "Maybe we could kiss till 'White Christmas.'"

"Surely, you don't mean for the next two whole days," she said raspily.

"That's exactly what I mean," he murmured, as if carols were the last thing on his mind. His palms roved upward on her back, pressing every last vertebra, then traveled down again, over her backside. Somewhere in the proximity of her thighs, he found her hand and his fingers twined with hers. "C'mon," he nearly whispered. "You haven't heard anything until you've heard me do 'Silver Bells.'"

Silver bells, she thought illogically, as he pulled her up the stairs. Her lips still felt damp and swollen, and for an instant, she was sure the bells he meant were of the wedding variety.

When they reached the room, her parents, Amanda and the others—Evan, Bob, Clayton and the members of the marketing and promo departments—were all looking pointedly at her and Santa. So were the four little boys who shared the room.

"I think we're in trouble," Santa whispered. He gave her a surreptitious pat on her rear end that turned her cheeks scarlet.

She playfully slapped his hand. "If you don't quit, you really will be," she whispered back as she glanced around the room. The boys looked clean, neat and well fed but, even so, Cyn felt suddenly sad. Paxton held out a large sack of gifts, and Amanda bounced up to each boy and delivered wrapped copies of *Little Amanda's Perfect Christmas*. Each boy also received a second gift, which Cyn had wrapped—footballs, catcher's mitts, baseballs, hockey pucks.

She glanced at Santa. They hadn't talked about his childhood for years now. Still she knew that part of Jake Jackson's history also belonged to Santa. He'd lived in foster care and had been in homes that were probably very similar to this one. He caught her gaze, saw her sudden sadness and seemed to know what she was thinking. His smile looked a little wan. Then he winked.

"Ready to sing the next carol?" Paxton asked as he closed the gift sack.

Analise smiled. "Now that Santa and Cyn have finally come from wherever in the world they were…"

"Now, now, Analise—" Santa caught Cyn's hand and squeezed it. "Save your breath for the songs."

"Let's sing 'O Little Town of Bethlehem.'" Paxton leafed through his caroling book. "Will you please start us off, Santa?"

"'O Little Town of Bethlehem, how still we see thee lie…'"

Once again his voice swept Cyn away. The notes were so true and perfect that the very air of the room seemed to expand, as if to make space for them. Everything seemed fuller somehow, including her heart. Maybe that could expand, too, and make room for Santa. Everything—from the kids' smiles, to the wrapped packages they'd delivered, to Amanda's Kelly green dress—seemed suddenly brighter.

"'In thy dark streets shineth the everlasting Light.'"

Outside, the night sky was dark and cold and clear. Great puffs of white steam rose from grates in the sidewalks. Across Central Park, twinkling stars nestled in clusters around the spires of skyscrapers, and all around her, the lights of Manhattan burned bright. Beneath the window in the Harrison House, a horse stamped its hooves and then, at the urging of a carriage driver, began its regular route around the park.

Just at that moment a light snow began to fall again, making the world seem fresh and clean and innocent. And yet, Cyn thought suddenly, if Santa was right, there was a kidnapper in their midst. Someone who knew Amanda. Someone who was pretending to be her friend.

Suddenly the words swam in front of Cyn's eyes. As if sensing it, Santa's arm gracefully nuzzled around her waist again. Her cheek brushed against his shirt as she gazed at his strong profile.

She wasn't sure but thought that Santa, who had no family of his own, might want one, even if he wasn't the sort of man to openly say it. She knew he wanted Amanda. But could she give him her whole family? Would she?

She raised her voice a notch. It wasn't nearly as good as his, but the two melded together as surely as their lips did when they kissed, or as their bodies did when they made love. They finished the song, gazing into each other's eyes. "'The hopes and fears of all the years are met in thee tonight....'"

"GOODBYE!" Cyn called repeatedly. "And thank you."

"See you soon." Santa waved with one hand and held Amanda's with the other.

"Merry Christmas and everything," Amanda murmured sleepily.

Outside, the air smelled like burning wood and freshly cut pine. A film of icy snow coated Fifty-ninth Street, and it shimmered under the white lamplights, as if the pavement had been strewn with diamonds. Just across the street, Central Park was blanketed in snow. Everything looked so clean and crisp and white that Cyn couldn't help but think of Santa's shirts. "Drive safely," she called again.

As the last caroler returned a final wave, she sucked in a deep breath—it was so cold it hurt her lungs—then blew it out, watching it cloud the air. For a moment, she, Amanda and Santa merely huddled together on the stoop of the Harrison House. Finally Cyn snuggled her hands deep into the pockets of her down coat and chuckled.

"Hmm?" Santa glanced at her, raising his brows.

"It actually smells clean out here," she said wryly. "For once."

"Not the usual in the city," he said smiling. "I'll grant you that."

"And cold."

"Then I guess we'd better hold hands," Santa said.

"We're holding hands." Amanda sounded as grouchy as she looked tired.

"I mean, your mother's hand."

"Oh," Amanda said. "Okay."

Santa chuckled as he sidled close and dipped a hand into Cyn's pocket. When she shot him a playful, censuring glance, Santa said, "Well, Amanda said it was okay."

Cyn smiled as he started to pull her down the steps. She realized he was headed across Fifty-ninth. "The car's over on Fifty-eighth!" she protested.

"True." Santa nodded just as they made it across the street. "But look at Central Park."

She laughed as she stepped onto the sidewalk. "What else *is* there to look at?"

"More virgin snow," he said persuasively.

"What's virgin, Mommy?" Amanda asked.

Cyn watched Santa bite back a grin. "Thank you, Mr. Santa Claus," she said.

Santa gazed over the top of Amanda's head and rolled his eyes. Then he looked at Amanda. "Virgin snow is the best kind for making snow angels, sweetheart."

Cyn never would have guessed it, but fatherhood suited the man. "Not a bad answer, Santa," she admitted. Looking at him, she knew he was suited for more than just parenthood. Under the streetlamp, his slicked-back hair gleamed with streaks of light. His seductive smile lifted the corners of his eyes, so they crinkled with tiny lines. His lack of concern about how his camel coat blew open with the wind made him look dangerously cavalier.

"What's snow angels?" Amanda asked.

At that, Cyn laughed outright. "I think you'll find the questions never end."

Santa swept Amanda into his arms, then headed down the stairs, leading into the park. "C'mon. I'll show you."

"It's dangerous out here!" Cyn exclaimed, scurrying after them. "And Amanda's pretty sleepy."

"I am not!" Amanda shrieked. The tone alone made it clear that it was hours past her bedtime.

"And we're not going to the reservoir or the pond," Santa reminded, over his shoulder. "Just to the first patch of snow." When he reached the bottom of the stairs, he swung Amanda around, then deposited her on the ground with a flourish.

"It may be virgin snow, but it's still New York City," Cyn protested. She glanced around, realizing with relief that they were still under a streetlight. "Are you two actually going to wallow around on the ground?"

Santa shot her a mock contemptuous grin. "Now, Amanda, the first thing you have to do is hold your nose."

Cyn's shoulders began to shake. "Don't listen to him! You don't have to hold your nose!"

"Sure she does," Santa said. "It's New York snow and all. Remember?"

Cyn rolled her eyes.

Amanda dutifully pinched her nose, and when she spoke, she sounded as if she had a cold. "Mommy don't do it right."

"I simply can't believe this," Cyn managed to say, but she obediently held her nose, too.

"Now, you fall flat on your back," Santa continued.

Santa sounded as if he were doing a commercial for cold medicines. Cyn giggled. *This,* she thought illogically, *is the father of my child.* In her wildest imagination she'd never have guessed that Jake Jackson would reenter her life. She certainly hadn't imagined him standing in Central Park on a snowy night, looking utterly dapper except for the fact that he was holding his nose. She clamped her chattering teeth together.

"Angels are serious business," Santa said in a low, lethal voice.

"Yeah, Mommy," Amanda said, looking like an angel herself. Her cheeks were rosy and a white knit cap pressed her curls against her forehead.

"Pay attention now," Santa said, as if he were about to present the world's greatest magic trick.

Cyn watched in astonishment as all six-foot-plus of Santa stood at rigid attention, then fell backward. If he weren't so handsome, he would have looked like an ironing board falling over.

Amanda was so awed that she quit holding her nose. Her brows knitted together as Santa began to sweep his arms in great, wide arcs. Finally she said, "That's fun."

Santa's belly laugh filled the air. "I think I broke my back."

Cyn laughed and strode toward him, feeling Amanda follow close on her heels. She stopped when her toes touched the flat soles of his shoes. "Told you so," she said.

He groaned. "Did you come to help me up or to gloat over my carcass?"

"Oh," she teased lightly. "I kind of like you that way." And she did. His hair had flattened at the back and lay against the snow, as if against a pillow.

"What?" he asked. "Completely out of commission?"

She grinned, stretched her hand down and made a show of pulling him up. "You could help!" she exclaimed breathlessly, backing up as he walked into her. He casually put his arm around her.

"Wow," Amanda whispered, staring at Santa's imprint in the snow.

"Make a few, Amanda," Santa said softly.

"Go ahead, honey." Cyn leaned against Santa's chest and glanced toward the stairs. "We've got to get you home soon."

As sleepy as Amanda was, she was suddenly whirling like

a dervish from one clean spot to the next. Within a few moments the ground all around Santa's imprint was covered with tiny Amanda-sized angels.

"We better go," Santa called after a few minutes. "We can make some more on the roof tomorrow."

To Cyn's amazement, Amanda didn't even protest but ran into her arms. She settled her daughter on her hip. As she ascended the icy stairs, she glanced over her shoulder, wondering why Santa had lagged behind. She realized he was right behind her, and she was pretty sure he'd remained there in case she might fall. What a guy, she thought, suddenly smiling.

At the top, they paused and surveyed the scene below. At least twenty tiny angels, with shining, glistening wings, took flight around Santa's large one. "It's strange," Cyn found herself murmuring, "but I feel like we're looking down on heaven."

"Heaven's in the sky, Mommy," Amanda corrected impatiently. "You said so."

"But sometimes, honey," Santa said gently, "you can actually find little pieces of heaven on earth."

Cyn glanced quickly at Santa. He was gazing down at Amanda, with clear eyes that looked full of love. After a moment he turned and headed toward the street. She began to follow but the snow angels caught her eye again. They seemed to beg the question of whether she could share her own angel, her baby.

"Santa's sleigh awaits, ladies!" Santa called.

Whatever emotion she'd just seen in Santa's eyes now seemed tempered by the humor in his voice. She whirled around and gasped. Santa was waving at her from inside one of the Central Park carriages. "We've got to go home!" *Home. Does he really want it to become both his and mine?*

"He'll take us," Santa yelled.

"But the car—" She lowered her voice as she neared him. "And I'm not even sure it's legal to go..."

"It's not, but I gave the man a heap of money." Santa leaped down lithely, then helped her and Amanda inside. "I'll get the car tomorrow," he continued as he climbed in next to her.

The driver called, "Go, Prancer!"

"Do you think his name's really Prancer?" Cyn whispered as the carriage moved forward.

Santa chuckled. "He looked more like Vixen to me."

"I want Rudolph," Amanda murmured, making Cyn smile.

For New York, the snowy night was quiet, and when the horse neighed in the silence, Cyn felt as if she'd been transported to another century. Amanda nestled against her and her eyes drifted shut. She seemed to breathe in rhythm with the steady clip-clop of the horse's hooves.

"Here, Santa," Cyn said softly. She disentangled Amanda's arms from her neck and shifted in the carriage seat. "Why don't you hold her?" *Your daughter. Our daughter.* "I think she's asleep."

Their gazes met and held in the dark confines of the carriage. Shadows flitted over Santa's face. "Are you sure?"

"She's a little heavy for me," Cyn lied.

He'd held Amanda many times, but this was different. Cyn wasn't giving her child to him because he was her bodyguard, but because he was her father. "C'mon, Amanda." He carefully lifted her from Cyn's lap. Amanda sighed deeply and curled against his shoulder.

The carriage seat was small—made for cuddling—and Cyn scooted next to Santa. She leaned against him and rested her cheek against his chest, feeling as comfortable as Amanda. She sighed softly as he put his arm around her. "I've lived in New York all my life but I've never been in one of these carriages."

"First time for everything," he said. Cyn couldn't really see but felt his arm curl around Amanda's back. His hand appeared over the top of her knit cap, and he smoothed her bangs.

A first time for him to be a father, Cyn thought. Through the carriage window she could see all the untouched snow in the park. Next to her, Santa's hand, which was so strong and yet so sensual, continued to smooth the hair over Amanda's forehead.

She had robbed him of their little girl. It was strangely ironic, since for so long she'd thought of him as the thief. He had stolen from her family, as surely as he'd stolen her heart. And yet, she thought now, maybe it was Anton Santa she'd loved all along.

No doubt her younger self had wanted the wild rebel she'd seen in Jake Jackson. But perhaps she'd sensed another man deep down inside. Perhaps she'd known there was a real man beneath—an Anton Santa inside Jake somewhere.

Thinking that, Cyn didn't feel like such a fool. Looking at Anton Santa now, it was becoming clear that she hadn't been one. This man made snow angels and said things about there being heaven on earth. He watched over her and her baby. And yet, for all that, she couldn't quite bring herself to invite him into her bed again or to let him tell Amanda he was her father.

If she did those things, her comfortably predictable world would become just like the virgin snow. Every day with Santa she'd take a thousand steps she'd never taken before. Mundane, routine things would seem as fresh and new as they did to Amanda. And her heart would feel so full…like it could break again.

"Still there?" he whispered. He leaned and found her lips, parting them in a soft, slow, heartfelt kiss.

"I'm just not sure I believe what's happened in the past week or so," she murmured when he drew away.

"Maybe this will convince you." He reached up and grazed his thumb and finger over her cheek, in what was more of a caress than a pinch. "It's real, Cyn. You, me, Amanda—everything that's happening to us is real."

Part 11

Chapter Eleven

Friday, December 23, 1994

"You didn't have to come with me to get the car." In the back seat of the cab Santa draped his arm around Cyn as if to indicate otherwise.

She tweaked his nose playfully as their driver pulled to a curb nearer the Fifty-ninth street entrance to The Plaza Hotel than to the Harrison House. "But we wanted to."

Amanda giggled. "Somebody's gotta protect Mr. Santa Claus."

"Oh, Giantelli's!" Cyn exclaimed, glancing across Fifth Avenue. One look, and her mouth started watering. She'd thought only Santa could make her drool like one of Pavlov's dogs, but she'd forgotten about Giantelli's. Stacked arrangements of cheesecakes, Key lime pies, tortes, tarts and bite-sized chocolate confections beckoned through the gleaming windows. "I'll make the diet my New Year's resolution," she murmured contritely.

Santa shifted his hips in the seat, dug into his pocket and peeled the cab fare from a money clip. "Hmm?"

"Why don't you get your morning papers while Amanda helps indulge my sweet tooth?"

"Why go across the street, when I'd be more than happy

to indulge it right here?'' Santa got out of the cab and offered her his hand.

"The day you're as sweet as Giantelli's," Cyn quipped, "is the day when you-know-where freezes over."

"Where?" Amanda asked as Cyn caught Santa's hand and stepped onto the sidewalk, pulling her daughter with her.

Cyn chuckled. "Just you-know-where."

Santa's eyes narrowed with sudden seriousness. "I should come with you."

"Mom and Dad'll be here any minute," Cyn said, hating the sudden reminder that they might be in danger. She nodded in the direction of the pastry store, where a policeman was mounted on his horse. "There's a cop right there."

"Well, it's just across the street," Santa conceded, glaring toward Giantelli's windows as if each cake were a villain in the flesh.

"You look so cute when you're concerned." Cyn cozied beside him and planted a solid smack on his cheek.

The kiss decided him. "I'll grab a paper and meet you."

Cyn caught Amanda's hand and headed across Fifth, saying, "It's a beautiful day, isn't it, honey?"

"Why can't you marry Mr. Santa like Beauty and the Beast?" Amanda returned in a complete non sequitur.

Cyn would have stopped in her tracks if the traffic light hadn't been about to change. When they reached the opposite sidewalk, she considered voicing a denial that would end Amanda's train of thought. "Would you like that?" she asked, instead.

"If we went to a wedding, would Mr. Santa be my daddy?"

He is already. Cyn cleared her throat and held open Giantelli's door. "I suppose so."

Fortunately, the shining glass cases of scrumptious treats caught Amanda's eye and she raced forward. "Mommy! We gotta get these Santa Claus cookies, 'cause Mr. Santa can eat them all. Lots 'cause he don't share."

"Won't," Cyn corrected automatically. She glanced over the counter, into a clerk's sympathetic eyes. "It's okay," she said. "We'll take a dozen." Her eyes dipped down, past the cheesecakes, to a number of chocolate cakes decorated with red-and-green-icing poinsettias. "And I'll take one of those and—" She pressed a hand to her heart and smiled. "And one of those incredible marzipan Christmas trees, please."

"Can I get a baby pie?"

Cyn squinted at the tiny round crusts stuffed with lime filling. "Three baby Key lime pies," she continued.

The clerk hastily boxed their purchases and secured them with string, then handed the boxes to Cyn over the counter.

"Amanda," Cyn said, "I can't carry these and hold your hand, so grab my coat pocket. Okay?"

Amanda immediately did as she was asked, and the clerk was nice enough to step from behind the counter and open the door for them. Outside, the air smelled as clean as it had the previous night. The morning traffic had turned the snow in the street to slush, but the day was glorious.

"Look! There's Grandmama and Granddaddy!" Cyn nodded across Fifth, while she and Amanda waited for the light to change.

"Granddaddy!" Amanda screamed. There was no way he could have heard at this distance, but Paxton waved.

Cyn felt a rush of pure happiness. She wasn't exactly sure where she stood with Santa, but the past seemed ages away. Now they were headed into the frontier of the future. As hard as it was to reconcile herself to sharing Amanda, Cyn knew Amanda needed her daddy. The icing on the cake today was that her mother and father had both agreed to meet them for brunch at The Plaza.

And maybe if Santa were really in my life, things would be as perfect as this day, she thought. It was nearly impossible to imagine him leaving. "C'mon, Amanda, our light's green."

Cyn heaved the cake boxes up, pressing them against her

chest, then started across the avenue, moving at Amanda's pace. The roads had been salted, but where the snow came only to the tops of Cyn's high heels, Amanda's boots were covered to the ankles.

"Grandmama!" Amanda yelled. This time when she waved, she nearly slipped.

"Easy there," Cyn murmured gently, glancing at the light.

Amanda came to a dead halt and stared down, to contemplate a pile of snow. "Can we wait till Santa comes and saves us?"

Cyn heard a nearby motorcycle rev its engine. "C'mon, Amanda, the light's going to—"

Suddenly Amanda tugged Cyn's coat with superhuman force.

My baby's not that strong!

"What the—" The cake boxes pitched violently from Cyn's arms as she whipped around, her body no longer moving of its own accord. *What's happening?* She wrenched in the opposite direction, and her fearful gaze darted to her coat pocket, just as a rider on a motorcycle lifted Amanda into the air.

"Mommy!" Amanda screamed.

He steered with one hand. Amanda was clutched beneath his free arm and her legs flailed madly above his handlebars.

But she still had Cyn's coat.

Her baby was holding on for dear life!

Cyn spun across the icy snow, out of control, with nothing between her and the kidnapper but Amanda's small, outstretched arm.

"Don't let go!" Cyn shrieked. She clawed at the air, reaching for the cycle, but when the man gunned the motor, Amanda lost her grip. As Cyn lost her footing one of her high heels flew off, spinning toe over heel. She tumbled across the snow in a ball of fur coat, like a round, fuzzy animal. Out of the corner of her eye she saw Santa emerge from the gold-framed revolving door of The Plaza and amble down the red-carpeted stairs.

Cyn scrambled to her feet just as the light changed. Cars and trucks bore down on her, horns blaring, showing no inclination of stopping.

Santa was now coming at a dead run.

Cyn bolted for Giantelli's, so fast that she lost her other shoe, and wound up slamming into the policeman's horse. "My daughter!" she screamed. "My daughter! My daughter!"

The cop dismounted and flipped open his notebook.

"Didn't you see? Didn't you see what just happened?"

"Ma'am, you'll have to calm down," he said gently.

But the cycle was fishtailing toward Fifty-ninth! Cyn shoved the policeman, threw her foot into the stirrup, then kicked the horse hard before she'd even fully mounted. She realized the cycle was taking a shortcut through the park, just as the horse reared on its hind legs and shook its massive head like the devil, trying to throw her. Somehow her flailing hands snatched the reins. Before the front hooves even hit the ground again, the horse was off at a sprint.

Cyn hunkered down in the saddle, galloped down Fifty-ninth, and when she saw a stretch of low guardrail, managed to jump it. Up ahead, the cycle hit a trail path. The man was headed uptown. Cyn reached around and slapped the horse's backside, screaming, "Faster!"

She hadn't ridden since high school and the freezing air and metal of the stirrups were painful against her stocking-clad feet. Her hat had flown from her head, her gloves were in her pockets, and her stinging eyes were tearing so much that she could barely see. She squinted against the sun and wind. Where was he going? The pond? The zoo? The Tavern on the Green, she thought illogically.

He headed for the reservoir. Cutting through a stand of trees, Cyn felt her heart soar. She was gaining on him. He had Amanda in front of him and he was steering with both hands, which gave him more control. She jerked the reins with all her might, forcing the horse onto the tree-lined jogging path around the reservoir.

"Get out of the way!" Cyn sat up long enough to yell, but terrified joggers were already diving off the track. Barren, snow-tipped tree branches dripped with icicles just inches above her head. She ducked again.

"You can't do this, lady!" an irate runner screamed.

"You're going to kill somebody," a woman shrieked.

"I've had it with this city!" a man yelled. "I'm going to move! I swear, I'm going to…"

Cyn barely heard them. She slunk so far down that her chest hugged the horse's neck. Even though his blowing mane and her own hair slapped against her cheeks in stinging strips, she hoped the horse's neck might protect her from the furious onslaught of the wind. "Amanda!" she screamed, wishing her little girl could hear her but knowing she couldn't. "Amanda!"

The cycle veered off, heading for the West Side. Good, she thought as he disappeared between trees. He was on fresh snow. She could see tracks. But where was he headed?

Just as the horse burst through a thicket, the cycle popped a wheelie and jumped a guardrail. By the time Cyn reached the spot, there was no sign of the motorcycle. And no sign of her daughter.

She kept moving. She was now trotting down a West Side sidewalk on a horse stolen from the police. Her eyes darted everywhere, but she didn't hear a motorcycle or see Amanda. Her stockings were in shreds and she could no longer feel her feet. When she looked down, she realized that one of them wasn't even in the stirrup.

She kicked the horse's belly, glancing down one street, then another, thinking that the motorcycle was blue and green. The man had been dressed in black and had worn a black helmet. On either side of him, she'd seen Amanda's two little legs kicking the thin air, as if seeking a foothold.

Over and over Cyn saw that blue and green bike pop its wheelie and jump the white guardrail, and she clung to the image. She'd just been thrown over a perilous cliff and that mental picture of Amanda was like the branch she'd caught to save her life. *I will see my baby again.*

Just as she darted down yet another street, the driver of a car slammed on the brakes. They squealed, then the vehicle hit a patch of ice and swerved in front of her. The horse reacted, leaping upward and resting his weight on his back legs. When he came down, his hooves missed the hood by a fraction.

Something inside Cyn snapped. "Get out of my way!" she screamed murderously at the driver.

The passenger door swung open. "Get in!"

It was Santa.

He didn't wait for her to dismount, but leapt out of the driver's side, then hauled her down into his embrace. Cyn's arms clung to his neck as he ran toward the car. She didn't know if minutes had passed or hours. But she suddenly felt something almost resembling relief.

"Don't worry." Santa reached across her and slammed her door. "No man escapes me for long."

"No woman, either," she murmured numbly.

"OFFICER BLANKENSHIP'S horse is at Fifth and Ninety-fourth." Santa clutched the car phone with one hand and the steering wheel with the other. Once he'd relayed the message, he hung up.

"The motorcycle was green and blue, and I think it was a man, but now I don't know—I just don't know," Cyn rambled. "He had black clothes and a black helmet and he jumped the guardrail."

"Where do you think he was going?" Santa demanded.

"New Jersey, maybe," Cyn said shakily. "But maybe uptown." Her voice wavered. "I don't know, anywhere."

"Okay." Santa tried to concentrate on driving, while his

eyes darted down the side streets and alleyways. That was better than contemplating the murderous things he was going to do to whoever had taken his daughter. He didn't want to think about how Cyn had looked on that horse, either. Furious, terrified, numb, lost. Oh yes, he'd kill the man who had done that to her.

It was all his fault. He'd been hired to protect Amanda, and at the crucial moment he'd gone to buy newspapers. He'd known he was doing the wrong thing, but when Cyn kissed him, there was nothing he'd deny her. She'd wanted to go to Giantelli's while he'd bought the papers. So he'd let her. Now, unless he got Amanda back safe and sound and soon, he'd never forgive himself.

He reached across the seat and squeezed Cyn's knee. Beneath her ripped stockings, it was like a knob of ice. "Here." He cranked the heat and trained the vents on her hands and feet. "Your shoes are on the floor. Your daddy got them."

"What are we going to do?" she wailed. She leaned forward and stared through the windshield.

"We're going to find her." Santa wished he felt as convinced as he sounded. "And you're going to start rubbing your hands together. You won't be much help to me with frostbite."

That got her moving. She began to vigorously rub her feet together, too. Then she quickly stripped off her stockings and slipped her bare feet into her shoes. "But she could be anywhere...."

"Don't worry," he repeated. "I got the plate numbers."

"You got the plate numbers!" she echoed, her voice leaping as if for joy.

"The cops are running them. I gave them the number in the car, too, and they'll call as soon as they have something."

"Oh, thank you." Cyn pressed both her hands to her heart. It was clear she was talking to God now, not Santa. Santa smiled reassuringly, praying he wasn't encouraging false hope. "There's more."

"You think you know who did it?" Her every word seemed to have "please" after it.

He shook his head. "But there was a guy from the *Daily News*, hanging out in front of The Plaza, looking for celebrities. He got a picture. Paxton bought the film, and he's taking it to an hour developer. He can get the results faster than the police."

"A photographer?" Cyn scooted beside him in the seat, her neck still craning in one direction, then another, as her eyes searched for the motorcycle. "If the story gets out—" Her voice suddenly caught, and she choked down a sob. "I mean, if there's a ransom— Oh no, if this hits the papers, somebody else could call in a ransom."

"The *Daily News* guy is the only one we saw."

"Where's my mom? What…" Her voice trailed off again, as if talking required too much energy.

Santa hoped Cyn could hang on and stay strong until they found Amanda. "With your father. As soon as they drop off the film, they're heading to your place. That way, if any calls come, they'll be there. They'll call us every half hour. If we haven't found her by the time we get the pictures, we'll get blowups. I'm sure it'll turn up something helpful."

He didn't really see, but felt Cyn cross her arms over her chest and hang her head. He knew exactly how she felt. "Cyn, it's way too early to give up."

"I'm not giving up!" Once again, she scooted next to the passenger-side window, her eyes scrutinizing the streets.

Good, he thought. He could handle anger better than despondency. As much as he wished he could take her into his arms, and that they could comfort each other, they had to keep looking.

"It's a motorcycle!" Cyn suddenly screamed. "Behind us!"

He jerked the wheel so quickly that the car fishtailed. Coming out of the spin, he did a U-turn in the middle of traffic, then laid on the horn and punched the gas. He'd passed two cars before he realized the cycle was silver.

He glanced at Cyn. Tears shimmered in her eyes and glistened on her lashes. "For weeks we've known this was a possibility," he managed to say. "It's why I'm here."

Cyn whirled on him. "Then why don't you do something about it?" she shrieked.

Her voice, so full of accusation, hit him like a blow. "She's my daughter, too," he said as he braked for a light. He turned in the seat and looked at her just as her mouth dropped open in astonishment and one of her hands flew up to cover it.

"I'm sorry. I am so sorry."

When she blinked, a tear fell, zigzagging a rivulet down her cheek. She slid next to him and pressed her face against his arm. "Aren't you scared?"

"Yeah," he said softly.

"How can you stay so calm?"

I have to be strong for you. "It's my job," he said.

And then Cyn began to sob, her fingers closing around his arm, as if she'd never let him go. He wished he were a better, smarter, tougher man. A man who could have kept her safe. Right now he would give his own life to place his daughter in her mother's arms again.

Yeah, this was his job, he thought. And he'd been in this position many times. He'd been forced to watch and wait, listen and investigate. But the object he sought had never been his own flesh and blood. Or the child of the woman he now knew he loved.

"ANGELO MAY HAVE TAKEN Amanda?" Cyn asked shakily, for the umpteenth time, as Santa pulled the car to a curb in Spanish Harlem.

Santa wanted to say that in such cases even one's best friend could be the culprit, but didn't. He surveyed the old tenement walk-up and shook out his fingers; they ached from clutching the wheel. He and Cyn had made loops through Queens, the Bronx and Jersey before a call had come. The motorcycle was a messenger bike from Too Sweet. And it was assigned to Angelo Garcia. "How well do you know him?"

"Just to look at."

Cyn's fury was barely contained. Her reddened eyelids were still puffy, but her eyes had regained a steely expression. The woman was nothing if not a survivor. From the look of her, Santa knew he'd have to kill Garcia pretty quickly, otherwise Cyn would beat him to the punch. "I want you to stay in the car," he said.

"No way," she snapped, pushing open her door.

He got out, then surveyed her over the hood. "Doesn't look like a great neighborhood," he said, glancing around. Down the block was a burned-out building. Across the street, a wheelless car had clearly been stripped. Graffiti marred every vertical surface.

"And so you're going to leave me in the car?" she shot back, almost sounding like her old self.

He circled the car and headed toward the steps. "C'mon— but stay behind me."

The outer and lobby doors were both wide open. In the hallways, paint peeled from the walls. All the way up to the fourth floor Santa kept wishing he had his gun. If Garcia had Amanda—which Santa hoped he did—all hell could break loose.

"Stand back." He paused at the apartment door and waited until Cyn was positioned behind him. Then he rang the bell.

After a moment a woman began calling questions through the door in rapid-fire Spanish. A twinge of pain touched Santa's heart; it had been years since he'd heard a voice so like his mother's. The woman was looking through the peephole and not seeing him.

"Delivery," Santa called.

When the door swung open, an elderly woman peered up at him. She was dressed in black, wearing an apron, and her long silver hair was piled on her head. "Delivery?" she asked in English. "What delivery?"

"I'm looking for Angelo Garcia," Santa said.

The woman's face lit up in smiles. "Come in, come in," she said, pulling Santa into the room. Cyn followed. Sounds of happy, chattering children floated down from the farthest reaches of the apartment. Just as the door closed, a twentyish man wearing running pants and a hooded sweatshirt strode into the room. He stopped in his tracks. "Ms. Sweet?"

With a sinking heart, Santa realized that the scene was all wrong. Amanda wasn't here. The place smelled of ham and turkey and strong coffee. A tree was thoughtfully decorated with beautiful handmade ornaments. The head of a hiding child suddenly popped up from behind the sofa. Angelo Garcia was looking at them with watchful concern. To find so much homeyness in such a bad neighborhood reminded Santa of his own childhood and nearly broke his heart. These were people who struggled to love each other, and who did so, in spite of the odds against them.

"We're trying to locate your messenger bike," Cyn finally said. "It's missing from the garage."

Angelo's lips parted in worry. "I parked it and turned in the key, like I always do." He shrugged. "There are always more robberies around the holi—" His eyes narrowed. "You've been crying. What's wrong?"

"We have to find your bike," Santa said.

"What happened?" Angelo's eyes shot between Santa and Cyn.

"We just—" Cyn's voice caught, but she quickly steadied it. "Hoped you might know something."

Angelo stared at them, with his hands on his hips. Then he started yelling in Spanish as he pulled a leather jacket from the closet. He shrugged into it, then dug a pair of sneakers from under the sofa.

He was just tying his laces, when the elderly woman—probably his grandmother, Santa thought—appeared again, now yelling at the top of her lungs and carrying two brown paper bags and a thermos. Santa remembered enough Spanish to get the gist. Without even knowing why they were looking, Angelo was ducking out of a family dinner to help. After some negotiation, the woman gave Angelo a set of car keys.

Realizing what was happening, Cyn said, "You don't have to do this. I mean, we appreciate it, but—"

"It's Christmas—" Angelo leaned and quickly kissed his grandmother. "And one look at you guys tells me this ain't about a lost bike."

At the door, the woman put her hand on Cyn's sleeve and handed her a bag of food and the thermos. "Everything is okay? No?"

Santa watched as those infernal tears shimmered in Cyn's eyes again. "I hope it will be," she whispered.

"WANT TO SPLIT THE LAST of the coffee?" Cyn asked as she squinted blindly through the windshield. Nearly all the lights in all the houses in Paramus, New Jersey, had been extinguished, and Santa swerved in a wide arc on the curving road with only the Christmas lights to guide him. The many trees on one large lawn had been strung with tiny white lights, but the trees themselves were invisible in the darkness. Looking at those lights, strewn like diamonds tossed against the black sky, Cyn couldn't help but feel as if Santa were driving through the air and above the chimney's…right into the sky and the stars.

"Sure," Santa finally whispered. "Coffee might be good."

Cyn nodded, then glanced at the digital clock as she poured from the thermos Mrs. Garcia had given them. Hours had passed. Each minute of each one had felt like eternity. Her body ached from sitting at attention, the pain in her shoulders was nearly unbearable, and her head was throbbing.

"Here, Santa." After he'd taken the cup, her fingers lingered on his sleeve for comfort. Then she found a foam cup and poured herself the dregs. She drank with one hand and kept the other on the car phone.

It was three in the morning. At nine it had been established that not even blowups of the photographs rendered anything useful. At ten, Santa had forced her to eat one of Mrs. Garcia's sandwiches. At eleven, convinced the person they sought was from Too Sweet, they'd staked out Bob Bingley's house. He'd arrived home in a cab, half-inebriated, with a tall redhead hanging from his arm like a stocking. Kidnapping had been the last thing on his mind. At midnight, it had officially become Christmas Eve. And at one, Analise had driven to Evan Morrissey's house to discuss what was happening.

It had been decided that only Evan would be told. Bob, ever the party animal, had been too full of holiday cheer to be of use. Clayton Woods already felt guilty enough. And Santa and the Sweets couldn't have cared less about how tomorrow's widely publicized promotion should be handled. They just wanted to keep the story out of the press and find Amanda.

When the phone rang, Cyn snatched the receiver to her ear. "Yes?"

"I'm calling from a pay phone off the West Side Highway."

She felt disappointment set in. "Angelo," she said to Santa. Pulling the mouthpiece closer, she said, "I want to thank you for all your help."

"No problem, but I've got to get my grandmother's car back to her now. She's working an early shift tomorrow...."

Cyn nodded as Angelo listed the territories he'd covered. He'd been down every street and alley in Brooklyn, Queens, the Bronx and Staten Island.

"Thank you so much, Angelo," she managed to say again before replacing the receiver. Somehow she swallowed the rest of her coffee. Just as she crumpled the cup, her bloodshot eyes met Santa's.

For hours neither one of them had wanted to say it. The unspoken words had hung in the air. "We've got to go home," Cyn whispered now. "We've got to sleep."

For sixteen hours Santa had remained as he was now—hunched over the wheel, his eyes roving from one side of the windshield to the other. *He loves her,* Cyn thought. Why hadn't she let him tell Amanda that he was her father? *What if he doesn't have the chance?* "Don't even think it," Cyn said aloud.

"What?"

Cyn shook her head. "Sorry, I'm just—"

"Beat," he finished.

"The police know what they're doing," Cyn said softly. "They're looking, too. They'll look all night."

After a long moment, Santa stopped the car, backed into a driveway, then turned around. He headed toward Manhattan again. As he did so, sheer defeat crossed his features. It vanished as quickly as it had appeared, but it made Cyn feel nearly as helpless as the fact that Amanda was gone. She slid next to him and rested her head against his shoulder. "Santa?"

"Hmm?"

Her mouth went dry and she swallowed around the lump in her throat. "No matter what happens," she said. "I know how much you love her and…"

"And?"

"And I love you, Santa."

He didn't say anything, just swallowed once himself. Good and hard.

SANTA COULDN'T BEAR to enter the apartment. Amanda wasn't there. Paxton was asleep in a reclining armchair, a plaid coverlet pulled over his suit. The phone was in his lap, and his hand still rested on the receiver. Analise was asleep on the sofa.

Cyn nodded toward the hallway. Before tonight, Santa couldn't have imagined Cyn looking less than perfect. But she did. Her hair was stringy from where she'd raked her fingers through it all day, and her eyes were more red than green. Tension made her face look tight.

He'd never needed her more. He stopped beside his door, reached out and caught her hand. "Good night," he whispered.

He didn't know what her eyes said in return. That he was a fool, maybe. That tonight everything was different. That they were too old and too tired to play games. "I need you with me," she said simply.

He pulled her close and hugged her, squeezing her tight. When he released her, he merely nodded.

In her room they didn't turn on the light but fell across the bed. "I feel guilty sleeping," she murmured in the darkness. "I don't think I can."

"You can," he said softly. He sat and slipped her shoes from her feet. "Where is your nightgown?"

"My dress is fine." Her voice was little more than a croak.

He rolled off the bed and headed for her chest of drawers.

"Second drawer," she whispered. He found something flannel and warm. Behind him he could hear her undressing. "Here, Cyn." He tugged her sleeves free, then folded the garment and laid it over the arm of a chair. Then he pulled her gown over her head. He mechanically stripped to his boxers, then slid beneath the covers and wrapped her in his arms. Her own circled around his neck. She settled on top of him, burying her face in his chest.

"I feel as if…"

Her voice trailed off and her breathing steadied, becoming even. Santa was sure she had fallen asleep. He needed her more tonight than he'd ever thought he could need anyone.

Even though she lay on top of him, she was the only thing anchoring him to the world.

"If..." she began again.

"What, Cyn?" His palms rubbed over the warm flannel of her gown, molding to the contours of her back.

"If I go to sleep," she murmured, "we won't find her."

"We'll find her." And they would. He would. He had to. "Can you sleep?"

"Yeah," he lied, knowing he couldn't. "I think I can."

"I've never felt so alone." Her voice was so low he could barely hear it. Any second she really would drift off.

"You're not alone," he said. *You'll never have to be alone if you don't want to be.* "I'm here. Right beside you."

She inched upward, and her lips sought his. He kissed her back slowly, feeling a comfort that transcended passion. Her lips said that bad things happened to good people, and that they were there for each other.

He wouldn't have thought it possible, but the kiss deepened, until that comfort only she could offer turned to passion. And yet, what he felt wasn't so much her lips and tongue, or how her belly curved against his aroused body, but her trust, her love, and her ability to give.

She moved slowly on top of him in the darkness and lifted her gown, while his hands slipped beneath it and slowly glided over her breasts. As she slid his shorts down his thighs, her nipples grew taut against his palms.

He kicked his shorts from his ankles, then pulled her fully on top of him. He shut his eyes, giving himself over to the sensations of her mouth on his. If their first kiss tonight had been of comfort only, this one was nearly feverish. Their tongues touched in an increasingly desperate desire to forget all that had happened.

Cyn moaned softly as her long legs opened and trailed down the sides of his thighs. His flattened palms curved around her waist and downward. Cupping her silken backside, he lifted her.

For just a heartbeat—when she touched him, to guide him inside her—his lips forgot how to kiss. As she sank slowly onto the length of him, he drew her closer and closer, inch by inch, until his arms tightly circled her waist.

He made love to her by barely moving. He nested inside the safe, warm haven she offered, until her breath became nothing more than catching sighs. He was sure he couldn't wait for her, but then she exhaled a soft sound of surprise that wasn't quite a moan, and rocked against him, over and over.

For the next minute all he could see was blackness. Then, in his mind, an arching stream of white-hot fire seemed to cut through the darkness. His muscles tensed until they were as hard and as rigid as steel. His hands gripped her backside and he drove her down on him, hard, as his hips thrust off the mattress to meet her. He exploded, feeling as if there could be no end to it. He so desperately wanted to savor this moment of forgetfulness.

"Oh, Cyn," he whispered, running his hands over her back.

She shuddered against him and brushed a hand over his head. She'd meant to smooth his hair but she was too tired, and her palm merely dropped onto his forehead. He wished he'd said something in the car when she'd said she loved him. All he'd been able to think was that he'd nearly had his family—only to lose Amanda.

"Cyn?"

He was sure she was asleep now. He said it anyway. "I love you, too."

Part 12

Chapter Twelve

Saturday, December 24, 1994

"Just let her sleep," Santa muttered softly. It was 10 a.m. He hadn't slept at all until dawn. Now he was out of the shower and already in his trousers. As he buttoned the newly laundered shirt he'd brought in from the guest room, he watched Cyn's shoulders rise and fall.

The sleeves of her gown were pushed to her elbows, and the spread was bunched around her waist. One of her feet peeked out at the foot of the bed. He could see only half her face; the other was pressed into her pillow. The tightness around her eyes had vanished, and her lips were curled into a near smile. She looked so untroubled that Santa decided to let her sleep, at least until he'd called the police station and picked up the newspapers.

He tucked in his shirt, still watching her and wondering what would become of their relationship. Then he shrugged into his jacket and headed for the kitchen phone. In the living room, Analise and Paxton had barely moved. *Nothing like a heavy sleep to cure us of reality,* he thought, as he strode down the hallway. He wished he was the proverbial sandman, and that he could send them all to the land of dreams until he'd found Amanda.

He wasn't hungry, but he grabbed a knife from a drawer

and a piece of fruit from a basket on the kitchen table. He was halfway through both dialing and peeling before he realized he'd gotten himself a pear rather than an apple.

"Officer O'Malley," he said when a receptionist came on the line. The man in charge of the case had the decency to answer on the first ring. *Good. He's been looking.* "This is Anton Santa. Any news?"

"We're still working on it. All we've got to go on is the bike, and it's so small it could be anywhere."

Santa wasn't surprised. If there'd been a break in the case, the ringing phone would have awakened the house by now. "I'm going back to Too Sweet," Santa said. "I'll start interviewing employees again."

"You'll find a Detective Black over there." O'Malley exhaled a cop's world-weary sigh. "He's been there all morning."

"Thanks. We appreciate all you're doing."

"This kind of thing's a real nightmare," O'Malley returned. "A shame on the holidays. We'll do everything we can to find the girl."

"She's my daughter," Santa found himself saying.

"I thought you were the body—"

"Yes. *And* she's my daughter."

"I understand, sir," O'Malley said gently, just before he hung up.

He didn't have a clue, Santa thought, trashing the pear core and silently heading down the hall. Just as quietly, he opened the front door and shut it behind him. As he waited for the elevator, his mind replayed the thousand times he'd looked into someone's eyes and said, "I understand."

Now the only one who understood was Cyn. They'd shared terror, grief and comfort. He'd never felt as close to anyone as he had to Cyn in the past twenty-four hours. But what had their lovemaking meant? Commitment or comfort?

He stepped into the elevator, without bothering to greet the operator, thinking that he'd been undercover, when he'd met her. He'd been so close to criminals that he could be mistaken for one. Hell, he'd even enjoyed pretending to be one. Four years ago, in the excitement of his undercover work, the only thing he'd regretted was not being able to tell Cyn the truth. But now, for the first time, he was truly on the other side of the law. The side where he was the parent of the victim.

"You okay, Santa?"

The doors opened. He glanced from the lobby to the operator. "Morning, Jim," he said gruffly. The man's concerned glance reminded him that he was usually more chatty. "I'm fine," he added as he stepped out. "And back in a second. I just need to get the papers."

"I'll hold the elevator."

Santa strode down the corridor and out the front doors. He dropped quarters into the machines at the corner and pulled out the papers: the *Times*, the *Daily News*, and *Newsday*. He shoved them under his arm and headed back inside. The temperature had dropped, and he found himself hoping that Amanda—wherever she was—wasn't outside. *Don't even think it.*

"You were quick this morning," Jim said jovially.

Santa nodded. "Yeah." As the elevator began its ascent, he pulled out the *Daily News*. He looked at the headlines and a familiar feeling of surety hit him so hard that he felt as if he'd been punched in the gut. It was more than a hunch. He'd found her. "Hurry up," he said.

Jim chuckled. "An elevator's only got one speed, Santa."

When the doors finally opened, Santa bolted down the hall. He pounded on the front door as he opened it. "Everybody up," he yelled. "Get up."

He bounded past Analise and Paxton, rushing straight for Cyn's room. "Cyn?" He leaned and shook her shoulder gently. "Cyn?" She rolled over and her green eyes opened in slits.

"I know where she is," he said quickly. "Get dressed."

She jerked upright. "Where?"

He was already halfway to the door. "Evan's, I think."

"Evan?" Analise yelled from the living room, sounding wide-awake. As Santa walked in, she jumped from the sofa and began wiggling her feet into her shoes. "But I was at Evan's last night. I didn't see anything that would—"

"Has either of you told anyone else she's missing?"

"No." Analise shook her head and brushed the skirt of her rumpled suit. "Maybe a policeman told someone."

"Of course I didn't tell anyone," Paxton said groggily. He squinted at Santa as if he couldn't quite remember what was happening.

Cyn scurried into the living room, her stockings trailing over her shoulders. Her eyes riveted on Santa's, she began to don her stockings, matter-of-factly and in front of everyone.

"It's in the paper," he said. He tossed the *Daily News* toward the coffee table, but Analise snatched it up before it even landed.

"That—that—*man.*" Analise's voice was so murderously hot it could have boiled water. Her head jerked up from the headlines and she stared at Paxton. "You never had an affair with Eileen, did you?" While she waited for a response, Analise staggered backward a pace, as if her mind were reeling and she couldn't quite keep her footing.

"Mother, we're trying to find Amanda!" Cyn shrieked.

"Eileen?" Paxton gasped. "My assistant? You think I had an affair with my—"

"Evan told me you—" Analise dropped the paper as if it had just scalded her skin. She reached over the back of the sofa and grabbed her coat. "I am going to go kill that man now," she announced with lethal calm.

"You're staying right here," Santa said smoothly. "Call the police. Tell them I'm at Evan's."

"Me, too!"

Cyn was shouting even though they weren't a foot apart. Santa was hardly going to argue. "Fine."

"He's the only one who could have told the media." Cyn ran back to her room and emerged with her and Santa's coats. "I don't know why he'd do this," she continued, her voice catching with relief. "But I don't think he'd hurt her."

"Why would he kidnap her?" Paxton asked, sounding confused.

"Because he wants to take over Too Sweet," Analise screeched. "That's why." She groaned. "And I'm the one who hired him! I thought his Wall Street background would—"

"Eileen?" Paxton asked again, clearly beginning to wake up. He shook his head. "I thought you were mad because I'd finally decided to track down Jake Jackson. While I was trying to protect Cyn during the trial, you seemed so upset about all the lies I told...and you said Jackson was Amanda's father, no matter what illegal activities he'd been involved in—"

"You knew!" Cyn gasped.

"Knew what?" Analise asked.

Paxton flushed guiltily. "You two better get going," he said. "We've got to find Amanda."

Santa grabbed Cyn's hand. "I suspected he knew," he muttered as he pulled her toward the door. "I asked you directly whether or not Jake was Amanda's father, Paxton," Santa called over his shoulder. "Why did you lie?"

"You two needed the chance to get to know each other again," Paxton replied.

Santa groaned. Under his breath, he muttered, "Your father is nuts."

"Call the cops," Cyn yelled at Analise as she went out into the hall. "You really think Evan has her?" she asked Santa.

"Sometimes I get a strong gut feeling," he drawled. "And I've never been wrong."

"So, you *know* he's got her?"

Santa put his arm around her, glad he wasn't lying this time. "I know he does, and she's just fine."

"THE BIKE'S RIGHT IN the damn driveway," Cyn seethed. Her eyes darted to the upper windows of the two-story house. If only she'd see Amanda's face peek out from behind the curtains...

"It's halfway behind a bush. Analise wouldn't have seen it in the dark." Santa pulled into a driveway two houses down.

Before they were even parked, Cyn pushed open her door and bolted. As soon as she saw Amanda safe and unharmed, she fully intended to commit her first murder. She didn't get far. Santa caught her elbow and she spun around.

"Keep your head," he chided softly.

A thousand protests shot to her lips, but she knew he was right. Looking into his eyes, she knew she could trust him. She'd shared the best moments of her life with Santa, and he'd held her tightly during the worst. "I just want her back so bad," she said.

"So do I." He steered her around a hedge that separated the lawns. When they got next to the house, they circled around, staring into the windows one by one. Through the cracks in the curtains, it seemed that no one was home.

"Where is he?" Cyn murmured. "And where are we going?" she continued, when they'd reached the front door again.

"This time we'll see if one of the windows won't op—" Santa nearly grinned.

"What?" Cyn asked urgently.

He nodded in the direction of the porch. "The front door's open. C'mon."

She did a double take, then kept close to Santa as he cautiously approached the porch. "Looks closed to me," she murmured. But sure enough, it was open an inch; there was barely a crack between the door and the frame. *Does anything escape this man?* She watched his lips part.

"Get behind me," Cyn whispered before he could say it. She dutifully took the backup position. He nudged open the door, then went in. She followed. Just in front of the door were the stairs. The place felt empty.

"Hello," Santa called.

Cyn nearly jumped out of her skin.

"You here, Evan?" Santa sounded so jolly that he might have been delivering Evan's Christmas gift. He glanced at Cyn and shrugged.

"Let's check the downstairs." She was already moving toward the dining room, on her right.

Santa frowned when they reached the stairs again. He glanced up them. "He's hiding."

"After you," Cyn whispered.

They moved stealthily, hugging the wall. When they were halfway down the upper hall, they heard a scraping sound. Cyn jerked her head in the direction of the farthest room. Someone was moving around in a closet. Those were hangers scraping over the bar. She ran toward the sound, close on Santa's heels.

"Amanda!" Cyn exclaimed. She tore through the bedroom so quickly that she banged her hip on the side of an ornate brass bed. The room was empty, but the closet door was shut, and a key was in it! Cyn quickly twisted the key and flung open the door.

"Glad someone finally showed up," Evan said drolly. He was seated on a footstool, in the middle of the walk-in closet, with his feet propped on a typewriter. A silver tray, laden with the remains of someone's breakfast sat on the floor.

"He doesn't have her," Cyn murmured, barely aware that Santa charged past her. A moment later she realized he was dragging Evan from the closet by the scruff of the neck.

"Watch my suit," Evan protested. Santa cuffed him to one

of the brass curlicues in the headboard, just as the phone on the nightstand began to ring.

"Where is she?" Santa demanded.

His drawl was so calmly menacing that Cyn figured Evan was about to die a slow, torturous death. "Spit it out, Evan," Cyn found herself saying, "or I'll kill you before he does. Where's my little girl?"

Evan's eyes narrowed. "I've heard the rumors about you and your burglar boyfriend, you know. And I'd like to inform you that your little girl clearly carries the genes of her criminal father." He smiled a sharklike smile. "Mind answering my phone?"

"Where?" Santa repeated. He advanced on his prisoner, murder in his eyes.

Either Santa's threat or the sudden wail of approaching sirens loosened Evan's tongue. "She was in the closet. This morning she kept yelling that she wanted breakfast. When I came in with the tray, she locked me in. The little creep took my wallet, too."

The phone was still ringing, and outside two cop cruisers squealed into Evan's driveway. Car doors slammed. "Why'd you do it?" Santa asked.

"Every time something bad happens to the Sweets, their stocks plummet." He flashed a grin at Cyn. "And I own more of them than you think I do."

The phone was driving her crazy. She snatched it up, prepared to say that the man of the house was under arrest. Then she realized that Evan might have a partner. She clenched her jaw, waiting for the caller to speak first.

"Is someone there?" Analise finally asked.

"Mom?"

"She's here!" Analise exclaimed breathlessly. "She's here!"

Cyn gasped. "Amanda?"

"Paxton just went to get her," Analise said in a rush. "She pulled right up to the store in a cab. After we called the police, we realized that Evan wasn't handling things here and— None of it matters. She's at the store!''

''Be right there.'' Cyn hung up, just as Officers O'Malley and Blankenship charged into the room and began reading Evan his rights.

''Is she okay?'' Santa asked.

Cyn nodded. ''She's at the store.'' Santa caught her in his embrace and swung her around high in the air.

IT WASN'T AMANDA, but Bob Bingley who met them at the door. A folded Santa suit, a wig and beard were piled in one arm. He clasped his free hand tightly around Santa's bicep, as if he meant business.

''Where's Amanda?'' Santa attempted to shake off Bob's grasp.

''Third floor,'' Bob snapped.

Cyn ran toward the crowded escalators. ''Bob, there are things happening here that you don't know about.''

Santa chased after Cyn. Since Bob wouldn't let go, he simply dragged the poor man behind him. He knew he could disengage himself, but he didn't exactly feel comfortable belting Analise's right-hand man. He wanted to hurry, though. He wouldn't believe Amanda was safe until he saw her. Up ahead, Cyn was already weaving through shoppers and climbing the escalator stairs. She whirled around.

''Bob!'' she screamed over the heads of the bystanders. ''Let go of him!''

''Sorry! Some of us are trying to ensure that this promotion runs smoothly!'' Bob tightened his grip on Santa as they took the first stair. ''But no one bothered to show up this morning—not you or Paxton or Analise or Evan—not even Santa Claus! He's sick again. Only Clayton came to work. So, Cyn dear,'' Bob railed, raising his voice to a shrill pitch, ''I need your bodyguard in exactly two seconds.''

''I can't believe this,'' Santa muttered. ''You want me to be Santa Claus.'' To appease Bob, he began pulling the Santa garb over his suit while they jostled customers aside and ascended the moving steps.

"You can't go up!" Bob exclaimed, even though they'd already reached the second floor.

"Give me the pants." Without waiting, Santa jerked them from Bob's arms and stepped into them as he walked. Cyn was nearly to the top of the next escalator.

"Not upstairs! The promotion's down here! The kids are waiting beside Santa's chair!" When Santa grabbed the wig and beard, Bob wrung his empty hands nervously. "Oh, no, those pants are falling down. Padding. I've got to find extra padding!"

By the time the three of them reached the third floor, Santa found himself dressed from head to toe in the red velour suit.

Bob was still pawing at his sleeve. "Put on that beard. It's got elastic in the back!"

"Mommy!"

Santa forgot Bob entirely. His little girl shot out from behind a Barbie display and ran toward Cyn in a blur of green velvet. He watched Cyn drop to her knees and catch Amanda in her arms. She stood slowly, still clutching their daughter, and then turned around and around in circles.

Santa bounded toward Cyn and Amanda—his girls—and reached them just as Cyn collapsed in an armchair. "Are you all right?" Her hands roved over Amanda's arms, legs and back. "Are you?"

Santa was barely aware that Analise and Paxton were standing near the chair. He only had eyes for Amanda, who now wiggled in Cyn's lap. "I get to wear the same dress for two days," she said happily. "And Evan didn't make me get a bath or anything."

When Cyn glanced at Santa, tears were streaming down her cheeks. A wealth of understanding seemed to pass between them. Regardless of where they were all headed, their baby was safe. *Sand,* Santa thought illogically, his eyes stinging. *Must have sand in my eyes.*

He blinked just as Amanda looked at him. "You're not Santa Claus!"

He sank down beside the chair, squatting on his heels. He felt so relieved he could barely breathe. His little blond-haired, green-eyed girl was the most beautiful sight in the world. She really was his, too. Anton Santa had really brought that kind of beauty into the world. He cleared his throat. "There's only one Santa," he managed to say. "I'm just a representative."

Amanda's eyes narrowed. They seemed touched by more sadness than a child could know. "You can't hear what we want?"

"You mean, what you want for Christmas?" he asked softly.

Amanda's face became a mask of forced bravado, and Cyn began rocking her, as if sensing something was wrong. When Amanda blinked, one round tear rolled down her cheek. How could his daughter smile gleefully one minute, then cry the very next? Santa wondered.

"I gotta see Santa!" she suddenly wailed.

"You can talk to me," he said.

His little girl's arms stretched for his neck. As Amanda fell from Cyn's lap onto his knee, Cyn shook her head in worry. Her eyes said, *Please fix this, Santa.*

A lump lodged in his throat. "So, what do you want for Christmas?"

"I don't want nothing. I gotta get a daddy," Amanda said in a rush. Then the floodgates opened. One minute she'd been talking; now she was sobbing against him. His chest constricted, and he rubbed her back. "It's all right, sweetheart," he soothed.

Finally Amanda sniffed. "You're nice," she said weakly. "Right?" She looked at him as if his eyes might contain the answers to all the questions in the world.

He nodded. "Yeah."

Words suddenly poured from her lips so fast that he

couldn't keep pace. "What about a girl whose daddy was so bad that he had to be a con-vic and then she stold money and didn't go where she was spose'd to—" Amanda stopped just as suddenly as she'd started and hiccuped.

Santa knew exactly which convict daddy she was talking about. He had half a mind to tell her the truth now, Cyn be damned. Instead he asked, "What money?"

Amanda hung her head and swiped at her cheek with the back of her hand. "The cab man counted, and he said he was spose'd to take fourteen to come home, and he said I took three hundred dollars 'cause it was at Mr. Mor'sey's house." A sob caught in her throat. "I still got the rest! I could give it back!"

"We know you took three hundred dollars from Evan's wallet, honey." The edge in Cyn's voice cut through Santa's heart like a razor. "But you had to, to come home. It's okay."

The words only sent Amanda into another fit of sobs. "He—he—"

"Who Amanda?" Cyn asked urgently.

"Mr. Mor'sey says—says I was mean..." Amanda sniffed.

"What, honey?" Santa ducked his head so he could hear her.

"'Cause my daddy is mean and me, too, like Little Amanda in our story and that's why I gotta get a new daddy," she whispered mournfully. "'Cause I steal stuff—" Amanda sucked in sharply. She pursed her lips, holding her breath, then exhaled shakily. "I steal Barneys and Barbies and Slinkys—and I'm a crim'nal!"

Santa had had about all he could take. He found himself glaring at Cyn. His eyes said, *let me tell her.* And Cyn wavered. He hated her for it. His little girl's heart was breaking, and he could do little more than have a staring contest with her mother. Even worse, Cyn won. He blinked first.

"Okay." Cyn sighed warily. "Go ahead."

He felt his heart drop to his feet. Did this mean Cyn would eventually be willing to let him into *her* life, too? "Amanda?"

"If I gotta go to jail, do I meet my daddy?" Amanda whispered.

Santa winced. "Amanda, this is going to be confusing, but I want to tell you something very important." *How am I going to tell her this?*

"Listen to Santa," Cyn said softly.

He wasn't sure, but he thought he heard Analise and Paxton nearby, urging him on. Cyn's hand dropped onto his shoulder. She squeezed, in support. Amanda stared at him intently and his heart started to pound. "This is going to be a little confusing."

Amanda's eyes looked murderous. "You said that, Santa Claus."

He opened his mouth, then shut it again. Cyn squeezed his shoulder harder. *Hell, just say it.* "I'm your daddy, honey."

Amanda looked nonplussed.

"I used to be a policeman," Santa continued. "That's what I was when I first met your mother." He watched for a reaction, but Amanda looked baffled. He didn't blame her. He didn't know where he was headed with this, either. "I was working undercover, so your mother never really knew my real name. She thought my name was Jake Jackson."

Amanda's eyes widened.

"I'm your daddy," he said again.

"You're my daddy?" she asked in astonishment.

"That's the main point," Santa conceded. Amanda wrenched around in his arms and stared at Cyn.

"It's true, Amanda." Glistening tears caught in Cyn's lashes. "He really is."

Amanda's mouth formed a round, perfect O. She turned around again and stared at Santa, as if she'd never seen him before. "When I went to Mr. Mor'sey's, you got married and had a wedding?" she asked slowly.

Santa was beginning to feel as if he were going to collapse. He glanced at Cyn, who averted her gaze. "No," he said.

"So, you gotta get a wedding now?"

His throat was so dry it was beginning to ache. "I suppose we *could*," he said gently.

Amanda wiggled in his lap. "You gotta, to be a daddy."

When Cyn looked at him, he wished he could read her mind. Tears shimmered in her eyes, as if she might start sobbing. Her lips were twitching, almost as if she might laugh. Her eyes had widened in surprise. He was a master at reading people, but he couldn't have second-guessed her if his life depended on it. And maybe it did, he suddenly thought.

Santa became conscious of the fact that they were in a corner of a crowded toy store. People milled around them, casting curious glances their way. Even so, they remained a blur. He'd found his inner circle—his family. He belonged with Cyn and Amanda. *Yeah,* he thought, *suddenly Christmas doesn't seem so lonely, after all.* "Cyn?"

She looked as if she'd guessed what he was about to say, but couldn't quite believe it. "What?"

"Will you marry me?"

She gasped. "Are you serious, Santa?"

"He's serious, Mommy." A pleading tone crept into Amanda's voice. "I can tell."

"Marriage is a lifelong commitment," she murmured, as if that might not have crossed his mind.

Was Cyn going to turn him down? Somehow he managed to smile. "That's the general idea."

Amanda tugged on his sleeve. "If we get married, do we all live in our house?"

He chuckled softly, his gaze never leaving Cyn's. "We do."

"Cyn!" Bob wailed. "There are a hundred kids downstairs!"

Santa glanced toward Bob. He was hovering nearby, holding two pillows and a belt. Santa sighed and looked at Cyn again. "I'd tell you to think it over, but I don't really want to wait until tomorrow."

"But who could say no on Christmas?" Cyn whispered.

"Exactly," Santa returned.

"It's not that I don't want—" She squirmed in the armchair, straightening her posture. "I mean, I do want to marry you. It's just—so many things have happened. I haven't really thought too much…"

He squinted at her. "But you want to marry me?"

"Oh, yes." She sounded shocked.

Amanda flung her arms around his neck. "You're my daddy!"

"She just said yes!" Bob exclaimed. Amanda scurried to the floor as Bob gripped Santa's elbow and jerked him to his feet. Cyn rose gracefully from the armchair. She was smiling, even though her eyes were misty. If she'd really said yes, it was the most convoluted yes he'd ever heard, he thought.

"I just said I was going to marry you, Santa," Cyn said, huskily. "Aren't you going to kiss me or something?" She reached across the space that separated them and gave him one of her trademark pokes in the chest. "Scared, Santa?"

"Oh, terrified," he drawled, catching her finger. He pulled her close, his lips hovering above hers.

"You're not really, are you?" she asked, snuggling against his chest.

"Me? Never." His lips grazed hers as he spoke and his arms tightened around her waist. "You want to know why?"

"Why?" she returned raspily.

"Remember that gut feeling I was telling you about?"

She gazed deeply into his eyes. "The one that's never wrong?"

"Yeah," he whispered, "I've got it right now."

"Mind telling me what it's saying?" Cyn murmured.

"That you're a sure thing, Mrs. Santa Claus." She smiled against his lips when he kissed her, just the way he meant to keep her smiling for the rest of their lives.

Epilogue

Epilogue

black helmet. On either side of him, she'd seen Severin's
big little legs racing for cover, as if seeking a warthog...

Epilogue

Sunday, December 25, 1994

"Get up."

Santa bit back a smile and kept his eyes squeezed shut. He'd meant to return to the guest room but had fallen asleep in Cyn's arms. Not that Amanda cared. She was now wetting her fingers, presumably by sticking them in her mouth, and then repeatedly wiggling them in his ears. When he suddenly opened his eyes, catching her in the act, she giggled naughtily. He smiled. "Merry Christmas, Amanda."

His daughter hovered over him. "You gotta get up, so maybe it will be," she crooned. Santa glanced down at his bride-to-be, who nuzzled against his shoulder and opened her eyes.

Cyn squinted at him, then at Amanda. Was it really Christmas morning? she wondered. And was she really lying here with Santa? It all seemed like a dream. "Merry Christmas," she murmured.

"Santa came," Amanda announced. She shifted from one foot to another in excitement, and fidgeted with her gown, tugging the front of it. "I know, 'cause he ate those cookies we left on the stool by the chimney."

Somehow Santa managed not to smile. They'd been chocolate chip. His favorite. "Why don't you go sit on the sofa? And your mom and I will be out in a minute."

Amanda bugged her eyes and pursed her lips, in an exaggerated show of pique. "Don't be a fem'nist."

Santa arched a brow.

Cyn giggled, feeling comfortably cozy nestled against Santa's rock-hard chest. "She means an annoyance, remember?"

"Ah." Santa grinned. "Your mother and I may be feminists, but the sooner you go, Amanda, the sooner we get up."

Amanda flew from the room. Over her shoulder, she called, "Okay, but hurry."

Once she was gone, Cyn squirmed upward and kissed Santa, still not quite believing she'd said she would marry him. Not that she had reservations. All she was mulling over was the date. She grinned. "Since you're such a feminist, Santa, why don't you go start my shower?"

He chuckled. "I'll even wash your nooks and crannies."

Cyn's whole left side turned a little colder when he rose from the bed. She rolled to her stomach, so she could soak up the warmth from where he'd lain. "Santa," she murmured sleepily. She told herself she had to get up, but shut her eyes and drifted for a moment. She just felt too cozy for a shower, even if it *was* warm.

It was thinking about Santa *in* the shower that finally got her moving. Just as she dragged herself into the bathroom, he emerged. "Hmm," she said. "Stark naked and dripping wet. It sure looks like I got what I wanted for Christmas."

He laughed and grabbed her, hugging her tight, thinking he had a whole lot more to give. "Just wait till I put that bow on my head."

"Oh!" she exclaimed, leaping back, just as the water from his dripping hair splashed her cheeks. She realized her gown had soaked clear through, and that they were standing in a puddle.

He grinned, hauled her into his arms again and playfully

swatted her backside. His hand lingered for a moment, grabbing a palmful of her soft flesh. "Last one to the Christmas tree's a rotten egg," he said as she slipped by him, pulling off her gown. He couldn't take his eyes off her. Cyn really was magnificent. When she coyly tossed her gown at him, he caught it. Even though she snapped the curtain across the rod and disappeared, he remained on the other side for a moment, smiling.

Then he went into overdrive. By the time Analise and Paxton rang the bell, Amanda was dressed and breakfast was in the oven. Usually Cyn made a full-scale brunch, but this year, she hadn't had time. The previous night, before they'd put out the remainder of Amanda's gifts and stuffed the stockings, the two of them had picked up scones, *beignets,* bagels and fruit. They'd made an omelet casserole from a recipe he'd found in one of her cookbooks. And it had been his first taste of relaxed, domestic bliss.

"Merry Christmas!" he called, emerging from the kitchen and heading down the hallway.

"Merry Christmas!" Paxton boomed.

"Morning, son-in-law." Analise hugged him and planted a smack on his cheek just as Paxton clapped a hand on his shoulder.

From her doorway, Cyn took in the scene. It was the homiest she'd seen in a long time. Her parents were back together. Apparently Evan had manipulatively tried to drive a wedge between them. And because her parents had their differences at the time, it had worked. Paxton had explained the whole story about Santa's past to Analise, too.

Where Analise didn't believe in keeping secrets and would have accepted Jake Jackson as Amanda's father—jewel thief and all—Paxton had wanted to protect Cyn. Later, thinking his lies about Cyn's marriage to Harry were the reason Analise had left, Paxton had done what he could to track down Jake. Instead, he'd found Anton Santa. Of course, Paxton had known Cyn wouldn't take kindly to the truth…at first. So, when the opportunity arose, he'd decided to both protect Amanda *and* play matchmaker. He'd hired Santa. And the rest was now history.

They were together again. A family. As her soon-to-be husband fiddled with the CD player, "It's Beginning to Look a Lot Like Christmas" began to play. Cyn grinned at Amanda, who was standing in front of the package-laden tree, with her hands on her hips. She was wearing her new appliquéd sweatshirt and, for once, it wasn't on backward. Santa Claus was in front, just the way he was supposed to be. Analise was madly snapping pictures.

"Mommy! Can I open them now?"

Analise and Paxton headed for the sofa, and Santa placed a cup of hot coffee in Cyn's hand. "Sure, honey." She'd nearly reached the sofa herself when Santa pulled her into an armchair and onto his lap. "My coffee," she murmured as it splashed.

"That's what saucers are for," he returned absently, his gaze riveted on Amanda. The sound of tearing wrapping paper filled the room, and the first bow flew through the air.

The adults sipped their coffee, snapped photos and listened to carols, while Amanda gasped and oohed and aahed. When she'd opened half her presents, Cyn noticed Amanda stacking some of them by the front door. "Honey, why are you carrying them over there?"

Amanda whirled around. "I'm gonna give lots of them to that Harrison House where we Christmas caroled," she said breathlessly. "Just like in our story."

Santa glanced from Amanda to Cyn and back again. It was such a sweet thing to do. But didn't his daughter want her toys? Just because the girl in *Little Amanda's Perfect Christmas* gave her gifts away didn't mean his Amanda needed to do so. "You don't have to," he reminded.

Amanda charged toward him and Cyn. "I got what I want." She giggled, wet her fingers again and stuck them in his ear.

"You did?" he asked in surprise, suddenly realizing he'd left his present for her in the guest room.

"A daddy for Christmas!" she squealed. She hopped up, kissed him on the cheek, then ran back to the tree, just as Analise snapped another picture.

Cyn chuckled. "Oh!" she exclaimed. "Your present's in my room, Santa."

He rubbed her hip. "You better go get it," he drawled. "Or else."

As soon as Cyn hopped off his lap, Santa rose and headed for the guest room. He and Cyn emerged at the same time, and within seconds they were ensconced in the chair again.

"Is that for me, Daddy?" Amanda asked, eyeing the three-foot-tall box in front of the armchair.

"Sure is," he said as she walked over slowly and plopped down in front of it.

"But first, you gotta do this." Amanda nervously handed Santa a flat, square box.

He smiled and gingerly opened his gift. When he saw it, he had to fight back a belly laugh. He should have known what she'd get him. It was an eight-by-ten green frame, with a red mat. Inside, was a glamour photograph of Amanda. Her dress was slinky, her hair was topped by a rhinestone tiara, and she had on enough makeup that she could have passed for thirty.

"She insisted we go for the glamour shot," Cyn whispered.

"I'm a knockout," Amanda announced. Even though she'd seen the picture before, she looked stunned at seeing herself so dolled up.

"You sure are," he said with a chuckle. He knew it wasn't in his best interest to tell his little knockout that he loved her just the way she was. Nevertheless, his fingers curled possessively around the frame, and he sighed, already dreading her teen years. No doubt, he'd be running off her countless suitors with his shotgun.

"Why don't you open yours, sweetheart?" he asked. This time, Amanda unwrapped slowly, running her small fingers beneath the paper folds and disengaging the tape. She solemnly folded the wrapping neatly when she was finished, too. Cyn leaned and helped her with the cardboard lid.

"Oh, Daddy!" Amanda murmured in awe, scrambling onto a footstool and staring inside.

Santa leaned around Cyn and pulled the gift from the box. It was a hand carved, delicately painted nutcracker soldier that was as tall as Amanda. Santa realized his daughter was staring at him with wide-eyed wonder, as if he'd discovered her innermost secrets. She gasped. "When I grow up, I was gonna get me a prince." She averted her gaze and stared into the nutcracker's eyes. "How'd you find out?"

"Just a lucky guess," he said softly.

Amanda inched toward the armchair, stood on her tiptoes again and kissed his cheek. "Thank you, Daddy."

"You're welcome." He smiled as Amanda seated herself next to her nutcracker.

"Analise," Paxton said. He sounded nearly as solemn as Amanda as he placed a box in his wife's hands.

"I bet I know what this is," she whispered happily, slowly opening the gift. Inside was a black velvet jeweler's box. Analise snapped open the lid and held up the contents for all to see. Sure enough, it was another red and green link for her lucky Christmas necklace.

She smiled at everyone. "Christmas, our wedding anniversary, and an engagement all rolled into one."

"It could have happened sooner if Paxton had just told me the truth when I asked him," Santa chided. He winked at Paxton.

"For all I knew at that point, you would have been on the next plane out of town!" Paxton chuckled.

Analise hugged her husband and reached into the pocketbook at her feet. She handed him a tiny box.

"Cuff links!" he exclaimed after a moment. "I've been such a mess without you, darling."

"But I'm back now," Analise whispered as he kissed her.

"For good?" Paxton asked.

"For good," Analise returned.

"Well, aren't you going to open it, Santa?" Cyn asked, poking Santa's chest. While he was watching Analise and Paxton, she'd surreptitiously put his gift in the very lap where she now found herself squirming. Santa glanced down.

"This looks promising." He picked up the small box, then gazed into her eyes.

Cyn smiled and wiggled her brows. She felt her heart beat double time as she watched him open her little package. The second she'd seen it, she'd known it was the perfect thing.

"A pocket watch." He gazed downward, feeling the heavy weight of the gold in his palm.

"I had it engraved yesterday," Cyn nearly whispered.

Santa unlatched it, his eyes roving over the tiny cursive letters of the inscription. "For My Husband," he read aloud. "In Memory Of The Time We've Lost—In Happiness For The Future We've Found." His voice suddenly caught. "Love Cynthia."

His hand closed tightly around it; he was still holding it when he handed Cyn her gift. "This looks pretty promising, too," she said huskily. Somehow Santa found it difficult to smile. He realized Cyn's hands were shaking.

"Tiffany's—" She stared into her lap and laid the shining gold wrapping paper aside. It had been days since she'd seen Santa inside Tiffany's. Had he already decided to ask her to marry him? *No. It couldn't be a ring.* She turned in Santa's lap and gazed into his eyes.

"Open it," he said.

"Open it, Mommy," Amanda whispered.

Cyn swallowed around the lump in her throat. *He was thinking about proposing before yesterday afternoon. But then, I've been thinking about marrying him since the day I was born*. With trembling fingers, she managed to open the box, then the jeweler's box inside.

"It's lovely." She cocked her head and gazed at her engagement ring. She was barely conscious of the fact that Amanda was now standing, and that Paxton and Analise were craning their necks. "Somehow, it looks like me," she murmured as Santa lifted it and nestled it on her finger. "Guess this makes it official?"

"Sure does." His arms tightened around her waist and he pulled her as close as he could.

Cyn's eyes roved over his heavily lidded, changeable brown eyes and his soft expressive mouth. *I'm looking at the man with whom I'm going to spend the rest of my life*. She ran a hand through his hair, then stretched upward. "Merry Christmas, Santa."

"Merry Christmas, Cyn," he murmured. Their lips met in such a soulful kiss that both knew their love was fated. And that nothing could ever come between them again.

✦ *Harlequin Romance*®

Delightful

Affectionate

Romantic

Emotional

Tender

Original

Daring

Riveting

Enchanting

Adventurous

Moving

**Harlequin Romance—the
series that has it all!**

HROM-G

HARLEQUIN PRESENTS®

The world's bestselling romance series...
The series that brings you your favorite authors,
month after month:

Helen Bianchin...Emma Darcy
Lynne Graham...Penny Jordan
Miranda Lee...Sandra Morton
Anne Mather...Carole Mortimer
Susan Napier...Michelle Reid

and many more uniquely talented authors!

Wealthy, powerful, gorgeous men...
Women who have feelings just like your own...
The stories you love, set in exotic, glamorous locations...

HARLEQUIN PRESENTS,
Seduction and passion guaranteed!

Harlequin® Historical

From rugged lawmen and
valiant knights to defiant heiresses
and spirited frontierswomen,
Harlequin Historicals will
capture your imagination with
their dramatic scope, passion
and adventure.

Harlequin Historicals...
they're too good to miss!

HARLEQUIN®
Makes any time special.™

Upbeat, all-American romances about the pursuit of love, marriage and family.

HARLEQUIN *Duets*™
Two brand-new, full-length romantic comedy novels for one low price.

Harlequin® Historical
Rich and vivid historical romances that capture the imagination with their dramatic scope, passion and adventure.

HARLEQUIN® *Temptation*
Sexy, sassy and seductive— Temptation is hot sizzling romance.

HARLEQUIN® SUPERROMANCE
A bigger romance read with more plot, more story-line variety, more pages and a romance that's evocatively explored.

Harlequin Romance®
Love stories that capture the essence of traditional romance.

HARLEQUIN® INTRIGUE®
Dynamic mysteries with a thrilling combination of breathtaking romance and heart-stopping suspense.

HARLEQUIN PRESENTS®
Meet sophisticated men of the world and captivating women in glamorous, international settings.